D0437208

Letters from an Age of Reason

Letters from an Age of Reason

NORA HAGUE

wm
WILLIAM MORROW 75 YEARS OF PUBLISHING
An Imprint of HarperCollins*Publishers*

 For information address HarperCollins Publishers Inc.,
10 East 53rd Street, New York, NY 10022.

HarperCollins books may be purchased for educational, business, or sales promotional use. For information please write:
Special Markets Department, HarperCollins Publishers Inc.,
10 East 53rd Street, New York, NY 10022.

FIRST EDITION

Printed on acid-free paper

Library of Congress Cataloging-in-Publication Data has been applied for.

ISBN 0-06-018491-4

01 02 03 04 05 QW 10 9 8 7 6 5 4 3 2 1

For my parents

ACKNOWLEDGMENTS

First and foremost, I wish to thank Douglas Tyskiewicz, without whom this book simply wouldn't exist. He, more than anyone, directly influenced its course and content; I am indebted to him in a thousand ways big and small. At one time or another, he served, tirelessly and skillfully, as my reader, editor, printer, researcher, moral support network, loyal cheerleader, ruthless critic, and, always, as my finest friend. His intellect, spirit, and seemingly limitless abilities have my utmost respect, and he has my utmost gratitude.

For everything, I thank my family: Mother and Dad, A., G., C., and N. They're always behind me—and sometimes way ahead of me.

I am profoundly grateful to E. L. Doctorow, who gave me the benefit of his instruction and his wisdom; he is a writer's writer and a teacher's teacher, without equal in either forum. I am so grateful as well to my wonderful agent, Jane Gelfman, for bringing her consummate professionalism, talent, and energy to this project. And I am certain I could not have invented a finer editor—particularly for myself, and for this novel—than Claire Wachtel; her smart and straightforward (but gentle) input made the editorial process a painless—even fun—experience. I also thank those über-assistants Cathy Gleason and Jennifer Pooley, for keeping the Big Picture centered and the details straight.

This book was also made possible by the auspices of my friend and fellow author, Alicita Rodriguez. Her kind invitation gave me a sanctuary in which to write, while her keen critiquing made the novel better—and shorter—than it would have been otherwise. My deepest and heartfelt appreciation goes to all the members of the Rodriguez family—Alicia and Ovidio, Nica, Karen, Alex, and Alexa, and, of course, Alicita—who so generously, and for so long, made me a part of their lives and their households.

The staff and students of New York University's GCWP provided me with guidance, support, and friendship. They remain some of my favorite people, and my favorite writers. My favorite reader, however, remains Ms. Jennifer Jordan, who stuck with this project from its inception.

Finally, I thank Max—Muse and partner in crime—for his unflagging belief in my abilities, for the nature and degree of his influence, and the depth of his insight. But mostly I thank him for being himself, and for his very being, alongside which so much pales so greatly.

Part one

chapter one

MONDAY, APRIL 23, 1860

Dear Journal:

I am beginning to think it may not be such a dull week after all, despite the cool weather and (to my mind) utterly premature war preparations which have made my usual entertainments almost too arduous to undertake. This morning I had a letter, and it seems I have been invited (or perhaps I should say challenged) by my cousin Constance to attend, tomorrow evening, a séance—my very first, as it were.

As I'm sure I've mentioned to you, dear companion Journal, these meetings of Spiritualists and their adherents, for the purpose of contacting the souls of the dead and conduiting messages to the living, have become quite popular of late. A number of prominent Mesmerists, Mediums, and Clairvoyants have been crisscrossing the highways all about New York State recently, and even our little town of New Parrish has not been exempt from their attentions. The event I've been invited to is being presided over by a lady Medium in Ithaca, but as that is just a step over the town line I suppose I may count New Parrish as being graced with the presence of this self-appointed liaison to the Departed.

If I sound skeptical, dear friend, it is for the best of reasons: namely, that I am, that such is my sentiment toward the entire undertaking. I simply do not believe in either the veracity or power of these so-called Mediums; I suspect they are largely misguided or deceitful, and I'd be willing to wager the latter is closer to the truth. There is much renown to be had for the price of a few rappings and tappings, so might not the temptation to arrange them prove overwhelming in some (if not all) cases? Oh, I do believe wholeheartedly in a Beyond—but surely God in His wisdom would not allow precious souls to be lost in the crossing over to Paradise, and thence reduced to thumping upon tables for the attentions of mere mortals. No; the whole Spiritualist business smacks to me of thoroughly un-Christian chicanery, and if Constance is willing to endorse it with wholehearted enthusiasm, well so she may, but I most certainly will not.

Of course, Constance *would* be one to swallow this particular fish whole. I've confided often enough to you, friend, my frustration at her wild-goose chases and silly indulgences. I am determined to be a woman of substance someday, rather than one of those vaporous creatures who faints at the drop of a hat, or a gullible swan drawn in by the flimsiest quackery—but Constance seems equally determined to be exactly those things! She is always on about something new but of dubious merit—it is her *wont*, as Mamee says, and I mustn't hold it against her, for she resembles Uncle Henry in that regard: her focus is a narrow one, and her attentions fickle.

But I do resent—although I try to be tolerant—that she holds herself above me, and uses her pursuits as a means to that end. Although she is little more than six years older than I, she acts at twenty-two like a matron of sixty, and insists upon talking down to me as if to a toddler in arms.

Most recently Constance has been consumed with this notion of the Spiritualist movement, and has taken it upon herself to informally sponsor a Medium, so that she and some of her Ladies' Circle members (you will recall these from my previous descriptions) might have access to the Netherworld every Tuesday evening, or whenever they feel the need to discourse with the Spirits. I wonder if her dear Thomas approves of the use to which his wife's weekly allowance is being put, but of course I cannot ask him without incurring Constance's not-inconsiderable wrath. So I have confined myself to smirking behind a hand whenever the topic arises, that is, whenever Constance has occasion to visit—this despite Father's warning that I mustn't be smug, as it is not an attractive trait in a young lady, and Mamee's insistence that Constance be humoured in her attempts to "better" herself.

Alas, I've succeeded so well at my humouring that Constance has invited me to one of her Tuesday meetings; or perhaps she merely suspects what is doing behind my dainty cough and well-placed hand, and is looking to prove me presumptuous and wrong.

I was certain Father and Mother would suggest that I offer Constance a graceful refusal, but to my surprise they did not. They both feel I should go. Father maintains it is "harmless," and Mother seems intrigued by the idea. And so I accepted, and must make ready to meet the Spirits—but at least it shall be an evening out, and Constance is not such bad company, once she has been allowed to expound at length on her latest pet project.

APRIL 24, 1860

Dear Journal:

Richard has been pulling a long face all day, and is following me about the house like a wounded puppy. He seems to think I'm off on some great adventure this evening. He's mightily perturbed that he cannot join me and even begged Mamee to allow him to be brought along, but for once she's refused to let him have his way. The invitation was to myself alone, she told him, so I am to be permitted to partake of an adult evening without a slippery thirteen-year-old brother underfoot. I am glad of this, although I wonder if Richard's antics won't be missed after a few hours in the company of the Ladies' Circle.

Now I must decide what I shall wear. I have the gray-and-white-checked gingham with violet trim; that might do. I wore it last week during my stroll with Mr. Jeffrey Price (how my hand enjoys forming those letters, and finds flimsy excuses to do so, although only You may know that!) last Friday. He said it set off the "extraordinary" dark of my hair, and turned me this way and that in the light from the windows of the inn. But now he's seen that dress, and as we may pass him in the carriage on the New Parrish post road, I think I'd be wise to choose something else.

I have been walking with Mr. Price only thrice, but feel there can be no mistaking his intentions toward me. There is certainly no mistake about my own intentions, although I would never let him suspect that. He is so *terribly* handsome! I have never seen eyes of such a rich amber, or teeth so white, or lashes so long. Of course, I would not allow myself to be swayed by these considerations alone—Mr. Price is a most eligible bachelor, and a pillar of the community as well. I've heard it grumbled that he is too stiffly conservative for some tastes, and has voiced some objection to our invoking the notion of war prematurely, but his detractors are more than likely jealous, and there can be no doubt as to his prospects. He is returning to Harvard as soon as his voluntary unit can spare him, and will complete his study of medicine. In the meantime, he serves selflessly as a helper to old Dr. Spofford, who can barely sit his horse long enough to ride in from the country for emergencies.

Still, it does not hurt matters that such a fine character comes presented in such a proper package. It is my hope that Mr. Price will ask me to the spring Cotillion, and that we'll be courting by summer; thus I wish to be always at my best when I may have cause to run into him. So—perhaps the indigo silk. It's awfully fancy, but somber and gracious too, and seems appropriate under the circumstances. Besides, my throat looks white against it, and my lips redder, not to mention the effect upon my "extraordinary" mane.

I must make some haste, for Constance will call for me in the carriage at six P.M. sharp—I hope Lucy is not so burdened with Mother's chores that she cannot help me set out the silk. And I must have Cook fix me something small, as I'm unsure of the refreshment the Ladies' Circle will be providing for us. What sort of victuals, after all, best complement an evening of conversation with the Dead?

TUESDAY, 11:30 P.M.

Well, friend, I've so much to report—I'm just returned from the séance, and must recount to you every second of this absurd evening.

Constance came, as expected, at six upon the nose, and I left to the accompaniment of Richard's sniffling. I could only soothe him with assurances that I would give a complete account of whatever transpired upon the morrow.

I had on the blue silk, and two good lace petticoats and my black shawl, and just as an added touch of sobriety I stuck Mother's jet brooch to my bosom. I dearly hoped we'd pass Mr. Price near Front Street, whereupon I'd be able to lean from the carriage and give him at least half the benefit of the outfit, but Constance told me we'd be bypassing the road through town and heading directly into Ithaca. The Medium is presently residing there as the guest of Constance's friend Mrs. Audrey Stanton; it was in her parlor that the séance was to be held.

Constance was upon me the moment I stepped into the carriage, pulling at my ruching and flicking my hair as if I were some prize cow she was conveying to the county fair. I noticed she was also dressed quite finely, and was glad I'd chosen as I did. She was all done up in green bombazine with black trim, her hair (which has more red than mine) pulled into ringlets at the sides of her head. There is no question that Constance is a beauty, and I do see why people say we resemble each other, although I feel the effect is lost when she opens her mouth and those pinched tones escape. "Now Arabella," she began in That Voice, "whatever your misgivings, I hope you will comport yourself as a young lady, and keep in mind that this gathering is of my closest friends, and that Madame Zunia [the Medium] has become a personal friend to me as well." I was tempted to ask her why she'd invited me, if she felt she had to warn me against acting the barbarian, but I held my tongue and simply nodded to everything she said. I was feeling, by this time, a twinge of excitement over the evening to come, and decided I would not give Constance any cause to complain about me. She kept up a continuous patter of "So-and-so said this" and "Madame Zunia said that" all the way to Ithaca, so in fact saying nothing was not a difficult feat for me.

We arrived at the Stanton home around seven. Constance's driver David brought the team and carriage to the stable, and we ladies were shown into the parlor by the maid, Christina. Poor Christina—she is a lively girl, an octoroon, pretty and quick, but it is well known that Mrs. Stanton beats her regularly, along with the household laundress, Colleen; and it's not for any infraction either, but for the way they attract the roving eye of Colonel Stanton, Mrs. Stanton's fat and pompous husband. Mrs. Stanton is the sort of matron that Constance may decline into being or perhaps aspires to be. Though only forty or so, she is huffy and stuffy and dull, quick to laud her own character and to point out the faults in others', but never able to see the similarities between the two. Her husband, the Colonel, is a cheek-tweaker and elbow-pincher, and from the looks of poor Christina and Colleen, probably a good deal more that is unmentionable.

At any rate, Mrs. Stanton greeted us in the parlor, which was beautifully appointed in apple-green and yellows—spring colors, and quite nouveau—and then Constance introduced me to the rest of the Circle. Miss Margaret Kinway was present; she is a spinster, although the reason for this escapes me, as she is kind and pretty, and is known to be quite rich, although not nearly so rich as Father or even Constance's Thomas. Then there was Mrs. Chamberlain, a young woman who, sadly, lost her firstborn daughter during last January's outbreak of influenza, despite valiant attempts to save her. And then Mrs. De Groot, an older lady I've known from my childhood. She used to make Mamee's long social visits to her parlor more pleasant by sending us children to the kitchen for slices of iced cake. I know Mrs. De Groot hasn't had an easy time of late, since her husband enjoys a drink and has embarrassed her thoroughly on more than one occasion.

Constance led me round the room and pushed me forward with a flourish, announcing at every turn, "Look who I've brought, my little cousin, Arabella Leeds"; and although I greeted everyone politely, I was actually busy inspecting the room for hidden wires, or closets holding accomplices, or other signs of the tampering I was sure had occurred prior to our arrival. Tea and tea-sandwiches were soon served, however, so we refreshed ourselves and chatted amiably for some minutes; and then Mrs. Stanton wafted off toward her dining room.

A moment later a hush fell over the guests, as Mrs. Stanton reappeared with a woman dressed entirely in black. I knew this was the Medium, Madame Zunia, and my first thought was that she looked every inch the part she'd chosen to play. She was not tall, but carried herself straight as a rod, so that she appeared imposing. Her black hair was drawn into a heavy bun, and her large dark eyes sat over sharp and prominent cheekbones. She had set her mouth in a faint smile, and carried in her left hand a black fan, such as Oriental ladies might use; this she clutched dramatically to her breast as she stood surveying us and weighing, I suppose, her effect upon us. I must confess that at first I was caught quite short by her regal bearing, but when I saw the way the other ladies fluttered and flew about her I resolved not to do the same, but to keep my eyes keenly open and my wits about me.

Mrs. Stanton presented Madame Zunia to each of us, in turn, and once again Constance hovered behind me, pushing me practically into the Medium's arms. "My cousin, Miss Arabella Leeds," she chirped, and I watched the woman take my measure, as indeed I had decided to take hers. I curtsied quite coolly, and said I was charmed, and then Madame Zunia said, in a strangely accented and musical voice, "It is I who am charmed. I have no doubt you will be a welcome addition to our table." Then Mrs. Stanton drew her away.

The introductions were completed, and Madame Zunia addressed us. "I bid you all follow me into the study, where a table has been arranged for our purposes. You are aware of what we are about to partake in tonight: a communion with the Netherworld of the Spirits, nothing more and nothing less. I shall serve as your guide on this journey, though you will hear the voice of my Spirit ally, who will speak through me. I must ask you to obey all of my instructions exactly, and to pose any questions or requests through me, as the Spirits are extremely sensitive and the door to the Other World a narrow one."

Then we followed Madame Zunia into Mrs. Stanton's study (which, I realized, had been conveniently kept shut during my prior inspection of the parlor). Madame Zunia instructed us to take seats around a large table covered with a dark cloth, pointing out where she desired each of us to be placed. To my surprise she requested that I sit to her right, while Miss Kinway was given the chair to her left. Mrs. De Groot was next to me, then Constance, then Mrs. Stanton, then Mrs. Chamberlain. Once we were assembled, Christina was put to blowing out all the lamps, save two upon the table. Then the little maid exited the room and closed the door behind her, and we were left very nearly in the dark; not a thing was visible past our circled faces, made grotesque by the candles beneath our chins. At once Madame Zunia began to speak.

"Let us all join hands!" she commanded in a sonorous voice, quite different from her previous tone. "Once these fingers touch upon each other, let them be undisturbed until I instruct it, let each one here resolve that they will not let go, whatever sights and sounds may assail them! To break the circle of energy is to invite the most dire consequences, so let any faint of heart leave now before entwining her life force with ours and entreating the Spirits to heed our calls!" She paused a moment, and I waited to see if anyone would flee, but none did. I felt Madame Zunia grasp my hand, and I joined hands with Mrs. De Groot. Then all of us laid our intertwined fingers on the table, where they were to remain until the conclusion of the séance.

All was silent for a moment, and a little shiver crawled up my spine. I felt a rush of air, then Madame Zunia spoke again. "O Spirit Guide!" she whispered. I glanced over and saw that her eyes were closed, her head thrown back and rolling onto her shoulders. "O Spirit Guide," she moaned more loudly, "it is I, Zunia, who calls you from your rest! O hear me, Sakajaweha! Hear me, and come to me! Enter my body, and speak to this gathering with my mouth! Guide us to the doorway of the Shadowy Realm, let our questions be answered and hearts set to rest! Let all from the Beyond who wish discourse come now to this table, to speak through Sakajaweha, and through Zunia!"

The Medium's torso began to sway from side to side; her hand, in mine, clutched tighter round my fingers. She started to wail, her closed lids fluttered, and I could feel poor Mrs. De Groot trembling to my right. I found I could not take my gaze from Madame Zunia (although several of the other ladies had shut their eyes); her wailing and rocking increased, and her chair began to jump beneath her. Just as I thought she was sure to topple it, her movements subsided, and then a great bass voice thundered out of her.

"WHO DISTURBS THE DEAD!"

I felt the other ladies startle, and Constance gave a shriek. Madame Zunia's eyes flew open, her face contorted, and she glared about the room. "I am Sakajaweha, Blackfoot scout and warrior! Who has dared disturb my rest?" We sat trembling, and I was poised to ask why the "warrior" had chosen a lady Indian's name, but Madame Zunia's head now set once more to rolling, and her normal voice reappeared.

"O Indian scout, it is I, Zunia, who seek your guidance. We are gathered here, most humbly, to ask of you the insight of the Spirits. Speak to us now, hear our entreaties!"

The bass rumble returned. "What would you ask of Sakajaweha?" There was a dead silence, til Madame Zunia's voice rasped, "Let any in the circle who have a question pose it now!"

At this poor Mrs. Chamberlain piped up from across the table. "O Spirit," she cheeped, her narrow chin quivering, "I beg of you, tell me—might there be in that realm where you dwell the soul of a child, a little lost girl named Niusia?" I could hear the tears in the woman's voice, and they shone on her cheeks as well. "It's my own daughter, you see, who was taken from me most cruelly just months ago, and who I hear in my dreams, calling and bidding me come to her!"

There was more rocking, and the bass voice replied, "The child you seek is here." Madame Zunia's eyes rolled backward, and then I heard a sound which made my hair lift from my neck. It was a high, thin wail, heartrending and frightening, and seemed to issue from somewhere around Madame Zunia. Then the Medium's mouth moved, and a tiny child's voice called, "Mama! Mama!"

Mrs. Chamberlain gasped and practically leapt from her seat, but the ladies held tightly to her hands. "Niusia! Oh, my baby, my poor lamb, is that you? It's Mama, Mama is here!"

"Oh, Mama," the thin, fine voice went on, "I'm so glad I found you! It's dark here, and cold, and there is evil all about me! Our family was cursed in life, that is why I sickened and died. Now the curse has followed me to the grave, and suspends me in this terrible place. But you can save me, you can lift the curse and speed me to Paradise! Help me, oh, help me!"

"Niusia! How can I help you? Tell me what to do!"

"Come to the parlor of Madame Zunia. Bring to her any precious objects that were mine in life, and then let her advise you from there, as she alone can intercede with the powers of evil that constrain me. No—do not reach for me, Mama—I will kiss you upon the cheek."

For a moment there was silence, and then I heard Mrs. Chamberlain burst out in great sobs. "Oh, I feel it! Your kiss, my angel! My Niusia!" She cried as if her heart would break, for a good two minutes. And partly I felt moved to cry myself, but part of me was wondering what my senses had just witnessed. As far as I could see, everything seemed to be issuing from the mouth of Madame Zunia. Mrs. Chamberlain claimed to have felt a kiss, but I had seen nothing, and felt nothing myself.

I continued to watch as the séance went on, and other questions were asked of the "Spirit Guide." Mrs. Stanton asked the content of her husband's will; Constance sought an appropriate name for her first child. Each time,

Madame Zunia underwent the most dramatic transformations, but nothing occurred which could not be explained in terms of drama. There were indeed none of the elaborate effects which I had been expecting—no banging, or floating heads, or tables lifted from the floor. Yet most of the other ladies seemed completely convinced that they were witnessing a possession by various entities; they also felt kisses or bursts of air when told they would feel them. I found myself wondering if those kisses existed anywhere except in the minds of the recipients, and in the mind of Madame Zunia, who had suggested they should exist. But I sat quietly, with my fingers still in their original position, as Madame Zunia swayed and rocked and spoke in the tones of the Indian, and then alternately, a Frenchwoman, a British soldier, and a Greek philosopher.

And then somewhere along the way, I got an idea. I cannot say where in the world it came from, as I'd never had one quite like it before (although Father has always maintained I am a scamp, or was as a tiny child), but it was a terrible and mischievous idea. Oh, I suppose it was wrong, but it was so much wicked fun I couldn't resist it! Perhaps I was just carried off in the mood of the evening—but no, in honesty I cannot justify myself in that way. The truth is that I felt I'd watched wickedness practiced on Mrs. Chamberlain and others, and I desired the chance to aim it at its rightful targets. If there was drama to be enacted, I wondered if I shouldn't be as good as any at it, and decided that I should be quite good indeed.

So I waited until an appropriate moment, and one came soon enough when Madame Zunia asked, "Is any other Spirit present who wishes discourse?"

I wasted no time. I gave a dramatic gasp, and then I began to roll my head and moan as I'd seen Madame Zunia do. I could feel everyone turning to stare at me, not least of all Madame Zunia, who appeared mightily surprised to see the Spirits choosing another vessel through whom they might speak. I swayed back and forth in my seat, and then I shut my eyes and began to mutter the first pieces of nonsense which entered my head. "Thor and Isolde! Psyche and Cupid!" I raised my voice to an old lady's cackle, then to a young man's bass, amazing even myself with my skill. I settled on a suitably eerie contralto to continue in, and then I addressed the circle. "O Circle, heed me! I am come from the great Beyond!" I could hear Constance sputtering, and then she cried, "Goodness, Arabella, what on earth are you doing!"

I was quite certain that at any moment Madame Zunia would give me a good poke, or a slap, or attempt to startle me and expose my fakery, but to my surprise she shushed Constance and turned to me. "O Spirit, you are one I have not encountered before. Who are you, and to what end have you come to our gathering?"

I thought quickly. "I am Iphiginia, come from Valhalla, across the mists of the ages!" I had no idea whether this made any sense, and dearly hoped none of the ladies paid too close attention to Norse or Grecian legend.

"Pray, continue, Spirit," Madame Zunia encouraged me, and so I did.

"I come with dire warnings," I rumbled. "Heed me, and mend your ways, or the gates of Valhalla shall close upon you forever!" I took a deep breath, and then called, in my finest banshee wail, "Mrs. Stanton! Mrs. Audrey Stanton!"

"I am here!" I heard Mrs. Stanton quaver.

"You who spare not the rod, desist and cease—for who wields the lash in this life shall feel it in the next!" This was nothing more than simple paraphrasing of Jesus' own words, and I hoped He would not mind my borrowing them in this pagan context, since they would be put to good use.

Mrs. Stanton gave a satisfying gasp, and I continued: "Let not the sins of the master be visited upon the servant"—and here I turned to Mrs. De Groot—"nor upon the mistress!" I gave the old lady's hand a friendly squeeze, for I intended to assure her that Iphiginia, at least, did not hold her responsible for her husband's drunken antics.

I was having a goodly amount of fun, and was giddy with the thrill of holding my audience rapt, so I turned my cannon to the next victim, and fired off a volley. "Constance Barry!" I intoned. Constance drew in her breath. "You who know all, know this! Your firstborn son is to be called Michael James—" (This had been Madame Zunia's—or Sakajaweha's—suggestion.) "—but your firstborn daughter shall be Agnes, after the Lamb of God!" I knew this was a name Constance particularly loathed, along with Bertha and Blanche, and I was gratified to note, through my narrowed eyes, her rather confused and disappointed expression.

I would have stopped there, for I had run out of ideas and was ready to let Iphiginia return to the "mists of ages," but then Margaret Kinway spoke, for the first time. "O Spirit!" she addressed me. "Is it possible for me to know—shall I be married in this lifetime, and where now is my future husband, if that man does yet live?"

Well, I was in a pickle here, it seemed, for I had no wish to mislead the poor woman, and of course had no idea of how to answer her. I suppose I could have rolled my eyes and maintained that my trance was finished, but then I thought, "What harm can it do," and so I replied to her with words that simply jumped into my head: "Your true love lies across the sea, and high are the waves you must cross ere you are to find him, but great shall be your happiness at the finding!"

And then Miss Kinway startled all of us by yanking her hands from the circle and clapping with delight: "Oh, I knew it, I knew it!" Whereupon I began my moaning exit, and Madame Zunia cried, "The circle is broken, the Spirits shall now depart! Quickly, call for the lights!" I laid my head upon the table, and Mrs. Stanton rang for Christina, and soon the lamps were restored and the room was abuzz with voices. I continued to lie still until Constance touched my shoulder, and then I sat up brightly, as if nothing had happened.

"Oh, have we stopped, then? I must have fallen asleep! Did the Spirits come?"

"Arabella! Do you mean to say you remember none of it!" I shrugged prettily, and said my good-nights to all the guests, who gazed upon me as if I were a ghost myself, and appeared amazed to find me still solid flesh.

All the way home in the carriage, I maintained this posture, as Constance fell over her own words describing to me the incredible doings and supernatural trance into which I had fallen. I let her go on for some time, but at last I could stand it no longer—my shoulders were shaking with glee, and I knew I should be unable to keep from laughing another moment. So I reprised the moans of Iphiginia, and called to her, "Constance Barry! Name your first daughter Agnes, and the next one Blanche, and the next Bertha!"

Now, I had expected she would take this all in the spirit of fun, as I had meant it, my barbs being mostly for Madame Zunia (whom I believed I had proved an utter fraud, since I was a fraud and yet had been as convincing as she). But to my surprise, Constance was livid with rage. She seemed to think that *she* had been made the butt of my joke, along with all the other ladies present. Try as I might, I could not make her see the humor of what I'd intended, nor could I force her to acknowledge that, if I had deceived her, and therefore humiliated her, then so too had Madame Zunia, who ought to be held at least as culpable.

Constance raged at me that I am an ingrate and a scoundrel, and that I have toyed with her one too many times, and then she fell to crying, and told me she shall never forgive me. Upon reaching our driveway she booted me from the carriage without even a "good night," and drove off still sobbing.

And so here I am, in my own bed at last, and not quite sure how I should feel; for I believe I had a good joke and exposed a faker to boot, and intended harm to no one. But I am truly sorry that Constance feels otherwise, and it pains me to think she believes I intended malice toward her, and is so thoroughly angry with me. I am very tired now, and believe I will go to sleep, and hope that Constance awakens with a new view of the night's proceedings.

APRIL 25, 1860

I need not have fooled myself that a good night's sleep would soothe Constance's temper any.

I was barely awake at nine this morning when I heard a frightful commotion in the driveway, and looked out of my window to see the Barrys' rig drawing away. Then Lucy came to fetch me, and told me Mother wished to speak to me at once.

Constance, it seemed, had rushed over to spill the entire tale, and then stormed from the house without even giving me leave to defend myself. Mother was quite distressed and wrung her hands a bit, but Richard seemed to think the whole thing quite funny, and circled round me making ghostly sounds and flapping his arms until he was shushed.

I thought I might explain myself, but to my chagrin Mother called Father in, and repeated a shortened version of Constance's story.

"Well, Sauce, what have you got into now?" Father asked, with a look he reserves for those times when he feels I've been cheeky or mischievous. I recounted what, to my way of thinking, had actually happened, including my own opinion that Constance was again building mountains of molehills, and that I had meant no harm. I thought that Father might chuckle over the incident and then forget it, but that was not to be—far from it. He shook his head and told me it was clear that there were some amends to be made, since I had acted quite abominably.

I confess I grew upset at this. What of Madame Zunia, I asked, what of her amends? In vain, I tried to describe her imitation of little Niusia Chamberlain, and my anger at the cruel way she had deceived the poor child's mother. Yes, I had used deception myself, but I admitted as much, and had done so only to expose the truth, which Father had always maintained was the most important aspect of any situation.

But Father shrugged and said that ladies often enter these diversions expecting to be tweaked if not outrightly hoodwinked, that fancy is the province of the female gender while the search for absolute truth is better left to science and therefore to gentlemen, and that I mustn't take things so literally.

Dear friend, I could scarcely believe I was hearing this, and even now I puzzle over the meaning of it. For it seemed not like my father at all, that father who taught me French and Latin at his knee and insisted I learn with as much intent and seriousness as any "gentleman."

But that was not to be the end of my humiliation—for then Father announced that by way of amends I should present myself to Madame Zunia to confess my little trick to her and formally apologize. And then I must go to the Barrys', to apologize to Constance, and hope that things might be set right.

I was aghast at this—at the notion of apologizing to that charlatan—but Father said, "It is your lack of manners for which you are apologizing, not for your opinion of this Zunia creature. Whatever your degree of disbelief in her, it is no excuse for bad manners. You insulted her, and more so Constance who brought you there, and also your hostess, Mrs. Stanton."

Then—oh, horrors—it dawned upon me that I might also have to confess to Mrs. Stanton, and acknowledge that "Iphiginia's" reprimand was in fact my own, that all of the "supernatural" insight I'd directed at the ladies was in fact based on the gossip and glimpses I'd formed my opinions from.

I implored Father not to make me go through with this, but he said sternly that here was his advice to me, that I was an almost-grown young lady but if I wished to be treated as one then I had better act the part.

So now I am stuck, dear companion, and am dreading the morrow, for that is when I must abase myself before that awful gypsy; and you have no idea how I wish I could truly raise the spirits and convince them to erase my prank from the annals of memory.

APRIL 26, 1860

Dear Journal:

I have just returned from Ithaca, having had the oddest experience, as if the travails of the last two days were not odd enough.

I rode to the Stantons' (upon my own beloved RainShadow, as I had no desire to be driven) to carry out Father's instructions to me. Luckily the Stantons were not at home, but Christina (whom I inspected for fresh bruises and gratifyingly found to have none) fetched Madame Zunia for me.

What can I say of this interview except that I feel I have fixed nothing, and am more perplexed than ever? I confessed to Madame Zunia that I had simply a bit of the actress in me and had conjured up my "trance" from imagination, and wished to apologize to her. But instead of accepting me at my word, she made this strange reply: "That is often the way it is when the Spirits choose to make themselves known to us, child—we are at pains to deny it, and to pass it off as imagination or a slip of the tongue."

I thought that perhaps she had misunderstood me, and so I repeated that I had without question made up all of what I'd uttered, and only wished to be forgiven and have the incident off my conscience.

To which she said, "I must ask you a question, my dear. From where do you suppose the idea came into your head to indulge in what you call 'acting'?" I told her I did not know, it was just a fancy which had overtaken me. "Just so," she said. "And what are these sudden fancies, which have never been manifested before, if not perhaps inspirations from another plane of being?"

Well, my companion, it was clear enough to me what she was suggesting, although *why* was entirely beyond me. I was in a quandary, for Madame Zunia went on: "I have every faith, my dear, that regardless of your wish to deny it now, your possession the other night was a real one, and I went so far as to express that conviction to the ladies after your departure." She smiled at me. "The advice of your Iphiginia was quite sage. Miss Kinway, for instance, was delighted with it, as she has a gentleman overseas and had been debating whether or not to break off her correspondence with him."

I was quite shocked at this, and sputtered that Miss Kinway must not make such a drastic decision based on some folly of mine, whereupon Madame Zunia said, "But you see, she could have made of your words whatever she wished, and was free to discard them, so it is no fault of yours if she did not. Rather, you brought her great joy, and I wonder what else your Spirit might care to tell us if we decide to contact her again."

I find that I hardly know what to think myself, now I am returned home. I keep turning it over and over in my mind, reenacting that moment when I decided to make my little show, and now I am quite at odds with myself, and wonder from where the idea did come, although I would swear it was mine alone. And I am fretting over what I shall tell Mother and Father, and what of my apology to Constance? But I see you have no answers for me, dear Friend, as you are quite a perfect listener, but not one for advice.

APRIL 27, 1860

I did not sleep well last night, as you might imagine. I tossed and turned, and awoke to find my pillow on the floor, where I assume I—or was it Iphiginia?—threw it sometime during the evening. I snapped at Richard at breakfast, and would tell Mother and Father nothing except that I did as I'd been bidden, and spoke to Madame Zunia yesterday. Father insists that I ride to the Barrys' today, and so I shall. I am clearer in my mind this morning, at any rate; I am quite sure that no Spirit has possessed me, whatever the gypsy chooses to believe, and I intend to make a clean breast of it with Constance and bury the whole matter once and for all.

FRIDAY EVENING

I never did ride to Constance's house today. I didn't have to, for shortly after noon she appeared at the door and asked to see me. I wondered what she could want of me, and didn't have long to wait for an answer, for no sooner were we seated in the parlor than Constance apologized to me for her rage of the other evening. I was too surprised to reply to this, so Constance plunged on, telling me Miss Kinway had called upon her yesterday and explained exactly what Madame Zunia had said to me: that the first encounter with the Spirits is usually a strange one, and the Medium may not know what to make of it herself, and may choose to laugh it off or deny its power. But it was plain to Madame Zunia—and she is an expert—that I am the real article, and so should be encouraged to pursue my gift for communicating with the Beyond.

I did not know then whether to laugh or tear my hair, since I felt I was foresworn whatever answer I chose to make. If I agreed with Madame Zunia, it would be under the falsest of pretenses, but if I disavowed her I would be compounding the original insult—and moreover, I got the sense that Constance did not want my disavowal, that this lie was much more credible to her than the truth, and that, whatever protest I made, I would not be believed. And so I was right too: I repeated once again that I had merely made a joke, and that I was sorry, and Constance said, "Poor thing, of course you are," as if I were a madwoman who didn't know her own mind.

APRIL 28, 1860

Dear Journal:

It is now apparent why Madame Zunia had taken such pains to defend me before the Ladies' Circle. Father arrived home this evening from a trip into town, and he carried with him a flyer which had been handed to him by a young boy paid to distribute them near the Town Meeting Hall. There upon the cover was an etching of Madame Zunia herself, and several quotes attesting to the "High Purpose of This Enlightened Spiritualist and Medium." And on the inside, beneath the title, "An Account of the Séance of Tuesday, April 24, Whereupon Communication With the Departed Was Established," there was a full description of the possession of Miss Arabella Leeds, a New Parrish girl of "spotless" virtue and Christian sentiment, and certainly a genuine conveyor of messages from the Beyond, as the Ladies' Circle in attendance will confirm.

The humiliation of it! I hoped that Father would advise me as to what I should do, but instead he asked me, "What happened, Arabella? What is meant by this?" I cried, and told him of my meeting with Madame Zunia, and with Constance, and asked him how in the world I should proceed. He said he would go over and wring the gypsy's neck himself. But Mother stopped him and said he should think about this, for he himself had advised me not to be so concerned with absolutes, and which was certain to hurt my reputation more—to acknowledge this claim, or deny it and admit that I took all of these prominent ladies for fools? I thanked Mother for her wish to spare me, but told her I wanted nothing more to do with this business, and would deny it at every turn. And so I shall, for I am determined to be honest, and will never, ever attempt such a foolish prank again.

APRIL 29, 1860

Oh, Friend, I am lost!

Today I met with Mr. Price in the street, and instead of hastening to walk next to me as he has of late, he brushed by without a word. I tried to convince myself that perhaps he was merely distracted, or rushing toward some medical emergency, but I fear I delude myself.

I cannot be certain of it, but I suspect some news has reached him of which he disapproves, for what else could account for such extraordinary behavior? Of all of my beaux, I had regarded Mr. Price as the most serious contender for my affections, and was thinking perhaps Mother has been right in her advice that I mustn't wait too long; for, as she says, a new crop of flowers blooms every spring, and a young man may forget last summer's fading blossom. But now it seems my chance is lost, and over something beyond my control, namely some whispered word of which I am unaware.

As if this were not enough, I was seating myself in church this morning when I heard, from behind me, a distinct hiss. I could not imagine what it was, and when I turned to look, elderly Mrs. Rowe, that harpy, did it again, all the while staring me right in the face. I was hissed in church! And by a neighbor who has known me all my life! I wanted to duck my head and run, but then I thought, of what am I ashamed? And so I looked right back at the woman, and seated myself, and sat as straight as ever.

Then as I was leaving I heard the crone's voice behind me: "Bound for the Devil she is, yet she prances into services just the same!" I turned round and stared hard at her again, but I am stung and wonder why me and not Constance—but then, Constance did not speak, her name is not on the inside of a flyer, and mine is. It is one thing to observe the Spirits, and another to maintain they speak through you; one is a harmless diversion and the other the work of the Devil.

As if to confirm that my soul is in some mortal danger, Reverend Gore stopped us in the church drive and asked Mother if he may call upon us this week. He barely looked at me, but I cannot help but feel I am the focus of his attentions, for he has never suggested such a thing before. We are a Christian family, but not an excessively pious one, and the Reverend's visits to our home have been entirely social, during Christmas balls and the like. Father went absolutely white-faced, and seems disgusted with this whole turn of events. But Mother allowed as that would be lovely, and would Friday be all right? So now there is that to dread, and Heaven knows what sort of lecture I may receive. And I was forced to ride all the way home with Richard hissing in my ear, and desisting just in time to be undetected by Father, who kept turning in his seat and scowling at us.

MAY 1, 1860

I have been loath to leave the house for fear of more hissings and snubbings, and thought it best to simply remain out of sight until this whole matter is forgotten. But now the latest wrinkle in this horror presents itself, as the mountain has come to Mohammed.

There was a knock upon the door this afternoon, and when Lucy opened it there stood the Fitches' cook, Bridget Harrod, and her daughter Aileen, a girl of fourteen or so. Lucy called my mother, but they maintained that it was I they wished to see, and implored Mother to summon me. So tearful was Bridget that Mother relented, and when I came down I was mystified to see who my callers were. I have barely exchanged a word with this pair and know them only from my calls to Judge Fitch's home, where Mrs. Fitch, who is a warm and cheery soul, presented them as if introducing her own relations. We made to sit in the parlor, Mother and I and the visitors, but then Bridget asked, in the most halting way, if they might not speak to me alone. Mother very reluctantly excused herself, and I asked Bridget what in the world she had to discuss with me.

Well, Friend, the unbelievable upshot of all this—which I came to only after a good ten minutes of roundabout evasions and euphemism—is that young Aileen was compromised against her will by some scoundrel. (I blush even as I write this, for I can scarce believe I am recounting such events on paper—I would surely be judged both worldly and shameless if these pages came to light.) She was struck ill sometime back with the same influenza which took the life of poor little Niusia Chamberlain, and while delirious in its grip was attacked in her very own bed, on the ground-floor servants' quarters of the Fitch home. She claims not to have recognized the man; she said nothing for days and would likely have kept her silence forever, but for her fear that Nature would take its course with her. Her mother Bridget suspects she's indeed in a family way—and wanted me to confirm it, and reveal the debaucher, by contacting the Spirits! The elder Harrod went on and on about my "divine gift"—quite the opposite of Mrs. Rowe—and told me that the community is abuzz with the news that I am some sort of saint. I could hardly speak for my astonishment, but when I did, I told her that she had been the victim of a terrible misunderstanding, and that I have no powers in this regard at all.

Poor Aileen (who had been most evasive and reluctant all along) now began to cry, and Bridget implored me please not to turn them away because they were not fine people such as I was accustomed to. But I insisted that this had nothing to do with it, and that they should go to Mrs. Fitch and explain all, as she is an open-minded person and would surely not turn them out. Whereupon Aileen gasped and fled the parlor and the front door, and Bridget followed, calling her and almost knocking Lucy over in her haste.

And then Mother rushed in, and Father, and when I told them what had happened, Father said that this is the final straw. He shouted that he will not have me ruined, exposed to such base and coarse goings-on, whatever the motive. He intends to send his solicitor to Mrs. Stanton's this very day to force Madame Zunia to retract her statements and cease her advertisements at my expense.

Oh, will there never be an end to this!

MAY 2, 1860

Well, I can be certain now that Mr. Price's behavior of the other day was no accident, as I was snubbed in the street again today. But I feel, besides the mortification, a cold anger coming over me. Whatever has caused his change of heart—and I'm sure it's to do with the Medium, and the vague whiff of impropriety which has attached itself to me—I know he did not bother to approach me and discuss it, or give me the benefit of the doubt by remaining friendly. And I find that his behavior infuriates me, and makes me question what superficial fancy drove him to court me in the first place, since it can be so easily dispelled by all this foolishness. If it was only my "extraordinary" hair which attracted his gaze, and no spark of my personality, then the Devil take him; I will cut off a few locks and mail them to him, and he may do with them what he will. Who is he to sit in judgment of me, if his character is so weak that his affections cannot withstand the slightest breath of air?

MAY 3, 1860

I was forced to leave the house upon some errands today, and find I cannot go anywhere without being either jeered or importuned; nor is there any predicting who will do which. A Negro butler crossed himself at me in the market, while at the tailor's the very proper Housemans accosted me, to say they would be delighted to sponsor a "reading" if at some point I wished to hold one.

But most disturbing to me were the women—large-eyed, furtive, rich and poor alike—who clutched at me on virtually every corner, whispering: "Miss Leeds, Miss Leeds, please, just a moment—" Or tried to press into my hand a note or invitation, while I repeated, again and again, that this is all a great mistake. I cannot forget their faces, and I wonder what misery has overtaken them, and how it is they have no one better than myself to turn to. I think of Christina's blackened eyes, and of Mrs. Stanton, who turns her shame upon her maid but dares not chastise her husband, and of how I made light of this, and believed I should solve it through some clever trickery. And what of Aileen Harrod, why should she fear her mistress's counsel and creep to my door like a leper, while her debaucher skips about without a care?

Worst of all is the disregard everywhere for the truth of this matter, for I am damned or exalted despite anything I say. Neither side is willing to accept my retraction; they close their ears when I tell them I am a fraud, and I can only imagine what hysteria I would set loose if I said I was not. My friend, it seems there is no one I can turn to for counsel, for in all times past I conferred with Mother and Father, and accepted their advice as Law. But now Mother seems completely at a loss, and what can I make of Father's construction of the truth—for he was, at first, more angered by my lack of manners than by the deceit which precipitated it.

I fear my moorings shall be completely loosed; but tomorrow I meet with Reverend Gore, and it is my hope that God's servant can offer me some comfort, and point the way back to the path.

MAY 4, 1860

Reverend Gore arrived at his appointed time today, and, as I suspected, it was indeed myself he was interested in speaking to. He took tea with my parents in the dining room, but when he had finished we proceeded to the parlor, where he shut the door behind us.

He sat down across from me on the settee, put on his kindest face, and grasped my hand. So I was not to receive a lecture, for which I was heartily grateful, although the prospect of it bothered me less than it had last Sunday. I was expecting, then, that he would advise me on the church's view of Spiritualism, and that I would be able to unburden myself to him and be put back on the straight path, and leaned eagerly in to hear his words.

And so he began speaking, but I discovered that the content was quite different from what I had anticipated. For while he made some gestures toward the state of my salvation, it soon dawned on me that what concerned the Reverend most was not the repercussions of my actions upon me, but how they would affect *him*—specifically, how the church would be affected in terms of revenue if I embarrassed him by making a spectacle of myself. He would be held responsible for my misdeeds, and his parishioners would question his ability to lead the flock; my parents would also be disappointed in him, and there might be an end to my father's hefty contributions, and those lovely soirees in the ballroom and upon our lawns.

He did not use these words exactly, but might as well have, as his meaning was clear; and he wrapped it all up with a ribbon by suggesting that I consult with him before indulging in any more follies, and that it would be wise for me to be more visible in church activities and to keep my distance from any whiff of the unusual, at least until this all died down.

He spoke at some length, and as I began to comprehend him I found my attention drawn quite away from his speech. I realized I had never observed him so closely before, and I found my eye singling out the particulars of his face, and his body movements. The pores on his nose appeared to me as craters, and the nose itself bulbous and laced with fine veins; his mouth, ceaselessly moving, was flecked with spittle at the corners, and his jowls flapped as he exhaled. I felt I was seeing, as if through a microscope, his very mortality, the frailty of his flesh, and then it occurred to me that whatever he was saying, it was a product of that flesh, of the mortal mind within it. And as I watched his hands moving about, and his eyes rolling heavenward now and then, I thought of the many times I had seen these gestures from the pulpit; I was reminded of something, and then realized with a shock that he evoked to me nothing so much as Madame Zunia, with her rehearsed theatrics and her claims of inspiration from beyond.

And what a frightening shadow, then, was cast upon the world, in the wake of this observation!

For what within that world now shall remain beyond scrutiny?

My thoughts race along, and down their inevitable path they draw me, but oh, how I wish I could stop them. For they have snatched from me a hemisphere of certainty, and placed me, far and alone, outside the safety of its confines.

MAY 7, 1860

Nobody has called on me over the last few days, for which I am grateful. Mother brings me news of the town's doings, chattering on at length, but I am not of a mind just now to care one way or another. She informed me this evening that Madame Zunia is abandoning New Parrish to resume her travels about the state. She also told me that Mrs. Fitch has discovered her maid's situation and has (as predicted) taken the girl under her wing to protect her from vicious gossip. And the Reverend has been asking for me—he seems to think he has brought about some great change in the set of my moral compass, and has congratulated himself quite freely before other members of the congregation.

I can only shake my head at these doings; my situation has moved beyond their power to affect it. I am quite taken up with my own concerns, and happy to retreat behind the front door.

MAY 8, 1860

My Dear Friend:

Blackest of days—I do not wish to write of it—but to be still is worse—only to you can I recount this. I will try.

I awakened today to find myself in the grip of some malaise which made me crawl within my own skin. I could not sit still, and yet when I rose and paced about the house, I was provided with no comfort. At length I realized I must have some sort of action, and so I embarked upon a harmless walk. ~~whereupon I discovered Mr. Price emerging~~

Oh, Arabella, stop that driveling fabricating this instant! This is not the truth, not precisely, and you know it well enough. If I start upon such a course as lying to myself there will be no end to it, no peaceful repose even within my own head.

So let me begin again. The truth, only friend, is that I did indeed awake in a foul mood, but the action I decided upon was quite a deliberate one. I have come to know the habits of Mr. Jeffrey Price rather well, you see, and so I set out today with the express intent of arranging an "accidental" meeting between us.

Why did I set myself upon such a mission? What did I hope to achieve? As with other moments over the past fortnight, I must reply that I do not know. I think I truly believed that, after the debacle which was my meeting with the Reverend, there was some principle to be put to the test in confronting Mr. Price, that my mind would be eased in the testing, and those ends which had been set to dangling either severed or bound. And so I finished breakfast early this morning, and packed my green velvet drawstring bag with some calling cards (to justify my trip, should needs be). I then walked the entire distance to Front Street, until I reached the spot where the Price town house stands, just between the Fitches' and the Rowes' own dwellings.

I know Mr. Price goes each weekday morning to the apothecary, where he is delivered of the daily newspaper and the medications his father uses. I determined to wait until I saw him leave upon his errands, and made myself fairly inconspicuous in a bit of shrubbery across the lane. My patience was rewarded, for as surely as the clock strikes, Mr. Price left his house at a quarter after nine or so, and turned left down the street on his merry way. Whereupon I vacated my hiding place and hurried round the corner in the opposite direction, so that we arrived at the intersection of Chestnut Street at exactly the same moment.

What can I say of that first glimpse of Mr. Price, except that my heart was pounding, and my fingers twitching, as I watched him approach? The sun was behind his shoulder, nearly blinding me; I almost turned and ran, but my own will would not allow it. I had come too great a distance to scurry away without accomplishing what I'd set out to do. And so as we came only a few feet or so apart, I said to him in the clearest voice I could muster: "Mr. Price! I should like to have a moment of your time, if you will."

"Miss Leeds." He drew up, inclined his head, his voice cold. "You must excuse me, I have errands to run and am rather in a hurry."

"Then I will walk with you," I said, and of course there was no gracious response he could make to this. We fell into step beside each other, although it was obvious to me that he wished himself away, and was determined barely to acknowledge my presence. At length he asked, in the most aggrieved tone possible, "Well, then, what is it you'll have of me, Miss?"

"Mr. Price," I began, "you'll excuse my being so forward, and suggesting such a lapse in propriety. But it would appear, though, I beg you, correct me if I am wrong, that you are avoiding me."

"I shall indeed correct you. I've no conscious wish to avoid you. I am a busy man, I've affairs of my own to tend to, and if this constitutes avoidance, then I must tell you that this is your own mistaken impression and no concern of mine."

"I see," I replied calmly. "I meant no insult to you. It is odd though, that just a few weeks ago you hastened to walk with me, yet recently you have turned away when we came upon each other, and proceeded to act as if I were a total stranger to you, which, by the way, you are doing even as we speak."

He surprised me by halting, in the middle of the walkway, and turning directly upon me. "If I were of a mind to avoid you, Miss, it is this—exactly this—which I would seek to spare myself. And how amazing that you cannot see it, that you persist in it even as you'd have some apology from me."

I could not make out his meaning, and so I countered, "In what, sir? In what do I persist?"

"In this coy attitude of cleverness you adopt, which nonetheless cannot camouflage a most unladylike assertion of will."

I had resolved to remain cool, but Mr. Price had rendered himself a good degree colder, and I felt my composure crumbling. "I hardly think it fitting that you scrutinize my manners, sir, when it is you who have ill-used me."

"How have I ill-used you, Arabella? Tell me that."

"I thought that we were friends, at least, and beyond that you sought to engage my affections—"

"And now I've chosen to disengage them. I owe you no explanation, I made you no promises, no formal declaration—"

"Indeed!" I heard my voice rising of its own accord. "Am I a lawyer, sir, come to sue for breach of contract, so that you lecture me about formalities and promises? What insult! I am a woman, and I shall ask for due consideration as one. Does our previous friendship count for nothing? Am I not entitled to know why you had this change of heart toward me?"

At this Mr. Price abruptly grabbed my arm. The gesture so surprised me that I could not make a response to it, and before I could protest he had yanked me from the sidewalk. "I'll not be forced to stand here in the street bawling like a common fishmonger," he hissed in my ear. He pulled me onto the green, toward the little vine-covered gazebo at its center. When we reached its relative seclusion, I drew myself away, my silk boots sinking in the mud.

"It was this business with Mrs. Stanton's Medium which caused the change in you, was it not," I asked, barely containing myself.

"I owe you nothing, no explanation, and I won't be entrapped, understand that," he snapped.

"You needn't worry," I replied, wishing I'd never begun the discussion. "I expect no resumption of our previous association. I wish only to know why you abandoned me, without even seeking out the truth of the matter."

"And what great truth would that be, of which you believe me ignorant?"

"Why," said I, "the truth of what transpired with the Medium. I assumed—I assumed you saw that horrid flyer, I assume you've heard these spurious rumors the gypsy concocted."

When he replied, his tone had gone still colder. "What I heard, Arabella, was that you appeared to undergo some sort of trance at the gypsy's séance, of which she took the fullest advantage in order to enhance her credibility with her featherheaded supporters. Whereupon you insisted that you had merely played a practical joke, which your cousin Mrs. Barry, among others, is loath to believe. That is the truth, as far as I know it. What points might you wish to correct me upon?"

I was caught short, puzzled. "You know I intended the trance as a joke?"

"I do."

"Then you do not believe me possessed, or think me to be in league with Madame Zunia?"

"Certainly not. I'm a man of science, after all."

"But—but if you know those things, then why did you withdraw from me?"

"Because you set out to deceive me."

I could not keep my mouth from gaping open. For of all the things he might have chosen to say, this was the very last I expected. "I—what?" I sputtered. "I *set out to deceive* you? How? In what manner?"

His brows seemed to draw together, and his face colored as he spoke. "I believed you right-minded, Arabella, your concerns befitting a young girl of your station. You conspired to present yourself thus. I believed you one thing, and then you revealed yourself to be quite another."

"But what can you mean—I merely engaged in a joke, a bit of humor which you yourself—"

"The circumstances of your 'joke,' as you call it, have nothing to do with it. Can you not see that? No, of course you can't, and that is precisely where the trouble lies. Perhaps I'm wrong in branding it a deception. It is more the revelation of a flawed character, in which case I'd do better to be disappointed than angry. If you were a child, then such a turn of mind might be acceptable, but you are long past childhood. You are on the verge of becoming a lady, at what point will it occur to you to start acting like one?"

I could not answer his question. I was able only to stare at him, my mouth still in the same astonished position, and so he continued on, stepping forward to face me directly.

"Do you think this is the sort of behavior with which any sane man would associate himself? You brought yourself into the public eye, evinced a disregard for simple decorum—you made quite a display of your cleverness, didn't you, shaming your neighbors so that you might look their smug superior—"

"But the Medium is a fraud—"

"It does not matter. She could be the Blessed Mother for all I care. What matters is this idea you have got of yourself, as if you'd be some defender of morality, possessed of the wherewithal to unmask her—a philosopher, a theologist, instead of a schoolchild whose mind should be upon the spheres for which she was designed—"

"You're angry because I had an *idea*?"

"Who are you to be conjuring them? Who will next demand serious consideration of her ideas—that little yellow wench of the Stantons' you defended? Or the Fitches' Irish baggage, who so revere you that they visit you in your home? What, did you think I hadn't heard about all that? Did you give a single, solitary thought as to how preposterous it is, your speaking on behalf of these lax-moraled serving girls whose misdeeds earn them their just deserts—better you learn the blessed art of keeping a civil tongue in your head—"

He was shouting, and then all at once he stopped, and leaned panting with his back to me upon the latticed siding of the gazebo. When he turned, his face was a doughy greenish-white against his shirt. "Even now," he said, from between clenched teeth, "you manage to force me into a temper." I had not moved or spoken, and on that basis I might have challenged this last assertion—except that I could not move or speak.

He straightened his collar—it had flown almost entirely round, I recall—never removing his eyes from me.

"You'll not have your way. There is still order, and I am bound and sworn to uphold it. There is no room at its top for you. And your own character will bar you from its midreaches." He raised his chin, and his gaze seemed to widen, passing over me with neither empathy nor recognition. "Perhaps you'll fall a little farther, though," he said. "And there would yet be a basis for seeking your companionship."

I stood as if the ground had grown over my feet. Some obstruction in my throat blocked both breath and speech, and my dry eyes seemed robbed of the relief of tears. His words were beyond comprehension or response. But then the meaning of the last became clear, and a feeling utterly alien rose within me, to possess me more surely than any strange Spirit might.

My urge was to do violence to him—it was such a pure, clear command, rising like a howl from somewhere other than mind—and I could not resist it, nor fail to realize that I ought, and in that moment of struggle my arm seemed to rise of its own accord. The velvet bag containing my snood and calling cards flew on the end of its silken wrist-loop to strike him again and yet again squarely in the face. My hand lost its grip on the cord, and the bag spilled open, the cards within spraying forth like so much confetti; my feet found their purpose restored, and in horror at my own self as much as at him I turned and began to run.

Immediately he gave chase. I could hear him behind me, shouting my name, and imagined I could feel his fingers at the very ends of my unfastened hair. But I continued on, resolved that I would drop rather than turn, although my breath was ragged and my stays cutting into the flesh above my ribs. I ran from the green to the end of Chestnut Street, and even then I did not stop, although I no longer sensed him behind me. I ran past the Meeting House, past the square where the three churches stand. I ran out onto the post road, where the houses rose up and died away behind me as I went by them—the Reverend's, the Housemans'—all familiar, all foreign, places which could offer me no comfort.

I ran until the entrance of our driveway appeared, and then I stopped, and turned into the grass. And there I disgorged the entire repast I had eaten only hours ago. And I thought I was finished, until I saw rushing before my eyes the picture of my own hand and the velvet bag leaving it; and then it struck me how wrong I had been, that there are ghosts, and truly I had seen two, the man I thought I knew and my own self. And then my insides heaved again, and the ground flew at me, and for a few moments I knew no more.

I scarcely recall my return to the house. I remember only that my boot had lost a heel, and so I limped up the steps, and Lucy glimpsed me there and screamed. I begged her to stop and ask me nothing, but deliver me to my bed, where I lie writing now, and from where I intend to move never again.

MAY 9, 1860

Over and over I recall the events from yesterday morning to this one. I cannot help it. They leap at me unbidden, like the stream of images moving past the window of a carriage. The days before them seem irretrievable. As indeed each day has seemed since the one on which I confronted the cursed Medium.

But even as I wish for oblivion I am interrupted. There are constant footfalls upon the hallway carpet outside—Richard and my parents glide past my door, whispering and tiptoeing, as if I've manifested some sort of deathly illness.

Perhaps I have.

MAY 10, 1860

This morning the Prices' stableboy arrived with a package addressed to me. It was the green velvet bag, wrapped in tissue paper. Inside there was a note.

These are difficult times which weigh upon me. I spoke my mind too freely. With regret, JLP

Mother delivered the package to me. She asked me again if I would explain what happened, but I refused. "Never mind," she said. "I understand. My poor lamb, how awful to have this burden descend on the heels of everything else." It was plain from her demeanor that she believes I've suffered a broken heart. I have no wish to correct her; it's easier to allow her this than to examine the true nature of all I believe to be broken.

He regrets. Not his actions or his thoughts, but only his inexplicable words, which were spoken too freely.

MAY 12, 1860

I am told that I must eat something or I shall soon waste away. Nothing would please me more.

MAY 15, 1860

How did I know him really, except for the exchanges we had as he accompanied me about the streets on our informal walks? He was courtly upon those occasions, but what reason had he not to be? Why did he aim such an outburst at me? What of him did I ignore, so that it would not interfere with my arrangements?

Had none of this happened, I should never have known what else existed within him. But then, had none of this happened, had I not provoked it, perhaps it should never have had cause to exist.

MAY 16, 1860

Father summoned Dr. Spofford today. He came with his unguents and ointments, his vicious and steely instruments, which he displayed like an old soldier arraying his weapons before battle. He blustered about my bed, poking and prodding me, muttering "hmmmm" and "yes, yes" at every turn.

I did not speak a word to him, and he seemed to have little desire to speak any to me. Instead, when he was finished, he consulted with Father and Mother in the hall. He did not bother to shut the door—perhaps he believes me beyond the reach of human speech—and so I overheard him explaining that I am in the grips of some hysteria, of the sort which regularly fells those of my age and sex, and must be left alone to resolve it, but not for an excessive amount of time. He assured my parents that my condition is not due to influenza or pox or any other airborne ailment, and then advised them that in the event of an emergency they should consult young Mr. Price, who resides in town and has been so helpful and who could ride here in half the time that he himself would take. And I felt the blood freeze in my very veins, until I heard Mother hastily assure him that she was certain this wouldn't prove necessary, but that if such a crisis occurred, they would carry me themselves to Dr. Spofford's doorstep.

MAY 18, 1860

I am uneasy—my thoughts race and I must hold on to them but cannot—the bed feels hard as winter ground. What is it that makes me thrash about so—it is surely him—but more—or everything, beginning with the night of the Spirits, and ending here.

MAY 22, 1860

i am so cold and hot what did i think what is it i forgot ignored failed to see it ran across my mind the day of the doctor the doctor at my bed occurs intrudes but i lose it

MAY 23, 1860

to write helps me to grasp it

doctors leaning over me and I so small where do doctors go to visit me in my bed in the sickroom where no one else can be when one cannot attend another must

when the old one cannot go the young one goes

to the beds of the neighbors with influenza the great and the small the ladies

and the judges and their servants too

the servant girls

serving girls he called them

the lax-moraled ones falling

to the ground floor
to writhe in fever dreams unspeaking
who else could it have been where no one else can go but he has business there it cannot be it surely cannot be my vicious mind spews vicious thoughts

MAY 24, 1860

~~it is only ideas bred of fever surely i should have some water~~

MAY 27, 1860

today Mother and Cook fixed me a bowl of lentil soup. it used to be my favorite. it sits in my stomach like lead.

MAY 29, 1860

I am awake now. I believe my fever has broken. I sat up upon the pillows today, ate a biscuit, and drank a pot of tea to the bottom. Such dark dreams I entertained in my delirium! Surely the light of day shall chase their shadow away, reveal all as it was, as I believed it to be.

MAY 31, 1860

It's very simple. Either I shall rise or I shall not. One way or the other life must go on: the bedsheets must be changed eventually. I believe I'll give Lucy a chance at them today; I'll descend to the parlor, where I'll be out of her way. At least there I can rest on the settee, should that become necessary.

JUNE 1, 1860

The better part of this rainy day was spent haunting the library.

I am certain I feel the stirrings of my strength returning and so I hastened here, to that realm of the philosophers and pedants, whose wisdom pushes errant thoughts from the mind and cleanses the spirit. Thus surrounded, I waited to be restored and delivered, disabused of the remnant nightmares of fever.

It has not happened.

The chant born of my delirium runs yet through my head. It has not fled with the clear light of day. I try to distract myself with needlepoint, with simple mending, but I cannot. I find myself marking time with it as I stitch; occasionally I realize I've been speaking it aloud.

It cannot be it cannot be it cannot be. All which was sensible rendered senseless.

And yet, if it were to be, would there not be newly explained so much which I found inexplicable?

JUNE 3, 1860

Now I understand his ire: it was his fear of what he thought I already knew, of what he believed I had been told. But at that point I'd suspected nothing. There were no pieces for me to reconstruct. He must have realized that later on, and so the apology, the note in the bag.

Why am I so cursed? Why is it given to me to conjecture, unravel, unmask? Would that I could forfeit the ability—or find ample reason to reject my conclusions.

But these last have withstood my scrutiny. Though born of fever and no doubt flawed, they are built of fact, and so endure. If I turn from them now, I turn from myself, and the evidence of my own mind; and I turn not because I believe myself incorrect, but because I wish not to see what I know to be true.

Such a turn I shall not—cannot—make.

JUNE 4, 1860

What should I do, what should I do? Around the question goes, but it reaches, always, this maddening end: there is nothing to be done. Or nothing I can do, which is not to say that some solution is not eluding me, dancing just beyond my present grasp.

There is no proof, only what I've drawn together, and in the absence of evidence, none would believe it. Surely Aileen assumed the same, and so it was that she sat upon our parlor couch with her lips compressed, swearing she had not recognized her attacker, and praying that no spirit would move me. She will not speak. How many others might be similarly silenced? I cannot bear the thought, the injustice of it. I am comforted only by the knowledge that she is provided for.

Now the day is changed for me in every particular. And so I must move forward to greet it on new terms. No Reverend, no Medium, no Spirits guide me.

JUNE 5, 1860

I find I absolve myself for those actions which previously pained me—the séance, the day of the velvet bag—for in a new context, some details take on a new significance, and others a new irrelevance.

Whether I can absolve myself for silence remains yet to be seen, even as I truly believe I have chosen the only course.

The worst of the lassitude seems to be behind me, but still my exertions tire me. So I bid you good night, dear Friend, and pleasant dreams, which is all I would ask for myself at this point.

JULY 18, 1860

I hope you will forgive the lapse in my attentions, but I have been so distracted I've had scarce time to write.

Mother and I have been packing and making ready for a journey. It was decided, in view of events here, that it might be a good idea to arrange a visit with some of the Leeds cousins who have been begging us for years to make the trip overseas. And so we are traveling to England, where we shall spend the better part of the year.

I have made it known that I prefer not to go, as this would mean turning tail on what weighs upon me here at home, but Mother and Father insist. Mother came to my room last evening and told me they are both still worried about me, about the state of my general health, since so many strange ideas had overtaken me of late and I seem not at all myself. I resisted my urge to laugh, and told her that on the contrary, I have never felt more surely myself. I maintained that there was no point in a journey just now, as the place of my birth seems as utterly unfamiliar as the moon, and I might just as well begin my renegotiation of the world with this spot. Mother replied that this is precisely the sort of thing that has so alarmed Father and herself. I longed to comfort her and assure her that I am quite well, but the words would not come; I felt I had explained my mind as I now see it, and something within me could not justify a halfhearted retraction.

I suppose, nonetheless, that I am to be made to take this unpleasant voyage, and so I must find in myself the will to see it through, however unpalatable it appears just now.

JULY 23, 1860

What a difference a few days make! Once again, I stand in awe of the antics of my own mind, but having decided that I am on to some new phase of my development, I am determined to follow it through all its twists and turns.

As I relayed to you, Friend, I was initially against the journey we're to make to the home of our Crown-subject relations. But over the days since the announcement was made, I've found myself piqued with curiosity about what England might be like, and the Continent as well. More to the point, though, is this question: who might I be there, and what might I uncover within myself?

If I feel myself wholly out of place here, then would not a change of atmosphere be advisable? And as for certain of my detractors here, why do I owe it to them to make myself miserable in their presence when I might just as well make myself happily free of it? Once I considered it, I realized an opportunity for great adventure had presented itself, and now I am quite excited by the prospect of the unknown. My only apprehension regards that which remains unresolved, if not in my mind, then outside it.

We are to leave in scarcely a week, and there is so much to make ready before that time. Lucy had been fussing over my traveling wardrobe—she insists that Parisian ladies are exquisitely fashionable, and that I must be prepared to hold my own should we undertake a trip to that luminous city. I quite surprised myself by telling her not to be bothered about the state of my toilette. I find I honestly don't care what the mademoiselles are sporting, nor what I do or don't bring to adorn myself. I told Lucy to instead apply her energies to the closing of the house, and the other more important chores which are no doubt waiting to be seen to.

I myself have been keeping busy by helping Richard to organize his things. His presence is somehow comforting; he seems the most himself to me, in these days when everything has taken on such a strange shape, and so I find myself doting on him in a rather quaint elder-sisterly fashion.

My own preparations will be few indeed. I will carry only a single trunk, as I wish not to be burdened with excess baggage during the course of the trip.

Tomorrow I'm to accompany Mother on a round of farewell visits. I expect this will entail a certain amount of awkwardness, but I'm rather looking forward to it. It shall be a fine test of my new resolve, and I am quite curious to see how I will weather it.

JULY 24, 1860

Tomorrow we set off!

Our good-byes are said, and although I was cold-shouldered and looked askance at in several of the houses we visited, I found the whisperings glancing off me as if off some steely protective shield.

My trunk is ready, my costume set out, and I am prepared for the voyage. There were but two things I had left undone, and so after brief debate I saw to them only an hour ago, at the last possible moment.

After we returned from our calls, I retired to the study and penned a long, exacting letter, which I sealed in an envelope and addressed in bold print. I was tempted to invoke the authority of the Netherworld to lend its contents some credence, but of course this would be hypocritical. It must stand upon its own merit, and if the best it can accomplish is to set the pendulum in motion, then so be it.

That task completed, I ascended to my bedroom, and retrieved from my armoire, where it has lain all this time, a certain deep-green velvet bag. This I put into a cake box purloined from the kitchen. Then I wrote out a second note upon another sheet of Father's heavy stationery, to be enclosed in the cake box as well:

Mr. Price: I have spoken my mind freely, to His Honor and Mrs. Fitch. Without regret—AL

Lucy has promised to deliver my parcels to the post office early tomorrow, before we depart. And so now I am finished. Whatever the outcome, I have done what I could—better late and in my absence than not at all—and am at peace. I will pack you in securely, my Companion, until we are under way, and hope you are no more prone to seasickness than I, and when next we meet I shall be on my way to a new point in my future. You shall be there to bear witness to it—to my follies past, present, and to come, and to whatever I am able to make of my chances in the seat of the Empire.

chapter two

(DECEMBER 15, 1862)

My Dear Granevangeline:

How ironic that these desperate and war-torn months are the very ones in which I seek to reestablish contact with you. I cannot know when I shall behold your kind and loving visage again, and am loath to consider all the years of my childhood which have passed since I did so. But I pray the few brief notes I've tried to send off to you since leaving the Southern territory have, indeed, reached you. Perhaps someday I shall lay claim to a permanent home so that some word from you may find me, but until then I shall do my best to let you know my whereabouts. I am sorry I have not explained myself at length before now, but please, Gran, accept my heartfelt apology and apply your generous understanding to the circumstances of my neglect.

I know that you know Mama's poisonings in my ear contributed to my seeming lack of attentiveness, at least while I still dwelled beneath the Paxtons' roof. More recently, the conflict in New Orleans and the flight I was forced to undertake from that region have kept me from going to you. Yet I have always held the memory of you close to my heart. Your letters to me are saved, every one, in their envelopes, and are the most cherished of those belongings I yet hope to set eyes upon again, and my visits with you linger in my mind as the sweetest and most pleasant intervals of my childhood. I recall the chinked walls of your cabin, which seemed to smell always of citrus or some other fresh fruit; I recall the statues of the Saints we painted with stains and brushes, the little leather bag containing your vodou stones, and the sound they made as they clicked about in your hands. I recall the fragrant bags of herbs lining the kitchen shelves, and the story of Little Brown Pup you read to me in French as we sat upon crates in the doorway, watching the horizon for thunderstorms.

If you—who created for me a humble paradise—could witness the circumstance under which I summon these words, you would doubtless be appalled. I sit upon a mean and filthy straw-tick mattress, on the plank floor of what passes for a rooming house on the east side of New York City; all of my earthly belongings are gathered into a single carpet-and-raffia bag, over which crawls a small army of vermin.

My window—it is not a window, but rather a slit in the brickwork that appears to have been hewn with a sledgehammer—faces out onto a bleak airless corridor; what's left to breathe is fetid beyond imagining. I sit wrapped in blankets—three of them, and they are neither clean nor well mended, but at least they are heavy—so as not to foul my few untattered garments. My only light comes from a small oil lamp I brought with me. I hesitate to burn it, though, as the bit of smoke it produces seems to draw the very air from my lungs.

Without light, I am constantly lured by the prospect of sleep, but one might just as well attempt to sleep in hell. The cacophony of shouts, whistles, moans, poundings, and other assorted expressions of misery rises up from the streets and penetrates the walls as if there were no boundaries between its authors and myself. And then there is the insidious cold, which blasts through my meager shutters and devours the small warmth from my stove before I can begin to restoke it. I think in my head, a thousand times a day, it is not New Orleans, it is not any place on earth that one can imagine without having experienced it.

Needless to say, only the most drastic progression of events could have brought me to this dismal turn, but there is reason and purpose yet in my choice. I am here because the docks are here, and it is to the docks, and to the departing ships within them, that I shall go to seek my salvation.

You have no doubt heard of the circumstances under which I fled Mr. Paxton's. Or perhaps you haven't—perhaps Mama hasn't seen fit to inform you of them. Or, more likely still, she has decided to break her years of silence and speak to you at last, only to regale you with her own version of the story. I beg you, Gran, do not judge me harshly. At least allow me to tell you the facts of the matter, in my own words, so that I may rest assured of your having heard them.

I must start with the occasion of my final visit with you. How long it will take to relay the details between that day and this, I cannot say, but as I have at last the dubious luxury of all the time in the world in which to recollect, I hope you shall humor me in the task of telling, by taking upon yourself someday the task of absorbing the tale.

I don't know what it was that began the argument between Mama and yourself that day. I recall only that I sat in the corner beneath your trundle bed, pretending to play with the two tin soldiers Thomas had given me, while the pitch of the discussion rose higher and higher. I remember Mama's raging was so loud the legs of the bed seemed to vibrate against my back, yet I held you equally responsible for the discord. You were repeating, over and over again, those words which so incensed her: "Can't raise up properly on lies, Onessa, can't raise up." To which Mama would launch into a fit of hysteria concerning your plot to interfere, and usurp her place as my mother.

This talk terrified me then, just as it always did when she embarked upon it at home. Particularly awful was the picture she painted of my leaving Mr. Paxton's city house to labor as a field nigger, which she swore would be the inevitable outcome of your secret plan to remove me to your own cabin. "Look down at your hands, Bree, and get them ready," she would moan, practically in tears. "Just think how they'll feel without a pen and pencil but wrapped around a hoe handle from sunup to sundown. Might as well bend your back over now, Bree, because after one season in the cotton it'll never be straight again."

When she talked like that, all I could think of was losing everything that was dear to me. I loved the long and magical afternoons I spent with you at the Old House, but Mama promised me that they were sublime only on their surface. Should you ever succeed in gaining custody of me permanently, the hideous truth would be revealed, a truth of drudgery and labor that would wear my spirit to the bone and undo all the good Mama had toiled to arrange for me. And once it revealed itself it would be too late—the die would be cast, and there would be no return from that hell upon earth, which even your gentle presence would not ameliorate.

Not even for your sake could I imagine myself without Mama, without Louella and Thomas and our lessons. I could not imagine giving up my recorder and my pony, or my feather bed, or any of the other things I was sure to lose as a result of those soft words you spoke which inflamed Mama's heart. And so, despite your devotion to me, my trust in you faltered. After all, Mama said, in pursuit of your own selfish aims you would risk removing me from the city house, with all its advantages; how, then, could I believe that you truly were interested in my welfare?

I fought the tug-of-war within me: the evidence of my own eyes versus Mama's rantings, your steadiness contrasted with her hot-and-cold. In the end, though, Mama always won. I did not know then what I know now—which of course was the issue between the two of you all along—and, given her ceaseless campaigning, it was inevitable that I should come to see Mama's side as my own.

That day, I remember her quickly reaching the point from which there was no return, when she began to shriek at you, "You are not gonna poison my son, Mama, you are not gonna have your way—" You were very calm, you insisted to her that this was not your intent, but that she could not continue along the same path. I trembled at those words—here surely was evidence of what she maintained was your agenda all along—and tried to wedge myself farther under the bed, but Mama saw this cowardice and turned the full brunt of her attention on me.

I don't know whether your recollection of what happened next will match my own, but on my part it was unforgettable, for it happened with a dreamlike slowness that imprinted it upon my mind forever. When Mama reached under the bed, screaming, "Just look! Just look what you're doing to him, you gree-gree witch!" I could think of nothing but retreating farther. I felt her pulling on my arm, but something in me resisted. The more she wrenched at me, the more I dug myself in beneath the trundle springs, until at last I was folded in so tightly I could barely breathe. I don't know how long or how hard she tugged, only that I could see your legs emerge behind her, and I could hear you imploring her to let go, because she was frightening me. Mama, of course, was yelling that *you* were the one I was frightened of.

By that point, though, I had decided that I would not come out into the presence of either of you, and that was the moment I chose to bury my teeth in Mama's fingers. I suppose I ought not fault her for her reaction. I drew blood, and hurt her dreadfully, I'm sure, and so when she applied all of her strength to the dislodging of my body, it might have been as a result of the same sort of animal urges to which I had succumbed myself. Whatever it was, I recall that the sound which my elbow made when it cracked seemed to deafen me; the boards beneath my nose, as I slid along in her iron grasp, seemed to take hours to pass before my eyes. Then I was out, and I have no memory of when I began to howl. Mama swung me up against her, and I remember only the sight of her contorted face, of the blood running from her fingers onto my limp arm, the sound of her screams in my ear. "You'll kill him, you'll kill him," she was shrieking over and over, and you were saying, "Dear God, Onessa, be still, he's hurt."

I recall her whirling and pushing you into the wall and how you fell there, and then the terrible jouncing as she ran carrying me through the door. My last sight was of you trying to run behind us, screaming to Mama to stop and calling, "Aubrey! Gran loves you, Bree," while Mama screamed without looking back, "Leave us *be*, goddamn you!" The pain in my arm was so encompassing that I could think of little else, but I remember too how my feelings of ambivalence were stoked into rage at that moment. Something in me was awakened, some awareness of wrongdoing, of subterfuge, embroiling me; it was this thing which I believe eventually led me to the revelation of the truths of my life and so to my present circumstance.

At first, Mama was able to manipulate this newfound perception in me to her own purposes. Of course you know we left your cabin that day never to return.

For days, weeks, and months afterward, Mama let loose a torrent of invective designed to make me brand you the instigator of the entire affair.

Even my arm, Mama told me while Lila set it that very night, was directly your fault. "If your grandmother hadn't scared you so, you never would have wedged under that bed like you did. If your grandmother hadn't shoved me, I never would have clamped down on you like I did," she said. At first, I was swayed by these arguments, and so I participated in Mama's boycott. I believed her when she told me it was best that I never associate with you again, that you were the biggest threat to our future happiness. She called you a liar, a vodou priestess, a prostitute, and an evil spell-caster, out to lure me away so that you could apprentice me to the devil. That was why I never answered your letters, or sent any of my own. Eventually, when your letters stopped coming, I assumed you had tired of your attempts to undo our family and were prepared to leave us alone.

Later on, however, I began to rethink this position. For one thing, despite her interpretation of the story, I never quite forgot that picture of Mama's fingers around my arm. It was *her* force which had been brought to bear on me, *her* strength which had snapped my bones in two. And over time there were other incidents which forced me to recall that picture in detail.

For my broken elbow was by no means the end of the injuries which seemed to befall me in Mama's presence. After we took our leave of you, her rages began to direct themselves more frequently at me, and I was less able to predict their onset or severity. I initially tried to behave as I imagined she wished me to, but often my mere presence seemed to provoke her into a fit of anger. After a while it occurred to me that I would be whipped or slapped regardless of what I did, and I confess that when this realization took hold, I began deliberately to provoke her, to tread that line which might earn me a swat or a beating, in the hope of creating in her exactly as much turmoil as she would mete out to me as punishment. I was never happy in these manipulations, however. I am still pained to think of them, and of the degree to which Mama and I both loved and tormented each other. It was strange—and is strange to me still—that Mama should have been as drawn to one polar course as another, that each was as convincing and absolute as the next.

Yet I recall that when she held or hugged me, when she sang into my ear, or when I lay upon the four-poster with her, drifting into sleep while she spun tales of our futures as freemen and merchants, it seemed that this was her true nature revealed, and that all of my other memories of her were distant and mist-shrouded, and never to be awakened again. And conversely, when in the next day—or minute or hour—she would turn upon me and knock my face round over my shoulder with her fist, and shake me and call me a shiftless yellow bastard and not her blood kin at all, it would seem that that was her truest self and truest opinion of me, and that the loving incarnation was a fantasy I had conjured in my sleep.

At any rate, after the day when we took our leave of you, Mama's fits became more passionate and more regular—in fact I have few memories of ever having witnessed them before that day—and contrasted sharply with her vigorous assertions that you were the source of evil in our lives. The final straw came when I discovered, some seven years ago, a collection of your letters in a brass box in the carriage house.

I knew Mama stored things there, in a little-used corner of the loft where only she had occasion to go. My curiosity got the better of me, and one afternoon when she was napping I stole off to the loft with her key ring, and discovered the set of locked trunks. I matched the key to the first one, and you may imagine my surprise when I found in it dozens—of course you know this—of missives sent to me in care of Amos.

I realized instantly that Mama must have talked the driver into handing them over to her and never saying a word. Amos was notoriously fond of my mother, practically swooned in her presence, and was not the brightest darky in the world in the first place. I read through only a few of the letters, and as I did so that sensation which I date, rightly or wrongly, from the day of my fractured arm, arose in me, and beat against the confines of my loyalty to Mama. I could not believe she could be so small, so heinously petty, as to keep what you intended for me from my sight. I had already agreed to her conditional rejection of you, what more did she want of me? Did she believe me so mercenary that even a few lines, a letter, would move me from her side to yours?

That was my first thought. When I read what you had committed to paper, my resentment and anger became even greater. For after years of being incited against you, what I saw there—quite clearly and with somewhat older eyes—was not the malevolent plotting of a selfish crone, but the loving sentiment which I had always witnessed in your actual presence.

I confess that I was not an adroit or clever spy. I could have hugged the knowledge of my discovery to myself until an opportunity arose to make use of it, but I succumbed to the impulse to confront Mama directly. I ran back to the house and threw a fistful of the letters at her as she lay napping on her bed.

Needless to say, that action provoked one of our worst confrontations yet. We argued at fever pitch for the better part of six hours, and several times she slapped me full-force in the face. But I had, at twelve, an awareness that I was no longer helpless against her. I was already somewhat taller than she, and I remember that for the very first time I was moved to raise my hand against her, although I did not carry through and strike.

It shames me to admit this, and to recall the reaction it inspired in Mama. She broke down in a way she never had before. She slid to the floor, gasping and splaying her fingers over her chest, and I remember that this sight was like a shock of cold water over my heated blood. When she recovered enough to speak, she told me I did not understand things as well as I thought I did, and that she might have been "cross" with me at times, but that I must believe that she loved me absolutely, and had always done her best to protect and provide for me. She promised she would deliver any further letters you sent me as well as any I wished to send back, but begged me not to reestablish contact with you until such time as she herself was ready to do it.

So moved was I by Mama's pitiful posturing that I agreed to do what she asked. But my faith in her version of events—not only those concerning you but everything having to do with our lives—was shaken, and it seemed more and more that we existed in a state of uneasy truce with each other. I began to long for the day when I might experience some freedom in the form of escape from her gaze, and set about trying to bring plans for this same to fruition.

It seemed I had found a way to manage this when I turned fourteen, and discovered that Thomas intended to bring me to New Haven when he departed for the campus at Yale a year hence.

Now, I doubt I need tell you this, but I had barely felt myself a slave during the years of my childhood among the Paxton household. Every particular of my life reinforced in me the idea that my family occupied a niche closer to that of the Paxtons themselves than to the realm of the other Negroes on the property. It was obvious to me in the course of our day-to-day living in the city that Paxton and Madame Eugenia regarded my mother as indispensable, more administrator than slave or bondswoman. I had witnessed the long evenings she spent in the library in consultation with Paxton, poring over the ledgers filled with her tiny, precise script, every penny, every doing in the household, meticulously noted and accounted for.

During these weekly meetings Mama always sat at the mahogany desk in a big leather chair opposite Paxton. She never stood or perched on a stool like an underling. And Paxton's voice when he spoke to Mama was jocular and familiar. I could see for myself how much he trusted her; she handled money and had a key to every room in the house.

I became used to thinking of the home on St. Charles Avenue as our own. Since the Paxtons were so often away, we had run of it to whatever extent we pleased. Our quarters on the third floor, rather than downstairs behind the kitchens—our parlor and sitting room, our two bedrooms with their enameled beds and carpeting—appeared to me to be miniatures—only slightly less grand—of the great house itself, and our position over the other servants reinforced the idea that Mama and I were lord and lady of the manor, in the Paxtons' absence.

Those occasions when we visited you in the country, before that final separation took place, did nothing to contradict these impressions. I never questioned the fact that you and I and Mama were permitted to move about at will, that Paxton, like his father before him, had supplied us with permanent passes which the patterollers never even asked to see. Likewise, I took for granted my fine and tutored education, and Mama's, and your own only slightly lesser proficiency at reading and writing. Nor did I wonder at the luxury of your cabin, or its placement far from the slave row: you were as removed from that circle of shacks as we were from those others—black Amos, Adeline, Cheney and David, and even Lila, to some extent—who resided in the city house, and that seemed right and fitting to me.

If at some point I required an explanation for any of this—and I don't recall as a child ever thinking there need be one—I could find it by looking no farther than the mirror. It was obvious to me that my life resembled the Paxtons' because I myself resembled the Paxtons: straight-haired, fine-boned, white-skinned, and light-eyed. I never felt any of myself—or Mama or you—reflected in the dusky color and incomprehensible speech of the typical house Negroes, not to mention that of the bestial and barbaric field niggers.

Instead I felt at home alongside the Paxton children. Louella and Thomas were my constant companions; we ate the same food, shared the same games, learned at the same table, read the same books. The bent of their minds became the bent of my own, and their expectations too became mine.

I believe that this was precisely what Mama intended for me, and yet when her intent became a reality and reached toward its ultimate conclusion, she held it to be my doing, as if I had betrayed her in some fashion, or taken up a new religion which utterly discounted her own.

When I announced at our dinner table one night that Thomas intended me to accompany him to Yale, I unleashed a storm whose brooding existence I had only recently come to be aware of.

The conversation began simply enough. I told Mama that Thomas had broached the subject of university with me. She looked up from her food and nodded, then looked back down. I waited for her to say something, but she did not, and so I continued. I would need some new shirts, I told her, and could she have some made out of the allowance she was given by Mister Paxton each week.

She replied that Mister Paxton hadn't mentioned anything about my going with Thomas yet, but when he did she was certain he'd tell Magdalene at the Old House to mend my old clothes and make them presentable.

I shook my head at this—no, I remember saying to her, that's not the point at all. I don't want these old things patched up and repaired. You have the money. Why can't you go into town and get the cotton, have Mister Paxton's tailor make it into shirts? He made your good dress, why can't he do this for me?

Mama placed her fork gently upon her plate and then stared at me. After a very long moment she said, "Bree, what is it that you think you need new shirts for?"

Her tone was odd, and I was wary, being well acquainted with her abrupt shifts in mood. But having begun the conversation I felt I had no choice but to answer her.

"For the classroom, Mama. For Yale. When I go with Thomas to the campus. It's a fine school, I'm sure everyone will be properly dressed, and seeing as he asked me—"

She jumped in on me then, an arrow closing upon its mark. She picked up her fork and used it to point at me. "No, Bree. Get one thing settled in your mind. Thomas didn't *ask* you. He *told* you. He didn't *invite* you to Yale, do you understand that? Who do you think you are, a fine city gentleman, Mr. Thomas's moneyed freeman acquaintance, and would-you-care-to-come-to-Yale-for-a-year-of-study-and-cricket? Is that what you think?" She continued to stare me down, her eyes growing narrower.

I swallowed, my face becoming hot, and snapped a reply back at her. "No, that is not what I think, Mama. Never mind. Apparently you are in a mood, so let us drop the subject. I'll buy the damned shirts myself, or I'll have Mister Paxton order them for me."

I guessed that this response would mightily annoy her, and so it did. "Let me tell you something," she said in a nastier tone. "You may believe—you with your lily-white skin, your fine manners, your arrogant disposition around this house—that you're stepping out right alongside Mr. Thomas, that you're headed into the world on the same footing. But that's not *truth*. I'll tell you what it is: it's *illusion*. Do you know what an *illusion* is, Bree? It's a fantastic thing, a dream which seems real but has no substance. You're under the *illusion* that you're a freeman, with choices to make and plans to lay. But the truth, Bree, the truth everywhere but within your own head, is that you're a slave. You are *Mister Thomas*'s slave. You are his *property*. If Mister Thomas tells you to go to Yale, you'll go, and not to study the textbooks either. You'll go as his manservant. You'll go to carry his bags, and blacken his boots, and see that his collars are properly starched. And when you're doing all of those things for Mister Thomas, you won't need new shirts.

You'll be doing dirty work, and for dirty work your old shirts will do. You are a *slave*, Aubrey, and for slaves old clothes will do."

Why would she say these things to me? Why especially when it was she who had placed those dreams, those illusions, as she called them, inside my head? Whatever the reason, the sight of her—her fork raised in the air, her long eyes narrowed—infuriated me, reminding me as it did that yet again I'd been impaled on that cold blade of her betrayal. Beautiful as I thought her, she became to me, in these moments, as ugly as the devil himself, and so I sought to strike back at her with whatever means was at my disposal.

"You're jealous," I said calmly. "You're jealous because I'm young and you're old, because I'm going to travel the world, and you have no choice but to stay here and make market and count pennies and order beef haunches for dinner until you drop dead. You're jealous because you were born a woman, and I a man, and I've been chosen for opportunities which will be greater than any of yours. That's what's put you in such a foul temper, isn't it, Mama?"

Of course I regretted these falsities the moment they passed my lips, but could hardly retract them.

I thought Mama would rant or fall to the ground in a swoon, but she moved not a muscle, only fixed me with that same level stare. "We'll see" was all she said—and I recall this frightening me more than any shouting fit would have done. She rose from the table, never taking her eyes from me, and then walked down the little passageway to carry her plate to the scullery. When she came back she stood in the doorway and addressed me.

"Everything you have, Aubrey, you have because of my intercession with Mister Paxton. You don't understand that because you've gone spoiled, living in this house like you own it, passing to half the white folks in town and dropping Mister Paxton's name on the other half. You keep pressing your luck, and soon enough you will find yourself without me to smooth your path. And mark my words, boy: if that happens, you'll be strung up or headed east on the back of a wagon faster than you can spit, just one more yellow nigger with nothing to his name but his swelled head and the shirt on his bloody back." Then she turned from the doorway and walked off, leaving me staring at my own cold plate of victuals.

The very next day Thomas told me that his father had vetoed the plan to bring me to New Haven. Thomas's explanation was that a Northern school would never allow a Southerner to bring a Negro slave onto the campus, what with the abolitionist furor gaining strength in New England and the threat of war imminent. Thomas himself had only been admitted to Yale, he said as he gazed at the carpet, because of his mother's prestigious family name. He was sorry, but there was no point in highlighting his father's contribution to his parentage by insisting upon my presence to the school officials.

I felt I knew better why Mister Paxton had withdrawn his support of the idea, but I said nothing. I could only wonder, first at the measure of my mother's influence over the man who owned her, and then at the perversity with which she destroyed her own hopes for me, and held me at her side so that we could be bound together in mutual discomfort.

I wondered also at myself, at the terrible disappointment I felt in knowing I should not be allowed to go. What *had* I expected of the trip? Did I really imagine that I would attend the university classes in any way that would make them meaningful or useful later on? Had I slipped so far into the coziness of my *illusions* as to think this was possible? Oh, yes. It seemed likely. I expected to absorb the university lectures just as I had our daily lessons with Sister Corinne, the Paxtons' tutor, when Thomas, Louella, and I were younger. And later on, I imagined, I'd put my education to use, when the second of my Great Illusions came to pass. I harbored the strongest hope—truly believed, there was no sense in denying it—that upon the attainment of my majority Mister Paxton would formalize what was informally understood already: the matter of my servitude was a mere pretense, my freedom papers would be issued, so that the question would be settled once and for all in a legal sense. Then I would apply my energies to joining that considerable class of Creoles and free people of color who operated so successfully within the trades and merchant communities. It all seemed so near, so very attainable.

But with the issuance of the decree barring me from Connecticut, the truth of my existence rose up to slap me awake with full force. It became apparent that those in charge of my fate had quite a different idea as to what it should be, and that my own fancies had forced them to confront me with this harsh reality. Rather than the increasing laxity which I had anticipated in advance of actual freedom, I was now met with the descending upon my shoulders of greater restrictions than I had ever known.

Within a few weeks of Thomas's telling me of his father's decision, the whole nature of the household's relations began to shift. I noticed the change first in Mister Paxton himself. Whereas before he had occupied the place of a surrogate grandfather for me—rumpling my hair with affection, chuckling at my precocity, bestowing a toy or trinket upon me on numerous occasions—he now became every inch the Master, his acknowledgment of me pared down to a nod, his directives issued in terse language. The matter of New Haven was never spoken of directly, nor was any confirmation of my change of station, but clearly all was altered.

I was now expected, Mister Paxton informed me, to take up some more strenuous duty around the house—I had lain idle too long, and clearly the lack of responsibility was telling in my character. He would leave it to Mama and to Adeline to address the question of where I should be placed. Regrettably, I could not be trained for the position of *majordomo* in the household—Madame had her own European servants, and one of them already occupied this highest post—but for the time being I could serve as Mr. Thomas's bodyservant, and in his absence take on whatever my mother determined proper for me.

I was stung at the iciness which accompanied this declaration, and felt keenly the withdrawal of Mister Paxton's affections, but I said nothing, and merely nodded my assent. Perhaps in time, I thought, my presumptuousness—or whatever it was that had caused this—would be forgotten, and those constants of my life which had been so altered would return to normal.

In the meantime, I wondered how this new definition of my proper place would affect the friendship between Thomas and myself. I did not have long to wait to find out. For from the day he informed me of his father's decision, we simply did not speak. Such an odd thing this was: here we were, abiding in the same house, and somehow managing never to come into contact with each other. By some unmentioned mutual agreement he kept to the great rooms and I to the back corridors, and when our paths chanced to cross in the kitchen or the rear entrance we nodded and mumbled acknowledgment of each other, and then turned away, our eyes never meeting.

Now, this development was even more excruciating than the cool behavior of Mister Paxton, for as I know you are aware, Thomas and I had been close beyond friendship for the whole of our lives. I was a cousin, a brother, to him even more so than a friend, for I lived intimately within his circle as only a relation can do. That I dwelled there as chattel was some sort of odd abstraction to which no mind was paid. When Thomas returned from traveling with his parents we would punch and hug at each other like puppies rediscovering a litter-mate. It was with him that I shared the activities I had come to enjoy, it was to him that I confided my innermost and untellable thoughts, and it was I who became his confidant as well. When my arm was broken by Mama, when the raging between her and myself filled the corridors, when the colorful result of those exertions appeared on my face, my shoulders, my ribs, it was to Thomas that I took what I could not dispel in any other fashion.

"Letting off the steam" was his expression for it, and we would retire to the barn and don his father's boxing gloves, there to pummel the hay bales, or the saddles, or even each other with our fists until I felt the fury drain out of me.

On other days we roamed the city and the outlying districts together, fishing in the swamps, searching for baby alligators—our favorite prey—or reenacting the Battle of New Orleans in a drama that went on for weeks at a time, with varying characters and chapter stories. We scandalized the citizenry, using the Cities of the Dead as makeshift parks, playing Go Seek among the elaborate mausoleums; we tripped along Decatur Street, calling to ladies upon their balconies and fleeing from the occasional irate shopkeeper or landlord.

In summers, when the Paxtons were in residence, the family and its loyal servants would venture to Lake Pontchartrain, from which trips we males would return brown and dirty (the ladies—Madame, Louella, and Mama—having retired under netting or umbrellas). At night Thomas would request of Mama that I be permitted to sleep in his room, and so I was delivered from the sweltering hell of the third floor to the slightly less hellish second, there to lie in the big four-poster beside Thomas, both of us naked and damp with perspiration, eager to catch any scant breeze from the open windows. We rarely slept; it was too hot, and at any rate there were too many games to be found in the tenting of the sheets, or the preparing of tin armies for war, or the endless giggling over some scatological reference or other.

In all of our games I was a contemporary: the fellow trickster, Jean Lafitte or the British commander, the boxing champion, the fearless 'gator hunter of the bayou. And wherever we went I was a contemporary there as well, for if we encountered white townspeople who knew us, then my status as Thomas's companion was accepted without question; and if we encountered strangers, I was assumed a white child myself, and treated accordingly. Thomas never betrayed the truth—perhaps it never occurred to him—and neither did I, at this point.

As time went on, however, I must admit that a sense of competition developed between us, well before the year of the university incident. I believe that when this was happening, I was at pains to deny it, because some deep part of me wished to have only the truest, finest bond with Thomas. But another part of me was sharply aware of it, and especially aware of who bested whom in the majority of these competitions.

I do not mean to be boastful. I have no way of knowing whether Thomas was a fit adversary or not, and perhaps among better competitors I would fall upon my face; but in direct conflict with him—be it physical or intellectual—it would not be an exaggeration to say that I usually emerged the victor.

After the age of eleven or so, I began that growth spurt which does not seem to have abated even yet; I stand a little over six feet now, and had reached much of that by thirteen, whereas Thomas remained three or four inches behind me. I am lithe, but faster and better muscled than Thomas, and it became evident that to outrun, outbox, or outswim him was no great feat at all.

And even before this I had noticed that, as we sped through our lessons, it was always Louella first, then myself, and then Thomas who captured the new concept, produced the right answer. In Louella's case this seemed appropriate, since she is the eldest, and a whip besides. But Thomas is older than I, by nearly two years, and so it was somewhat a wonder to me—and an irritation to him—that he seemed to lag so in his schooling.

But what came to needle him most, I believe, was the attention we drew as we grew somewhat and attracted the notice of young ladies of the neighborhood.

At twelve or so, I cared nothing for girls. Louella I regarded as a sister, an annoying and haughty one at that, and the frequent butt of my and Thomas's practical jokes. Other girls were simply in existence or in residence, with no more import to me than similarly situated old men or babies. Thomas, however, from the vantage point of his two added years, had begun to find the province of the female sex quite interesting. He inveigled to enter that province by whatever flimsy excuse he could fabricate, so that he might observe its natives at closer range.

On these excursions, as on all others, I was his constant shadow. I was bored at first with the visits he undertook to neighboring parlors and lawns, but I could not help noticing that I had become rather a favorite among the little ladies, while Thomas struggled to hold even the lesser share of their attention. I cannot say why this was. Perhaps it was some mysterious quality I'd developed as a result of my forced companionship with Mama—one which Thomas lacked, not having spent his childhood tethered to a woman's whims. Or perhaps, it has been suggested, my appearance contributed somewhat to the regard in which I was held. I cannot fathom this myself. In my own reflection I see what I imagine anyone might see, each feature in its proper place—two eyes, a nose, a mouth—but none of them appear particularly distinguished to me. I will admit, however, that I've witnessed the effect and degree of Mama's loveliness, and I can identify the stamp of her countenance upon my own.

Thomas, on the other hand—and Louella too, although she is not under consideration here—seems to have inherited the worst characteristics of his least-attractive parent. I'm sure you've noted the prominent nose, crowded teeth, and mousy hair bequeathed him by Madame; it often pained me, back then, to realize that Mister Paxton's great handsomeness seemed to have missed his children entirely.

Whatever the cause, though—be it comeliness or personality—I found myself the focus of certain feminine scrutiny, while Thomas stood outside of it, doing his best to appear undaunted. This was an untenable and regrettable situation, and I tried mightily to diffuse it. At that point, Thomas's esteem was more valuable to me than that of any girl's, and so I would tweak and tease my admirers while attempting to draw him into the joke.

In time, however, I found that I no longer had need of these ruses, as Thomas himself had discovered a means by which to level the playing field. He began simply to introduce me, at the earliest possible moment, as precisely what I was.

"This is Aubrey, our house servant," he would announce to the ladies and anyone else present, and the sidelong glances and gigglings would cease as utterly as if they'd never existed.

It was absolutely necessary, of course, that he do this. We were growing up, and even I was aware of the danger which could arise from the mistaking on the part of some young white creature of myself for a white gentleman. It was easy enough to do, since I appeared so often and so casually in Thomas's company, and hadn't the bearing or duties of a servant. I had no desire to bring that sort of calamity onto my own head or Thomas's; I had no desire to shame the innocent girl who happened to be in error.

But it was impossible not to wonder if deep within himself, Thomas did not derive a measure of satisfaction from deflating me thus. I came to dread that moment when my station would be revealed, I dreaded the suspicion that this was the inevitable end of any competition between Thomas and myself. I dreaded the instant when the sparkling eyes of the parlor guests, the shopgirls, the fresh-faced daughters—those green and blue and hazel eyes—would glaze over, flatten and dull, when those sentences escaped Thomas's lips.

So I developed the habit of speaking the words myself. This somehow diffused the power of the declaration for me, for I had control of it then, and could at least predict and arrange the moment of my undoing for myself. I allowed no mystery to build as to my origins. As soon as I noted a smile, a coo, a butterfly-flutter of lashes aimed in my direction, I would calmly announce with a bow, "I am Aubrey, Mister Thomas's manservant, Mademoiselle," and watch the performance come to an end.

I believe Thomas must have felt somewhat guilty for the way this necessity intruded itself upon our friendship, and for whatever glee he partook of as a result of it, for after months of reenacting this same scene with changing female faces, he attempted to compensate for it by finding a new outlet for our youthful energies.

Thomas presented me with the idea that there might be a venue for female company in which neither my color nor my station would prove a handicap (and, no doubt, where his own deficits would be unremarked upon as well). I had never visited the famous brothels of New Orleans proper, but I had, like every other denizen of the city, heard the rumors surrounding their existence. It was

Thomas's plan that we should acquaint ourselves with them thoroughly, as it was one of the many prerogatives of gentlemen to indulge themselves in whatever lascivious tastes they wished.

I thought this, initially, a ridiculous scheme—perhaps because I had only the vaguest notions of what it might entail. I was fourteen years old; I had seen dogs breeding and pigeons chase each other about, but what happened beyond that, between men and women, was a great burning secret in which I longed to be instructed. For once, Thomas was ahead of me as befitted his age. It was he who explained to me the precise mechanics of physical relations. His descriptions, although at first beyond belief, acted as pitch upon a fire, for no sooner had I accepted them than I was possessed of a mind to experience them for myself. In fact I could think of little else—that single-mindedness which had overcome Thomas now hit me full force, and I could scarcely wait to indulge it and be initiated into the more ignoble of my gender's pursuits. The faster we availed ourselves of a bawdy house, the better, although the thought of what awaited me there was as frightening as it was thrilling.

One thing was certain: we would seek out the sort of establishment where I would be made as welcome as the son of my owner. I listened, wide-eyed, while Thomas informed me that there were indeed such places, where all shades of black, brown, and pink mixed without comment, where fine white gentlemen could bestow upon a favored Negro servant not only the pleasures of a whore, but those of a *white* whore. I recalled my gingerly stepping around even some unknown young miss in the street, and shook my head in dissent; but no, Thomas said, I was wrong, those houses were real, and often the very statesmen who would have me strung up for gazing too boldly at their ferret-faced wives could be seen there, buying luscious golden harlots for their pitch-black butlers. It's a gentleman's prerogative, Thomas said, it's different in the gentlemen's clubs, and the women there are not ladies, but whores.

I found I cared little for the idea of a white prostitute over a black or yellow one. The thought of access to *any* female was good enough for me, and I had long been able to find in the myriad presentations of feminine face and form the pleasure of variety.

But Thomas shrugged; if a little forbidden was good, then a lot must be better, and if a lot could be had, then I should have it. He would see to it himself. Of course the Negro so favored must not look the part of a slack-jawed field hand, but I would have no problem whatsoever in this regard, he assured me. I did not feel it necessary to add that I knew this already. We had only to unearth the addresses of these establishments, Thomas went on, and the bliss within would be ours for the taking.

The organizing of this trip became an obsession between the two of us, and did much to wipe away the residue of ill feeling which had accumulated over the last few years. We plotted and planned, exchanged notes, compared schedules, all of which served to draw us close once again. Thomas was finally able to secure directions to Frank Herbert's Camellia Inn establishment, the most notorious of the whorehouses which catered to all colors and all tastes. And so on a summery Thursday evening around midnight, I brilliantined my hair, pulled on a fresh shirt, stole from my room, and tiptoed down the servants' staircase to meet Thomas at the rear doorway.

We raced from the house, and once clear of it, whooped with glee in the roadway. Thomas flashed the roll of paper money he'd brought for the occasion, and then offered me a pull from a silver flask of whiskey he had somehow light-fingered from his father's collection. Thus fortified, we made our way to the much-maligned tenderloin of New Orleans.

We had wondered whether we would recognize the whorehouses when we came upon them, but even two spoiled bumpkins such as ourselves could scarcely have missed the doings of the French Quarter. As soon as we turned a single corner we knew we had crossed into some foreign and exotic territory. The entire Quarter, by night, had become a vast playland of lewd entertainments. The usually gracious buildings now were teeming with activity: women hung from the upper floors and called to men from the balconies; I heard gunshots from one direction, and the shouts of a brawl from another. Up and down the streets, doors were open, noise and light and figures spilling into the night, music and the biting scent of Creole cooking drifting over the heads of the men strolling the sidewalks. In darkened corners or under street lamps, more women lolled or beckoned, and occasionally two figures could be seen transacting business right there upon the roadway.

I gaped and gawked, pointed and sputtered at Thomas—I was awed, fascinated, repulsed, invigorated all in the same instant, and we hadn't even yet reached our destination. I kept yanking Thomas's shoulder, but he shrugged me off, saying this was nothing compared to what we would behold at Mr. Herbert's pleasure palace.

When finally we found it we were not disappointed: it was indeed everything which had been promised. The building itself was set away from the worst of the district's trade, on the corner—suitably enough—of Royal Street. It was wrought of red brick, and French doors complemented each of the rooms on its topmost stories. Most of the doors were closed, but one or two were open, with a half-naked girl languishing at the wrought-iron balcony, tantalizing us with glimpses of breasts or calves. The ground floor of the building was not open to the street. Two large men, one black and one white, stood at the scrolled door, undoubtedly to exercise discretion in admitting patrons to the house.

I could not believe we were to be allowed entrance to this corrupt and wonderful dreamworld. But here Thomas's breeding asserted itself. Although peach-cheeked and skinny at sixteen, he nonetheless walked directly up the steps, tipped his head to the two thugs, flashed the roll of money, and stood back, as if the outcome were never in question. And wonder of wonders, he was successful—the men exchanged smirking glances, but they opened the door for us, and stood aside to let us enter.

The downstairs rooms consisted of low-lit parlors, and bars at which whiskey or beer could be purchased. Wandering through the halls and arrayed upon the flocked sofas were prostitutes of every description, and in every state of dishabille: there were black women and white ones, brown and yellow and even Oriental; some were older, some were children younger than myself. There were bony girls and fleshy ones, rounded breasts and breasts barely present, all displayed in lamplight turned low so as to enhance the mood of the place. And there were boys there too, and men, appearing not as patrons, but as prostitutes themselves.

This I was thoroughly unprepared for, and mightily distressed by. But Thomas merely handed me the whiskey flask and told me to cool myself, and to look for a girl who caught my fancy, and not to bother about what caught other gentlemen's fancies.

We ourselves were stared at and pointed at as much as we stared and pointed. The other patrons guffawed and poked each other as we passed. The women—especially the older ones—shrieked with delight and called, "Cherry pickin's" to their friends, or grabbed at our posteriors. I was glancing all about so as not to miss anything, and generally found eyes—male and female, young and old—glancing back at me. But I paid no mind, as Thomas had instructed, and instead stole sips from the flask, and also picked up for myself a half-full glass of bourbon discarded on a side table by some other patron.

One thing I could not help noticing, however: there were—just as Thomas had said there would be—truly dark black men here, at the sides of their masters no doubt, but here nonetheless, enjoying without worry what, out on the street, they would have been tortured and executed for witnessing.

I was considering the wonder of this and guzzling my drink when I noticed a ravishing blonde woman standing by herself against the dark wood of the bar. She appeared to be perhaps twenty-five or thirty, she had a tiny black clover painted by her mouth, and her open bodice revealed full sloping breasts, each with a pink budlike nipple protruding. My heart pounded at the sight, the glass literally stopping in midair. Thomas noted my stare, and offered to buy her for me, but I quickly dissuaded him—she was far too sophisticated, and I was terrified that she would scoff at my inexperience.

Instead I hastily downed the rest of the liquor, and suggested we make our way into the next room, where a floor show was in progress. I was desperate to move, before my legs gave out on me altogether and plunged me in a quivering heap to the floor.

Thomas was eager to make a selection, however. He glanced around the room, then singled out and corralled a mulatto girl of maybe eighteen or twenty. I remember little of her except that her teeth were very white, and flashed when she smiled. My head was reeling by this time. I heard Thomas in my ear urging me, "Go ahead, pick somebody," and so I decided I had better do just that.

The girl I selected was likely the tiniest "adult" female on the premises. She told me she was sixteen; she looked more like eleven. She also had a deformity, a strange cleft lip which gave her mouth a piquant, pursed expression. When she smiled I realized her front teeth were missing and that the cleft extended to her palate as well.

But she had smooth, blue-white skin and very blue eyes, and I chose her because Thomas was leaning into my ear shouting, "Come on!" and because of all the women standing near us she seemed the one least likely to laugh if I approached her.

Thomas took one look at my selection and let loose an amazed cackle. "My God, Bree, she's *hideous*!" he roared. "Do you mean to tell me that in the midst of all this beauty, *this* is the creature you elect to pay for? Have you lost your frigging mind?"

I then found myself in the curious position of being embarrassed on the girl's behalf. It further perturbed me that Thomas—who deeply resented the rejection incurred as a result of his own physical shortcomings—should nonetheless be the first to take aim at another for the same reason. So I defended her angrily, and maintained that yes, this was my choice, and if he didn't like it, then bugger him, he could go to hell and take his own whore with him. This set both girls to laughing, to my surprise; then Thomas joined in, and a moment later I was laughing myself, no doubt from the whiskey and the tension of the whole unreal situation.

At length our purchases pulled us toward the stairway, where we were to pay the whoremaster for their services and then be led to rooms above. Here we received a surprise, for while Thomas's girl cost twenty dollars for the evening's romp, my own was priced at thirty-five dollars. "You're bloody joking," Thomas said to the man, a moustachioed giant in shirtsleeves with arms the size of my own thighs. But no, the man said; my girl—whose name was Clara—was a "fancy," and therefore more expensive. It was the lip, he continued. Men paid extra because of the lip. I could not see what a lip had to do with the business at hand, and had expected Clara to be the cheapest—and therefore most grateful and willing—girl in the house, but I looked at her now with a renewed respect; and Thomas did as well, and paid the thirty-five dollars without protest.

We were taken to the next landing, and here we received another surprise—for while the downstairs and the upper rooms from the street had looked quite gaudily ornate and very much in keeping with our fevered expectations, the plain plastered spaces into which we were ultimately led were so mundane as to be on the verge of squalor. The hallway was dim and painted a dark green, with a faded cabbage-rose runner on the floor; wall sconces every ten feet or so provided the only illumination. As Clara and the mulattress led us by the hands, we could hear assorted grunts, groans, and squeals from behind flimsy makeshift barriers on hinges, and even, in one case, from beyond a curtain upon a rod.

Finally Clara stopped before a grimy white door and said, "This is mine." Thomas continued past me, led around the corner by his girl, and he turned to flash me a drunken smile and yell, "Good hunting!" before he disappeared.

As we stood there in the hallway the enormity of what I was doing pulled at me for the first time. Clara opened the door and showed me into a tiny cubbyhole barely ten feet by ten. In it were a cot with a thin sheet—stained gray at its center where bodies contacted it—a straight-back chair, and a side table with an ashtray and a dim lamp upon it. I felt a sudden sobering clamminess rising up in my cheeks at the sight of the furniture—I don't know why—and immediately sat down upon the bed. Clara walked over to the side table, opened its only drawer, and pulled out the stub of a cigar. "When it's down to here," she said, indicating the cigar's midsection, "your time is up." She lit the cigar and set it in the ashtray, and its thick foul smoke immediately began to fill the room. Then she sat down next to me, and even her slight weight upon the mattress made the springs sag and my stomach clench.

I had pictured it so differently—the girl hoydenish but somehow intended for myself alone, the bed high, velvet-covered—and now here was the reality, far meaner, and here was I, also not the being of my imaginings, for I had no idea as to how I should proceed.

I was close enough to Clara now to catch, over the smoke, the faint unwashed scent which wafted up from her neck; she smelled of some sort of rose water underlaid with stale perspiration. Her hair at least appeared clean. It was an ashy brown and very shiny, rolled into long pipelike curls and pulled from her face by two lavender ribbons. She was wearing a pinafore such as a child might wear, and beneath it her arms and legs were bare, her tiny bosom free. Her skin, so white that it was blue and nearly translucent, was heavily powdered, and her strange parted lip was painted crimson.

She turned to me and gave me a bizarre half-smile, apparently under the impression that I would take the initiative in some way. When I failed to do so she cleared her throat and asked, "So, how would you like it, around the world or straight or what? You want the special? I bet you want the special, right?"

"I don't know," I said miserably. The terms, obvious as they were, were quite beyond me. I could think of no way to explain my sorry state except to reveal it, and so I said, "I'm fourteen."

She stared at me, her blue eyes expressionless, her lip curled. "It's the same to me," she shrugged. "There's eight and nine and ten working the floor downstairs. You want younger, is that it?"

"No!" I said, appalled. I stared at her, shaking my head, and finally she seemed to take my meaning.

"Oh, now," she said. She began slowly to undo the buttons on the pinafore. When she was finished, she stood, and the dress dropped to the floor. Beneath it she wore only a white boned corset, which was quite unnecessary: her ribs were evident, her tiny breasts barely jutted out over the topmost grommet. She turned and faced me, and my skin burned; I was unable to look up at her. Instead I stared at a spot on her calf, where, I recall, a brown and yellow bruise bloomed.

"I'm glad it was you," she whispered in a different tone.

I mumbled, "What?"

"I'm glad it was you. You that picked me, and not your friend. You are the prettiest I ever had here. You seem nice."

I am not nice, I wanted to say.

"Here, now." She reached down and picked up my lifeless hand, placed it against her blue thigh, moved it along the muscle toward the cleft above. I stared at my fingers, my own skin so barely darker, barely yellow, against hers; yet beneath mine the Negro blood pulsed, and this amazing thing was transpiring, that the blood of a Negro should lie this close to white flesh, preparing to violate it utterly. It seemed such a foolish distinction, such an irrelevance, though, as it had always seemed when I was growing up—especially now as another part of me was breached, engaged, and mesmerized. I moved wherever her fingers said I should, and then finally looked up at her, all notions except the most immediate driven from my head.

She knelt down before me, allowed me to touch her breasts, to circle the nipple with a forefinger, which I did with my eyes shut so that my fingertips would remember the sensation. She loosened my shirt, and then placed my hands at the buttons of my fly so that I might undo them myself, and when I was separated from my clothes she whispered, "You're grown for fourteen." I recognized her joke and smiled, surprised that I was able to do so. Then she lay down beside me on the bed and pressed the length of her body against me, handled me gently and then a little harder, and I found myself gasping in her ear, "Will you kiss me—it's your kiss, isn't it," and she didn't kiss me but instead rolled away and said, "No, that's not it, I'll show you," and knelt upon the floor, and pulled me to the edge of the bed where she did indeed show me.

This took only the briefest of minutes, the shock of it coupled with everything else. I was transported and returned before I had any notion that I could or should have drawn it out, and I sank back upon the bed, my heart still hammering.

She smiled at me, from her knees, and I tried to return her smile. Then she rose to pick up the smelly cigar and take a good pull. It had barely begun to ash on the end; a good three-quarters of our time was left. She offered it to me and I took it, dragged upon it too deeply and coughed out the excess in a cloud. She giggled and lay down beside me, and I felt infused with a deep, satisfied warmth, all my misgivings and apprehensions having been drawn away.

"You were my first cherry," Clara told me, snuggling against my chest. Her speech had a strange whistling nasal sound, and her consonants were mangled almost beyond recognition.

"You were my first anything," I told her back.

"Your talk's so pretty. You must be a fine gentleman, got lots of learning. Are you a Spaniard, maybe, or Frenchie?"

I felt a chill at my neck. Nonetheless my training asserted itself, even without my wishing it to. "I'm a colored servant," I replied. "I belong to that white gentleman you saw me with."

"You ain't said!" She whistled softly at this, but gave no sign of alarm. "I would never of thought it, white as you be."

I closed my eyes, relieved, then found myself saying, by way of a change in subject, "It's a blessing, isn't it?"

She mumbled, "Hmmm?" and shifted against me.

"Your lip. It must have seemed a curse to you but it's really a blessing."

She looked up at me, and her face seemed to open, unfurl itself, as if its expression a moment ago had been a scrim arranged to conceal the set stage.

"I'll tell you the truth, pretty sir, so's you don't go falling for every sort of shit you're fed in a whorehouse. The lip don't make it no better. That's just some old wives' tale what got started. Any girl with teeth as knows what she's doing can do just as well. But the men hear a story and they think, well, that's new, and then they have to try the harelip too, so they line up, and one boasts of it to another, and it's like the tale of the Emperor's clothes: no one wants to admit that it weren't no different, that they laid out extra change for a freak." She sighed. "It's novelties, sir. Every house has 'em. Girls with three tits, or a tail growin' out of 'em, or half-men half-women. All sayin' it's the best you'll ever have, when really it ain't no different." She paused a moment. "It ain't no blessing. If I hadn't of had it I might've been a proper lady with a husband somewheres, instead of poked fun of and ended up here. I don't get none of the extra cost, you know. The house takes that."

This candid reply rather deflated my sense of goodwill. I lay by her quietly then, and said no more. I wanted to close my eyes, and did so, not bothering to pull the sheet up about me. I was in this position, upon the cozy edge of napping, when there was a sudden loud banging from the hallway.

Clara jumped up and went to the door. She opened it a crack and hissed, "I'm working! Who is it!"

I heard a female voice mumble something, and then Clara replying, "No you can't, I have it for an hour and it's only half up." I gathered they were discussing the room. It occurred to me that it was to Clara's advantage to hold on to it, since her business with me had concluded before the time ran out and she could now relax if she wished. I didn't dare hope there would be further business to conduct.

But the woman outside was persistent. I could hear the hiss of her voice rise and fall, and then Clara sighing. Finally she said, "Oh, all *right*," and slammed the door shut. Turning to me, she said, "Now pretty, would you mind, we can go sit in the parlors if you like, I'll even buy you a drink."

I rose up on my elbows, groggy. What with the intrusion and the return of my other faculties, I was feeling less comfortable, and more agreeable to the idea of leaving. I wondered where Thomas was in his debauch, and whether I would have to wait long before he joined me, so that we could travel home. I hastily pulled on my clothes while Clara did the same, and when she saw that I was ready she took my hand and led me from the room.

The woman who had interrupted us stood waiting just outside in the hallway. Older she was but not in any sense more lush; rather, she was thin and slatternly, with reddish hair and an angry turn about her mouth. She was also, I noted with a start, dressed in men's clothes. A bowler sat upon her head, she was in shirt-sleeves, and—most amazingly—breeches clung to her legs. I had barely taken in this sight when I became aware of another creature standing before her, pulling on her hand and pleading softly. This was a child of about waist-height, dressed as such in a frilly baby-girl pinafore and stockings. Blonde ringlets shook as she whimpered at the older woman's feet. "For God's sake, Mama, I'm tired, can we just go to bed. Please, Mama."

The woman hissed a response, and I realized with a stunned rush of queasiness that this was no act: they really were mother and child—mother and child whores. And then the queasiness rose to full-blown horror when the child, chastened, turned its painted body, and I was able to see the cutaway front of the dress, which revealed quite clearly the wearer's male sex. What unspeakable act—what revolting display—had they been purchased to perform? And where was the brute responsible for this grotesquerie?

I was never to know, for Clara led me away with a firm grip on my hand. But as we passed, the boy, behind his rouge and powder, gave me a look at once so pitiful and so comprehendingly adult that I was moved almost to physical illness.

I now wished only to be shed of the place and its business. When Clara motioned me toward the bar in the lower room, I bowed and declined, and instead told her that she had been wonderful company, and would not be soon forgotten, but that I must now take my leave. Never mind Thomas—I had sneaked out and could sneak back in, and although the wad of bills he held would have bought my cab ride home, I was content to clear my head with the walk. I gave Clara a final nod from the big front doors of the establishment, and watched as she faded back into the din. Then I was out upon the lawn, the sounds of the dying night surrounding me, the moonlight illuminating the road before me. My hair and clothes seemed dirty and fouled, reeking of cigar smoke and strange perspiration. I drew the fresh air into my lungs in an attempt to reorient myself.

Retracing my steps through the whore district, I made for the most direct route home, and had gone perhaps a quarter hour in that direction when I heard the clop of hooves behind me. I turned, and there I saw a hansom cab, and Thomas leaning out of it, his collar open, his hat perched comically on the crown of his head.

"There he is, the bloody idiot! Stop, you dunce!" I gathered he was shouting at the driver, and presently the cab stopped, and Thomas held the door wide for me to clamber in.

As we started off, Thomas and I faced each other. He grinned at me, and then I began to grin too, both of us posturing like survivors of some great battle, and then Thomas leaned into me and began to scream with laughter. "Jesus bloody Christ," he swore, "I feel like a king's ransom and a dirty sink of dishes. How the hell do *you* feel, Bree?" I couldn't answer because he was laughing so maniacally, but eventually he stopped long enough to ask, "What in the hell did you do with that little monster, was she worth it?" His eyes glittered. "Come along, you bastard, tell it! Was it heaven?"

I began to laugh myself, in the spirit of the thing, and allowed as it *was* heaven, but mainly I hadn't expected the manner of my death, and was therefore taken by surprise. I went on to relay my conversation with the whore, and

Thomas guffawed. "She was plying you for a tip, no doubt, giving you her sob story. And you were right in the first place, she ought to be grateful, because if it weren't for the lip she'd be spending all her time on her back, and then she'd have to worry about pox."

Instantly I blanched—I hadn't even considered the pox, hadn't for a moment let the idea cross my mind.

"Don't look so spooked," Thomas laughed. "You aren't going to get the pox from *that*."

"What about you?" I asked.

"Don't worry about me. I checked my girl, she was clean. And besides, she told me she only serves gentlemen, not dark Negroes or trash."

"Well, then," I said, with more conviction than I felt.

"She was *spectacular*, though," Thomas whispered hoarsely, and then he regaled me with a moment-to-moment rehash of what the girl—who called herself Sissy—had performed upon him. At one point, where he described the way she'd perched on him and lowered her breasts onto his face, and how he'd almost stopped breathing and begun to choke, we roared and fell against the walls of the cab.

"It's the life they've got there, isn't it," Thomas said, shaking his head and wiping the tears from his cheeks. He leaned back upon the upholstery and shut his eyes, still smiling, while I tried to formulate a response.

But instead, in that moment, the picture of the bowler-hatted woman and her painted son chose to leap into my mind, so that my own smile vanished into the black of the evening. I was suddenly aware again of the oppressive staleness which clung to my clothes, and so I stuck my head from the window and gasped in the moist air.

Thomas noticed nothing—he had begun to snore with a contented grin still upon his lips, and we passed the rest of the trip in silence.

When I saw that we were nearly home, I woke him, and we stopped the cab just beyond the borders of the Paxton property. Thomas paid the driver, and then oh-so-quietly we made our way to the rear entrance, and stole in.

It was nearly five; pinkish light was already creeping about the horizon and staining the windows within the house. On the first-floor landing, Thomas tottered against the polished brass railing, clapped me on the back, and bear-hugged me. "We did it," he whispered. "Have a good sleep, you lucky bastard!" I hugged him, then shoved his arms away; we stifled laughter against each other's shoulders, and I felt my euphoria return. United in the glory of our dubious achievement, we left each other, he for his tremendous bedroom on the second floor, I for my own on the third.

Mama was not awake—although she would be in less than an hour—and I reached my bed without detection. Once in it, though, I found my high spirits evaporating yet again. I discovered I could not sleep; my mind insisted upon recounting every moment of the evening to my fevered eyes—and the moment it chose to reprise most exactly was the one when I'd passed the whore and her little boy leaning against the doorway. More so than Clara, more so even than my own bliss, that scene had imprinted itself upon my memory, and I could not dislodge it.

The only tableau I could evoke to combat the vividness of this apparition was of my second-long feinting contact with Thomas. It was clear that something momentous had passed between us this night, to tie us in a way that nothing before had. And I found, in the weeks to come, that this wondrous something became the talisman which I summoned not only to dissipate the memory of the whores in my mind, but to comfort me in other moments as well. I had never felt myself more a man among men than at the instant when Thomas hugged me upon the staircase, and my step and carriage rose with my spirits whenever I considered it.

That very week Thomas suggested we visit the tenderloin district again, but I had no wish to, and we never did. Instead he began spinning tales of what Northern women were like, and how we would experience every variation on the feminine theme if we could only make our way to the great cities of New York or Chicago. We'd get there, he assured me—we were a traveling team, and scoundrel kin, and if we were wicked, well, we'd do our time in hell together, side by side. No doubt you are wondering if I am bound for that place, Gran, and if I can be your own beloved blood who undertook such activities, and I apologize for sullying your ear with the tale of such great sins. But you who have seen and heard so much must surely understand my feelings. At the time, I thought nothing of any vile deed I might do or of the punishment I might receive, so long as I would share it with Thomas Paxton.

It was this spirit of near-brotherly enthusiasm which marked our dealings after the night at the Camellia, and this spirit which was in place when Thomas received the news that he had been admitted to Yale University, and planted in my head the suggestion that I should accompany him there.

And it was this camaraderie that failed utterly, and plunged me into the depths of misery, when it was withdrawn after my New Haven plans turned into debacle.

The stony silence which followed the collapse of my Yale aspirations lasted throughout the summer. Thomas and I exchanged not a word; no further explanation or acknowledgment was forthcoming from him following the delivery of his father's edict. He was more frequently away from the New Orleans home than in it, for which I was grateful, and when present he undertook to avoid me at all costs.

Our separation was complete until he sent for me one hot afternoon by way of Adeline. I trudged up the two flights from the kitchen to the bedroom, wondering what next step was to occur in our stalemate, and whether it would weigh upon or lighten my heart. If he'd only said, those months ago, *My father forbids your going but it's not my doing*, if he'd only indicated in some small way that this new and hideous protocol put in place would not create a complete rift between us—but none of that had transpired. I could know nothing of what he was thinking, or indeed whether his thoughts rested with me at all, having had no clue in either direction.

I found Thomas seated at the desk in his bedchamber, penning a note. I entered with a small commotion, and cleared my throat so that he might know I was there. "You sent for me?" I addressed him coldly. I was determined to betray nothing until I'd gotten a sense of where his feeling lay.

Thomas turned in his seat. His eyes swept over me and reverted to the floor, then darted back to meet mine again. "There's to be a small supper dance at the Pinchots' tomorrow evening," he began.

I waited, part of my mind anticipating that he was building up to an invitation of some sort. Countless times in our younger years I had accompanied him to a birthday party or tea, and I assumed he might be planning to thaw the ice between us by arranging another shared social occasion.

I was preparing to refuse coolly, so as to even the score a bit for the torment he'd inflicted on me these past weeks, when he continued.

"You're to attend me. And I'll need you to ready my evening clothes. You can set out the tailcoat tonight, and please see to it that my gloves are brushed."

I stared at him in astonishment. I could not help it, the idea of any of it was so preposterous. Surely this was a feeble joke, which in a moment would be suspended by a crooked-toothed grin, a clap on the shoulder—a drunken embrace upon the staircase, for a partner in sin. He could not be serious.

I would have said as much, but I saw then the expression in his eyes, and it stopped me cold. Awkwardness there was, and a certain abashedness, but there was relish too—and challenge, which made his pupils and the corners of his mouth dance.

I saw how it was, then: he was practicing. Testing his ability to master. This was the lure held out to sway him from comradeship, and he had swallowed it utterly.

"Look here—" He tilted his head, assumed a patrician air. "A certain—*parting of ways* is inevitable—" *Whose words are those,* I wanted to ask him, but I said nothing, my gaze still locked with his. He attempted a new expression, meant to convey that he need not provide explanations, then he turned away. He sat and resumed his scratchings at the desk without another word to me.

It is perhaps fortunate that I found myself briefly unable to move, for had I followed the pure and sickening rush of my instincts, I might have struck him. In the end it was all I could do to turn upon my heel, my eyes unseeing, my face on fire. I managed to climb the stairs to my own chamber and close the door behind me before I allowed the thought to hit me fully—*So this is how it's to be between us, for all time ever after, and this is who I'm to be*—and then I began to cry, taking pains to hide it, covering my mouth with both hands as if to force the weakness back to whence it had come.

I did not hide it well. Mama knocked upon the door almost immediately, and opened it without my leave. "What did he want," she asked from the doorway.

In an instant my tears ceased, and I felt again the most undiluted wash of hatred, only this time it was not toward Thomas or Paxton, but toward Mama, who had engineered this entire outrage. She had said it herself, that soon enough I would be blacking his boots and carrying his books, and she had seen to it that her prediction came true.

"Get out," I snarled, and she took my meaning and shut the door.

What would they do, I wondered, now dry-eyed, if I refused? What *could* they do? *Beat* me? *Sell* me? Either of those choices was open to them, and yet so insane, so beyond my experience, were they that I considered defying my instructions just to see if they would be resorted to.

In the end, though, I hadn't the heart. What scared me most—more than any vague notion of punishment, the likes of which I had never witnessed among the Paxtons in my entire life—was the idea that I should fall still farther in the esteem of Thomas and his father, that any chance of the present horror's blowing over might be lost to me forever. And so that night I went about my tasks in a nightmare of fumbling confusion.

That I had never performed such duties before only added to my misery. My humiliation was complete when I had to ask Adeline for advice on how to remove lint from a coat, and how to brush the nap on gloves. I cringed when I saw the astonished look on her face, at the sight of me handling Thomas's apparel like some soft eunuch of a butler.

The next night it was Amos's turn to be astonished when I came marching behind Thomas wearing my own scratchy version of the butler's evening clothes, bearing Thomas's cape, top hat, and walking stick in my arms. Thomas seemed to turn every which way except in the direction that would force him to see me. I could barely focus my eyes, could barely keep them from Thomas's back as we entered the carriage, could barely keep every muscle in my face in the rigid, frozen mask it had assumed since that afternoon. The ride to the Pinchots' was deathly quiet. One would have thought us two complete strangers, except that between strangers no comparable tension would have existed.

When we arrived at our destination I was given to see fully, for the first time, what the terms of my new status in society were to allot me. Thomas threw his gloves at me once we were inside the door, and I stood there, openmouthed, wondering what to do—what had I seen other servants do once an occasion had got under way? I could not remember—the truth was, I'd never noticed, or given a goddamn, what the other servants did.

I would have stood there in the foyer all night except that one of the maids, a huge lumbering brown creature I recalled seeing but had never once addressed, tapped me on the arm and bade me follow her. She too seemed bemused at the fall in my fortunes, but she said nothing, only led me to a corner against the wall of the Pinchots' huge, gaily lit, and decorated ballroom where other Negro (and a few white) butlers stood, their hands behind their backs, awaiting the moment when they might again assist their masters.

All through the preliminaries I had occasion to watch Thomas drink and laugh, flirt and chuckle, often flashing the expression I'd seen when he'd spied Sissy the mulattress at the Camellia; but never once did he look in my direction. And neither did even one of the ladies, from the youngest to the oldest. The quartet played, a fine fiddler was summoned for reels, the liquor was consumed, the guests toasted, and I stood outside it all like a bit of mist, a ghost condemned to watch the progress of life without ever experiencing it. I had become disembodied and invisible, even to myself, whereas previously I had been human flesh and bone—in Thomas's eyes, and so in mine.

Finally the music ceased, and the thirty or forty guests sat for dinner at the long tables. Now the waiters and house servants could take over, and I found myself following the other butlers to the kitchen—where, I knew well enough from the Paxtons' own soirees, manservants and ladies' maids ate while their betters dined. The white servants occupied a bright corner of the large yellow-tiled room, while the blacks sat at a long plank table, and here I found myself confronted with a new problem. With whom was I to sit—with the whites, who had nodded to me outside as to a fellow, obviously thinking me one of them, or with the blacks, with whom I most certainly belonged, but who even now were staring at me stonily and waiting for me to pass so that they might continue with their bantering and gossip? There were yellow skins among the blacks, even high-yellows, and familiar faces in that crowd too, but not one of them came forward to offer me a kind word, or a place at table.

In the end I felt such a sickness in my stomach that I did not sit down or eat at all, but instead walked outside into the courtyard and leaned against the doorway, and stayed that way with my eyes closed until I heard the sound of the plank benches being scraped across the tiled kitchen floor.

Here then was a truth—not an illusion; Mama would have been proud of me for discerning the difference: that I belonged nowhere, being neither fish nor fowl, but both and nothing at the same time.

Dizzied and near ill, I stole in from the comfort of the evening, and passed back into the ballroom. There I chanced to catch a glimpse of my reflection in the enormous gilt mirror which hung over the main fireplace. I was shocked at the expression I wore, which I had adopted without even realizing it. For there it was, beneath my pasty green-gray complexion, the damp hair that hung in my eyes: that opaque stare which says *Go ahead, do anything before me, I see nothing, I'll tell nothing*, that look which I had seen on a thousand Negro faces, often brought on by my own presence, and surely by a white person's chance appearance. I recalled in an instant my many encounters with variations on that look, and realized that this was what I had read in Clara's blue eyes as she said, "Here, now," at the Camellia—it had not left her until the moment I'd called her cleft lip a blessing.

I am nothing, therefore you needn't fear me.

And now I had become one with this expression, and could know whereof it emerged, and of the emotion which bubbled just behind it.

I wish to recount no more of that night, only that it passed as if someone else lived it, but not soon enough, and I found myself once more at the door of my own quarters. The only kindness I received all evening came from Amos, who must have noticed my keen distress on the ride home, and who placed his big hand on my shoulder and held me back a step as Thomas exited the carriage. "Don't take on, my friend," Amos whispered into my ear; and I repaid his kindness by throwing his arm off me—its pressure, its familiarity, an offense to my senses—and stalking away.

The days after the party were no better, being spent in a sort of shocked delirium on my part. Each morning brought some new indignity which either Thomas or his father felt obligated to inflict upon me so as to test my acceptance of the new status quo. Each night brought silent meals which Mama insisted I share, she watching me with her narrow eyes, but offering me not one word in relation to what she must have known was occurring within me, and I staring silently, ragingly, back at her, while I endeavored to touch not a single bite of food.

But then at the summer's close came the long-anticipated news that a civil war was imminent. And with it came a new letter from Yale University—which I read myself, in Mister Paxton's study—stating that Thomas would not be welcome in New Haven after all.

A change of plans was quickly put into the works by the senior Paxtons. Yale was forsaken for Oxford, which Thomas entered only by the skin of his teeth, once again relying on his mother's connexions—this time on the hook of her useless title, which Mama had always maintained she sold to Paxton for his money.

By September Thomas had been whisked away to England, his father on his heels. Madame was still at her ancestral home in Aix-en-Provence, in southern France, and Louella was traveling from her boarding school outside London to the Oxford campus so as to be with her brother. The entire brood was gone, in other words, and I was left in my stunned state in New Orleans, with Mama and the usual skeleton crew of servants with whom to share my misery.

And so approached the winter of 1860, and with it that incident which it has taken me all this time to reach the telling of, the one which led to my quitting New Orleans forever and arriving here, where I sit relaying all of this pathetic journey to you.

It began with an event none of us had even the slightest awareness of. Mister Paxton, in direct opposition to the stated Unionist-abolitionist position, had purchased another slave that summer.

I say this tongue in cheek, as you can no doubt guess; I know full well that Mister Paxton was not regarded as a true Southerner at all, and certainly never thought of himself as one.

But it was like him to be perverse in his dealings—witness his liberal treatment of us, which so outraged some of his neighbors—so that he acquired this new flesh on the eve of war, perhaps as a last indulgence. I did not know. In fact I knew nothing of the slave herself until she was deposited upon the doorstep.

Her arrival was preceded by a period of the most extreme tension between Mama and the Lord of the Manor. After what had occurred regarding myself and Thomas, I assumed that Mister Paxton and my mother were more than ever of one mind—she, of course, had set the ball to rolling toward my annihilation, and Paxton had picked it up and played it. But despite my own abject misery that summer, I could not help noticing that the cordiality between my tormentors lessened following the incident over New Haven. Frequently I'd overheard chuckling and joking exchanged during the weekly domestic meetings between Paxton and Mama, but this now came to an end. The meetings were shorter, and Mister Paxton seemed only slightly less cool with Mama than he was with myself. When finally the white Paxtons left to see Thomas off to England, Mama appeared as relieved as I—we were both looking forward to a period of solitary quiet in which to lick our respective wounds.

The silence was broken, however, by a letter sent to Mama, saying that she should be on the lookout for a girl arriving by coach in mid-January. Between the fifteenth and the twentieth, the letter instructed, she should send Amos to the depot to see if the woman had landed; the instructions could not be more specific, Paxton wrote, because of the unpredictability of the shipping line which was bringing the girl from Jamaica.

Jamaica! Immediately Cheney and Adeline began speculating on who this creature might be, and why she was being sent to New Orleans, which had no need of another live-in house servant. Why, Cheney wanted to know, hadn't Paxton ordered the woman to yourselves at the Old House, where a new acquisition would more logically be accommodated and trained? Adeline was curious as to when he had bought her, and she and Cheney calculated that it must have been the previous summer, which was the date of Paxton's last foray to the West Indies.

Whenever it was, whatever the reason, the new girl appeared at the coach depot on the eighteenth of January, and was borne home by Amos in the back of the dray cart.

Her name, as you have doubtless guessed, was Faith. She carried nothing with her save a homespun shawl, tied at the corners, to hold her belongings—a shift, a kerchief, a rag in which to wrap her hair—and was dressed in some sort of pinafore, which was more like a sack with holes in it than an article of clothing. Her shoes were brogans with brass toes, and appeared several sizes too big for her feet. She was thin and pasty-faced, drawn from her journey no doubt, and seemed as dazed over her arrival in New Orleans as we were at seeing her arrive. I recall my first impression upon meeting her: here, I thought, was a creature who looked as bereft as I felt, and perhaps with much the same cause.

For Faith was the whitest Negro I had ever laid eyes on—besides myself. She was so unarguably white that at first I thought her an indentured servant rather than a slave, but Mama corrected me on this point. She was a Negro, Mama assured me, bought and bound as surely as were we ourselves. And she was pretty—very pretty, although at that point her prettiness was not in the least obvious, and at any rate was of little import to me. I had begun to connect the decline in my fortunes with the sin of lust committed at the Camellia, and had no thought of being distracted by the charms of this girl or any other. So I noted without interest her wavy deep brown hair, hazel eyes, and the splash of freckles across her cheeks; and I saw Mama expressionlessly do the same.

Faith spent her first few weeks in New Orleans either in tears or on the verge of them. She appeared to miss Jamaica mightily, but would say little about how she had come to lose her position there. Much of what she did say was unintelligible to me; it soon became apparent that she was not an educated person, having acquired neither reading nor writing, and her speech was a jumbled patois spiced with accents of the Deep South. I pitied her, but felt no lust or affinity toward her. She moved into the downstairs quarters, and had been handed over to Adeline for assignment to some duty when she recovered her wits, and so initially I had little cause to interact with her beyond superficialities.

For the first few weeks after her arrival, I seemed to meet up with the girl only in the kitchen, where she took her meals with the rest of the servant household. I would say a quick "good morning" or "good evening" to her, and she would bow her head and reply, "Mawnin', suh," in her strange marble-mouthed dialect. Sometimes Mama would be with me, and then Faith would add a "Ma'am" to her greeting. It took some time for me to realize that she believed us to be white overseers or "massas" of some sort; I at last overheard Mama tell the girl that she need not address us as "Mistuh Aubrey" or "Miz Onessa."

Once this formality was dispensed with, Faith began to perk up a bit, and recover a measure of good humor despite her homesickness. She seemed amazed by the doings of the Paxton household, by its wealth and the status accorded ourselves, the live-in servants of the New Orleans home.

She had been given new clothing shortly after her arrival. Amos had been dispatched to the Old House to ask Magdalene for some appropriate petticoats, skirts, and chemises, along with an old boned corset. Plain as the garments were, one would have thought them satin and lace from the pop-eyed bliss with which Faith received them. She spun about, smoothing the skirts, throwing her hair over her shoulder, inspecting the sleeves of the blouse, which was, she said, the first she'd ever owned. She was also given lace-up boots, hand-me-downs from Adeline, which delighted her even more than the blouse. They fit her, for one thing, and enabled her to walk without tripping, and she cooed over their comfort and the softness of their leather lining.

Too, she now had her own washbasin, soap, and towels, although at first she had to be coaxed into using them. She appeared quite surprised at the regularity with which we bathed, hygiene apparently having been unimportant to her previous owners or their charges. Once she became accustomed to the idea, however, she reveled in the feeling of cleanliness, and could not stop exclaiming at the luxury which even she, the lowliest of the house servants, was to be afforded.

I, in turn, was kept amused by her inflated opinion of us, and her wonder at the life I presently found so dismal and devoid of pleasure. She came to be my distraction, and in time I welcomed this, and the respite it gave me from my thoughts of Thomas Paxton and my own misery.

"I never seed niggers live in no massa's house widdout no oberseer," Faith confided to me one afternoon. We were doing a leisurely job of cleaning the pantry together, checking the put-up preserves and bottled pickles for signs of rot. "Every one a y'all lives jes like white folks." She thought a moment, then shrugged, "Course, y'all almost *is* white folks. Nothin but yaller all roun dis place, dat fer sure!" She laughed and held out her own creamy forearm, a keg of jam dangling from her fingers, to prove her point.

"Not true," I said, teasing her a little. "You forgot Amos. He's black as the ace of spades. How do you account for him?"

"Dey ain't no 'countin for any a dis," she said. "Dis ain't like bein a nigger a-tall." And then she fell silent for a while.

Presently I found myself asking, "What was it like where you came from, then?" I had little interest in knowing—as little as I had in anything just then—but we were working side by side, it seemed polite to inquire, and conversation kept my mind from my troubles.

It pained me to see tears leap into her eyes almost at once.

"I ain't like Jamaica much," she began. "I was jes fiel han dere, on dis big plantation what growed sugarcane. Jes choppin, jes shuckin, workin de new plants whilst de mens cut de stalks wid de big knives. Mawnin to night, jes de same ev'y day, 'cept Sunday when us gits a half-day to frolic some. Dere was hunnerds a niggers, I ain't even knowed all dey names, jes de ones as I worked 'longside. I belongst to Massa Bennett dere, an he am de one what sol me to yer Massa Paxton."

I was intrigued. "How did Mister Paxton come to lay eyes on you if you worked in the fields?" What I really wanted to know was why on earth he had singled her out of the hundreds of slaves he saw everywhere he went, and why he had decided to purchase her.

"He come to look roun de fiel one day, and Massa Bennett call de oberseer, dat ol' devil, ol' Devil Cross hisself, to line us gals up so's we can look sharp fer de gennamin guest. An I sees yer massa lookin at me, and he axe me, step fo'ard, girl, an Massa Bennett say do it. Dey ain't say nothin else, jes walk roun lookin at me some, den Massa Bennett jes walk away, and ol Devil Cross say git back to work. An I don' see Massa Bennett agin fer long bout six month. Den Devil Cross call me to de Big House—it so far, dem fields so big, I got to ride dere on de donkey—an Massa Bennett say, Gal, ye member dat gennamin come to look roun, an I says which one, cause Massa always bringin gennamin roun to see de fields, an he say, Dat one as look ye ober, an I says yes even tho I ain't recall, an Massa say,

He done pay good price fer you an you sol. You leavin, goin to New Orleens, come summer. An I'se real happy, cause it mean I git to leave dat sugar farm, even if I ain't know what New Orleens is, nor what ah'm gonna do dere."

I nodded, although I am reproducing only about half of the story here, the rest of it having been beyond my means to decipher. "Well, tell me then, why are you so sad and homesick? If you didn't mind leaving Jamaica, if it was so awful, why do you miss it so?"

"I ain't miss Jamaica," Faith said. "I miss Georgia. Georgia where I'se borned."

"Georgia!" This was Deep South, regardless of where it lay on the map in comparison to Louisiana; it was a land of horrors to my way of thinking, as alien—and far more forbidding—than the unknown of the Indies.

"Yessuh, dat's where I'se borned and bred. Georgia's where I'se sol from, 'fore I goes to Jamaica. Dat where my peoples is."

"How is it," I then asked her, "that you came to leave Georgia for the Indies?"

"Well, das a ol' story, one as I s'pose y'all can guess at, if you ain't awready."

I replied as I hadn't guessed at all, and would she care to fill me in on the details of what the "old story" might be.

Faith shrugged, shook her head, indulged in a variety of twitches and tics before arriving at some point whereupon she could continue her narrative. "Oh, y'all know how it go," she sighed. "My ma was de house nigger fer dem no-'count Bakers, Ol' Missy Sally an Mistuh Hal Baker, outta Lynn Creek, Georgia. White trash if dey ever was. Dey own thirty acres, five niggers, an two mules, an damned if dey don' work ev'y one of 'em t' death. Anyways, Ma real high-yaller, an done take up wid yaller han dere, name a Richard, an had my brudder Jim an den me. Soon's I kin walk good, Ol' Missy put me up inta de house to be house gal 'longside Ma. I'se gonna sweep de floor, an tote water, an comb Ol' Missy hair out at night. She say she glad to have us'n, as she ain't trus no coal-black jungle niggers.

"Well, I'se workin right up dere in de big house, tho it ain't no big house really, not nothin like Massa Bennett's or dis here place. But I'se dere, ev'y day, year in, year out, an afta while I sees dat trash Baker be lookin crookedy at me, slippin past me on de porch, rubbin all up on me, an me only ten, 'lebben year ol'. Ma see it too, an tell Pappy, but what dey gonna do? Cain't tell off no white massa, cain't say no if white massa decide he gon have de nigger gal. But Ma git so riled, she decide to tell Ol' Missy, an when de Missy hear of it she pow'ful mad—not 'cause she care none bout de niggers, but 'cause her ol devil husban makin her look de fool in dey own house.

"Ol' Missy git so mad she tell Baker one of us got to go, an ain't gonna be her.

She make ol' Baker pure miser'ble til he say awright, he gon sell me off. Ma an Pappy begs him not to do it, an I says to Ma I do anything he want, even be he nigger slut. She say don' say sech things, but I don' care, an I tells Ol' Massa dat to he face, an Ol' Missy hear it an come down de steps an cut me a lick in de mouf wid her wooden spoon. I'se so crazed, I git my hand half-up, like I aims t' cut her right back. An den dat's de end, Massa see dat an fetch the spec'lator right dere, an dat same day he come an take me away from Ma an Pappy an Jim. He sell me on de block in de big town in Georgia wid a big mess o' udder niggers, den I goes 'cross de water in de big boat what make me puke, an all dis time I ain't stop cryin for nar a day. Dat's how I comes to Massa Bennett's, an den here, an I ain't seed my fambly from dat day to dis."

Throughout this tale, Faith kept her eyes straight ahead, neither looking at me nor turning toward me, but when she finished it was plain that she was crying once again. Her nose was running, and in one of those moments of surprising indelicacy which had come to be her hallmark, she wiped it with the back of her bare hand, then wiped the hand upon her dress. Had it not been such a lovely nose, and such a lovely hand, for that matter, I should have found the gesture disgusting, but as it was, my heart went out to her, and so I laid my own hand upon her slender wrist so as to offer her some comfort. My action, however, seemed only to deepen her pain, or perhaps to unleash it, for she responded by lowering herself to her knees, and sobbing aloud as a child would do. "Law, Law," she repeated softly, rocking upon the ground. I took her words literally and could make no sense of them until I realized they were simply her peculiar pronunciation of the term "Lord."

I felt I could give her nothing better in that moment than a sympathetic ear, and so I stood by and waited. Presently her tears ceased, and she rose and straightened her dress with great dignity, and then turned toward me. "I ain't mean to put dis on yer mind, Bree," she said, now looking me directly in the eye. I fumbled for some appropriate response, but found I could make none, and so I grasped her fingers and smiled at her with all the reassurance I could muster.

So that I might bring us round to pleasanter topics, I endeavored after a few minutes to tell her about my own family and past. I spoke gently, so as to distract her; I spoke of you, Gran, of the Old House and your cabin there, the education I had enjoyed under your tutelage, of all that made you irreplaceable in my heart.

"Our family has always belonged to the Paxtons," I explained to Faith. "Jean-Tomas Paxton, the master's grandfather, built the Old House, and bought my great-grandparents. Leland Paxton, our master's father, owned my grandmother, and she and my mother lived at the Old House until just after I was born. Right around then our master finished building this place for his wife, and asked his father for my mother and me along with a few other servants. Old Leland made a gift of us, and died a little while after we moved to the city, and Mister Paxton inherited the Old House and all the slaves on it. That's how he came to have two properties. The Old House was a cotton plantation once, but Mister Paxton hasn't much interest in farming it seriously."

"Dat right," Faith said, vaguely. I wondered if I might not be boring her, or at least failing to turn her mind from her own troubles, and so I jumped to what I thought might prove a more interesting topic.

"My grandmother is a fortune-teller," I said next. "She practices vodou, although my mother doesn't hold with it much."

"Vodou!" This caught her ear; Faith rolled her eyes, wiped away the last remaining trace of tears, and tested a smile. "I sure seen some a dat in de island! On'y dey call it 'obeah' in Jamaica—dey say 'vodou' de Haiti way a sayin it. But it de same thing. Cuttin de throats a birds an sech, an crucifixers, an prayin to dem Papist Saints, and Af'ican haints—an zombies! Plenny talk a dem zombies! Vodou man git you an make you a zombie, you like de livin dead, gotta be slave to de vodou man an sleep in de grave. How bout yer gran'mammy, she ever conjure dem zombies up?"

I smiled. "No, she never did anything like that. Maybe Adeline does, though—she's a conjure woman too, although she's not as learned as my grandmother."

I saw Faith's eyes widen, and laughed. "Not to worry, Faith. Adeline must oversee Cheney and David, I doubt she has time to raise up any other zombies." I grinned at her, and she made a little chuckle.

"My gran used to speak of the Living Dead sometimes," I went on, "but these were only legends, stories to tell me when she wished to spook me or make me behave. She had a crucifix and a big wooden rosary, though, and plaster statues of the Holy Family and the Saints. We painted them with dyes she took from the spinning woman. Some of their faces were black—like Mary, the Virgin—and others were brown or white. She tells fortunes with little stones, and she is the herb doctor at the Old House—she knows every tree, every leaf and toadstool, in the forest, and what ills they can alleviate."

"She soun like de righteous woman. When ye s'pose I gon meet er?"

I raised my head. "What? Oh—it's a very long drive to the Old House. I'm sure some one of us will be making it—soon."

"Awright." Faith shrugged. "Ye know," she said, "I seen some a dat healin wid de herbs mahsef. My mammy weren't no vodou lady, but she doctor de niggers so de white doctor ain't gotta come an see after us. She learned me some, though I'se mostly fergit it now." She paused for a moment. "It been a long time since I seen Mammy so's she could tell me. It been long time since— Law. It been long time since lots a things."

Her fingers had ceased moving over the stoppered jars. When I glanced at her, I could see that her recollections had led her right back to the moment of that terrible parting from her family—exactly the opposite of my intent—so that her face clouded over once again.

And as for me, my own story had led me back to the moment of my abrupt parting from yourself, Gran, so that I found I had no more to offer to the conversation than did my poor companion. I brought my eyes back to my own business, and we returned in silence to our checking and sorting, both of us feeling, I imagine, deeply moved, by the telling of our stories and the hearing of them, and the witnessing of those emotions which accompanied them.

After that day, I did not look anymore upon Faith as an amusing bumpkin. Rather, I recognized in her all of the spirit and suffering such as I myself might lay claim to. Though she had not the words to express it, her situation was not unlike mine, her rude awakening in the servitude of her owners not dissimilar. I vowed to treat her with more affection, to make her transition to life at the New Orleans home as welcoming and smooth as possible.

I mentioned my plan to Mama, and was met, for my trouble, with a small smile and a shake of the head. "So you're kindred spirits, eh?" Mama chuckled. "Yes, I can see how you'd share her pain. How similar it is after all to the wrenching turmoil you've encountered here."

But I was not to be discouraged from my course of action. I embarked upon it that very day. I was soon rewarded with such confidence as Faith possessed toward anyone at this point, and with an outpouring of sincere feeling and appreciation such as I had never experienced. Upon seeing me, Faith would break into the most rapturous smiles and a flutter of curtsying and skipping. I had never been so blatantly the object of anyone's affections before, and the sensation evoked in me was a heady one. I was also surprised to note how the improvement in Faith's spirits vastly improved her appearance. She seemed to evolve from mere prettiness into radiance, so that to encounter her became a pleasure for my senses as well as for my spirit.

Even her odd mannerisms took on a charm and piquancy of their own. Where previously I could not have imagined being more than neutral in my feelings toward her, I now wondered why I had overlooked the ample evidence of her appeal, which included those aspects I had formerly found off-putting, or at best rustic.

She had, for example, a repertoire of little songs she indulged in while doing her chores. Most of them were tuneless ditties whose lyrics hinted at the circumstances she had endured in Georgia. There was one favorite which I recall well:

What you gonna do when de meat give out?
What you gonna do when de meat give out?
Sit in de corner wid my lips pooched out!
Lawsy!
What you gonna do when de meat come in?
What you gonna do when de meat come in?
Sit in de corner wid a greasy chin!
Lawsy!

It was the "Lawsy!" which I enjoyed most; Faith would give a little nod whenever she came to that part of the refrain, so that waves of shiny brown hair danced down her back. It wasn't long before other members of the household picked the expression up, and soon some of us were marching about flavoring our speech with outbursts of "Lawsy!," accompanied by Faith's little head toss, whenever a point needed additional underscoring.

There was another song she sang too, though, one which was not nearly so endearing or inspiring:

Run nigger run, de pateroller git you
Run nigger run, de pateroller come!
Watch nigger watch, de pateroller trick you,
Watch nigger watch, he got a big gun.

None of us wished to store this one in our memories.

I enjoyed Faith's performances, and her company at odd little jobs about the house, for the better part of the spring, until it became apparent that some more useful position would have to be found for her. She was Mama's responsibility, Mama being the head of our household in Paxton's absence, but Mama declined to take on what might shape up into a monumental task, and promptly handed her to Adeline for training.

Her first assignment was light mending and seamstressing. But that was abandoned when it was discovered that she had no affinity for sewing, her bruised thumbs and needle-scarred forefingers bearing silent witness to the fact. Adeline next placed her in the kitchen, but Lila took offense to those habits which

I had imagined to be "rustic," and gently suggested that perhaps she'd be of more use elsewhere in the house. Finally it was decided that she would assist Cheney, our maid-of-all-work, by taking on the duties of the downstairs parlor maid.

You no doubt recall, Gran, that Madame Eugenia had certain fixed notions regarding the formality of a household. She was always in favor of a European-style servant system, complete with uniforms for the various stations. And so, upon being placed in her new position, Faith was issued a suitably somber raiment and collar and starched hat, which over her pretty and lithe frame seemed particularly offensive. She was assigned the simple task of cleaning and polishing the furniture in the front hall and dining room, and straightening the parlor itself. Should guests call at the front door, it would be Faith who would receive them, and notify the proper party of their arrival. And in the event of the Paxton family's return to the New Orleans house, it would fall to Faith to maintain the English-style afternoon tea service, since Madame enjoyed her "spot of" at precisely four o'clock each day.

Even in the absorbing of these small tasks, however, Faith seemed uncomfortable, and made mistake after mistake in their execution. Cheney commented that she could hear the wind whistle into one side of the girl's head and, with nothing to stop it, come whistling out the other side a second later. But Faith was not stupid—she was only uneducated and unused to our customs, and as such should have been accorded a bit more leeway than she received in those first weeks.

Part of the problem was her high color, combined with the strange circumstances of her purchase. Cheney and Adeline—Creole and high-yellow though they were—seemed grudging and jealous, particularly Cheney, whom I'd always regarded as having a vicious tongue. (Matters were not helped any by David's obvious appreciation of Faith's charms, which Cheney noted at once.) It was not long before rumors were set to flying: that Faith's mistakes were in fact purposeful, and born of a resentment over having to work for her bread when she was so nearly white; that she thought herself above the rest of the household and its duties; and, most disturbingly, that she had been purchased by Mr. Paxton so that she might function as his mistress, the successor to Madame (and God knew who else, Cheney said) in his bed.

The majority of these grumblings caused me no anxiety, as I knew they were untrue, but the last one weighed upon my mind. Could it be that in some devious fashion Mr. Paxton had acquired the girl in order to make a concubine of her? Would that not explain her abrupt arrival, the seeming lack of forethought which had gone into her purchase? I had never known Mr. Paxton to indulge in such wretched tastes, but the practice was common enough, and often surreptitiously undertaken. In fact had it not been this very issue which had led to Faith's dismissal from her Georgia home—how appalling if her deliverance here was to be a reenactment of the same awful scene!

I said as much to Mama, with considerable distress, but she scoffed at my fears. "I can tell you this, Aubrey: Mister Paxton does not believe in race mixing. He never has, and I doubt he ever will. If he has mistresses—and perhaps he does, for all any of us know, Bree—he's taken them from among his own class and color. Besides," she added, "even if he were to develop a taste for yellow flesh, why would he go on to *buy* some little backwater fool when he could have had her in Jamaica as many times as he wished and been done with it? You see, once you think it over, it doesn't add up. Mister Paxton didn't bring that child here for his own benefit. That's just Cheney shooting off her big mouth with nothing behind it, as usual."

I was relieved to hear this and let out my breath with a sigh. But Mama wasn't finished; she picked absently at a nail, waited until I was ready to rise and depart the room before adding, "I'll tell you what does add up, though."

I turned to look at her. "What?"

"Perhaps Mister Paxton brought her here for *your* benefit."

I might have considered that startling idea at more length had not other circumstances intervened, which took my considerable attention off Faith and my involvement with her.

By this time, the rumors of imminent war had escalated, and tension was evident everywhere, especially in such dealings between whites and Negroes as we were forced to have. Wherever one went in the formerly familiar city, one was met with icy stares, with scuttling and whispering, and with the coldest demeanor on the part of white folk. Each loophole by which the Negro might have brought some pleasure into his mundane and mean existence was tightened, and then closed. Passes were required for the slightest venturing off the owner's grounds, visits between neighboring lovers ceased. Prayer camp meetings came to a halt, practitioners of vodou were persecuted. All of this, I suppose, was designed to prevent our getting it into our heads to foment some sort of revolution or, at the very least, abandonment; but it seemed to me that most Negroes had no thought as to either—they were as terrified of the Yankees and the idea of conflict as their white masters.

The increased restrictions did not affect the Paxton Negroes as much as they did our neighbors. We were able to write passes at leisure, and come and go with the same frequency as before. Yet this very fact called attention to us: although we were not field hands, we were not white folk either; we were not freemen, yet presumed to act as if we were. And if this had been tolerated in peacetime, it seemed that in view of imminent war it was to be found considerably more offensive.

The afternoon came when there was the sound of a horse's hooves upon the roadway, and then a knock at the door. I was upstairs in our own chambers, which faced the yard, but I stalked quietly down into Louella's former room and lifted the curtain there. I thought I recognized the horse tethered to the wrought-iron fence outside—a bay gelding with deep black mane and tail—although I could not see the owner beneath our balcony.

Presently, though, I heard the door open, and realized Faith must be answering it. A moment later she was racing up the stairs, tripping on the hem of her uniform and calling in a hoarse whisper, "Onessa! Miz Onessa! Bree!" I stepped into the hallway and caught the back of her arm just as she was about to hasten up the final flight to Mama's rooms.

"What is it, Faith? What's happening?"

"Dey a man downstairs. Say he de sheriff a some sech. Say as he wanna see de massa, o yer mama, an right now."

I knew then who the man must be. The distinctive bay belonged to a *gendarme* named L'Heuron, a tall, cadaverous Cajun who, despite his lack of wealth, had wangled a position within one of the parish's white citizens' guilds. I imagined him, fresh from his dismal quarters and swamp-rat wife, gingerly treading up our flagstone walkway, shifting in his ill-fitting boots as he stood before the Paxtons' great front door.

But what could he want here? As far as I knew, every member of our small household was minding its given business, obediently going about the upkeep of the Paxton property with the degree of loyalty and dedication it had always previously exhibited. Neither I nor anyone else had been about causing trouble, or seeking it out.

I ran up the last flight of steps myself, but Faith had already called Mama, who was on her way down. I met up with her just as she had reached the second-floor landing, and was stunned to see her descending the stairs with one of Paxton's old muskets slung under her arm. "Mama—" I whispered, but she put a finger to her lips and brushed by me.

I grabbed Faith by the hand and proceeded to the back staircase. By slipping through the kitchen and the dining room we would be able to get into the parlor unseen and overhear whatever was said at the front door.

L'Heuron was the first to speak. "Well now, Onessa. Lookit you. I surely hope you aren't intendin' to blast my head off with that thing."

"Monsieur L'Heuron, sir," Mama demurred, "I *am* so sorry." I could not see where she held the musket at this point. "There is a new girl here, she told me only that there was a stranger at the door, and I had no idea it was yourself. I meant no disrespect. I was only preparing in case it be someone intending Mister Paxton's property ill—things have taken such a desperate turn, sir, if you know what I mean. This old piece doesn't even shoot, sir. It's merely decoration." Mama's voice was music, and I could picture the languid stretch of her neck, the peek from under fluttering lashes, which she delivered as she spoke.

"We surely are in desperate times, Onessa," the deputy replied, but not with any warmth. "And it does my heart good to see a darky willing to defend her masta's property. But a yella gal with a gun in her hand is like to be a dead yella gal before too long, so decoration or no, you are gonna put that musket back where you found it, aren't you, now?"

"Of course, sir," Mama purred. I could hear L'Heuron brushing by her to enter the foyer, and at the same time she said, "Sir, I must tell you, Mistuh and Miz Paxton are traveling right now, there's nobody here but myself and the other servants."

"I know that, Onessa. It's you I'm meanin' to have a talk with anyway."

I felt my heart jump in my chest. A moment later Mama was leading L'Heuron to the front parlor. Faith and I scrambled to exit that space and rearrange ourselves behind the sliding door of the formal dining room, but from this post we could make out only the muffled crescendos of conversation, and not a word of what was said.

After perhaps ten minutes, I heard the click of Mama's little heels on the parquet floor. A moment later came the creak of L'Heuron's boots, as he prepared to take his leave. He clomped back toward the foyer, while Faith and I crept behind at a safe distance.

"When exactly is your masta expected?" I heard him call back to Mama from the front steps.

"I'm not sure, sir, but I will write and tell him of your visit, and perhaps he can contact you himself."

"No need for that, Onessa. Just so you know to keep your place, until all this bad business blows over. We'll lick 'em, if it comes to that, and you can look forward to a long life peacefully serving your masta and missus, just as you always have."

"Yes, sir. I surely do dream of that, sir. I thank you again for your concern, and for stopping by. Good day to you, sir."

She closed the door upon him so gently that I did not even hear the latch click. When I stepped into the foyer, I found her with her back still turned, the musket propped in a corner beside her, where she must have placed it some minutes before.

"Mama?" I called.

Faith had crept in behind me, and now she spoke in a small voice. "I heerd you, ma'am. Sayin as I were new. Did I do wrong, ma'am?"

Mama turned around. "What? No. You didn't do wrong. I'm sorry to have used you as a scapegoat, Faith. Your performance was perfect."

"Oh." She seemed puzzled, and it occurred to me that she was wondering what sort of beast this scapegoat might be.

"Mama?" I said again. "What's happened?" She wore those narrow, feline eyes which I recognized as the prelude to some of our less pleasant days together.

"Aubrey, tell everyone in the household to be ready for a meeting tonight before suppertime. I am going upstairs to write for a bit. If you need me, I'll be in my room."

"Yes ma'am." I watched her sweep out of the door and up the steps, boot heels again clicking on polished wood, the ancient musket now clutched tightly in her right hand. It was a lie, I knew, which Mama had told L'Heuron regarding the gun: that musket shot all right, and the ammunition for it lay in a rough wooden box in Mr. Paxton's study; and Mama as well as I knew how to load the thing and how to take it apart and grease each piece so that it might remain in perfect working order.

I did as I had been bidden, and at promptly six o'clock the entirety of our small servant family sat gathered in the kitchen: Cheney and David, Lila, Amos, Adeline, Faith, and myself. Mama sat at the head of the big oak-slab table, a general before her troops. She had drawn the coarse spirals of her hair away from her face, and she twirled one distractedly about a finger. When all of us had settled ourselves, she began to speak.

"We had a visitor today. In case any of you hadn't heard. Monsieur L'Heuron came to see me." There were furtive glances exchanged across the table. "I've been informed that our position here has become most precarious. Very likely there is gonna be war, and as of now we are a group of slave Negroes alone in a house without any authority to mind, while all around us our betters prepare to do battle with those forces who would see us freed. Naturally, some of the parish's citizens have developed a degree of ill feeling toward us. And being as Monsieur L'Heuron is wholly sympathetic toward us, and knows we are good and loyal niggers, he has taken it upon himself to give us suggestions as to how to conduct ourselves, so as to avoid accidentally stepping out of place and incurring the further wrath of certain nameless individuals hereabouts."

She eyed each of us in turn. "Make no mistake: L'Heuron and his ilk have got a skittish finger on the trigger. We could very well be dead in a week because some swamp-bottom bastard gets it into his head to make an example of us.

"For that reason I thought it best to post a letter to Mister Paxton. I've explained the situation, and I've asked him to respond, and possibly to return here to help us handle it. In the meantime, I believe that our most prudent course of action is to follow whatever rules are forced upon us, until there is some realistic hope of defying them." She halted, as if expecting somebody to interrupt her, but none of us did. So she continued on, explaining what the new laws of the land were to be, obliterating our few opportunities for pleasure and leisure with swift and well-placed strokes.

"Monsieur L'Heuron and his associate Monsieur Calvin are watching us closely. They will be stopping in each day, to assess our comfort and well-being. They shall provide a pass for me to make market when I need to. We are no longer to write passes ourselves. And all other travel is forbidden."

She turned to Amos. "I'm afraid you are gonna have to do without Berta for a bit." Amos visited his laundress wife at the home of her owner, Monsieur Cassout; I wondered how he would take this news, but his face was expressionless.

"And for the rest of us, no more gree-gree—" (She glanced here at Adeline, our vodou expert in your absence, Gran.) "—or revivals—" (This was directed to Cheney.) "—no more moonshine, card nights, and so on." (This dispensed with everyone else except me.)

"And Aubrey," she said at last, "I trust your one excursion to the Quarter was enough to satisfy your curiosity. Your tomcatting days are over, for the time being." I sat rooted to my seat—how in the world had she known about the Camellia?—then blushed to the tips of my fingers, and turned away.

"Now, I realize this seems harsh. But it's the wisest course, until we determine which way fortune is going to go. Let us pray it brings the Union to our door, for then I shall be the first to take up arms and fight. Meantime, anybody sees fit to disagree with what I've done, give a suggestion, now is the time to speak your piece." No one did. From Amos all the way down to Faith, we were silent.

"Well, then," Mama said. She pushed back her chair with a long, slender hand and sat smoothing her skirts over her thighs.

That appeared to be the cue for the breakup of the gathering. There was a small commotion as the participants left their seats, but no one addressed Mama, no one looked in her direction—not even Amos, who certainly took advantage of Mama's presence, on most occasions, to look as much as she would permit.

I watched them rising to go, and noticed, seemingly for the first time, a certain stiffness between some of these members of my servant family and Mama, the way they glanced sideways at her and slipped by with rigid mouths, as if seething beneath the weight of her authority but lacking the wherewithal to challenge it.

The thing was done, though, the authority wielded, and the upshot of it was that the entire household now lived as if under a form of martial law. Each night after dinner one of our self-appointed overseers arrived on horseback and requested that all of us show ourselves at the gate; otherwise we could barely leave the house. The end of our sidewalk might as well have been the end of the earth for all that we could see beyond it. Amos at least had the refuge of his little room in the carriage house, which he shared with Soleil and Lumi, the dapple-gray carriage team. And David tended the yard, he trimmed the stately chinquapin tree that grew just outside the gates, and invented a million other outdoor chores so as to remove himself from the domain of his wife.

But the rest of us were stuck together in the house, which seemed to grow smaller each moment that we inhabited it. Mama noted our sniping and grumbling, and took the trouble to tell me that she hoped Mr. Paxton would not be too long in answering her letter—then perhaps some relief would come. My own feelings about such a deliverance were decidedly mixed. I dreaded the return of Paxton with or without Thomas, and so I dreaded—even as I knew I should hope for—that moment when Mama would receive the response she awaited.

When I was not too preoccupied with dread, though, I noticed sorely my lack of entertainment, and was forced to make my own—an arrangement which, in the face of my recent circumstances, could not come to any good. Whereas before my primary enemy had been misery and an intense weighted sense of sorrow, I now found myself principally plagued by boredom. And the devil, true to form, quickly found work for my idle hands, and the idle mind which controlled them.

Despite my repudiation of the carnal sin that had led me to the Camellia, it was not long before lust once again overtook me, and led me to contemplate anew the charms of our most recent arrival. As soon as our "house arrest" became the status quo, I began to dwell again on that suggestion of Mama's which had preceded Monsieur L'Heuron's visit: namely, the idea that Faith had been intended as an oblique gift to myself from Mr. Paxton. In the back of my mind somewhere came the warning that were this true, it would amount to no more than a sop offered to distract me from the question of my heinous maltreatment by the Paxtons (and doubly so, since, by contrast with Faith's, my circumstances could not help but appear much rosier); but what was that in the face of the creature herself, who, if a sop, was certainly a glorious one? I was flattered to think that in some way Paxton had acknowledged my incipient manhood, and had chosen so carefully for me, at least in terms of the physical if not the cultural or intellectual.

For it was the physical that now primarily consumed me. Observing Faith at her chores, it was hard not to imagine that she wanted me to observe, to see her as she showed herself to her best advantage. Dusting the Limoges figurines in the parlor cabinet, she bent languorously left or right, or to the floor, her breasts toppling forward in her shift, or displacing the bib of the white apron of her uniform. Sweeping the hearth, she switched her buttocks beneath her skirts, whilst the petticoats caught at the ankle to reveal an inch or so of satiny skin each time she took a step. Or she would push her hair with a hand from her forehead, that hair which she wore loose and streaming down her tapered back. Her arms were plump and curved, her wrists tiny, her collarbone firm beneath her curved neck; her eyes were a translucent golden brown, and her lip, unpainted, rosy. I could not glimpse any of these features without imagining how I might exploit them—how I might sit her atop me so that those breasts leaned forward to graze my chest, or grasp her from behind and pull her against me, or wind my fingers into that hair as her lips sought mine. Each gesture she made seemed designed to throw me into a fit of desire, so that on more than one occasion I was forced to excuse myself, or turn or sit, lest my indecent state be obvious to the entire world.

I could imagine all that I would enact upon her, but I had no notion of how to suggest it, and so my actual attempts at contact with Faith were both ridiculous and frustrating. At first, when we worked together (at the repairs and busywork Mama had dreamed up to keep us occupied), I found even the slightest of my advances rebuffed. If I brushed her hand (accidentally, of course), she would push me away with a smile. If I inveigled to squeeze by her, she would make a show of shrinking into the wall. This infuriated me, as it seemed a contradiction to the smiles she flashed me, and the display she made of herself. Yet when we spoke, I felt a tenderness and a kinship toward her that squelched my anger, and in other moments she was as forthcoming, as glad for my company, as ever.

So I kept up my clumsy feints and passes, and in time I noted a change in her response toward me. Slowly but surely, she began to allow greater liberties, which I quickly took advantage of. My hand was permitted to linger a bit longer on hers, and sometimes she would even find an excuse to touch my shoulder, or my face. She began to devise as many reasons as I to be caught in the narrow servants' staircase, or in the pantry, where we would have to brush by each other with barely a hairsbreadth between our bodies.

At last one day I knew a perfect opportunity had presented itself when Mama sent us into the bath beyond the master bedroom to clean the huge claw-footed tub therein. We were armed with lye soap, with hog-bristle brushes and rags, and we wore our lightest clothing, as it was a humid day and the job a tedious and laborious one.

In the bathroom we made awkward circles round each other, as if knowing that some resolution of the tension between us was inevitable. "Well, guess we bes git down to de job," Faith sighed at last, leaning against the tub onto her elbows. "I suppose so," I replied, as nonchalant as she. I shrugged and turned away, pretended to be occupied with the water bucket, although I could observe her movements easily enough in the glass.

She busied herself, seeming not to see me, dipping the coarse bar of soap into her own bucket and working up a lather on one of the brushes. Then she caught her skirts with a hand, drew them up, and tied her apron over them about her waist, so that they formed baggy pantaloons—and left her calves and knees bare. Lastly she got down on all fours in the tub, grasped the sopping brush in both hands, and set to work scrubbing—pushing and pulling, her body rocking rhythmically, hair and breasts swinging, rump poised in the air.

This, combined with the sight of her naked legs, was simply too much. Surely she could not be innocent of the effect she was having, and surely I could not be blamed for being affected. I stepped into the tub behind her, knelt, and leaned over her neck. "Let me help," I said, thinking myself very clever, and placing both hands over hers on the brush.

"What you doin, Bree," she giggled.

I was no poet; the romantic inclination I wielded was more club than rapier. I spouted no witticisms, but giggled myself and nuzzled her cheek with my own, and when she did not pull away, I allowed more of my torso to rest against her, and ran a hand up the length of her arm. She stopped moving, and I saw her shut her eyes; thus encouraged, I kissed her cheek, then pushed the heavy hair from her neck and kissed her there. She inclined her face toward me, and gathered her legs beneath her; I leaned back to allow her to turn, and she knelt facing me, her eyes wide.

I realized then that she had placed me in command of the action between us. She might be the one to direct—or forbid—it, but it was obvious from her demeanor that she expected me to take the lead. How different this was from Clara's efficient conduct, and how much more alluring! Whatever I knew or did not know, I was secure in the certainty that she knew less, and that therefore my own inexperience would not be the focus of attention. Encouraged, I leaned in toward her; I ran my fingers over her nose and lips, and then I closed my eyes and kissed her lightly upon the mouth, and when she allowed this, I did it again, this time opening my mouth a little to see if she would respond in kind.

She did—and a second later, we were wound about each other, panting, our tongues searching, our fingers busied negotiating the layers of fabric that separated our bare skins.

This kiss—I hardly knew how to manage it, where to place my lips, whether to use my teeth—it overwhelmed me, having a force beyond even that delicious moment in the Camellia when I'd spent and fallen back upon the bed. I could think of nothing but to prolong it, and along with it the freedom to explore. Wonder of wonders, I managed to slip my right hand beneath Faith's skirts, and felt the flesh of her thigh burning against my palm. She wore no petticoat today; dizzied, I attempted to pull the skirts out of the way, my mind knowing not where to focus: upon my mouth, where her tongue played over my lips? upon the sensation of her breasts crushed against me? upon my fingers, unerringly seeking their prize?

I was lost, and only the intervention of the object herself pulled me out of the ether.

I felt a tugging at my hand, and I was aware that the press of Faith's body had been withdrawn. Then her mouth was at my ear. "Naw," she was saying, "naw, Bree, don', don' do dat."

I stopped and sat back, my breath ragged. She was gasping as well, her mouth looking raw and bruised. "You cain't," she whispered.

"I *can't*?" I blinked stupidly. "Why not? You don't like me?" I was puzzled: had she led me to the edge of this precipice only to cruelly deny me, or had I assumed too much interest on her part?

"Yeah, I likes ye. But I don' know yer mind. Ain't courtin ye, I means. Cain't let jes anybody have at it, ye see? Specially not no fine gennamin, jes funnin wid me, an gonna walk off soon's he's had his way." She cowered back in the tub, yanked the skirts down over her ankles.

"What ye want wid me, Bree? I cain't spell or do no sums. Ye got fancy talk an learnin, ye must t' thinkin I'm jes li'l pickaninny right out de fiel, cain't say no to de likes a yose'f. Ye half-right den—if ye gonna force me I cain't hardly stop ye, but I ain't no slut, whatever ye hearin bout plantation niggers."

I sat back, chastened. I had not meant to force or to judge her, only to infer her willingness; nor did I presume myself a "fine gentleman"—in that, at least, she was mistaken. But in a sense she had pegged me correctly. I did assume that most plantations were hotbeds of promiscuity, from whence she could not have escaped with her virtue intact. Thus any claim of maidenhood was mere pretense, and any frolic with me a mere secondary offense. What could she care, in the long run, about what was a bit of poke between us, if she was already so compromised?

But now it struck me that perhaps her reticence was no affectation.

After all, she was so nearly white.

Her moral sensibility would surely have been formed accordingly; she might therefore have fought with vigor to defend her honor. And too it would have been unconscionable for an owner to leave one of such high color and attendant greater refinement at the mercies of rapacious, dark-skinned Negroes. So she just might have escaped unsullied, a fair flower poking its head above the mud.

I felt a wave of that fellow-feeling which so bound me to her, and I was transformed from ravisher to protector, and rather nearly glad that she had stopped me thus, for now I knew her to be a creature of some quality. I touched her face. "All right," I said, struggling to exert some control over myself. "It's all right." I bent to kiss her again, but softly, with closed lips. She thought herself a lady—her rusticity, her speech, aside—and so I would indulge her. She sought to be wooed, so I would comply, knowing she wished it. The idea of this pursuit gave me almost as great a pleasure as the thought of conquest.

When she saw I meant to respect her limits, she placed her arms round my neck and peeked out from beneath her lashes. "Ye still like me?" she asked.

"Yes," I replied, honestly, "I like you very much. Very much, Faith. You possess grace and charm—and character, of which sums and spelling are no measure." Her eyes grew misty and huge. *Aubrey,* she fluttered, and nestled against my shoulder.

I wished I might sit like that, her buffer against the world, forever; I thought suddenly of my drunken embrace with Thomas upon the stairs the night of our debauch, and realized I had not felt so full, so large within myself, since that moment. "Yes, I like you," I said again into Faith's sweet-smelling hair, and she snuggled more firmly into me.

She desired courtship, and so I endeavored to find out what said courtship might consist of. My venues for research were somewhat limited. I did not, of course, ask Mama—why leave oneself open to ridicule—nor did I think David (whose most frequent request of his wife Cheney was that she "shut her big lips") or Amos (who had courted Berta with the gift of a spittoon and chewing tobacco) would have anything of use to contribute. I thought longingly of Thomas; I imagined the splendid adventures he must be having, the extravagant gifts laid before young ladies, the extravagant caresses granted in return, and all of it experienced through a sweet haze of perfume and candlelight. He would certainly know how I should proceed—but would he laugh at me for bothering, when the "young lady" was a slave late of a cane field, who could neither read nor write, and had never seen a drinking cup before coming to New Orleans? "She shouldn't be hard to impress," I could imagine Thomas chortling, "just take off your boots before you have at her, and she'll no doubt be grateful."

But I did not long allow myself to think of Faith thus. Whatever she was, she was beautiful, and she was before me, and thought the world of me. And thought enough of herself to demand more than the removal of my boots before I deflowered us both. She deserved better than Thomas's sneering sarcasm, and I banished him with a shake of my head.

I decided I could best appeal to her with those gifts bestowed through education, the exposure to which Faith so sorely lacked. She had been astonished when I told her one day that I could actually read the leather-bound books in the Paxton library; an exhibition of this skill, I decided, might be a fine place to start.

I set aside afternoons in which I met with her in the study, or the pantry, or the carriage house—wherever anyone else was not—and recited to her those works I thought would cast me in the best light while holding her interest. Thus was she availed of the sonnets of Shakespeare, the comic intrigues of Molière, the elegant theories of Newtonian physics—all the subjects, in short, which had bored me to tears during my years of servitude under the good Sister Corinne.

"Law!" she would swoon, after each performance, "dat is de prettiest soun I evuh heerd! All de words! What it mean?" And then I would explain—to the extent that I was able—and watch as she struggled to find some point from which she might springboard to understanding. I discovered, through these tutorials, that she was not in the least dull-witted or coarse, but rather simply unfamiliar with the idea of abstract thought. She had spent her short life running away, mourning, surviving, and had not had time even to imagine the niceties of art or philosophy. Once exposed, though, she was not only appreciative but hungry, consumed by her glimpse of this feast of intellect from which she'd been barred.

That I should provide her entrée to the banquet earned me, of course, the very favor I had been seeking. And I traded upon that favor, careful not to overstep myself, but persistent nonetheless. The more eloquently I made love to her through speech and recitation, the more of her flesh I claimed for the purpose of exploration. Each inch of access was a hard-won battle, but once won, the territory was mine for good. Romeo's speech to Juliet upon her balcony earned me a kiss, with my hands outside Faith's wretchedly full skirts. Ephesus Dromio's condemnation of his master put the hand beneath the skirts up to the petticoat. And a thorough overview of the concept of gravity resulted in the placing of both my palms beneath her bosom, from whence I was permitted to roam that terrain at length. (Not even a fine excerpting of *Lysistrata*, however, was enough to convince Faith that she ought, at some point, to caress me back.)

Of course my forays into the library did not go unnoticed. Mama saw me either entering or leaving on several occasions, and shot me a withering glance. Certainly she knew what I was about—as she'd known, after all, about the Camellia, as she herself had been the one to suggest Faith as a match for myself in the first place. Yet I imagined her disapproving, or more likely sneering, for whatever reason, and somehow this made the idea of the match all the more compelling.

The groping segment of our lessons usually took place in the carriage house, where Faith and I arranged to meet in the small hours of the morning. Amos had resumed his nightly forays to Berta's, not a week after Mama had expressly forbidden it, and so we were afforded our privacy in the little outbuilding. The tack room where Amos had his cot seemed too mundane a setting to me, and so we used the loft, climbing the ladder through the hatch, spreading quilts upon the hay, setting a very trim lamp upon the crossbeam. Beneath us, the horses snuffled and munched, and an occasional mouse skittered over the bales, or over us.

After about a fortnight of these surreptitious meetings, I decided I would surprise Faith with a present.

During my forays into the crannies of our house, I had come upon an item left behind by Louella, in her nearly empty chest of drawers. It was a dusty velvet jewelry pouch, which likely had not seen daylight in a decade. There were several orphaned articles contained therein, and I decided (as the other servants did now and then) to arrange the disappearance of some of them—in this case an old pair of garnet earrings. They were quite lovely, with stones set in silver, and that deep maroon hue which would so flatter Faith's skin. I pocketed them, and brought them to our meeting place that night, slipping in before Faith was able to sneak out of the downstairs quarters.

When she arrived I pulled her up into the loft, and kissed her. "I've something for you," I said, breathless, as we untwined from each other. I made her shut her eyes, and then I took hold of her hand, opened the fingers, pressed the earrings in, and closed her fist around them.

"Go on, look now."

She opened her hand, and her gasp of surprise filled me with pleasure. "Jewels!" she cried. "*Jewels!* Y'done got me *rubies*!"

"No, they're not rubies," I chuckled, "only garnets. But at least they're not glass, as far as I know."

She paid me no mind. "Jewels!" she crooned again. "Dey so *purdy*! Ain't never seed no jewels on nigger gal. Even Ma never had no jewels! Law, even Ol' Missy Baker herse'f never had no jewels!" She glanced from the trinkets to myself, then flung her arms round my neck and squeezed me nearly blue. "Oh, Bree! Oh, thankee! Y' done got me jewels! I'm like t' feel jes like a queen!"

"A fitting title," I smiled, but I was thinking that even without it she was too good for me: I felt a distinct pang of guilt knowing I had purchased her simple adoration with the castoffs of another, finer lady.

But she was holding the prizes up against her cheek with delight, and they were as flattering as I had imagined. Faith tossed her head this way and that, and dangled the earrings at arm's length.

She then examined them with that feminine precision reserved for objects of adornment, and squinted. "How I'm gonna put 'em on, Bree?" she asked, her brow knotted.

"What do you mean?"

"Dey got li'l wires. Dey fer ears wid holes in 'em."

I knew nothing of wires, or ears with holes. No wonder Louella had never worn them, I thought; ear piercing was a fad favored by Gypsies.

But Faith's dark beauty lent itself to such affectations. She unfurrowed her brow and grinned. "I kin put de holes mahse'f," she brightened. Before I could object to this, she jumped up and scampered down the ladder, and soon returned with a sewing needle, which she'd likely found among Amos's effects.

I was squeamish enough at the idea that she meant to pierce her lobes with her own hand—I recalled her lack of skill during her seamstress training—but when she placed the little silver needle in my palm and said, "Awright, Bree, make sure ye git 'em even," I felt positively faint.

"I'm not sure I can," I balked. "I don't know how. What if I hurt you?"

"Ain't gonna hurt me none. Go on now, jes do it quick-like, don' drag it out."

I took the glass shade from the lamp and held the needle to the flame to clean it. Then, swallowing hard, I bent Faith's neck back, pinched her fat little earlobe between my fingers, and drove the point in. She flinched, and I felt a sickening resistance to the needle, but I did not stop, and at last the sharp steel emerged from the other side. Faith's eyes streamed with tears, her lower lip trembled, but she handed me one of the earrings. "Put it in," she whispered, so I withdrew the needle, which seemed to pain her even more, and worked the wire through. She wiped her cheeks, then turned and bent her neck to present the other ear, and I repeated the process. Only this time the shaft of the needle drew a drop of blood, and when I inserted the wire I realized the earrings appeared to be made of the same substance—drops of blood, which dangled alongside her lovely neck from gossamer silver threads.

She turned to face me, the garnets leaping to life in the lamp glow. "How dey look?" She smiled through her glittering lashes.

"Beautiful." It was quite true. "You are so beautiful. With or without the stones."

She lowered her head and raised her eyes to me. "Dis mean I yer gal, Bree?"

I considered my response, but not for very long; after all, what other girl was nearby extending herself thus? And how binding was such a question when all around me, Negroes bred on the slightest pretext, and "marriage" consisted of jumping over a broom before one's Master? Of course Mama would never sanction such behavior, but then Mama was alone, with only me, her "yellow bastard," in tow, my own high-yellow father long since having been sold away, or perhaps merely having fled.

"Yes. You're my gal," I told Faith, the act of claiming her inflating me tenfold. She kissed me of her own accord, and then ran the back of a smooth hand over my chest, beneath the buttons of my shirt, which she proceeded to undo. And as I watched her, unblinking, she took both my hands and placed them around her waist, and bade me lift her chemise, and then undo the corset, so that she sat before me, a gift, her breasts free, bluish veins snaking beneath their tawny skin. I removed my own shirt and embraced her, felt her tongue pulse in my mouth, felt for the first time my flesh contact hers, unobstructed—felt her hand squeeze along my thigh, where it did not tarry long, felt sensation smash into me like a fist, so that the discarding of the rest of our clothing passed for me in a blur, until we were naked upon the quilt. Inflamed now, I could only rush headlong into the experience—finesse and modesty forgotten, the universe contracted into the contours of Faith's body beneath me, my fingers reaching, seeking, coming away moist, she putting them to her lips, then to mine, she guiding me, and then guiding me further; resisting, her breath in shallow gasps at my ear, and then yielding, her hands scampering over my shoulders, my back, urging me into her rhythm.

My own sound in my ears was unrecognizable to me, and stunningly loud, and perhaps that was why I did not catch any noise which might have chanced to rise from the street to our eyrie. I stood poised at the brink of momentary insanity, where even Faith's pained whimpers could not penetrate, and when I fell from this precipice I was oblivious.

It took me several minutes to recover myself. When I felt I could control my body, I raised up onto my elbows, and stared down at my conquest. Faith's eyes had once again filled with tears. I wiped these away, and chastised myself—the animal, the beast—for not having been more considerate a paramour. "Did I hurt you much," I whispered. She shook her head, and I found myself, perversely, just a tad disappointed. She was still crying, though, and she bit her plump bottom lip with her teeth while her eyes overflowed. Her weeping stirred every protective instinct in me.

"What is it?" I cradled her in my arms. "What is making you so sad?"

She wiped her nose, her hand trembling. "You de first," she sniffled. I had supposed this, but was hugely gratified to hear it confirmed. A long moment went by, during which I debated speaking, but then decided against it. Eventually she drew in a breath and continued.

"Dese years been so hard, Bree. Sometimes I wunner should I go on, worry whut de nex day bring—I could be daid, so why take on if one a de mens come afta me. Why not jes pleasure mahse'f, save mahse'f de battle. But I couldn never do it. Goin off wid jes anyone, passed like de bottle from one to de nex, an chillen comin widdout I'm knowin who dey daddy is—I couldn do it. I done fit off mens since 'fore I's outta shirttails, 'fore I even gotten titties, woulda mebbe fit off my own brudder an pa, like de other gals do, if de massa ain't sol me 'way first. I git chased ever place I been, got slapped down plenny, an have de mens at me night an day. But some way I'se saved, Aubrey. Fer you. I knowed ye was comin—don' axe me how. I jes knowed dey be betta out dere fer me. Now I done been had. Ye gotten me. I on'y hope I done right, not waitin til de broom be jumped or de preacher come."

I was about to reassure her—once I'd discounted Clara, who after all had been a whore and merely Frenched me to boot—that this was also my first experience, for which I felt only gratitude, and not remorse. But my tongue caught, as the implication of her words became clear. At her mention of preachers and brooms I found myself wondering just who had had whom.

But I could not fault her—was her fortitude not admirable, and her untenable situation not unlike my own? I had respected that fortitude even as I was its undoing, and now it was time for me to bear responsibility. This was not difficult, gazing at her in the lamplight, and so I touched her face, and whispered, "Of course you did right. You are a lady, Faith, whatever your circumstance, you were meant to come upon me here," or something equally melodramatic. The sentiment was genuine, though, and Faith appeared to sense as much; at length her tears dried themselves and she even managed a hopeful smile.

Those rocky moments out of the way, I now let myself enjoy the sight of her displayed before me, the wonderful languor that followed our defilement of each other. Faith's spirits returned; we mouthed endearments, toyed with each other's bodies, partook of all the guilty pleasures of stolen affection.

But after we had lain for a time in this torpor, I found myself suddenly, oddly, recalling the whisperings that had followed her to the Paxton house, those rumors begun by the other servants, which Mama had so roundly scoffed at. Hard on the heat of possessing her, I now felt another, a jealous smolder which could be allayed only by hearing her deny for herself the accusations aimed at her.

"Faithy," I whispered, for I had come to call her this, "I must ask you something." I rolled onto an elbow to look down at her.

Her eyes went wide with expectation, which made me wish I had phrased the statement somewhat differently.

"What I mean is, there is something I wish to know about your past circumstances, the time when you were summoned here from Jamaica."

"Jamaica!" she exclaimed, her eyebrows rising. "What you wanna know bout dat fer now? Dey ain't much to it, like I tol you."

I took a breath. "Please don't take on at this, or read insult into it. But I must ask. There was a rumor—it was said"—how to phrase it delicately?—"it was said that perhaps Mr. Paxton had brought you from Jamaica so that he might—enjoy you this way. So that you might be his—his—"

"He nigger whore?"

I blanched. "Yes—no! His *mistress*. So that you might be his mistress."

Faith closed her eyes and began to chuckle. "Oh Law, Aubrey. What a mind fer stories dem yaller house gals has! You believe dat mess? You think Mista Paxton gon fool wid de likes a me?" She shook her head. "He ain't even look at me, 'cept dat once in de sugar fiel, an den he jes look like he pickin a pum'kin or a apple from de barrel. Like he don' see me none. Ain't never talk to him, not dat time nor no time afta. He pinin ta have me fer his mist'ess, he got some funny way a showin it, cause dis de firs I hear bout it, fer sho."

"You're certain he never approached you? Never said anything untoward?"

"He never said *nothin*. Not backwa'd, fowa'd or towa'd neither." She smiled and stroked my face, and I let her ease me against the quilt as I prepared to be relieved.

"Don' worry none, Bree," she said as I lay back. "I ain't afta yer pa. An he ain't afta me. He wid yer ma, got de fine lady mist'ess, an de fine wife too, however he manage it."

I sat up again.

"What are you talking about?" I asked her.

"What? I'm talkin bout what ye axed me. What're *you* talkin bout?"

"I was talking about Mister Paxton, Faith. The master of the house."

"So'm I."

"No, you said 'pa.' And something about my mother."

"I said *yer* pa. Dat's who I means, Massa Paxton."

"Mister Paxton is not my father. We only share his name because we're his servants, just like any other held slave."

"I *knows* why ye got his name, Bree—same reason I got it. Dat ain't nothin to do wid him bein yer pa."

I was staring at her, my mouth formed into a perfect gaping *O,* but now I shook my head in astonishment.

"Where did you ever get such an idea?"

"What—ye tellin me ye *ain't* got dat idea, smart as ye is? I don' believe it, Bree. Ye gotta be blind as a day-ol' coon if ye ain't seen dat." She laughed playfully, then raised her hand to stroke my hair again. "Ye don' gotta hide it from me. Dere ain't no shame in it. Ye think I'm gonna talk bad bout you an yer mama, wid all dat I seen white mens take afta nigger gals, 'specially high-yaller ones?"

"It isn't true," I gasped. I yanked her hand from my face.

"Law, Bree, anybody kin see it true jes by lookin at y'all. I on'y see de massa oncet, an dat all I need to know ye his chile first time I set eyes on ye, jes as sho as ye be yer mama's chile."

"It isn't true."

Her smile was fading. "Good Law, Bree, ye ain't funnin, is ye? Ye ain't never been tole, ain't never seed it?"

My ears rang; the ocean, the swell tide of the Mississippi, had roared into the room, and I could barely discern her words.

"Who ye think yer daddy is all dis time?"

I forced my throat to perform. "Hired man," I croaked. "From the Old House."

"Who tole ye dat?"

"Ma—my mother."

"What she say happen to 'im?"

"He left her. She never. Never said."

"An ye ain't *axe*?"

No. No. I had not asked. Or rather, I had given up asking, because of the excruciating pain it seemed to cause her, because she had requested that I not ask, telling me only, he was the great love of her extreme youth, she did not blame him, such things happened. They had happened to her own mother, after all, with a white overseer—my mother's father, my grandfather, whom neither of us had ever met, since he dropped his Negro dalliance as soon as he discovered she was pregnant.

"An you *believe* dat mess? Dat mess a baby see clear through? All dis time?"

Had I? Had it never entered my mind—the privileges, the special status we enjoyed, Mama's laughter behind the study door—had I never sought an explanation for it all in the most obvious, the most apparent, instead of taking refuge in the most dubious of tales?

I could not say. Could not recall whether I had never entertained the thought or pushed it from awareness, again and yet again, until it no longer dared attempt entry there. But it battered at my fortifications now, the whole of my certainties turning inside out in its wake. I sat, stared into the darkness, unmoving and unseeing.

"Aubrey?" Faith was whispering. "I'se sorry. I ain't meant to shake ye none. Aubrey?" I barely recognized her voice or my surroundings, had no idea whether this was her first call or her twentieth. "Aubrey?"

Speaking as if through cotton wool, I pretended I had just recalled the hour and suggested we should return to our beds.

We pulled our clothing back on, then crept from the loft, not laughing now or grabbing at each other, Faith leading down the short path and turning once or twice to look at me. When we reached the rear door I kissed her woodenly, and in so doing noted the swinging earrings behind her hair. "You'd best take those off in the house," I said dully. They would be remarked upon at once, I knew, and even in my present state I had no wish to risk accusations of thievery, or to reveal just yet the extent of my involvement with Faith. I watched as she slid the gems from her ears, and concealed them in the deep pocket of her skirt.

"I a'ways gonna carry 'em," she told me, "even when dey ain't in my ears, 'cause dey makes me think bout ye."

"It's lovely of you to say so," I intoned.

Her face fell, and she took my hands. "Law, Bree, I ain't meant nothin—fergit what I said. I jes guessin, an prob'y wrong at dat. Say we gonna talk tomorry. Den I makes ye feel betta, awright?"

"All right."

She threw me a luminescent smile. I stared at her as if she were a ghost, and dropped her hands. Downcast then, she squeezed through the front door and along the hallway of the lower servants' quarters. I started up the rear steps, my head spinning, my stomach a vile pit of nausea and tumult, and fell into my own bed, where I descended into a dark and dreamless sleep.

It was nearly ten o'clock when I awoke the next morning. I was amazed that I'd been undisturbed, that Mama had not barged through my door at sunrise to determine whether I was ill or merely lazy. I lay on my back, paralyzed, the weight of consciousness returning to me in stages.

What had happened only hours ago—oh yes, I had shed my long-unwanted virginity. I could hardly recall what the moment of surrender had felt like. It was as if I clutched at the strands of an old dream.

What else—oh yes. Faith had spoken it aloud, that unspoken fact, which was apparent to everyone but me.

Mister Paxton is my father. I considered the words, wrote them inside my eyelids, repeated them under my breath, until they began to blend into senselessness.

That is what she so wanted to keep from me, isn't it, Gran, that was the secret that lay between you and Mama, the one you threatened to reveal, which made you accuse her of raising me up on a pabulum of lies. The one which caused her to wrench me from your grasp, wrench my arm from its socket, on the day I played with the tin soldiers.

My owner is my father.

What sort of insane blindness had overtaken me my whole life long that I hadn't seen it? Even now, my brain struggled to disavow it, to find those flaws in the heavy stone of its reality that could make it untrue.

How could it be so, I thought, when Madame Eugenia was often here in the city house at the same time as her husband, and would have noticed in an instant any attentions he lavished upon Mama? This was no plantation, with its ready-made dens of iniquity in the form of outlying slave cabins. In this house we were obligated to share quarters, to be within each other's sight continuously. Even from behind the doors of the study, where Mama went over her accounts with Paxton, sound readily escaped; and never could I recall an interim in which the *lack* of sound had caused me suspicion.

Nor had I, from childhood, ever noted my mother's absence at odd times, or witnessed any impropriety between Paxton and herself. Paxton was warm and cordial toward Mama and me; he was not overly solicitous. If he had been, would Madame Eugenia not have suspected? And if Madame had suspected, would she have been cordial toward us, as she had always been? To turn a blind eye toward one's husband's bastards roaming a slave quarter is one thing. To have the bastard and his mother installed in one's sight and made pets of is quite another. Madame would not for a second have tolerated this, and I especially would have been well aware of her intolerance.

Which was not to say that it could not have happened only once, at my conception, to be forever afterward regretted, and our present circumstance an attempt to rectify that mistake. But then, why not just send us both away, out of sight, why not sell us, or free us, or pay us to disappear from view? Or banish us to some field, to work out our days in solitary misery?

Why why why. What did it matter?

My owner was my father.

Which meant that his treatment of me—so benevolent toward a servant—was merely a horrific reminder of his failure to acknowledge me as his son. As Thomas was his son—my brother in blood—as Louella was his daughter. Just the same, but not the same at all.

How could he have done it, how could he have pretended all these years, borne the sight of me, even indulged me? I recollected whole days from my lost childhood—Thomas and I at play in the yard, Mister Paxton's head appearing out of the lead-paned library window—

"Lower your voices out there, you monkeys, you'll raise the dead. Thomas, get down off Timothy and give Aubrey a turn. Aubrey, don't kick him in the ribs, that's no way for a proper horseman to treat his horse. No, you may not take Timothy into the road—ask Lila for iced cake, it's nearly four . . ."

And so on, all so normal, so typical of our lives.

How could he have borne it?

And how, later on, could he have turned about so mercilessly, condemning one son to wait upon the other, allowing his own flesh and blood to be viewed by black and white alike as common chattel?

But then, my station could matter little in the face of his own reputation. What was I to him but an accident of nature, to be disavowed? And was his betrayal really any worse than that of my own mother, who in a sense had put him up to dismissing me so, with her hearty permission?

Ah, *Mama*. Now my thoughts turned to her, and that red veil returned to blind my eyes, that red poison to rush through my veins and induce my fists to curl. Mama: liar, hypocrite, whore.

Always her actions had left me reeling, being contradiction piled upon contradiction, but here perhaps was the explanation: that unbearable tension between herself and her lover which my presence created, the longing for both freedom and servitude to her beloved, the unbearable choice between her child and the father whose wish is to deny it.

And she had chosen him.

All that she had done, all the pain she had caused me, had been executed so that she might protect him, ensure herself against the loss of him, remain in his favor. It was so grotesquely apparent.

Mama. My hatred of her was a palpable, acid bile which rose into my throat.

But I was not so foolhardy as I had been as a child discovering your purloined letters. I would not reveal my newfound knowledge to her, would not confront her until the moment was right for the unsheathing of this weapon. I would wait; I could be as crafty as she, I too could hold my secret within me. Never again would it leave my consciousness, but for now I must keep it at a distance, so that I could resume the basic functions of my life. I shut my eyes and attempted to force the bile back from my throat, the blood from my fingers.

I sat so for nearly another half hour. When I felt somewhat more calm, I arose and lifted the small curtain so that a shard of listless sunlight fell upon the bed. I dunked my hands in the basin, splashed water over my face. Then, slipping into coveralls, I made my way down the steps, intending to find myself some leftover scrap from breakfast, although in truth I felt no hunger at all.

I rounded the corner of the silent hallway, padding along on bare feet, meeting no one. When I passed into the formal dining room, though, I came upon Lila, seated alone at the head of the huge cherrywood table. Her presence there struck me as odd: despite our being alone in the house, Lila kept close to her kitchen domain; she rarely availed herself of the main rooms, and looked distinctly out of place here, her broad posterior arranged upon one of the high-backed, horsehair-covered dining chairs. Strangest of all, though, was her expression, for she stared straight ahead, her mouth a faint purse of surprise, her hands grasped tidily in her lap.

I had no wish to inquire after her, as too much weighed upon my mind already, but my conscience would not allow me to pass by without a word.

"Lila?" I called to her.

"Oh, Aubrey. No one woke you. Oh my goodness."

"Lila, is something the matter?"

She turned her head to look at me. "Aubrey." The tears she must have recently wiped away now resumed flowing. "Amos was beaten last night," she said.

I felt my stomach heave; it surely would not bear another shock. "*Beaten?* Is he all right?"

"No. He isn't. He is in David's bed. Your mama and Cheney are tending to him now. We've taken turns. It seems his legs have been broken."

I shut my eyes, sweat tingling beneath my armpits. "Who did it? Where did it happen?"

"We don't know where it happened, as Amos is still asleep and can't talk. But David found him this morning outside the gates. They must have thrown him there after they were finished with him. As to who it was, we don't know that either."

"Oh certainly we do."

I turned. Mama stood in the doorway in an apron, which was spattered with blood. She was drying her hands on a towel. "Don't be foolish, Lila," she said. She turned to address me. "The war's begun, Bree, the news is everywhere. Shots were fired in Charleston, South Carolina. Just a day ago. The Confederacy has captured a fort. If you want to hear our neighbors' call to arms, stick your head out the window. Someone is bound to ride by screaming or shooting off a rifle. They took Amos to make an example of him, to punish him for disobeying. To punish all of us for shedding their sons' blood. It's that simple."

Lila shook her head. "Hush now, Onessa, just hush! Not a bit of that is certain. I cannot believe we would be deliberately singled out for mistreatment. Anybody might've done this—Amos could've been set upon by robbers, or maybe he had a grudge with some other darky, or maybe it was speculators out to try and snatch him. It could've been anybody."

"Don't delude yourself," Mama said again. "It makes things no easier." She patted her cheeks with the towel. Lila was still shaking her head, and now she was quietly crying in earnest, although she did not bother to wipe her face.

Mama turned to leave the room. "Come with me, Bree," she ordered over one shoulder. "I forgot all about you, but now you're awake you can make yourself useful." I shot Lila a sympathetic glance, and then I followed Mama, my stomach roiling, my eyes boring into her back.

In David and Cheney's tiny room I found the rest of the household, clustered around the pushed-together mattresses where Amos lay in a faint. I realized from his slack-jawed appearance that he must be drugged, and when I glanced at his lower limbs, I knew this was just as well.

Amos had been hobbled. Some heavy object like a mallet or stone adz had been used to crush his shinbones just above the ankle. I knew when I glimpsed the blood-soaked bandages—which caused my entrails to clench still tighter—that Mama had been right: this maiming was surely a message.

Lila obviously had seen to the difficult job of setting the shattered bones. I recalled her handiwork upon my arm and wished Amos the same fortunate outcome. His legs were splinted, neatly bound to wooden boards with strips of cotton, but the strips oozed mightily, and a sick smell pervaded the room. Cheney leaned at the foot of the bed, her bilious yellow face hard, daubing the blood from the soaked bandages with a clean cloth. David sat in one corner upon his stool, his rubbery limbs for once at rest, his face devoid of its usual half-grin. At Amos's head stood Adeline, fingering her crucifix and muttering incantations as she gazed toward the ceiling. Her arm was around none other than Faith, whose bruised and puffy eyes met mine when I looked in her direction.

"How long do I have to do this, Onessa," Cheney snapped when she saw Mama enter the room.

"You've been at it fifteen minutes. You have forty-five left. I suggest you shut your mouth and conserve your energy."

"Go to hell," Cheney breathed, just loudly enough to be heard.

"Mind your tongue" was all Mama replied. I was surprised she allowed this insubordination to pass so easily, but perhaps she was distracted by the gravity of the situation.

"This is doing not a damned bit of good," Cheney went on a second later. "I am wiping soaked rags, what's the sense of it?"

"At the end of the hour Lila will change them. In the meantime they must be kept clean. Speaking of which, Adeline, will you please take this bucket outside, and rinse and hang these used rags. Bree and Faith, go through the servants' linen, please, and see if there are any mended or tattered sheets we can tear into bandages."

"We wouldn't be put through any of this if the goddamn fool had done like everybody else," Cheney muttered.

"We're all upset, Cheney. Now isn't the time for recriminations."

"He drew attention to us. The *cochons* will be watching all of us now, looking for an excuse to torment us. Because of *him*."

"How is that you aim more of your vitriol at one of our own than you do at the people who attacked him?" Mama asked sharply.

"How is it you're not angry at him for disobeying you, but you're angry at *me* for stating the truth?" Cheney shot back. Her voice rose with indignation. "I did everything you told me, and I'm not going to be punished for someone else's mistakes. I'm not paying for an old woolly-head's stupidity." She splashed the rag in the bucket, and then applied it with such force to Amos's shin that he groaned and settled in his stupor.

"That's enough," Mama snapped. She stalked across the room and grabbed the rag from Cheney's hand, pushed her from the bedside. "Get out. Find something to occupy you until you've come back to your senses." Cheney stood fuming, then glanced around the room at all of us, but no one met her gaze except David. Chastened, she turned on her heel and swished through the doorway, still blowing her breath out in huffs.

I caught Faith's eye and nodded toward the hall. I wished to be gone. The blood-smell was overpowering, and the tension in the tiny space unbearable. We slipped from the room and made our way to the linen closets just before the pantry. I recalled, as if from another life, how often we had used this site as a trysting spot, to steal a kiss or arrange a secret meeting. But today romance seemed as dead a notion to both of us as last night it had seemed alive, and the only worthy pursuit on earth. We stood facing each other without touching, and then Faith began to shake her head.

"Oh Gawd, Bree, it were pitiful," she whispered. "Seem like I'se jes in de bed an shut my eyes, when Cheney come in shoutin fer Adeline to git up, somethin awful done happen. She ain't call me so I stays dere til I hears 'em all outside. Den I goes an looks out de back, and dere's eve'ybody carryin 'im up de path on a board, blood eve'ywhere, an cain't tell whether he livin or daid. Yer mama tell me git de sheet off de bed in Cheney room, an I runs ta do it, an dey brings 'im in dere so's Lila kin set de laigs. He start ta moanin an groanin, an yer mama feed 'im medicine so's he go to sleep. But all de time we doin dis we hear de mens ridin by on dey hosses, sayin it's war, an 'death ta de Yankees' an 'death ta Lincoln an long live de Sesesh,' an we so skeered dey gonna come right up on de house fer us." She gazed at me, huge-eyed. "Oh Law, Bree, what we done? What we done?"

"What have *we* done? Who? What do you mean?"

"You an me—if we hadn't a been in de hay—*sinnin*—we mighta heerd 'im, coulda got 'im inside 'stead a him layin out dere on de cold groun til de sun come up. If he die, how we know it ain't 'cause a dat, ain't our fault? God punish us fer bein wickedlike, and po' Amos got to suffer in our place."

"That is *ridiculous*," I hissed at the girl, shaking her by the shoulders. "If we hadn't been in the hayloft, we would have been in our beds, where we would have heard nothing anyway. We don't know how long he was out there. He might have been lying there before we got to the loft, or he might have been thrown there after we went to sleep."

I said this, but I did not believe it; in my heart of hearts I knew Amos had been tossed in the ditch at the very moment of my most extreme ecstasy.

"We had nothing to do with this," I assured her nonetheless, "and you mustn't let yourself keep thinking that we did. No god is so unjust that he'd knowingly punish an innocent for another's crime."

She dried her eyes. "I try to 'member dat, Bree. On'y I pray he git better, den maybe I believes you."

I wished heartily for the same outcome, not only for Amos's sake, but so that I might believe myself.

But Amos did not get better. He was asleep or groggy with laudanum for the better part of a month, and when finally he awakened, he remembered nothing of the incident which had crippled him. His legs began the long process of healing, but it was plain he would never be without a chair or a cane.

His mind, moreover, had been affected. He had difficulty forming his speech, and rambled from one topic to the next, appearing scattered and giddy in the manner of an imbecile. Mama thought this might be due partially to the laudanum, which was the only thing enabling him to tolerate the terrible pain in his legs, and we held out hope that at some point, when freed of the drug's grip, more of his faculties would return. I tried my best to be of use to him—it wrenched me to see him in this state, for I had always regarded him kindly, despite the distance that seemed to yawn at times between us, and I had not forgotten his kindnesses to me. But when I approached him, he would wrap his arm about my waist, pull me to him, and whisper in my ear the most incredibly lewd or absurd comments, not a few of which concerned Mama or the other women in the house. This was so unlike him: taciturn he had always been, appreciative but respectful. It seemed another spirit had come to inhabit his flesh, and the thought of this horrified me so extremely that I found myself dreading entrance to his tiny sickroom.

It was almost a relief when he began to lapse slowly into silence. The urge toward profanity left him, and he retreated into some sort of ether-haze, from which he could distract himself only to eat, or to pass along a mundane comment or two. I found it easier then to visit with him, to take my turn, along with everyone else, bringing him a meal and sitting with him while he ate it.

But the person who attended him most faithfully was Lila. She and Amos and you, Gran—you have been Paxton slaves all your lives, have seen three generations of his family and your own rise up alongside each other. How I pitied Lila, for her eyes moistened each time she left the invalid's bedside. "He was a *good* man," she told me over and over. "*Good*. And strong—fifty-three years old, and strong as an ox. So many years left." She ignored his ravings, and once they ceased, sat him up in bed to shell beans or chop vegetables on a board so that he might feel useful; and they spoke a wordless language to each other, of small familiar gestures.

The rest of us moved about the house as if behind the walls of a fortress. We were haunted within by Amos—a ghost reposing beyond the kitchen walls—and threatened without by unseen enemies. There was no resentment now of Mama's iron-fisted dictates. She had assessed the situation better than any of us, and even I was forced to grudgingly respect her judgment. In the aftermath of her vindication, we took whatever precautions she insisted we take. The doors were kept always locked, and none of us were ever in the yard or the carriage house alone. The musket stood against the wall in the dining room, loaded and ready for the appearance of an enemy from either side. When Mama went into town to market for us, she took David or myself with her, and returned well before dark.

Wherever we dared go—followed by the hateful stares—the talk was of nothing but war: which mile had been gained by whom, what town had fallen, how long it would be before the Sesesh routed the Yankees for good. Flyers were posted in storefront windows, warning of the dire consequences for any Negro who dared be seduced by the false promises of Unionists. Twice I saw L'Heuron pass by upon his bay gelding, and he actually turned toward us and tipped his hat, and Mama inclined her head, just as if Amos did not lie mutilated upon his bed with a bowlful of beans to shell, just as if the musket did not lie loaded against the dining room wall.

I had gone to bed sobbing over my paternity and awakened in another country.

As for Faith and myself, all amorous activity between us ground to a halt. It was as though the night in the carriage house had never happened, although several times I caught a ruby glint behind her hair, and knew she had slipped the garnets into place. No one else appeared to notice them, and I was not sure whether she intended that I should notice either. Were they donned to chastise me, or were they to serve as a reminder of our one night's abandon? She did not tell me, and I did not ask. We seemed to be waiting: for Amos's recovery, for the force of her statement about my parentage to loosen its grip, for the war to end—whatever the outcome—so that we might resume our lives in some normal context.

Mama was waiting too, though, and her vigil ended before either of ours did. Her letter—long anticipated, and long in coming—finally arrived, the various stamps and official markings bearing witness to its journey from Aix-en-Provence in southern France.

"Read it," Mama said, handing it to me. I took it, loath to touch her fingers. Mama gave me no clue as to its contents; her face was without expression, although her fingers trembled.

The letter was written in French, in Paxton's strong hand, and began without greeting.

Onessa:

I am aware of the worsening situation in New Orleans and have taken steps to dissolve the family's assets in that city. Madame Eugenia and Mademoiselle Louella will be arriving to see to the closing of both town and country residences. Upon the completion of that task, they will be issuing documents of emancipation to all servants presently bound to myself. Regrettably, there are few positions overseas for said servants, but I invite yourself, your mother Evangeline, and your son to continue on in our employ here. Should any of you have become engaged or betrothed, your spouses will also be provided for.

I ask your assistance in readying the other servants for liberty and self-determination. I shall provide for them monetarily to the extent that I can, but will rely on you to guide them in their choice of employ or new locale. Needless to say, they must be removed from the Secessionist territories as soon as possible, as must yourselves. This will be difficult to accomplish in the face of outright war, but rest assured that every measure will be taken to see that it is done. In the meanwhile, I have also sent word on to the city authorities that you are not to be interfered with, but you must not rely on any influence of mine to secure your safety. Rather, remain as inconspicuous as possible until the arrival of your mistresses.

I leave my wife and daughter in your capable hands, and you in theirs. I will advise you further as more information becomes available, and ask you to obey without question any order delivered by myself, Madame Eugenia, or her advisors. Your well-being, and that of your compatriots, is uppermost in our minds.

God be with all of you—

Louis E. Paxton

My first thought was of his extraordinary cowardice, his callousness in sending his wife and daughter into the fray of civil war rather than risking the necks of himself and his son.

And then in the next moment, a thousand incoherent and whirling emotions overcame me: great joy at the idea of freedom, of being reunited with you at last, Gran, great sorrow as to the fate of my companions, however I might feel toward them, ambivalence as to whether or not I wished to be a minion to my own father in a foreign country, although never to see him again would be unimaginable. And Thomas, what of Thomas, was he approving of this venture or disapproving, and what would transpire upon our first renewed contact with each other?

My second clear thought—which screamed at me above my mindless yearning to believe every word Paxton had written—was that he meant none of it. How could he, when he had spent the previous year reinforcing the reality of my servitude? What about-face, what trickery, was this? It made no sense. Was not to be trusted.

I glanced up at Mama, expecting to see my own doubt confirmed in her face. But instead she gazed back clear-eyed and triumphant, a fevered glow in her cheeks. Of course—it struck me like a slap: how else would she look, standing now upon the brink of obtaining all she could desire—both freedom, and the promise of continued servitude at Paxton's side?

She snatched the letter from me and crushed it to her chest, her eyes wide, her voice emerging as a hiss of breath: "Don't say a word to anybody else. Not a word, Aubrey, do you hear me? Not until it's all settled and done."

As the letter had promised, Madame Eugenia did indeed disembark some three weeks later with considerably more fanfare than had accompanied Faith's arrival. I was required to meet her at the dockside dressed in stiff livery (this duty of Amos's having fallen upon myself), so that I might bear the brunt of what were sure to be her material excesses: the endless stream of bags, the hatboxes and trunks, perhaps a little long-haired lapdog tottering about drunkenly, its land legs not yet returned, pissing upon every surface in sight. And heaven knew what else.

The dockside was in chaos. Passengers—no doubt used to finer lodgings—spilled from their mean accommodations upon those vessels still willing to risk running the North's port blockade. I thought I should have difficulty locating her, but here at last came Madame, in one piece and an absurdly large bonnet—and, I was delighted to note, here too was her daughter.

I had not seen Louella in nearly five years, but I spotted her even as I sat atop the carriage driver's seat. I jumped down, waving my hat, and she turned toward me, leaving a puffing porter to wrestle with her baggage. I gaped to see the changes those five years had wrought in her. She was tall—nearly as tall as I—and thin, dressed smartly in a suit of some iridescent pinkish material, with a cap of black-and-white ostrich plumes upon her head. If she was not quite pretty, she was certainly handsome and impeccably groomed, and with an air of confidence and practicality which earned immediate respect. She was, in a word, the polar opposite of her mother, who shared only the raw and irregular bone structure she had bequeathed to her daughter, with none of the attendant dignity.

"Louella," I beamed, and then corrected myself. "Mademoiselle." I inclined my head. She stared at me. Then her face burst into a tremendous grin.

"*Aubrey?* Little Bree? *Mon Dieu*, is that you? I would never have known it! You're absolutely *enormous*, a grown man! Look at you, how handsome you've become!" She inspected me at arm's length, and then suddenly, unexpectedly, drew me to her, kissing me upon both cheeks, and embracing me.

I was taken aback. I had not dared hope Louella would remain untouched by the sentiments which had overcome her father and brother, but here she was, affectionate as a long-lost sister.

And in fact was that not what she was, the horrible thought struck me—at which point I colored and drew away, mumbling, "I'll see to your things, Miss."

But she caught me by the arm. "What's this, are we going to act as strangers after all this time? You needn't stand on ceremony for me, Bree. In fact I won't have it. No fawning and bowing, am I understood?"

"Yes—" I stammered, flustered past words. "Yes—" I could not imagine from whence her largesse had sprung, nor had I given a thought as to how it would affect me, in light of what I had learned of my origins. I glanced to where Madame Eugenia now came down the gangplank, squawking directions to a procession of laden underlings. She turned toward her daughter, and I could make out even at this distance the scowl with which she regarded Louella's hand upon my arm. I felt a little wave of nausea, and gulped a deep breath of the salty air. "It's easier if I'm consistent in my manners, so as not to confuse myself, Miss," I said quickly. I hurried off before she could reply, partly so that she would not guess my state of mind, and partly because her mother had commenced flagging me down.

When I reached her, Madame peered at me closely, and without recognition. "*Aubrey*, Madame," I reminded her, bowing low.

"Heavens," she said in French, "weren't you just a child last I saw you?"

"Yes, Madame. I've grown a bit since then."

She pursed her lips, no doubt at my barbaric accent, and then shrugged. "Understandable enough. Time marks us all equally—or perhaps not. Where is the other one, then, the dark man who usually drives here?"

A vision of bloody sheets flashed before me. "He is ill, Madame."

"Ah. Well, you then, help Monsieur Dolley with our belongings, and if you please, find another taxi, for I doubt there will be room in the carriage for the luggage and all of our party too."

There would certainly *not* be room. True to form, Madame had come with a profusion of bags, and with endless lead-lined, dead-weight trunks filled with foodstuffs and casks of her beloved French wines. And if there was no dog, there was instead a standing cage and its occupants, a pair of green lovebirds. In addition, Madame was traveling with two maids and her *majordomo*, the prissy Englishman Vivien Dolley.

I had seen Dolley perhaps twice in ten years, and each time I liked him less. He barely glanced at me as I dragged the first of Madame's trunks to the carriage, and I decided to put things on the right foot by asserting myself immediately.

"Madame wishes an extra taxi. You might find one over yonder," I said, pointing brusquely with a thumb. If he expected obsequiousness as a result of either station or color, he would not find it here. He was a servant, paid if not bought, and I felt in no way obliged toward him. He eyed me narrowly, then set off to hire a rig. When he had gone Louella sidled up to me and whispered, "Let's make certain he rides in the taxi, Bree. I cannot bear the thought of being trapped with him all the way to town." I allowed the corner of my lip to curl as I nodded my acquiescence.

The travel arrangements were soon settled. I managed to fill the back of the barouche with boxes and lovebirds, so that Madame and Louella could barely squeeze in, which left Dolley and the maids—two pasty, giggling Provence girls—to ride with the trunks. Arranging the packages, I found myself staring up into Louella's face, and the width of her green eyes, the animation there, was so achingly familiar—and yet so far beyond acknowledgment—that I had to turn away.

We set off, and as I drove I was mindful of the ladies chattering behind me, but I dared not listen. There were few topics I cared to hear discussed, and I feared that my eagerness for certain words would cause them to magically evaporate. *Documents of emancipation*—not only the pass to liberty, but the acknowledgment of kinship, the closest, perhaps, that I would come to a declaration of love.

But Madame was commenting only on the appearance of the countryside, and how she did not recall New Orleans being so warm this time of year. By the time we reached the gates she was fluttering her fan, and gasping as she handed herself out to be helped to the curb. Louella climbed down unassisted, and then I set to removing the baggage from the rear seat. The taxi pulled up a moment later, its draft horses heaving, and Dolley emerged, brushing at his morning coat as if he'd been soiled.

Our bustling roused everyone within the house. A little crowd spilled out of the front doors, and was briskly arranged into a reception line before Madame. No expense had been spared by Mama in anticipation of this moment. She wore her black dress with the striped bodice and tight sleeves, a ring of keys at her waist, and her hair was pulled back in a contraption like a net. Lila practically glowed in immaculate white muslin and a clean apron; Faith, Cheney, and Adeline resembled three Roman sisters in their black skirts, white aprons, and starched white caps. David wore a butler's uniform, shiny at the knees but a uniform nonetheless. Only Amos was missing, but his clothing pinched at my shoulders, and I took his place in the line.

When we were still, Mama stepped forward. She gave a charming curtsey. "Welcome back, Madame," she said in her lilting French. "We're delighted to be at your service after your long absence." On cue, the rest of us gave a small bow. Louella looked on, bemused, while the Provence girls giggled, and exclaimed too loudly that they had never before seen people of such exotic countenance. Dolley silenced them with a glare, and then rearranged his features to sneer at us.

But Madame applauded her delight, and I saw Mama's shoulders go limp with relief.

We were all relieved as well, knowing firsthand as we did what had gone into the preparations for the mistresses' arrival.

Under Mama's lash, we had been driven into a frenzy of cleaning, rearranging, and practicing service drills for two full weeks. Mock meals had been prepared and sampled, table-waiting, maid-serving, and butlering skills mercilessly critiqued and fine-tuned. I'd seethed as I participated in this nauseating rigmarole: it was nothing more than Mama's attempt to curry favor with the very woman she was cuckolding, and her performance was both brilliant and awful to watch.

Madame, on the other hand, was thoroughly charmed by it. Dinners went off without a hitch. High teas were flawlessly served, bedclothes turned back, the two Provence maids integrated into the workings like bees in a buzzing hive. The only fly in the ointment was Dolley, who, having nothing to supervise, instead searched for ways to undermine our efforts, or else skulked about looking miserable.

Louella and Madame ignored him. They congratulated Mama, and lavished praise upon all of us. They both undertook to visit Amos, and the sight of him bore witness to our plight far more eloquently than any well-planned speech could have done. Madame stood in his doorway with a silken sachet at her nose, to combat the smell of laudanum, dried blood, and the chamber pot. Her eyes overflowed, despite Amos's slurred assertions that he was on the mend and grateful for Madame's concern. Louella spoke little, but she sat by the bed all morning, watching as the invalid took his medicine and became by turns euphoric, then sleepy, then cranky, as the pain overtook him once again. We did not know what to make of her sitting so, but Amos seemed unselfconscious and unconcerned, and so none of us attempted to dislodge her. We heard them speaking quietly, and later that day, Louella ordered David across town to Monsieur Cassout, to deliver a letter inquiring after Berta, and whether she might be for sale. We greeted stone-faced the news with which David returned. Berta had already been sold, Monsieur Cassout wrote, as punishment for having conspired with Amos in his disobedience. A slave of questionable loyalties would not be tolerated anywhere on his property, now least of all. Louella read the letter, then stuffed it into the hem of her sleeve without comment. When she retreated into Amos's chamber, only the heaviness of the silence told me the information had found its mark.

The next morning, when Monsieur Calvin rode up upon his horse to take his informal census, Louella was waiting for him by the wrought-iron gate, a taffeta bed robe thrown over her gown, her hair drawn back beneath a sunbonnet. And in her fingers she clutched a weapon, but it was no ornamental musket, no antique piece. This was a six-shooter, pearl-handled, glinting and greased. The hand which held it trembled—I'd seen that when she passed me—but held on nonetheless. Madame stood in the foyer, peeking from the narrow window, her long bony nose silhouetted against the glass. Adeline and I crept out the kitchen door and around the side of the house, from whence we could watch the proceedings.

"Good morning," Louella called, without a smile, from behind the locked gate. "You are Monsieur Calvin?"

Calvin attempted to remove his hat whilst controlling the horse upon which he sat. "That is correct. And you might be—"

"I *am* Louella Paxton. Monsieur Paxton's daughter, and one of the mistresses of this house." She stepped out another step into the road, allowing her arm, the pistol extending from it, to dangle freely.

"I'm recently arrived from the Continent," she said. "My servants tell me you've been kind enough to look in on them each morning."

Calvin made as if to reply, but Louella went on without waiting for his answer. "I thank you for your interest, Monsieur. I'm sure you were most thorough, despite one of our men being badly beaten by hoodlums. Of course, one can only do so much, but I'm certain your office is in pursuit of the guilty parties."

If Calvin made a reply to this, it was too garbled for us to decipher.

"At any rate, your services will no longer be needed, seeing as Madame Paxton and I are now in residence."

We heard him speak now, his power of speech restored. "It distresses me some to think of you all in this house by yourselves, with no suitable—*person*—about to see to things."

"You needn't worry yourself." Louella's tone was sharp. "We require no further assistance, as you've done quite enough already. We are capable of handling our house, I assure you. We are armed, sir"—here she raised the pistol, and I saw Calvin flinch—"and have no intention of being surprised. And we have our servants to rely upon. We shall call on you if need be. Good day." And then she turned and walked back up the path, leaving Calvin to compose himself and yank the mouth of his nervous animal, who had begun to chomp upon the bit.

After a few days passed without further incident, we grew more confident of our good standing with Madame, and relaxed somewhat. We even managed a joke or two with the new maids, who were jolly enough and quite unaffected by our status as slaves, beyond being merely curious.

Louella saw to the running of the household, much more so than Madame ever had. She quickly became everyone's favorite, not only because of her confrontation with the deputy, but because she inquired after us sincerely, spending portions of each day speaking to the servants and observing our activities.

Yet when she attempted to engage me in private conversations, I found myself resisting, withdrawing upon any excuse. A strange unfamiliarity had overtaken me of late, an awareness that Louella—despite her kindness—was no longer the playmate of my youth, even as I recognized her as kith and kin. I grew uneasy whenever I met her alone upon the stairs or in a chamber, and so I endeavored to appear formal and aloof before her, or sought the presence of another soul whenever I might confront her.

It pained me to act so, though, for I had come to know the extent to which she truly meant us well. A few days after the incident with Calvin, Mama had cornered me in our chambers and sat me down at the edge of the bed for a chat, confiding to me that there was even more to Louella's investigations than met the eye.

"She spoke to me this morning regarding the family's plans for the future," Mama said. "She seems to believe we've been treated abominably, all of us, and has prevailed upon her father to correct the situation as soon as possible. Conditions shall only worsen here given the tenor of the war, she says, and so there's no point in delaying our liberation until the closing of the houses is completed. Rather, she shall see to some business about the region, and then when she returns shall bestow upon us what she feels should have been ours all along."

I said nothing, although my mind leapt at these words. So the letter had been sincere, and here lay the explanation for Paxton's reversal. The pleas of his daughter—rather than any enlightenment on his part—had turned his heart.

But what had caused Louella's own epiphany? I recalled her behavior toward me upon the pier. My God, had she somehow discovered the kinship between us, was that the reason for the preferential treatment Mama and I and you, Gran, were to be meted out? She had always been the smartest among us, smart enough to see beyond the tales I'd been fed to satisfy my curiosity. But it did not follow that such a discovery would cause her to worry over the fortunes of the Negroes, and my family in particular. Should she not have been happier to see all of us banished, to trouble her mother no more?

It was a question worth pondering, but Mama was already moving on to how our shift in status should be accomplished.

"Dolley and Louella will be leaving in about a week or so for the Old House, and then for Baton Rouge, and Texas. The family has holdings of land, there are solicitors to see, papers her father wishes to collect, and so on. When she is finished she intends to return here, at which point she will speak to the other servants and advise them as to what is happening." She paused. "She mentioned again the offer of continued employment in Provence. Of course, that would extend only to yourself, your grandmother, and me."

"I see," I said. "How convenient. But I wonder why they have chosen to so favor only us?" I skated over thin ice here, but wished to read her face as she answered.

She looked back at me, unblinking. "We'll fare well in France, Aubrey. We speak the language, we are educated, we are accustomed to the family's habits.

Heritage is regarded differently there, as you'll see. As for the others—" She lowered her eyes. "They would be much more difficult to integrate. The family has no use for field laborers, and of the house servants, only a few are fluent in French, and none can read and write with any proficiency. Louella assured me that everyone will be provided for, and that she shall not rest until she's secured safe passage for all the servants out of this godforsaken place, and up to the Northern states."

"And you believe she will do this."

"I do." Mama paced the floor. "She seems eager to detach her family from the entire enterprise of slaveholding, and Paxton has given her permission to do it. Of course I would have thought Thomas, or maybe Madame . . ." Her voice trailed off, and she shrugged.

"But what of the rest of the household? They surely will suffer," I interrupted. "What of Adeline, and Cheney, and David? Where is Amos to go? Who is to care for him now his wife is gone? What about Lila, she's belonged to the family as long as Gran has. And what about Faith, did Paxton purchase her simply to remove her to some other dire situation?"

"I understand your distress, Bree. And I've ideas of my own on that subject, besides Louella's assurances that everyone will be cared for. But we must think of ourselves . . ."

"Oh yes, ourselves, by which you no doubt mean *yourself*. It's you you're so worried for, isn't it, you've plotted and planned, and now finally it's about to bear fruit, and damn everyone who isn't in your fortunate shoes. Isn't that right?"

She strode up to where I sat, then bent to twist a lock of my hair in her fingers, pulling my ear to her mouth. "Now listen well, boy. I have worked and waited all of my life for this moment. I have dreamed every night of our emancipation, and *none* of it ever had to do with what I wanted for myself. I have been selfless as I'm gonna be. Our moment is here, and I will be damned, *goddamned*, if we will fail to seize it, whatever the consequences to anybody else. God owes this to me," she hissed. "He owes it. Whatever arrangements He makes with the rest of the world is between Him and them, but this He owes to me." She bent closer to my ear. "Cry all you want over Cheney and Adeline. But know that we've gotten what we deserve, what I worked for, whatever the reason. And take it when it's given, Bree, because the chance at it may not come again."

She released my hair, and the lack of tension caused me to flop back on the bed. I had barely righted myself when she turned to face me again, her narrowed, feral eyes telling me she was busily drawing a bead upon new targets.

"Besides, boy, I told you I had ideas of my own. Since you're so concerned about Faith, you'll no doubt be glad to know you can step in and save her yourself."

I stared at her.

"There is the provision, remember, that allows all of us to bring a spouse or betrothed with us. I believe Paxton put it there specifically for you. After all, who would two crones like Gran and myself be marrying? But I'm certain the restrictions could be stretched somewhat to include whoever is dear to us, in which case Gran would take Lila, and I could take Amos. And you could take Faith. After making her your wife. Doesn't that appeal to your keen sense of altruism?"

I felt my throat go dry.

"What's the matter, boy? You claimed her, didn't you? You wanted her badly enough to take her. If you believe she's bound for some terrible evil, why not step in and deliver her?"

"Why should you wish me to," I spat. "You were so disdainful of her, why do you foist her on me now?"

"I'm foisting nothing upon you. And never have. The choice is yours, I am merely attempting to ameliorate your guilt. And so that you might know it, I was never disdainful of Faith—it was *your* behavior with which I took issue."

I should have known as much.

"Why is it, Mama, that you manage to find me perpetually in the wrong?"

"It's not a matter of right and wrong. *Le coeur a ses raisons que la raison ne connaît pas*, Bree. And the reasons of the body are even less informed by reason than the heart's, especially at your age. You're a young man, with a young man's sensibilities. Which makes you dangerous to a simple and ignorant child like Faith, whether you're my son or not. I should have known you might use her to your own ends—now you need reminding that she is not a plaything. If you pretend concern for her well-being, then be man enough to act upon it. You wed her in body, now follow through, claim her, and deliver her from whatever you fear will befall her."

"But why must I marry her—why can I not merely ask that she be taken?"

"You were hardly discreet—the entire household knows how far it's gone between you. Given the loose lips hereabouts, it shan't be long before Madame does too. We are not field hands. Madame will not sanction Faith's removal to France so that she can serve as your harlot."

I thought of our one evening's passion, and of how we had barely conversed since; I felt not so much an aversion to Faith as a great confusion. How could I imagine marrying her, taking her to wife—I had never intended this in the innocence of our romp, it had not occurred to me, which was not to say that it never would have. But to consider it now—I am so young! I thought. And there is so much of my life I have not yet lived, so much I hoped to experience, especially now, with the right to self-determination within my grasp.

As if reading my thoughts, Mama added, with apparent nonchalance, "You would not necessarily be forced, you know, to honor the commitment to the letter."

I glanced up at her. At first, I could not read her meaning, but then it occurred to me what she might be suggesting: a marriage or engagement of convenience, enough to justify to the Paxtons the expenditure (and propriety) of bringing the girl with us. And in this she had a point—if Faith had done me a turn in the giving of herself, then could I not do one to reciprocate, at least until we reached the coast of France and her position was secure?

I was about to ask Mama if this was indeed what she had in mind when Madame's quavering call was heard from the foot of the stairs. "Onessa! Onessa, do come, I must give you my marketing list for today." Mama gave me a grim smile. "Duty calls. And when it calls, we must answer." Then she pressed her lips together and exited the room without another word to me, so that I was left to consider this new dilemma for myself.

It did not take me long to make up my mind concerning Faith. I determined that she should go, but that I would wait until Louella had made her announcement before saying anything to the girl. I feared she would become so flustered in anticipation of our flight that she would fail to perform her duties properly and somehow earn Madame's undying enmity.

Yet despite my best exertions, this very thing came to pass.

Even as the rest of the household visibly relaxed, Faith became more and more nervous, especially around the ladies. She appeared to forget a greater number of her chores than she remembered, and I noted the dithering, scattered way she performed them, a swipe with the feather duster here, a swish with the flannel there, and then on to the next thing, until she realized she'd left the last half-done. She seemed terribly distracted, and I wondered if she had not got wind of the plans in the offing, perhaps by having listened at the doorway to Mama's chambers. Several times I made as if to question her, but before I could do so she skirted by me to exit whatever room I entered.

This went on for several days without explanation. Finally, though, she came to me of her own accord.

I was out in the carriage house oiling the tack—yet another of Amos's responsibilities which had fallen to me—when I sensed a presence behind me, in the doorway to the tack room. When I turned, there stood Faith, in her homespun skirts and half-laced boots, her hair untied, her arms hanging by her sides. She was the very picture of misery, and I could not help contrasting her appearance on this day to that on the other, happier nights on which we'd visited this place. I was moved to pity for her, and it was clear she wished to speak, so I ended the silence between us at last, walking toward her and leaning against the doorway so that we might converse.

"Faithy," I began. "I have tried—I have noticed of late that something is amiss, and I feel we should resolve—ah, at least attempt—"

She broke in without preamble. "Law," she whispered. "Oh Law, Bree."

"What is it, what is troubling you?"

She shook her head. "I got ta tell ye. Got ta, an it gon kill me." I waited while she swallowed, wiped cottony spit from the corners of her mouth with the back of her hand. "Ain't seen no blood in nigh now six Sundays. *Law*."

I was puzzled. "What are you talking about, Faithy? What blood? Amos's? Is that what has upset you so? Go on, you can tell me."

"Naw. Not Amos. *My* blood. Ain't seen *my* blood." Her voice rose, flat, toneless. "I'se knocked. Ain't seen no blood, I'se KNOCKED. Oh Law, ah'm in de trouble now."

" 'Knocked'?" I asked gently. "What is 'knocked'?"

It is hard to believe, in retrospect, that I'd never heard the term, but perhaps I'd heard it and forgotten it, or wished right then not to understand it.

But Faith cleared the matter up succinctly. "I'se wid a chile, Aubrey. Gonna have a baby. Wid you. Your baby."

I froze where I stood, my whole body contracting into itself. *Oh dear God*, I called inside myself. *Law*.

"How? How can that be? Jesus Christ, how did it happen?"

"How you think it happen? Same's it happen for eve'y other slut."

I felt a tremor pass through me, taking with it my leisurely plan for that act of redemption, the betrothal without strings. Hadn't Mama warned me she was not a plaything?

"Why didn't you take care," I raged at her. "How could you allow this? Or perhaps it was deliberate, is that closer to the truth?"

The tears began to well in her eyes, but mostly I saw anger there—anger at *me*, when—or so I thought—I was so definitively the victim here. "How kin you axe me dat? Ain't you got no feelin a-tall fer me? What I tell you, 'bout havin babies widdout no man to raise 'em up? Mah whole life, I been afeared a dat, an now here I be, jes like in de worse bad dream I evah had. God punishin me fer sinnin, pleasurin wid you when we ain't wed. Ain't nothin I axe fer. Ain't even *think* t' make sho I don' have no chile. Nevuh had no man 'fore ye, how I'm supposed t' know what t' do?"

I leaned against the doorframe to steady myself, my eyes shut. "I know. I spoke unjustly, Faith. I am sorry."

"You done had more wimmins den I had mens. Why ain't *you* did nothin, ye knows so much?"

Why indeed. Was there nothing for which I was not responsible—seeing as I knew so much?

I raised up to look at her. "You must give me time to consider what to do."

I thought of you, Gran, that if only I could reach you, you would surely have some potion, some secret elixir, to induce her menses and extricate us from this horror. "I need time to contact someone—"

"Naw!" Faith rasped. "Cain't tell no one! 'Speshly not here! Gwine mebbe git me sol a worse, de missy find out I'se knocked!"

"It wasn't Madame I was thinking of telling," I replied. "And anyway, you're wrong—she may well wring her hands and deplore your condition, but she'd not sell you off for being with child. The Paxtons have never done such things." I then added, somewhat flippantly, "She'd more likely sell you for performing poorly than for having a baby, so please, Faith, leave this alone and concentrate on your work, and let me think upon it."

I had not meant this last to be taken to heart, but Faith's complexion paled even further. "She think I'se doin' po'ly? She say dat?"

"What? No—of course she didn't say that. I was joking—for God's sake, don't be so literal. Nobody is to be sold for any reason—"

But she had gone a pasty yellow, and begun to twist her fingers, bringing the knuckles to her mouth as if to bite them.

"Law, whut ah'm gonna do, whut ah'm gonna do," she muttered, "I jes knowed she don' like me, could tell somethin gonna go bad de minute she come through de do'. She lookit me jes like she know mah mind, an what in mah belly too, know I ain't better'n a common slut, havin dis po' baby outta God's sight. Might even git ta thinkin it a whi' masta's chile I carryin. She gon turn aginst me, I feels it. Gon sell me, sell me souf, or—oh Gawd—sell de baby soon's it's borned, 'way fum me like I been sol 'way fum my fambly, an mah chile gon live an die in de fiel pickin an hoein, an runnin fum de whip jes like I done—"

"Oh, for the love of *Christ*," I snapped, unable to listen any further to her dire predictions. "Will you leave off, Faith—nothing of the sort is going to happen. In the first place, I doubt Madame even cares that you exist at this point, nor, as I've already told you, have the Paxtons ever bought or sold servants arbitrarily. And such a thing is even more improbable now, because on top of all that—" I began, and then caught myself short and went silent.

"On top a all dat, whut?" Faith cast her bleary, weeping eyes up at me, hanging now upon my every word.

In an instant I saw my mistake—I had vowed to say nothing, knew I could only be leading us farther into the mire—but I went forward. "On top of that," I continued, because I was distracted, because my desire to calm her, to be the bearer of good news, had briefly overcome my better instincts, "on top of that it is Mister Paxton's plan to liberate every one of us, and to bring a few of us—yourself included—to work for him as freemen in the south of France."

She peered at me. "Where in de souf am France? I ain't heerd of it."

"Yes you have, remember Molière?"

She looked at me blankly; Molière was a thousand years past, in another lifetime. "France is not in the south of the United States," I sighed. "France is another country entirely. It lies across the water, in Europe."

"*Law,*" she whispered. " 'Cross de water!" Then, suspicious, "It ain't like Jamaica, is it? Dem big plantations?"

"No. It's not like Jamaica."

"An' de massa wanna bring us dere? An set us free? Pay us'n de wage?"

"Yes."

She pondered this, then looked at me again, shaking her head. "I ain't scarcely b'lieve it. Ain't wanna push ye, but how ye hear dis? An how come on'y some of us goin?"

"I first heard through a letter Mister Paxton sent to my mother. And Louella is here to make the arrangements, she told Mama so herself. As to why only some of us are going—" I hesitated, but what was the point, it was too late now. "—it's because the offer was extended only to my mama, my grandmother, and myself. We were told, though, that we could bring along a spouse or a betrothed, should we have one. As my mother and grandmother are unwed, they will likely take Lila and Amos. And I had planned to announce an engagement between us, so as to take you."

Now it leapt into her face: that pure, transforming adoration, as if I were a god whose aura bathed her in sunshine. I had not realized how much I'd missed that expression until this moment. "Ye takin me!" she gasped.

"Yes."

I thought she might swoon from sheer joy. But a moment later her face fell. "What ah'm gonna do bout mah ma an pappy, an mah brudder Jim? Always done thought ah see 'em agin, 'speshly if dis war be lost. I go 'crosst de water, how ah'm gonna find 'em?"

"You'll be free," I reminded her. "You'll be making a wage. You can return to search for them, or you can buy their way over, so that they might be with you." I did not bother to mention how unlikely any of this was, regardless of the war's outcome. She seemed satisfied with my answer, and gazed up at me once again.

"You wantin t' go to dis France, den? Fer sho?"

"Yes."

"An you wantin"—I could feel her hesitate—"wantin t' claim dis chile? Marry me proper?"

I could not look at her. For what I wanted, in fact, was to rid her of the pregnancy, so that our engagement could revert once more to the status of a tolerable and temporary ruse. Then my position as saviour would be assured, while the marriage itself need never come about. What I said, though, was: "Yes. Of course. Only I shall wait a bit, until Louella has gone and returned from clearing up some other matters, and has discussed her plans with the rest of the servants."

She regarded me, her head cast down, her chin quivering. "I ain't meanin ta pester ye none, but why ye gotta wait, Bree? Why cain't ye marry me now? Ye sure ye gonna do it, an not change yer mind later?"

"Certainly I'm sure," I sniffed. "There is no rush—if the child is mine, it is mine. If I'm to claim it, if it's to happen, what does it matter whether it's now, before Louella goes, or after she returns?"

I could feel her trembling as she grasped my hand, twined her cold fingers around my own. "Jest don' want nothin t' go wrong, is all, Bree. I'se so skeered, skeered a de missus, an 'fraid to tell you all dis. Been rasslin wid de blankets in de night, cain't hardly think straight in de day. I on'y axe dat ye do right by dis chile, Aubrey, an den I be de best gal to ye. I come 'crosst de water wid ye, an make ye de good wife. Jes wanna be wid ye, Bree. I know ye know it, dat ye be more t' me dan mah own life."

She paused then, as if waiting for me to repeat those sentiments back to her. But I could not bring myself to comply. Sunk in my intrigues, I hesitated, then stammered, "I know how you feel, Faith, and you know what I feel for you, I am only overwhelmed—" and then fell guiltily, miserably, silent.

She understood that silence only too well, I am certain now. In the end she broke it by saying, her eyes to the ground, "Law bless ye fer takin us'n on yer shoulders. Jes git us 'crosst de ocean, Bree, an I ain't make ye regret it." She shook her head. "O dear Law Gawd, I on'y pray de missus ain't hate me so much, or find out 'bout de chile an say I cain't go."

I could only repeat to Faith that I knew she was in no danger, and need merely be up to the rudiments of her work to consider herself safe.

But she replied, "You ain't been where I been, seen how dese whi' peoples do, 'speshly de whi' ladies." She continued to appear downcast and subdued, and nothing I could say subsequently seemed to rally her. She clasped me to her bosom, but her face remained pale, her skin clammy. When she turned to leave me, I saw the flash in her ears beneath the tangle of her hair, and I thought to mention this, but forgot, in light of the circumstances, almost as soon as it occurred to me.

I did not rest that night. I lay upon the covers of the bed, staring at faces in the plaster ceiling with which I had been silently conversing since childhood. I felt overcome; exhaustion pulled at me, but the fancies in my mind—of Thomas upon the stair, of Faith beneath me in the hay, her smile incredulous (*"You mean you ain't axed?"*), of her wide eyes (*"Knocked!"*)—assailed me. I heard Amos moaning from his room upon the first floor, his opium calm disturbed, or perhaps it was some sort of malevolent spirit, fleeing the Cities of the Dead, envious of the troubles of the living.

I have to tell Mama. She would find out soon enough, whether I told her or not, of course.

And oh, the withering contempt with which she would eye me, her every assessment of me confirmed! I dreaded her judgment as I would my execution. I, the plunderer of virgins, the ravisher, the fiend. Mama had offered me redemption through her sham marriage; now it was no sham, and she would hang me upon its hook and hold me there. But the point of telling now was that there might be something she could suggest before it became too late.

On the other hand, surely if there *were* something, she would have used it upon herself to avoid introducing me into the world.

God. *Law*.

Had I really thought myself bereft when Thomas betrayed me, when I discovered the secret of my parentage? Had I thought I would savor even the hint of freedom's sweetness upon my tongue? How naive I had been!

I assumed, at least, that Faith's demeanor would be altered, that my disclosure of allegedly good news would induce a change in her perceptions once she'd thought on it.

And so it did. By the very next day, she was far, far worse.

What could she have been thinking in the dead of that night, when we both likely lay awake upon our mattresses? Evidently she had not been rejoicing over the possible change in her circumstances, or my description of Aix-en-Provence, or the happiness that might lay beyond this infernal moment. No, instead she had seized upon some remote flaw in the facets of the jewel, some flickering which held her entranced: the idea of Madame's malevolence toward her, the one thing she imagined might prevent her leaving, or threaten our unborn child. Who can know why a woman in such condition feels or observes as she does?

That next morning, she appeared, whey-faced and puffy, in the parlor, and became so unhinged in Madame's presence that I pulled her aside and offered to make an excuse for her in the dining room that night. "Naw," she rasped, rattling the knickknacks upon a side table as her foot caught in the legs. I had not the chance to argue with her, for I was wanted in the kitchen, where Lila was cleaning up the remnants of breakfast.

At any rate, we were all needed that evening for the dinner service. Lila had prepared a roast goose, and Madame wished, as usual, to have served some of the delicacies she'd lugged across the ocean, as well as several of the regional French wines. Louella was seated in the place she had always taken on the table's left, while Madame occupied one of the heads. "I expect to leave on Monday," Louella said as I poured Madame a glass of some potent fumé blanc. "I'll need Cici"—one of the Provence maids—"and tell Dolley to be ready, since we must go over Papa's paperwork together."

Madame's lips turned down in displeasure. "Must you take Dolley?" she asked. "Can you not take one of the other men, one of the Negroes?"

"You perhaps might bear in mind, Maman, that the country is engaged in a war at least in part over the fate of the Negroes. I doubt that any of them will be anxious to escort me. And besides, I must have Dolley—much as I'd prefer not to—to authorize the transactions. I cannot affix my own signature, you know, being merely a woman." Her voice dripped with sarcasm, and her mother's pursed mouth registered disapproval.

"Let us not cover that tedious ground again," Madame said. "Why you wish to intrude upon the vulgar business of men I cannot imagine, but if you intend to usurp the order of things, then disharmony will be the natural outcome."

"I could not avoid *intrusion*, Maman, even if I wished to, seeing as every venture tied to the world beyond my front gate has been requisitioned and held hostage by our benevolent lords. To me that is most unnatural, and I pity you that you cannot see it. As for disharmony, there are worse things than the upset which follows the overthrow of tyranny."

"Enough!" Madame said, rubbing her temples. "I am eating, I will have no more of this nonsense at table. If you must lose your mind, kindly have the grace to do it elsewhere, when I am not digesting."

Louella patted her mouth, her cheeks reddening, but said nothing more. I moved behind her to fill her glass, but she covered the goblet with her hand and wrinkled her nose, giving me to know that she did not share her mother's taste in wine, as in so many other things.

Just then Faith staggered into view beneath a tray of asparagus in butter sauce, which she was required to serve with ornamented silver tongs. I held my breath, but not a slimy one of them missed the plate, and I exhaled as she withdrew from over Madame's shoulder.

But in the next moment she straightened, exposing her neck and the still-slender line of her jaw. Madame peered up, and in the midst of my exhalation I heard her say to Louella, in French, "It seems we have a thief among us."

I caught myself mid-breath. I had finished pouring; I stood stiffly against the wall, my hands behind my back—and a lucky thing it was that I was in this position, for I felt my legs weaken a tad beneath me.

"What?" Louella followed Madame's nod. Faith could only halt where she stood, knowing she was being spoken of, but unable to understand a word.

"A thief." Madame nodded again. "Are those not Grandmother Denis's earrings, there in that girl's ears?"

Louella glanced over, then shrugged. "I'm sure I don't know, Maman. I left half of those atrocious old things behind when I departed this house, and I've quite forgotten what they looked like."

Again I felt my breath catch in my chest.

"Come over here, Miss," Madame said in English. She gestured, and I saw, with a still heart, Faith's head turn, so that the garnets were fully visible beneath the loose braid of her hair. She walked as if a rope pulled her in the other direction, as if she could barely force her poor feet to propel her forward. She stood trembling before Madame, and croaked, "Yes'm?"

"Where did you get those jewels in your ears?" Madame asked. Louella breathed a loud sigh.

Faith's skin paled further. She seemed puzzled by the question—she cast about, her gaze found me, and an eternity went by while I wished that we both might be swallowed by the earth and disappear. "Dey's a gift," she whispered, her eyes returning to Madame.

"I see, a gift. Would you mind removing one?"

She laid the tray down on the table and did as she'd been bidden, and Madame examined it, then said in French to Louella, "These are certainly Grandmama's. They go with the sterling necklace, and the bangle bracelet."

"I'm happy to hear it, Maman. At least someone is getting some use out of them, ugly as they are."

"That's hardly the point," Madame snapped. "A gift, she says! They are stolen from us, and she has the effrontery to wear them in our very presence! The stupid creature! Well, I'll not abide it. I'll not have thieves under my roof."

"Oh, don't be so dramatic. Perhaps they were a gift, how do you know they're not?"

"If they were," Madame huffed, "it means only that some other robber remains to be dealt with. This could be only the beginning—today it's whatever's lying about unused, tomorrow it's the silver, or the jewelry from our very persons!" She gestured again at Faith. "Who gave those to you?" she asked in English.

Now Faith turned round to face me, and there was nothing else to be done. Much later than I should have, I stepped forward. I nudged the girl out of the way and made a low bow to Madame. "Madame Eugenia," I said in French, "forgive me. It was I who gave them to her. I found them whilst doing a thorough cleaning inside Mademoiselle's drawers, I did not realize they were of value, as they'd been left behind. I apologize profusely. I intended no disrespect."

Madame gave me a sour stare, but Louella clapped her hands with delight. "A romance!" she cried in English. "A fine, romantic gesture! Bravo, Aubrey, well done!" Faith appeared hopelessly confused, Madame glared at her daughter, and I kept my head bowed, wishing that Louella would be quiet.

"You will remove those at once and give them to me," Madame said to Faith. "I will dispense with you later, sir," she addressed me. Faith slowly removed the other earring, looking crushed and mystified.

But as she was about to hand it to Madame, Louella said, "Bring them over here, please." Faith hesitated, Madame's furious gaze still upon her. "All right then," Louella said, rising. She strode over to the girl, tweaked the earring from her fingers, and picked up the other on the table. Then, as Madame looked on fuming, she opened Faith's hand—just as I had once done—and placed the garnets inside. "Here," she said, smiling. "I make a gift of these to you. They belong to me, you see, and Aubrey took them from my rooms, that's what all the fuss is about, dear. But as they are returned to me, they are mine to do with as I wish. And I wish you to have them." I closed my eyes; Louella no doubt meant the gesture kindly, but she seemed not to consider how Faith might be made to pay for it later on.

Madame's face remained pinched. Faith stared at the earrings in her limp hand; then she sobbed, "Please, ma'am, 'scuse me," and fled the room.

I straightened at last. "You, sir—" Madame began, but Louella cut her off.

"That's the end of it, Maman. He took them from a drawer, he meant no harm, they're trinkets I cannot use, and I've given them to the maid. That's the end of it."

But it was not. Faith moved about that evening like one of the legendary zombies, and when dinner ended she cornered me and threw the earrings upon me. "Take 'em," she said, wild-eyed once more. "Don' want 'em roun me no mo'."

"I am so sorry," I began. "I never meant that you should be blamed—"

"Ye lied," she interrupted me. "Ye ain't git 'em fer me, ye stole 'em. Ye done won me wid thievin. Don' want nothin stolen in mah hand. Ev'ything go bad de minute I put 'em on, I shoulda knowed it." She thrust the jewels at me once again, and said in a gentler tone, "I know ye ain't mean harm, Bree, but jes take 'em, bury 'em or burn 'em, and mebbe de evil eye be lifted offn' us."

"But they're yours now," I stammered. "There is no evil eye, I explained my own fault to Madame. No one suspects you of wrongdoing—"

"Don' matta none. De missus' eye on me now, watch ev'ything I do, cotch ev'y mistake now, no matta what ye done said. Dat whut anybody git wid stealin, de eye on 'em one way or t'other, jes like I say 'twould be!"

She whirled away from me, back down the hall, and I had no choice but to put the earrings in a pocket, where their sharp wires pierced the material and pricked the skin of my thigh.

Louella left three days later, despite warnings from the newspapers that travel was ill-advised, as all the Southland's resources were to be poured into the glorious war effort. The Confederacy was winning, or so we were continually assured, what with General McDowell having ceded Bull Run, near Washington, to the Sesesh troops. Nonetheless, we were encouraged to stay at home, since unfinished roadwork, infrequent stagecoach arrivals, and diminished law enforcement were the prices exacted for our victories.

Madame begged Louella to postpone her trip, but the girl was adamant: this business must be concluded *now*, so that all of us could depart upon her return. Nothing would happen, she assured her mother. The papers were merely doomsaying, the war was a world away, and if not for the blockade of the ports, no one in New Orleans would feel its effects at all. "You'll be fine," she told her mother, as they reviewed her itinerary. "You're left in the best of hands." Madame looked dismally back at us, her mouth drooping beneath her long nose.

Cici the maid and the miserable Dolley accompanied Louella, as promised. Everyone was relieved to see Dolley go; I was glad to see Louella depart as well, for I no longer knew how to act in her presence. I found I could barely think straight, so much swirled in my brain at any given moment. I had still said nothing to Mama about Faith's condition; the girl herself strode about more disoriented than ever, and—true to her prediction—Madame seemed to be watching both of us with annoyed eagle eyes. She would have only Lisabeth, the other French chambermaid, in her rooms, and when forced to accept meal service from either Faith or myself, refused even to acknowledge us. Naturally, she mentioned the incident of the earrings to Mama, who, naturally, took it upon herself to chastise me.

But Mama was not so hard upon me as she might have been, considering. She merely told me that Madame had made a fuss, and that I ought to be more clever in my thievery, and that the matter was bound to be forgotten in a few days. Faith and I should stay out of Madame's reach, Mama advised me, until she found something else to preoccupy her.

I happily agreed to this, and passed Mama's comments on to Faith, but they did little to lift the girl's spirits. In addition to her mental torments, she was now suffering physically as well, in a manner typical to ladies in a family way. She dragged through her duties, and spent portions of the day discreetly running to the privy, where I imagined she was vomiting up what little food she was able to take in. I wondered if there was not something more I should do—but then, I doubted she desired any advice, however well intentioned, from me.

Rather, I caught glimpses of her in earnest conversation with Adeline—and even, on occasion, with Cheney. I said a prayer that she'd not decide to fall in with the latter company. My own counsel would have been more objectively delivered, as I had rarely known Cheney to be interested in the outcome of matters whose beneficiary was not herself.

And then—were all of this not enough to trouble the mind and spirit—about a week after Louella's departure, Madame Eugenia fell ill. She appeared at first to have caught a touch of stomach influenza, her symptoms being a mild nausea after eating and a subsequent lethargy which induced her to take to her bed. She was convinced that the problem lay in her diet, and spoke to Mama and Lila about making changes in the menus which might better suit her tastes.

But after a few days she appeared no better—in fact she had gotten considerably worse, much to everyone's distress. She was nauseated not only after but before meals, and for a good part of the time in between, and had begun to be troubled by severe headaches which even Mama's tincture of opium could not relieve. By the fifth day of her illness she had retired to her rooms upstairs, where she was forced to take her supper upon a tray.

She was not the only one in the household to be so affected. Lisabeth, the Provence girl, began to evidence symptoms shortly after Madame, and followed her mistress to the sickbed only a day later.

Mama decided then that it was time to summon a doctor. Whatever the trouble, it would not do to have the only two white folk on the premises languishing untended to, and so she sent David for the nearest physician, Dr. Chambliss, whose home was about a quarter-hour's ride from our own.

The doctor at first refused to come. Of course he mentioned nothing regarding the annoyances the war had inflicted upon us, which many were hoping to avoid by departing until the Confederacy prevailed. No; rather, the doctor was preparing for a short business trip, he said, and could spare no time for new patients.

But David for once took Mama at her word when she told him not to return alone. He camped out upon the veranda of the Chambliss home for an hour, then two, patiently pleading his case each time the owner appeared to throw him off the grounds. At last Dr. Chambliss agreed to come, on the condition that, whatever his findings, we utilize another physician should any more calls prove necessary.

Arriving at the Paxton residence, he could not have been more perfunctory. He hastened Madame through a description of her illness, and sighed with impatience as Mama translated, from French, Lisabeth's account of her own condition. Then he diagnosed the problem as some sort of female trouble, a response to the ladies' delicate systems having to adjust to the unfamiliar New Orleans climate. He prescribed willow bark tea, which he dispensed on the spot, and a poultice of onions for the chest, and then he hastened from the house, as if from a burning building.

"Leaving, no doubt, for fairer pastures," Mama murmured, watching him hurry away from our drive. She followed the doctor's instructions to the letter, but neither Madame nor Lisabeth appeared to improve much after their treatments. They had progressed to a state of high fever, and regular bouts of vomiting, which lasted even after they had expelled the final morsels from their stomachs.

The rest of us were forced to listen to their exertions and to wait upon the invalids, so that our house now resembled a sanitarium. Amos was ensconced downstairs, where Lila divided her time between the kitchen and his care; Madame was upstairs, and Lisabeth was contained in the tiny dressing room just off the master bedroom. All day now, the healthy members of the household were kept busy changing and washing the sheets, blankets, towels, chamber pots, dressing gowns, and undergarments. We were also expediting three meals a day to every corner of the building, and cleaning up afterward. The work was ceaseless, to say nothing of the anxiety we all suffered wondering which of us would be the next to fall ill.

Only Faith seemed willing to care for Madame on a regular basis, which amazed me considering her own condition, and the fear she had of anything which might jeopardize our unborn child's health—not to mention her fear of Madame herself. Yet she volunteered to sit with Madame at night, to apply the poultices readied by Lila, and perform a thousand mundane chores required for the comfort of the patients. I wondered if this was not because she sensed an opportunity to ingratiate herself; but it was also true that there was no one else who could spare the time Faith had to devote to the invalids.

For Madame had insisted on taking extra measures to ensure her recovery. She did not trust the doctor, whose attentions seemed cursory even to us; she placed no faith in his poultices and teas. She wanted instead special mixtures made from the food she had brought with her from Provence: fresh bread to go with the various cheeses, glasses of wine heated into toddies, tinned and jarred dainties opened and arranged as best Lila knew how. We were expected to supply these delicacies on demand, in addition to our regular duties and the strain of caring for the ladies. Mama insisted that all instructions be followed to the letter; she was taking no chances with the health of Paxton's wife.

"Do you think their condition so serious that all of this is necessary?" I overheard Cheney ask, shortly after Mama had implemented the doctor's special orders, as well as Madame's own.

Mama was brooding, stalking the halls in her silent and predatory manner. At first she didn't answer, but when the question was posed a second time, she replied, "I am thinking everything is serious, at this point. Let us treat this as though it is, for we have nothing to lose by being cautious."

Yet despite our most exacting ministrations, Madame and Lisabeth seemed to worsen by the hour—particularly Lisabeth, who began to bring up a quantity of blood with every bout of retching. Faith noticed this first, being the one most immediately in contact with the patients. She came down to the kitchen one evening with the chamber pot in her hands, and one would have thought from the pallor of her skin that it was her own blood drained into the porcelain bowl. She displayed the contents to Mama, while the other women peered over her shoulder.

Now Mama was not the only one alarmed. This was surely no climate adjustment, no passing ague. She turned to Adeline. "There's an end to that fool doctor's medicines—we must handle this ourselves, as it's plain he hasn't the slightest idea what the trouble is. So think now—what's to be tried next?"

Adeline's stunned expression was replaced by one of intense concentration. "Charcoal," she finally suggested. "Plenty of water, whatever she will take. And cut a fresh apple, let it brown, and we'll feed her that with boiled lemon and sugar. That should be a start, if pray God the blood's just the result of irritation, perhaps from the constant puking."

"All right," Mama said. She, Adeline, and Cheney set to preparing the remedy while Faith returned to the sickroom. I realized the girl had taken nothing to eat for herself all day, so I put some biscuits, fresh butter, and cold preserves upon a plate and proceeded up the steps.

In the master bedroom I found her seated in a small chair near the door of the cubby where Lisabeth slept. From this vantage point she could see Madame's bed as well, and Madame in it, breathing heavily. But Faith was not paying attention. She sat with her fingers clutching at each other, her eyes shut, lips moving. "Law," she was whispering, so that I could just discern the words, "take de fever fum dese here Christian wimmins what love an serve you. F'give me mah sins, O Law, an heal us in yer name—"

"Faith," I called. Her eyes flew open, and she turned. "You must be hungry, I brought you something small to eat."

"I don' want nothin."

"You mustn't sit here amidst sickness without any food to give you strength. Come, have just a bite."

She stared back at me, and for the first time it truly struck me, that it was my very flesh the girl carried within her, which tied us irrevocably whether I sanctioned it or not.

"Please." I offered the plate again.

"Naw. Ain't want no food." She shifted away in her seat, her posture dismissing me. I waited a moment to see if I could prevail upon her, but when her head did not turn again in my direction, I sighed and withdrew.

Mama and Cheney and Adeline were just then entering the room with their apple-charcoal remedy, and so I halted by the door to see what the outcome of the treatment would be. "Lisabeth," Mama called, "we've medicine for you, come now and be a good girl, eat it all up and you'll soon be feeling better." The maid opened yellowed eyes in her flushed face, and shook her head. "Look here, it isn't bad," Mama crooned, holding up a spoonful to show her. When she did not turn away, Cheney attempted to prop her up against her pillows into a position which at least would enable her to swallow. Adeline then tried, with trembling fingers, to pour the noxious-looking mixture into the girl's mouth. I was shocked to see how weak Lisabeth was—so much so that she could not lift her head, nor raise a hand even to refuse the medicine. She took a feeble swallow, but the liquid oozed from her lips and down her chin; and I turned away, feeling I was somehow violating her by witnessing the intimacies of her care.

I returned to the laundry downstairs, and busied myself folding the mountains of linens which had been washed and hung the previous day. They now sat in baskets, wrinkling—a detail which would have sent Mama into a rage in normal times, but which these days merited barely a glance from her.

A half hour later, I heard Mama and Cheney descend the steps, their portion of the maid's treatment completed. When I heard Adeline emerge an hour or so after that, I strode to the foot of the banister to ask upon the girl's progress.

Adeline stared at me as if I'd slapped her, her black eyes wide under their thick brows. "What is it? What do you want?"

"Only—" I felt myself stuttering, taken aback by her manner. "—I only wished to know how Lisabeth is faring—"

"She's a strong girl," Adeline interrupted me. "She's sure to recover. I did everything—" She stopped abruptly, stared at me for a moment, and then turned, rushing down the hall until she reached the kitchen.

I watched her slam through the double doors as if the devil himself chased after her. And I wondered how long it would be before sheer nervous prostration caused every member of our household to lose his or her wits, and fall into the grip of complete insanity.

I finished my chore and returned to my room exhausted, intending to examine a portion of Madame's newspaper, which she was presently unable to negotiate. But I fell asleep instead, and when I woke it was nearly eleven o'clock, and the candle by my bed almost burned away. I decided I would read until the nub extinguished itself, so that I might gather the latest insights as to the war's urgency.

I was halfway through a sickening description of the Bull Run victory when I chanced to hear strange noises emanating from the second floor. They sounded like an argument of some sort; there were screams and shouts punctuated by pounding, and then silence.

No one else in the house seemed aware of the commotion. At least, no one else was responding to it, probably because they were all asleep. I hesitated a moment, wondering if I was only imagining the sounds, but then the pounding came again, the thud of something heavy striking the floor beneath me.

This time I did not hesitate. I ran down the steps from my quarters to the hallway below. I entered Madame's rooms without knocking, and there I came upon a horrible sight.

Madame lay perspiring in her huge canopy bed, her fever raging so hot that I imagined I could feel it from where I stood. She was alternately croaking Mama's name, babbling nonsense, and thrashing about beneath the damp, rumpled sheets.

To the left of her bed, where the doors to the other rooms opened out, was her maid. Lisabeth had crawled from her tiny closet into the vast bedchamber. She lay writhing on the floor crying and moaning, and trying to clutch at herself. Clinging to the front of her white dressing gown and staining the polished floorboards beneath her was a puddle of gooey, blood-streaked vomit.

And kneeling over Lisabeth's head, making the most noise of all, was Faith. She appeared to be in some sort of mystic trance. Swaying from her waist, she let her outstretched hands fall to slap the floor near Lisabeth's body, while her voice rose in a howl that shook me to my depths.

"Law Gawd! Don' let de sins a de guilty tech 'pon de innocent! Show de mercy, Law Jesus, yer servant Faith am beggin ye! Heal dis chile, O Law! And bring 'er fum de edge a de pit!"

She brought her hands down with such force that Madame's perfume flacons danced on the vanity. Lisabeth cried out and rolled away, and then fell into a violent bout of vomiting, expelling a torrent of fresh, bright red blood. And Faith raised up again to begin another supplicating wail: *"Law, maker of de world, dis am yer servant! Chase de evil fum dis house—"*

I rushed forward, calling her name, to grab her before she injured either Lisabeth or herself. But at the sound of my voice she screamed, as if I wielded an ax and intended to use it upon her; she rose and shrieked, her red, raw hands clutching her hair, her face distorted and stained with tears. "Let me be! Naw, let me be, Aubrey! Don' tech me, don' tech me!" I tried to lunge for her, but my bare feet slipped in the bloody mess, and I slid forward, saving myself only by grabbing onto the post of Madame's bedframe. Faith backed into a corner by the wall and stood there crossing herself as the Catholic sisters do, again and again, while muttering imprecations.

I heard footsteps on the stair outside, and a moment later Mama entered the room, followed closely by Adeline and Cheney. Mama took in the scene in an instant. "Mother of God," she gasped. She rushed to Lisabeth's side, and turned back to me, her eyes frantic. "How long has she been doing this?"

"I don't know—Faith was tending to them—I heard shouting—" Mama now turned to where Faith cowered in the corner, noticing the girl for the first time. She glanced back to the doorway, where Adeline and Cheney were still huddled. "One of you see to Faith, it's clear she's overwrought." Neither of them moved. Finally Mama addressed herself to me: "Go on, take her out of here, Bree."

"Faithy," I called, edging toward her, "it's all right, come with me now." I extended my hand, but she did not even look in my direction, instead staring straight ahead as if at some other landscape. I continued to move closer, until I was able to grasp her arm and give it a gentle pull. Then I walked her past Adeline's and Cheney's stunned faces, and guided her into Louella's room, and up onto the big feather bed. I sat beside her, placed my arm about her shoulder. "You'll wait for me here, all right?" She gave no sign of understanding. "Everything will be fine, Faithy. You needn't worry." I eased her onto her back, drew the cover over her, while she made no sound at all. Then I left her, and hurried back into the master bedroom.

The women therein had begun a flurry of activity. Mama and Cheney were attempting to help Lisabeth stand, but she pushed their hands from her and curled into a ball upon the filthy floor. Madame was ranting beneath her coverlets while Adeline struggled to feed her some water.

After a moment, Mama turned to me. "This is no good," she said over her shoulder. "Go get David, Aubrey. Tell him he has to ride to the Old House and fetch your Gran, right now. And if you can't rouse him in one minute, saddle up and go yourself."

I was turning on my heel when Madame's shriek caught me short. "*No no no!* Don't you dare leave me in this house! Don't you dare send for some heathen medicine woman, I won't have it! Louis? Louis! Where is Thomas? Where is my daughter! Where is Louella! Dolley! Where is Dolley!"

"She is delirious," Mama said to me, but Madame overheard her and cried, "I am *not*! I am mistress of this house, and I bid you *stop where you are, do not take another step or I will sell you all off on the next wagon!*" I froze, and Mama rushed to Madame's side.

"Madame Eugenia, Lisabeth is very ill, you must let me send for my mother. She may be able to help, at the very least let her try, before the girl's condition worsens."

"No, stand off her! Give her some wine—I forbid it! No one is to leave the house!" Mama looked back at me, but each time I moved, Madame took up with another earsplitting wail of protest.

Just then Lisabeth's convulsions began again in earnest. "Please," Mama begged Madame. But the mistress shook her head, put her hands to her ears. "No no no—I'll let no heathen touch my Lisabeth—"

Mama placed her hands on Madame's shoulders. "Listen to her, Madame! Don't you hear—" She had begun to shake her, and I found myself yanking at Mama's arm, and then Mama slapped me away—"Get off me, she must listen to reason"—and Madame slapped at Mama. I had managed to wrestle Mama away when we heard Cheney give a gasp.

We turned in the same moment, in time to see Lisabeth project a river of blood onto the floor. It dripped from her nose and from her mouth, it spattered Cheney's forearms, which were around the girl's waist. She seemed to undergo some sort of paroxysm, which began with contortions of her face and continued all the way down her body. She foamed at the mouth, flailed and jerked with amazing strength, her arms flying outward, her heels drumming against the floorboards. Finally she lay bent over Cheney's arms like a poppet, her sticky hair matted over her face. Cheney stared at us wildly, then made as if to release the girl, but Lisabeth made no attempt to catch herself. Her head lolled on the end of her neck like a weight, her arms hung limp. Cheney set her down as gently as possible, cradling her head with one hand.

She lay on the floor, not moving. Cheney pushed the hair back from her face. She was ghastly to behold, her skin as blue-white as milk, the flesh about her eyes black, patches of sticky blood caked about her nostrils, outlining her mouth like a grotesque rouge. None of us moved either; rather, we stared at her, each praying silently that the moment would pass and she would cough or breathe, or open her eyes.

But we had tarried too long in our arguments. And now there was no need to hurry for Lisabeth's sake, for it was obvious that not even you, Gran, could be of any use to her.

"Dear God," Cheney breathed.

I found that tears leapt into my eyes out of the sheer impact of it, rather than from any great depth of feeling. For at that moment I felt nothing at all, seeming to have moved outside my own skin.

Mama had put a finger to her lips, and threw a glance at the bed where Madame lay, still moaning and clutching at the air. "What is it, what's happening!" Madame cried. She was trying to raise herself so that she might see over Cheney's back. I rushed toward her, between the bed and the scene upon the floor, so that her view of Lisabeth might be blocked. I know not where the instinct for this action came from; I was as detached as if I watched myself from some other room.

"Madame," I began in my most soothing tone, "you must not rouse Lisabeth, she is sleeping and must be taken to rest—" Out of the corner of my eye I saw Mama and Cheney lift the girl from each end, and I stared into Madame's fevered eyes, willing her gaze to remain upon me while they crossed by the foot of the bed to the door. Madame peered around me, but seemed not to realize what had happened; only I noticed the sickening force with which Lisabeth's head hit the doorjamb as Mama swung the girl's torso round the corner and into the hallway.

I waited until I heard no sound from the hall, and then I eased Madame back onto her cushions. When I saw her eyelids drooping, I went into the bath, with its claw-footed tub—the very one which Faith and I had cleaned, where I had kissed her for the first time. I stared into the glass there, and saw upon my cheek a spattering of blood. Then I stared down at my feet, and saw that they too were covered with blood, and with vomit, in which flecks of recognizable food—a smear of lemon pulp, a bit of apple—were still evident. In a sudden rush my spirit came to inhabit my body once again; nausea overtook me, and I collapsed over the bathtub rim. With my eyes shut I pictured the girl's dead face upon the floor, and I retched uncontrollably, while Madame muttered in her fever from the other room.

I lay upon the tile floor, my cheek against its coolness, my eyes closed, until I felt I could reach the pitcher, rinse my mouth, and clean the tub. Then I staggered out, ignoring Madame's ravings behind me, attempting not to see the bloody pools and footprints upon the floor. I passed Louella's room, and there I saw Faith sitting up in the feather bed, staring straight before her, her body still as a statue's. I kept going, and found myself at Thomas's door, which was shut. I turned the knob, my fingers icy, and entered.

They had laid Lisabeth on the floor, upon a bedsheet which they were now using as a winding sheet. I could not bear to watch them. How could they do it, I wondered, be so hard as nails when the poor, poor girl had been alive only an hour ago—but then I saw that Mama was on the verge of tears.

Cheney's eyes were dry. She worked with a fevered concentration, barely glancing up as I entered the room.

When they were finished, Mama turned away, then rose and walked to the desk, where she buried her head in her hands. "Dear God," I heard her whispering, "Mother of God."

Cheney rose and stepped behind her. "What are we going to do?"

I wondered what she meant, and then it occurred to me: if Lisabeth were to be given a Christian burial—any burial—there would be authorities to notify.

"Who are we to tell?" Cheney asked again.

"Let me think," Mama said without turning around. She was breathing deeply; I could see her ribs expand and contract beneath the corset stays. "Madame is not fit to make decisions. We must send for Evangeline before she gets any worse. And we must attempt to reach Louella."

"There isn't time for that," Cheney said. She was staring at Mama's back, her eyes hard. "Suppose Madame goes next, what's to become of us then? How shall we explain it, two misses dead, and the rest of us here in perfect health, and blessedly alone?"

"What would you suggest, then, that we call Calvin, or L'Heuron?" Mama snapped.

"I do suggest it," Cheney said. "I suggest you tell Madame what's happened, whether she understands or not. Then let the *gendarmes* come and see Madame for themselves, let them dispose of the child's body, and we will wait here until Louella can be found."

Mama closed her eyes. "I must have time to think," she said, rubbing her temples with her fingers. "Leave me be tonight. In the morning I'll tell you what we're to do. For now I believe we must concentrate on getting my mother here quickly, to minister to Madame."

But Cheney shook her head. "No, that's pointless. Worse than pointless. It'll only work against us should she—should the worst happen, and Madame not survive. We'll be blamed, do you understand, so better to let them see her now, fetch their own doctors, witness for themselves that it's none of our doing. Besides, she won't have Evangeline touch her. You heard her ranting clear as I did."

"In another day she'll not have the strength to rant. Then perhaps she won't mind our nigger doctoring quite so much."

In the end they agreed to wait until daybreak before sending for anyone, since, at any rate, travel in the darkness was too perilous to be chanced. This left us with Lisabeth to tend to, since we could not simply abandon her upon Thomas's floor.

"Take her head," Mama ordered me. "I'll carry her from the legs, and we'll bring her to the carriage house."

I bent to place my hands beneath the shrouded shoulders, and then stopped and straightened, clutched at the wall.

"What's the matter with you, go ahead," Mama barked.

I swallowed hard past the stone caught in my chest, yellow sunbursts dancing before my eyes. Then I bent again and did as I'd been bidden, only to discover the corpse still warm beneath my fingers, although the limbs were growing stiff as lumber. There was a splintering sound as Mama lifted the ankles; the hips would not give, they cracked instead, the deadweight of the torso pulling them down.

We proceeded slowly, laboriously, to the carriage house, pausing every few feet for breath, while Cheney opened the doors and lit lamps for us. In life the poor maid had been a plump and pretty creature, but now she was as heavy as cement, and as unwieldy, her rigid limbs refusing to move through the hallways, her stiff dead feet banging against the banisters.

We passed David in the servants' quarters, dressed already in his skivvies. He shrank against the wall as we brushed by, and widened his eyes at the sight of the bloody shroud. "Where have you been," Mama panted from under her burden. He shook his head. "Never mind, go on upstairs and look in on Faith and Madame. This here is Lisabeth, and she's already dead." David's skin paled appreciably, and he looked at his wife as if for further explanation. But Cheney only snapped, "You heard her, the girl's dead, go on upstairs and see to the other two."

In the carriage house we laid Lisabeth on Amos's old cot—he had no need of it now—and then wiped the perspiration from our faces. I glanced over at Mama and Cheney, and they appeared to me as two succubi straight from hell, their taut mouths and wide eyes illuminated in the yellow lamplight. But Mama stopped to make a cross over Lisabeth's forehead, and close her eyes in a quick prayer.

Then we proceeded back to the house, where Lila was now waiting for us in the kitchen. "David just woke me," she began, and then stopped short at the sight of us. *"Mon Dieu,"* she breathed. She rushed into the dining room and returned with the whiskey decanter and three glasses. She poured us two fingers each, and we drank it down in a single gulp, the liquor searing my throat and causing my stomach to seize up in revulsion. A moment later, though, I felt a heat coursing through my limbs, and was grateful for it.

We fell upon the benches at the kitchen table, and Mama spoke to Lila, filling in the details of the last hours. Then she began to delegate tasks, although I was numb beyond reason and could barely lift my head to listen to her.

It was not until she had counted off all of us in turn that something seemed to occur to her, and indeed it occurred to me in the same instant, although I did not speak it. But Mama paused and peered around the table at us, as if to make sure she had overlooked nothing. Then she asked—expecting no answer, I'm certain—"Where is Adeline?"

She was gone.

When we rushed to the room she shared with Faith, it was apparent. The pegs which held her clothing were empty, her drawers in the one dresser bare as well.

"Perhaps she's gone to get Evangeline," Mama said. "She heard us discussing it, after all." I volunteered that this was the last place I'd seen her, hours ago: by Madame's bedside when Mama was suggesting we let you doctor her, Gran.

"She'd never do that," Cheney scoffed, "knowing how dangerous it is, when she could have sent one of the men. No. You know what she's done, Onessa. She's run off."

Lila was wringing her hands. "Run off! But why? Why would she leave now? What's to be gained?"

"What's to be lost is the better question," Cheney muttered. "Perhaps she had good reason to run."

"What are we to do?" Lila asked Mama.

"There is nothing we can do, for the moment. At least let us wait until morning to see if she returns. After which—"

"Are you crazed!" Cheney interrupted. "Wait until morning! No! I'll tell you what we're to do, it's obvious. She's run because she's involved with all of this, with Madame being sick and Lisabeth too. Or else she knows who's responsible, and now the girl's dead she's left their blood on our hands to save her own neck. What we're to do is call upon L'Heuron *tonight, this minute*, before any of this is discovered in some other fashion."

"And risk having him blame all of us anyway—which you know he very well might? Or send him after Adeline, when we know nothing for certain? To get her caught and possibly killed—Adeline, your friend?"

"She isn't my friend who'd leave me to hang for her dirty deeds."

"You know nothing," Mama seethed. "Nothing except your own fevered imaginings. What has she to gain from such a foul act as killing those two? Not a thing, and it's not a bit in her character. Besides, how would she accomplish it?"

"With poison—roots, herbs, some foul concoction—isn't that apparent?"

"When, with either Faith or Lila overseeing the women every moment? It's nonsense, I'm telling you."

"Yes, that's right, Adeline was nowhere near the food," Lila put in. "That much I know."

Cheney whirled on her. "Goddamn what you know, it doesn't matter! What will anyone care for our explanations when we're caught here, one white woman dead, another dying, and one of us run off unreported! We'll hang for sure. What did you tell us, Onessa, to lie low until it's all ended or the moment comes to fight—and I've obeyed every word you said, only to be undone by these bastard fools, who'd have my neck wrung before I get the chance to defend myself!"

Mama was about to reply to this when we heard a shout from the hall. It was David, standing at the top of the second-floor landing and calling any one of us to come.

"Onessa—Cheney—somebody, get upstairs here, it's Madame!"

Mama breathed, "Oh, no," and then all of us moved at once, tumbling through the double doors on each other's heels. I felt the most sickening dread overtake me as I hastened to mount the stairs behind Lila: this night had rushed beyond our control, there would be no reining it in now, and the dawn would see every familiarity irrevocably altered.

I passed Thomas's room, the door still open to reveal the bloody floor; I passed Louella's room, and saw Faith upon her knees by the bed, her shoulders heaving, her head flung back. I arrived in Madame's room, and here there was only stillness, for Madame lay upon the bed in an attitude of such abandon—her arms outstretched, her face waxy white, her dressing gown thrown open, with one flaccid breast protruding from it—that we knew quite certainly she must be dead.

"God help us," Lila moaned, and I saw her plea echoed in all our expressions. For a moment none of us spoke. Then Mama walked over to the corpse, so recently Madame Eugenia. She lowered its arms, closed the eyes, drew the gown over its forlorn bosom. "Jesus save you," she whispered. Then she leaned upon the wall to steady herself, and turned to David.

"You," she said, "you must go to Baton Rouge to find Louella. Right now. I will get the itinerary and a letter of permission, but you must find her, even if you must knock upon every door in the city."

Cheney opened her mouth as if to speak, but Mama turned on her, her face pale as death. "No," she said. "Don't. Not a word. Not now, unless you'd have me go mad upon you."

David skulked from the room, and Mama turned to me. "Aubrey, go see to Faith. She is ailing. Pray God she is not sick as well. Cheney and Lila, please attend to Madame. Rinse her and dress her, and when you've done, wrap her and leave her upon her bed. I must go write the letter for David." She exited the room without looking at any of us, without waiting for us to move. I saw Cheney staring after her, and then she caught my eye as well, her expression stony; but I cared not a morsel, and stared back at her until Lila gently touched her arm and nodded toward Madame's twisted form.

Faith had not risen from her knees in all this time. She was still muttering her crazed prayers by the bedside when I entered Louella's room once again. I did not attempt to speak to her but, rather, guided her from the floor back up to the high bed. Then, beyond caring, I lay down beside her on the coverlet, taking no notice of my bloody clothes or filthy bare feet.

I shut my eyes, and somehow fell into a poisonous, wretched sleep—the kind which does not refresh, but only invades like a fever, leaving the mind clouded and the body stiff.

When I awakened it was to weak dirty light through the drapes, and voices outside upon the stairs. I struggled to my feet and opened the bedroom door. Perhaps, I thought—and hoped against hope—Adeline had come back, and brought Louella or even you, Gran, with her.

But it was David. He had returned after only a couple of hours. "It isn't no *use*, I'm telling you," he was saying to someone, probably Mama. "Every highway is blocked off. I showed the letter, but they chased me back, the soldiers did—said get home or next time it'd be my neck."

"Did they know you, did you recognize them?" Mama asked him.

"Naw. They were just soldiers, ones I haven't seen before."

"Did they want to know why you were traveling?"

"Yeh, but I didn't tell 'em nothing, except that my mistress was needed, and I'm sent to Baton Rouge to fetch her back home."

"Maybe we'll have some time, then, before someone comes checking upon us," Mama said, half to herself. "In the meanwhile," she addressed David, "you must try again, perhaps on foot—" But David cut her short before she could finish.

"No. No. I'm not trying no more, Onessa. The streets're just full of soldiers and deputies, you can't hardly move out there, and I don't doubt they're telling me true, they'll have my neck the next time."

I closed the door, having little need to hear Mama's reply.

Turning back to the bed, I saw that Faith had raised herself up, and that her dulled eyes were peering out at me with at least some semblance of comprehension in them. I came over to sit beside her, resting my forehead upon the heel of a hand.

We remained like this for some moments, and then Faith said, without expression, "Adeline am gone?"

"Yes."

"An Madame done died." Her tone made it a statement, rather than a question.

"Yes," I said, equally tonelessly, "she has died."

Her tears were silent, profuse, and I wondered that she had any strength left to cry them after the fit which had overtaken her most of the previous day and night. She fell back upon the pillows, and I fell back beside her; and there we lay apart, motionless as two corpses ourselves, staring at the ceiling as we waited for the wrath of this day to overtake us.

Then Faith said, "It wa'n't Adeline."

I assumed she had reverted to gibberish once again, and so I ignored her.

"It wa'n't Adeline," she repeated softly.

"What? Are you speaking to me?"

"Yeh. I am tellin ye, it wa'n't Adeline dat kilt 'er. 'Twas me."

I turned my head slightly to look at her. "Don't blame yourself, Faith. You couldn't have saved them, no matter what you did."

"Ain't blamin. 'Twas me. What give de mistis de pizzen. I got it fum Adeline, but 'twas me what give it to 'er."

I felt the hair stand along my forearms. I wondered if she had lost her mind, but I could see that her face was composed, her eyes focused. "What are you saying?"

Her tears began again, overflowed, and I sat up upon the bed, grabbed her beneath her arms to sit her up as well. "What are you saying, Faith?"

" 'Twas me, Aubrey."

"Oh, no."

" 'Twas."

"Oh dear God."

"I done it. I git de pizzen fum Adeline, 'cause you tole me she de conjure woman too—"

"No. Don't say any more, don't tell me."

"—on'y I tells her it fer me, dat I got de bilious an de liver trouble wid de chile, an need to purge some. An I takes it t' test it out, an it work some, make me sicklike, pukin an nasty, so I puts de dose—all she given me—in de tonic what Missus drink at night. An she git sick right off, so I don' give 'er no mo', but de young missy, Lisabeth, she git it too, musta drunk de tonic herse'f. Den I'se waitin fer de sickness t' go 'way, but dey don' git no betta, jes git wuss an wuss."

"But why," I cried at her, "why in Christ's name did you do this?"

"So de missus—oh Law—so she see dat I'm good. I takes care a her, y'see? An den she find I ain't no thief, am de righteous gal, an be good gal fer ye. An she let me have de chile den. An come wid ye 'crosst de water, to France."

"France." I wiped my eyes with the back of my hand. "To France."

"Oh Gawd," she sobbed, "I done wrong—done wrong—I ain't mean fer nobody to die, ain't mean no harm to nobody—Adeline, she musta run 'cause she know I lie to 'er, an dey find out de mist'esses be pizzened, an figger out it me, an den mebbe I lies an blames her, or jes tell de truth, dat I git de pizzen fum 'er, an den she hang too. Oh Law, Aubrey. Dey gwine kill me. An I ain't meant nothin, ain't wanna hurt no one, I sw'a'n."

I turned from her and pressed my closed fists into my eyes. Dear God, transport me, I prayed, to awaken in another day, one long before or long after this one, to hear no more of her tortured gasping: "He'p me, Aubrey, oh Law Jesus, he'p me, he'p me—"

I grabbed her shoulders once again. "Be quiet," I hissed at her, but it seemed I could still see her lips move, imparting horrors of which I wanted no knowledge. So I shook her again, shouted louder, "Shut up shut up shut up," until she was silent and still, and my own panting was the only sound between us.

But her eyes were still fixed upon me, tremendous and black-ringed. My fury abated at the sight of them, and I fell upon her shoulder. "What did you do," I said into her hair. "What did you do."

When I could sit up, I asked her, still shaking, "Who else knows of this?"

"Nobody. Adeline. An now you."

I buried my face in my hands so that I might think.

What was to be done? Whatever it was, I would, in part, be responsible for doing it. I had to be. I had fathered the child she carried. I was her downfall. And she mine.

Our mistress and her white maid were dead, but was there any way to prove it had been poison? Would it not be better to do as Cheney said: call the deputies, let them believe us honest in our reporting of natural death, let them bury Madame and Lisabeth, and take us into custody until Louella's return?

But that was no good. Because of Adeline. If we notified the deputies, we would have to account for Adeline, and it was too coincidental—the mistress dead, a Negro run off the same night. And Cheney would betray her to the deputies immediately. Whereupon the shadow of suspicion would fall over us all—Cheney was mistaken if she believed that it would stop with Adeline, to leave the rest of us untouched—and sooner or later squeeze the truth from Faith.

And if Adeline was caught—this would be the worst scenario, for she was sure to betray Faith, and the game, for the girl, would be lost for good.

If only Louella would return!

But then, what could I expect of her? Her mother was dead, and two in the household guilty of plotting against her, to whatever extent. What measure of clemency could I anticipate under such circumstances?

I would have to deliver Faith myself. At least until some of the variables had settled themselves. Until I knew whether Adeline had made good her escape. Until Louella returned. Until we decided what to do with the bodies of the women.

Faith would have to be hidden—but where? I thought at once of the Old House, but that was no good. It was the first place anyone would look, and would only have meant involving more innocent people in our intrigues.

I sat, waiting for an idea to form itself.

And slowly it did: I would take her to the swamps. I knew them well enough—their channels and islands, shanties and alligator nests—from my forays there with Thomas, during the long-dead days of our childhood. They had for years provided a worthy hiding place to runaway Negroes; they would now become Faith's haven, giving her refuge from her enemies, black and white.

I would take her to the swamps.

And then what? What would happen next?

Perhaps I could smuggle the two of us northeast, across the battle lines, where we could throw ourselves upon the mercy of the Unionists. Perhaps wait here and beg Louella for forgiveness when she returned. Or hide both of us until we could make good an escape at some future point.

If only someone could advise me as to which option was most worthy.

But someone likely could. I had to acknowledge it: Mama. Mama would know.

Whore, hypocrite, harpy—yes, but she was still no less the wisest of us.

I raised my head.

"You must get away from here. I'll help you. And then I have to tell my mother."

"Oh Gawd. Oh no."

"Listen to me, will you—she'll know what to do, she'll figure something out."

"She'll hand me t' dem—"

Would she? Would she run the risk of our being tainted by guilt as well? No, she wouldn't do that—especially if she knew the girl carried my child.

"No. No she won't, I won't let her. She'll believe you, and she'll help us."

"Naw."

"You must trust me, Faith," I said to her. After all, I had to trust Mama, and what could have been more difficult than that?

The household slept all that day, or at least had retreated to its various chambers, the horrors of the previous evening having taken their toll. Outside, a steady rain fell upon the city, discouraging all but the most necessary travel.

I had determined that we should leave that very afternoon, before the situation developed any further, before anyone—particularly Cheney or David—could awaken and ponder a next move, or question us. I had no idea how we would fare in the streets which David had found impassable just hours ago, but I had concocted a flimsy ruse to sneak us past those white citizens who might take notice of us. Said ruse involved an old suit of Thomas's clothing, some official-looking documents I had written and wax-sealed myself, and Faith's old pinafore, the one which had accompanied her from Jamaica. I intended that we should appear to be a white gentleman trader and his female chattel, on our way to or from the transaction of a sale. With any luck we would meet no one who might recognize me. Once at the edge of the city, we could take a back route deep into the swamps, where I would deposit Faith in one of the fishing shanties that ringed the water.

Then I would return home. I would inform Mama of what had transpired, and ask her advice. Perhaps in time the others could be told, and when we were once again thinking rationally, we could come to a decision as to what to do, so long as we agreed that no harm come to Faith.

It was Cheney whose reaction I worried over most—Cheney and her lackey, the doltish and slavish David. I was surprised at the skill with which she'd deduced half the story, the fact of the mistresses' illness having been intentional, and of Adeline's involvement in the scheme. I doubted it would take her long to unearth the other half—she had to suspect that someone else in the house had participated in the poisonings, for Adeline had nothing to gain by them for herself. The most obvious conspirator was Faith; Cheney had overheard the exchange concerning the earrings, she had seen Faith blundering about in Madame's presence. What she did not know she could infer, and I was sure what her response would be: let the guilty parties be brought to justice so that the rest of us would be spared.

But perhaps if it were put to her in a different fashion, explained in its true terms, she would understand, and be willing to help implement a plan which might save the lives of Faith and of our child. We were all crazed just now, after all. Crazed at the notion of death within our own house, at the implications for all of us. Surely in a day, or two or three, if we could escape discovery by the white authorities, cooler heads would prevail. Or so I sincerely hoped.

I bade Faith wait until early that evening, until I had determined that no one was about within the house. Then I led her by the hand down the front steps, moving carefully in Thomas's too-tight suit, avoiding the kitchen and the ground-floor servants' quarters just beyond it. I took us out the front door, from which I intended to sneak back around to the carriage house. There were certain items there which I knew we would need when negotiating the fringes of the bayou: a lamp, a machete, a good thick blanket, a jar of pitch to keep the mosquitoes away. I had already secured stolen cash upon my person, not only for food or supplies, but for a boat, and for bribes, should the need arise.

Faith carried a bundle of her own. Against my wishes, she had insisted earlier upon going to her room—the one she'd shared with Adeline—and fetching those objects she felt she could not leave behind. They were now hastily tied in a ragged piece of checkered homespun; I told Faith she could better secure the package once we were beyond the main house.

We stepped quietly along the edges of the gravel drive, and made our way into the carriage house. Soleil and Lumi, surprised at their hay-nibbling, raised attentive, large-eyed heads and snuffled at us. I wished suddenly that I could exchange places with them—become a simple animal, guileless and dumb, unaware and uncaring of human machinations.

I led Faith past the stalls and into the tack room. I heard her gasp as she caught sight of the wrapped figure on Amos's cot; even in the slate-gray half-light the white shroud was plainly visible. "Shhhh," I whispered to her, "don't mind her, she's at rest now."

I found the lamp and lit it with a phosphorus match. In the grotesque shadows—the same ones from which Mama and Cheney had stared out at me only half a day ago—I watched Faith undo her bundle, and set out before me its precious contents.

Displayed there on the dirt floor were the dress, chemise, and corset she'd been given upon arriving in New Orleans, and next to them the brogans she had brought with her from Georgia. Inside one shoe was a piece of purple grosgrain ribbon, which Faith wound about a finger and shoved farther into the toe. "Chris'mas gift fum Ma an Pappy, de year befo' I'se sol," she said softly. In the other shoe were three other items: a wooden cross made from twigs and bound together with a dirty piece of leather thong, a needle and thread, and a loop of straight and shiny blue-black hair, sewn inexpertly to a scrap of cloth.

I recognized the hair at once. It was my own.

She saw my expression and whisked the items from my sight, and then they were gone, those sole traces of her mean and troubled existence. I did not watch as she tied the checkered cloth carefully by the corners, and then slung the bag over her shoulder, resting it against her thickening waist. I only saw her out of the corner of my eye as I collected the things I thought we would need, and made a bundle of my own from one of the horses' blankets.

"Time to go," I whispered to her when I was finished. We left the tack room, clicking to the horses to soothe them as we passed their stalls, and stepped through the double doors of the carriage house into the misty drizzling dark.

We were about to round the corner of the building when I heard the voice, soft and flat, directly in front of me.

"Where you think you're going, Bree."

I recognized the tone without seeing its owner, recognized the menace, the implied threat.

It was Cheney.

I felt Faith freeze beside me. I grabbed her hand, having no intention of retreating.

Now she came into view, emerging like a malevolent spirit from the shadows of the drive, where she had no doubt been waiting to accost us. David stood silent behind her, still hidden in the darkness, and at Cheney's side, clutched firmly in her right hand, was Paxton's ancient musket.

"Where you going, Bree," she said again.

I stopped and stared her down. "We're walking. Stand off us. Leave us be."

"Where you walking to, by yourselves in the rain? Don't you know it's dangerous in the streets? You wouldn't be planning to run off now, maybe follow Adeline wherever she went to? If you are, you best turn around and think this through."

"Leave us be," I said again. "It's none of your affair."

She narrowed her eyes at me. "Why'd you do it, Bree," she crooned. "Why'd you kill that innocent girl and our own mistress? And now you run off like this, leave your own mama who raised you up to suffer in your stead. I never would of thought it of you, Bree."

I backed away from her, confused.

She slowly raised the gun to her shoulder, closed one eye so as to aim. "I can't just let you go, boy. You know that. I don't want to shoot you like a dog in the road, but you're a goddamned murderer, is what you are, and if you can't even tell me why, then I got no choice—"

I felt Faith trembling beside me, and only then did I grasp the purpose of Cheney's bizarre accusations. For Faith's hands flew to her head, she clutched at her hair, dropping her bundle, and cried out, "Oh, Law, don' shoot 'im, don' shoot 'im—he ain't had nothin to do wid it!"

I saw the triumphant set to Cheney's chin as she lowered the gun.

"What would you know about it, girl?"

"Be quiet," I barked at Faith.

"Nothin," she sobbed, "I don' know nothin—on'y dat Bree ain't done no wrong—"

"You know more than nothing," Cheney said, "and we can wait here all night, or I can march you to the sheriff, or call him here to see those poor dead ladies, unless you start telling me more than nothing."

"Go ahead," I said to Cheney, calling her bluff. "Fetch whomever you like. You'll fall down with the rest of us, if it comes to that."

She turned away and began walking, and again she had taken Faith's measure correctly.

"Naw!" the girl cried. "Don' go—"

"Shut your mouth, Faith!"

"—'twas me! 'Twas me, I done it!"

"You, girl?" Cheney turned slowly. "You telling me you are responsible?"

"Oh Gawd. Yes, ma'am."

"How'd it come about, girl? Tell me now—Adeline put you up to it?"

"Don't talk to her," I shouted at Faith, yanking her backward.

But she pulled her arm away from me. "Naw, Bree! De trufe got to come out.

Cain't let ever'body else be blamed for whut I done." She turned back to Cheney. " 'Tweren't Adeline, she jes give me medicine, an I slip it to de mist'ess. Ain't mean ta hurt 'er. Ain't mean ta—" She was crying once again, her voice breaking between sobs.

Cheney held out a hand. "There, now," she crooned, "there. Come on over here, girl. Come with me. Right this minute. You done good. We'll go to the sheriff together, and we'll tell what happened, and I will vouch for your story. They'll go light on you if you turn yourself in, and then there'll be an end to all of it."

I had not figured Cheney's angle until this moment, but when I heard these words from her, I knew that the worst I could imagine was also the most likely. For I knew that she would never be fool enough to believe her own statement, or consider going to the authorities alone. She was as aware as I of the mood of the city, and of what she could expect even if she merely accompanied the Negro murderer of two white women to her confession: they would both likely be lynched on the spot, no fine distinctions made. And as for vouching for Faith's story, even in the best of times Cheney's word was worthless—that percentage of black blood which allowed Paxton to own her also made anything she said irrelevant in a court of law.

She was lying, and it came to me in a second what her true motive must be, so that I lunged for Faith's hand and cried, "Stop!" But in the same instant David sprang toward us, and now I saw my suspicion confirmed—they had not been sleeping either, this long day, they had been awake and madly conspiring even as we had been—for in the lackey's hand was a length of rope, already tied and made ready.

David reached Faith at the same moment I did, and yanked her so ferociously that she was torn from my grasp. She began to scream, but Cheney grabbed her other arm, hurled her down into the dirt, and smashed the butt of the musket into her cheek. I swung at David mindlessly, but he caught me full in the face with his fist, and this was no Thomas, no mere stripling—his punch had force enough to knock me onto my back. In the few seconds it took me to recover, he had run back to where Faith lay writhing on the ground. He slung her under one arm like a sack of potatoes, dragging her along even as she tried to flail at him and scream through her bloodied lips.

Now Cheney followed him, turning to aim the gun at me, and shouted, "Get back—go on! Don't make me kill you, Bree, it's this here one is the cause of it—" But I ran straight at David, intending to push him off his feet. I leapt at him, and as I passed, I saw Cheney follow my track with the musket, and then there came an explosion, and a bright flash of light.

I felt only a heat near my shoulder, at the back, and I continued on, throwing myself at David. But Cheney pulled at me, and now there followed a searing pain, and I realized the shell had found its mark. I could not help doubling over for a moment, and in that time they drew farther up the drive, so that I could only hear Faith's screams echoing back to the spot where I stood.

"Oh Law Gawd he'p me—oh Gawd, I'se wid a chile—please Jesus please no—oh don't oh no—baby Jesus he'p me—Aubrey—*Aubrey*—"

I staggered after them, around the carriage house, until I reached the front yard, and there I saw them ready to make use of the rope they had so carefully prepared. David slung it over the lowest branch of the chinquapin tree, and drew it through a loop at one end.

The other end, the noose, swung over his head.

Cheney had dropped the gun and held Faith about the body, pinning her arms; now David tied her hands behind her with another length of rope. She kicked at him and spat, she howled and shrieked—"No! Gawd! No!"—even as blood poured from the gash in her lip.

I ran toward them, my shoulder now causing me such torment that it seemed to steal the very breath from me; but I screamed to them, "Jesus, don't do it, don't do it, she's pregnant—"

"She's a murdering *whore*, then," Cheney screamed back. She reached and held the noose steady, and David lifted Faith straight up into the air, where she struggled and writhed so fiercely that the rope could not be placed about her neck. So they lowered her, and Cheney picked up the gun, and swung the butt with all her strength at the girl's head, and Faith staggered, dazed, in a circle. Then they lifted her again, she not moving now, but only swaying heavily, and I pulled myself forward, but the noose slipped over her hair, and then it was about her throat, where Cheney pulled it tight. And then David released her body, and stepped from beneath her.

She dropped. The rope pulled taut with the weight of her, and I knew from the twist of her neck that it was broken. But she did not die. There was no mercy, no deliverance from the *Law*; she hung there, strangling, her feet kicking, her shoulders flailing, her eyes mad but *knowing*—I could see them from where I had fallen to the ground.

I made a sound in my throat which became a word—"Why why why"—and my sight seemed to narrow into a single point before me, roiling clouds gathering at the edge of my vision as I crawled forward on my hands and knees. But even as I moved, I felt a force behind me, pulling me back, and then I heard Mama's scream in my ears: *"Goddamn you! Lunatics! Murderers! What have you done—what have you done to the child!"*

"Get away from me," I sobbed, "I didn't do it," and I tried to free myself, but her hands were viselike about my shoulders. Then she threw her body atop mine, and I fell to the ground; the darkness which threatened me rushed in upon me, and the last thing I saw, before it overtook me, was Faith's body, twirling slowly at the end of the rope, one yellow foot bare, the other caught in the laces of the boot which dangled beneath it.

When I awakened, it was many hours later. I found myself in blackness as thick as that which had so recently overwhelmed me. It seemed I had no flesh except that which pained me, it seemed I had no thoughts except for pictures which dropped unbidden into the void that had opened within me. I raised myself upon one elbow, but this caused the other to throb so mightily that I was forced to lie down again. I stared into the darkness, and as my eyes adjusted, I came to recognize my surroundings.

I was in the tack room of the carriage house. Who had brought me there, and why, I did not know—still do not—but they had seen fit to close the door, hence the absence of light. I was lying on Amos's cot, so recently the resting place of Lisabeth the maid, but I now saw that she had been laid upon the floor to make room for me.

There was no sound, either about me or from the distance. Presently I attempted to sit up again, and this time the pain seemed less consuming. I raised my right hand to feel my left shoulder; it was stiff with blood, but that blood was dried, and my arm had normal sensation all the way to the fingertips.

I looked over at the tack room door. I could tell from the way it met its frame that it was locked from the outside. But whoever had shut me in here had not thought very carefully. There was the ladder which led into the hayloft, which itself opened out over the horses' stalls. I had only to climb up into the loft—if I could do so one-handed—and then jump to freedom.

Even the small effort of sitting up had dizzied me, however, so I eased myself back upon the cot once more. Minutes passed, and they were as vapor to me—swirling, gray, without form but encompassing—as indeed would be so many of the minutes and months which followed the death of Faith.

But slowly one substantial thought came to realize itself in my mind: I vowed as I lay there in the blackness of the tack room that I would never enter the Paxton house again. I knew as surely as I still had breath that I must leave, and not in a day, or in a week, but now, that instant, wound or no wound, regardless of what lay beyond the door waiting to assail me.

I would not wait here, meek as a lamb, to discover what end my captors had in store for me. Nor would I force myself to look again upon those walls which had so long contained me, or upon their inhabitants—whichever of them survived, or remained. For all were guilty, if not of one sin then of another, and mainly they were guilty of yet living while Faith and the child she carried were gone.

But it was I who was guiltiest of all of the crime of existence. I who had brought the girl to this turn, failing her at every juncture, until I had failed her ultimately, even as she screamed out her life from the end of the rope. It was therefore myself I most sought to leave behind, for arising within me was a sense of horror at being stuck within that self, attached to that in me which was repugnant—a sense so powerful as to carry over into a physical pain, rivaling, even surpassing, the pain of the hole torn in my shoulder.

And even as the throbbing in my arm bade me rest, this other pain, stronger, more palpable, bade me rise and make good my vow.

And so I did.

I left the carriage house, laboriously, by the method previously described. Then I stepped out into the drive, making no attempt to hide myself or soften my footfalls. I met no one, never once looked back for a last glimpse of the woman who bore me, never glanced at the house to see whether lights burned there. I took nothing save the bloody clothes on my back, I made no plan, had no destination, set no goal. I wandered out toward the gate and the front lawn, and I could not keep my eyes from turning toward the chinquapin tree; and there I saw the cut end of the rope on its lowest branch. I put my back to the tree, to the house, to all the familiarities of my life, and I started down the street, my body and soul weighted and empty, both in the same instant.

Of what occurred next, I will recount only brief particulars, those I remember.

Of tottering all the way into the city, to the edge of Esplanade Avenue, and collapsing into a stage—still in Thomas's fine if bloody clothes, with the wad of bills and the forged papers in the jacket's inner pocket—and demanding to be taken to the next eastward coach.

Of riding, night into day, uncaring as to whether I lived or died, was caught or uncaught—which perhaps is why no one bothered to question me.

Of arriving at the very border of Louisiana only to collapse at last from the pain in my shoulder.

Of being borne by two coachmen to a miserable backwater hospital in a tiny town called Chopin, there to be mistaken for a wounded white civilian.

This hospital—it was little more than a house, where three or four patients languished in each of the four bedrooms. The local doctor, an elderly Frenchman named Pétain, resided there, and insisted upon treating me himself, particularly after seeing the fat wad of bills I carried in my bloody jacket. He questioned me as to why I'd fled the city and how I'd come by the wound—I remember this—but I found I could not answer him. When I tried to speak, the sounds backed up in my throat, my mind became blank, and I stuttered incomprehensibly.

My treatment was begun nonetheless. The doctor dug out the fragments of shell from the ragged hole in my arm, then endeavored to sew the edges shut, all without benefit of morphine. Despite the agony this caused me, it seemed a good solution; he bandaged me, and I prepared to convalesce, wordlessly, hoping soon to be on my way. I wanted only to travel east, and then north toward Washington where, behind the Federalist lines, I imagined I would at last feel safe.

Within days, however, it became apparent that Dr. Pétain's ministrations were proving inadequate. The first sign was a worsening of the intense pain in my shoulder. Then came ominous red streaks which reached toward my elbow, and a great swelling which bloated my arm to nearly twice its normal size.

The doctor informed me that he would have to remove the bandages. He picked at them, but they had become embedded in the thin scab formed atop the injury; when Pétain finally pulled them off, he pulled away tissue as well. I thought I might swoon—particularly when I beheld what had become of a portion of my own body. The wound beneath had festered, opening into a pus-filled depression twice its original size. The sutures were lost among the rotted, whitened flesh, which stank like something dead. Pétain reared back, then set to digging out the stitching with his needle—again without any trace of morphine in sight. This time the resultant pain knocked aside the last of my resistance. I fainted, mercifully, and when I awoke my arm was covered once more.

That night I begged the doctor for laudanum—it took me minutes to get the single word out in a whisper—but he replied that he hadn't any, as medicinal supplies were being diverted to the war effort, and what little there was had become prohibitively expensive.

There was nothing for it then but to lie there, and this I did, crying half the time, writhing in pain and near-delirium the other half, while outside that evening passed, and then another and another, and fall inched imperceptibly into winter.

I did not heal. Instead I wasted, infected and rotted, with alternating periods of sweating and chills which soaked my bedsheets. Pain was my constant companion, robbing me of any interest save its cessation. I could not eat; I lost even the base pleasure of a good piss—the activity resulted in an excruciating burning sensation, and the urine emerged brown as muddy water. Pétain wrung his hands and treated me with ointments, he bled my extremities with gleaming razors; used white-hot irons to cauterize the deadened flesh. In time I began to scream before he laid even a finger on me, the mere sight of his instruments being enough to push me to the edge of my sanity.

The day came when I was carried over that edge. And if I cannot pinpoint it exactly, I can recall the manifestations which tell me now that it had come and gone.

I had had a bed of my own up to this point, but around the middle of winter I received a bedmate, an innocuous fellow named Bailey who had crushed his leg beneath a cartwheel. He was a chinless young man, a simple farmer. But from the moment of his arrival, my mind, afloat now in some poisonous soup, ran over with black and vile ruminations as to how he'd been sent to do away with me.

Not a little of this concerned the fact that he often brushed against my festering arm on his limping trips to the lavatory. I would be wrenched from my stupor by blinding pain, and would howl for all I was worth; after the first such brush I miraculously recovered my lost voice, and instead of simple screams, began to curse and revile Monsieur Bailey in two languages. *"Murderer! Assassin! Shit-eating pig! Who sent you—Onessa sent you! She let you fuck her so that you'd come here and kill me!"* In the next instant I sobbed on his horrified shoulder, "I did nothing, I did nothing, I cannot go back," and then subsided into silence.

Within days Monsieur Bailey had—happily for him—fled my bed for another somewhere in the "hospital." But his removal did little to reverse my own deterioration. From Bailey it was a short jump toward recognizing that the real culprit, the real assassin, was none other than Dr. Pétain himself. After all, who else was it that came to my bedside to torture me with every conceivable sort of implement? My intent now became to fend the traitor off by whatever means necessary, and so I began to shriek for help when he entered my room, to hurl pitchers and dishes of food at him, to bite him when, despite my exertions, he attempted to approach or—worst of all—touch me.

So, naturally, there came a day—or night, I have no idea which—when I found myself being removed from the hospital, there being nothing more Pétain could do to treat me either in body or soul. I was first cornered in my bed by three huge white brutes, who turned me upon my stomach, pinned me down, and then—despite the bloodcurdling screams with which I responded to the bloodcurdling pain—wrenched my arms behind me and tied them behind my back. I was next lifted onto my feet, and dragged (as I could not walk) from the room, while poor Pétain clutched his hands in the hallway and reminded them that I was injured, as well as in a fevered delirium from infection.

I was outraged enough at all of this, but worse was to come when I overheard Pétain directing the thugs as to where I should be taken. For my destination was to be a makeshift soldiers' hospital, staffed by a friend of the doctor's, whose experience and location within the great city might offer him better resources with which to treat me.

I was to go back to New Orleans.

This was a kindness, I see now, on the doctor's part, for he could have simply removed me to a public madhouse. But in the moment I saw it only as the most horrendous betrayal. I kicked and screamed more violently than ever, spat at him as I passed him, assured him that my death would be upon his conscience forever.

Then I was dragged out into the chilly twilit air, and hurled into a closed cart with a barred window in its thick wooden door. I landed on my side upon the raw plank floor. There was nothing in the cart save a blanket, which, in my rage, I at once endeavored to destroy by pissing on it. I had no clothing; this had been wrapped in a bundle by the doctor, along with the much-depleted roll of money, and handed over to my abductors for safekeeping.

So it was that I returned to the awful port which was Louisiana's pride. I arrived looking every bit the half-mad villain I was: naked, with hands shackled, wrapped in a foul, reeking blanket, pus and blood oozing from my shoulder to form rivulets along the side of my body.

I was taken to Pétain's associate and to the makeshift hospital, and here soldiers lay all about me, white faces behind bloody beards, some lacking legs, or arms or hands, covered in butternut or gray or gangrene. Most of these men were from far-off battle sites; they had extraordinary injuries which they had survived long enough so that the physicians here could amputate their limbs properly. Not a few of them were also raving lunatics, but whether this had predated their war injuries I did not know or care.

What I did care about was the stockpile of morphine, which was finally administered to me—for the first time in six months—so as to relieve my pain. No sooner had I been treated with the blessed substance than my fury lessened, the violent impulses drained from my mind like so much black and viscous poison. But drained away too was the power of speech, so that I was left again in my silent state, unable—and unwilling now—to undertake communication of any sort. The treatment of my shoulder was begun anew, and I watched it dispassionately, speaking not a word, not to anyone: not to the doctor who cut away my infected flesh, not to the milky-skinned nurses who washed me, dressed me, fed me the magical opiate, soothed me when I screamed.

I recollect the dreams I had, dreams of explosions which were in fact explosions, gunfire which I awakened to find was gunfire, and other dreams which repeated themselves, every night the same players, but different roles assigned to each. Faith was there, always, and Mama, and Thomas and Paxton; and they were joined, not infrequently, by the denizens of the Camellia.

Eventually, my cast of characters came to visit me in the light of day, so close and alive, I felt I could reach forward and clasp them to me. At times I tried—I watched myself lean into the empty air, desperate for solace, wretched when it eluded me.

And I would laugh at this terrible joke, or scream, and the women would come with more morphine.

"I am a Negro," I would tell them—another tremendous folly, at which I howled with laughter—and they would push me onto the pillows, and eventually I would realize that no sound had come from my lips.

When the war came to our doorstep that April, when the Yankees arrived and the battle for New Orleans was finally fought in earnest, along our own shores, and upon our own soil, I was abandoned by my benefactors, left with those who were believed insane or unsalvageable. We languished there—some seventy of us, from what I recall—for three days before a posse of Union soldiers broke the door down, possibly expecting the warehouse to hold munitions, or food, or other valuables.

What they had not expected was the sight of us: a vast hall of wandering idiots, or half-men on cots, waving stumps and ranting in fever, all of them urinating or defecating where they stood or lay, gnawing on the few provisions that had been left in the hasty departure, on the verge of gnawing upon each other.

I do not recall how the soldiers evacuated us, whether they took all of us, or how I was chosen to go if in fact there was a selection of any sort. What I next remember is arriving at a prison beyond the front lines, a prison which was not a jailhouse but a plantation whose cabins had been requisitioned for the storage of wounded enemy. At some point, we were to be separated into civilian victims and soldiers, but in the meantime I lay in a single room with eleven other men, lice-infested, babbling, some unable to walk. I was given only a pallet on the ground, since my injuries were not considered extensive enough to warrant a cot or a blanket. There was little to eat: corn mush, collard greens, every now and then a watery soup made of beans. A pitch-black mammy did our cooking. I took a tin bowl before her each morning and night, and watched as she wordlessly filled it from huge pots hanging out-of-doors. Union soldiers in uniform, still flushed with the thrill of their victory on the Mississippi, stood with bayonets and rifles at the ready, to fire upon us should we become ornery.

I soon realized that the cooking mammy was living in the Big House, and that the other Negroes—the former residents of the cabins—were living there with her. The Union soldiers had taken a fiendish delight in turning out the white owners of the property. These unfortunates—a wounded former Confederacy soldier, his bony wife, and their two small sons—were housed in a chicken coop behind the kitchen. I saw them now and then, hauling laundry from the Big House, for the soldiers were garrisoned there with the Negroes to wait upon them, and the white family was situated to wait upon the Negroes. I noted the abashed looks the old mammy gave her former master, as if apologizing for her new station in life, while she handed him her petticoats for washing.

But one of the young men—the mammy's son, I presumed—delighted in throwing his clothing wherever he could upon the lawn, and calling to the white people as they ran about beneath the bayonets, snatching the items up: "Looka dere, Mista Maxwell, ye done missed dem *pants*, gotta git dem pants *clean*, so tell de missus scrub 'em real good!"

And this Mista Maxwell, to my surprise, would look back at the young man and laugh. "Charlie, you lazy black son of a bitch, your pants never been dirty from a hard day's work in your life, so what do you care how they're washed?"

I wonder still which were stranger, the things I dreamed, or the things I believe I truly saw.

After a time the soldiers decided that it would be both practical and amusing to put the alleged prisoners of war to work helping the beleaguered Maxwells. Two or three of the more mobile of us from each cabin were rounded up at gunpoint and hustled to the laundry, or to the kitchen for scullery duty. A skinny Union boy yanked me off my pallet and pushed me into line. He did not bother shouting orders at me, for it was assumed, because I was mute, that I was deaf as well.

I was to work in the laundry, but I never completed the journey there. For as I shifted on my feet in the line, uncaring as to where I was to go, I heard a cry from behind me.

"You! Nigger! Yes, *you*, you nigger bastard! Goddamn you, you yellow wretch—" I wondered who could be the object of this rain of curses, and from whom they came.

I turned to look, and there stood none other than Felix L'Heuron, the former deputy, two men behind me in the line, his left eye and ear shot away, but his good eye singling me out at once. His finger pointed wildly at me as he continued to shout invectives.

Our skinny guardian walked over to him. "What's the trouble with you, you goddamn fool," he asked, sounding more amused than stern.

"Nigger!" L'Heuron sputtered. "That one! He's no white man! He is Louis Paxton's nigger, out of New Orleans! Thinking I don't see him—I see you, you bastard—"

The white boy looked over at me, his eyebrows raised. "He can't hear you," he told L'Heuron with a nasal snort. "He's deaf as my grandma, so you may as well shut up and get back in line."

"Deaf my ass, he is Paxton's smart-talking nigger—"

"Nigger! What, are you blind as well as a coward? He's whiter than you, you dunce."

"Horse*shit* he is! He's high-yella is all he is, the little son of a bitch!" It was interesting, I thought, to note the change in the good *gendarme* which his misfortunes had wrought: his courtly manners, so well displayed the day he had come to our door, had disappeared, as they had from the repertoires of most of the men I was imprisoned with. It was a threadbare thing indeed, that chivalry and Christian humility which cloaked the Southern gentleman's heart.

The skinny boy, perhaps sensing an opportunity to break the monotony, sauntered over to me, seemed to be deliberating as to how to communicate with me. He glanced back at L'Heuron. Then he pantomimed writing with a pen, pointed at me, and waited expectantly.

And I, for whatever reason, looked back at him and mumbled my first words in weeks: "I can read and write if you like. But it's not necessary."

"You ain't *deaf*?"

I shook my head. The boy was flustered for a moment, but then he began to smile. "Well, shit, I guess nobody actually asked you, did they." I shook my head.

"You hear that crazy man over there?"

I nodded.

"Hear what he said about you?"

I nodded again. Then I said—knowing clearly for the first time since the hospital that I was saying it—"The man is correct. I know him, and he knows me. From New Orleans, where we both lived. I am a Negro. I am Mister Louis Paxton's Negro servant, Aubrey." The words seemed stilted, false; my throat felt rusty, having lain too long unused.

L'Heuron went practically mad, his finger jabbing straight into the air. "You see! You see!"

The boy stared at me, then whistled. "Well, I'll be damned." He thought for a moment, then appeared to have an idea. "Come here," he said, walking toward L'Heuron and beckoning me to follow. When we halted, L'Heuron glared at me in triumph, his good eye narrowed, his nostrils flaring.

The boy removed a handkerchief from his belt and gave it to L'Heuron.

"Wipe his boots off," the boy said, jerking a thumb at me.

L'Heuron stared, and the glinting blue eye registered first shock and then the most profound rage.

"You Yankee shit-eating fool. Here to make the world right, are you—" He hawked some saliva back, and then aimed a perfect gob of spit at the young soldier's face.

The boy drew his pistol and cocked his arm. The next instant, the pistol butt cracked across L'Heuron's bad eye in a sharp backhand. He howled and clutched his head in his hands, and the boy grabbed me by the elbow.

"Get moving. You're going to see the captain."

The captain's name was Block—Quincy Block. It was a penny-press sort of name, and the man himself lived up to it, looking every bit the kind of rawboned, humorless elder we'd heard sprang from New England's rocky soil.

The skinny boy marched me to the officer's study in the Big House's parlor, and explained straight off what had happened.

"The other one, he claimed this one is a Negro, a slave. And this one says it's true, though that's the first thing I've heard him say since he set foot here, and I've half a mind not to believe it just looking at him."

I stood silent, uncaring as to what the incident and my admission would cost me.

Captain Block stared at me with lidless watery blue eyes set in a skull whose skin seemed stretched to the breaking point. The man's veins, his very bones, were apparent beneath that taut canvas, but his expression was unreadable.

"What is your name, boy?"

"Aubrey Christian Paxton."

"Are you a soldier, Aubrey?"

"No."

"How did you come to be housed with these wounded white men?"

I explained my journey from the corner of Esplanade Avenue to his doorstep, leaving out a few irrelevant details, along with the ones I could not remember clearly.

"Is it true that you are a former slave?"

"Yes."

"You understand, that's hard to believe."

"My mother is high-yellow—that means, very light-skinned. My father is—he is a white gentleman—"

"It's not strictly a matter of color, boy. You sound like an educated man. How'd you come by that, exactly?"

"I was taught by my owner's tutor. The same as taught his oth——his own children. He insisted upon it. He is very liberal-minded in such matters, as was the rest of his family."

"And where is he now?"

"Aix-en-Provence. Southern France." *France*. The single syllable stung my tongue.

"What, he didn't care to make his stand here and shed blood for the Confederacy?"

I gave no reply, only stared back at him.

He sighed. "Have you no papers, then, boy? No proof of your identity?"

"No. I was injured running away. I took nothing but what I still wear." I glanced down at the rags Thomas's suit had become. The shirt's left shoulder was missing a sleeve; it had been torn off back in tiny Chopin to permit better healing of my wound. The captain followed my glance, and nodded.

Our interview resumed, and went on for the better part of an hour. Who was the man who had revealed me, the captain wished to know. Was he a soldier or civilian? What did my master do for a living? Where were my relations, why had I left them behind? I told him all that I could as forthrightly as possible, without revealing the actual circumstances under which I had quit my home.

At the end of the hour he sat back in his chair and regarded me. "What are we to do with you, then?" he asked.

I did not answer.

"Plainly I can't put you back among the injured population, as you might be attacked there. And there's no reason for that, really, if your story is to be believed. But I'd not feel right housing you with these Negroes—" I shook my head to indicate that I did not wish this, either. "So what's to be done?"

After a few moments of silence he appeared to arrive at a decision. "Private Fletcher!" he called through the door to the skinny boy, who entered the room again. "This young man is to be removed from his quarters and housed in the kitchen with yourself. He'll be your responsibility from now on, so I'll thank you to keep an eye on him." Fletcher gave me a curious stare, then saluted the captain with a smart "Yessir!"

Turning to me, the older man said, "If you're thinking of trying any fancy business, boy, I'd think again—I've cut you a square deal, the best you're likely to come by. You'll stay in the house with the regiment. I'll look into your story myself while you're recuperating, and if everything is as you've explained it, you'll be free to go. You can't get much fairer than that. It's not our intention, you see, to harass civilians, especially them what are to be emancipated."

I nodded, wondering whether Captain Block considered his treatment of the Maxwells to be harassment, and also how free I'd be when he discovered the murder of my mistress and her maid, the facts of which must surely have come to light back in New Orleans.

But I said nothing, only followed Fletcher from the study to my new quarters in the former kitchen.

By the end of that day I'd been led about the house, while the soldiers and the other Negroes cast suspicious eyes upon me; and I'd been supplied with new clothing, and a pallet near the fireplace, where the cooking mammy kept a kettle and embers perpetually lit.

I spent my first evening—the first in which I felt nearly rational—becoming acquainted with my new guardian, who proved amiable enough, if perversely curious about my habits as a Negro. He took a specific interest in my relations with women, having heard amazing tales of black male stamina and black female promiscuity from his Northern cohorts. I feared I would sorely disappoint him in that regard, having few ribald sagas to share, but when informed of this he hiked a shoulder, and said that, after all, I was hardly representative of the purer members of the race. Then he blew out his candle, mumbled a nasal "g'night," and rolled over on his pallet, leaving me to wonder in the dark about the nature of the freedom he and his compatriots hoped to bring to the Negroes of the Southland.

Shortly after my removal from the incarcerated population, the camp doctor determined that I should be removed from the succor of morphine as well. My shoulder was now healing nicely, he said, and the worst of the pain was past. I agreed heartily with this decision at first. I recalled the state in which Amos had found himself, being wed to the medicine, and also the weeks of my delirium, traceable, I assumed, to the same source.

But from the very first day, the reduction of my dose of opiate proved a torment, and kept me confined to my pallet with such wretched illness as I had never before experienced. My face burned with fever, my head pounded, I vomited until there was nothing left to disgorge. The muscles of my body seemed to be contracting, so that I could not keep from stretching them, from yawning, twitching, contorting, so that I might relieve the discomfort. But at the same time my skin had become so sensitive that a puff of air pained it, and so all those movements only caused me greater distress in the long run. My stomach heaved and cramped; sleep was impossible, and the sensations of light, sound, and touch unendurable.

Worst of all, though, was the mental anguish I suffered, for all that I had avoided in the previous weeks now overtook me. Every nuance of blame, of doubt, of self-loathing, came to assail me in extra measure, so that in my rare moments of dozing I was tormented by nightmares, and when awake I cried almost perpetually, too sunk into misery to care who saw or heard. My ceaseless sobbing—without explanation, for I felt I could articulate none of it—caused my guardian to weep as well, for the memory of his family at home in Rhode Island, and for the bitter deaths of his friends (which events he *did* articulate, in the greatest and most demoralizing detail).

And so I passed the blackest weeks, weeping, retching, and tormented. Many times I wondered if the end of a rope would not serve me as well as it had Faith, and if I did not deserve it thoroughly; many times I prayed for the energy to do away with myself, so that the image of that yellow, dangling foot might be erased from my memory. At least my hosts—or rather, my captors—were kind enough to demand nothing of me during this interlude, to leave me be upon my pallet, interrupting me only to offer food. But at the end of this period, when I had relearned the art of sleep, and the anguish had diminished somewhat, I was told by Fletcher that the captain had news for me.

I prepared myself for the worst, although I doubted I could bear it. But when I was again brought before the leather-faced Captain Block, he said simply that he was prepared to fulfill the promise he had given me: he had followed up my story by some means, had determined it true as far as he could tell, and was ready to pronounce me free to leave, pending the completion of some bit of paperwork.

It had to be a mistake, I thought. Or a trap—the "paperwork" an indictment, the soldiers waiting outside the door to shackle me, Mama and Louella ready to point accusing fingers: *Ravisher. Murderer. Coward.*

But the captain's demeanor suggested none of that. He was riffling through the documents on his requisitioned desk. When he found what he was looking for, he raised his head to address me once again.

"Now then." He cleared his throat with a phlegmy rattle. "Listen up, lad. Five days ago, the President issued what he calls a preliminary Proclamation of Emancipation. As of the twenty-second of September, all slaves residing within United States borders are freed as a matter of Federal policy, meaning that wherever the Union army holds sway, the President's edict shall as well. Of course, strictly speaking, you were liberated the moment you were got behind our battle lines, but now it's official. Or rather, it will be when a final issuance is made. I suppose I could hold off until then, but I see no point in doing that, and I'll admit"—his thin lips stretched into a smile here—"I rather look forward to placing another rankling burr beneath the asses of your Rebel massas. So—by the power of the Federal Government of the United States and the Commonwealth of Massachusetts, I am pleased to decree you an emancipated Negro under the following provisions—" And then he named them, while I stared at him dumbly, too astonished to do more than that.

"I am also authorized to issue you emancipation papers," the captain went on. "These may entitle you to some sort of pension eventually, and at any rate shall make moving about much easier. You need only provide me with a few pertinent pieces of information to secure them. Agreed?"

I regained enough presence of mind to nod my consent. But I did not hear what he asked me next, for I'd had a flash of inspiration upon my comprehension of his news.

I would have *papers*. Papers on which to travel. I could go to you, Gran, to find you and take you with me, if I wished to traverse the dangerous way back to the city.

But I dispensed with this idea almost as fast as it occurred to me. After all, you were free as well by now, whether by Louella's hand, the Union army's, or the Federal Government's. And you were safer at the Old House or with Louella than with me. I might yet be facing criminal charges in New Orleans, which by some miracle the captain had not discovered, but from which no presidential proclamation would free me.

No. It had been a foolish fancy, which could benefit no one.

I was returned to the business at hand by the tapping of Block's pen against his desk. "I say, lad. I should like to complete these forms sometime today, if you don't mind."

I startled. "What—I'm sorry, sir. I was distracted for a moment."

"I was asking you, if you please—name of father."

I debated a wretched instant, then managed to reply "Unknown."

The captain jerked his head up, then shook it in disgust—if not at me, then at the institution which had produced me. "I see," he muttered, writing my answer upon one of the pages.

"Name of mother?"

"Onessa Lee Paxton."

"Date of birth?"

"August sixteenth, eighteen forty-three."

"Place of birth?"

"New Orleans, Louisiana."

There were a number of other questions, and so it went on this way for a quarter hour more, and then the captain prepared to finish up.

" 'Issued in the name of,' " he said. "*Aubrey Christian Paxton*, I believe." He bent his head, his pen moving swiftly over the paper. "Will that do?" He asked this peremptorily, without looking up.

Before I could think about it, I heard myself say "No."

The pen ceased its motion, the lidless eyes rose to meet mine. "Eh? What's that?"

"I mean—I do not wish to carry the name of my former owner," I managed to stammer.

The captain's eyebrows rose. "Oh? You wish to register as something else?"

"Can that be done?"

"I can do whatever I please, boy, so long as I record it here for posterity."

"Yes—yes, that's what I wish to do."

"Very well. Whom would you be known as?"

I thought for a moment, trying to recall the surname Faith had mentioned those long months ago. Then it came to me, and I heard myself blurt, "Bennett. Put that down, if you please, sir. Aubrey Christian Bennett."

"So shall you be," the captain said with a flourish of his pen. He dipped it into the pewter inkwell, and put it to the paper. With a few strokes he created me anew, meticulously noting in his daily log, *"Freed: Aubrey Christian Paxton. One Part-Negro Youth, eighteen Years of Age, sound, formerly Servant of Mr. Louis Paxton, New Orleans, Louisiana, now to be known as Aubrey Christian Bennett."* He handed me only those documents with the latter name printed upon them, and a serial number by which I had registered myself as a freed slave.

I picked the papers up and perused them, feeling a breeze blow through my soul, allowing me perhaps the most slender hope that I would survive to somehow put right my part in the death of Faith.

"Where will you go now, young Aubrey?" the captain asked, not unkindly, as he leaned back in his chair and studied me.

I looked up at him. I was surprised at how quickly the answer escaped me: "I wish to leave the country."

"The Southland, you mean?" he asked. "This Southern country?"

"No. America. The United States, if they're ever to be united again."

The captain leaned even farther back and smiled. "Oh, we shall win, boy, you needn't have any fear of that. Your old massas can't hold out forever, no matter the battles they win here and there through sheer grit. Don't worry—these States shall be united in time for you to leave them. That's quite an ambition, though, boy, for one who's never been fifty miles outside Louisiana."

"Yes, and if you were myself, how do you imagine you might accomplish it?" I realized I had turned some corner: there seemed nothing I was unwilling to say, whatever fear quaked in my belly as I said it.

The captain let out a short bark, his version of a chuckle. "You're one for the books, all right," he said through his stretched lips, "when it's all we can do to push most of these Negroes off their masters' plots and out into the world, where they might make their own way. I'll tell you this much, though. Were I in your shoes, I'd get myself to a seaport, hire myself out to work aboardship, and pray as one of them dumped me near where I wished to go. It's rotten work, and dirty, and dangerous, but you're a stout lad, and you've got learning. So you might fare well, and you'd reach some foreign shore without paying a ha'penny."

I considered this, and thanked him for the suggestion.

"Not at all, lad, I wish you well." He paused for a moment. "You know, were you to fight for the Unionist cause, you would earn yourself an army pension as well—" But then he shook his head. "No, you'd best see to that shoulder, it'd hardly serve you under harsh conditions. Be off with you, then."

"Thank you," I said. With wholehearted gratitude, I shook his dry hand and, with the papers he'd given me clasped to my breast, saw myself out of his office.

I then returned to the kitchen, where Fletcher was waiting, ready to grill me about the proceedings which had taken place behind the locked study door. I relayed a shortened version of the events, and upon hearing of my good fortune, he suggested a drink of whiskey to celebrate. I accepted; whatever my opinions of him to this point, I was grateful for his sincere pleasure in the outcome of my travails. We toasted, with two tin mugs of mash, our respective futures. And when Fletcher cried, "Here's to Aubrey Bennett, wherever he may go," I felt the next phase of my life truly launched.

I discovered shortly afterward that the same information resulting in my liberty had provided others with a similar reprieve: ten or so New Orleans prisoners—diehard Rebels all, no doubt—had their civilian status confirmed, and so were set loose that very day.

Mr. Maxwell's Negroes were also granted their freedom papers. Many of them, true to Block's comments, opted not to depart at all. Others spent the day celebrating, and the more ambitious of these set off that very week for new situations, unaware of or undeterred by the notion of the white prisoners' having been turned out to cross their paths with further evil.

But I myself wasted no time pondering these double-edged workings of Justice. Rather, I was obsessed with the information the captain had so casually provided during our final interview. He had tossed his suggestion out with little forethought. But it entered my head and lodged there as a plan with merit, and I found myself determined from that moment on to seek out precisely that situation which he'd laid before me: a seaport, one in the free and unblockaded North, from which I would secure a job aboard ship.

And I knew where I should go, should the opportunity arise: to France, there to confront the father who had disavowed me, to wrest some acknowledgment from the one parent who might provide it.

Mama I would leave—unforgiven—to the ghosts, to the Cities of the Dead.

And somehow—when I knew I could think of it without being overtaken by darkness and inaction—somehow I vowed I would avenge Faith's murder and the murder of the child she carried; somehow I would happen upon Cheney, and then, my soul restored, I would mete out the justice she so richly deserved.

But in the meantime, I would seek my solace in the world of men. I would leave behind the murky doings of women, the twisted, needful skeins in which they snared me. I would disavow my own lust, as distant now as infancy, and disdain the prissy notion of romantic love, which I did not fool myself into thinking I'd ever experienced or could even now be capable of.

I would put it all aside—all but you, Gran, although I wonder in my heart if I recall these events with any real hope that they shall reach you, or whether I tell them to myself to give them voice, substance, some semblance of order.

Thus it was, having set forth a plan, however vague, that I determined to leave the camp. I had opportunity to go when Private Fletcher advised me that a ragtag group of soldiers would be passing through, to take with them any discharged wounded who wished to make the journey as far as Maine, by way of a northerly, then easterly, crossing behind the battle lines.

When the party arrived, approximately on schedule, Captain Block agreed to speak on my behalf to the attending officer, a Lieutenant Wade. I stood by as the introductions were made, waiting for the moment when I—the emancipated slave working his way north—would be called forward, but that moment never came. Instead Captain Block said, "This is Aubrey Bennett. He's late of New Orleans—has kin there—but he's one of ours. He's looking to go along as far as New York, perhaps, or Boston."

And that was all. Almost of their own accord the words rose in me—*"I am Mister Paxton's Negro servant Aubrey"*—but then I realized: I was not. I was nobody's servant. For the first time in the whole of my life, I served no master, need ask no permission, sought no white man's favor. And as for the question of my race, it was obvious to me that Captain Block's failure to mention it had been intentional. He gave me a long, level glance after he had spoken, and I returned it, hoping that my expression would communicate the gratitude I could not put into words.

So it was that I left with Lieutenant Wade and his band, after making appropriate good-byes to the captain and my guardian, Fletcher. I asked him, should he have the chance, to post a note to you, Gran, and was asked in return to post a letter to his family in Rhode Island when I was north of Philadelphia. This I agreed to do—wondering all the while what would transpire between now and then, and where my journey would reach its conclusion.

I cannot describe the sensation that filled me when I started down the plantation drive on horseback. I had never seen the outlying countryside beyond the cabins, having been drugged and raving upon arriving, nor had I imagined that I would be leaving it this way, as a free man, with a destiny before me which was mine to mold and shape as I might see fit. The sorrowful weight upon my back, of Faith, of Mama, of you, Paxton, Thomas—it lightened a tad, resettled itself, at this, the start of my emancipation.

Our route took us northeastward first, and at every turn I was given to see what I'd been spared, both in terms of my upbringing and, more recently, in terms of the devastation the war had wrought. Wherever we passed, I saw my countrymen, black and white alike, living in conditions beyond imagining: in houses made of blankets over poles, or tin bathing tubs pounded into sheet-metal covered with twigs. Some of the black and brown and yellow faces greeted us as angels, liberators; others assured us that life beneath the lash had been a paradise which they had no thought of leaving. None opened to me as to a brother, or compatriot. The white faces met us with stony stares or desperate offers of appeasement; in every gesture we could read the history of their losses, or their hatreds.

We slept most often in barns or abandoned buildings, or beneath the open sky. On our last night in Louisiana, we made camp in a meadow, tethering our horses and rolling out coats and blankets into makeshift beds. Two boys went off with our skins toward the gurgling sound of water, but a moment later they were running back toward us, their voices baying like hounds upon the scent, their eyes wide. The rest of us rose to follow behind them, along a trail which led to a bright and bubbling stream.

There beside the water, on a bed of needles, and beneath an undulating blanket of flies, we discovered the naked bodies of two men, both yellow-skinned, both upon their backs, and chained hand and foot. Their faces had been worked into mottled black pulp. Their bloated limbs were crosshatched with welts, were missing coin-size bits of flesh here and there where the forest creatures had begun to snatch morsels from them. And their penises and scrotums had been neatly removed. Something in the decaying palm of one of the men winked in the late-afternoon light. A boy from our band bent to examine it, and discovered a burnished metal crucifix upon a piece of leather entwined in the fingers.

Without a word, two of the band began to dig a makeshift grave, but the hole filled and refilled with water, and after an hour or so the effort was abandoned, the bodies along with it.

At the outset of the journey, I had been intent upon listening for those inflections which had distinguished Faith's speech, and, when I came upon them, asking their owners if they'd heard of a town called Lynn Creek in Georgia, and if so, near what great city it might lie. But as we drew farther into recently won territory, I found only hostility aimed toward this meddlesome Yankee with his strange questions, and I received few replies to my inquiries, none in the affirmative. At last I acknowledged to myself that I'd had only a hopeless dream of finding the town where Faith had been born, after the wretched war was ended, and bringing some news of her—and some deliverance—to her family. Whatever was to become of them, it would not be given to me to know, and with that recognition came the gradual diminishing of the vows I'd made to myself upon leaving Captain Block.

By the time we reached Washington I was forced to admit that I would probably never see Cheney or David again so that I might take my revenge—and the lust for that revenge itself seemed to have waned, being replaced only with a profound sorrow. I realized that in fact I might never see Mama, or you, or any familiar New Orleans visage for the rest of my days. Despite all I had done to arrange it thus, I was plunged into melancholy at this thought, a melancholy which has not lifted to this day. For I have no compatriots here and now; I am reinvented, but as alone as any newborn unlucky enough to be orphaned. I am as an orphan in other respects as well, having no past upon which to stake my future, no family name to carry forth.

I decided upon New York as my final destination after long talks with Lieutenant Wade and the other members of the band. It is one of the busiest seaports, they told me, and likely to provide me with work fairly fast. My lack of experience would be less noticeable there too, as it's a large city, filled with transients offering themselves for a variety of positions.

I was content knowing I might soon be off to the shores of another country—for what else have I to look forward to but more of what is unfamiliar—but I questioned my decision to travel so far north when the weather began to change. I had never known it could get so horribly, definitively cold, so that the cold becomes a substance which invades the clothing, and then the skin, and finally the mind itself. I had never known, although I'd heard as much, that snow could fall for days at a time, and accumulate to become a substitute for earth upon the ground, a blanket which made the landscape sparkle but which rendered travel impossible.

Yet we continued on, often miserable now despite greatcoats and other supplies given us by the military outposts. And depleted were our numbers too, for many of our companions had reached those places they knew as home, and quit us accordingly. When at long last we crossed the border from Pennsylvania into New Jersey—after mile upon mile of green trees set upon rolling hills—there were a mere six of us left, including the lieutenant.

This good man took his leave of me at the edge of the great city of New York itself, for none of the others were stopping there, and the party hoped to make a town due north on the Hudson River by nightfall. So I was left on my own, with a crude map, a hastily scribbled list of names, a few dollars, and some well-worded warnings, to negotiate the metropolis. I took a ferry in a town called Hoboken; from its shores I could see the flat outline of Manhattan, interrupted by buildings and by streets laid out as cleanly as sand between bricks. This pristine view was deceptive, however, for when I reached the dock on the New York side I was given to see what was not visible from only a quarter mile or so away.

As I have said, Gran, there must surely be no place quite like this one, or at least I hope there is not—for I cannot imagine two cities producing such a depth of depravity and human misery. Wherever I went that first day, I was confronted with assaults upon my senses: with sights of wealth and grandeur which only underscored those of abject poverty, with the stink of waste beneath my feet, the feel of it beneath my boot heels like some slippery carpet, the piles of it—horse manure, old fruit and foodstuffs and the like—attracting steady trickles of rats. There were the sounds of endless confusion, and human enterprise many times that of New Orleans: the horse hooves, chants of street vendors, shouts and whistles of pedestrians passing this way and that. The road traffic is incredible, being negotiated at high speed whatever the risks, and the subsequent accidents are bloody spectacles by which the population seems more entertained than horrified. The language here is a harsh mauling of the gentle tones of English I am accustomed to, and it is delivered in double time, close to the face, by someone who is more often than not harried, irate, in a hurry.

All this I regard as a uniquely depressing facet of this infernal city, but then there were those tribulations which would have visited me anywhere because of my sheer ignorance. I had no lodgings, no food, and no idea how to acquire these things; I had never before made such decisions on my own behalf. The simplest transaction was a mystery to me. How, for example, did one purchase a loaf of bread? I had seen Mama do this and tried to recall the steps in detail—did she give over the money before or after the loaf was in her hand? Did she choose from among the varieties offered, or did the baker choose for her? Alas, my attempts at recollection came to naught, for the fact was that in New Orleans,

Mama made market in those establishments which knew her by name, and knew precisely what she would require at each ordering.

And as for money, I knew that I carried twenty-seven dollars with me in different denominations, but I had only a vague idea how many of each made up the next largest, or how much coinage equaled this or that paper bill. I recalled Clara the prostitute, and wondered that I'd never given a thought to what the price of my pleasure with her had actually meant. I recalled my fine education, and marveled that such practical matters as money had never been a part of it. But then, why should they have been? I could amuse my master with readings of Shakespeare, but what use would I have for money?

That first day, I landed at the pier on West Street, and walked inland for a block or so until I came to a bakery with a crowd of seedy-looking customers filing in. I was reduced to watching them as they posted their orders, then thrust bills at the counterman while he handed over a brown paper cone with a hot fresh loaf nestled in it. I was ravenous; I could barely contain myself until the line thinned and I found myself at its head. "What'll it be," the counterman barked at me, and I barked back, "Rye!" as I'd heard the others do. "How many, boy? Two bits'll get ya four," came the reply. "No—only one," I answered, shaking my head, and I handed over the quarter, trusting the man to complete the transaction honestly.

On the street, the loaf steamed in its wrapper; I ate it piece by piece as I continued walking inland, searching for the address Lieutenant Wade had given me. I discovered I had landed at a point exactly opposite from where I wished to be; I made a half-dozen requests for directions, which sent me down a long thoroughfare called Canal Street and over to the East Side of the island. At last I found the building: a decrepit brick edifice on the corner of Catherine and Henry streets where would-be sailors took lodgings by the week while waiting to be called upon to work. I managed to negotiate the price of the hovel I now inhabit (again by handing over the bills and trusting the landlord to treat me honestly, which I later discovered he did not), and I set up such housekeeping as I could, given my few possessions. There were several hooks pounded into the brick, and these I moved above the slit in the wall, with its warped shutter board, so that I might hang my greatcoat over it at night. There is a small wood-burning stove, and I spent many subsequent freezing days scrounging for material to burn, so that I might avoid being overcharged by vendors. Meals were and are a mean affair; I can afford only bread and occasional beans, and have not been above plundering the better neighborhoods for recently discarded food. I had never paid much mind to squalor, because it had not been my lot to witness it firsthand; but I discovered that first day and night precisely how it drives the light from the spirit and drains its energy. When I looked around me I wondered if freedom had been worth the price, and I half-envied those dull-witted slaves who nonetheless had had the presence of mind to stay with their masters.

The day after my arrival in New York, I set about finding the offices of the Golden Star Line, the shipping company which the captain and the lieutenant had advised me to approach. At their headquarters I met a scarred and shaven-headed man who introduced himself as Shanley, the booker of unskilled crew for the line.

He conducted a brief interview, which established that I was literate, healthy (excepting the injury to my shoulder), and neither criminal nor drunkard. But when he asked for my qualifications, I found I had woefully little to offer, as I've no experience with manual labor, and have never been nearer a boat than to stand at the dock. At length Shanley shook his head. "I mayhaps could getcha on board as an assistant cargo checker. There's some general shipboard duties, harden them mitts a yours right up, but mostly it's counting boxes, settin 'em right in the hold, lookin over bills a ladin' and somesuch. It don't pay much."

I allowed as the money was not important, so long as a position might come open soon.

"Well, I wouldn't hold my breath on that point either," he warned. "Not too much call for extra hands a your sort, what got no experience. Check back every other day in the afternoon, and bring your identification papers with ya if ya have any. That's the best I can do for you." He offered me a paw to shake, then dismissed me curtly by looking back down at his own work.

I took Mr. Shanley's advice and reported to him religiously, but weeks went by without any sign of an opening. I used the idle time to wander the city, to haunt the homey and quaint neighborhood surrounding Washington Square Park, to wonder at the wealth of Broadway's elaborate manses, and the poverty of the tenements on the Bowery, near my own decrepit neighborhood.

And I made a friend—my only one here.

Upon waking and leaving my quarters to search for food, I would often come upon a huge blonde man either entering or going from the building. As we met frequently in the dim, rank hall or at the doorless stoop, I took to nodding to him—mainly so as to feel that I was worthy of communication with another human being, communication which did not depend on the transfer of money or some official business. The blonde man nodded back from the very first, and we continued on in this manner for some time.

One day, however, I met up with him at the establishment of a coffee vendor I'd discovered. He entered after me, and the occasion seemed to demand something beyond the usual nod.

" 'Morning," I said to the man.

"Goot morning," he said, in a strange, accented voice, bowing his head with its long and curly yellow locks. We waited to have our orders filled—I had brought my precious tin mess-kit mug with me—and as we stood in line the man moved to my side. "You are sailor?" he asked—and I was so grateful that he had spoken to me first, in a friendly manner, that I turned to give him my full attention, and the first genuine trace of a smile I had managed in weeks.

"No, I'm no sailor," I replied. "Only trying to be one. Only looking for work."

The man nodded, allowed his own lip to curl a little. "You go where? What line?"

"Golden Star Line. With Shanley."

"Ach. No work there. They take only who they know, and then for money, bribes they pay to get aboard."

I paled at this—I had no money for bribes, having barely enough to buy my room for the next few months if I spent nothing on food. The man must have noticed my expression, for he said, "Look, Oha get you names. Go with you. Get other work here if you need it, before you sail."

I wondered about this "Oha" he referred to, then realized he was speaking of himself in the third person; it crossed my mind then that he might be about some sort of trick—but I decided, what did it matter, I had to trust someone, and smiled my appreciation at the man. "Yes, yes, that would help me. Thank you for offering."

The man extended a very large hand, at the end of a muscled arm. "I am Oha," he said. "Sven Oha. But called only Oha mostly. From Tromsö, Norway."

I am Mister Paxton's—"I am Aubrey Bennett. Bree, if you're a friend. From New Orleans." I shook his hand. "Look, would you like to drink this somewhere?" I gestured at my tin mug. "I've had no company in a long time, if you'd not mind talking a bit—"

Oha did not even answer; he simply started walking away, turning to make sure I followed. Outside the door, he looked for an appropriate stair stoop and settled himself upon it, unconcerned by the passage of people in and out of the building.

And no wonder—even sitting down, he was an impressive physical specimen. I think of myself as tall, but Oha was some four or five inches above me, placing him closer to six and a half feet than six. He wore woolen britches with red suspenders; beneath them his thighs bulged, while his shoulders strained the corners of his cotton shirt and the woolen coat which refused to close. His features were angular but even, dominated by an aquiline nose and wide-set, icy blue eyes, and full lips which hid straight white teeth. His hair was so blonde that it was almost white, and curled down to his shoulders. His eyebrows and eyelashes were also tipped with blonde, something I had never seen before. But there was little gentleness in his eyes; I knew right off he was someone with whom I should not like to tangle. He seemed weighted with his own afflictions and carried them close to the surface, a man who had suffered much and intended not to suffer more—and should that course be interfered with, he would let you know it.

I nonetheless sat beside him on the stoop, and sipped at my coffee while he noisily slurped his. Eventually, he turned a little to ask, "You are gentleman's son? Rich man?"

In normal times I would have laughed; as it was I ducked my head in astonishment. "Rich—what, me? What would give you such an idea?"

"The hands." He held one of his out, and gestured that I should do the same. The difference was obvious, his large fingers bearing countless calluses and scars about the thickened knuckles, the skin chapped, reddened, peeling. My own hand was well shaped and still well groomed, the nails clean, the palms smooth. The hands of a fop. Or a house nigger.

I frowned. He saw this and let out a harsh laugh, and I was forced to smile despite myself. "I grant you your point," I said, "but what else besides the hands would make you think me a rich man?"

"Your talk. Schooled talk. And fancy manners. Look how you hold the cup and drink." I looked down: I held my battered cup by its handle, while Oha had both hands around his, lifting it to sip with a loud sucking noise. I thought painfully of Faith. "You are schooled," Oha continued. "Maybe run away from your father, maybe lose money in the war and come here now, but you are not born to this. Oha iss right, no?"

"Yes," I said. "You're right, in a manner of speaking. But if you think I've money for you to steal, I'd advise you to look elsewhere."

He ignored this. "You are foreigner. Northern Spain. Maybe Portuguese."

"Wrong. I was born here in the United States."

"Then you have Indian blood, or Negro."

I felt my mouth go dry. "No," I said. "Wrong." I turned away.

"Arab, maybe, then." Oha rudely ignored my attempt to end this phase of the discussion.

"No," I said quickly, "none of those." I tried a deft change of focus. "But what of you, what's your circumstance?"

He shrugged a reply. "Norwegian, full blooded. No schooling did Oha get. No riches. Reading and sums, he teach himself. At sea many years now. The sea make a good life. You will see." He stopped and added no more to this, and I figured it was as good a place as any to let the conversation conclude. I finished my coffee and rose to leave. As I did so Oha looked up at me and said, "Remember, Oha come for you. Tomorrow we go and Oha help you." I had not expected the offer of assistance to be quite so concrete, and so I stammered another thanks, and added that I should be in my "room" on the third floor of our residence, should he wish to seek me out.

Oha was as good as his word, both on that day and on many others since. He did indeed call on me, registering me with a number of crew foremen whom he knew personally, securing a job for me carting garbage from some of the store-fronts to a dumping ground off the docks. The work was heavy and difficult, and paid me two dollars a week, but this was two dollars more than I'd had, and so I was grateful. Oha is clever and cunning, if rough about the edges; his advice spared me that bitter trial and error which I would have otherwise experienced, and his company kept me from being completely isolated in my new surroundings.

I am not sure still what to make of him, although I've come to know him better as winter has settled upon us in earnest. I know he is very much the loner, having few companions and eschewing the social groups of sailors which form and disperse regularly. He spends a goodly amount of time and money (rather to my disgust) in the prostitutes' districts west of us; he is inclined to talk freely on the subject of women, and I find his tastes therein as strange as other of his attributes. Oha has no sweetheart, no wife, no children, nor does he expect to have any. On this point I agree with him, since I seem to bring nothing but calamity to members of the fair sex, while they do likewise to me. But he avails himself regularly of the whores, and not with any sense of pleasure, but with a contempt and bitterness that are beyond my understanding. Whores are the only honest women, he says; all the rest are equally as calculating, as grasping, but are unwilling to admit it, claiming virtuousness because of the ring upon their finger or the husband's name they are able to attach to their own.

I'm sure I disagree with him, for despite what I know of Mama, there is also what I know of Faith, and of that sad creature Clara with the harelip; but he is so adamant that I say nothing, not wishing to embroil him in some fruitless argument. I add only that I am disinclined toward female companionship myself, for other reasons—and that my disinclination most surely extends to prostitutes.

Of Oha's past I've discovered little, except that the land he left was even more frigid and unforgiving than this one. It is dark as night six months of the year, and lit by a cheerless tepid sun the other six; the population survives on a steady diet of dried fish, and little else.

It sounds wretchedly awful, as do the particulars of Oha's upbringing. His father appeared to me a stern and angry disciplinarian, although Oha merely called him a "man of men," whatever's meant by that. His mother is deceased; it was her death that resulted in his taking to the sea, although the details of this event are unclear to me. At any rate, he left his home at eleven years of age and never returned. He is now thirty, and has spent most of his adulthood at sea. Because he is a skilled sailor with numerous contacts, he is usually assured of work, but the war has upset trade mightily, while an incident on board another ship prevents him from seeking out his last employer.

Oha has made it clear that he would like to see both of us aboard the same vessel, and I am inclined to agree. He has taken me under his wing to a large extent, and given all I do not know about life at sea, his presence can only help me there. He is certain that we shall sail before long, and I dearly hope so, for I doubt I can survive many more months of the bone-chilling cold in this godforsaken ruin. The money I earned from the garbage collection is nearly gone, and I wish never to rely upon such deplorable, filthy work again. I am sick to death of stench, of foulness, of poverty, of gnawing hunger, of bad drink and worse food—all the particulars of my existence here on the edge of the world, in this place so unimaginable to me just a year before. But what I left is itself dead, so here I reside, poised to discover whether there can be any experience beyond misery left to me.

And so, Gran, I have brought you up to the present moment, to the very second just past. And having done as much, I release my mind from its troubled recollections and beg you once again to look upon me with understanding, to forgive me any transgressions, and to keep me close to you.

I no longer recognize my life as such, for all the joy and spontaneity have left it, and it has become mere existence, from hour to hour and day to day. So the life of my mind has become that much more vivid; it is where I spend most of my time, my forays into the physical world via Oha notwithstanding. So flat are my experiences, so dead my observations, that I wonder if I retain the capacity for feeling; but then I escape into my thoughts, and happen upon some gold-tinged moment which reminds me of my humanity, and I experience all over again the pleasure of recognition and the sorrow of loss.

I know not what shall become of me, but I pray for the day when I shall look upon you once again, and hope that moment shall be one which touches the deepest well of happiness within you.

I love you always.

chapter three

JANUARY 15, 1861

One would think that after enough experiences of a particular bent I'd have learned my lesson. After all, I am not a naive girl or a dull one, as everyone here so continually reminds me. But no—I insist upon butting my head against the same brick wall, just to see if this time it shan't hurt.

Thus I sat at table this morning, chewing the usual inedible crumpet, and mentioned to Cousin Henry that I'd seen a lovely pheasant fly up from its roost yesterday, among the heather and bracken in the north field. As soon as I'd said it I could have bitten my own tongue off. After all, I've watched the grounds of Leeds Hall become slowly denuded of rabbit, grouse, and fox, primarily because of previous revelations on my part that I'd spotted one of these creatures at such and such locale; it is inevitable that, having been apprised of a thing of beauty within his domain, Cousin Henry be inclined to go out and shoot it. Now I've doomed the poor pheasants with my attentions, and as I say, you'd think I'd know better. Perhaps I am simply so overcome with boredom that I forget myself.

Ah well—at least we'll be leaving this dreary plot of marshland for the relative excitement of London. We—the entire family, including Cousins Anne and Persephone, alas—are to travel to the town house tonight so as to be ready for a party on the thirtieth of the month. It seems that some Americans whose children are attending the colleges of Oxford University have seen fit to throw a ball of sorts, for other similarly placed Americans lonesome for home. Cousin Edward mentioned to the hosts—some people named Rogers—that his relations from the States are visiting, and they were kind enough to include us in the invitation. It's to be a huge affair, and I'm sure Richard will be mightily impressed—he has got Oxford upon the brain since Edward's admission to medical school—but I would just as soon forget the whole undertaking. It's sure to be another evening of banalities and superficialities, with Anne and Percy struggling to outdo themselves at sartorial splendor, and both of them smugly outdoing me. Aunt Josephine is no better than her daughters, and I've seen the strained look upon Mother's face when she's attempting to smile through yet another detailed description of fabric shopping or button choosing.

Although, admittedly, the strained looks on the faces of both my parents appear most often in my presence nowadays. They will not let the subject of Mr. Price drop, although neither do they confront it directly. Instead they partake of that ritual of hankie twisting and sideways glances which I so deplore.

It matters not a morsel that all of my accusations were borne out, once Mrs. Fitch insisted that the matter be pursued. No—Mother and Father dwell instead upon the uproar proceeding from the public revelation of the facts. How grotesque it is, they whisper, to see New Parrish sullied so, and once again divided. (For that is what has happened, friend: half the town has rushed to defend the sterling character of Jeffrey Price, mainly on the basis of his aged father's character, and the lack of same in his accusers. The other half, led by Judge Fitch, has sought—in vain—some form of legal action against him. The two camps have had it out upon the very street corners, I am told, and lifelong friendships have faltered as a result.)

On one issue, though, much of the populace has managed to stand together, and that is in roundly condemning myself. Constance and Thomas and many of our family's friends have written to join my own parents in their hand wringing: why would I choose to create such a scandal, and how came I to deduce the truth? As if my reporting of such tawdry acts is a crime, while their commission is not.

It boggles my mind, and makes me further seethe in Mother and Father's presence—especially when I see the attempts they make to keep the incident from Aunt Josephine and Uncle Charles. Perhaps they're afraid I'll be ostracized, being as I might corrupt Anne and Percy (not to mention the boys); perhaps they're afraid my cheek will reflect badly on them. Whatever the reason, though, I heartily resent this duplicitous silence, and assert at every turn that I am ashamed of nothing, that Price deserved to be revealed, that the facts of Mrs. Fitch's vigilance and the other women coming forward should convince anyone that I am no troublemaker, and young Aileen Harrod no liar.

But why should I be surprised at my treatment when the villain himself has escaped virtually unpunished?

I thought I had learned enough of justice not to be bitterly disappointed at how it is meted out, but it seems I have only begun to fathom that lesson. My education continues, and a sad one it is; but I refuse to be beaten by it, for if I were, then *he* would triumph, and all like him as well. And that I shall not countenance so long as I breathe.

JANUARY 25, 1861

The Knightsbridge house is a change from the drafty, damp stone walls of the estate, but frankly I can hardly bear either locale, and wish only to be off to some other place—Italy, perhaps, or Spain, where the sun shines brightly. No amount of sophistication can make up for London's extraordinary dirtiness, or the chasm between its well-established denizens and its destitute. There is an undercurrent here, of twilight-dwellers and furtive activity, that all of the pleasures by which I'm surrounded cannot ameliorate.

I admit to having quite given in to this shadowy melancholy; I have taken, over the last days, to exploring the city and its outlying districts, both on foot and by coach, during daylight hours and after twilight, and my travels have led me, not occasionally, into those neighborhoods which I would ordinarily shun. All of this is far preferable to being trapped within the town house to endure the scrutiny of my family. It has become something of a ritual, despite the harsh looks and whisperings which follow me whenever I indulge myself thus.

Two evenings ago, however, I wandered farther eastward than I'd ever been wont to do, and found myself lost, well after darkness had settled, in the vicinity of Whitechapel. I had never heard of this district before, and did not care for it. It was bleak, impoverished beyond description, and despite the cold, teeming with shadows and scurrying figures, with shouts and calls from precarious windows along the narrow, reeking streets. There were several uninviting public houses from which a great deal of noise and light spilled, but of course I could not avail myself of them even to ask directions, being a lady alone (although I saw not a few single ladies, and ladies in pairs, enter the establishments, or leave them, reeling). Rather, I stumbled about, tracing and retracing my steps, and then decided I should wait upon a stoop at the most well-lighted thoroughfare for a hansom to happen along.

I was sitting thus, my hands frozen and stuffed into my muff, when I first noticed the shadows slipping furtively over the little footpaths and down the cobbled alleyways. They alarmed me terribly, as I imagined them to be thieves or ne'er-do-wells; but then I recognized the dainty, measured footsteps, the kind only women are capable of making, and at last I saw the silhouettes which revealed the owners' sex. I thought perhaps there was one woman, or two, traversing the short distance from a neighbor's house to their own, maybe meeting somewhere in the middle to pass each other. But the footfalls echoed, died, began again. The shadows grew too numerous to be made by a pair colliding upon some errand, and the women showed themselves, finally—first pairs, then a handful, and, within a half hour, a dozen or more. They eddied about in doorways, congregated on the street corners, some in finer dress, some in little more than fancy rags. They walked with elaborately careful steps over small areas, circling, then returning, stopping, reversing.

The tremendous cold seemed to have slowed their progress; they moved as if through water, their breath pluming behind them. I must have been frozen as well, for only when the first carriage abruptly stopped and the first lady, beckoned, disappeared into it did I realize what and whom I was looking at.

It stunned and shamed me to think I had found them, that I had even inadvertently wandered into their domain—but how could I have avoided it, as the very streets teemed with them? Could every single female truly be about here for the same purpose? From the manner in which men began to circle the area and light upon this one or that, from the increasing volume of conversation in doorways and alleys, from the thickening carriage traffic, I had to conclude that this was indeed true. Of course this spectacle had eluded me, for until recently I had rarely been about after dark within the city, after the time when the privileged classes have departed the parks and the gardens and markets for their suppers. And when I had been about, I had mistaken these painted denizens, these promenading ladies, for ordinary women on their way somewhere. I had a terrible urge to run, to flee the place before its taint inched, borne on the cold, through my fur collar and fur muff, onto my skin, where it would become a patina visible to anyone who glanced upon me.

Yet I could not move, for where should I go, not knowing my way—and besides, I was terrified that I should encounter one of the creatures, be forced into acknowledgment, or perhaps attacked, undone by her to whom nothing is too base for consideration.

So I continued sitting, immobile as if I were encased in ice, even as my heart pounded hotly within my chest.

One of the women passed out of the darkness and slowly made her way down the sidewalk toward me. She ambled along, and with each of her steps my nails drove farther into my palms. Happening upon me, she turned and slowed, and I had no choice but to remain motionless and thus view her, as the act of averting my eyes would have been the more obvious and provocative gesture.

She was perhaps a few years older than me, with dark hair pulled into a mass of curls at the nape of her neck. She wore a proper jacket and skirts, and a wool shawl, but her bosom was bare; she had outlined her eyes with some dark matter, but her skin shown pale and lightly freckled. At the very moment when she should have passed me, she looked pointedly down, and in one dreadful instant our eyes met; and then she opened her mouth to speak.

"Wish I had me one a them" is what she said, softly, the edge of her mouth curling as her gaze sought something lower than my own face. It was my muff, I realized. It was my fur muff to which she was referring, since her own hands were wrapped around her body, beneath her inadequate shawl. The remark, had it come in a normal manner between fellows, would have been one of those which required only a nod of the head; given the circumstance, I could not manage even this.

What should I have said—"How dare you address me"? Why should she not when I sat before her inside her familiar territory's boundaries, for all she knew—my God—one like herself. What should I have said—"You deserve it, the pain of your cold hands"? What would this serve, except to reveal that I knew enough of her to judge, and therefore should be subject to judgment myself?

In the end my silence was absolute, and it caused her to look again into my face, whereupon a variety of expressions crossed her own: confusion, realization, and then a stiffening of the mouth, a turning forward of the eyes, the arms tightening about the body, the measure of her step returning. She walked out beyond the circle of the lamplight and into the blackness ahead, and then I heard the resonating of her heels in a stone tunnel beneath the road as she continued her promenade.

I had survived. I felt myself blessedly unchanged, but wasted no time upon a prayer of thanks; rather, I offered one asking that a taxi should happen upon me soon.

The carriage rolled around the corner at exactly that instant. It slowed as if the driver had seen me, and I lifted my arm to hail him, but then I saw that it was already occupied, by a gentleman whose top-hatted face filled the window. Still the wheels continued to decelerate as if they should stop completely, and I did not pause to consider, but assumed the gentleman to be alighting here.

I rose, and hurried toward the door, which was opening. "Sir, if you haven't need of it, might I have this taxi—I'm rather lost, I'm afraid," I gasped into the frigid air, attempting a smile with the rush of words.

The gentleman stuck his head through the door and peered at me. And upon his face I read that strange progression of curiosity to awareness—familiar expressions only because I had seen them mere moments ago—followed by shock, and a quick closing of the door. A heartbeat later the carriage jolted forward, and then set off at a brisk pace.

I stood upon the road, numbness reaching from my fingertips to my toes, and not entirely on account of the cold. I was oblivious to the insult I had suffered at exactly that moment. Rather, I considered the countenance of the gentleman—the man I had presumed a gentleman—and thought, he could be any man, any well-dressed man of means, young and comely—he could be, perhaps, Jeffrey Price—and could I not, in fact, have been any girl to him—the girl who admired my muff, or any sort at all . . .

The footfalls came again, from the direction where the shawled woman had disappeared, and I realized I had misjudged the space between us. She was not beneath me. She was merely down the road a short distance, a distance of no import to the man in his carriage. I heard the horse's hooves come to a halt, and I wanted to call out, not to the man but to her. But another set of hooves came clattering around the corner, and these did indeed belong to a steed pulling an empty taxi, so I waved frantically, and the driver, stone-faced, looked me up and down, quoted me a price, and then allowed me to enter.

So I was driven home, where I was able to slip into the house and its life unnoticed, since the adults were gone to some dramatic event for the evening. I made only mumbling, perfunctory excuses to the servants who admitted me and saw me to bed.

I observed my face, pallid and drawn, in the dressing room mirror as I prepared for sleep; I realized I should have liked to speak to someone just then, but to whom could I recount my adventure, and in what manner?

I am afraid, but no longer of her. And of that I am more afraid.

JANUARY 26, 1861

There is at least, to London, the refuge, the daylight grandeur, of the city museums. This is humanity too—I must not forget it: the art and literature, the great music and soaring architecture, wrought by human minds and hands. This is what is possible.

Today I attended a touring exhibition of Rembrandt's later works at the South Kensington Museum. It was a revelation—the artist's genius, offsetting his frailties, struck me with enough force to knock the breath from me.

Yet I am not to be distracted or rendered speechless. Yesterday morning, for example, I gently suggested to Uncle Charles that the weather, which has turned even colder since that night, must prove a great tribulation for that population which dwells in the streets with little access to shelter.

"My dear," he answered me, drawing upon his pipe and crossing one meaty leg over the other, "being a physician, I can assure you such people are a hearty breed. There are not so very many of them that their plight should distress you, but Jesus reminds us that there will be poor always. So the best we can do is be grateful for what we have, and tithe a fair amount to charity on their behalf."

It seemed a pat answer—although granted, mine was a pat comment—and it rankled me mightily, containing falsity, truth, and justification all in the same breath.

I dare not ask Uncle Charles whether the women in Whitechapel will have heavier and more encompassing clothing to don during the harsh winter, or whether the donning of it shall affect their livelihood.

JANUARY 27, 1861

I need not have thought my nocturnal wanderings would go unnoticed. This morning I received a lecture from all of the adults in the household, while my cousins looked on smirking.

Mother began it. "Arabella, dear, have you taken to venturing about after nightfall for some reason?" she asked as we ate breakfast.

"Yes, Mother. I'm only walking, as I assumed the fresh air would do me good."

"But my dear," Aunt Josephine said, cocking her head, "you roamed positively out of the neighborhood. Last week your Papa and Uncle Charles went searching for you up and down four streets, and you were nowhere to be found."

"I must have only missed them, Aunt Jo. I do sometimes get carried away."

I looked up in time to see Mother and Father exchange a look across the table.

"You wouldn't be riding about alone, would you?" Uncle Charles asked innocently. "In a taxi, perhaps?"

I knew perfectly well what he meant: someone had seen me, or else they'd simply guessed at this, having no doubt been informed of my late arrivals by the servants. But I sensed I was being given an opportunity to squirm out of the incident gracefully, and so I took advantage of it. "I might have once, Uncle Charles," I said, "but it was only for the sake of a change of scenery and a tiny adventure, and of course I daren't go far out of the vicinity."

There were more looks across the scones and eggs. Then Uncle Charles spoke again. "Nonetheless," he said sharply, "you'll not do so a second time, is that understood? If you wish to walk, you've all the daylight hours to do it, and if you care to go out at night, any one of us will be more than happy to accompany you."

"You must realize," Father added more gently, "the streets are no place for a young lady by herself, Sauce. Even in New Parrish one can't anticipate everything, and in London—well. Let us leave it at that."

"Surely we can provide enough to entertain you here, can we not, dear?" my aunt simpered, ringing her little bell to call Lydia for more tea. "We've a most erudite reading group which meets each second Tuesday of the month, and there is Miss Taylor's embroidery circle which Anne and Persephone have recently joined. And of course you are welcome to ride all you wish out in the country, if you promise you'll make use of the sidesaddle."

I could only picture all this: the crashing boredom of the "reading group," which was no doubt an excuse for gossip; the tedium of embroidery, with yet more gossip; and the riding upon the ridiculous sidesaddle, whose only benefit was that at least it was an activity that could be undertaken alone.

But I replied, "Thank you, Aunt Jo. I have quite a lot to do, you are right. I did not mean to imply that I'm not busy. I am only used to a great deal of exercise, as it was my custom at home to take it."

"Well, you needn't stalk about here like a lumberjack," she clucked, and Percy sniggered into her teacup. "You can stroll a bit on the sidewalks, but no young lady needs to tramp miles on end."

"Yes," Mother added, "you're in excellent condition, and you'd not want to strain yourself with too many exertions. See if you don't enjoy something more calming—you know, I loved embroidery as a girl. I made a number of items for my own trousseau."

She smiled at me, and Father did as well, and I thought to myself that really, it has been very cold lately, and I could do with some more sociable pursuits. And so I promised I would end my walks, or confine them to more reasonable hours or locales.

But it annoyed me to think I'd been rather bullied into this, and it especially annoyed me to see the looks on Anne's and Percy's faces—not to mention Edward's and Henry's—as if some satisfaction had been bequeathed them by the curbing of my pastime.

I thought it a very good thing, though, that I had never revealed to anyone where I had actually gone or what I'd seen. I can imagine how horrified they all would have been, and how inexplicable they would have found my actions. Another oddity, I imagine them exclaiming, undertaken by that terribly odd girl. I find I do not wish even to share my feelings regarding the art exhibits with my relatives; it would somehow taint my recollections—although I regret saying this—as I doubt anyone would have the slightest understanding of my thoughts.

JANUARY 30, 1861

I am glad to be able at last to report something undilutedly positive. I'm just returned from the Rogerses' ball, and it was far more enjoyable than I'd anticipated.

The evening got off to a typically stuffy start: as predicted, Anne and Percy argued for the better of an hour over a particular green silk dress, and no sooner did Anne—being the eldest—claim it than she decided she wished not to wear it at all, thank you. She ended up choosing, from her dozens of gowns, an atrocious draped pink thing, while Percy settled on a light blue satin with a smattering of artificial rosebuds. Seeing as the green dress was left to languish in the pile of rejected garments, I picked it up myself, intending to make good use of it—whereupon my charmless relations began the argument regarding its possession all over again, this time aiming their vitriol at me. Only Aunt Josephine's interference ended the battle. She entered the room to declare that, as emerald green suited neither of her daughters' coloring, they might as well rest with their previous choices and allow me to wear the item in question.

So I was offered the leftovers, but Mother nonetheless heartily approved of my selection. Or perhaps she was merely thrilled to see me at last making an effort at some activity presumed to be "suitable" for the proper creature I doubt myself to be.

At any rate, we were at last all dressed, and the broughams were brought round to the front of the house. I climbed into the first one with Mother, Father, and Richard, and thus was spared the presence of my aunt and uncle, as well as Edward, Henry, Anne, and Percy; they followed behind us in the second carriage, no doubt arguing all the way to the party in that terse English style which consists more of silences than of words.

The ball was held just outside the city at Mersy Hall, a huge estate belonging to some member of the vast English nobility. There was a tremendous commotion at the front gates as some several hundred guests attempted to dismount from carriages and make their way to the entrance; things were further complicated by the lack of space in which the stream of vehicles had to turn and park. It was raining—what a surprise, in this dismal country!—so we were forced to crowd about the enormous front door, where servants were waiting to announce us to our host and hostess.

Finally, though, all of us were escorted inside, there to pass down a long receiving line, which seemed to consist mainly of doddering American Oxford alumni. I offered my hand to so many hiccoughing old men that I expected to find my gloves soiled, but I reached the last octogenarian relatively unsullied, and was shown into the vast halls where the festivities were under way.

These were very much as I'd expected them. A suitably subdued orchestra played popular waltzes, while uniformed servants stiffly offered hors d'oeuvres and tall flutes of Champagne on covered silver trays. Orders were taken for stronger spirits, and the guests set to filling out the room, which was decorated with tapestries and Grecian-style pots of trees and exotic flowers. Our hosts, the Rogerses, circulated about, welcoming the small clots of visitors and introducing one set to the next, while trying their best to make these introductions seem spontaneous.

I was duly bored throughout these proceedings, and throughout the long, many-coursed dinner which followed in the adjacent hall; I thought I would lose all patience when at the conclusion of the meal one after another of the alumni made his way to a carved podium to address the future scholars. The third of these was just beginning a wheezing preamble when I decided to abandon my seat and saunter to the back of the room for a breath of air.

I discovered that I was not the only one to be so motivated. Some of the men had gathered discreetly near the far end of the tables or had wandered off into the ballroom, and several groups of girls my own age had moved their dining chairs into little huddles out of sight of the podium. I stood stiffly against the rich mahogany inlay of the back wall, barely listening as first one gathering and then another commented upon the proceedings.

But then a young woman cut through the twitter with a remark that engaged my attention.

"I should like to know what entitled *this* one to his Oxford diploma," a clipped, cool voice said rather too loudly; she was no doubt talking about the silver-headed orator at the podium.

I wondered whether the girl was merely rude, or had some personal quarrel with the speaker or the event, and so I inclined my head to catch what she might say next.

Instead I heard another voice reply, "Oh, I doubt it was much besides gender and title—or maybe it was his *speaking* skills." There was the barest hint of a laugh from the pair.

I thought the comment a little cruel, but had to admit it amused me; the man at the podium *was* a bore, and unskilled at elocution to boot. I turned to see who might have made such an observation, and found myself looking at two girls of about the same age as myself, dressed impeccably in the English manner, but seated with a certain lack of stiffness which confirmed that they were Americans. One of the girls was an angular creature with a long, prominently boned face; the other was roundly pretty, with exceptionally lovely blue eyes. They noted my gaze, and I turned away, coloring, while they went back to their discussion.

"How goes your brother's progress?" one of the girls asked—I knew not which one, since I could not turn to see them.

"Oh, well enough, I suppose, for a dolt. He's been accepted *with conditions*, as they say. It doesn't matter, though. He could suck his thumb and wail for all anybody cares. He's our precious scion, he's titled; thanks to Maman, his seat at university's bought. So whatever those *conditions*, he need only rise to the level of mediocrity and avoid outright failure to assure his advance."

"Ah," the first girl sighed. Then she said, in a more serious tone, "Such is the way of the world."

"Yes," the second girl said. "Such it is . . ." she trailed off.

"Don't tire yourself," her friend whispered. "You needn't go on to me, of all people."

"Perhaps," the second girl said in an artificial tone, "we'll meet wealthy beaux hereabouts, and marry them!"

Then they both burst into laughter.

It was one of the oddest conversations I'd ever heard, and one of the most intriguing. I could not decide whether they were serious or playful, and at which junctures they might have been either. They soon went back to commenting on the speechmaker, and I strained to overhear them.

At one point, as the windbag was enjoying a round of tepid applause, one of the girls noted, "If he doesn't finish soon, we'll be too tired to dance."

Whereupon the other replied tartly, "If he doesn't finish soon, we'll be too *old* to dance."

I could not help letting a sudden burst of laughter escape at this, and because I attempted to block it with a hand, it became something between a chortle and a sneeze. As I recovered myself I heard from my right one of the two girls say, rather more loudly, "You needn't laugh. You'll be aging right along with us." I realized, mortified, that she was speaking to me, and I wondered if I dared turn, thus acknowledging that I'd been eavesdropping. But when I did I saw that the girl—the one with the bright blue eyes—was smiling at me, and patting an empty seat beside her. "Come sit down," she said in a loud whisper, "it'll be more convenient when you fall asleep."

I smiled back at her, and, having detected no malice toward myself in her tone, took the empty chair she'd indicated. As soon as I was seated, she leaned over to offer me a hand. "Caroline Beckwith," she said, by way of introduction. The angular girl then reached around her friend to similarly greet me, and whispered, "Louella Paxton."

"Arabella Leeds," I said, grasping their fingers in turn. "A pleasure to meet you both."

"And probably the only pleasure you'll have tonight," the girl named Caroline said, which set us to smiling again.

Having dispensed with these introductions, we pulled our chairs into a tighter circle, ignoring the disapproving glares from guests in front of us.

"Well, Miss Leeds, what brings you to Mersy Hall? Have you a relative attending university?" Miss Beckwith leaned forward so that I might hear her without too much trouble.

"Yes," I said. "A cousin. What of the two of you?"

"Brothers," said Miss Paxton sourly. "Caroline's can lay claim to being a scholar, at least. Whereas mine—" She rolled her eyes.

"I take it yours is the aforementioned dolt," I said.

Both girls opened their eyes wide, and then laughed loudly.

"My apologies," I shrugged. "I couldn't help overhearing. Especially not once I'd set my mind to it."

"Nicely done, Miss," Louella Paxton said, "and you're quite correct as well. My brother is indeed the dolt."

"Oh, Louella, he's not so dreadful. Just barely hideous, if you ask me," Caroline said.

"Perhaps, but he hasn't the intellectual mettle to spell his own name, now has he?"

Caroline gave her friend's arm a soothing pat. "From whence do you hail, Arabella?" she asked me, probably as a means of changing the subject.

I replied that I'd been born in upstate New York, and lived there all my life, until my visit here. "And yourselves?"

"My mother was born in southern France," Louella said, "but my father is an American, late of Louisiana."

I startled a little at this, for here was a native of the renegade Southland right before my eyes, and there sat I, a decided supporter of President Lincoln—but Louella caught my glance and reassured me. "Not to worry. Caroline and I are both staunch abolitionists, among other things."

"Correct," Caroline added, "my own family hails from Chicago but my mother is a Quaker by birth, and has been an opponent of slavery from the outset."

We fell then to discussing our respective backgrounds, and I discovered that, while Miss Paxton's family still held Negro servants, she had taken it upon herself to convince her father of the necessity of liberating them, as a war to decide this issue—among other things—seems increasingly to loom on the horizon. As for Miss Beckwith, her own father is neutral on the subject of the Negroes, but her mother is deeply involved in the emancipation movement, to the point of having supplied runaways with hiding places and material goods during their flights from the Southern states. Both of the girls were enthusiastic supporters of the President as well—although, as they were quick to point out, they had been unable to express their support through political means, having been deprived of the ability to vote.

The conversation turned next to our present place of residence, and on this point too we were largely of one mind. We all agreed that England was a terrible disappointment, that its climate was as dreary and oppressive as the cultural mores of its people, and that we should be glad of the chance to return to American soil. That last is dependent upon the outcome of the turmoil between the States, of course, but none of us appeared to have any doubt as to how it would go: the seceded South cannot possibly wage war against the industrial North and hope to win, and are they to attempt it, victory is sure to be quick and decisive—for which we three, at least, will be exceedingly grateful.

We were just ending this phase of our conversation, when a round of applause ensued, signaling—at last!—an end to the speechmaking. Almost as soon as the noise subsided, my eye was caught by the figure of a young man approaching us from the front of the room. When I turned to look at my two new companions, I found that they were frowning at each other, and then Caroline breathed, "Well now, speak of the Devil and he waltzes right in."

The young man reached us a moment later. He was a gangly youth of about my age, his head shorn in that abominable stubbled style which has become all the rage, and I realized at once, from the set of his green eyes and the shape of his nose and jaw, that he must be related to Miss Paxton. And I was correct, for Louella then said politely, if somewhat coldly, "Hello, Thomas. I trust you're enjoying yourself."

The youth looked down at us. "Good evening, ladies." He gave a little bow that was rather too formal. I noted that he had Louella's features but not her bearing, for she possessed a dignified handsomeness, while nothing in his expression suggested this.

"Good evening, Thomas," Caroline said, as coolly as Louella had managed it.

"Ah, the lovely Miss Beckwith. Will tonight be the night you grant me the pleasure of a dance?"

"No, it won't. Not unless you've a pistol to hold to my head. And maybe not even then." She dismissed him by looking away, as if the subject were closed.

"Methinks you doth protest too much, Caroline," Thomas said.

Whereupon Louella snapped, "Oh, do stop being such an insufferable ass, Thomas, or else go away."

"Not until you tell me who this charming creature might be." I realized he was looking directly at me, and so I did my best to smile, although in truth I wished he would take Louella's suggestion.

"Miss Arabella Leeds, allow me to present my brother, Thomas Paxton." Louella's voice had taken on rather a caustic edge. "There, Thomas, you've been formally introduced. Now take your leave, please. We're attempting to have a conversation here."

"You'll get nothing but bile and vinegar from these two," Thomas said, directing the comment to me. "Old maids, they're determined to be, with all their dull *nouveaux* ideas. Don't sit too close, Miss Leeds, or you may catch what's ailing them."

As I made no reply to this, he peered at me more closely, and said, "Perhaps the warning comes too late, then."

"Go *away*," Louella hissed more loudly, and at last her brother took the hint, and retreated with another smug bow.

Louella rolled her eyes after him, and then we returned to our discussion, whilst the other guests made ready for dancing and frolics in the ballroom.

We explored the various attributes and deficits of every partygoer who passed us, and Caroline provided us with hilarious little thumbnail sketches of their families' assorted scandals. Then we moved back to the subject of impending war, and from there to the habits of the British aristocracy, to which I contributed my tale of Cousin Henry's shooting sprees. We reviled the English cuisine and named our favorite dishes, complete with recipes; then we invented new concoctions based on my cousin's conquests (fox-ear omelette was one of these offerings). And at last, when I felt more at ease than I'd felt in an age, I related to them the tale of my great adventure in New Parrish, the evening with Madame Zunia the Spiritualist. I went only so far as the end of that night, being unable to speak of the rest of it, but I surprised myself even in this, and they roared with laughter at what I told them, and pronounced me a sage and a wit, and a great good table-turner as well.

So involved and lively did our chat become that I was scarcely aware of the hours passing, and it was not until I saw Mother signaling to me from the entrance to the ballroom that I realized the party was nearing its conclusion. I rose to take my leave, and my companions did also. As we sauntered toward the door, I exchanged addresses with both of them, and promised to send a note or calling card as soon as I arrived home. I was saddened to hear that Miss Paxton may be departing soon for the south of France, where her father is presently residing, but Miss Beckwith assured me that she at least will visit, as she is situated just outside London and expects to be there for the better of the upcoming weeks.

Thus we parted, with several kisses upon the cheek. I went to our carriage feeling decidedly exhilarated, and was little bothered by Mother's comment that I had been rather unsociable, ensconcing myself in a corner instead of making myself available for a waltz or two. Father asked me who my new acquaintances might be, and I answered him, but said nothing about the sensation which had stolen over me: namely, that at last I had met two kindred spirits, after these many months of feeling quite alone in the world.

FEBRUARY 1, 1861

My situation has eased up somewhat with the departure of my aunt, uncle, and cousins. They returned to the country yesterday, leaving my own little family in relative seclusion at the town house.

I should feel better, and yet I find myself seized by a curious restlessness. I date its arrival from the evening of the ball, but what could have caused it, I do not know.

I've sent short notes off to Caroline Beckwith and to Louella Paxton, but of course I've had no reply as yet; I shall not even start expecting one til the end of the week.

Perhaps I shall read awhile, although I doubt my aunt and uncle have much in the way of literature that can interest me. Aunt Josephine collects only cheap novels whose theme—unbearable, unrequited love—is always the same, while Uncle Charles prefers scientific journals, and the medical textbooks which are necessary to his practice as a physician.

Oh well; I am certain that between the two of them they can supply me with something either vapid or dense enough to lure me into sleep.

FEBRUARY 12, 1861

I have still had no word from Misses Beckwith or Paxton, but as my birthday shall arrive in two days I am distracted from thoughts of them by a certain amount of furtive fuss going on in the house. I believe everyone is trying excessively to prepare for this occasion, as if to lure me back from some precipice they imagine me standing upon.

I would not mind this if I were unhappy, and if my own unhappiness provided the motive for their attentions. But the reality is that I believe I'm intended somehow to perch here upon my ledge; it is they who don't like me there, and it is their own discomfort rather than any true assessment of me which drives their efforts. I intend not to speak of this, though; I have no doubt that Mother and Father would be terribly hurt, and would not take my point at all. Instead I will try to put on a pleasant face, and to accept whatever comes as a loving, if misguided, gesture.

At least I have found an antidote to the restlessness I mentioned days ago. I've discovered Uncle Charles's journals to be quite fascinating, and can lose myself in them for literally six and seven hours at a time. I attempted

Aunt Josephine's novels first, I'm sorry to admit, and thus wasted a good ten minutes of my existence on the turgid doings of some maiden named Kathleen, who pined for someone called, improbably, Brockman. What nonsense Josephine engages in! She reminds me of Constance, and as that young lady is a Leeds—her father, Henry, being Father's and Charles's youngest sibling—I must only imagine that Josephine's and Charles's offspring come by their penchant for silliness from both sides of the family.

FEBRUARY 13, 1861

I cannot believe the confusion I'm in the midst of, just one day before my birthday.

It all began when I excused myself after luncheon, and took to my bedroom in order to peruse the latest issue of *The Lancet*. I'd begun an interesting article regarding the use of salts as an anti-septic, and wanted to finish it before taking a walk. I mentioned as much in the dining room, and went off to secure the journal and settle in upon my window seat. But no sooner was I opening up to that spot where I'd left off than Mother knocked at the door. "*Entrez*," I called, although I hoped she would simply tell me whatever she needed to and depart. But the door opened wide, and Mother stepped in, closing it behind her.

"May I sit down?" she asked me, indicating the armchair.

"Of course," I said, a bit crossly—for it seemed obvious that whatever she meant to impart was not to take a mere matter of seconds.

"Berry, dear," she began pleasantly, and my suspicions were at once aroused: Mother uses my favorite nickname only when she wishes especially to get on my good side; being the result of Richard's babyish mangling of my name, it is something too sweet-sounding for when she's interested in being stern. "What is it that you've taken up here to occupy yourself?" I figured she meant to make conversation, and so I said, "Nothing, Mother, only Uncle Charles's *Lancet*, as I told you. I'm midway through the most fascinating discussion of—"

"May I see it, please?"

I hesitated, only now realizing that this itself was the issue at hand.

I could imagine what Mother would make of my diversion, for besides the article that interested me, there was also a segment on syphilitic symptoms in nomadic South American tribes, as well as a question-and-answer letter column whose topic, this month, was the ongoing problem of grave-robbing for the purpose of delivering cadavers to science.

Nonetheless I handed her the journal. What else could I do, after all? I waited, knowing perfectly well where she was headed, while she pretended to scan its contents and come spontaneously upon whatever was sure to dismay her.

She gave a little gasp of horror, and then closed the pages and looked at me. "Berry, dear. You know Papa and I wish to set only reasonable limits on your behavior, and that we would deny you nothing that could satisfy your curiosity or widen your interests in a healthy manner. But certain things"—she hefted the book for emphasis—"certain things are merely a dark indulgence, thoroughly unsuitable for one whose character is still forming. Some topics are better left discussed and explored by experts, Berry, and I think you'd have to agree that medicine and science are among those. If you do not understand them, you will come away misinformed, and given the—well, *position* that you've presently taken I feel that subjecting your spirit to these demoralizing discussions can only harm you irreparably."

"I see, Mother. So what are you telling me, precisely?"

"I'm *telling* you nothing, dear, except what conclusions your father and I have reached after some consideration. Surely there must be something else within the library that interests you. I am simply *asking* you to forgo any more material of this kind, at least for the time being."

"Very well, then, as you are only asking me, I wish to exert my right to refuse." It pained me to say this—I know I am often short with Mother these days, and an ungrateful wretch—but I felt I had no choice. Imagine, attempting to censor my reading matter! And here on the eve of my seventeenth birthday!

Mother heaved a deep sigh, but made an effort to retain her composure. "Bella, dear," she began again, this time using that most repellent of nicknames, which she knows I abhor, "what I am asking of you—"

I found I could not hold my tongue. "What you are asking of me," I interrupted her, "what you are *demanding* of me, as usual, is that I pretend. Yes, that's it, Mother, that I *pretend*—that there aren't such things as syphilitics or dead bodies in the world, that I *pretend* not to have read the journal and understood it." I paused for breath, and saw her about to cut me off, so I jumped in before she could do it, giving scant thought to what I was saying. "And it goes beyond the journal, doesn't it, Mother, for you'd also have me *pretend* a multitude of other things, and live in some sort of netherland where I agree to being benighted and deluded—"

"Heavens, that is quite enough," Mother interjected, but I ran over her words.

"No, it is not enough. You would have me lie—lie to myself, and lie about much of the world as well, and defend that lie at the expense of acknowledging what's true—well, I will not—"

"For goodness' sake, Arabella, leave off, will you! Stop making such a drama!" She sprang to her feet. "There now, I hope you're satisfied, you have me screeching like a barmaid." In a quieter but no less harsh tone she continued: "Since when have you become an expert on such lofty subjects as 'truth' and 'the world'? Do you think you're the first schoolgirl to indulge in these adolescent ravings? You believe you know everything, Miss, and—think of it!—you've been only sixteen brief years on the planet. Well—perhaps with some patience, you'll gain the wisdom you'll need to see that you're quite mistaken—"

"No, Mother, *you're* mistaken. I don't think I know everything. I think I know nothing, and that you'd be content to keep me that way, so that I might be the more like all of you."

She stared at me and pressed her hands to her temples, and at that moment I felt so horrible, so contrite, that I wished only to reach out and fall upon her shoulder. But she turned before I could do this, and left the room without bothering to look at me again.

I tried to recover my composure, but it was useless. My tears brimmed over my lashes, and I pulled a handkerchief from my sleeve to wipe them. I was just in the act of doing this when I heard footsteps upon the stairs; and a moment later, Mother reentered the room with Father on her heels.

I could tell by the look on his face that he'd donned his Disciplinarian mantle. Usually these stern moods of his blew over quickly, but I had the feeling that this one would not.

"What is all this," he fairly shouted, "how dare you challenge your mother so abominably? What has got into you? You've been told to make a very mild concession to the happiness of this household, and you act like this? Well, you shall make it, Arabella, we're of one mind about that. We are responsible for your welfare until you leave this house to begin your own family, and then—"

"—and then I'll be someone else's responsibility? Is that what you're telling me?" I cried. "No, I'll make no concession! Not in this matter."

"It is our duty to determine what's best for you, and pull you back when we feel—"

"When you feel I'm doing other than what you did. Isn't that it? When you feel you don't understand, and so it's necessary to force me into some position you *can* understand!"

Father began to rub his forehead, just as Mother had massaged her temples a few minutes ago. When I looked more closely I saw that his eyes were red, and that there were tears in them.

This sight reduced me to stillness. My own tears were one thing, but the idea of Father crying bespoke a matter whose gravity was unimaginable. However our argument had distressed me, I thought myself more petulant than anything else, and surely petulance could not be the cause of my father's weeping.

The three of us were silent for a few seconds. Then Father said in a low voice, "We are at our wits' end, Arabella. We realize you have suffered a number of great shocks over the last months, and we ascribed this change in your temperament—the adopting of this persona—to those shocks. We meant you to recover here, to become once again your old self, but it seems that was a naive hope. I'm left to wonder if perhaps you should not have gone someplace more—structured—someplace where better-trained experts could see to your convalescence."

I felt the air squeeze out of my lungs. Then a tiny voice I barely recognized as my own said, "This is what comes of my reading a journal? *You would put me away?*"

Mother stepped toward me, her hands—of course—twisting each other. "No, no, of course not, we meant only that perhaps we cannot provide the peace and quiet you need to fully recover yourself, but we've decided nothing."

"You would put me away?" I repeated.

Father's mouth trembled. "We are at our wits' end."

"You've discussed this, then."

Father walked to the edge of my bed and sank down upon it. "Arabella, this is nothing to do with such trivialities as journals and reading matter. We see you taking a course for yourself which may have tragic consequences for you in the future. It goes beyond mere adolescent rebellion or high spirits. These silences, these moods, the rides alone into the city—we know of those, you see—these strange unhealthy interests, your thrusting of yourself into the center of the most unimaginable scandals—we are at a loss as to how to respond to all this. We ask only that you cooperate—that you attempt to show us you are capable of heeding our advice, which we give only out of love for you. If you cannot, then what choice do we have but to see to our duty as parents, to interfere on behalf of your best interests? Perhaps there is some organic problem—I've discussed the possibility with your Uncle Charles—"

"Uncle Charles?" I sat with my shoulders slumped forward, my head reeling.

"Please, Berry dear, say you will try to abide by our limits. We are not so unreasonable, we have only your future in mind—" Mother approached me, and the look in her eyes was so wrenching that I quite forgot my own pain for a brief second.

But the instant passed, and I saw instead what my choices would be if I held to my convictions. I tried, I truly tried, to see the matter through their eyes, but I felt in that moment only the most profound sense of betrayal, as if the last rock to which I'd clung in a stormy sea had just disappeared beneath a great wave. How had I moved beyond normal "high spirits"? What imperceptible line had I crossed? Oh, I had known my parents' feelings and my own were often at odds, but never had I imagined they would turn upon me so absolutely, and twist matters so horrifically.

"You wish to imply that I've lost my reason because I differ with you, to treat me as a lunatic when you know that I am not. Well, if I am insane, then my promises are worthless, are they not? And if I am not insane, then it's merely for the sake of punishment that you threaten me with a sanitarium—is it not?"

"No, no." Father shook his head with vigor. "We had discussed only a private spa—you are making much too much of this, and you must not think of it in those terms, they are not what we intended at all."

But that is what it amounts to, Father. I said nothing, however. I felt it would accomplish nothing. A very long moment passed, and then I looked up at both of them.

"What is it you wish of me?"

The relief which flooded into their faces was palpable. "Only that you try to observe the limits of respectable behavior, and avoid those things which are contributing to this poisonous state of mind," Father said.

"Yes," Mother joined in, too cheerfully, "that won't be so difficult, will it? Good health feeds upon itself, that is our point. You could find some companions—I know you don't get on with Anne or Percy, and I can't say as I blame you, but what of those two girls you met at Mersy Hall, perhaps you could arrange some entertainments with them. I would be happy to help you, dear, you know that. And there are several young men who have been asking after you—Mr. Carter Forbes-Spencer, you must recall him, he noticed you the other night, and Mrs. Rogers advised me of it—"

"Whatever you wish, Mother," I said, with as much enthusiasm as I felt.

She fell silent. The three of us sat there through one of the most awkward minutes I recall ever living, and then Father said, "Perhaps we've discussed this enough for one afternoon."

"Would you like to be alone now, dear?" Mother asked. I sensed she simply did not know what else to say.

"Yes. I would, if you don't mind."

They rose, and Mother leaned to give me a soft kiss on the forehead. Father followed her through the door; he turned back to me before he closed it. "Everything shall work out, Sauce. You'll see. You'll soon be back to your old self."

I could not force myself to agree with this, and so I remained silent, and they retreated down the stairs.

So there it is. Little did I know how far things have gone. They've asked me to try to behave differently, and so I will. Perhaps they are right, in a sense—perhaps I have let gloom and heaviness overtake my spirit, and would be better served by new activities. But they wish me also to give up the presence of mind which I feel I've gained, and that I refuse to do. Nor will I give up the enterprise of learning, simply because the subject matter does not suit them.

"Those two girls from Mersy Hall" indeed! I wonder how anxious Mother would be to foist me upon them if she had overheard even a scintilla of our conversation.

FEBRUARY 14, 1861

Today was my birthday. It was, nearly as I can tell, the most unhappy one of my whole life.

The cousins came for the event, which of course meant Aunt Jo and Uncle Charles—he of the "spa" discussions—too. The atmosphere of false gaiety was so depressing as to make me wish to cry. How could they all skip blithely about like fools—especially Mother and Father, and their conspirator, Uncle Charles—after what transpired yesterday?

Everything they did infuriated me, from the childish decorations they hung to the overdone pomp with which they regaled me. Mother insisted on crowning me with the little rhinestone tiara she's used on my birthday since I was five or six; Father sang "For She's a Jolly Good Fellow" as he's done every year, but all of it struck me as false and strained. *Go along with it*, they seemed to be saying to me, *show us you are your "old self."*

Then it was time to open presents, and eat the cake Lucy had prepared.

I am grateful for the gifts—I wonder how long it would take any child abandoned to the streets of this city to gladly exchange places with me—yet I could not help but feel provoked at some of what had been chosen for me. Certain of the givers appeared to have made their selections based more on their own tastes than any of mine.

Thus I received from Aunt Jo and Uncle Charles a set of the Carmody Twins Adventures books, which are aimed at a reader of approximately ten years. From Anne I received a pink crystal necklace, which she shall no doubt be asking to borrow in a day, since I will never put it on, and by Percy I was given none other than the green dress I wore to the ball the other week. "It suited you so well," she fluttered. *And also, coincidentally, did not suit you,* I thought, knowing that if she'd liked the dress even an iota she'd have cut it to ribbons before seeing it in my possession.

Edward gave me a silver watch, with which I could find no fault; but Henry gave me—he actually wrapped it in paper and put a ribbon round it—a pheasant which he had murdered and stuffed himself. When I opened it I could not help screaming and flinging it across the table, and then I prepared to pound Henry over the head with it. But when I saw his crestfallen expression, I realized that he truly was so dense as to think he would please me, and was mystified as to why he had not. I promised him I would put it in a special place—I have the underside of the bed in mind.

Father and Mother gave me a large bottle of French perfume, and a lavender silk dress they'd had made from a Parisian pattern, with matching boots, gloves, and jacket. Mother had also collected a sample of deep crimson fabric, with which she promised we'd make a formal gown. I tried to reconcile this with the fact of their discussing my removal to a hospital or asylum, but the two pictures did not come together. I wondered if they'd intended that I should wear the nice new red gown in the halls of Bedlam, and so my thanks, when I gave it, was unsteady and muted.

Only Richard seemed to have been thinking purely of what might suit me. He gave me the collected works of Jane Austen, and a copy of Mrs. Shelley's *Frankenstein*, and also an original edition of the writings of Thomas Paine, which he'd managed to find at a bookshop. I looked over at him and saw him duck his head with unusual shyness; overcome, I ran to the end of the table and gave him a tremendous hug and kiss upon the cheek. He screwed up his face and blushed, but winked at me in complicity, then set to attacking his cake. I must look at Richard every now and then to recall he's the same child who boarded the boat with me a few months ago. His voice has deepened, he has shot up several inches, and acts much more the man than the little boy. Yet I feel closer to him than ever. He is no longer a plaything or a nuisance but very nearly an equal, and my ally at that.

When the cake was done, the party sat about sipping cordials and coffee and indulging in Aunt Jo's favorite topic: other people's lives. But I wished only for the day to be over, and so I excused myself, and took to my room after thanking everyone.

So I am now seventeen. I wonder if any other person of the same years has ever felt as alone as I. When I recall the celebration I had last year, I could fairly weep; I remember the party at Constance and Thomas's house, with my friends Sarah and Diana there, and how I stood up to toast my guests after tearing through the beribboned boxes with glee. I remember I gushed that a finer group of people had never been assembled, and that come what may, I would always regard everyone in the room as my loving family, and be eternally grateful for their presence. How far away it all seems!

I cannot help wondering what shall transpire by the time my next birthday celebration rolls around, but that it cannot be more miserable than this one I have little doubt.

FEBRUARY 16, 1861

Today I received what can only be regarded as belated birthday gifts. My new friends, Misses Beckwith and Paxton, both responded to me with letters, which I tore into eagerly upon being handed them by Lucy. So as not to have to read them before the whole company, however, I took them up to my room, shut the door, and lay upon the bed to peruse them in privacy.

Miss Paxton writes that it was a great pleasure to meet me, and that she looks forward to seeing much more of me when she returns to England. But alas, she has indeed set off for southern France with her mother. She has gone to confront her father, and to demand—beg—"use any means necessary" was her phrase—that he allow her to return to the United States before war becomes a reality, to see to the evacuation and dispersion of her family's holdings in Louisiana. I was aghast at this. How can she even consider it when it seems we were all mistaken—hostilities could break out at any time—and moreover, how can the men of her family allow it, when it is they who should be incurring this risk?

I found my questions answered in the next paragraphs, for Louella went on to say that she recognizes the danger, but cannot rest until she has pulled every string, made every argument, so as to be allowed to go herself. It is purely her idea, which her father will no doubt oppose; but what may carry the day was her point that, as women, she and her mother need not fear being conscripted into the armed forces should the worst come to pass. They will have much more mobility as civilians than either her father or brother.

As to why this mission must be undertaken at all, Louella says it is the fate of the family servants that concerns her most. She has designed a plan whereby a number of them are to be offered positions here, while the rest must be gotten to safe free states. But they must be removed *by* somebody, they are powerless and in danger on their own. I think it is truly admirable the way Louella has taken on the fate of these people as her responsibility; whatever I in my ignorance might have been inclined to believe of the citizens of the South, she has turned my mind with regard to herself.

She has engaged Miss Beckwith's mother, with all of her precious contacts, to help her with the arrangements, and hopes that within not too much time she will have convinced her father to allow her to go, and be on her way back to Europe, having dissolved the family's assets in Louisiana and seen to the rescue of the slaves.

After relating all this, she asked after me, and suggested that despite the newness of our acquaintance I might wish to send her a letter as often as I could manage, so that during her absence she would have plenty to read, and be brought up to date on my activities.

Next I opened Caroline Beckwith's letter, and discovered that it began much in the same vein as Louella's. She too heaped praise upon me, and exclaimed at what a fortuitous thing it was that I had found myself in the same place as they at the same time.

Then she went on to summarize what I'd already learned of Louella's activities from her own letter. Caroline added that she thinks Miss Paxton is making a grave mistake and putting herself and her mother at terrible risk, but her friend will hear none of it. Caroline has even suggested that the abolitionist group of which Mrs. Beckwith is a part can arrange the escape or protection of the slaves themselves, and keep them safe until the end of any hostilities which break out. It is ridiculous, she asserts, for Louella to travel to the recently dis-United States, when there is little doubt that there shall be a conflict—one which may trap her within the confines of Louisiana indefinitely, and result in disaster for everyone concerned.

But Louella insists that this is not reason enough not to try, and that at any rate, if no one goes now, before an actual war erupts, all of the property and holdings her father has in Louisiana may be lost. Flimsy excuse! Caroline retorts. Louella's family is extremely wealthy and would hardly be hurt by losses in the States. The truth, she maintains, is that Louella is fanatical on the subject of the slaves and would risk her own life to save them herself. After heaving a figurative sigh on paper, Caroline expressed wishes for our friend's safe return, and moved, with some reluctance, on to other topics.

She endeavored next to tell me a little about her own activities to date. From the weighty subject of Miss Paxton, she jumped to one rather lighter, though no less intriguing in its own right. She mentioned that her mother, Hester Beckwith, was present in Seneca Falls fourteen years ago, and is making plans to reconnect with some of the ladies she met there who have fled the States and are presently traveling in Europe. I cannot attach significance to this, as I have no idea what "Seneca Falls" refers to, or what happened there; I must ask her to clarify this for me.

She also mentioned, in a different vein, that she raises puppies, cocker spaniels in a variety of colours. She thought I might like to see them at some point, and added that one of her finest breeding females has just had a litter. She even offered to make a gift of one should I desire a pet; she does not breed them for sale, but as presents for her family and friends.

Lastly, Caroline told me that a young man named Carter Forbes-Spencer had indeed been asking after me the night of the Rogerses' ball, just as Mother reported. It seems Caroline's family is friendly with the Forbes-Spencers, so Caroline came by this information firsthand. What Mother did not know, however, is that young Carter asked after another young lady as well, meaning that I was not the only female to catch his attention that night.

"Carter is not the most sterling of characters," Caroline writes, "but I don't suppose he is the worst sort, either. If you are interested in nothing too weighty, perhaps a friendly meeting, a carriage ride or pleasant entertainment, you might arrange to respond to him in some manner. I'd be happy to relay the response, so that you can meet him and judge for yourself." She will be quite busy over the next few weeks, she says, but hopes to make time for a visit, and will surely write, as she hopes I shall do.

I must make busy myself and send an answer at once, and I shall try not to seem too downcast in reporting my own news of late. At least I am comforted knowing I have made potentially good friends in this desolation at last, and that they are as close as the post service, willing me their good wishes.

FEBRUARY 20, 1861

The gods certainly have their peculiar sense of humor—we can rest assured of that, as I found out from Aunt Josephine that the second young lady Mr. Forbes-Spencer noticed at the party was none other than my cousin Percy. I must admit this inclines me against him on principle. I loathe the idea of being trapped in any category with Persephone, although I cannot deny that she is pretty, and therefore does catch the eye, if not the discerning mind. Thank God the other girl did not turn out to be Anne—for then I should have been classed with true homeliness as well as a dull wit.

As it is, I had to put up with Percy's fuming, she being as insulted as I at finding us rivals. She proceeded to huff and sigh as if I myself had had something to do with engaging Mr. Forbes-Spencer's attentions, while in fact I did not even know at the time that he existed. She managed to work in the comment that it was a lucky thing she'd passed the green dress on to me—as if it had walked about by itself at the party, without me in it. Then she added that I may amuse myself as much as I wish with young Carter; he is of no interest to her, being only nineteen. She, at fifteen, has decided that no one under twenty-five has the material means necessary to win her affections.

Sadly, this merely opens the door for me to respond to Caroline's offer, whereas had Percy remained in the running I would have had ample reason to pass. There is a part of me which longs for the thrill of being courted, but there is as much a portion which mistrusts the enterprise, and tells me I should defer. I shall try to make a decision soon; perhaps it would not be such a terrible thing to have him visit the house, and no doubt an outing with him is an outing of which Mother and Father would approve.

FEBRUARY 23, 1861

We are alone again in the town house. Yet despite the decline in prying eyes, I still sometimes have the sensation that I am a beetle beneath a magnifying glass, or a field mouse being stealthily stalked by an owl. Father, Mother, and Lucy keep me quite in their sights, although they try mightily to appear unconcerned.

They are not so clever as they seem, though, for I have managed to slip some reading matter into my private lair, by sandwiching it between two of Aunt Josephine's ridiculous novels.

But this mention of sandwiches makes me hungry. I think I shall tiptoe to the kitchen, quiet as a mouse, and see what one of the owls has prepared as a snack.

FEBRUARY 24, 1861

It has been cold and blustery for nearly a week now, and so I am loath to leave the house. I'm quite content to sit in my alcove or beneath my blankets and peruse my contraband.

I must admit that Mother may have had a point, however, for today I am finding *The Lancet* to be extremely rough going.

The article which has me alternately gasping and rereading is entitled "Examination of the Female Orgasm and Its Connexion to Reproductive Incapacity." It took me some time to figure out what any of this meant before I attempted a single line of the text—and even now I am not sure I've deciphered it correctly. As nearly as I can tell, "Orgasm" refers to a muscular contraction experienced by women while in the midst of the act of passion. In fact it seems this sensation is the reason why passion is passionate—or at least partly so. The "reproductive incapacity" named in the title refers to the inability on the part of some women to become with child. The apparent connexion between the two, the author asserts, is the stimulation provided by the pleasurable Orgasms, which if experienced in excess may lead to mental unbalance, a weakening of the body's systems, and subsequent failure to conceive. Well-to-do ladies may find themselves more prone to this syndrome, he concludes, since they are by nature delicate, and unable to withstand repeated shocks to their organs and persons, whereas the women of the underclasses are of heartier stock, and coarser in nature, able to flourish despite these descents into carnal dissipation.

The article caused me to swing between blanch and blush as I read it, containing such explicit phrases as I have never laid eyes on before. There is a precise drawing of the private parts of the anatomy along with their common clinical Latin names; thus the male organs of reproduction are labeled the Penis (with its Vas Deferens, Foreskin, Glans, and Shaft), Scrotum, and Testicles, and the fluid emitted is known as Sperm. (Yes, I am writing these words, truly, and daring myself to keep a steady hand as I do so—to imagine myself a lady scientist, perhaps penning an article of my own for some future *Lancet*.) I have not viewed a Penis at close range since Richard's babyhood ages ago; I recall finding the attachment rather odd and silly then, and I cannot say the illustrations herein altered my opinion considerably. It is fascinating to note, however, that during the act of passion the Penis fills with blood, assumes a much larger size than when at rest, and becomes stiff as a broom handle, thus readying it for insertion into the woman. The female organs are labeled as well: the Vulva, the Vagina, the Clitoris, the Labia Majora and Minora, the Uterus, and the Ovaries. The external organs of the woman also swell during passion, but not to the degree which the man's do.

The text explained in minute detail how the Orgasm occurs physiologically, and what function it may serve in terms of procreation.

I did not know whether to be appalled at this information or to rejoice. What I do know is that I feel I've been provided an explanation for a dozen facets of my fellow humans' behavior which previously left me baffled. I am somewhat surprised to realize it, but much as I knew that the act of love is essentially the same for humans as it is for our pets or for breeding horses, I did not understand the precise nature of what drove it along. Of course there is emotional love and romance, but of the physical manifestation of that emotion known as Sexual Congress—well, why bother with it?

Why do animals seek out this contact when they cannot know it leads to the increase in their numbers? And what elusive prize—it is surely not romantic love—drives men into the arms of mistresses or prostitutes, or into the company of their wives? Is it the same prize in each instance? In marriage, for example, there is the obvious appeal of progeny, but this incentive is hardly present with anyone with whom one does not desire a family, so what is the point of undertaking the act with them? (That act, by the way, is referred to here as Intercourse, a common enough word which reminds me of two mingling rivers, although it seems a bit detached.)

As I now discover, that prize is a physical sensation so grand as to be overwhelming, and it occurs in both the male and female of the human species. In the male the moment comes during the release of the Sperm into a woman's body, and is a part of Intercourse so long as that release occurs. For the woman it may occur at any point, but usually happens after a protracted contact with the man. Sometimes, for reasons the article did not explain, women do not feel the Orgasm at all. But God's wisdom in arranging its existence is obvious: whether we know or not that our passion shall lead to offspring, we shall continue to engage in Intercourse, because there is this wonderful moment of bliss to be had at its completion.

Of that last I had been given not a shred of information, despite the many talks I'd been subjected to regarding the joys of family life. I recall, upon my first experience with my monthly time, being told by Mother that, wretched as this flow was, it was a sign that my body was ready to bear babies for my future husband, and that I must now be told how that wonder would come about. I had already an inkling, but as she described it, a husband places his seed into the body of his wife by using the private part designed for that task. The couple undertakes this act in the full expectation of having children; it thus becomes a duty of marriage, as the completion of accounts or the settling of a home is a duty. It has little to do with the pleasure of a kiss or the holding of a hand—although men, being by nature more brutely physical, are actually able to derive enjoyment from it.

I recall imagining the discussion which might surround this task: the husband and wife, having decided the time is ripe for a baby, agree on a date; the husband prepares his private part, the wife prepares hers, there is a second or so of concentration and contact while the "seed" is delivered, and then they return to the study to read or discuss the day's events. Or else, if the husband is one of those "coarser" individuals, he indulges himself, while his wife waits patiently for him to finish.

Of course I had seen cats and dogs chase each other about with a great deal of screeching, writhing, and yowling on the parts of both, but as they were mere beasts, I assumed the act they performed must be different in sensation, if not in mechanics, from what human beings experience.

At any rate, Mother went on to tell me that under no circumstances must that act be undertaken with anyone other than a husband, and with him it *must* be undertaken, however unpleasant it may be. At the time I wondered why on earth she felt it necessary to explain this, for that it was both necessary and unpleasant was obvious, and therefore why would anyone except a wife, desiring children, undertake something so grotesque, messy, and embarrassing?

There was no talk that day or any other of Orgasms (although later I heard talk, and felt the stirring, of feelings other than disgust for the act of Intercourse). What a difference this phenomenon makes in my understanding of why we undertake courtship and marriage, and why such forceful emotions tug at men and women! There is not only the love of the heart with which to contend, there is also the love of the body for the body of the other, which bestows this gift. That is the dual combination which results in passion; it is a heady and irresistible mix, as one need only look about to see.

What I do not understand about the article in question, though, was why its author seemed to believe that Orgasm for the woman leads to mental unbalance. This seems plainly ridiculous to me. After all, why would God endow us with such a wonderful capacity if it were not to be enjoyed to its fullest? How can it be "overused"? I should think that men would suffer more from its "overuse" than we women; after all, with every Orgasm, they lose a bit of their bodily fluid, which I assume, like blood, must be replaced. Yet fathers of huge families seem quite healthy to me, and no one suggests that they risk being otherwise in producing their offspring.

But there are truths, facts, things that can be applied and experienced consistently regardless of outward circumstance—you throw the ball into the air and it returns, whether you are in Greece or New York—and then there are conventions, are there not?—and it seems to me that the notions we attach to the body and its functions fall among the latter.

I knew when I listened to Mother's talk—as I settled beneath a hot-water bottle, and bore that deep, but somehow comforting, ache within me—that her words were meant not only to instruct me in facts, but to instruct me in the convention of how I should view those facts. She meant me to know that I'm to *pretend*—look, see how early that notion entered into my training—to find my husband's attentions unpleasant, *pretend* to regard them as duty, whether I truly feel this way or not. I'm to do this for the same reason I was to squeal at the sight of frogs and insects although in fact they fascinated me, for the same reason I was later to feign disinterest in food and lace my corset as tight as I could stand it. I have experienced such pleasure in my ability to pretend these things well, to feel myself one with my female companions. But there is such a thing as pretending not in spite of belief but until one believes, and somehow I could not—cannot—accomplish this. Why? How is it done? What has caused me to fail, and does every lady fail inwardly yet hide it perfectly, even from herself?

Whatever the answer, I recall the moment when I admitted it to myself, when I allowed myself to know that I had indeed failed in this regard: it was the first time I strolled with Jeffrey Price and feigned a calm aloofness, while meantime the inches of skin where his arm contacted mine burned with pleasure. I recall now how this bewildered me, how I wondered if I were the only one that could not erase the element of fakery from her correct demeanor. Yet—further proof of my perversity!—I wanted for nothing so much as to have that touch upon my flesh again. I realize that I have waited all my life for the wink of Mother's which would bind us in the complicity of fakery, reassure me that I am not the only one so divided. But the moment never came.

So I am left to think that perhaps I am indeed alone in these duplicities, these chasms into which I have fallen, and which, worse still, I am unwilling to wrench myself out of. Is that fact not further evidenced by the writing of these words, the reading of this material, the unearthing of what is surely of no interest to the true-born lady, namely the precise nature of passion?

Now I have discovered it, though, in this cold and (to my mind) wrong-headed piece designed for the attentions of physicians; and in *my* wrong-headedness, I do not back away. Rather, I feel I have been cheated, and I revel in what I have unearthed. Yes, I revel in it, I imagine the poetry of it, the grandeur. Somewhere beyond the bloodless page, the Vas Deferens and the Labia Minora, there is this primal and magnificent realm. We enter it alongside all the birds and beasts, I think, as much its slaves as any of those creatures—and yet this does not offend me, but suggests to me the oneness of everything which breathes beneath the Sun. I dearly hope I shall reach that place hand in hand with a beloved, to be captivated by its music, the ballads of passion, to dance beneath its spell and sing those lusty songs the animals sing.

FEBRUARY 25, 1861

I must endeavor to find a safer hiding place for you, friend, as the information I am about to impart would surely be enough to convince anyone who happened on it that I am indeed deranged. I wonder it myself—shall I find the mettle to write it, or shall I shrink from the task? No, I shall write. But afterward, I shall perhaps place you within the deepest pocket of my traveling trunk, which I can then secure with a lock and key.

To recap, though: as I reported yesterday, we are undergoing a frightful cold snap here, and as the weather is impossible I have not moved from the confines of the house. I was bored beyond belief, and even considered going along when Mother and Father announced that they were treating Richard and Lucy to a view of the fabled Tower of London. (Uncle Charles would be aghast—fraternizing with servants is unheard of here—but Mother maintains that Lucy is a second mother to us all and has earned her outing. Good for Mother.) But luckily I remembered in time that, as all of them were undertaking this adventure, I would be left blissfully alone, except for Uncle Charles's house servants—a rare occurrence. Besides, I have little interest in seeing that monument to the cruelty of the British Empire, except perhaps from an architectural point of view.

So the family departed, and I had my solitude at last; the question then was how I should best take advantage of it.

I found myself thinking of the article which had so rocked my foundations yesterday. I desired no more reading, but I could not keep my mind from resting on the anatomy drawings. My curiosity got the better of me, and I realized that if it had been years since I'd viewed Richard's unclothed body, it had been even longer since I'd inspected my own—because I had never done so in my life.

So I went to my bedroom and locked the door, and then found in my drawer my little bone hand mirror, which I laid on the bed. Then I stood before the full-length glass and removed my clothing.

I confess I was confused by the image I saw there. I peer down at my own body every day, each time I dress and each time I bathe, and yet I never inspect it at length in its natural state. I admire it when it is clothed and perfumed, but without adornment, I suppose, I take it for granted. So I looked—really looked—at what the glass revealed to me, and found I was unable to decide whether I was very ugly or very beautiful.

My body seemed long to me, although I am not tall; my waist is small, and the suggestion of musculature indents my stomach, which is flat. This muscled appearance does not appeal to me. It seems too mannish, as does the curve of my bicep and the sinews visible in my flank. I would prefer the dimpled elbows and rounded thighs I have seen portrayed in the classical paintings, although I should not like to have so much excess flesh as would interfere with the wearing of my own clothes, or moving about with ease. I approve of my unmarred skin, though; it is pale and without blemish, and the flesh beneath it firm. I like my hips, which curve nicely from my waist, and my buttocks, which are suitably full and feminine. And my breasts appear beautiful to me; they slope more than I recall them doing when they first announced themselves at around thirteen or so, but my nipples are small and pinkish-purple, and the dark area around them even and distinct. Between my thighs, I saw that the patch of hair is more coarse than that on my head, but still reddish, and that it describes a precise triangle outside of which not a single strand grows. How does it know to do this, to appear in one spot and not another? And what function does it serve? The rest of the hair on my body is so fine and white as to be unnoticeable, yet these patches at the thighs, under the arms, and over the eyes are smart enough to grow in differently. An amazing thing.

Finished with the body-length glass, I then lay on the bed and picked up the small mirror. I confess that my hand trembled as I did this. I, like every child, I imagine, have been instructed that one's own privates must not be touched or examined. And I have on occasion disobeyed that edict—I wonder if in this I am like every other child, or if, again, I am alone in my perversions—although only recently have I acknowledged this to myself. The touching of this area produces pleasurable sensations—and thanks to my reading of the article I now understand why—and so I've indulged in it halfheartedly and with an effort not to think too much about it, but never have I undertaken to consciously view myself.

I lay on my back so that I might examine the region known as the Vulva. (I am the scientist, remember, and a scientist does not shrink from the thing itself, never mind the mere naming of the thing.) Beneath the hair, I found the plump lips of my Labia Majora; these I nudged aside to see the pink Labia Minora within. At the farthest point from the crease of my buttocks I saw the little hooded button known as the Clitoris, and beneath that, the opening known as the Vagina (which is where the Penis is inserted), and within that the Urethra, which is used for evacuation. I must say it is rather handy that we have a passage and opening for every function of the body. I should not like to be a man, and know that from the same spigot is delivered both body waste and the Sperm fluid.

I was relieved to see that all my parts were in place just as they'd been illustrated in the journal. I had not expected to find that I was abnormal necessarily, but a little question lingered, given as I have never had a chance to compare myself to any other woman. I have viewed my cousins and family members naked, but never at great length, and never in so intimate a pose. Everything I saw in my hand mirror appeared quite lovely to me—the flesh had a fresh pink color which deepens to rose or purple at the lettuced edges, and was formed of intricate prominences which disappear into themselves—but again I wonder if this is only because I have not viewed anyone else. Do we all look the same, or is there—as I would imagine—as much variation as there exists among faces, and hands, and feet?

At any rate, once I had gone this far it occurred to me that I should test out the premise of the Orgasm as I'd seen it described, although I have no doubt that this is far more serious a transgression than the viewing of my privates. Certainly I know of the Biblical injunction against self-abuse, the spilling of one's seed by one's own hand; but Onan was a man, and the seed of women is contained within them, and besides, the whole incident was part of the Old Testament, when the having of children was vital to the Israelites, and was never broached in the New.

I decided that I would begin with the familiar and pleasurable activities I've engaged in before, and simply continue until something unusual happened. So I lay back upon my pillows and placed a tentative hand at my Vulva, drawing the fingers lightly across and around it. I had never done this with such deliberateness before, and the act made me terribly self-conscious. And so I stopped, feeling both immoral and immodest, and wondering whether God and a phalanx of long-dead ancestors were frowning at me from above, condemning me as a lewd, coarse creature with bestial appetites.

But then, for some reason, the story of Jesus at the wedding in Cana popped into my head. Jesus was no hedonist, but neither was He crabbed and rigid in His self-mortification. He enjoyed life in its turn, and the sensations of His physical being, and did not deny that these things form a vital part of existence. So I tried to imagine that, were He watching, He would probably approve of this activity (our own modern sensibilities aside)—particularly as He in His wisdom had designed our bodies to perform it.

So I began again, this time letting my fingers work farther down into the folds of my flesh. It occurred to me that Orgasm was discussed in the context of Intercourse, so that perhaps it was necessary to engage in something which mimics that act; I therefore placed my pinkie finger at the opening of my Vagina, and pushed it in a little.

This was not pleasant. My muscles responded to the strange intrusion by clamping up and refusing my finger admission. I stopped at once, and returned to the activity of stroking the outer parts of my privates. I recalled the article's assertion that the Clitoris plays a role in female Orgasm, and so I rubbed the tip of it gently. This was quite pleasurable. In fact, within a few moments I noticed that my fingers fell into a rhythm which the little button of the Clitoris seemed to be directing by herself, without the interference of my brain; slowly but surely the resulting sensation moved beyond anything I had heretofore known. I allowed my mind to drift, to summon pleasing images, or romantic ones, or even recollections of the yowling cats and dogs; I thought even of Jeffrey Price, or rather, of the person I had believed him to be, and the sensation became a heaviness in the whole region of my privates which seemed to demand that I touch more diligently. But the more I did so the more the feeling increased, so that I reached a point where I forgot my self-consciousness, and strove to give my body what it demanded; and this became easier and easier, for I was supplied with a moist slickness beneath my fingers which kept the friction from hurting.

I continued on in this way for some minutes until I was moved to yet another plateau in the experience, whereby I felt ready to burst and yet eager for that point at the same time. All the thoughts now flew out of my head; my focus narrowed to the sensation between my thighs. I can describe the feeling as akin to having an itch, and the release of scratching it, or having to sneeze, and the relief of doing so, except that this was far, far more intense than either of those things. Just when I felt I could not move any faster, or stand any more of that blossoming fullness, a flutter arose somewhere inside of me, ending at my Clitoris, and at the entrance to my Vagina. Wave after wave of it followed, as if my Vagina were swallowing, or drawing in whatever might be at its entrance—the tide of my summer-holiday recollections, relentlessly pulling the sand from under my feet. The Clitoris demanded my attentions until, like that aforementioned scratched itch, the relief outweighed the provocation, and the heavy sensation subsided. Through all of this I felt transported, as if every fiber of my being had become an extension of my fingers and the flesh beneath them; if anyone had called to me, or battered down the door, I should not have noticed.

When at last the intensity waned a bit—it took only seconds, although it seemed to last interminably—I became aware again of my surroundings, and of a tingling sensitivity in the little Clitoris. She seemed to want no more of my rough fingertips, and so I closed my eyes and lay still against the pillows, my breath coming in shallow gasps.

This, no doubt, was the Orgasm—at least, I hope it was, for if the body is capable of something even more overwhelming, I should be almost afraid to know it. At least I can be sure now that the phenomenon exists, and that I can produce it within myself—although God alone knows of the deviant bent of my mind which would cause me to want to—and I would like to write to the author of the *Lancet* article, a Mr. Acton, that I am experiencing no physical ill effects, and that he should keep his observations to himself, especially since he can never know this particular subject matter firsthand.

I admit to a residual mental discomfort with what I have done, however, and perhaps this is the danger with which Mr. Acton ought be concerned. Such activity is so foreign to everything I have ever been taught regarding the province of my body and my nature as a woman. Again, I am of two minds, chaste and unchaste, but at least I know I am not alone in my fragmentation, my fraudulent claim to propriety. What of Madame Zunia, and Jeffrey Price, what of the business of Chapel Street? It would seem from those examples that every age and every being creates for itself the need to live in two worlds: the one it professes to believe in, and the one of its actions as they truly are.

I refuse, therefore, to give in to shame, but it was mightily hard to hold to this view when the family arrived home from its tour of the prison tower.

"What have you been about all day, dear," Mother asked me as we sat before the fire in the study and waited upon dinner. I could not help colouring considerably. My corset was laced, my peplumed jacket and skirt arranged with care, but I felt I was sitting before her naked as the day of my birth. "Nothing earth-shattering," I replied, that being the first phrase which popped into my head.

Then Father entered the room, and I felt myself fairly glow with heat. I could not even look him in the eye—I thought it a lucky thing that whatever limits Mother and Father may place upon my movements, they cannot enter my skull unless I will it, that there is one territory which I still control absolutely.

Then it occurred to me that, whatever sensation I had experienced this day, Father at least had had some taste of it, for did not that very act of Intercourse complete with Orgasm produce me, who now sat before him blushing crimson? That led to a hideous but mercifully brief mental image of my own parents engaged in my production—and then my mind slammed the door shut upon this confounding vision. I've tried returning to the picture just to see whether it still shocks me—and it does, although I know that it is the lady and not the scientist who indulges in this sentiment. Every person on earth began life in the same manner, whether we view it with distaste or not, and it's a foolish world—and a foolish girl—who attempts to hide from the fact.

Oh, how happy I should be to see the world less foolish, to see our enlightened age dispense with its conventions of distaste, so that I might not be the only one to look at them askance! But—then again—might not some other postures arise in their stead? Perhaps some equally false immodesties, or frantic forms of sensual indulgence? I doubt the world should be much improved by such a substitution; rather, I think I should find it very like a place where strawberry shortcake is to be had every day, until one grows bored with it and forgets that once it was special, even whilst declaring it wonderful out of mere conformity.

FEBRUARY 26, 1861

I attempt to reread what I've written over the last few days and wonder if demons haven't come to possess me and cavort about your pages with my pen. For what other excuse can there be for the prurient and disgraceful entries which I see rendered in my own hand? I must be insane, a madwoman divided into two, the fair and dark comingling in one brain.

In moments such as this one, I am stunned at myself, and penitent, and I wish only to stay that way, to renounce this other creature who mocks every tenet of the moral code which all civilized society holds dear.

Yet I know the heart of that other creature, I know I am she, and in an instant I am back upon her side of the fence, looking over at my former self and crying, "Fraud!"

For I was never wholly the innocent, as you know, but rather a *pretender*, desirous of the smiles and approving glances with which my fine actressing was rewarded. That is one world—and then there is the other I inhabit as the Wild One, where no one smiles, where I transgress and offend seemingly with every movement, but where inside myself, I feel deliciously exhilarated with every breath. Those are the choices. There is no middle ground, no safe bridge over or under for me to straddle.

Oh, why can I not choose to be good! And the answer mocks me: if I were truly good, there would be no need for choosing it.

MARCH 13, 1861

Today I had a social call, one made all the better by its being unexpected, as this is not the afternoon on which we normally receive visitors.

Miss Beckwith and I have been exchanging letters with regularity, yet in none of them did she mention that she would be in the vicinity of our Knightsbridge address, or that she planned to add our town house to her visiting itinerary. So you may imagine how shocked I was when the door chimed, and I was called to it a second later. There stood Miss Beckwith, resplendent in pink and white brushed flannel which perfectly complements her fair hair. She carried with her a little basket, which I discovered, to my delight, to contain a tiny cocker spaniel puppy.

I gasped a greeting, and then we adjourned to the sitting room, where I introduced her to my family. While they beamed approval, I invited her on a tour of the rest of the town house, which she readily agreed to.

When we reached my room I suggested we sit, as here we would have the opportunity to chat uninterrupted. I offered Caroline the armchair, while I took my favorite post at the window. There was a bit of initial awkwardness—after all, I have spoken to Caroline in person only once, and then exchanged letters with her—but this was soon overcome, and in not very much time we were conversing away like old friends. I asked after Miss Paxton, and Caroline said she's had no word as yet, but prays that everything will go smoothly and that she shall soon return to the Continent.

We discussed our respective families, and I explained that Leeds Hall, where my cousins are ensconced at present, is our ancestral property, to which Father donates a hefty sum for upkeep. The town house here belongs to Uncle Charles, but as he felt we might wish to have some variety during our stay, he and Josephine are happy to switch back and forth with us. Leeds Hall is open to us—and to any of our extended family—whenever we wish, and although I am proud that it remains in our hands, I cannot imagine myself ever seeking to establish residence there, as it is as medieval, drafty, and foreboding a manse as was ever erected.

Caroline told me that she has no relations in England, at least none of which she knows. She is here because her family has come to see her brother Harlow into university. She is staying at a property of some family friends called Linton Manor, which she says is large enough to encompass a small village. This seems to be the British norm—at least among the aristocracy. Bigger is better, and more space denotes more status. Neither Leeds Hall nor Linton can compare to Mersy Hall, and I am certain that Mersy Hall, in turn, could probably fit into some other palace as yet unknown to me. It is a mystery to me why there is so much animosity between England and the States, since it seems that in fact they share many of the same sacred notions.

At any rate, Caroline expressed her preference for the city to the country, and for her home in Chicago to any part of London. I have never visited the western section of our nation, but from Caroline's wild-and-woolly description of it, it seems a good bit less dull than our present address.

We talked on in this vein for a time, and when we felt we were thoroughly reacquainted, we looked about for another diversion. Caroline caught me eyeing her basket, so she reached inside and removed the puppy, who seemed eager for a diversion of his own. He peeked about the strange surroundings as if discovering the edge of a new world, and soon had us laughing at his preposterous antics. He's a darling little creature, gold-colored and with a short, wide-eyed face like an otter's. First he snuffled about the rug, then investigated in turn the bedskirt, the chair legs, and my feet. After a thorough tour of the room, he pawed at Caroline to be picked up, and soon fell contentedly asleep in her lap.

Then Caroline asked me what is new with me since my last letter. I almost hesitated, but thought, how shall I make any friends if I fail to trust them with my true sentiments? So I recounted to her the conversation with my parents regarding my removal to a "spa." She confessed to finding the whole thing barbaric and incredible, and I felt an obligation to present it to her fairly, so that she might not judge Mother and Father and Uncle Charles too harshly, and so I started back at the anecdote I had relayed at the Rogerses' party, the tale regarding Madame Zunia, and continued up to the present month, with my investigation of *The Lancet* and the confrontation which then ensued. I left out nothing of the altercation with Jeffrey Price, nor did I spare Caroline the sights and sounds I voluntarily put before myself during my forays into the city at night.

I spoke at some length, and then fell silent, wondering whether my would-be friend would exit the room in disgust, or make some polite excuse to leave, or simply say that she wishes no more of my company.

Instead she peered at me with her exceptional blue eyes. "I thought you a wit at the party, Arabella, but that's hardly all of you, is it?"

I replied that offensive as it all seemed, it was in fact consistent; I had done what my heart demanded I do, which for me makes the response of all of those in my circle even more inexplicable. "I am not bold, or a libertine, or a debaucher," I finished, staring at the floor.

"No." When I looked up I found that Caroline's eyes were still fixed upon me. "No, you are not. You are quite the heroine, and I congratulate you."

These were such effusive words of praise, so unexpected and firmly delivered, that I felt the blood course into my cheeks. I am sure Caroline noticed it, for she went on kindly, "No doubt, dear, your set is ill-used to a lady who seeks to know her world and become mistress of it, but, that being the case, who shall yield? You—with the whole world before you—or they?"

I replied that I had never considered the matter in this light before, but that perhaps in some sense I would have no choice except to yield, as I had now been presented with an ultimatum by my parents.

Caroline arched a brow. "You may yet yield in behavior without yielding in spirit. That is often the way with such things—we find a means of working within our bonds until the day comes when we are free to cast them off. Our own Negro populace is proof of that particular lesson."

"Oh, you mustn't think it's as bad as all that. They are only my family, after all, and I assure you, you needn't fear that they beat me with whips or harness me to the dray cart. It's only that perhaps—well, that I should like to move about now and then without a chaperone, or a shadow who pretends not to be there."

"But surely there are outside activities which would win the approval of your guardians without requiring their presence, no?"

I sighed. "Yes, but none that I have even the slightest interest in. Embroidery classes and discussions of cheap novels—I think I should prefer to stay inside if those are my only choices."

"Ah," Caroline smiled, "but that's where you are mistaken. They are not your only choices." I widened my eyes at her, expecting her to explain this cryptic statement further, but she put a finger to her lips. "Say no more. Only follow my lead when we return to your sitting rooms." I nodded my assent to this odd request.

"Now then," Caroline breezed on, changing the subject, "what of that other matter under discussion, the one concerning Mr. Forbes-Spencer? Have you given any thought to it, and should I be the instrument of your introduction, or have you decided to pass him on to your cold-blooded cousin?"

I laughed heartily at this. "Miss Beckwith, how dare you—how come you to presume that my cousin is cold-blooded? You've met her but once, as far as I know."

"One needn't always bite the apple to know that it's rotted at the core. Persephone's reputation precedes her, I'm afraid. Lady Forbes-Spencer was less than thrilled to hear that her darling had set his sights upon her, seeing as Percy is rumored to be an ambitious bit of baggage. She confided as much to my mother, and so the intelligence was passed on to me."

"I see." I was still smiling. "Well, I can confirm it for you. Percy has declined the gentleman for the very reasons his mother feared. He hasn't enough in the way of prospects yet to pique her interest. But as for me—" I shrugged. "If you can assure me that he is at least worthy company, and not a total bounder, then I suppose I'm game, as I have little else to do."

"Lady Forbes-Spencer will be relieved to hear it, although I'd guess your being an American will curb her enthusiasm somewhat. Nonetheless, I'll pass the word on, and you must let me know what ensues from there."

I agreed to this, and then we took note of the time and decided we should return to the parlor, after which Caroline would be on her way. As we descended the stairs, she asked me whether I should like to have the spaniel pup for a gift. I would have loved to say yes, but as a dog is near to an infant in terms of its care, I think this is an indulgence I must pass up for the moment. I told Caroline as much, and thanked her for the offer. Whereupon she replied, "Not at all. I'm happy to know you are so diligently responsible." Then she turned on the step and whispered, "Now remember what I said—follow my lead when I make ready to depart, and we'll see if we can't arrange a reward for that fine character of yours."

We reached the parlor, and sat making polite conversation for some minutes with Mother and Father, while Richard stared at Caroline as if she were a fairy vision landed upon our sofa. When Caroline rose to leave, Mother escorted us to the front door, whereupon Caroline turned to inquire of her, "By the bye, Mrs. Leeds, are you at all interested in the habits of tiny creatures? Small animals?"

"Small animals? Well, I am fond of certain pets, but it should depend on the variety—what sort of small animals have you in mind?"

"Oh, for example—insects. Beetles. Earthworms. That sort of thing. And amphibians—toads and the like. Living ones, of course, to be studied at close range."

Mother's lips pursed. "Heavens, no—I've no interest in such beasts. In fact, I imagine I'd find their proximity quite disturbing."

"A shame," Caroline said, "for I was discussing with Arabella a new study group which a naturalist acquaintance has begun. She cultivates these creatures in artificial environments, you see, and notes their habits, and has begun a small circle for the purposes of discussing them. Arabella is quite interested—aren't you, dear—" And here she raised her brows at me, and I recalled her instruction that I follow her lead. "Oh yes," I piped up, and she continued without pause. "—so I have agreed to ask her whether she has an extra chair available for the duration of the group. Were you interested, Mrs. Leeds, I should try to secure one for you, but as you are not—well, I'm sure you won't mind if Arabella participates."

"I suppose not," Mother said, "so long as the instructress comes recommended, with appropriate qualifications."

"You may rest assured that she does. In fact, you might ask your sister-in-law Mrs. Josephine Leeds about her—Miss Elizabeth Ashe, the lady's name is, and she's tutored members of the royal family."

"How lovely," Mother fairly beamed. "If it interests you, Arabella—"

"Oh, yes," I chirped again, feeling like a shuttlecock between two rackets.

"Well, then, it's settled." Caroline stepped onto the porch. "I thank you for your hospitality, Mrs. Leeds, and please do relay my thanks to your husband as well. It has been a pleasure." She turned to me. "Arabella, would you care to see me to the corner so that I might find a hansom?"

"Of course," I said, and then Mother shut the door amidst more wavings and good-byes.

When we reached the end of the walk, I burst upon Caroline in a torrent. "*Insects*, Caroline? Toads? I am sorry—you may think me a terrible ingrate—but compelling as they are, I don't know that I'm prepared to spend an evening in the company of *toads* just now."

"Hush, Arabella, and give me room to explain myself—"

And so I hushed. And so did she explain, at some length, as we walked toward the end of the path so that she might find a cab.

And that is all I shall tell you of that conversation, friend, for now.

MARCH 15, 1861

Aunt Josephine is apparently quite perturbed that her daughter has passed up a chance at Mr. Carter Forbes-Spencer. It seems he is better situated than Percy imagined—two of his female relatives are Ladies-in-Waiting to the royals—and would have been quite the prize catch, had Percy in fact caught him. Aunt Jo is trying to appear valiant in the face of disaster, but it's clear what her fondest wish would be: she would have me relinquish my own claim upon the young man, refuse him so that Percy might reenter the race—she has boldly hinted as much, without saying it outright.

But I have no intention of accommodating her. Miss Beckwith has passed my goodwill on to Carter, and I am quite looking forward to a bit of company, not to mention masculine interest—at least I know this to be the sort of which my parents wholeheartedly approve.

Aunt Jo, knowing that I mean to frustrate her, has resorted—as is her wont—to disparaging my new friends before Mother. I am amazed to report that she was able to dig up no dirt concerning Caroline—being new to the Empire, the Beckwiths are outside the range of her prying. She managed only to discover that the family raises cattle, and has acquired a good deal of money through the enterprise, in addition to what Mr. Beckwith brought with him to the marriage. Mrs. Beckwith is both a Quaker and politically active—disturbing facts to Aunt Jo—but she is also quite well regarded among those British nobility who share her somewhat modernist sentiments. So there is little to be gained from attacking her, although that has rarely stopped Aunt Jo in the past.

Louella Paxton, however, was quite a different story. For here is a family well known in London, its foibles on view before the entire population. It seems that Louella's father is an American by birth, his own family having owned property in Louisiana for several generations. But Mr. Paxton is an eccentric and an international; he appears to have had no use for the settled life of Southern gentry, and instead has been traveling the globe since coming of age. He met his wife, Louella's mother, in Paris, and fell at once to courting her. She is titled, and in possession of a great deal of land, but her family's working cash was dwindling, and so her match to Mr. Paxton was a fortuitous one for both parties. Aunt Jo maintains that Mr. Paxton is a rake and an upstart—he is reputed to be very handsome, and to have applied his considerable charms to wooing Mrs. Paxton so that he might have a pedigree affixed to his wealth. Mrs. Paxton, on the other hand—and again according to Aunt Jo, whose word must be swallowed with a teacup of salt—is said to be something of a featherhead, but not so much so that she did not see the advantage of securing fresh capital for the upkeep of her estates and vineyards in southern France.

This is the union which produced Miss Paxton and her brother, but Aunt Jo's formal report did not conclude there. She proceeded from a discussion of the parents to one of the children, and here she found her true mark. For Louella enjoys something of a reputation among those who know the family—and there are many among Aunt Jo's set who do. Louella is "odd," Aunt Jo took the liberty of informing Mother. She is far too bold for the tastes of even her own mother, who has made no secret of her frustration with her daughter. Louella's father, however, seems to indulge her when it is convenient to him: his decision to let her travel to the States to conclude the family's business there is an example of the careless application he makes of his authority.

Louella's brother Thomas—whom she called the "dolt," and who gives every indication of being one—is considered by Aunt Jo's set to be the family success. This amazes me, as the difference in quality—not to mention intellect—between the two siblings was obvious to me after only one meeting.

But Thomas is just the sort whom that group would find appealing. He struck me as pretentious and facile, wise enough to defer to the British sensibility and play along with it, all the while laughing behind his hand at its conventions. Oh, perhaps I am being unfair, but I cannot help thinking what a fine match Thomas Paxton might make for my own cousin Percy. The two of them are adroit social climbers, and pretenders to gentility, which to me is not a matter of blood but of character. Though they are full siblings, Louella possesses that noble quality—it is evident in her spirit—while her brother merely mimics it.

I hope such fakery will not sway Mother before she has even had a chance to meet Louella and judge for herself, but already she is warning me against my association with Miss Paxton, dropping rather pointed hints that perhaps I, with my present troubles, had best avoid a girl known to be at the very least unconventional.

MARCH 22, 1861

I hope you will excuse the lapse in my attentions, friend, but I have been most busy of late, and have had scant time to bring you up to date on my activities. Let me recap briefly, and promise you that I shall try not to let so many days pass in between my visits to your welcoming pages.

I've wrestled with the question of whether or not to commit to paper the incident I am about to relate. But considering the precautions I've taken thus far, I think the risk is an acceptable one, and so I shall go forward.

Shortly after my last entry, I contacted Miss Beckwith to let her know I wished to accept her kind offer regarding Miss Ashe's "naturist study" group. Part of me was atingle even as I sat before my tablet, but I forced myself to write the words, and asked that she send reply by the messenger who'd carried my letter. She did so, with the result that I found myself bound for a meeting with Miss Ashe only a day later.

That distinguished lady keeps apartments quite close to Hyde Park, not so very far from Uncle Charles's own home, and so Caroline and I hastened there by hansom, after Caroline oh-so-gaily assured Mother that I should enjoy this tutorial mightily. She led me from the house with a dazzling smile and a toss of her blonde curls, and Mother smiled after us benevolently; but I wonder if Aunt Jo's troublemaking has not set her to being uneasy somewhere in her heart.

At any rate, we were soon arrived at Miss Ashe's, and I was quite surprised at the splendor in which this supposed mere governess dwelt. I was escorted into a large town house whose foyers dwarfed many conventional parlors. They conveyed a sense of subdued wealth and rarefied tastes, what with their crystal chandeliers, marbled floors, and ornate mouldings. The formal dining room, the grand parlor, the hallway—where I am certain the artwork is the genuine product of Old Masters—only served to enhance the impression of old and well-bred fortunes. Caroline ignored my insolent eyeballing, and led me through the entirety of the house to a yard beyond the back anteroom's double doors. There I saw an elaborate glass-and-iron greenhouse, where our hostess was to be found tending to her pastimes.

Miss Ashe turned out to be a tall and imposing woman with blondish coarse hair pulled away from her face. Her features were regular but undistinguished, although she wore a pair of spectacles on her nose, which gave her light eyes an owlish cast. I would have guessed her to be somewhere in her forties, despite the taut skin and high color which made any true assessment of her age difficult; she had one of those faces which might as well have been thirty as sixty. She greeted us—or, I should say, me—with a gaze that was at once interested and imperious, and then she gave Caroline a nod, and invited us in.

Her greenhouse was heated to a junglelike steaminess. It was a wonder of climbing foliage, exploding blooms, and the hums and twitterings of various forms of animal life. The naturalist label is no understatement on Miss Ashe's part; she had created within the latticed glass sphere behind her house a world approximating some exotic tropical paradise, and she must have done so only out of the profoundest devotion to her pursuit.

She spread her arms wide in a gesture of welcome, and as she did so I saw a huge transparent-winged darning needle whiz past her hand and disappear into the greenery behind her.

"Miss Ashe," Caroline said, unruffled, as I ducked frantically, "may I present to you Miss Arabella Leeds, the young lady I was telling you about when last we spoke."

Miss Ashe tilted her head back to peer beneath her specs, and gave me a thin smile. "I take it you wish to join the naturalist circle," she said, in clipped British tones.

"Well—yes, please, I do," I replied, wondering whether this was the proper answer. Perhaps there was some sort of password I was expected to employ so as to legitimize my interest.

"Follow me, then," Miss Ashe beckoned. "I should like to show you about my habitat." She stalked off, her apron ribbons fluttering in the moist breeze. She wound about so many potted plants and rooted trees that I feared losing her even within this small space, and was able to keep up only by following the sound of her voice, which floated back toward me through the heavy air.

"The temperature in this sphere," she was saying, "is kept at a regular eighty degrees. This is accomplished by piping warm air in from several stoves. But it is also necessary that there be moisture, and so water is drawn constantly, and sprayed from spigots in the frameworks. It is essential that the balance between temperature and moisture be maintained, for without it everything here would die."

I was so intent upon listening to her that I was startled by the shrill call of a bright-green parrot, gazing down at me from a vine. So there were birds, too, in this extraordinary dwelling, I thought, and hardly had I gotten over my surprise at this when a small snake of some sort slithered past my feet into the undergrowth of ferns.

Finally Miss Ashe came to a stop, and turned to face me.

"This is an artificial world, you see, although it mimics the real one very precisely. Everything here is a question of balance. Each form of life depends on another for its survival. The birds depend upon the smaller creatures—the toads, the frogs—for the occasional meal, although I feed them seeds and nuts as well. The frogs and lizards depend upon the insects. The insects depend upon the flowers and plants. And the plants depend upon the insects, who pollinate and fertilize them. All are needed, none are greater or less."

She paused, and I realized she had stopped before a small wooden box which reminded me of a layer cake, with its several horizontal divisions. It took me but a moment to recognize the apiary, and had I had any doubts, the drone of bees zooming in and out soon would have dispelled them.

Miss Ashe regarded the little box for a long moment, while I eyed my clothing for signs of errant bees lighting upon it and possibly crawling within its folds. Then my hostess continued, in a strangely distant tone, "Behold the hive, Miss Leeds." I followed her gaze, and beheld. "Notice the freedom with which each tiny worker sweeps from the doorstep into the air, then whisks away upon gossamer wing to pollinate and gather food."

I made some appreciative noise, wondering what on earth the woman was getting at.

"Notice how each negotiates the circumference of this enclosure as if it is the world entire, without the slightest knowledge that beyond lies a greater, vaster world, and that they are kept captive here by forces they little suspect. And notice, too, another thing about those workers, Miss Leeds: they are all of them sisters, born of the same mother; they run their universe efficiently and effectively, and they would make the finest use of freedom, but they are prevented from utilizing it by what they do not know." I nodded, in what I hoped was a polite fashion, then looked behind me for Caroline. Sure enough, she had followed me to where I now stood; I pursed my lips and widened my eyes at her, so that she might know I was finding Miss Ashe not a little odd.

I had thought the gesture subtle enough, but Miss Ashe caught it even before its intended recipient, and turned to me with a hard set to her mouth.

"I see you wish to make light of your first lesson here, Miss," she said. I felt myself blush pink, but she cut off any reply I might have made. "That's well and good. It tells me you have no reason to take life too seriously, that you have never suffered the most dire consequences of whatever behavior served to bring you to my doorstep. I sincerely hope that this shall remain the case, that you shall always be able to greet new situations with humor, my dear. But I must warn you that some things must be accorded extra weight, and your admission to this circle must be one of them."

She fixed me with glittering blue eyes, and I felt myself pinned in place like a specimen upon a board. "I must know before I accept you here that you understand the ramifications of what you undertake. If you would be attached to my good name and reputation, you must prove yourself capable of comprehending and following my edicts to the letter."

"I meant no disrespect, Madame," I murmured, gazing at the floor. For once I found myself without either witticism or defiant air; Sauce, it seemed, had forfeited a goodly amount of her pepper.

"Not to worry," Miss Ashe said a little bit—a very little bit—more gently. "My expectations are not so great as to preclude you from meeting them, once you accept the necessity of doing so. I warn you harshly only for your own good."

"I understand, Madame," I said, my eyes still aimed at the ground.

When she had decided that I appeared contrite enough, Miss Ashe launched into a long dissertation on what would be required of me if I were admitted to her secret society. I kept my gaze fixed upon her throughout the duration of this speech, although I was mightily distracted by the sensation that I was being assessed—nay, stalked—by pairs of eyes, both warm and cold, which were hidden from my view. At the end of her lecture Miss Ashe asked, "Have you any questions?"

I shook my head, and replied that I did not.

"Well, then. Should you think of any, I'm sure Miss Beckwith can assist you, but in the meanwhile I should like to welcome you, and wish you well wherever your flights shall take you." She held out her paper-skinned hands for me to grasp, and squeezed with a surprising fervor. Then she turned on her heel, and beckoned both of us to follow her into the main dwelling, so that she might give me certain papers to review and keep.

Within ten minutes we'd concluded our business, and Caroline and I were again standing outside before the town house's grand doors. I shook my head as if to clear it of the odd impressions my visit with Miss Ashe had placed there. Caroline chuckled and put a hand upon my arm, and gave me a wink as well.

"I'm sorry if you were caught off guard, dear—I couldn't warn you ahead of time, as I've given my word to Elizabeth that I'll let her do the questioning and explaining, and say no more to candidates than is necessary. But you've passed muster, you're accepted—I hope you shall forgive me the ordeal."

I frowned at her, but I find it is impossible to be angry with Caroline, particularly when she is standing before me, and within another moment we were laughing once again and falling upon each other's shoulders.

"My God, what a goblin of a woman!" I gasped. "It's no wonder she's fond of lizards and insects—no human would have her company!"

Caroline demurred. "She's a strange one, I suppose. But very wise, and so well traveled—you shall see. And you charmed her, Arabella—no, really, you did—she doesn't grasp just anyone's hand. And see, she instructed me to give you these."

I looked down and saw, in Caroline's outstretched palm, two ornate iron keys.

"All of Miss Ashe's protégés have these—you'll need them to exit and reenter the property. This smaller one opens the atrium door, and Miss Ashe's garden gate. You exit that way, and follow the alley behind her house to the wrought-iron door on the next street. You let yourself out with the big key. When you return, you follow the same route, and end up back in the atrium.

"Never, ever use the front door of the house, except when you first arrive for the evening. That way it all looks quite normal to anyone escorting you. Only obey the time constraints, and use your common sense—for remember, if you are caught at some illicit entertainment, Miss Ashe shan't provide an alibi. She'll claim to be as shocked as any at the use you made of her noble enterprise. That's how she's managed to keep her reputation untarnished all these years."

"I shall do nothing to embarrass her, I assure you—I wish only an evening's innocent privacy, nothing more."

"Of course you won't, Arabella. I am only warning you so as to feel I've done my job thoroughly. Now, I believe we should celebrate your success, by taking full advantage of your first night of freedom!"

Although I doubted I had "charmed" Elizabeth Ashe, I did agree that some sort of milestone had been reached, and that celebrations were in order, so I set off with Caroline to see how we might accomplish them.

Despite the heady sense that we were at liberty to come and go wherever in the city we wished, we did nothing that night which might have compromised our good names. Rather, we walked past several sweet shops and purchased bags full of chocolate petits fours, which then required mugs of steaming hot chocolate to wash them down. We ate and drank on the sidewalk like beggars, our breath freezing behind us, the warm liquid giving off clouds of steam. Passersby scowled at us as if we were mad, but we ignored them and proceeded along, arm in arm, laughing boisterously as if we were the only two inhabitants of the world. What a sensational feeling it is to walk along the street, fearing nothing, with the conviction that any place you choose to visit is in fact your rightful place, without judgment or restriction attached to it! What would it be like, I wonder, to walk so to the greatest extent, to enter any theatre, any pub, any shop, without perusing eyes and upbraiding tongues following along behind?

We took our pleasure somewhat, at least, on this night, and Caroline dropped me at my door promptly at ten o'clock. Mother was still awake, and inquired as to the lateness of the hour, but Caroline smoothly explained that Miss Ashe had held us for a time after the lecture, as is her practice. Then she bade me good night, and I saw her out and kissed Mother on the cheek—with a little guilt, perhaps—and retired to my bedchamber with no one any the wiser regarding the evening's activities. How deceitful I felt, and yet how aglow, how enlivened by possibility! Only when I recognized this sensation and named it did I realize how long it has been since I've felt it, and how greatly I have missed it.

Two days after my inspection by Miss Ashe, I was contacted by Caroline regarding yet another meeting arranged by her hand: this one concerned Mr. Carter Forbes-Spencer, my admirer from the Rogerses' ball. Having gotten my go-ahead, she had apprised him of my willingness to see him, and had suggested a date one day hence, for which she needed my confirmation. When I agreed to the evening in question, she informed me that Mr. Forbes-Spencer had secured tickets to the opera—*The Magic Flute* was to be performed—and that he and I would be joined by herself and a companion. This pleased me greatly, as it would make the occasion much less awkward for both my escort and myself. I asked Mother and Father for permission to go, and this was readily granted; as predicted, they were more than happy to see me off with Mr. Forbes-Spencer, and it was not necessary for me to schedule my meeting during one of Miss Ashe's tutorial nights.

On the day of the opera I waited for Caroline's arrival with not a little trepidation. I would have felt so anyway, at the prospect of meeting a potential beau, but in addition to this a rather terrible thought had crossed my mind just that morning: suppose I was not one of the two girls Carter Forbes-Spencer had spied at the party? Suppose a mistake had been made, and he was expecting to meet another young lady entirely? How humiliating it should be were he to take one look in my direction and mutter, "Who the devil is this, and where is the real object of my affections?" Imagining this absurd scene used up not a little of my energy, and I was feeling rather drained by the time I'd completed my toilette, dressed in my new crimson gown, donned my brooch and gloves, and had my hair arranged by Lucy.

When Caroline's carriage pulled up and three figures stepped down, I further strained myself at the foyer window trying to discern who might be whom. There were two young men, one of them Caroline's escort—but which one? I was relieved to note that either would have been acceptable appearancewise. They were both tall and blonde, one having a sober, long face with a noble nose, the other a mischievous handsomeness and somewhat lighter hair.

When they arrived at the door and the introductions were made, my questions were answered, and doubts laid to rest. The noble-faced, sloe-eyed gentleman was Mr. Spencer; I knew it at once because, happily enough, he lit up upon seeing me, and said gallantly, "At last, I set eyes again upon my inamorata, thanks to Caroline Beckwith!" So I was not the wrong girl after all.

I was surprised to learn, however, that the other young man is not Caroline's beau but her brother Harlow, the same one as is studying at university. Once I knew this I felt I should have guessed it, as he looks so much like her, having the same compact features, upturned nose, and twinkling eyes. He also has that American casualness which I've so missed; it was apparent even in the way he leaned against the doorframe upon an elbow, crossing one long leg over the other at the ankle as if he were dressed in coveralls rather than evening clothes. Caroline, by the way, looked absolutely radiant, again in the fresh and healthful way only Americans can; she was wearing a gown of off-white with a white fur cape, against which her lips shone pink as berries.

We set off for Covent Garden, and all the way Harlow kept us entertained by making up hilarious and absurd histories for the landmarks we were passing. He did this with such skill, at the same time weaving in truth with his outrageous lies, that we were hard-pressed to know one from the other. Although he aimed a few swipes at the English gentility, Carter took it well in stride, smiling and glancing at me with a wink when Harlow tossed off something particularly witty.

At the hall itself we made our way to what turned out to be the Spencers' box, and I was surprised to see that we were pointed at and whispered about as we passed the other patrons—or at least Carter was. I had no idea his family was so well placed; no wonder Aunt Josephine was wringing her hands over Percy's hardheadedness. As for myself, I enjoyed being at the fringes of this limelight, but as it had nothing to do with me, I could hardly feel flattered by it.

The four of us took appropriate seats in the velvet-draped loge, and I noted that Carter used the excuse of stretching his limbs in order to drape an arm along the back of my chair. I was not sure whether to allow him this liberty—after all, it could have been strictly a matter of comfort, and to push him away might have appeared overly presumptuous, and even rude. Then again, I'm sure young men have been using this ruse for eons so as to gain access to the proximity of young ladies, precisely because it is so ambiguous a gesture. At any rate, I did not move his hand, not least of all because I realized it should be the more interesting for me if it stayed where it was; but this decision did not suit me entirely either, and I spent the first act in an anxiety as to whether I was expected to push away the offending limb (or discreetly move my chair) or not.

This dilemma was not the only source of my discomfort. Although I'd noticed nothing amiss upon putting it on, the crimson gown had begun to feel somehow constraining from almost the moment I'd sat down. Confined to my chair, not moving a muscle, I found myself becoming more and more bothered: the dress's fabric caused me to itch, the bodice determined to squeeze the very breath from me, the tip of a stay drove into my rib. Each adjustment I made only worsened the situation, placing some other means of irritation in contact with my body, until I thought I should either jump up or be driven to distraction.

At last I could stand it no more, and so, just after good Tamino had begun his ordeal within the Temple of Wisdom, I excused myself and blundered down the back steps, into the ornate parlor reserved for ladies in the loges. Once inside, I checked to make certain no one else was about, and then I stripped off the bodice, and loosened the corset grommet by grommet. Then I indulged in a delicious stretch, reaching my arms up over my head and balancing on my tiptoes, as if to touch the dizzyingly high and sparkling chandelier which hung from the ceiling. I twirled before the mirrors, studied my face in various degrees of light, and arranged myself upon the settees, which were strategically placed to accommodate the frequent faints and spells of Englishwomen.

Of course the gown seemed even tighter when I donned it again, but at least my few moments of freedom had provided me a measure of relief.

I re-dressed with care, and could, at this point, have rejoined my companions, but I did not—at least, not right away. For on this evening even the heavenly music of Mozart had lost a portion of its charm, the drama striking some irritating and discordant note within me. *Oh Arabella, you are becoming such a cross and contrary creature,* I berated myself, but nonetheless I stayed put in the parlor, examining the potted ferns and wondering if Miss Ashe would know their names and origins, as well as how to care for them—for these ferns were brown and stunted, unlike that lady's own robust and verdant ones.

At last, knowing my absence should be remarked upon if I delayed any longer, I made my way back to the box. When the final note of the opera was sung, I rose up from my chair, ready to depart—only to be forced back down again by an endless procession of curtain calls.

Finally, though, the performance was truly over. The lamps rose on the spectators, and we were released from our duties as audience members. It took us fully another quarter hour to reach the street, however, for at each turn Carter was assailed by jewel-clad ladies hallooing, or gentlemen in evening dress piping up with a throaty "I say there!" Caroline, Harlow, and I were duly introduced as "friends from the Colonies," and although no mention was made of it, I could feel the eyes which focused upon me, I being, no doubt, Carter's companion for the evening. I was glad to escape the hall for the fresh air of the street, although it was now drizzling, and a damp wind had begun to blow about.

As soon as Carter had located his landau and driver among the throng, we climbed in, and the top was raised to shut out the evening chill. "Wasn't that a fine job they did onstage tonight!" Carter exclaimed. "If there's anything more sublime than Mozart's vision of romance, I shouldn't know what it is." I was discreetly scratching at my wrist and did not answer him, but I saw Caroline throw a look to her brother, who frowned back at her and then announced, "I'm famished, Carter, what say we drive to that little tavern—what's it called, the Ramsbottom Inn—for some mutton stew and a pint?"

"Are you mad, Beckwith—slumming, in good dress?"

"Not at all, what better way to slum than in a top hat?"

"Oh, honestly, Harlow! I'll not go dragging these skirts over a floor covered in sawdust, if you don't mind," Caroline scolded her brother.

"Well, it's the best I can do, mutton and so forth, as I'm a poor student now, and must count my pennies."

"In the first place," Carter broke in, "it's called the Lamb's Hock Inn. In the second place, it's insufferable, as you well know, so suppose I treat us to some real lamb, and Champagne, and you can reimburse me when you're a famous scientist, Sir Beckwith."

Harlow grinned. "That was the idea all along, old boy! What say you, Miss Leeds, will Champagne meet with your approval?"

"Actually," I said, making my eyes as wide as possible, "I should like to see the Ramsbottom."

"Would you indeed," Caroline smirked, and then Carter said, "It's the *Lamb's Hock*, my dear," and the four of us burst out laughing.

We were seated immediately at the plush hotel restaurant Carter had chosen, and although the gaiety we'd felt in the carriage still pervaded the party, we were forced to rein it in somewhat, as the dining room was filled with terribly proper diners, all going about their terribly proper business.

We had made our way through a meal of wonderfully butterflied lamb and were nibbling tarts when Carter launched into the final anecdote of the evening, a story of how the previous summer he'd called for his manservant, then searched him out up and down, only to find him bathing in a river on the grounds quite naked—as was the young housemaid he was frolicking with. According to Carter, the lad had been so startled that he'd grabbed the first thing at hand with which to wrap himself—and this happened to be the poor girl's skirts, which left her stranded in the river with no choice but to scream and curse her companion from the water.

We laughed at this, and then Carter, shaking his head, declared, "Ah, the common man, he'll outlive us all, and have a jollier time doing it, I believe. I should have liked to dive right into the water myself that day, it was one of those which makes the very leaves droop on the trees."

"Why didn't you, then?" I asked him, shrugging. From the corner of my eye, I caught the faint mirthful curving of Caroline's cheek.

"Is this another of your jokes, Miss Ramsbottom? We cannot all be Papageno, dear girl"—we were back to *The Magic Flute*, I noted—"and immerse ourselves in the sensual. Some of us must be Tamino, and take on the guardianship of civilization."

"All of which means you should rather perspire on a hot day than jump into the river for a swim."

"I should rather perspire as a gentleman and do right by my heritage as one, you obtuse vixen, than descend into the fleeting pleasure of a life lived moment to moment."

There was a pause, which Harlow broke by heaving a protracted sigh.

"Alas, Spencer, you should have been such a pleasant distraction in your maid's set of skirts."

On this absurd note, the dinner was ended. The bill was tendered and we left the hotel, driving home in the same frivolous mood which had marked our departure from the opera—and if the crimson gown still pinched and clawed at me I was able to push it from my mind, knowing I should soon be able to throw it off.

When the carriage arrived at my door Carter asked if he might escort me inside. On the way up the path he asked to be permitted to see me again, and I agreed, although I wondered why he wished the company of an "obtuse vixen"—as much as I wondered why I had behaved as one. He suggested we plan on the following night, and told me he would enjoy visiting a bit with my parents, if I had no objection to this. I did not, and so the date was set, for a half past five on the evening hence.

That next night Carter passed the better of two hours chatting with Mother and Father, while I delighted Mother (and caused Richard to roll his eyes) by sitting demurely upon the couch and concentrating upon some needlework. I suppose I was feeling a bit guilty for the way I'd run out at the opera the previous evening, and for the "vixenish" barb I'd aimed at Carter over dinner. It was all quite tedious, particularly the interval during which Carter and Father excused themselves to partake of ancient cognac and smelly cigars in the back study. I made light of my boredom to Carter when we were at the door bidding good night (although I could not be loud about it, since of course Lucy was on hand to chaperone us), but to my surprise Carter maintained with a straight face that he'd found the evening quite interesting, and my parents delightful. I assumed he was attempting to be polite, having just met my family, and when he requested yet another outing with me, this one in the afternoon two days hence, I again readily accepted. Mother later hinted that perhaps I should have refused, so as to make myself appear busy with another prospect, but I discarded that suggestion, and the plans were set.

On that afternoon excursion, we arranged ourselves under woolen blankets and took a surrey along the Thames, which must have been a scenic and lovely river in Shakespeare's time, but which now is at various spots a reeking cesspool afloat with waste. We tried our best to enjoy the vistas while ignoring the pollution, and Carter bemoaned the sad state of his island's natural treasures.

Then he asked me questions about that vast, untouched heathenish wilderness known as the United States. He has a kind if somewhat intense manner, and his notions of America are quite comical; I rather do enjoy talking to him, despite the conservative bent in his thinking which becomes downright stuffy at times.

I know that I should never trust him at this point with the episode involving Jeffrey Price, though, nor would I dare confide to him even a sliver of what I confide to you, friend, or to Caroline Beckwith. But perhaps that situation can change, considering we've only just met. Perhaps I am underestimating Carter somewhat.

At any rate, I know I am taken with his serious gray eyes, and I have a fantasy—again, I confide this to you alone—of winding a curl of his fine ash-blonde hair around a finger, to discover whether it's as soft as it looks. I do as well like to lean upon his shoulder, which is strong and wide; he somewhat dwarfs me, but this is not an unpleasant sensation. Best of all, Mother and Father approve of him so wholeheartedly that I have been given *carte blanche* to travel unchaperoned, so long as Mr. Forbes-Spencer is my escort.

On the whole I am quite enjoying my association with Carter, despite the rocky start, and I have little doubt that he feels likewise, as he surely would not bother soliciting my company otherwise. He helps me to curb what I suppose is that excessive sauciness which I simply cannot suppress, and when in his company I feel myself partially the girl I was a year ago. Perhaps there can yet be a meeting between Miss Ashe's most recent pupil and the lady upon Carter's sturdy arm. He and I have been apart for days now, but are scheduled to see each other tomorrow night; to that meeting I look forward with keen anticipation.

MARCH 23, 1861

This is the end of my association with young men. I cannot figure them one way or the other; I cannot behave with them as I know I should, and to behave otherwise invites nothing but torment and censure. I should know better, and now I do, so let there be a finish to it all; if I must spend my days alone and die a spinster, I shall not mind it in the least.

Tonight I kept my appointment with Carter, as planned, and we took in a local chess tournament in which he professed to be interested. It was a pleasant enough evening, as we had dinner at one of the social clubs to which he belongs; the tournament was entertaining, if not so thrilling as the races or even a good game of Bridge. Afterward, Carter suggested that we visit one of his family's lesser estates, and I agreed, thinking it high time I met some of his relations, as I have not yet had the opportunity to call on them formally.

The home to which he took me was lovely indeed. It was not so large as Leeds Hall, but cozy and exquisitely decorated; the only odd thing was that it appeared to be empty. The door was opened by one of those mouldy septuagenarian butlers England seems to produce in abundance, but aside from him and a similarly slab-faced parlormaid there seemed to be not a soul in residence.

I was ready to comment upon this, but then I realized that of course Carter knew the house to be empty, and had spirited us here for just that reason. There was an instant when I considered refusing to enter. Certainly a year ago I would have refused. I knew that Cousin Constance—and Anne or Percy for that matter—would have turned right round and climbed back into the carriage, but I am not any of them, nor the girl I was, and so of course I crossed the threshold, figuring on the rapport Carter and I had established to make this dubious decision acceptable. It thrilled me to think perhaps he had just a bit of the scamp about him as well, that perhaps we were more of one mind than I'd realized.

He drew me into a sitting room where the lamps were so low as to throw the faintest glow upon the furnishings; everything in the room appeared to be covered in either green or red velvet, with dark hardwood effects. It was the perfect setting for a romantic tryst, and of course this was exactly what Carter had in mind. He opened a bottle of lively Champagne, downed a quick glass, and handed me one. Then, when I had composed myself upon a *chaise longue*, he knelt before me, loosed my fingers from the glass's stem, and took my ungloved hand in his own.

For a frantic moment I wondered if he did not have a marriage proposal in mind. I had no idea what I should do if this were the case—I was fond of him, but did not love him, and although my mild ardor might later be fanned into flame, this was no wager upon which to build a lifelong union.

I was not, however, forced into confronting that difficulty. For what Carter intended was not a proposal, but the beginnings of a seduction, which so intrigued me that I made no move to halt it.

Kneeling before me, he used his free hand to reach forward and tilt my face toward him. "Arabella," he murmured a tad drunkenly, "you do so entrance me. You have uniquely compelled me, my little vixen, from the moment I saw you."

I was not yet feeling the effects of the Champagne. "Well, that's not quite true, Carter. I do recall my cousin Percy compelled you as well. So whatever your feeling upon viewing me, I would say it is improper to describe it as 'unique.' "

"Ah, you are so refreshingly literal," Carter said, shifting on his knees. He let go my hand and replaced my Champagne flute in it, and rose to sit beside me. Then he leaned into me with a little wisp of a smile upon his lips. "All right, O Aloof One. Tell me, how can I convince you that you occupy a special space within my heart?"

"I don't know," I replied. "How can you?"

"Puckish girl!" Carter exclaimed, pinching me upon the cheek, and I wondered why indeed I was being so "puckish" when only an hour ago I'd felt quite the sedate and proper lady by Carter's side. I realized I was teasing him, and enjoying it as I had all along, and saw no real reason to desist, as I meant no harm.

He refilled my glass with Champagne, and now I did indeed feel the warmth of the alcohol making its way to my head. Two glasses is rather more than I usually partake of, but the sensation was not in the least unpleasant.

"Now, tell me how I shall win you, Arabella, and make your request outrageous—in fact, the more outrageous the better."

I thought for a moment. "If you insist—I suppose I can dig into my brain to see what might be an acceptable token of your esteem. Let us see . . . First, Carter, dear, I should have a lock of your hair—but from the forehead, not the back—so as to prove that you are not vain beyond any woman's vanity regarding its prettiness." I waited, giddy, to see what he should do, and to my complete amusement he grabbed a letter opener from the nearby desk, and sliced through a twist of his mane right there, leaving a shorn portion above his left eye.

"Here," he said, bowing as he handed it to me, "keep it close to your heart, and never say I neglected to make myself look the fool for you."

I was giggling, and Carter's eyes danced as well; it was a game, of course, but a good one, at which I thought we should both prove adroit players.

"What else would you have me do? Order away, cruel and wicked Salome, any prophet's head upon a platter is yours for the asking."

"Even though I've not danced for you?" I winked. "You do flatter me, sir. Very well, then—if you would have me keep your locks close to my heart, you must guess the color of the chemise I wear, under which I shall put them." I knew this to be quite risqué of me, but where would be the point in supplying only tame requests?

Carter glared at the carpeting, cogitating. Then his head popped up. "Blue!" he cried.

"No, sir, you are wrong. It is white." And then, to prove I did not lie, I reached a finger into the top of my bodice, and pulled a piece of the chemise through for him to see.

At this his eyes fairly popped, and he smacked a hand to his forehead to affect some posture of torment. I thought this a rather excessive reaction to a bit of plain cotton cloth, but I am no expert in the vagaries of male passion and what excites it. Carter seemed to fall into a semiswoon, and then, before I knew quite what was happening, he lunged almost atop me and began pressing his lips to my neck.

"You cherub—you little tart—just a kiss—that's all I ask, but I must have it—" he gasped between assaults on my flesh. Yes, this was the moment when I should have pushed him away with all my might, when I should have fled his attentions and confusing endearments. But the truth—before God, the sad truth—was that I was enjoying them, and I cannot claim I was won over in ignorance, for I knew where he wished to lead me, and trusted both of us that it should be a point mutually agreed upon, and safely withdrawn from. Yes, I was enjoying myself, so much so that I did not object when he backed up a bit, took my face in his hands, and kissed me upon the lips.

In fact I was feeling such a pleasant heat over every inch of my skin that I decided I should like to raise its temperature a notch. I had read of a technique in one of Aunt Jo's novels which was not mentioned in Mr. Acton's *Lancet* article, but I thought I might try it anyway, and so, when I felt Carter's mouth contact my own, I opened it a tad and ran my tongue lightly over his lips, and then inside them. Yes, I did this, knowing I played with fire, but again relying on the understanding between us to countenance this liberty.

Ah, well! Had I been thinking as Constance or Anne or Percy would have been (but then, they should never have been in this position in the first place) I should have anticipated the reaction this provoked. And believe me, Friend, it was not the one I intended. Carter reared backward. His hands sprang away from me as if from hot coals, and one of them flew to his mouth to wipe it with a sleeve. "What are you doing!" he cried, aghast. At which question I could only start in astonishment, for what on earth did he suppose I was doing?

"I was kissing you!" I said, when I'd managed to find my voice. "It's a Venetian Kiss, I came across it in my reading and—"

"I know perfectly well what it is," he cut me off, still shrunk into a corner of the chaise, "but it's the gentleman who ought introduce it to the proceedings, if you'd not mind being patient."

"I *beg* your pardon?" I felt my confusion growing by the second, although I attempted to lighten the moment with a bit of humor. "Really, Carter, you mustn't speak in riddles, we American girls are inclined to be blunt."

But Carter answered with haughty seriousness. "You American girls are inclined to be forward too, and I can't say as I find it terribly inspiring."

Now my confusion sharpened into irritation. "Are we back at the chess tournament, then? Must we each move in turn?"

He winced. "I'll thank you, Miss, to refrain from being crude, although perhaps from your performance I should guess it is your wont."

"Why—you hypocrite," I gasped. "You bring me here knowing it improper, yet when I abandon myself somewhat, and take the tiniest step toward indulging my own affection as well as yours, you accuse me of impropriety. Accuse yourself, sir. You are as guilty as I, and I am as entitled to my feeling as you."

I folded my arms and turned forward in my seat, knowing not what to say—waiting for what, I wondered to myself, an apology? a sign of comprehension?—and he sat similarly, staring straight ahead. Thus did a minute or two pass, in disagreeable silence.

Then Carter sniffed, "I do not understand you, Arabella, and I doubt that any sane man would." I did not reply and after another moment he spoke again, but now his tone had changed, softened. "You merely surprised me, is what I suppose is at issue. I am not used to presuming that a lady's affections translate necessarily into the physical. After all, you divine women are creatures of the heart, whereas we men are creatures of the flesh."

"How very convenient." I still did not turn to look at him.

"Now now, Arabella." From the corner of my eye I could see him shift his shoulders toward me in a conciliatory gesture. "Don't let's argue, when we were going along so agreeably. You surely must understand my position, but if you wish to defy the laws of nature and advance upon the realm of the sensual, who am I to stand in your way? Let us put our altercation behind us and continue."

And then he placed a hand against my thigh, but this time—unlike the one in which he'd draped his arm over my box seat—there was no question as to his intent. The pressure of his fingers and his leering grin made that quite apparent, and it went well beyond anything I'd sought to arouse with my kiss. I did not flatter myself, moreover, that his renewed interest was contingent on my charms or our mutual pleasure; he had simply recognized an opportunity for his own lust's satisfaction—whose object might have been any willing female.

So that there should be no mistaking *my* intent, then, I picked up his hand and threw it into his own lap. "You may take that back, sir, as it is not desired in any region of mine, and particularly not where it has strayed."

He responded with a nasty little smirk: "Oh, it's a tad late in the game for such coyness, I think. After you've crossed one line, my dear, you oughtn't presume you may hide behind others."

And that, of course, decided it. I leapt up from the chaise. "I believe I have had enough of this exchange. I should like to go home. Right now. This minute."

"Oh, for Heaven's sake—what sort of two-faced tease are you—"

"If you don't care to take me I'm certain I can arrange my own transportation."

"Honestly, this is so unnecessary—have another sip of Champagne, and let us forget this fuss—"

"I don't want any more Champagne. What I want is to leave. This instant."

"All right—if you intend to be stubborn—good, you shall leave."

"Good."

"Good."

I stood and gathered my things, then marched out the way I had come, not bothering to wait for him to light the lamps along the way. I then climbed into the carriage myself, as soon as his ostler had made it ready.

"I shouldn't wish to inflict my presence upon you on the drive home," Carter said as I prepared to shut the brougham's door.

I did not acknowledge the sarcasm implicit in his tone. "Thank you for your consideration. You may give your driver my address. That shall be sufficient." I banged the door closed, and a moment later I was under way; I did not bother turning to see whether he looked after the carriage, or simply went inside before I'd passed beyond the drive.

Naturally, when I arrived home, Mother was sitting up in the front parlor, maintaining the pretense of reading some piece of literature or another. As soon as she saw me enter the foyer alone, her face fell—where was the illustrious Mr. Forbes-Spencer, she no doubt was wondering—but I squelched this inquiry before she made it. "I was taken home by Carter's driver. Carter is not here, as he did not escort me." I marched right past her toward the circular front staircase, but she called after me anyway—and a little too shrilly, "How was your evening, then?"

"Divine!" I barked, mounting the steps. "It was a little taste of Eden!" Not waiting to hear what she'd make of this, I swung open the enormous carved door of my room, entered, and then heaved it shut, with rather a bit more force than necessary.

So—that is the end of Carter Forbes-Spencer. I wonder if I am overreacting, but then I realize it doesn't matter, for whether I am right or wrong, whatever affection I felt for him has flown from my heart almost completely. Imagine, the nerve of him—the hypocrisy, the self-righteousness! He makes me feel a fool, and look one. Surely the fault is partly mine—he would no doubt say I acted the debaucher, and so got what I'd asked for—but what of him? Is he alone permitted to explore his own desire and set his own limit? And must I alone fear censure for doing so? Surely *he* is not pondering his behavior right now—no, he is very likely collapsed on his divan, descended into smug, inebriated sleep.

Oh, good riddance to him then, I say—although I cannot help but wonder if ever I shall feel the draw of true likemindedness, or whether I shall remain alone for want of a companion who shall find the twist in my character acceptable. Why, oh why, is it given me to desire such unladylike explorations!

Why me, dear Friend, why me—or is the problem not myself, but rather this modern era into which I've been thrust? Would it have helped had I been born either earlier or later, would my strange nature have found itself welcomed—or disparaged in exactly the same manner—a hundred years ago or hence?

MARCH 28, 1861

I had barely risen from bed two mornings after my break with Mr. Forbes-Spencer when a letter arrived from Caroline, via messenger. Written upon the envelope were instructions either to send a reply back with the same courier, or at least to respond before evening in another manner. I knew I should not be able to compose an answer quickly, and so I sent the messenger away, then took the missive up into my bedroom to read it in peace.

It began with a huge scrawl across the top: TELL! WHAT HAS TRANSPIRED B'TWN CARTER & YOU? As I read down the page, Caroline went on to say that she had got wind of some trouble through none other than her brother Harlow, who had lunched with Mr. Forbes-Spencer and Louella Paxton's brother Thomas the day before.

What has happened? Caroline queried me, in her fine slanted script. *Harlow was furious when he arrived home. He maintained that Carter had disparaged you, implied you to be bold and loose, an allegation which caught that rake Thomas's attention immediately. Harlow argued your defense, and an altercation ensued between Carter and himself, so that they are now no longer on speaking terms. Please tell—and forgive me for being the instrument of your introduction to Carter, I thought him a gentleman and fair companion, and could not know he would act as neither . . .*

I immediately wrote back to Caroline, describing the evening's events, and assured her that I did not hold her to blame for the outcome of my involvement with Carter—but that it pained me to know—and it still does, by the way—that he would stoop to disparaging me. What I wanted to say was, "I send him to the Devil," but I was attempting to rein in my anger; it would take another day's time for the sentiment to escape my lips.

What brought *that* sad moment to pass was the call I had the displeasure of receiving the very next day: Mr. Thomas Paxton, of all people, come to sniff about after the easy quarry Carter Forbes-Spencer had no doubt assured him I would be. God knows what wild yarns Carter spun, but there was Thomas Paxton—whom I've set eyes upon exactly once—standing on the doorstep, leering up at me, and explaining that he had happened to be in the vicinity when he recalled that his sister had mentioned my residing here. He was quite breezily confident until I asked him how he had enjoyed the lunch he'd had with Carter and Harlow Beckwith two days ago; then his face reddened, but he stood his ground. He shrugged his shoulders as if to say, "You cannot blame me for trying you out"; and that was when I gave voice to my suggestion that he walk straight to the Devil, and invite Carter Forbes-Spencer along with him, and that, by the way, he might find that a reputation as a would-be rake is not all it's cracked up to be. At this he got an altogether vicious sparkle to his eyes, and replied that I needn't worry over his reputation, and turned to leave the property. I managed to retain my composure long enough to shut the door after him, but then I leaned against the inside of it, and allowed myself the luxury of tears. "Perhaps you shall fall a little farther," Jeffrey Price said to me, and it seems I cannot stop myself from falling. Whether I leap or am pushed, the results are the same.

And now I have no doubt made an enemy of Louella's brother, but as she considers him a dolt in the first place, I hope she shall not be offended.

JUNE 20, 1861

The lines have been crossed, my friend, many at a time.

The American States are at war. A little over two months ago Secessionist soldiers—they call themselves the Confederacy Rebels—fired fifty cannons upon a South Carolina Federalist fort called Sumter. They captured it and flew their own abomination of a flag from its pole, prompting President Lincoln to issue a call for militiamen and order a special session of Congress on the Fourth of July.

I recall the militia in New Parrish—which I took as being so much childish posturing—and wonder if they are even now headed down the coastline, ready to draw and shed blood. There is still a slim chance that this will be a smattering of isolated skirmishes, or so the newspapers here tell us, but I dare not believe this. I was blithe and optimistic once upon a time, but can muster no more of that foolish sentiment.

I cannot keep my thoughts from my family, estranged though I felt from them when we departed. What of Uncle Henry and Aunt Tina, Constance and Thomas—what of Grandmama Van der Waal, and Mother's sisters? Shall they be safe? I take some comfort in what I have heard over and over again: that even if the conflict should last more than a year, the chances of the Confederacy are slim, and the chance of actual fighting reaching as far north as New York almost nil. My main concern is that there will be deprivations, shortages if the fighting goes on, which may affect my family in some unforeseen way.

I dare not even imagine what should transpire should the pundits be wrong, and the Confederacy, by some hellish miracle, able to overcome the vast resources of the Federalist States and win the war.

Oh, I cannot be glad I am here, an ocean away from the possibility of danger; rather, I am furious at my entrapment, which is not voluntary, and which now is certain to go on for an unknowable length of time.

Which is not to say that travel back to the former United States is forbidden. European ships are carrying on as usual—or near usual—in Northern waters; and despite the blockade of Southern ports, there are still means by which to travel into the Southland, particularly from England, which after all is the greatest power in the world. I doubt the U.S. Navy would wish to fire upon vessels flying the Union Jack and risk a conflict in *that* arena as well.

All of which facts have made possible the disheartening and burdensome letter I received from Miss Paxton last month, stating that, incredibly, she intended to travel back to New Orleans, Louisiana, despite the start of an actual and undeniable war—in fact, because of it. The fate of her servants had now become a most dire matter, she said, and there could be no escaping moral responsibility. Besides, she had been assured that she and her mother were in no real danger. They would be traveling to Ireland, so that they might sail upon an English ship; the fighting is well away from New Orleans, the scramble to set the blockade in place will give them time to arrive—and there is always the chance that by the time they do so the entire affair will be ended.

She must have arrived by now, as she was to sail at the end of May—but of course in the States the entire affair is not ended. And there is no way to know how she fared, whether she crossed successfully, or was turned away—or worse.

Louella is a friend I met only once, by chance at a party, many months ago, yet I feel as if I've forged some profound attachment to her which I am now in danger of losing. How I should love to seek out Thomas Paxton and ask him what has happened, if there has been word, how his father could bear to allow his wife and daughter to place themselves in such jeopardy! I regret my enmity toward Thomas only because it prevents me from knowing the fate of his sister. Why, I should also love to ask him, did he not abandon his cozy accommodations here, and accompany the women of his family back to Louisiana? Why did he and his father not act as men and go themselves, the cowards?

Caroline is as distraught as I over all of this—more so because she has known Louella for a longer period of time, and has cultivated a far deeper friendship with her. She has found out no more than I myself; Harlow continues to be on the outs with Carter Forbes-Spencer and Thomas Paxton, so that Caroline has had no means by which to question the latter about his sister's whereabouts.

In addition to this, Caroline has relations in the States, although her immediate family is here in England. Her grandparents, aunts, uncles, and cousins are still scattered throughout Illinois and Pennsylvania, and while it seems unlikely that they are in immediate danger, there is the chance—particularly for her mother's relatives outside of Philadelphia—that the war could eventually place them in harm's way.

So there is much to worry over, and little to rejoice upon, and isn't that always the situation, it seems. So great is the scope of these present worries, however, that all others pale beside them, which is why, my friend, I must take a short respite before I resume. For, having relayed the tale of the great lines crossed and great worlds put asunder, I feel awkward and self-centered descending into the realm of the immediate. Yet I desire to turn the magnifying glass upon my own small existence, governed by no great President's hand, but only by my own; but where, still, battles have been won and lost, and territories ceded and conquered.

I have much to tell upon that subject, but as I have already rambled on at length, I shall save that task for the morrow, and dedicate the day—which I shall no doubt need all of—to completing it.

JUNE 21, 1861

You may just as well settle in, Friend, and find a comfortable spot, for here as promised is the continuation of my exploits (which I warn you ahead of time have been many, and will be lengthy to recollect). Thank heaven I had the wisdom to secure you in my trunk earlier, for if there was reason for it then there is all the more reason now. I think I fantasized that at some point an imaginary reader might peruse your pages, and therefore I hoped to be always at my best grammatically and so forth, but in the last months I have slowly let go that fantasy, and now I know it is for myself alone that I commit these words to paper. So there is no need to be clever or coy, to bother about painting an accurate—or flattering—portrait of myself. Rather, it is essential that no one discover you—or I should say, discover me—and so my attention shifts not to making this journal presentable, but to the task of keeping it inviolate.

You will forgive me if I hasten through certain segments of this story; there is a good deal to write, and I shall no doubt strain my arm to the breaking point.

To tell it then:

After the end of my flirtation with Carter Forbes-Spencer, I began to see quite a lot of Harlow Beckwith. I liked him from our first meeting the night of the opera, I might actually have preferred his company had it not been prearranged that I was to be escorted by CFS. After his falling-out with that rascal, Harlow paid me a visit along with his sister, and circumspectly answered my questions regarding Carter's disparaging of my reputation. Mr. Forbes-Spencer had spoken precisely as I'd thought he'd done, puffing himself up into the master seducer and reducing me to a devouring w——e, although he stopped just short of declaring me ruined; and Harlow still seemed disturbed by it, even as he hesitated to reveal every repugnant detail for fear of inflaming me even more.

Caroline could only shake her head and apologize. "I should never have encouraged you," she said, pulling at her gloves. "I knew little enough of Carter. He enjoys playing the libertine, but it is callow play; there is not an idea or sentiment behind it with which I should have found sympathy. I thought him harmless, though, or I should never have made his interest known to you."

"I told you otherwise, Carrie," Harlow broke in. "I told you that first evening they were ill-suited to each other, for I know Carter's type, I know how they think of American girls—fast and loose, not to be taken seriously, but jolly good entertainment. I think he was caught quite short by you, Arabella. You engaged his affections to a greater degree than he expected, but he's had too much training in the duties of his station to consider you as other than a passing fancy."

"I am only glad neither of you has taken his side against me," I said.

Caroline appeared shocked. "Why in the world would we?"

"I did not behave at all virtuously myself."

I heard Caroline's intake of breath, but it was Harlow who answered. "You did nothing wrong, so far as we are concerned. You know we are a racy set ourselves, and so you needn't worry that we'll judge you harshly, or at all."

"Thank you," I replied quietly. "I only fear that Carter will brag of his exploits to everyone he knows, or that your other companion, Mr. Paxton, shall do so for him, and then it shan't be long before my Aunt Josephine has another nail to add to the coffin my Uncle Charles is constructing for me."

"Whatever either of them says," Harlow said, "we shall be there to testify as to Carter's fondness for embellishment, and we shall defend you against any slurs."

"Yes, it's the least we can do for you, considering all the trouble I've caused you. Now, do not worry yourself, only say you forgive me." Caroline leaned forward in her seat. "Please say it, Arabella, I shan't rise from this chair or leave the house until you do."

"Then I'll say nothing," I smiled, "the better to hold you here."

The next day Harlow called upon me by himself. As it was our regular receiving day, I was quite prepared for visitors, but surprised to see him nonetheless, as I'd spent several hours in his company the day before. Today, however, the entire family was on hand for callers, and so there was little of a personal nature to be exchanged between us. We sat in the parlor while Mother and Father and Richard stared at Harlow; and I could practically hear Mother thinking, *Where is the other one, the charming Englishman, and who is this strange American come to call upon you alone*, for I have never given her a detail further as to what happened to CFS. No doubt everyone is wondering whether I shall next reveal Carter to be an ax-killer or a strangler, thus going Mr. Price, that odious toad, one better, but if there is anything to be revealed about Carter besides his being a monumental ass I shouldn't know it. Harlow is not so charming as Carter, though—or rather, he is, but in his own humorous, racy, and far more genuine way, which I could see he was quite underplaying for my parents. Thus he comported himself as rather shy and introverted, although I know this to be hardly the sum of his character. At the end of an hour, he rose and bid me good-bye, and asked at the same time if he could call upon me for a carriage ride the next morning. I was free, and so I agreed, and Harlow next turned to Mother and Father to ask their permission.

Mother looked up at him with raised eyebrows, and then, with a most syrupy grin, replied, "Why, yes, I should think that would be delightful. Richard would likely enjoy an outing too, wouldn't you, dear?"

I turned, and something snappish rose to the tip of my tongue, but in Harlow's presence felt I could say nothing, and so I glared with all my might. *Why do you protect me from the wrong people, in your blindness!* I wanted to shout, but Richard spoke before I could say a word.

"I believe I'll be *busy* at that hour, Mother," he said, glaring at her almost as hard as I. Father sat by watching this exchange, oblivious as to its implications; he is a fine one for stepping in at the point of crisis with a great blustery fanfare, but the subtlety of Mother's machinations often eludes him.

I ground my teeth and could see Richard doing the same, but Harlow laughed agreeably. "I shouldn't be insulted either way," he said to Richard, "but do please come if you can, and let's make a proper outing of it." I gave him a grateful look, and Richard—no doubt still feeling himself a trapped rat—halfheartedly agreed.

Then I rose to see Harlow to the door, but Mother jumped up ahead of me. "Allow me to show you out, Mr. Beckwith," she cooed. I was seething, but Richard brushed by me as he exited the parlor and whispered, just loudly enough for everyone to hear, "I like him much better than that other awful snob."

The following day we took the carriage ride, and I managed actually to enjoy it, for I felt myself neither constrained into acting a role which did not suit me nor compelled to fulfill one created for me by the preferences of my companion. I was wary, however; I could not erase from my mind the thought of Thomas Paxton's visit so soon upon the heels of Carter's betrayal. In some frightened part of myself, I wondered if Harlow—despite being Caroline's brother and therefore accountable to some extent for his treatment of me—were not similarly inclined, if all of this were not merely a game intended to lull me into complacency, whereupon a more intricate seduction might be attempted. So I allowed him to set the pace of our exchanges, and kept my senses alert for any false or discordant note he might strike.

But none emerged. Rather, the day passed blessedly free of rain, sunny and on the verge of true spring warmth. Harlow drove us out beyond the limits of the city and into the countryside; he is adept with a team, and we were able to open the barouche top so as to enjoy the air. Richard sat behind us, and far from pestering, added to the generally relaxed air of the party. "I am sorry," he'd apologized to both of us, when we were finally off and beyond Mother's hearing. "I'd rather not have come, but—"

"Oh, never mind. Mother is being impossible, and it's just as well, for whatever's made of our riding together, you're here as a witness."

"Yes," Harlow added, "you've a job to do, I only ask that you go lightly on me, as I'm a mere scholar and not up to any fisticuffs." He grinned at Richard, and Richard grinned back, then asked, having been set at ease, "What is it you're a student of, exactly?"

"Science and mathematics. I'm particularly interested in the study of the stars, and the configuration of the planets."

"And you attend Oxford?" Richard's voice dropped reverently as he spoke the sacred name.

Harlow hesitated a moment. He looked off over the horses' shoulders. "I've completed a year there," he replied.

"Why do you put it that way?" I asked. "Completed a year—what of the next year? Do you mean to say you don't intend to return?"

A few seconds passed, and I regretted my tactlessness. The subject was obviously causing him considerable discomfort.

"I've tentative plans to return to the States, while it's still feasible to travel."

He said this in a tone which plainly indicated that he had no wish to discuss the matter further. I turned in my seat to look at him, but as he avoided my glance I said nothing more.

Later, however, when we'd stopped along a lane to consume the picnic he'd generously provided, I had the opportunity to question him alone.

Richard had gone off to attempt some rudimentary branch-and-string fishing in a nearby pond, and Harlow and I were seated on the grass, our stomachs satisfyingly full of cold chicken and fresh bread.

"So, what of these tentative plans?" I asked him. "I don't mean to pry, Harlow, and you may feel free to rebuke me if I am doing so. But why are you thinking of abandoning your education?"

He peered at me, and then sighed. "I'm sorry I mentioned it, Arabella. I have no wish to burden you with my difficulties."

"Not at all, I should not have asked if I were not interested."

He sighed again. "I believe I was in error, fancying myself a scholar, imagining I would come here and study the stars, earn my diploma, and then settle myself into academia. Quite frankly, I feel I don't belong." He stopped, and I was about to reassure him, but sensed that he was merely debating whether to go on.

"Besides—" he continued, "besides which—there is the matter of a girl."

I found myself both reassured and saddened at these words. Reassured, because his melancholy over a lost love most likely precluded him from having some nasty game of seduction up his sleeve, and saddened, because I wished Harlow no ill.

I decided to address the first comment first. "Why should you not belong here?" I asked him gently.

"Oh, I don't know—it's the queer sensibility about this place, for one thing. I feel I've entered a stagnant pool instead of a social milieu. It's thoroughly oppressive, and rubs me quite the wrong way. Although—" He shrugged. "I cannot say I'm totally at home in my own country either, as the modern sensibility rankles me too, and that seems to be very nearly the same, at its core, from one continent to the next. I sometimes wonder if I should not have been happier had I been born earlier in the century. Natures then were not expected to be so refined, and societies not so stratified—a state of affairs which we've come to quite deplore in our own day."

I gazed at him, surprised and keenly interested, for did his discomfort and his conclusions not mirror my own? To test the notion, I probed a bit further: "But are there not aspects of that modern sensibility with which you should not like to do without? For example, do you imagine life was any easier in some backward time? And would you have us return to the rusticity of speech and manner that marks our grandparents' generation?"

Harlow laughed. "No. I do not believe that a lack of luxury or convenience is inherently noble—or particularly fun. And I'd not have us eating raw beefsteak with our fingers, and exploring our lavatory habits over dinner, and fornicating with impunity, if that's what you mean. I'd only require a greater degree of honesty about the subject of lavatories and fornication in general—a greater degree of acceptance for what is natural to the body and to the spirit, rather than this oppressive dictate that the two be completely separate, and the former abhorrent while the latter is divine."

"I heartily concur," I said.

"I thought you would." Harlow grinned. "I knew it the moment you branded Carter a fool, with his notions of 'perspiring like a gentleman.' "

I flushed a bit at the memory. "So long as you did not take the remark to be some callow romanticizing of life at the bottom of your stagnant pool."

"No—I rather thought that to be Carter's own ill-taken point. But then, we mustn't be too harsh with him, the poor dear—after all, he has a lot upon his shoulders—the weight of the Empire, and Lordship of Creation, and all that."

At this we both laughed outright.

Then Harlow grew sober once again. "But I wander from your question, Arabella."

"It's all right, you needn't feel obligated to continue."

"No, no—I should prefer it, it helps me to hear my sentiments voiced out loud. I was saying—oh yes, on the subject of my leaving—there are other reasons too, besides my awkwardness amidst the English. It's my own nature as well, I should admit that straight off. I am no academic, Arabella, I haven't the drive for it. I gaze at the heavens, do the calculations, and thoroughly enjoy this, and yet when it comes to self-promotion, to ingratiating myself with administrators and professors—well, this is how university posts are decided, and awards given, and so forth, and if I cannot enter the fray, then what is the point? I may just as well return home, and enter into my father's beef-bludgeoning business—there are numbers involved therein, of dollars and cents, which seems to be what life comes down to."

"But you should surely be unhappy with such a life!"

"My mother was convinced of the same thing, which was why she insisted I be permitted to come here. Of course she is furious that Caroline cannot attend a premium university alongside me—and I confess I've come to see her point, it's an unjust thing, and Caroline should have made so much better a scholar than I—but still she fought hard for my entrance because she knew how torturous I should find my father's plans for me. Yet now I am here, I believe I shall never find my niche, and so all her hard work on my behalf was for naught."

"Surely not, Harlow, for you haven't left your studies yet."

"No, but I almost certainly shall. Especially since—well." He gazed off into the distance, cleared his throat. "As I mentioned—"

"Ah, the matter of the girl."

"Yes. Well."

"You know, you needn't—"

"Yes I do, I do need to. I need to convince myself of its truth, and perhaps if I tell it to you, it shall be the more real, for being real to someone else. That is, if you don't mind being burdened so."

"Certainly I don't, you may speak as you like."

He was silent for a moment; a blue jay swooped in, cawing, and a breeze ruffled our hair. "As you've no doubt gathered," he finally began, "there was a young lady. I had not come here with the intention of seeking a wife, or involving myself in a courtship. To be honest with you, such pursuits are difficult for me. So few ladies catch my fancy—I mean no disparagement, it's only that I rarely meet one with whom I feel I have anything in common, and a certain likemindedness is important to me. And then when I do spy a prospect, I am besieged by all sorts of doubts. I imagine she will not take to me, or that I may be making a mistake, and before long manage to talk myself out of the enterprise completely." (I wondered about all this, staring into Harlow's sky-blue eyes. I could scarce imagine any girl refusing him on account of either character or comeliness. I think him as handsome as Caroline is pretty; whether he knows it or not is another question, but it might be the better for the female population if he does not.)

"On this occasion, though," he continued, "I saw my interest through at least far enough to reveal it to the girl. And wonder of wonders, she returned my attentions. We found in each other a mutual appreciation, which for myself, at least, turned into what I had always expected of romantic love: I could actually envision her traveling through life by my side. So I took to courting her seriously, which I thought she understood, and had tacitly agreed to. But no sooner did I voice my intentions and my desire to wed than—well." He took a deep breath. "She abandoned me. Completely. She maintained that she was fond of me, but that I had too much 'growing up' to do, if you can imagine. She accused me of a certain—aimlessness. And frivolity. And then she disparaged the whole idea of love and matrimony in general, and said she might perhaps never wed, and that she'd enjoyed my company but that now we must part. And part we did, as she would not accept my visits, or any gifts or tokens from me, and sent my letters back unopened."

"Oh, dear," I said, "I am sorry, Harlow."

"Ah, well, it hardly matters. That fickle creature—so what of it, that she tore my heart from my chest and left me unable to commit it to love again? I'll go through life a soulless and unfeeling debaucher, exactly what women most fear encountering—but I'll accept no blame, for now I know that heartless men are only what women have made of them."

I couldn't help smiling at this. "I doubt you'll do well as a soulless debaucher, Harlow. If you were so inclined, you'd not be sitting here bereft over the loss of one lady—you'd be out perpetrating heinous acts upon another. You're far too fine a creature for that, I can tell it. Nor can I agree that every heartless man is only the result of woman's mistreatment, or every heartless woman likewise. And finally your own young woman doesn't seem so very heartless to me. She simply told you the truth about her sentiments, which she is entitled to do, however harsh that truth may have been."

He frowned at me. "What was I thinking, asking the viper to take my side against the snake?"

"Oh, you don't truly think me a viper, do you? And besides, your lady love may have a point, may she not? You did just tell me, after all, that you're uncertain as to your future, and what you wish to do with your life. Perhaps she was only trying to spare you the difficulties of a hasty decision, or perhaps she is hoping you will come to some conclusions, and make her another offer, which she may accept."

"But I'm uncertain in part because of her, Arabella. Her remarks caused me to further question my capacity for serious study, and it is mainly her suggestion that I grow up which makes me think I should take on the adult duties of a businessman."

I was ready to make a response to this when I saw Richard meandering over the hill with his fishing string in his hands. I put a finger to my lips, and Harlow turned and caught sight of him, fell silent, then gave a cheery shout of greeting.

"How are the fish today, Saint Peter!" he called through cupped hands.

"Hiding or dead," came Richard's reply. Upon reaching us he tossed his string in the carriage, and flopped down in the grass beside me.

There was therefore no more talk of personal subjects that day. We passed the rest of the afternoon discussing the war at home—it had already begun, but we did not know that at the time, and were still speculating on whether it would become a reality. When it began to grow cooler we gathered up our things, reharnessed the horses, and arrived home at a time deemed quite suitable by Mother.

So successfully did this first outing go that Harlow took me on four or five others during the daylight hours; twice we were accompanied by Richard, and once by Caroline, after which Mother relented and allowed me a few hours' respite with Harlow alone. Each occasion was a delightful one. We engaged in both silliness and the most sobering conversations, and I resolved not to hold back an ounce of my character, but to act exactly as I wished. Harlow responded in kind, and we had that rare experience of feeling ourselves uniquely connected while at the same time true to our own natures.

It was inevitable, I suppose—one of nature's most consistent and successful tricks, played upon any man and woman with a rapport and sufficient time to expand upon it—that our interest in each other began to move beyond a desire for mere companionship.

So it was that despite my great resolve, despite everything I'd said or thought regarding Jeffrey Price and Carter Forbes-Spencer, that sensation rose in me once again: the desire to run a finger along the edge of Harlow's perfectly moulded lips, or to sample the softness of the skin at the nape of his neck, and to have him notice me in a like fashion. And he, in turn, seemed to have developed a similar yearning. He found excuses to place a hand over mine when lifting me into the carriage, or to prolong such moments of contact, he found reasons for the smoothing of my hair, or the brushing of my cheek with his fingers, he displayed himself to me, I believe, that he might provoke my interest as I hoped to provoke his.

It is a strange thing, but with Harlow I felt this activity wholly mutual and without strategy, one inspired on his part by my whole self rather than mere itinerant lust, and certainly unlike the incidents with Jeffrey Price and Carter Forbes-Spencer which preceded it. I felt the need for neither fear nor subterfuge. I did not question my own motives or his, I read no censure or presumptuousness in his air toward me. I did not force myself into maintaining a facade of suitable disinterest, and I did not torture myself for not having done so. The more I gave in to my flawed nature and its manifestations, the more Harlow seemed to take to me, and so we went on in this manner for several weeks, until one day Harlow asked to see me alone, and at night.

I wondered if I were not tempting the fates, after my narrow escape from ruination at Spencer's hands. But I wanted so to say yes. I shook myself sternly, I lectured myself: "Do you never learn, Arabella?" But none of these things could overcome my inclinations. What is the use in restraining myself, I thought, if I am not naturally inclined toward virtue?

So in the end I determined that it was time for me to begin my studies with Miss Ashe in earnest.

Father, of course, insisted upon accompanying me to Miss Ashe's door on the appointed evening. He sat with me in the brougham, while Philip, one of the servants on loan from Uncle Charles, took on the task of driving. Once at the house, we mounted the front steps together. Father waited patiently as we were announced and the maid fetched Miss Ashe.

That good lady appeared completely unruffled by the impromptu inspection. She invited us into the parlor, spent some minutes explaining her methods of teaching to Father, offered him tea (which he was good enough to refuse), and then graciously saw him out. I waved him off from the window, watching as he closed the door of the carriage upon himself. Then I heard Philip cluck to Paulus, Uncle Charles's elderly roan gelding; the horse's footsteps clopped mournfully on the cobblestones before fading off into the distance.

Harlow's carriage, on the other hand, made a terrible racket as we clattered down the streets of Knightsbridge at breakneck speed not a quarter hour later. "Where are we going?" I managed to yell in between being thrown against the walls and doors.

"Make a guess!"

"I've no idea! How should I know what to guess!"

We were heading away from my own neighborhood; it wasn't until I recognized the shabby and overgrown outlying street down which we'd turned that I suspected what our destination might be. Sure enough, we came to a halt before a squat stone building of three stories, over whose door hung one of those ancient wooden signs now prized for their quaintness. *Lamb's Hock Inn,* the carved relief read, and between the words was a rendering of the animal in profile, with its head bent to a foreleg as if to nuzzle the hock itself.

"Madame Ramsbottom," Harlow said, "your banquet awaits." He bowed low, playing the scene to its fullest. I did not smile. I merely crooked my fingers and intoned, "You may rise." Arm in arm, we entered the tavern.

Inside, it was not so bad as I'd expected. It was rather cheerful, in fact, with paneled pine walls, a stone hearth, plank tables, and a long bar. There were benches along the bar, where men sat nursing spirits; there were women in the establishment as well, but all were no doubt working class, and they gave some hard stares as we made our way to a table. But once I was seated Harlow went straight to the bar, and flashed a white-toothed smile at the barmaid, whom he knew by name. "Well, now, Margaret, it's been a while, hasn't it?"

The woman's round flushed face broke into a grin. "Ah, good Harlow Beckwith. It has indeed. It's gone I thought you were, to fight your war back in the Colonies."

I thought I saw him stiffen at this blithe reference to our home, but his humor did not fail him. "It's just barely a war, Meg, and I shouldn't be the one to win it if it keeps going."

Harlow ordered us two pints of stout, and two bowls of the infamous mutton stew. When Margaret came to deliver the food, she raised her eyebrows at me, but I placed both elbows on the table and gave her a straightforward smile, at which she smiled back. I was quite impressed with myself—here I was, drinking stout in a tavern, on a young man's arm! I fancied myself the boldest, most bohemian girl in London—that is, until I looked around at the faces of my fellow diners, and realized that they frequented this place regularly, and not out of any sense of adventure but because their everyday lives brought them here—and those lives were not bohemian in the least. "Slumming," Carter had called it, and I suddenly felt it the smug and shabby indulgence it was.

Either eat and keep a low profile, I told myself, *or leave. And stop congratulating yourself for being here.* I raised my glass of stout to Harlow's. "To your continued scholarship," I said. He ducked his head and blushed, but touched his glass to mine.

I sipped—and nearly spat the vile liquid into my lap. I had never tasted stout. I imagined from its color that it would have a sweet, molasses sort of tang, or perhaps one like a root beer, and was therefore nastily surprised by its bitterness and bite. After this, I was reluctant to eat, but Harlow had begun and so, hesitatingly, I picked up my spoon. I took a tiny bite from my bowl and discovered it to be—

—delicious! It was hearty and rich, the meat tender, the carrots, apples, and potatoes all blended together in a pungent sauce. The only meal comparable to it was to be had at the hotel Carter had taken us to, where all the chefs and all of the recipes are, of course, not British but French.

Our excellent stew was followed by excellent apple tarts swimming in cream, which we washed down with more stout—which I was now coming to enjoy—and then some good hot tea.

And all through these humble and wonderful courses, we talked and talked, over the china and around the rims of the thick mugs, and between the morsels balanced on the iron cutlery. We discussed the war; I mentioned Louella Paxton's trip to the United States, and Harlow stopped eating and went quite still. He shook his head, and said we could only beg the fates to protect that dear girl.

We then mulled over the intentions of President Lincoln, and before long we had moved on to our respective upbringings, and every other topic beneath the sun. Harlow told me that his mother is an advocate of women's civil liberties as well as an Abolitionist, and I found myself mightily intrigued at the notion of this woman's various pursuits, and eager to view her in the flesh.

It was over the tea that I brought up the subject of Jeffrey Price to Harlow. I did not know what Caroline might have told him of me, and as it turned out she had revealed nothing. So, with many of the same feelings which had accompanied my first telling of this tale, I relayed the entire thing, pausing at the end to see whether he should bolt from the table or simply turn from me and withdraw his affections.

Again, to my surprise and relief, he did neither.

"I am sorry for you," he said soberly, "and sorry that such a creature calls himself a man, and taints all of us by association."

I stared at him, feeling the warmth of the stout in my cheeks. "Tell me, do you think you might have done the same?" I asked suddenly.

"What? The same, when?"

"To the child. The sick maid. Had you had the chance, and known you would not be discovered, might you have done the same? Might any man?"

He did not hesitate. "I cannot answer for any man. I can answer for myself, and my answer is no. I doubt I could bring myself to an action of that sort, the issue of being caught aside. I have no stomach for it. I should not wish to gain by force or deception what I could not win on merit." He returned my gaze without blinking.

At that moment we were interrupted by the barmaid, who bent to remove our bowls and cups. Harlow now looked away from me to take a discreet peek at his pocket watch. "We had better be leaving," he told me, "although I'm loath to interrupt us at such a critical juncture."

I did not admit it, but in fact I was relieved: I did not know what had provoked my question to him, and was just as happy to be distracted from the entire issue. "No, no, you're right, I must be back before Father comes to collect me."

We left the Lamb's Hock, our conversation forestalled if not forgotten, and clattered back over the route by which we'd come. I was prepared to breathe easy, for we had arrived at our destination a quarter hour or so before Father was due to arrive.

But as we passed by Miss Ashe's home I saw, beneath the glow of the lamp, a familiar shadow diagonally across the street from her front door: it was Paulus, the roan gelding, harnessed to his rig, his head drooping, his distinctive white blaze quite visible in the gaslight. And lest there be any question, there was Philip, huddled in the driver's seat, looking as forlorn as his charge.

"Don't turn and look," I said to Harlow, "it's Father's carriage!" I realized he must have waited there all the hours since he'd dropped me off. *Spying!* I said angrily to myself, and then in the next instant I thought, *The poor thing*, my poor papa, for of course he could not have seen me go and would not see me return, and all his vigilance was for nothing.

We trotted past the house and turned onto the street behind Miss Ashe's; Harlow drew to a stop before the little iron gate set into its archway. Through this I would go with my keys, to the rear of the property and then into the garden and Miss Ashe's atrium, with no one watching her front steps any the wiser.

But before this, there were good-nights to be said. I sat quietly in the carriage, feeling a tension so thick, so grand, I wondered if the breaking of it could possibly be grander.

"I thank you for the meal," I said.

"I thank you for the company, which was far more enjoyable."

"As was yours. Truly."

"Good night, then, Miss Leeds."

"Good night to you, Mr. Beckwith."

His hand was upon the door of the carriage, his intent likely being to come round and help me from my own side. But before he could descend, I turned in my seat and smiled, knowing, I think, what effect this should have.

And so I was not unduly surprised when Harlow let got the door handle, picked up my fingers as if to kiss them, did so delicately, and then, without releasing my hand, bent forward to kiss me upon the mouth. He hesitated; I could tell it in the tentative way he pressed against me; I had not the desire to hasten the moment along, for it lacked the urgency I'd felt with Carter. Rather, I wished to prolong the state we were in, that of the briefest, sweetest contact. His lips were warm, and tasted of fresh lemon—from the tea, perhaps—and the faint scent of spearmint clung to him. My fingers, grasped by his, could detect the steady rhythm of his heart; I had shut my eyes, but when I opened them, the dark line of his eyelid with its fringe of lashes was blurrily before me. And all of this I observed minutely and recorded in a second, in the instant before his mouth pressed harder against me and then drew away.

"You know I mean you no insult," he whispered, his face still inches from mine, his pink lips parted to reveal a hint of white teeth. The smooth sheet of his blonde hair caught the lamplight, dully reflected it.

"I know it."

"You will see me again?"

"I will."

This time it was I who went forward, with no fear of doing so, and this time, in our kiss, there was that mutuality I'd so desired with Carter, so that our lips, our tongues, our bodies, were engaged. And if there was not the rushing fervor, there was a languor, as though we moved in sand, with the carriage and the street and the passing minutes compressed around us, narrowed to nothing, without motion. I felt Harlow's hands abandon my own for my waist, and a portion of my awareness, aside from that which was relishing his kiss, now moved to the flesh beneath my breasts and at my back, to delight in the press of his fingers there. With yet another new sense, I measured the contact between our bodies, how many separate inches of our skin sought the comfort of the other's; my hands, meanwhile, concentrated upon the wide ridge of muscles on either side of his spine.

All this, a lifetime of sensation, volumes in the telling of it, over in a minute or less.

Harlow leaned away from me.

"You are beautiful," he breathed. "There is so much you cause me to forget, or at least to put aside for a time. You raise my spirits each time I see you."

I began to speak; he placed a finger over my lips.

"Do not say it, I won't believe it—I lift no one's spirits right now, but perhaps I shall, if you can only wait for my own to lighten."

I put his finger to my mouth, kissed it, released it—but he was quite correct, he did not necessarily lift my heart, and yet I stirred somewhere, and so I said, by way of an offering of honesty, "You are beautiful, though."

His eyebrows drew together; then he smiled, and then laughed, shaking his head now, and I laughed with him.

Even when I had made my way to the carriage to sit beside Father, the faint scent of lemons seemed to cling to me.

"So—was your lecture enjoyable this evening, Berry?" Father began as Paulus pulled off at his usual lazy trot.

"Oh yes, quite. I hope you were not too inconvenienced, having to rouse yourself to return for me."

"Why, not at all. What was the subject of the lesson, exactly?"

"Bees."

"Bees?"

"Yes, bees. You've heard of them, perhaps. They're small striped creatures with a nasty sting—"

"Yes, Sauce, I believe I've run across a description of them in my travels. What interesting information did you receive regarding them?"

"Well, Papa, did you know that bee societies are ruled by a single queen? And that all of the bees in the hive are sisters, mothered by their queen?"

"All sisters? My, that's fascinating—but where is the queen's regent? There must be papa bees, surely, or there would be no little ones to carry on for Her Majesty."

"Oh yes, the papa bee is called the drone. He takes flight with a new queen when she is about to found her own hive, so that he can father all of her children."

"And when he's done with that task what becomes of him?"

"He falls to the ground and dies."

My next visit with Harlow came under the simplest of pretenses: Caroline invited me to spend an evening at her home, even offering to send the Beckwiths' driver round to fetch me. I was eager to comply; I looked forward to seeing Caroline again, and also to meeting the bold and fascinating Mrs. Beckwith. But when I arrived at Linton, I discovered that Mrs. Beckwith was still traveling with her hostess. (Of Mr. Beckwith I heard very little, either through Caroline or Harlow. I knew only that he was now bearing the wartime havoc in Chicago, having been unable to visit his son at university with the rest of the family.)

I was disappointed, but not nearly so much as I would be after noting Caroline's demeanor toward me. She was cool and haughty, evoking a picture of herself as she'd been at the Oxford ball, the first time I'd heard her voice. "So that you know," she said, barely looking as she addressed me, "it wasn't I who requested your presence here. Harlow asked me to invite you."

I had never been the object of this chilly blast before. I felt my mouth go a little dry at the shock of it.

"But surely you'll stay, so that we can visit—"

She brushed by me to mount the stone staircase which divided the house in two. "I've things to do. The puppies need looking after. I'm sure Harlow has seen to arrangements for your entertainment."

This was simply too obvious a cut to be borne without protest, and so I followed her up the stairs, and caught her by the elbow.

"Caroline—"

She wrenched her arm away, and whirled around to face me. "Did I not ask you to excuse me!"

"You did, but I shan't, until you explain what's come over you. Why are you behaving so coldly toward me? Have I done something to offend you? Are you angry that Harlow asked you to invite me here?"

Her eyes flashed, and then I was surprised to see them fill a little; but in the next instant she had blinked back her tears and turned away from me.

"I am sorry, Arabella. You must forgive me. I am only worried, and overwhelmed—you know, it's the war and such—and I'm feeling a bit—melancholy, perhaps, is the word. You mustn't think it has to do with you." Of course this was precisely what I thought. I had come between Caroline and her brother, and now he had asked her to act as a liaison between the two of us; perhaps she was feeling left out, or imagined I preferred Harlow's company because of its romantic dimension.

Whatever the reason, I wished to reassure her, and so I kept my hand upon her arm. "You must know how I treasure our friendship. If this has anything to do with me, anything at all—you must tell me—"

She looked down to give me a wan little smile. "Thank you. I treasure our friendship as well." She seemed about to say something more, but then turned away again and continued her flight up the steps. "I shall see you presently. I have only to do some chores, and then I shall join you. Go on downstairs now, dear, Harlow is waiting for you in the library. It's to the left of the trophy room."

I had no choice but to obey her. I found the trophy room, with its rich-looking furniture and a bewildering array of animal heads sprouting from the walls; it was attached by a sliding paneled door to the library, which I entered to find Harlow lounging upon an overstuffed divan, a book of Lord Byron's poetry conspicuously in his hand, his bare feet hanging over the armrest. We greeted each other with a nod, and then with a tentative kiss upon the cheek, and then brought each other up to date on the doings of the few days since we had been together. Finally I managed to work the conversation around to Caroline. "You know, Harlow, she seems upset at something. I thought perhaps she resents being asked to posture for us—"

He interrupted me with a graceful toss of his head, which flipped the blonde locks out of his eyes. "Oh, you mustn't take Carrie's turns too personally. She's always in a snit of one kind or another, I'm surprised this is the first time you noticed it."

"She's never been anything but gracious and charming with me."

"Then you've obviously not spent enough time around her. Really, I don't know what overtakes her, but she's a moody one, is our Miss Caroline. She'll come out of it, though, just leave her be for a bit."

He invited me into the dining room, where a table was laid and the servants ready to serve dinner.

We ate, and then returned to the trophy room, where Harlow urged me to remove my shoes and be comfortable. This I did, and we were lying about (on the tigerskin rug, which was laid over the Oriental and which I found quite novel, for it still had its poor stuffed head attached) when Caroline opened the double doors and entered. She carried with her a little black leather valise, which I thought might contain equipment related to her dogs' training.

"I thought I'd find you here, engaged in some decadent pursuit," she said, smiling at us. I was relieved to see that her good humor seemed to have returned.

"Indeed," Harlow answered her. "I haven't begun the evening's descent into decadence yet. Is that what you've come for, or have you perhaps brought the means yourself?"

She shrugged coquettishly. "No, not decadence, Harlow, you scamp."

I confess much of this went quite over my head; I thought it primarily meaningless banter. But then Caroline placed her little bag on one of the ebony side tables, and set to removing its contents. I was fascinated, for the items had nothing to do with the training of puppies. There were, among other things, glass and metal hypodermics, and phials containing both clear liquids and small whitish pills.

I peered at the collection, my brows knit. Finally I asked, "What is all that, exactly?"

"Morphia," Caroline replied. "It's similar to laudanum, but free of any dangerous effects. We inject it regularly, for the treatment of ills. I use it particularly for melancholia, which it dissipates in an instant, as nothing else can."

"Is there no danger of acquiring an appetite, as with laudanum?"

"Oh no," Harlow said. "Hypodermics of morphia are quite safe in that regard. There is no swallowing, no ingesting, and so no appetite. Morphinism is quite a different matter than the recurring hunger for laudanum. Our own doctor in the States assured us of it when he prescribed a supply for use by the family."

Caroline had made two of the hypodermics ready, filling the glass syringes with clear liquid and attaching steel needles to one end. "Would you," she said lightly to Harlow. She handed him one of the instruments, then sat down on a divan and pushed the sleeve of her frock above her elbow. Turning away, she offered her pink forearm to Harlow. He expertly pinched the skin there and flicked the needle in, then pushed the plunger down. I watched, curious as to what effect this would have upon Caroline, but it seemed not to affect her unduly; her mood merely lightened further, and after the needle was withdrawn she said brightly to Harlow, "Bring the other here, then." He fetched the second syringe, and sat next to her, his back to her, and she repeated the procedure he'd used upon her.

"Does the needle hurt you?" I asked, having never been given an injection.

"No, it's only the barest prick," Harlow said. He sat very still for a moment as Caroline pushed the plunger. "Would you care to try?" he asked me presently.

I refused, having an instinctive mistrust of substances similar to laudanum, with which the English dose their children liberally. It seems to me that, rich or poor, one can always tell which children have been quieted thus: they are scrawny and yellow-skinned, and very still, as children ought not to be still. But I did take Harlow's point that this morphia is different. The injecting of it certainly indicates to me a more modern, clean, and medically sound approach.

Harlow and Caroline wished to rest a short while after their injections. Soon they were feeling quite well, though, and we played several hands of cards there in the Trophy Room. Caroline next moved us to the parlor where a splendid piano sat. She played while we sang, and then I tried my hand at playing, while Harlow howled like an old Southland hound dog, and we had quite a merry time, until all of us were happily exhausted.

At nine o'clock I declared that I must back home, and Harlow called upon the driver to make ready a coach. On the way out, Harlow asked me if I would return again in two days, this time for a longer visit. Caroline maintained that she would not mind supplying the invitation and coming for me herself. "Say yes," Harlow said with that droll smile of his, "and I'll have something special to surprise you with."

"Lamb's hock stew?"

"Perhaps—or perhaps better."

I agreed to see Harlow two days hence. Of course, I asked Mother for permission once again to visit Caroline, this time for an overnight stay at her home. I was truly surprised when she said she would allow it—this was the second time we had used the same ruse, but Mother never asked after Harlow's whereabouts. I thought perhaps she had forgotten that brother and sister would most probably reside together, but then I began to suspect that she merely hoped I would forget—about Harlow, that is, so that perhaps Carter Forbes-Spencer might return to pay homage at my shrine.

At any rate, Caroline picked me up in the carriage at a bit after one o'clock, but when we arrived at Linton she did not dismount. "I'm going on," she said. "I'll be home presently, but in the meantime, go in, and keep Harlow company."

I ran up the walkway to the enormous door, and rapped the bronze knocker on its metal base. I expected to be received by the same pinched parlormaid who had admitted me two days past, but to my surprise Harlow came to the door himself. He peeked out, and then said briskly, with his usual half-grin, "We needn't any new governesses, thank you, Miss Eyre. The only job we've available is watching the attic."

"Oh, open the door and stop pranking," I scolded him. "I'm being eaten alive by gnats out here!"

When he admitted me, I looked about, and had the sudden sensation that I was back at Carter Forbes-Spencer's apartments: there was not a soul in sight.

"It seems you have quite a few jobs available, Harlow, as there seem to be no servants on the property."

"You're quite right—I gave them a holiday for the afternoon. They're not to be back until this evening."

"How grand—your mother traveling, the servants sent away. Tell me, are you taking lessons in seduction from Carter, and should I construe the obvious?"

"Don't be silly. After hearing Carter's fabrications, I'd hardly bother with lessons—I'd likely believe I had only to lie helplessly in the road and wait for you to pounce upon me."

"All right then, you rogue, why are the servants gone?"

"Because I've a surprise for you, and I didn't want them to see you arrive, nor do I wish to have them interfering in it."

"Shall I put my own case away, then?"

"No, you needn't do that. Leave it in the closet in front, and you can see to it later."

He led me through the house until we had reached the kitchen. There was a rear door here, and by it sat two large leather bags, secured with buckles. He picked them up, and urged me to follow him outside, and down the path that led to the stables.

"Do you ride?" he called back to me from beneath his bundles.

"Of course—at home I ride a stallion, the only one in our stables. His name is RainShadow." I felt a sudden wave of anxious sadness: what might be happening, at that very moment, to the house in New Parrish, to the horses, the grounds, the servants left behind? To banish these thoughts I spoke again: "Although I must tell you, Harlow, I prefer to ride astride, so if you've only a sidesaddle you may as well let me go bareback."

"Didn't I know you would say that! Certainly I've a proper saddle for you."

"We're going riding, then?"

"We are, but that's only the means to the end of our journey."

He made ready the tack and saddled two horses, my own being a lovely long-legged chestnut mare with what I anticipated would be a good soft mouth. We set off at a gallop over low fields, crisscrossed by stone dry-walls and barriers made of formidable brambles. The sun shone, the new green grass flew beneath the horses' hooves. I gave the mare her head, guided her into the fences, and delighted in the thrill of being airborne as she easily cleared each obstacle. "You're quite the steeplechaser," I heard Harlow shout behind me, and then he was galloping past, urging me to follow. We slowed the horses to a canter perhaps a mile from the main house, and then Harlow abruptly turned right, into a cluster of trees which stood at the base of a large hill. A path wound therein, and the horses picked their way along it, seeming familiar with its twists and turns.

I had assumed we were to have a picnic dinner, but we had passed a dozen perfect picnic stops, and were now climbing this gloomy forested hillside, so plainly Harlow had something else in mind.

Presently we reached the summit of the hill and the trees came to an end. A clearing, grassy and flat, greeted us—and set upon it, invisible from below because of the foliage, was a most unusual building, which I now assumed was our destination.

Harlow waved his hand, and pulled his gelding up. I came to a stop beside him. He was smiling, but I was still puzzling over the building, whose odd shape gave little clue as to its use. The ground floor was a squat square, made of stone, with latticed windows all around. At one end was a stone chimney, but at the other was what looked like a turret stolen from an ancient castle. It rose straight and windowless to its top, where it was fitted with what appeared to be a glass-and-metal cap much like Miss Ashe's atrium.

"It's beautiful," I said to Harlow, "but what is it?"

"You'll see," he said mischievously.

We stabled the horses in a tiny shelter with three straight stalls, and then Harlow took me inside.

The ground floor of the cottage was a single large room, but it was much more inviting within than it had looked from the door. The walls were covered in whitewashed plaster, and dark beams crossed the flat ceiling. At the chimney end was the most enormous fireplace I had ever seen. Its mantel was of carved ebony and black Italian marble, and so huge was the opening beneath the flue itself that I could stand inside whilst barely crouching. The andirons reached my waist, and wood with kindling had been laid across them. Directly in front of the fireplace was a high sleigh bed with a canopy; it was fully made, the bedclothes turned back. At the other end, in one corner, was a sitting area with cabinets, shelves of books overhead, and well-stuffed furniture. Oriental carpets covered the plank floors, and thick drapes were tied away from the windows. In the other corner was a carved ebony table with side chairs; the table was set with silver and candelabra. A small door led off into the pantry, and another, larger door led—I assumed—into the strange round tower.

It was obviously a spot often in use. And, just as obviously, Harlow had specially appointed it for our visit.

I was eager to know what our day was to consist of, but Harlow simply guided me through it, and I soon gave up attempting to guess what was to happen, as he had evidently gone to a great deal of trouble to both put me at my ease and delight me. A full dinner awaited us, no doubt cooked at and laboriously transported from the kitchen of Linton's main house. Harlow served me himself, and we dined upon cold pressed duck, salads, fresh berries, and cream. We laughed and chatted throughout the meal and afterward, and I wondered whether I should not inquire as to when we were returning to the main house, but in truth, I did not wish to return, and so I said nothing.

At last it began to grow dark. I knew at this point that we should already have departed, for how would we find our way over the treacherous fields at night—but I thought, what does it matter, I am safe here, Mother and Father believe me to be with Caroline; there is no one about to censure me, no servants to slip off and confide to a master or mistress. It occurred to me to wonder if perhaps the one source of danger here might not be Harlow himself—for beyond matters of propriety (and was I not well beyond them, given that I was here?) it was true that I was alone, with no one knowing my true whereabouts, and therefore completely at the mercy of my host.

But when I glanced up and found him eyeing me with his gentle and slightly bemused expression, I realized how absurd this was, and banished the last traces of suspicion from my mind.

Harlow carried our plates to the scullery himself—he insisted, although I offered my help—and then, seeing the last rays of the sunset, he lit a fire in the fireplace. Finally he unpacked one of the bags he'd brought, and removed a flannel blanket, and a carry-lamp. Lighting the lamp, he took my hand, and then led me through the door into the tower room.

Inside the round space there was nothing save a metal winding staircase, like that of an oubliette. It was quite black, and I could see only the steps beneath my feet; I found the effect quite eerie, and clutched Harlow's hand rather too tightly. We ascended endless steep stairs, reaching what would have been the fourth or fifth floor of a normal building. At last we were at the top, and the steps ended at a hole in the ceiling. Harlow reached the landing and turned back to shine the lamp for me; when I was standing beside him, I saw that we were in a large round chamber whose waist-high walls ended to become a glass ceiling.

Then I saw the telescopic equipment, and I realized what the building was used for, and wondered why I'd not guessed it before, given Harlow's studies at university.

"It's an observatory!" I clapped my hands, delighted. I had never been in one, and the effect, there in the dark, with the stars shining over our heads, was already spectacular. The hill we sat on was higher than it had seemed and, coupled with the height of the tower, gave us a stunning view of the countryside below. In the twilight the fields appeared to be vast blankets, and the foliage which dotted them green cotton wool. "Such an old building," I exclaimed. "I should not have known it would be put to such modern use!"

"It is very old. It was originally part of a fort from which the whole estate could be defended. Now it belongs to Sir Gilliam, the owner of Linton. He is a great aficionado of the sciences, and had the place refurbished in order to accommodate the most up-to-date equipment. Which is one reason my mother prevailed upon him to play host to our family."

Harlow was smiling in that flushed way I've seen boys do when they are showing you something—a chipmunk's nest, or a battle of tin soldiers—which especially moves them. But then he caught himself, and glanced at the floor. "I hope I've not disappointed you—my interests may not be yours, and I wished only to show it to you, but we can go now in just a few moments—"

"Oh no," I said, "you've not bored me in the least. Please, explain all of it to me—it's wonderful. And wonderful too that you have a passion for it."

He laughed. "I described it only as an interest. You mustn't mistake that for passion."

"You are not so disaffected as you try to appear, Harlow. Put aside your Lord Byron and stop wallowing—you've already kissed me, and unless you are a complete fool you no doubt intend to kiss me again tonight, and if you are kissing, then you cannot claim to be completely devoid of passion." I paused a moment, quite enjoying the worldly tone I'd adopted, and enjoying Harlow's blushing laughter.

"My God, you are shameless, Arabella," he gasped. "You'd bring blood to the cheeks of a corpse. You've found your subject, speaking so."

I frowned. "I think not. I don't know that it's clear to me what my own passion is."

"You've a passion for inhabiting yourself, most certainly," Harlow said.

I shook my head. "I doubt that is enough."

"It's more than most have."

I shrugged, so as to change the subject, and then I turned my attention to the equipment. The walls were lined with circular shelves, full of books, maps, and sextants. There were two mounted telescopes, and two chairs upon wheels which were designed to roll across the space. There were windows in the glass, I saw, so that the scopes could be aimed outward. I sat at one of the chairs and put my eye to a piece, but I could see nothing.

Harlow said, "I'll focus it for you in a moment." He seemed to be waiting for something, and then he took me by the shoulders and turned me in the opposite direction. "Here is what I wished you to see."

I looked down over the blanket-fields, following his gaze, and then I saw the yellow glow at the edge of the horizon. It was the moon—but such a moon as I had never beheld. It rose, enormous and full, over the countryside, and seemed so close that I imagined I could throw a stone and hit it.

I gasped at the beauty of it, and then Harlow fixed one of the telescopes upon it and guided my eye to the eyepiece. If I had been impressed a moment ago, I was now practically dumbfounded, for the object which jumped into my sights in no way resembled the familiar moon I'd expected. This was a complete world, a landscape, with channels and mountains and round pock-marked areas which looked like enormous bowls on the surface.

"Good God!" I breathed, unable to take my eyes from the sight.

"Keep looking," Harlow said, and then he guided the scope into a new position, and adjusted my shoulders to follow it. Now I saw another segment of landscape at the edge of the planet, and the brightness of nearby stars jumped into view at the corners of my vision. Harlow moved me again, and the night sky filled my gaze, so near, so blindingly brilliant, that I felt I had left the earth to roam the heavens at will. How vast it was, and the globe I inhabited much smaller than it had seemed an hour ago.

I swung my attention back to the moon. "Harlow"—I clutched at his arm without looking away from the eyepiece—"do you suppose there is anything alive on that surface, perhaps staring back at us?"

He chuckled. "There are certainly those who think so. I've seen scientific journals and penny novels alike filled with descriptions of moon-men, our lunar counterparts, with whom we'll soon be in communication."

"Why, what absolute arrogance, to imagine they'd be just like us. As if God is no more original than that."

Harlow laughed aloud at this, but I kept my eye pressed to the telescope, afraid I might miss something. Presently he sat down beside me and began to identify parts of the moon's scarred surface. He explained the craters and mountains to me, and told me the names of different regions, of which my favorite was the Sea of Tranquillity.

I watched for another quarter hour, until the moon had ascended into a higher point in the sky and assumed more usual proportions. Then, the celestial drama over, Harlow and I returned down the spiral staircase, and made ourselves comfortable once again in the main room of the observatory building.

Harlow offered me some claret and sweets, which we enjoyed whilst we talked, our discussion again roaming far and wide among topics both weighty and frivolous. We passed a pleasant half hour in this manner, and then Harlow rose from his place upon the well-upholstered couch and stretched. Excusing himself, he sauntered to the other end of the room, and fetched the second bundle he'd brought with him from the main house. He opened it, and I was surprised to see him remove the black bag containing the hypodermics and morphia—but as Caroline had praised the substance's euphoric effects I didn't wonder that Harlow might wish to partake of it again tonight.

I did wonder, however, if this was to be the final amusement of the evening. I realized that, although I had teased Harlow about our stolen kiss,

I did truly hope there would be an encore to that particular performance, but thus far he had made no move beyond the tentative greeting we'd given each other. And while I now knew myself to be a bold creature—with Harlow's unqualified approval, it seemed—there was that portion of me which sought to be desired as well as desiring, so that he might be the one to suggest a continuation of our activities. Not that I wished him to leap upon me as if at a wrestling opponent, à la Carter Forbes-Spencer—I wished only a signal, an unmistakable sign, that our forwardness in the carriage was not to be a singular occurrence. But I recalled how he and Caroline had napped following their injections during my last visit, and thought that, should the same prove the case this evening, there would be little time left for the pursuit of romance. So it was with a measure of disappointment that I watched him ready his syringe.

He drew liquid into the glass phial, attached the needle to the end, inserted the plunger. But then, rather than put the equipment away, he began preparing a second injection, and turned to me as he worked. "I'm making this one up for you, Arabella, should you wish to try it. You'll find it quite pleasant, I think, although at first I suffered a bit of nausea, which is fairly common."

I had not considered imbibing the substance myself, but now I found my interest piqued. After all, if Harlow were to partake, what should there be for me to do but observe? That would hardly be amusing, I thought, so perhaps in the immediate absence of more kissing I ought to join him and see for myself what the "milk of Morpheus" might be like.

"How does it feel, exactly?" I asked Harlow. "Is it something like sipping a glass of Champagne?"

He shook his head emphatically. "No. The finest Champagne in the world cannot match morphia for its calmative effects. It's quite indescribable, especially the first few times one tries it."

I shrugged. "All right then—but if I become disgustingly ill, you must look after me, and not tell anyone how I embarrassed myself."

He chuckled. "I give you my word."

After rolling up his shirtsleeve, Harlow slid the needle carefully into a protrusion in his forearm, and then sat still for a moment, as I had seen him do on my visit to Linton two nights previously. A few moments later, he picked up the other syringe from the side table and bade me offer up my own arm. This I could not do without unfastening my jacket and baring one shoulder completely, the sleeves being too tight to push above the elbow; and so I wrapped myself in one of the lap blankets, undid the jacket, and slid my forearm out from beneath my coverlet. I stared at the ornate mantel of the fireplace, having chosen not to watch as Harlow expertly slid the steel point into my flesh.

He was quite correct—I felt the barest pinch, the needle hurting me hardly at all.

A moment later I experienced a sensation unlike any I had previously known.

In terms of the manner in which it overtook me, the surge of the morphia equaled or surpassed even the Orgasm, although it was not concentrated only in the region of my sex. Instead it was like a warm bath encompassing body and mind, transforming them in an instant. I was no longer solid flesh and bone. I became pure feeling itself, and I can describe that feeling only as bliss, the undulating mantle of bliss with which God wrapped Eve in the Garden, and the angels in Heaven.

A minute passed—a minute which seemed to divide itself into the tiniest components of time possible. I had never known such happiness, such completeness, such a sense of absolute rightness with the world. I was love itself—I overflowed with love for my surroundings, for my fellow human beings, and not least of all for myself. For the first time I saw myself clearly, as if I had risen to look down upon my form from above, and what I saw delighted me beyond words. I was the perfect child of God. All of His children, I realized, are in fact perfect, all of them good and fallible in the same instant—evil does not exist, only ignorance.

If only the world could join me up here upon the exalted ceiling and realize how trivial its busywork was. If only I could make it see as I saw—

All at once it was clear: I must not struggle any longer against my unique nature. I had been born into perfect understanding, and perhaps it would be given me to impart a sense of this perfection to all of humankind.

But if I would do this I must disdain those conventions which stood between myself and that destiny.

The obsession with virtue was one such convention—it was so obvious to me now. The guarding of that virtue merely distracted one from larger issues, for what truths could I pursue if the most fundamental physical autonomy eluded me? I had no need of this or any other social constriction. I was beyond all of it, need never question the fact again—

I drifted back into the arms of the sofa, a feather gently come to earth; I snuggled into the chenille blanket, and thought how perfect its texture was, and how I should be content to sit here relishing it for the rest of my natural life.

A shadow passed between my closed lids and the lamp's flame, causing me to open my eyes. Harlow was seated at the edge of my chair, smiling down upon me.

"Are you quite well?"

I sat up and stared at him, my cheeks flushed with happiness.

His own smile lingered, then disappeared. Slowly he leaned forward to place a gentle kiss upon my lips. I turned toward him, and when next he kissed me I took his face in my hands.

He must have recognized something in my expression, in the intense pressure of my hands, for he took my fingers from his cheeks and held them. His voice was a gentle whisper: "You mustn't take those first moments of exhilaration too seriously, Arabella, or necessarily follow where they lead you."

As an answer I leaned into his face, and he kissed me once again, this time with more fervor and less reserve, and I felt myself melt into that languid space which Harlow himself seemed often to inhabit, so that my movements were slow, and their progression dreamlike. I knew then what my intent should be, and pressed my own body into his, and he seemed to be waiting for me to change my mind, he seemed uncertain as to whether he might move forward without censure; but at last, convinced, he returned my ardor with that languor that now defined us both, his body radiating a warmth that touched me even through heavy wool and gabardine.

I longed to dispense with the intrusive fabric, even as I could sense how his hands longed for me beyond the constraints of buttons, stays, sleeves. He undid my peplumed jacket and drew it from my shoulders; it proved just as simple for me to free him from his vest and collar. We sat so for a moment, and then he pulled me gently to my feet. I placed his hands at the laces of my stays, giving him the ribbon to undo. His fingers fumbled, confused, at the tangle of grommets and material, and although I smiled my amusement, I proved little more adept at unbuttoning his shirttails. Wordlessly we compromised: he slid the shirt from his back, and I loosed the corset and drew it, not entirely daintily, over my head. My flesh immediately turned to goose bumps, as much from the situation as from the chill I experienced, standing bare-armed in my chemise; Harlow, his torso bare as well, drew me to him, and I rested my forehead against his warm skin. After a moment, I pulled away, and placed his hands beneath my skirts. This time he seemed more certain of himself. He quickly drew the petticoats down, sinking to his knees so that I might step out of them, and then he rolled the stockings slowly down my legs, and smoothed each one past my feet. I closed my eyes as he ran his hands up my calves and thighs, then opened them again in surprise when I felt him lightly kiss me above my left knee, his tongue liquid and hot. Then he rose, and placed my hands at the buttons of his fly, where again I proved hopelessly unskilled. Once he'd helped me, I eagerly pushed the material down past his buttocks, until he stood in his underclothes. His arms drew around my waist, he lifted the chemise over my head, undid the buttons of my skirt; and then the last of our clothing yielded, fell away from us, unwanted and unnecessary, flower petals or October leaves which drifted into lazy heaps upon the floor.

I was naked before another human being for the first time in my memory, and yet I was overcome not by shame but by the most profound calm. I could not take my eyes from Harlow's form, for he was naked as well, his flesh golden, the ridges and hollows of his muscles smoothly defined in the lamplight, the beautiful Penis—it was not in the least foolish, I thought, in its awakened state—at last freed and visible. We caught each other's eye—caught each other's stares—and smiled our delight, and then he was pulling me toward him, his mouth at my neck, my breasts, while my hands explored the unknowns of his muscled thighs, his sex.

Then, to my surprise, he drew back and shook his head.

"No, no—"

"What is it," I whispered.

"I did not intend—I am not—"

"I know you did not, nor did I—but it's right, I'm certain of it."

I didn't add that I knew myself at that moment to be Supreme, and incapable of error.

"It's the morphia," Harlow was saying, "you are not in your right mind, and I should be an animal were I to press my advantage."

"You also partook of it, are you not in *your* right mind?"

"I'm accustomed to it, it hasn't the same effect on me anymore."

"Harlow," I said. I rubbed my cheek along the curve of his bicep, reveled in its firmness. "I am not accustomed. But neither am I intoxicated." This was quite true—every instant was clear to me, I felt none of the distortion of time or space which accompanies too many glasses of claret. "You must believe me. Never have I felt surer of what I want."

I looked up at him, and he returned my gaze, and then shut his eyes. "Neither have I, God help me," he breathed.

I ran my finger over his lips, traced the curve of his throat, and then he sank to the floor, pulled me with him. He was upon me, the weight of him delicious, his scent and the salt-taste of his skin filling my senses. He paused to gaze down at me, as if to memorize the appearance of my flesh; then he rolled away from me to explore with his fingertips and the back of his hand the expanse of my belly, the curve where my hip joined my thigh, the roundness of my nipple, the splayed hair over my shoulder. I watched him as he did these things, as delighted at finding myself the object of his admiration as he appeared at being the admirer.

He rose once more, but only to lead me to the bed before the fireplace, and here we coiled round each other with abandon. I felt his fingers between my legs and pushed myself against them, I reached between his thighs, and heard him gasp his pleasure. The surface skin of the Penis slid over the stiffness beneath where I grasped him, and I tested this novel effect until Harlow placed his own hand over mine and drew my arm back to my side. Then he rolled atop me, moving slowly at first, and I moved with him; we were two sleepy and slippery serpents, and then one creature, one in intent and intensity, each of us sensing the other's ultimate readiness.

Yet it was not exactly as I had imagined it.

At his first entrance into me I gasped, for as eager as I'd felt myself, the pain and the foreignness of it caught me short. I ceased moving, I felt my body go rigid; and Harlow felt it too, for he also became still.

But after we had lain quietly, I grew used to him, and stirred once again; and then our movements resumed, synchronized. I had expected something deafening, explosive, a thunderstorm, but instead we were as water flowing round and against each other, gentle as rain. And this lasted many minutes, until I heard Harlow breathe "my God—" and then lay quiet once again. When he lifted himself, just slightly, so as to lie next to me rather than upon me, a hot trickle seeped out from between my legs, moistening my thighs where they touched the sheets.

I allowed my spine to go limp, my limbs to relax, and lay back upon the mattress. My breath was still quickened; I'd felt the beginnings of that yearning which preceded the Orgasm, but had not risen near to that height myself. Perhaps, I imagined, this had to do with the pain, which had been not tremendous, but unexpected. Yet despite it, I felt at peace. I felt the keenest desire to continue my exploration of Harlow's body, to wrap myself about him, whisper and laugh with him. His foream lay across my breasts, and I looked over to find him staring at me, his expression wondering and bemused.

"You are unique in all the world," he said.

I thought of my grand destiny, so recently revealed, and was about to agree, but realized there was still a place for modesty in my repertoire. "Surely not," I smiled. "I'm certain I'm by and large like any other woman."

"Not like any other."

"All right then, if you are a man unlike all others."

"I should hope so."

I giggled, and nestled against his chest, enjoying the tickle of the hairs which grew there, and the sweet, rich scent he exuded.

"Are you all right," he whispered.

"Oh, yes. Quite all right. Beyond all right, in fact—quite happy."

"As am I."

I could feel my eyes closing, and Harlow's even breathing lulling me to sleep, and then I gave in to it utterly, and rested.

I was awakened the next morning by strong sunlight falling upon my face, through a crack in the heavy drapes. My head felt heavy, a dull throb beginning behind my eyes; my stomach was tender, and cramping slightly. I sat up, at first uncertain as to where I was, and how I had come to be there.

Then I turned and saw Harlow, still naked and rumpled and entwined with the bedsheets, and realized in the same instant that I was naked myself.

Dear God. It was my next thought, slamming the breath from my chest like a great hand. *Dear God, what have I done?* In the barest second it all returned to me: the precise nature of what I had done.

The shedding of false Virtue and the salvation of Humankind.

The warm, gold-tinged glow of the previous evening had dissipated completely. Now, in the glaring morning sunlight, I beheld with horror the wreck I had made of my life in an hour's time.

Spotless half a day ago, I was now irrevocably stained. I had fornicated with abandon, like the lowest of trollops. I was ruined. Sullied. My sin sure to be apparent like the mark of Cain upon my forehead—and however far I ran I should not be able to escape the implications of my behavior. I would never be able to give myself freely to a man in marriage—would never wear the snowy white of the bridal gown—indeed, no man would now have me—unless it was in that way which had been already suggested: I should become at best a mistress, a tawdry plaything, used and then abandoned, or at worst the companion of the woolen-shawled girl in Whitechapel, selling myself to the evening's highest bidder—my children would be bastards, with no man willing to claim them—and my parents—oh, my poor Mamee and Papa—how ashamed they would be! How I would give anything to spare them this, to reverse this tragedy I had wrought—which Harlow had wrought, Harlow who would first scorn and then laugh at me when he came upon me in the roadway—I would give even my life, which was now worth nothing anyway, yes, I should even prefer death to this mortification, this debasement, this—

"G' morning."

I heard Harlow's sleepy snuffle, and then his hand landed gently upon my naked shoulder, causing me to scream aloud and leap from the bed with the top sheet wrapped about me like a winding cloth.

"Let me alone!" I cried. At which he sat up in bed, looking mightily confused, and rubbed his eyes with a fist.

"What in the world's the matter, girl? You look as if you'd seen Cromwell's ghost."

I could not answer him. I tried, but nothing came from my lips but a stifled gasp. The more I sought to hide it, the more it forced its way through. At last I could endure standing still no longer, and I turned, tottering toward the pile of clothing by the chair—oh, horrid reminder!—sifting through it and gathering up every item which appeared to be mine. Behind me Harlow called, "Arabella, are you ill? Are you in pain? For the love of Christ, will you answer me?"

"Don't curse at me!" I shouted at him. "Don't think you can take the liberty of cursing before me because you presume me no longer a lady! I won't have it!"

Now he rose from the bed and strode over, still completely naked, and turned me by the shoulder. "Here now, what is all this? What's this business of ladies? What's happened?"

"I'm undone by my own choice," I stammered, "I admit it, you needn't gloat, it was my doing—and now I—I wish—" I could continue no longer, the sobs I had held back now broke through in earnest, and I wailed into the pile of clothing I held.

"I don't understand," Harlow said, placing his arms about me. "Last evening you were brave and certain and trusting and—wild—and today—"

"Last evening—" I began, and then stopped. Last evening, what? Every real thing had been altered. It had been the morphia, surely, just as Harlow said. Yet I remembered every detail of my own delusions—how far away they seemed now!—I recalled every instant of our wantonness. And my own part in it. How convenient it would have been to blame Harlow, blame the injection, but no—I had been affected, but not intoxicated. My mind had been transported but clear, my decisions my own. I shook my head, robbed of words.

"Arabella." Harlow tilted my face upward. "I am truly sorry if you have regrets over what occurred between us. I must tell you, though, I have none, for I have never—been with anyone, and now I shall have the most wonderful experience to recall as my first."

I shrugged his hands from me, shook my head. "You lie," I gasped.

"What do you mean, it was splendid—"

"You lie about your innocence! There must have been others. Romances. *Whores*." I spat the word aloud; what did it matter, now that I was a step from whoredom myself? "Every man has them, and has them blithely, it is only we women who must guard our virtue—"

"Oh, for God's sake." It was his turn to shake his head. "You've a point, Berry. There are both whores and hypocrites walking the world. But please, spare me the insult of placing me among them. I've no desire to sample the first and die of pox, and don't aspire to becoming the second. So I shan't hold against you what I've partaken in myself." He smoothed my hair, and such a soothing effect did it have upon me that I allowed him to continue. "I haven't Carter Forbes-Spencer's pedigree, you know. I'll not condemn or abandon you—I'd leave such behavior to him and his noble ilk. Perhaps we're exceptions, Berry, we are not the common breed and we may well rot in hell someday, but I doubt we are the only ones who think with more liberty and dare more than is common and acceptable. Let us enjoy it, as we were willing to do last night, instead of falling into self-reproach and defeat."

I recognized in his words a glimmer of the spirit I had so embraced the night before—and so rejected this morning. "It's not you who shall be followed by whisperings and condemnation all the rest of your days," I said quietly.

"Whisperings from whom? Lest you forget it, Berry, there is no one here but you and me, and I'm surely not about to open my mouth regarding the conduct of either one of us."

I looked up at him. "But we know of it nonetheless."

"Yes, and what of it? Do you feel compelled to warn the rest of the world of your pollution, so that they might avoid you and retain their own purity?" He said this with an irony that almost caused the corner of my mouth to rise.

"But such a transgression must reveal itself somehow, whether I wish it or not."

"Now I know you're not thinking clearly, Miss Ramsbottom. What have we done that was evil—it's transgression only if you regard it so. And let us hope it never becomes so simple as you think to tell the transgressors from the virgins. Else there will be few sanctified marriages, and even fewer wedding anniversaries, as the previously virtuous are revealed in all their debauched splendor."

This time I really did smile, despite myself. I felt my mettle returning, and recognized my earlier waking panic as exactly that. Yet I remained uneasy, for I could not bear the thought of a future as perpetual liar, reduced to tale-telling about this most vital aspect of my history.

I felt suddenly drained, overwhelmed, and requested of Harlow that he accompany me home, as I wished only to be alone for a time to sort out my confusion. He agreed—that gentle and good soul who had done much to calm me. He asked only that we stop at Linton Manor first, so that he might retrieve my travel case and prepare a carriage for the drive.

"Oh no," I cried, "you mustn't!" I realized with a start that this would involve exchanges with both Caroline and the household servants, and in my present state of mind I could not endure the thought of it.

But Harlow insisted that the distance to Knightsbridge was too great to be undertaken astride, and besides, what had I to fear from his sister—my friend—or the hired help? "I took you to the observatory. We dined, and I left you to sleep in the cottage while I tended the horses and bedded down upon the hay. Is it not that simple?"

I supposed it was, and at any rate I could not return home without my belongings unless I did truly wish to arouse suspicions. So I unbound the sheet from about me, and requested (out of what foolish modesty?) that Harlow turn away while I dress what he'd already beheld at great length. I smoothed my suit as best I could, and arranged my hair before the body-length glass, and then we set off for Linton.

Caroline was at home and greeted us at the door, and I could tell from her too cheery inquiries that she would brook no nonsense regarding horse-tending and beds of hay. I feared a repeat of her cool performance of the other evening, and indeed I saw a flash of it—but surprisingly, it was directed at Harlow, and not at me. I was standing in the foyer, waiting for a butler to fetch my bag; Harlow and Caroline had retreated to the kitchens, where Harlow intended to down a quick mug of tea. As they passed through the hallway I caught Caroline's angry whisper: "Why do you not find your own companions, and stay away from mine—?" followed by a muffled but quick retort from Harlow.

When she returned Caroline was as solicitous of me as she'd ever been—and was absolute ice toward her brother, as she suggested that for propriety's sake she would drive me home herself, and would he please make himself useful supervising the horses' harnessing. It was evident that Harlow had not expected to wave me off so quickly, but Caroline was adamant: no, he must not come with us. He managed to corner me by the doorway long enough to ask, "When shall I see you?" but I could only shake my head, and so he departed after giving me a squeeze upon the fingers and a fervent glance.

During the trip home, I sat folded in upon myself, my arms hugging my own body. My head pained me yet more, and the jouncing of the carriage made the bile rise in my throat. I was beginning to feel snappish and moody to a degree quite unlike my normal self. Caroline and I spoke barely at all, but I caught not a glimmer of reproach in her eyes or manner. Mostly, she gazed upon me with concern; I knew she knew what had transpired between Harlow and myself, if not in detail, then in essence. Each time she caught my eye my pale cheeks burned, but finally I felt I had to address her harshness toward her sibling.

"You mustn't think I was dragged off into the woods," I began. "Your brother is a gentleman, and a fine one, and any plan we undertook was mutually agreed upon—"

"Oh, Arabella, you needn't explain. I know it. I am only annoyed at Harlow, he is so lax in his thinking at times—but were he a scoundrel in any measure, I should have warned you long ago, brother or not. As it is, I know he adores you, you have quite interfered with his grief over another broken romance. And I am annoyed only because he steals you from my own company, although I suppose that's silly." She smiled a sad but radiant smile, and I felt compelled to hug her—despite the discomfort it caused me—which gesture she returned with fervor.

When I stepped from the carriage, she kissed me upon the cheek and whispered, "You mustn't worry, dear. Promise me you shan't."

I knew precisely what she meant, and replied shakily, "I shall try not to."

Thankfully, when I opened the front door, I was greeted by Uncle Charles's maid Lydia rather than Lucy. My parents and Richard had gone calling, she informed me in her barely comprehensible Cockney, so I was left blessedly to my own devices. I washed thoroughly, then went directly to my room and curled up into my window seat, and wondered how I should feel after pondering alone the events just past.

I was surprised at the answer. For the more I considered it, the less distressed I felt, whereas I'd imagined just the opposite outcome. I was able to recall (unfortunately without the accompanying bliss) those ideas which had led me to abandon myself with Harlow, and although they had seemed distant and insane to me that morning, I now felt them to be nonetheless truly the product of my consciousness, perhaps the grandiose conclusions which my waking mind, freed—or contorted—by the powerful morphia, had allowed to rise to the surface. Extreme though they were, I felt strengthened recollecting them, and discovered I was able to relive with pleasure rather than horror the moments of my "debasement," and to feel a great tenderness toward Harlow, who had proved himself a being of uncommon character.

I took stock of myself. I felt changed—not tainted, or polluted, but certainly different. A part of my childhood, my unknowing, lay behind me in the little observatory cottage; I was not now stained or evil, but *fuller*. And blessedly, I found that, regarding myself in this way, my acts became simply another piece of my history, rather than its defining moment. They were rendered a matter between Harlow, myself, and the Divine, who alone would judge us.

My fear of censure and sin was thus reduced. But the one fear which I could not dispel was of the worst and simplest consequence of passion, which has nothing to do with mere recriminations: it was the dread that I might become with child, in which case a separate being would surely suffer for my actions, whatever attitude I chose to take toward them. But I had long known Lucy's rustic opinions regarding the order of Nature: death comes most often in the small hours of the morning, when the soul's moorings are loosed; births are more likely during cloudy weather than fair; conception happens midway between one menstrual flow and the next. I had only finished bleeding a few days before. I prayed that folk wisdom would prevail, and spare me further turmoil.

I vowed I would not worry, as Caroline had advised me, and presently I made my way to my bed, and lay down upon it. Staring at the paneled ceiling, I found my discomfort waning a bit; I drifted into a state of calm not unlike a mild version of the morphia's effect, and I pursued this until at last it led me into a deep and dreamless sleep.

For three days I had no contact with either Caroline or Harlow. I found myself, in this interim, pondering that question which, for another girl, might have arisen much sooner than later: what was to become of my relationship with Harlow from this point forward?

What were we to be to each other now? That he would neither "condemn nor abandon" me seemed evident, but beyond this, what should I expect, and what did I want? Were we now courting? That would be an irony, I thought—that we should court after consummating courtship first. Were we friends? Paramours? Did I wish to repeat the act of passion—did he?

Did I love him?
Did he love me?

The afternoon of the third day was warm and humid, with dark clouds scudding about overhead and threatening rain. I sat in the garden behind the house with Richard, water-coloring landscapes and fanning myself a bit. Mother was at the dressmaker's, supervising the tailoring of a new yellow summer suit to offset her hair; Father was at Leeds Hall with Uncle Charles, playing cricket, or some other such gentrified nonsense.

It was Lydia who called me to the front foyer, and I was loath to go, as I wore only a cotton skirt and blouse with a paint-stained pinafore over them. I was even more upset when I saw—too late to change clothing—that the visitor upon our steps was Harlow, come to see me unannounced.

I gasped a little "Oh!" of embarrassment upon glimpsing him, but there was nothing to be done except to let him in. "You must excuse me," I said, "I was in the midst of painting—" but he cocked an eyebrow as if to say, "Do you forget who it is you're speaking to?" and I smiled and fell silent.

"Is there someplace where I may talk to you privately?" he asked, his tone—a rarity for Harlow—serious.

I led him to the rear of the house, then whispered in Richard's ear that Harlow wished to speak with me alone, and could we borrow the garden for just a little bit. Richard sprang up and gathered our pads and brushes, then honored Harlow with his usual mock bow as he passed into the house.

Harlow watched him depart, amusement in his eyes; then I seated myself on a small cushioned iron bench, and Harlow reclined next to me.

"I am not sure how to begin." He examined his hands in his lap.

I sensed something momentous on its way, and my heart began a steady thumping, although whether to anticipate good news or bad I could not know.

Harlow turned to look at me. "Arabella," he said, "I did not expect to be making this speech at this time, or indeed at any point in the near future. But I've given it a good deal of consideration, and in view of the—well, the circumstances—I should like to tell you what conclusions I've come to."

"All right," I said, with more composure than I felt.

"We're not a pair to mince words," he continued, and here I glanced up to make sure there were no witnesses to our lack of mincing.

"We've already consummated a marriage, in a manner of speaking, and I should like to do right by my own principles, and by you. If you will have me, I should like to ask you to be my wife."

My heart stepped up its frantic drumming. Here it was, the one opportunity I might have to reverse myself, to undo my decision, or at least legitimize it in the eyes of the world. Safely married to my illicit paramour, I would be beyond reproach, neither liar nor adulteress. I would have Harlow as a husband, and Caroline as a sister—what more delightful arrangement could befall me than this? Indeed, one might ask, had there ever been such a twist of fate, in which a woman might be *rewarded* for her indiscretion?

"You needn't think you must answer me right this minute. Please, take all the time you want, I must be certain you thought your decision over as carefully as I thought out my proposal."

I turned to examine him: this kind man who possessed not only the knowledge which might truly undo me, but also the grace not to make use of it. What made him so different from the ones who would have slandered me over nothing?

It was now my turn to stare at my captive hands. I could tell him to leave me until tomorrow—and indeed my cousins, and perhaps even Mother, might have counseled this course—or I could give him the answer which I knew would not change, however long I was permitted to think upon it.

"There is no need for me to ask you to wait." I took in a great breath of air, to steady my trembling voice. "I am more flattered than I can tell you to think you would consider me seriously." I paused.

Harlow gave me a tight half-smile. *"But—"* he said, as if he knew already what I was about to tell him.

"But—" I breathed deeply again. "I am afraid I must refuse your gallant offer."

Again I paused, and Harlow made no reply to me. We did not look at each other. A damp breeze stirred the leaves of the wizened apple trees over our heads, but besides the rustle of the greenery there was not a sound between us.

After a moment Harlow said, "So. I am to be twice dismissed as a suitor. I wonder, have I set some sort of record? Is there some laurel I can collect somewhere?"

I turned to look at him. He was staring ahead of him, his face as bemused, as quizzical, as it had been the moment he entered the door.

That expression—or perhaps the lack of change in it—told me in an instant everything that I could have hoped to know: that I had made the right decision, that the facts I had summoned to help me reach it had not been ill-, or quickly, considered but correct.

For had he truly desired me with any intensity, he might have tried to change my mind, or at the very least request a reason for my answer, and demand a chance to reply to my doubts or otherwise influence me.

But he did neither, and it was evident that despite his goodness—and oh, Harlow, how good you are, how true and fine a friend!—some depth of feeling was lacking, perhaps only for me, but perhaps—and this I had considered at length over the past three days—for most things which another young man might approach with seriousness and a sense of import.

"You mustn't think my decision is made lightly, or that it implies some lack of regard for you," I told him.

"No, I should think you inform only the best of your beaux that they may go hang." His mouth curled in the teasing, familiar way, but now I saw a touch of genuine sadness in his eyes.

"The trouble is, Harlow, I know I am not your first choice, and suspect that you come to me out of a sense of duty, and that is not enough upon which to build a happy life. You do realize as much, don't you?" I said nothing about my other suspicions regarding his nature.

"Not necessarily. I know lives that are built upon much more questionable foundations. And you are wrong, Arabella, you are not some mere substitute in my eyes, and I am not simply repaying a debt as your seducer. I do not feel myself a seducer, quite frankly, so much as a co-conspirator."

The blood rose into my cheeks at this, but nonetheless I pressed on. "Harlow, tell me—how much time did you spend courting your lost love?"

"You mean the first one I lost?" He caught my eye. "Very nearly a year. I had known her for many years more, actually, during which it had always seemed inevitable that we would be paired together someday. But—"

"You see," I interrupted him, "you are one to weigh your options, to be certain of your feelings before plunging into marriage. You have known me only a matter of months. I have no doubt of your sincere affection for me, Harlow, as you needn't doubt my own toward you. But you do not know me well or long enough to be certain that affection could sustain a marriage."

"But I know you in a way that I did not know my first love."

I was surprised to hear myself say, "That is a different matter." This sounded so detached and unfeminine that I wished for some way to unspeak the words. But after a pause I went on: "You warned me not to act upon the exhilaration of morphia. I suspect you should also not act upon the exhilaration of—of passion. Once married, you know, we would not be spending all of our time entwined in the bedsheets, and what of the rest of our lives together?"

He shook his head. "You are so refreshingly frank, Arabella, didn't

Carter say that of you? But you mustn't inflame a suitor when you're in the midst of throwing him over, my dear."

I was thinking that Harlow would have been much less inflamed had I worded my speech in the way I would have liked: his experience and my own had rather differed in degrees of pleasure and pain, and so my perceptions of our Intercourse, while still wonderfully moving and full, were not so clouded by eagerness to repeat the act.

We sat silently for another moment, and then Harlow said, "We have perhaps put the cart before the horse, but if you are saying that you should trust my feelings after a greater amount of time had elapsed, can we not continue to court—without the distraction of passion, as you call it—and see where we are led?"

How I should have liked to avoid that question! For it cut through all of my excuses regarding first choices and seductions, being the one I had wrestled with most in my deliberations.

Alas, the conclusion I had reached on my own had been confirmed for me this day. I could only view my feelings for Harlow in terms of what they were not. I loved him, but did not feel *passionately* toward him, the act of passion aside, and I recognized that this was mainly because of the fatal absence of that combustible quality in him. It was the teasing, languid indifference he adopted, not only toward his endeavors but toward his own worth, which told me that although our friendship might be deep, our connexion as lovers could not lead me to happiness. It was his—what had his lost love called it, it pained me to find myself recollecting her term—his *aimlessness*, which made him fun, gentle, careless, and amusing, and certainly honorable, but not . . . I struggled to define it for myself . . . not fully formed, not fully *present*. If this was to change in a month or a year of courtship, well and good it would be—but if it did not, what a sad bargain I should find myself in the midst of, and how miserable Harlow should be for having made it.

There was only one answer I could give, and so I gave it.

"We have a great and undeniable friendship, Harlow—perhaps this is where we should fix things for the time being, so that we are free to consider every choice without assumptions being made regarding our intent."

"In other words, *no*. In other words, time will change nothing, you wouldn't have me if a hundred years passed." This time there was no mistaking the bitterness in his tone. "It seems I flattered myself that we shared some profound communion three days past," he said quietly.

"You did not flatter yourself."

We sat for a time without speaking; it was just as well, for I thought I might cry.

Finally Harlow said, "I shall be on my way, then, Arabella. It seems I've run short of conversation." I reached without thinking for his hand; he saw the gesture, and deftly avoided it by rising. "You must forgive me if I choose not to indulge in the pleasure of our friendship for a time," he said. "I think I should find that rather too difficult." He retreated slowly toward the garden gate.

I wished desperately not to leave it at that. "I am sorry—" I blurted out.

He turned, and perhaps he considered some cutting retort for a half second; but being Harlow, he did not voice it. "Don't be sorry. I'm sure to come around in a bit, and return to my usual jolly self." Then he disappeared through the gate, and into the gloom of the awning-covered porch beyond it.

I did not move for what may have been a quarter hour. I did not even cry, for indeed, now that I had the privacy in which to wail as loudly as I wished, no sound came forward. The sky continued to darken, and then huge, fat raindrops began to splatter the tree leaves and the flagstones of the garden; but still I sat, unmoving. I watched without interest as the droplets stained my dress and bounced from my forearms. I felt them strike my hair and then become a steady downpour, until my skin was quite soaked. I might have sat there forever had Richard not come running through the gate. He rolled his eyes, then pulled me up off the bench, grabbing the chintz cushions in one hand and my sleeve in the other, and dragged me into the house.

I have not seen Harlow in nearly a week, and do not know if I should expect to see him any time soon. The tears I could not shed that afternoon have certainly made their appearance, at night and at the oddest moments, and at endless times during the writing of this saga. How I miss him, and wish I could have repaid his gallantry with something other than harsh dismissal! I did not mean it so, Harlow. I only felt it the right thing, and in that I have not wavered. I think every day of our outings together—how good it felt to laugh unrestrained, to speak my mind and find my opinion respected, how drawn I was to so much of your character. I think especially of that evening in the observatory; I linger over each scent and sound, but had we continued it, I feel certain we should have come to no good.

I wonder if I should have waited to explain this to him, though; I wonder whether I handled it properly, or made it that much worse for him to hear by speaking immediately, as if I required no forethought in order to do so. But what is the use—I cannot take it back, what's done is done, and I can only hope that in time he shall forgive me, that he shall understand I intended no malice toward him.

I also cannot help wondering how Caroline will react to all of this. She and Harlow tease and disparage each other with impunity, but—much on the order of Richard and myself—they are actually quite close. How would I feel toward a girl who so rejected my own brother's advances? Why, I should be tempted to slap her, I think; how dare any girl assume herself too good for Richard, and for my family? But then, it would depend on the reasons for her refusal—I surely would not be so quick to pass judgment if I had not at least heard the girl's side of the story.

May Caroline be so inclined.

I think of contacting her, but then I tell myself that this would be an imposition on Harlow. He no doubt has little use for me at the moment, and might interpret my approaching his sister as an inconsiderate interruption of his privacy.

One thing which crossed my mind and then quickly left it was the notion that Harlow might, out of anger, choose to betray me, and brag to whoever might listen of his exploit concerning me. I had even conjured up a blessedly brief image of Harlow sitting about the Lamb's Hock with Carter Forbes-Spencer and Thomas Paxton—and why not Jeffrey Price, why not have him miraculously fly across the ocean to add his own tarnished penny's worth—while each of them in turn discussed my various merits and debits as a paramour.

But I know somehow that he will not do this. It is out of character for him; it would debase us both, and I believe that Harlow—despite everything—treasures the memory of our knowledge of each other as much as I.

Ah, to have someone with whom to share the details of that knowledge, someone with whom to rhapsodize or laugh over it, or merely express my feelings as they shift about. But again, as upon so many occasions, I find myself at a loss. Here am I, having passed one of the great milestones of my existence, and there is not a soul who can know of it, no confidant who can counsel me. Harlow and Caroline should have been my first choices—what a shame that Harlow is also the subject of the confidence! My own parents do not even merit consideration, for imagine what the response should be were I to inform them of my lost maidenhood. And while I believe I could trust Richard with my secrets, I fear I would be burdening him unfairly, since I've no idea of his level of sophistication in such matters, or his opinions regarding them.

So I am left to myself—how familiar a sensation!—to view my "indiscretion" in whatever light I choose. At least once a day it occurs to me what a secret I hold within myself: I feel more intensely feminine, yet separated from others of my age and sex, by knowing what I shouldn't, and what they don't. There is, for me, no longer any mystery regarding the events of the nuptial bed. Whereas other girls may titter over them, I have experienced them firsthand. I could inform the titterers of any number of things: of the beauty of a man, and how it compels; of the fact that his touch leaves not an outward stain, but changes forever one's inner awareness, how the act connects one not just, or always, to the man involved, but to oneself. How odd it is that maidenhood is mourned as that which is taken away, when through the knowledge that accompanies its removal so much is gained!

Yet I know I shall never go to a future husband's bed as one chaste and ignorant—I shall never experience the wedding night as my first encounter. I don't mourn this for its own sake—for do we suppose that one who has eaten a single bite is spoiled for the joys of appetite and food ever after?—but surely this truth severely limits the chances that I might wed, for I will not lie and be ashamed, and how many men's affections shall withstand my revelations?

Ah, well—there is always the chance that I may marry later in life, to one not so eager to make a match for convention's sake. After all, every day, in every church, banns are announced between those in their fourth or fifth—or more—decade of life, between widows and widowers, presumed spinsters and confirmed bachelors—all of whom should, according to popular wisdom, be excluded from wedded bliss forever. Perhaps I shall be one of their number, doddering up the aisle upon an ivory-headed cane, smiling my toothless smile at my beloved, whose decrepitude will not bother me because I will be too blind to clearly see it.

So—my great Romance is over, and with it has gone my claim to Innocence in the eyes of the world. I have "transgressed" by the greatest means possible—but I know what it signifies, and what it does not. I must follow my nature, without that division of mind which has characterized me thus far, where it shall go.

JULY 1, 1861

I know now that an unexpected child is not to be my future lot, for a few days past I felt the familiar tugging and twingeing within me, and then my monthly flow began in its usual manner. I was, above all, greatly relieved, but

I confess I was a tiny bit saddened as well, for here was the evidence that my body considers little of import to have happened to me. All is more or less as it was, the blood attests to that. There have been no monumental changes, save those which have taken place in my head.

I have still heard not a word from Harlow, nor have I dared send him any word of my own. But I miss him mightily, especially now, with the last traces of our tryst erased from within me.

JULY 16, 1861

Today was our regular calling day, and I was first delighted—and then a little frightened—to see Caroline's card among the several we'd received. I almost considered feigning sickness, but I knew I would have to face this moment sooner or later, and so it might just as well be sooner, and gotten over with.

As it is, this was a wise decision, for—to my considerable surprise—Caroline seemed to bear me no ill will at all, despite what I was certain she'd seen as my callous dismissal of her brother. Rather, she embraced me the moment I met her at the door, and declared that she was glad to be able to come. She hadn't wished to rub salt in Harlow's wounds, but, well, how long should she be reasonably required to abstain from my company?

Caroline greeted my parents warmly when I led her into the parlor, and made pleasant conversation with them for a quarter hour or so. She is adept at this, and had brought several little German seed cakes as a teatime offering, which of course pleased Mother immensely (Mother has always enjoyed Caroline, despite Aunt Jo's twitterings, and the disadvantage my companion has incurred by being Harlow's sister).

Richard, on the other hand, was pleased by the position Miss Beckwith assumed on the side chair nearest him, and by the crossing of her delicate little ankles, from which he could not take his eyes.

When I thought a respectable enough amount of time had elapsed, I oh-so-politely interrupted the banalities, and asked Caroline if she wouldn't like to come outside and see some blossoming plant or another. Much to Richard's disappointment, she took my meaning and accepted, and I hurried her out toward the rear entrances.

"I hope you shall both forgive me," I began, as soon as we were seated in the garden. "I should have given anything not to be hurtful, for I love your brother—"

But Caroline breezily interrupted me. "Oh, you needn't explain. I understand the situation completely."

"He told you the entire story?" I asked cautiously.

Caroline stared me straight in the eye, as is her wont, and said simply, "Yes."

"I see."

"And as I say, you needn't feel it necessary to make apologies to me, for I understand your motivation. You refused him, and no doubt for the same reasons Louella did when he proposed to *her*."

I jumped a little in my chair, as one will do when truly and profoundly startled.

"Louella!"

Now she glanced away from me, rather quickly. "Yes, of course. That was Harlow's other tragic involvement—don't tell me he didn't discuss it with you." She seemed just a tad too surprised as she said this.

"He told me—but never once did he mention that the girl in question was Louella."

"Well, it was. It seems Harlow would have no romantic life at all if not for the parade of young ladies I supply him with. At any rate, Louella turned him down because she thought him unsettled and immature, as you no doubt did."

"Actually—" I began, but Caroline cut me off once again.

"Please, you mustn't feel any obligation to speak of it. I ask nothing in the way of justifications; in fact my own opinion is that the matter should remain between you and Harlow, so that it does not interfere any further with our own friendship. I'm rather tired of running between the battle lines, waving a white flag, as you may imagine. So let us put it behind us, shall we?"

I wanted to agree with her, but I felt somehow uncomfortable with this, as it seemed accomplished too easily—and besides, I was still reeling over the revelation that Louella Paxton had been Harlow's first love. I did not know whether to be furious with him, or to feel even sorrier for him—and more regretful of my own quick refusal of him—than I already did.

No wonder he had not named his lover, I thought. Knowing she and I had met and begun a friendship, what atrocious behavior that would have been!

But hardly more atrocious than skipping from her affections directly over to mine, and during the time that she'd left for the danger of the United States, of all things.

Yet he hadn't disparaged her either, or betrayed her by revealing the secrets of their history to me, however tempted he might have been to do so.

And I recalled his expression at the Lamb's Hock, soon after the war had begun, when I'd mentioned Louella's trip. He'd gone as white as if *he'd* seen Cromwell's ghost. No wonder—what a unique pain it must have caused him, to feel both the greatest resentment and concern over her, and to have no clue as to her whereabouts.

And to think I had chided him for his Byronic melancholy, which I'd assumed to be mere affectation!

It then occurred to me—I couldn't help it, since she sat right before me—that Caroline had been less than honest with me in this matter as well. In all of our exchanges concerning Louella, she had not once before today mentioned Harlow's involvement with her. It was curious, and it made me wonder whether I should also be angry with her—

I decided that this was one question, at least, to which I could seek an answer.

When I posed it, it was Caroline's turn to look distinctly uncomfortable.

"Oh dear," she said, with a little grimace. "Didn't I know this would come back to haunt me. You mustn't think I wished to intentionally deceive you. Originally I said nothing out of respect to Louella, because I should have been telling tales out of school by simply blabbing to you that she'd been courted by my brother. But then as time went on—as Harlow's regard for you became apparent—I felt I could not mention it out of loyalty to him. He asked me not to, in so many words—although he intended no deceit either—he simply felt it wouldn't reflect well upon him, that you'd perhaps decide to cut him off rather than step between him and a girl you're acquainted with."

"I should have liked to make that decision for myself, Caroline."

"And I should have liked you to make it too," she muttered, and then added, "You mustn't think Harlow did wrong on Louella's account. She had dispensed with him long before you entered upon the scene, and his failure to name her had more to do with concern for her than bad intent toward you. I am heartily sorry, though, if you feel mistreated, and were Harlow here, I am sure he would say the same."

Knowing Harlow, I certainly believed this; I only wished I might have been treated with more honesty by both siblings.

I was prepared to remain irritated, but Caroline was pulling me back into the present, and she is a hard one to resist when she is determined. I pray she never takes up poker, as she is one of the most easily read people I've yet to meet: when she is happy, she bubbles over like a saucepan on the stove, but when she is not, she has the downward cast of a condemned prisoner, or the surliness of an angry cat. Now I could see how eager she was to reestablish our trust. She talked on blithely, and with frequent laughter and squeezes upon my arm, so that I could not help falling into the rhythm of our old association.

Presently she said, "Miss Ashe has been asking after you. She wonders whether you've grown bored already with liberty."

"Not so much bored as simply without need of it at the moment, I'm afraid."

"Ah, we shall have to do something about that. It sounds quite unlike you, and quite unhealthy as well."

"You are a horrid influence upon me," I told Caroline sweetly, "and yet amazingly adept at appearing so wholesome."

"I regard it as my gift," she replied just as sweetly. "Now, I should also tell you that Miss Ashe suggests you come round anyway, even if you've no need of her primary services, and actually spend some time with her—she really does provide lessons on all manner of things, you know, and is a fascinating woman, once you get past her thorns."

"I cannot imagine spending half an hour with Miss Ashe, never mind an entire evening," I said.

"I know she is somewhat intimidating, Arabella, but really, she's been a family friend for as long as I've been alive, and I can swear to you that her bark is far worse than her bite. Don't be so quick to dismiss her—you can't spend all of your time in the bosom of your delightful family, or on gaddings-about with your charming cousin Percy. You'll no doubt need Miss Ashe when you desire privacy at some point in the future, and you'll appear the more consistent if you've been trekking to her home regularly."

I told Caroline I would consider Miss Ashe's offer (mainly just to change the subject), and then our conversation turned to other, more sobering topics. Louella's name arose once again, not surprisingly. There has still been no word from her, and we hesitated even to speculate on the reasons for this, although we both know precisely what they might be. There is little question that the war is going badly for the Unionists, the Rebels proving far more difficult a lot than any could have anticipated. God only knows how our friend has been affected, where she is, and how she fares—but we quickly agreed that we must assume the lack of news to be in our favor, for had she been injured or—God forbid it—killed, we surely should have heard of it second-hand, through her long-winded and loudmouthed brother.

What neither of us dared mention is that perhaps there has been no secondhand gossip, because no one at all has heard from Louella—not even the doltish Thomas. Perhaps she is enduring conditions in which all communication has become impossible—and so it may be going for others among our relatives and friends as well, for their missives are slow to reach us, and often contain news long since old or rendered irrelevant.

We could not continue with our speculations for long; they were too painful, with too many questions left unanswered. Instead we embarked upon lighter subjects, and then, two hours or so later, our visit drew to a close. Caroline said she must be getting back to Linton. Her mother and their hosts are expected within a matter of days, and Caroline wishes to be certain the house is in good order.

I asked her, upon seeing her to the door, if she would convey my good wishes to her brother, and although she agreed, there is no assurance that it will make any difference in the present state of affairs between us.

But it is good to know I've Caroline's favor to count upon nonetheless—I can only hope that Harlow will soon reach some point of equanimity within himself, whereupon this sad and needless stalemate shall be ended.

OCTOBER 9, 1861

At last I can feel an ending has been writ to the story of Harlow and myself.

He came to see me today, unexpectedly, and asked, as if it were months before, whether I should like to go for an impromptu carriage ride. Of course Father gave his consent; he and Mother have come round to the opinion that, while there is some measure of impropriety involved in my hacking about with Harlow alone, he could never hope to become a serious prospect for my hand, lacking as he does the glamour of Carter Forbes-Spencer. They are now blissfully oblivious where Harlow's comings and goings are concerned, and seem unaware as well of the mad pendulum-swings of my moods, and of any connexion between the two circumstances. But perhaps the fault is not entirely theirs—perhaps I have only become better at hiding my feelings.

At any rate, Harlow and I were soon off, and our trip began with a palpable awkwardness between us. I cleared my throat several times, and then announced I'd begun the collected works of Chaucer.

"You've my sympathies," Harlow replied.

"And yourself?"

"I've begun classes again."

I was genuinely delighted to hear this. "Did you! I congratulate you. It's for the best—I know it is, you were not intended to return to the States just yet."

"Apparently not, but I hope God isn't dragging the damned war on just so that I might stay here."

We then moved on to the topic of the weather, exhausting it in perhaps a good twenty seconds. At last Harlow managed to break through this brittle surface ice.

He was still driving when he said, without turning to me, "I should like to apologize to you, Berry. I've behaved like a spoiled child over the last few months, and I am sorry."

I had the urge to hug him then and there, but I refrained, confining myself to a mere spoken expression of my feelings. "No, please don't apologize. Your actions are quite understandable, and I did not mean to rush you back into a friendship before you'd settled matters in your own mind."

"You'll be relieved to know that I have, to some degree." He breathed a long sigh. "I believe you were correct. Our—evening together—" (It seemed this was to be the agreed-upon euphemism between us.) "—grand though it was, was not the basis upon which to begin a courtship. Had we entered into one there should have been expectations by both our families that we carry through on it and wed, whether we were ready to or not. I honestly thought at the time that this was what I wanted, but now—well, with the privacy to reflect upon it, I realize that I'm far too unsettled within myself to have properly committed to anything, including you. My affection for you is unaltered, I assure you, but I've come to the conclusion that it is not enough in light of my uncertainty. I'm sure you saw that quite clearly, but I didn't wish to see it, as I'd already been accused of it before."

"By Louella Paxton." I could not resist it.

He looked away. "Ah, yes. Caroline saw to it that you'd have that tidbit of information, didn't she."

"I should have preferred to hear it from you."

"I know it. But it seemed improper—unfair to Louella—to mention it at first, and then later—I suppose it was self-serving of me, but I intended no malice. Anyway, it's true, she refused me on exactly those grounds, and I suppose I wanted to challenge her, to show her I could yet fulfill another girl's vision of manhood."

"For goodness' sake, Harlow, you surely did not fail me so entirely on that account."

"No? I'm glad to hear of it."

He paused for a moment, and it occurred to me that he might be waiting for some more elaborate reassurance concerning his masculine charms; but I remained silent, feeling this was not the moment for that particular discussion.

"At any rate," he continued, "I believe I was hoping to prove to myself that I was not entirely without appeal to the fair sex. And in addition . . ." He trailed off, and for a moment there was only the sound of the horse's hooves striking the soft earth of the road.

"In addition, I was overcome by you. I did not expect to be moved by any girl so soon on the heels of Miss Paxton's departure, but I became convinced that you'd been placed in my path to give me a second chance at romantic bliss. Particularly after—well. But of course you refused me. And then I came to believe that you'd been placed in my path so that I might trip over you and fall on my face, while the Creator laughed himself silly at my vanity.

"But now I've given it some thought, I realize the Creator has more on his agenda than to toy with me, and that everything has happened for the best. And I have admitted to myself how greatly I miss your company, and how I should like to be back in your good graces."

I did not have a chance to reply just then, for we had reached our favorite picnic spot, the one we'd visited a few times with Richard. Harlow stopped the carriage, and we sat for a moment, while the horse, its reins dangling, set to munching an outcropping of grass.

I took a breath and exhaled it slowly. Then I began: "I cannot tell you how relieved I am to hear you say these things. I've missed you too, and you don't know how much I've hoped we would reach this pass. I regret nothing which has happened between us—only that perhaps it happened sooner than it should have, before we were ready to make the best use of it. But maybe we can come to terms with it, we can make a special place for it. As you say, we are not the common breed, nor the type to mince words, so let us not start now, but rather continue that tradition of honesty which we've established between us."

It sounded rehearsed, this speech of mine, and indeed it was—for hadn't I spoken it a dozen times, to the glass as I dressed, to the canopy above the bed, to the empty air in front of me as I wandered about our little garden in a daze. So that he might know it was nonetheless heartfelt, I turned to look in his eye and smile at him. He did not avoid my gaze, but smiled back, and there in his expression I beheld all the warmth I could have wished for.

"I would like that," he said.

We spent another hour or so talking in the carriage, but this was mere addendum. The most important portion of our conversation was done with, and I believe we both felt we'd successfully completed it; all that now remained was to test the boundaries of our new relationship, to see how pleasantries and comradeship—as opposed to intimacies and courtship—might suit us. We came to some silent consensus that this too had gone well, and so, with some purchase for our feet safely established, Harlow interrupted the horse's grazing and prepared to deliver me home.

It is an odd ending to an odd story, but it is no doubt the best one, the only one possible under the circumstances. I can think of many others less appealing—in fact, I have spent any number of predawn hours imagining them—and so I suppose I should feel lighter at heart at the resolution we have reached, and if I do not just yet, well, I must expect that it shall come with time.

9:30 P.M.

But not in time for tonight.

Tonight—once again—I am crying. Only a little and quietly, but still, how can this be? I haven't a handkerchief, I am using one of my everyday gloves to wipe my eyes, it has already taken on the consistency of a damp washcloth.

Perhaps my tears have moved past "a little."

I am as miserable as on the night I first turned him away.

Why does this happen now, Arabella? You have got everything you wanted. You wanted his forgiveness; you now have it. You wanted him to share your conclusions, and now he does. You wanted him to be unhurt, and now he no longer hurts on your account, apparently.

And so, where does the problem lie?

I know I made the correct decision in refusing his proposal. I know I was relieved today to hear that he understood it.

And yet how my heart dropped at that news. At his having come to the same conclusion as I.

Admit it. Say it now. There is no shame in it. Admit that you care deeply for him. That you would have enjoyed being forgiven but pined over for considerably longer, because your affection for him did not end with your refusal. Admit that you were so consumed with making the correct decision, with being certain you did not step mistakenly into marriage, that you paid little attention to that affection. You did not celebrate it or mourn it properly, because you felt it had no future. Acknowledge it all now, so that it may be cried over, and then swept aside, since it is too late for it to matter.

Admit that you would have liked to see him throw himself into his studies, vow to overcome that deadly nonchalance which immobilizes him, and then return in a year or two, a changed man, but still smitten, ready to declare his ongoing love for you.

And after that admission, be sure to remind yourself that were he to change, he might immediately have made his way back to the woman he knew and loved well before myself.

Louella is not here, though, to be returned to. No one knows where Louella is.

Oh, stop it.

Stop it and find the other glove, and blow your nose in it, for it's running.

Harlow and I are friends once again. Let that be the sum of it, let it go where it ought.

May God protect Louella, and good night.

NOVEMBER 11, 1861

I have arrived at your final page at last, good Book. What changes you have witnessed, what tumultuous secrets you guard! Or perhaps they are not so monumental, or only so to me. Nevertheless, I shall regard you as the Book of Transition, for when first I began you I was one creature, and now I am thoroughly another. You have been a loyal and dear friend, and I shall keep you safe and protected always; may your successor bear witness to happier times than have been our lot over these past two years. I wish I had something of more import to leave you with, but I have been keeping quietly to myself; I feel I am in the midst of a period of waiting, and no unsettling adventures have broken that stillness as yet.

Our family is making ready for the holiday season—and with it the inevitable return of my cousins, and the tedious back-and-forths to Leeds Hall—so I may not have the leisure within which to begin another journal until those somewhat dreary exertions are past. I look forward to Christmas, as always, but I am still amazed to find us spending another Yuletide in this wretched country, while our own country is yet deep in the bloody midst of civil war.

May the new year bring some form of resolution to all of us.

chapter four

(JANUARY 1863)

My dear Gran—it seems inevitable that the freedom of the colored populace shall be made the law of this land at last.

The papers are full of the news of the President's final Emancipation Proclamation. I made a quiet celebration in my dismal quarters, and offered first a prayer of thanks, and then another for the Federalist troops, that they may triumph and extend Mr. Lincoln's jurisdiction to every cursed inch of the Confederacy. I prayed too that liberty has brought to you, Gran, the happiness of which bondage deprived all of us. If you yet remain amidst the Paxtons, you do it with the knowledge that your Government has sanctioned your freedom, and that shall make all the difference in the undertaking.

The other great news here concerns my own undertakings, for it appears I am to be off upon the journey I have so long waited to make.

On the one hand I am filled with what, in my present circumstance, passes for excitement. On the other hand I am consumed with dread, and profoundly hope that the boat sinks in the harbor, so that I am never compelled to set foot on it.

If it does not sink—and I would wager my tin mug that it will not, as it is brand-new, just launched out of Ireland the previous summer—I shall wave farewell from its decks to the country of my birth, to my entire life here—and who can say if I shall ever return, or when, or in what condition. It is an awesome prospect; each time I imagine myself walking up the ramp—is it called the gangplank, or is that term in use only among pirates?—and stowing my few belongings onboard, I feel a dryness in my throat, and I wonder: will I really do it? Really commit myself to this journey, from which there can be no going back once the anchor is hauled up, and the dock out of sight? Or will I run for the shore at the very last second, leap from the decks into the sea?

Oha has found work for us aboard a steamer vessel which carries not only cargo but passengers across the Atlantic. The ship is called the H.M.S. *Artemis*. It flies the Union Jack—or perhaps I should say she flies it, for Oha has informed me that a ship must always be referred to as "she." (I made the mistake of inquiring why, and he replied, in his typically pedantic way, "Treachery. The boat iss treachery. Like the vooman. Must have the firm hand at the helm or it shall dump the man into the sea.") He has never been employed by this particular captain before, but he knows the line, it has a fine reputation, the labor is said to be fairly easy, and I have a spot secured, despite my lack of training or seamanship.

We are ready to go, but I cannot recall why I wished to do this, or what I expected to gain. I was given exemption from the draft because of my shoulder, I need not fear the war or conscription, so what is the point of leaving the country? I remember what I intended, of course. It is only that my intent no longer seems important.

But then, what does?

I wonder how I shall fare alongside Oha for the duration of our travels. I have discovered a good deal more about him in the weeks since our first meeting, and much of it I would rather have remained ignorant of.

I know now, for example, that—even compared to myself in my present state of mind—he is utterly lacking in humor, having cultivated no sense of the absurd whatsoever. His brilliant blue eyes maintain a suspicious squint, the hard set of his mouth is uninterrupted by a smile. His laugh—or at least I assume it to be a laugh—is more of a bark, a quick exclamation of satisfaction, and is reserved for instances of cruel irony rather than those moments which strike me as genuinely amusing.

He is also fond of pontificating on a variety of subjects. He talks in a stilted, halting monotone which is almost unbearable to listen to—but hardly more unbearable than the contents of the lectures themselves. Oha's favorite topic is the relationship between the sexes, and the fair one rarely escapes a vicious drubbing at his hands.

"Da vooman iss . . ." he will usually begin, shaking his blonde head slowly and staring downward to concentrate upon the wording. I know then that a lecture is coming; it might have been precipitated by almost anything, but its subject is bound to be stultifyingly familiar. "Da vooman iss . . . pollution. Da blood which run each month . . . iss da sign from Gott that da vooman is cursed ond unclean . . . Da man iss da child of Gott . . . Da man iss sun ond light, ond de vooman iss . . . darkness . . ."

I've heard these sentiments echoed—in a milder form—elsewhere, for what man, suffering at the whims of love or lust, hasn't cursed the power of woman's allure and decried her as proportionately fickle in nature? But in Oha's mouth such oaths reach a point of sheer madness, at which they are understandable to no one but himself. They tinge his every perception of the universe; they entangle him in webs of superstition and groundless wariness. He is oblivious of this, however; he is certain that his view is in fact not only correct, but the one held close by the entire world, and so he is consistently surprised when I challenge him.

This I do less and less frequently, since I haven't the patience necessary to endure his rebuttals. But there was a time when I took issue with every inanity he uttered, mainly as a means of amusing myself. When he explained to me the reason for the ships' feminine sex, for example, I sought to tease him by replying, "The boats keep men safe from the sea. Don't you think perhaps that's why they prefer to imagine their ships as benevolent ladies?"

Oha's response was swift, and far from bantering. His eyebrows drew together over his eyes, and the shaggy head commenced to swaying in earnest. When he is bothered, his speech increases not in speed but in volume, and now his reply fairly boomed out at me, in that same measured cadence, all the more annoying for being disturbingly loud: "NO. NO. Oha tell you—vooman iss TREACHERY. Boat too—sea too. You see, Aw-bree. Man—must—put his hand—to them—"

And so forth, until any thought of amusement had long since left my head. "All right," I finally barked at him, "leave off, already, I take your meaning." He immediately fell silent, hanging his head and looking sulkily out at me from the corners of his eyes. He pouted like a child—a huge, hulking Viking of a child—for the rest of the day, and I resolved then and there never to attempt a joke with him again, and never to bother insinuating myself between Oha and his madness. It's simply not worth the trouble, and it alienates him as well, which is something I'd not want to do—for despite his lunatic conception of the world, Oha has remained a loyal and good-hearted friend to me, one I should not like to dispense with too quickly.

I worry, however, over the toll which close proximity shall take upon our friendship. Onboard the vessel, there will be few places to escape from his didactic dullness when necessary, and the reminder that familiarity breeds contempt looms larger and larger in my mind as the day of our departure draws near.

I should add that I've taken to looking the part of a sailor, even as I refuse to have anything to do with its nomenclature, its social etiquette, or the skill of sailing itself. I've grown my hair past my shoulders, as Oha wears his, and have taken to tying it behind my neck in a knot so that it shall not blow about in my face. I occasionally go a few days without barbering, and on the whole appear quite dirty and dangerous, which suits my purposes just now. Of course any eye for detail will no doubt pick up the fact that I prefer to keep my hair washed and clean, as opposed to lousy and filthy, but that is a point of hygiene which I refuse to concede.

I have also undertaken the getting of a tattoo, which places me outside the bounds of polite society forever, I suppose (although enough of the demimonde sport them to make them novel, and therefore racily acceptable, among some sets). I had never seen one, until Oha showed me his bare left arm. There on the biceps was a picture of a tiger, facing outward, running toward the viewer and looking lifelike enough to leap at any second. It was a masterful piece of work, done in bold blues, blacks, and reds, and when I inquired as to where he'd got it, he told me that the artist is an ancient Oriental residing right here in our seedy corner of New York. I decided I wanted to have one as well, and Oha took me to the Celestial's little shop, where we agreed upon a price and I described the design I desired.

I sat down and bared my arm, watching while the artist—a shriveled raisin of a man who must have been at least in his seventies—prepared the inks and other materials necessary for the procedure, laying them out on small mats made from some sort of paper. I confess to feeling a twinge of nervousness as he went about his business; the one thing which reassured me was that his little shop, minuscule though it was, was as spotlessly clean a room as I had ever come across.

The man placed next to me a thin hollow dowel of wood which rested on a spring and fulcrum; it had a hole in one end, into which was inserted vertically a hollow metal needle wrapped in thread. The design on my arm was traced first with an ink fountain pen. Then the artist dripped ink onto the needle and thread, put the needle to my skin, and gave the dowel the barest, fastest taps. This set it to quickly rocking, springing up and down, piercing my skin with every downstroke. It produced an itchy, irritating sort of pain, like the vicious sting of insects. *Tap tap tap tap*—the Oriental's fingers fairly flew as he deftly worked the fulcrum with one hand and guided the needle with the other.

Including the frequent stops for the wiping of blood, the reloading of ink and so on, the process took about two hours, after which the design was permanently etched in my skin. When the master decided it was done to his satisfaction, he held up the mirror so that I might see it.

I looked, and there upon my upper bicep I saw a small, shining, stylized sun. It shot tongues of fire, its rays bursting forth in red; it parted floating clouds of blue edged in black. The single word, which ran through the sun, leapt out in a clear, black script: *FAITH*.

"You are man of Gott?" Oha asked me, puzzled, when he finally beheld my shoulder in all its completed glory.

"No," I said.

The tattoo artist grinned at me through his toothless gums. "Is name, eh?" he said slyly. "Name of sweetheart woman?"

"No."

The little man's face registered puzzlement as well, but I did not care to enlighten him further.

I have told no one of the circumstances under which I quit my life in Louisiana. I did not care to have either Oha or the little Oriental know that Faith was not the woman I loved, but rather the woman I had failed to redeem with love.

Although, as I've said, I've been notoriously uninterested in most of what comprises seafaring culture, I've made a lone exception for the sailors' superstitions. They amuse me, being senselessly complicated, and I've made a sort of hobby of collecting them.

The first and biggest piece of superstitious nonsense is that, despite all the feminine references and namesakes sailors bestow on every seagoing article, an actual woman aboard ship is believed to curse the vessel and the journey (although solvent female travelers, whose money pays the sailors' salaries, must be dealt with in a civil fashion). On this point, it seems, many sailors are as rabid as Oha. They prefer women to be banned even from the docks, so that they will not bring evil to the whole endeavor of sailing.

I tend to believe that this tradition is rooted not in the luck or lack thereof which accompanies women, but in the behavior of the men when out of their sight. So bawdily and atrociously do we comport ourselves when alone that we should be ashamed to have women view us; we might also be forced to rein ourselves in, and there would be an end to the raucous good fellowship that exists among men by themselves. Quite frankly, I tire of certain aspects of that fellowship rather quickly—there is only so much one can take of the exuberant drinking, cursing, loudmouthing, boasting, and pummeling, not to mention public pissing, farting, belching, and vomiting, which are part and parcel of such a milieu. After an evening or so of merely witnessing this parade of insults upon the notion of gentlemanly behavior, I am happy to leave it behind.

There is no mere pretending to raucousness here, as at the Camellia, where gentlemen descended to what, in their sheltered imaginations, was barbarism. The dockworkers and sailors behave truly like beasts, and without any self-consciousness, or wry awareness of it. I find their lot and their company wretched and pathetic; they live out their allowed time like draft animals, slaving all the daylight hours, and seeking to forget their burdens in nights of liquor and excess.

Uneducated and sodden-brained as they are, it is no wonder that they are fertile soil for all manner of ridiculous notions. The jinx associated with women is only the beginning; among the other *verboten* items are the number thirteen, the eating of pork, the mention of pigs, the color blue—the list is endless.

I will be watching closely to see how the observance of such foolish lore affects our journey—although I'm sure I can set down an accurate prediction from dry land: if the trip goes well, everyone will forget that someone let slip some mention of "pig," or wore blue shirttails, or allowed a woman to pass through the crew's living quarters or decks; if things go badly, every instance of transgression will be noted by the pious pagans, and blamed as the cause of all ills. So it works among the ignorant—but I cannot say that the educated remain unmoved, for I imagine that in very little time I shall be counting "twelve plus one" and eschewing bacon alongside the lot of them, simply to avoid being labeled the source of a jinx myself.

We are aboard and under way at last.

The news came eight days ago that we would be departing on the twentieth, and that we should make ready to sail on that morning. Oha immediately bade me collect those items I might wish to have with me on the trip, for the ship supplies few necessities—and no luxuries—to its loyal crew. What might I need, I asked him, and he suggested extra razors for barbering, extra blankets and bedding, towels and soaps if I so desired them, and tobacco, liquor, and so on, if I cared to have some delicacy beyond the swill we shall no doubt be served in the galley. He had secured all of the above for himself, along with a deck of playing cards and some dice, so that we would not lack for entertainment in between completion of our duties. I had little money to spare, but I managed to invest it as he'd told me, for the thought of being stranded at sea without the barest amenities repulsed me as much as had the conditions I endured on Catherine Street.

Most of the items I am now in possession of are secondhand, while others are frankly stolen, but I try to push this from my mind. I have two straight razors, a brush and bowl, two bars of lye soap, and a towel with monogram (which was obtained through an acquaintance of Oha's working as a bellhop in an expensive hotel. The towel was paid for with cocaine; I have no idea how Oha came upon *that*).

I took with me from Catherine Street my tin mug, my single blanket, the greatcoat, and two changes of clothes. In addition to Thomas's suitcoat (which is now unrecognizable despite my attempts to wash it at the pump), I managed to cadge a shirt from the Temperance crusaders who haunt our district, seeking to woo the whores and pimps from alcohol to Christ. I did not smell of spirits, and appeared well spoken and not a foreigner, so one of them invited me back to her mission house, where she presented me with a cotton rag, worn out beneath the arms and patched in several places. I eyed her fur collar, her cunning hat and silk boots, and had a sudden desire to laugh in her face or spit in it; the more so because, as she handed me this treasure, she fairly glowed with righteousness, as though God were patting her head at that very second. I restrained myself, however, and now I think of it I wish instead that I'd told her I'd be trading her largesse for a good pint of whiskey. That likely would have cut her more than anything else.

I also have a pair of workpants, obtained through the most basic sort of thievery: I stole them from a tailor shop whose door the proprietor had foolishly left open while he stepped out. I suppose I should feel shame, and do in some part of myself. But my conscience is as deadened as the rest of me, and I cannot find it in my heart to pity too greatly a tailor with a dozen pairs of breeches, and rich clients to pay him for a dozen more.

I wrapped all of my belongings in my greatcoat, and on the appointed morning four days ago I left the hovel at five A.M. (not having paid the rent for the week—that was the sweetest pleasure). Oha and I made our way west to the docks, and there I first set eyes on the *Artemis*, tied in her berth and awaiting her crew. What a magnificent monster she is! I have learnt nothing from Oha's endless descriptions of barks and sarks and cruisers; I only know that this ship is iron, as opposed to wood (and Oha says that soon all ships shall be made similarly, and the metal-sheathed wooden hull will be a thing of the past), and that she is big. We strolled the dock as we awaited the captain's perusal; the regular crew were allowed to board, but we itinerants were to be checked over and lectured regarding our duties before setting foot on deck.

While we waited I took a moment to glance at the other men milling about—my fellow workers, with whom I would be in intimate contact for the next two weeks or so. Closest to us were a Negro so dark he appeared almost blue, and a swarthy, shorter man speaking in what I recognized as Spanish. When Oha turned and saw them, he nodded in a somewhat friendly fashion, and I was given to know that he had sailed with them before. I was intrigued. I've had little desire to make the acquaintance of the few Negroes I have observed in New York, but the one behind us had an exotic air which piqued my curiosity. Oha, however, said, "Ghanaian," when he turned back to me, and I assumed this meant the man came from Ghana, in Africa; at that moment, the black one began babbling to his companion in some unintelligible language, which I knew I should never decipher, so I turned away again.

After a few minutes, Oha became restless, and told me to hold his place in the line, as he wished to go search out a bit of bread or coffee. I was standing by myself when I heard a voice behind me say, "Eh, boy," in English. I realized I was being addressed, and so I turned. The speaker was the blue-black man. He appeared to be perhaps fifty, with a musical voice, and crinkled skin about his black eyes, and he wore a little skullcap with a nubbin of material at the crown. His friend was younger, long-haired, bearded, and white, but with eyes equally dark.

"You goin on the *Artemis*, first time?" the black one asked me in his strange accent.

"Yes. Yes, I am." I felt an immediate sense of familiarity with the man: he reminded me—in terms of his age, his color, and his sharp features—of Amos.

"Sven Oha's friend, eh?"

"Yes."

"Good friend?"

I shrugged. "We boarded in the same house. He found me this position."

"You don' soun like a sailor, boy."

"No. I am not. This is my first voyage."

"First with Sven?"

"First ever."

At this the younger man gave a knowing nod and said something in Spanish, and I turned to look at him. But the black man shot me a half-grin, and repeated his companion's statement himself.

"Aurelio says, you watch your Sven Oha. Aurelio tell you, there's a name for that one. Is *el mosquito muerto*, Aurelio says."

" '*El mosquito muerto*'?" I drew my brows together. "A 'dead fly'?"

I could deduce, from my fluency in French, enough of Spanish to understand the words, but they had no meaning for me, as my command of idiom in the latter language is nonexistent.

The two men broke into laughter at my question, however, which irritated me somewhat, as I assumed it had to do with my ignorance.

"You know Oha?" I asked the black one, hoping to clear up the joke.

"Yeh, yeh, I sail with him three times, Aurelio done so twice. Always mercenaries, all of us, goin here, there, one way, then off to someplace else. Never steady crew. He's good sailor, though, good worker."

"And so what does that mean, what you called him, a 'dead fly'? That's your word for a mercenary, is that it?"

The African translated my question into Spanish, and the other man gave another, heartier chuckle. The African shook his head at me.

"Nah, nah. Ya know how it go, with the dead fly. He lies there on his back, all innocent and still, lookin' harmless as a snowflake. And then just when ya turn yourself roun', that dead fly, he fool ya—buzz buzz, got plenty buzz in him after all, an maybe even fly up right in ya face."

I stared at the African. His explanation had hardly made the comment clearer. But I could ask him nothing else, because at that moment Oha returned, and indicated to me that the captain of the ship was ready to speak to us.

We gathered in front of the crates, where the captain had taken a seat. He was a rotund man, pink-faced and crease-eyed, somewhere in his fifties. He wore his dress uniform, and carried a printed roster in his hands. His name was Worth—Robert Worth—but I'd heard the crew had a nickname by which they addressed him, affectionately, even to his face. They called him "Hatpin Bob," as opposed to Captain Bob, for it seems the captain dotes upon his wife, and purchases for her a bonnet or some sort of head covering from every port he drops anchor in. Hatpin Bob's wife is alleged to have an astounding collection of headdresses, skullcaps, beanies, top hats, scarves, and the like—but her favorite port is that of Marseilles, for at least when Bob docks there for a few days she's assured of a present she can actually wear.

Hatpin Bob gave a good-natured sigh. "All right, gather round," he called in his clipped British accent, "let's see what sort of motley lubbers we've managed to collect this time." He gazed at the little band of us; we were about ten altogether. There were Oha and myself, the African and his Spanish friend, two pasty-white muscled and mustachioed men in their thirties (who spoke yet another unintelligible language, and gave me long, strange stares when I happened to look back at them), and a few white American boys, younger than myself, who evidently were leaving behind nothing of value in their homeland. We were the itinerants, those last-minute hirelings working for half-wages at the worst positions aboard, and signed on for only one segment of the voyage, from New York to the Continent. We were at the bottom rung of the ladder, literally and figuratively: the captain, the line's own permanent crew, and the passengers all outranked us, and I was certain the distinction would become more obvious when we were shown our accommodations on board.

Hatpin Bob drew another sigh, perhaps elicited by the sight of us. "For those of you who have never sailed before," he began, "I'll start by listing the ship's rules. They're not many, but you'll obey them, for the first rule is that a ship is not a democracy. It's a kingdom, and as captain, I am the king."

He then proceeded to enumerate the edicts: liquor would be portioned out to the crew, but only during nonworking hours. Anyone caught drinking or drunk during duty, or, worst of all, during watch, would spend the voyage in the hold under arrest, and await discipline when we reached the shore. Tobacco was to be smoked only on the outer decks, never in the crew's quarters or in bed. Brawling and fist-fighting would not be tolerated. The passengers were to be provided with polite, exacting service at all times, even by those of us whose jobs did not involve seeing to their comfort.

And so on.

After about ten minutes, he concluded the address by wishing us a *bon voyage*, and good health. That would be all, officially, until we docked a fortnight hence.

Upon the fair shores of Southampton.

In Britannia.

Up to this point, I had been half-listening, half-observing both the captain and my fellow crew. But at the sound of the word "Britannia," I felt a kick in the pit of my stomach, and I whipped about to stare at Oha.

For—from the very first discussion of our plans—I had repeated over and over to my companion that I wished to set sail only for France, and he had nodded his huge head as if in perfect agreement. And in all the time since securing our passage on the *Artemis* he had never once mentioned that the ship was not only flying the British flag, but heading for Great Britain as well.

"Britannia?" I whispered loudly, while the captain shuffled among his rosters. "What in hell does he mean, *Britannia*? We are supposed to be docking in *France*."

Oha refused to turn and look at me. I refused as well to turn away, and we might have rotted there, locked in those positions, had not the captain begun to speak again.

"I shall take you one by one now, to give you your assignments," he called out to us. We queued up before him, the American boys first.

Oha and I awaited our turn, and I continued doing my best to shout while actually whispering. "We're going to England—why? *Why?*" I knew I'd be wise to control my temper. After all, the Norwegian had done me a favor, securing me this job, and there had been other favors as well. Besides, he might have a reasonable explanation for all this. But I was almost shaking with anger and disappointment; I wanted to shake Oha as well, and only the presence of the little crowd prevented me from doing so.

"Why?" I rasped again.

He still did not turn toward me. Instead he answered, looking straight ahead all the while, "Who are you? What sort of sailor? Where will you find work, with no experience, knowing nothing? Oha found you job. Goot job, on goot ship. She take you close to France. This is finest you will get. You do not want it, turn around now. Go home. Oha can go alone, to England." He stopped, and set his lips in the stubborn, grim way he did after making what he felt was a nonnegotiable point.

I glared at him, disgusted. It was too late to turn around now; Oha certainly knew that. My room on Catherine Street was gone; I had no "home" to return to, no choice except to let the procession carry me forward, toward the captain and *Britannia*.

"Of course it had to be *England*," I hissed, when I could stand to resume speaking again. "Of course you choose the last place I'd have picked, the one country in Europe's vicinity cut off from France by a body of water, which I must now find the means and the money to cross."

"Iss only the Channel that keep it from France," Oha grumbled back. "Iss not an ocean."

I made no reply to this. I had never seen the English Channel, of course, but from the role it had played in that nation's wartime history I imagined it as a sea of molten lava, as difficult to cross as the Atlantic. Besides, what difference did it make whether it was a thousand miles wide, or a thousand yards—it was the principle of the thing, the fact that he'd betrayed me, letting me believe, until this very second, that I was headed for another place entirely—the only place where any purpose for undertaking this journey awaited me.

I stared resolutely straight ahead, and Oha did as well; when the line moved again, I maneuvered myself in front of him, so as not to have to bear him at my side through the rest of our wait.

At last the captain had dispensed with the four youths, and then it was my turn to step forward. I handed Hatpin Bob my papers, and he looked up at me with an appraising glance.

"Well," he rumbled, "and what sterling and finely honed talents will you be bringing to this undertaking, Master"—he checked the papers—"Master Bennett?"

I knew, with some irritation, that Oha stood directly behind me, well aware that I would have little to offer in answer to the captain's question.

"I am a trained butler," I said, without apology. "I am skilled at formal tableside service, among other things."

"Formal tableside service," the captain repeated. He peered more closely at me, took in my hair and three days' growth of beard. "You're a bit rough around the edges for a formal servant, aren't you?" He shrugged. "Ah, well, not much call for that here anyway, I'm afraid, unless you're good at keeping the plates right side up in a rough sea. Table-waiting is a plum job, my boy, and there's little need for it aboard the *Artemis*. We carry but twenty passengers, and the senior crew members have the soft task of seeing to their comfort." He glanced down at his roster, and scratched his head. "Ehhhhhhh, let us have a look here. Any seagoing experience?"

"No."

"Machinist work?"

"No."

"Do you navigate?"

"No."

"Cook?"

I bridled; I had puttered about the kitchens back in New Orleans, but had never prepared a whole meal on my own. "No," I said at last.

"Ehhhhhhh." The captain rubbed a bald spot on his crown, and shut his eyes. Upon opening them he said, "Well, I'll place you in the galley kitchen, you can assist the cook. If you can serve food, you can prepare it. High time you learned. You'll take on general duties as well, maintenance and night watch in rotation, for which the crew will draw numbers. Agreed?"

"Agreed," I said—for what else could I say? I was to be trapped in the scullery or the galley, at the most menial task of potato-peeling or turnip-slicing, but how could I refuse?

"Let us take peek at the rest of this, then, shall we?" the captain said next. He quickly flipped through the documents I'd handed him—the ones Captain Quincy Block had supplied me with. Midway through the first page, he glanced back up at me, so that I knew precisely where amidst the information his eyes had gotten stuck.

"It says here in this paragraph that you are a former slave."

"Yes." As had become usual for me, I offered no information beyond what had been asked for.

"A *Negro* slave?"

I stood very still, imagining Oha behind me, hearing the questions—and the answers—quite clearly. I had never mentioned the emancipation papers I carried, had in fact been reluctant even to bring them with me, but had been afraid I would be refused work if I carried not a single piece of identification. Now I realized I need not have worried; the young men ahead of me had passed muster without a scrap attesting to any part of their existence. Too late it was, though, for recriminations.

I said, "Yes," in answer to the captain's question, as softly as I could. I gazed past him, feeling the burden of heritage settle itself among the others upon my shoulders.

He spoke again, and I forced myself to look at him. "I beg your pardon?"

"I said, you may collect your wages at journey's end. And I wish you good luck."

"Thank you, sir."

He held out his hand, and I grasped and shook it, then turned away, feeling myself in a daze.

I wished that I could simply walk off, extricate myself from the entire episode, but I was caught. There was no place to go, no place even to seek some privacy until we were permitted to board. I could not know what Oha had heard of my interview, but between that and the revelation as to where I was headed, I felt completely drained, and hadn't the slightest desire to see or speak to anyone. I sat down on a crate a short distance from the remainder of the queue, and hoped that Oha would have the good sense to leave me alone.

Of course he did not. Upon finishing, himself, with the captain, he walked over to me, and began the laborious struggle for words which told me I was in for a diatribe of some sort.

"England . . . iss . . . goot country. Goot place for young man, gentleman, like you. You stay there, maybe find work, maybe use wages from this boat for travel. From England, you go anyplace, sail across Channel to get to France, you see?"

This was his way of apologizing: not by saying he was sorry for deceiving me, but by justifying what he'd done.

"I know all that, Oha," I sighed. "None of it is really the point, though."

He stood there towering over me for another moment, and then he turned upon his heel, collected his bags, and walked off toward the ship.

I watched him go. As I did, I noted the two very pale fellows, the ones with the moustaches, glancing at me once again, from their place just behind the Spaniard in the line. They were the last to see the captain. They seemed less focused on him, however, than on me. I stared back at them, and the larger one locked glances with me, his face expressionless, for several seconds. Then he looked away, and he and his traveling mate fell to talking, and ignored me.

I saw the African look over at me too. He was finished with Hatpin Bob, and threw a grin back at me before strolling off toward the ship.

Finally all the interviews were completed, and I rose to follow the others toward where we would be boarding. At the railing the first mate checked us off individually, and then allowed us to pass. Apparently no chances were to be taken with stowaways, or with reluctant landlubbers mulling over second thoughts as they took their first steps onto the decks of the *Artemis*.

Once aboard, I discovered that our accommodations were not quite as bad as I had anticipated, but nowhere near as good as those provided the line's regular crew. There were no steerage-class passengers on board this ship. Instead, their substandard quarters had been reserved for the bottom-ranking crew members: namely, ourselves.

We were to be housed on the below-most deck, in tiny cubbyhole berths arranged much like straight stalls in a stable: cubicles containing two bunks apiece, an upper and a lower, lined either side of a narrow passageway; each cubicle was separated from the hall by a burlap curtain, and from its neighbors by walls of tin. Within each space were two small footlockers, now crammed with a thin blanket and small pillow; once we arranged the hammock-style bunks, the trunks would hold our few belongings. There was one latrine for the ten of us. I dreaded the confusion of slop jars and chamber pots that would ensue, and wondered how we would choose an order not only for bathing and washing each day but for emptying the latrine barrels.

On the opposite end of our deck, just beyond the galleys, were the larger quarters occupied by the regular crew. In addition to their size, these comparatively luxurious accommodations featured their own washbasins and glass, and one latrine for every four men. Lucky souls, those career sailors—but not so lucky as the captain, his first mate, the ship's officers, and the passengers, who were housed on the upper deck in spacious staterooms, each containing its own washroom facilities. The *Artemis* had been built as a showpiece; she was meant to carry not only cargo but dignitaries and other important people from one coast of the Atlantic to the other. Her finest accommodations were fine indeed—rivaling those of any ship upon the seas, I imagined.

But I was to know little of that luxury, except secondhand, for Oha had claimed a berth for us—a dark, cramped little space, but one near the stair, and with fresh air, at least—and this was to be my temporary home until we put to shore in Southampton.

I sat down upon the bottom bunk, and as I did so, I felt the ship roll ever so slightly upon a swell. Even this small motion nauseated me, and I closed my eyes. Oha was testing the top bunk. I wished he might go elsewhere, so that I could sit and sort out my thoughts.

But it is Oha's way to worry a topic like a dog with a bone. He now picked up precisely where we'd left off after the interviews with Hatpin Bob.

"England iss . . . goot . . . country."

Dear God.

"I know that," I said through my clenched teeth.

"You do not be angry then with Oha."

I did not answer. I was afraid to allow even a small measure of my anger to escape, for fear that the larger measure would overtake me—which, sooner or later, it generally did.

"Oha knows this will be good journey, you must trust Oha."

Now I felt myself burning, the acid taste in my mouth. For are not the most untrustworthy usually the first to demand trust, or declare their love too fervently?

I drew my hand across my eyes, resisted the inclination to shout. "I do not trust you," I said, "because you deceived me."

He did not pause even for an instant, but replied, "As you deceived me."

"As I—*what*?" I could scarcely believe his temerity. If the floor had not been moving, I would have stood up to confront him. "As *I* deceived *you*?"

"Yes, yes: you lie to Oha. Oha ask you, have you Negro blood, first day when you speak to me and we drink coffee, you remember, and you say no. Never tell me you were slave. Never tell me who you are. Lie to Oha. You are deceiver too, Aw-bree."

A sudden pitch of the boat caused my outrage to catch in my throat; I was glad I had not eaten, for here we were—sitting in the harbor in a dead calm—and already my stomach was rising into my mouth.

When I could speak I said, as evenly as I could, "Do not play with me, Oha. I did not tell you the story of my origins, you are correct. I'm sorry if you take insult with this, but it was my history to reveal or to hide, and you are none the worse for not knowing it. You, on the other hand, took it upon yourself to deceive me regarding a decision I entrusted you to make upon my behalf. You know quite well that the two things are not equivalent."

"You must not have shame because of Negro in you" was Oha's response to this.

I could only shake my head at his typically deft changing of subject. "Thank you for your reassurance—" I began, but Oha ignored my acid tone, and cut me off.

"You are welcome, Aw-bree—you are fine man. Fine man. It is no shame you have Negro inside. Maybe someday you tell Oha of it, where you come from. How it is to be slave-man. Not much different from the sailor, or the poor man, Oha think."

I put my chin in my hands, for what was the point in continuing the argument? I was closing my eyes and attempting to control my stomach when a whistle blast pierced the thin curtain across our doorway.

A moment later a man's baritone rang through the hall. "On deck! On deck! What, did you think you'd signed up for a pleasure cruise? On deck, all hands—yes, yes, *you*!" I could hear the owner of the voice pushing aside the curtains on the other cubicles and herding the occupants out. Oha and I scrambled from our bunks and fell into line behind our companions.

On the topmost deck, we discovered that the richly timbred voice belonged to Giovanni Delillo, the first mate. He was a tall, slightly balding fellow, with pince-nez and a face as mild-mannered as the captain's. It was Delillo's place to give us our daily work assignments, and to keep the more ignorant among us from sinking the ship—he actually said this, and I imagined he looked directly at me when he did so. He took a roll call, and now for the first time I learned the identities of my shipmates.

I already knew the Spaniard to be Aurelio; the African was called Ibrahim. One of the pallid white men was a German named Josef Beck; the other was an Irishman called Francis Dunleavy, or Francy for short. The four American boys were Tom, John, Lucas, and Will. Their faces were as nondescript as their given names, and I could hardly tell one from the other.

After ascertaining that all of us were accounted for, Delillo pointed to each man and gave him a number. I was eight, Oha was three. Delillo wrote our numbers on slips of paper and put them in a bucket. He swished his hand about, drew two scraps out, and read them. "Latrine duty tomorrow," he announced. "Number four, and number eight." I swore under my breath. One day at sea—not even at sea yet—and I was already consigned to hauling filth. I looked around; the African, Ibrahim, was number four, and he gave me a shrug which said *What can you do?* The other men smirked, whereupon Delillo said, "Go on and laugh, boys, it'll be your turn soon enough. There's plenty of shit to go around."

Next Delillo drew numbers for the hours for watch, and from this my latrine partner and I were exempt. While the first mate wrote down the watch order, Ibrahim sauntered over to me. "Ya, we get the worst business first, get it outta the way."

I did a fair imitation of his shrug.

"Where they got ya workin?" he asked me.

"In the galley with the cook. And you?"

"Equipment maintenance, topside."

"I suppose it pays to know ships."

He nodded. "Yah. Get a good job that way. But yours is good job too."

"Oh? I wouldn't have thought so."

"Wouldn't ya, now, Mister Fancy-talk. Ya next to the food, ain't ya think of that? Can always finagle a little here and there, if ya quick about it. A man get hungry, whether he know ships or not, and ain't no harm in bein in a position to do somethin about it." He gave me a white-toothed smile and a wink, and walked off.

Oha had drawn watch from four to five in the morning. He was also to work in the engine room, as he, along with Ibrahim, was one of the few of us with excellent shipboard credentials. The rest of the men had also been given their places on the nighttime watch roster. Each night, the line would move forward, so that the last man on duty, from five to six A.M., would switch with the first, from ten to eleven. Everyone would therefore have a chance at the best and worst of the shifts.

When this business was concluded, Delillo announced that we were soon to cast off. The passengers had boarded, the cargo had been loaded; the professional crew was now to see to launching us safely. We transients were to have no part in this activity, although we were invited to stay on deck and watch. A small crowd had gathered to see us off, and some of the paying clientele, mainly elderly couples, had gone out along the starboard side of the ship to wave to them. I declined to participate in the festivities, however, preferring to stand quietly at the stern, where I could view the still horizon and steady myself against the railings.

It was a lucky thing for me (and for those standing about me) that I was so inclined, for seasickness has turned out to be the plague of this excursion where my physical constitution is concerned. Who could have thought I would suffer so grievously from it—I, the Pirate Captain of the Bayou—yet I do, and did, from that first moment within harbor. My farewell to my home country was made whilst draped over the rail of the stern, dry-heaving (for I had eaten nothing all day) into the steely waters of the Hudson River.

And when I had recovered somewhat from that ignominy, I was left to cope with the extraordinary sight of the island of Manhattan sliding past me, and the vast, strange waters of the Atlantic beckoning in the distance. It was as well that my face was already wet and streaming, for nobody then noticed that I cried; the fact that John and Tom (or was it Will and Lucas?) were similarly moved was little comfort to me.

For what could they know of what I knew?

That night, in the cramped, fetid cubbyhole, I lay awake hour after hour as Oha snorted and wheezed above me. My loneliness assumed weight and form, settled upon my chest, and crushed the breath from me.

Behind me lay my existence of eighteen years, and every soul I had come to know in those years. Not a one of them knew what had become of me; did any among them care? Ahead of me lay Louis Paxton, and Thomas, and if once I had burned with the conviction that they should be made to acknowledge their blood tie to me, now I wished mostly to behold them as the only family I presumed to have left. I was not heated with anger and dreams of vindication so much as I was seized with longing, the longing to be who I had once been, to gaze upon the faces I recognized—even Thomas's, even Paxton's—if only to see in them a recognition of me.

I tried to imagine myself a year hence, and could not do it. I belonged nowhere and to no one, a flicker of life so insignificant that I could be extinguished in an instant, and to whom would it matter?

When I managed to shut my eyes, I fell deep into blackness, and my dreams came to me as they had during my long convalescence from the wound in my shoulder. Once more I was in Faith's company, all of her end yet before me to undo, or in Thomas's, our great companionship resurrected, or in Mama's.

In any case, I returned to wakefulness shaken and miserable, cast into despair upon realizing all over again that the dead remain dead, aching for that intangible thing my fingers had sought while I lay in a sleep as profound as death.

The next day, I awakened at dawn to the ship's bell, to latrine duty and my post as the cook's assistant.

Upon rising, I stumbled up the stairs to the upper deck, and there I received the shock of my life: there was water around us everywhere, and absolutely no speck—not even a hint—of land. I had known enough to expect this, and yet to behold it was something else again, as I had never been sailing upon the sea. In some corner of my mind I had pictured us within sight of the shore at every moment, the east coast of America behind us at the stern, and the west coast of Britain ahead. But around us now there was nothing—absolutely nothing—except mile upon mile of water, which looked exactly the same in every direction. How, I wondered, did the navigators manage to guide the ship on any particular course, or tell one stretch of sea from the next? I felt a new respect for them, and for the sturdy ship herself. Formerly just a tub of metal, she was now our protection and salvation, the only appreciable thing between us and the foam-flecked green depths.

When I recovered from my amazement, it was time for me to go below, and face the first morning rush for the latrines and the barrels of hot bathing and barbering water. I was barely able to splash my face and shoulders, for everyone had arrived in the washroom ahead of me, carrying cups, bowls, and mugs to supply themselves with water. But Ibrahim was the most creative of us all: he had brought with him a goatskin wine bag, and had done a leisurely job of filling it from the heated tub. When I arrived he was kneeling upon the floor in a corner of the room, wrapped in some sort of gown, pouring the water over various parts of his body. When he had finished, he noted me looking at him, and told me he was performing a religious rite, one demanded by his faith, which is called Oslam or Muslin or something along those lines. I have never heard of it, and am still not sure he isn't making it up simply to hoard more than his share of bathing water.

When I was washed, I reported to the galley to eat my first breakfast, although my stomach was as tender as a newborn's from the boat's ceaseless rolling motion. The sight of the food we were to consume did not help matters any. The cook had prepared a porridge, but so gray and full of lumps was it that I could barely force the first tasteless mouthful past my tongue. I made do with tea, thinking that if this was the quality of the meals we were condemned to eat, I would be taking Ibrahim's advice and sneaking as much on the side as possible.

My next task was to meet my superior, the creator of the lumpen porridge. This man was the exact antithesis of what one might logically expect in a cook. He was neither fat nor jolly nor inclined toward sensual pleasure but, rather, was a stooped, skinny, worried-looking fellow named Albertus Goodman. Goodman, far from being a connoisseur of food, seemed to have a positive aversion to it. He approached a meal with the idea that it should be gulped down quickly, and enjoyed as little as possible. To this end, he had devised a method whereby he could render any edible item a tasteless mass: he simply boiled it into oblivion, whether it be beef, or fish, or vegetable. Boil it, his instructor must have counseled, until it falls apart, so that the diners needn't even chew it—lest they savor it too much.

Of course I didn't know this on the first day; I assumed that the huge vats of water on the stove were to be simply a *part* of the meal-preparation process. I stood in the middle of the galley floor after breakfast, looking about and waiting for Albert to acknowledge me. He rushed past me, crabbed and hunched, pausing every few seconds to bring his hands to his temples in a gesture of pained concentration. Finally he appeared to notice me.

"Who're you?"

"Aubrey, sir. I'm to be your assistant." I said this looking down at him, as he was a good head shorter than I.

He stared back at me through his thick spectacles. "Oh. Well. What do you know about cooking?"

"Honestly, nothing much, sir. But I'm sure if you explain—"

But Goodman had already turned away, and was addressing the ceiling. "Nothing, he says. So why is he here? Idiots! Why do they send me some dandy who's never been about a kitchen?"

"I'm sure I can make myself useful with a minimum of instruction," I said, my tone cool.

"What? Oh—yes, we'll see about that, won't we. Here. You can start with this." He grabbed an apron from a peg and handed it to me, then gave me a little paring knife. Leading me to one of the huge pots, he indicated an equally huge pile of turnips. "Peel these, and dice them. Set them on some water for lunch. I have the passengers' meals to see to."

My guess had been correct: I was to spend the duration of the voyage denuding and dismembering vegetables.

When I was done with the pile—an hour and a half later—Goodman set the whole lot boiling, then took a side of mutton from the cold-locker, hacked it into pieces, and threw it into another pot. And that was lunch for the crew. Boiled mutton, and turnip mush—no salt, no spices, no flavoring. Hatpin Bob, Delillo, and the passengers were treated to tea and sandwiches, which luckily couldn't be cooked, but which did not look especially appetizing. I heard a good deal of grumbling from my nine lowly companions, and Oha—with whom I was still barely speaking—nudged me to ask, "You made this?"

"No, I did not. I only helped, I had no control over how he fixed it."

Oha gave a sour grunt, and the other men's faces revealed similar sentiments.

I went back into the galley for the next round, and found that the pile consisted of potatoes, and the meat was beef; aside from that, dinner was the exact same affair.

This time there was more than grumbling. My shipmates turned positively surly, and asked me what in the hell was happening in the goddamn galley and couldn't I exert some influence over the bloody bastard who was feeding us like dogs. I skulked away from the mess room, thinking that at this rate I'd be dead in another day, done in by my own furious and starving compatriots.

And from there I went to the latrine shift with Ibrahim, who pointed out that our change in duties would be hardly noticeable, since the meals had looked and tasted like shit.

"Go to the devil," I said. "There is nothing I can do about it. Go talk to Goodman yourselves, if you're so dissatisfied."

He shrugged. "I just tryin to tell ya, plenty a mutinies start at the dinin table."

"Oh? Well, I'm sure plenty of them start in the washroom, when certain people feel entitled to more than their share of hot water."

"Ya got to understand, boy, that's no bath. It's praise of A-La."

"How convenient that your gods demand you be clean."

He shrugged again, and I frowned back at him, but I felt even then that Ibrahim was a good sort, and I did not really begrudge him his strange ritual.

We started our task with our own washroom, dragging the big metal cisterns out from beneath the privy seats. We capped them, but there was still the chance they would slosh about, and we had to carry them one by one, a man at each handle, up the steps and onto the topmost deck, to be lowered overboard on snaking ropes and washed clean in the sea. After replacing the tubs, we proceeded to the regular crew's quarters, upon whose toilets we performed the same operations. It was miserable, reeking work, and yet I did not mind it; I'd never imagined I would come to find labor anything but burdensome, but I now know that it can be an anodyne for misery, as it keeps the hands occupied and the mind blessedly empty of the thoughts that assail it in leisure moments.

Eventually, though, both Ibrahim and I were eager for a rest, which we undertook before tackling the privies of the upper berths.

We arranged ourselves on a coil of rope on deck, and then Ibrahim brought out his carved pipe, to make ready for a smoke and a good long chat.

"So, Bree Bennett." He leaned back and lit his tobacco, exhaled a thick white cloud. "Some color-blind fool make a slave outta you, is that what I hear?"

Well, of course he had heard it, the whole world had, and I should have known I would be confronted with it sooner or later. But I was caught; there was nothing to do but tell the truth. "There was no decision on anyone's part. I was born to a quadroon mother, who was a slave. And she claimed my father to be either mulatto or quadroon. And so I am black enough by American law to be enslaved myself." I made my words as clipped as possible, so as to show that the subject was not a pleasant one for me; then, to turn it, I asked him, "But what of you? You have never been so burdened?"

Ibrahim grinned widely. "I am never any man's slave. I am a free man, from when I leave Africa to this day."

I had never met an African black. I asked him what it had been like there, and how it was different from the other continents he'd come to visit.

"I left Africa at twenty years. I am Ewe—E-W-E—Ewe tribe, from West Africa, that's how Africans live, in tribes, and the tribes make villages. I left when white men came through my village, looking to trade for food. They weren't slavers, just traders, wanderin about like fools. I know they gonna be dead or et up in a day, the way they carry on in the wood, or out on the plain. So I say to my pa, I'll show 'em about, travel with 'em west, to the coast, which is where they was headed.

"My pa and the chief, they say no, don't trust 'em, even though there been no slavers about for a long time. But I figure, what I got to lose? I wanted to leave. The village was small, an every day the same, an I don't want to be a farmer for de res of my life. Besides, my folk carryin on about the white man come and taking slaves, but two miles down the road is chiefs who once sell they own people off widdout a thought, or raid they neighbors an trade 'em.

"So off I go with the men, an we hear tell of some Brit bastards up the coast, trying to sneak a few Africans out even after the trade is outlawed, but these who I take up with are honest enough. I lead 'em west, an stay there, learn they tongue, an when it come time for their boat to sail, I say, I want to go. So the men take me, they give me papers for when I get to England, sayin as I'm a free

African, an right away I start work on the ships. Never had a question after that. It's a sickening thing, how a thousand Africans leave in chains for every one as leave a free man, and no difference between us except time an luck."

"Do you miss it, ever?" I asked him, the topic of homesickness being near to my heart just then.

"Ya, ya, I miss it all the time, miss the people, my ma and pa. I went back an saw 'em, and then I leave letters fer the traders to read, whenever I sail to the west coast, an after one voyage I get a message saying my ma die, so I go back an see my pa, and he so broke up he follow her two month after. My pa never take another wife, got no children but me an my sister, an my sister, when he's passed, she say to me, go, ya never gonna be happy here. And I couldn't be, neither. Africa is beautiful, so beautiful ya cry to see it, but once ya get a peek at another kinda life, great cities, London an Paris, big houses an modern things, it's hard gettin back to the mud huts an dirt floor, like how we build the houses in the village. So I go back on the sea. Never did marry, but I got a few sweethearts scattered about." He winked at me.

I smiled back, but I was trying to absorb the idea of villages full of black people, with their own chiefs, their own strange religions, their own rhythm of life. It was a charming picture—though I wondered if it should tempt an American Negro, for a freedom yielding only mud huts and dirt floors so closely resembled the lot of a slave.

I might have sought Ibrahim's opinion in this regard, but it seemed he'd had his fill of answering questions; he instead—to my chagrin—resumed asking them, having somehow decided it proper to do so.

"Speakin a sweethearts, boyo, ya got any?"

"No." Again I attempted to discourage his inquiries with the briefest of replies.

"What's your ma like?"

"She was a house servant. And educated. She kept books." Which was as much as I cared to say on *that* topic.

"She comely too, I bet." Ibrahim grinned. "Because ya good-lookin boy. Musta had all the young puss ya could catch." Luckily I didn't have to respond to this, because he continued right on. "And ya pa, what's he like?"

I did not even think first. "My mother's yellow lover is an invention. I think it's obvious that my father is a white man, and I believe he is the same one who owned us. My former master is my father."

I had never voiced the suspicion aloud to anyone, and now it came out so easily, slipping past my facade of reserve and into the ears of this near-stranger, as if it were the most natural thing in the world to acknowledge.

Ibrahim's expression did not change. "What ya think bout that?"

I could not restrain myself. "I hate him for it. And for his silence, which condemned me to the lot and status of a Negro. As his heir I should have laid claim to whiteness. Whereas now I may only aspire to it."

Ibrahim appeared to choke on his pipe.

"Aspire?" He coughed out a lungful of smoke in a huff. "To whiteness? What-all ya *aspire* to? How ya been done, how ya own daddy do? That what ya reachin for?"

I felt my cheeks flush. "I am not referring to the *behavior* of particular white men, Ibrahim, but to the broader *culture*, to the ethic it embodies, which is to say, what it *stands* for—"

He gawked. "What's it *stand* for, boyo? What's a skin stand for, when ya don't ask for it, don't earn it, can't change it—and when them as got it are such fuckers, eh?"

I had not meant to speak, and now had the perfect excuse for desisting, my tongue having tripped on my mind's logic. I thought of Faith in that moment, as often happened; I remembered how I had doubted her chastity because of her exposure to black field hands. When in the end it was I who had deflowered her with insouciance.

Ibrahim was shaking his head and smiling. He gave me a light punch on the shoulder. "Oooooh, I would sure enough hate to be you, Bree Bennett—ya, ya, much too complicated up there in ya head."

He rose from his position and slapped me on the back. "Come along, my brother, we got one more dance to do with them shit buckets." I followed him, and we attended to the upper-deck quarters, moaning with envy at the luxuries accorded the captain, his first mate, and the paying passengers.

But my mind was buzzing with the leftover implications of our conversation, and I could not throw myself into our manual exertions with quite the same fervor I'd managed earlier.

I was tired, and glad enough when we had done with it, and were heading back to our own berths for our night's rest. Ibrahim shook my hand at the foot of the stairs before departing for his own cubicle, which he shared with Aurelio. "Good workin with ya, boy, you're good partner," he said. "Now, just ya turn that galley around, and everything be fine, right?" He grinned, so as to show there had been no animosity intended in his earlier jibes, and I smiled back, to indicate that none had been presumed. I had thought the same of him, actually—that he was a good working partner, and if he caused me to reshuffle my assertions to some degree, it was not the worst that could happen.

The next morning, I faced Albertus Goodman with rather a different countenance. I was prepared to duel with him over the addition of certain niceties to the cooking process, and if he branded me an arrogant pup, it was too bad—better that than to bear the animosity of my comrades.

I did not bother asking; I strode into the cold-locker, and removed two fat slabs of butter from its chilly depths. And then I searched out the hiding places of certain basic condiments—sugar and salt, which Albert seemed not to realize were there for actual use—and measured some out. He came upon me while I was engaged in this latter activity; he had already set the huge vats of porridge to boil.

"What is all this," he blinked, as I proceeded to sift the salt into the bubbling mass and stir it. "What are you doing—here, what are you putting in that?"

"Salt," I answered. "Sugar. Butter. You use them to give the food *flavor*, Albert."

He exhaled loudly. "Nobody appointed you cook, Mr. Bennett, as far as I know it."

"I am merely assisting."

"You're out of your place, sir—I shall see to the food preparation, if you don't mind, and you shall assist at whatever task I appoint you to."

I turned to face him, still holding the ladle. "Look here," I said, pointing the wooden utensil at him, and shaking some porridge on the floor in the process. "I know this is your domain, Albert, but everyone aboard is complaining, and I'm only trying to avoid a full-scale riot. I don't mean to usurp your authority, but quite frankly, your cooking is inedible, and lacking in any sort of skill."

I saw the little man's lip quiver, and wondered whether he was about to cry or strike me.

"How many voyages have you attended as cook?" I asked him, to diffuse the moment somewhat.

"This is my first," he snapped, "and I didn't ask for the assignment. The regular bloke is ill. Anyway, don't think I don't hear the ingrate bastards grumbling—what do they expect—goose livers? Roast duck? I can only do so much with what I'm given."

You could do a good bit more, I wanted to say, *if you put even an ounce of thought into it*, but I remained quiet. I wondered if Hatpin Bob was faring any better foodwise than we had; I somehow doubted it.

"Besides," Albert went on, "meals are not meant to be some sort of feast for the senses. Food is nourishment, to be consumed and excreted. There is no point in making it more complicated than need be."

"I'm afraid your shipmates disagree with you on that account. The crew works hard, and there's not much to enjoy here besides eating, while the paying passengers expect at least a modicum of effort to be involved in the production of their meals."

Albert threw me a stiff, outraged glare from behind his glasses; then he briskly untied the apron around his middle and hurled it at me. "Here! Suit yourself. I'd no wish to do this job in the first place, you may consider yourself appointed."

"I cannot do all of it alone," I said, "and besides, I'm not certain I'm that much better suited than you. I only know what I've picked up here and there. I'd rather hoped we could go at it together."

Albert gave me a last exhalation. "Did you now—how gracious of you. I'll think it over while I'm relaxing in my bunk." He stalked out of the galley, leaving me to wrestle the two huge pots alone.

There was no question, however, that breakfast on this morning was astronomically improved. I served the porridge with cream, and the men were overjoyed. "Ya, that's more like it," Ibrahim said, while Oha nodded in his usual phlegmatic manner and declared, "Goot."

I fed the regular crew and the upper decks the same meal, with simply a bit more flourish and garnish, and even *they* were appreciative. Delillo told me to pass his compliments on to Albert, who seemed to be picking up the knack, and I promised that I would. For lunch I made fish-paste, and a cold salad, and biscuits; I silently thanked Lila for all the times she had pressed me into service in the kitchen, although I'd sulked and complained through every session. This time, Delillo came down to give Albert a clap on the back, but as my superior was pouting in his quarters, I told the first mate that he was off planning that evening's repast. I passed all of the commentary on to Albert, however, and managed to give the impression that somehow he really was responsible for the excellent efforts. In this way, I managed to win him grudgingly to my arguments. He appeared in the galley in the afternoon, telling me he'd had beef in mind for dinner again, and what should we do with it. I told him we'd make a stew, and set to showing how it was done, and this time he was on hand for the accolades which accompanied the effort.

And while I believe this whole process of planning and creating and enjoying is simply too indulgent for his spare tastes, he's become a good deal better at it, and works alongside me comfortably enough, even acknowledging to the crew that the better part of the labor is done by myself. So we get on well, and certainly our shipmates have given up any notions of mutinous attack, or of tossing us overboard to become dinner for fish schools, which follow the *Artemis* over the waves.

(FEBRUARY 1863)

I know now a good deal more regarding the habits of *el mosquito muerto*, the dead fly.

On the start of our journey's seventh day, I was roused from my sleep by the usual need for a late piss. It was past midnight; the quarters were dark and quiet. I made my way to the washroom and the accompanying privies (chamber pots are not permitted, as I discovered my first night, for there is too much chance they will toss about and overflow), stumbling along in the blackness. I was naked, but did not bother to take my blanket, as I expected to be back abed within a minute.

I entered the toilets, guided by the faint ember-glow in the stove which heats the wash water. I heard a voice mumble, "Who's it?" and recognized the questioner as Francy Dunleavy, the Irishman, whose turn it was for watch that hour.

"Aubrey," I replied sleepily, situating myself before one of the open privy holes. I attended to my business, finished quickly, and took a moment to let myself dry, thinking that I was not nearly so fastidious in this matter as I used to be.

I was ready to turn about and leave when I felt a whiff of air at my back, and something brush my shoulder. Immediately I tried to spin round, but a forearm caught me square at the neck, while a hand yanked my left arm behind me. In a bare second I was immobilized, being able neither to struggle nor to scream. With my right hand I attempted to dislodge the arm at my throat, but I had no leverage, and the more I fought, the more my attacker twisted my injured left shoulder, so that I was forced onto my toes.

"Shhhhh," Dunleavy's whispered brogue insinuated itself into my ear. *"Calm yourself."* His bare flesh beneath my jaw smelled of machine grease; the feel of it awoke such a fury in me that I could not stop twisting and attempting to yell, even with my mind instructing me that I should quiet myself.

"Hold still, will ye, we only want a word with ye."

I heard a sound to my right, and assumed I was about to discover the identity of the second person comprising the "we." Sure enough, a new voice said, "You take it now. Then we gif you that boy Lucas, you get him first," and the accent told me my second attacker was Josef Beck, the German; but his words made no sense to me.

I waited for one of them to speak again, but no further sound came. Rather, my right arm was now grabbed and held. And then I felt another sensation, of something pressing against the small of my back.

I thought at first it was a hand. But it was not.

It was Dunleavy, it was the front of his body, the stiff prominence there drawn across my buttocks as he shifted slowly, rhythmically, behind me.

I was not thinking in the usual sense of the word when I next acted. Turning slightly, I picked up my left foot, and brought the heel down as hard as I could on Dunleavy's toes behind me; I threw my whole body forward, and then back again, so as to dislodge him. He swore, his hand came from around my throat, and I used the leverage I had to back toward him, so that he was thrown off balance, and his grip on my left arm loosed. I twisted free, and heard him swear, "Jaysus!" as he fell upon his back. I was pulling Beck along with me; he still held my right arm fast, but once freed of the Irishman, I ran straight at him, surprising him. I pushed the heel of my hand into his face, and he let go my arm with a cry.

"Jaysus, are ye crazy, we're only tryin ta have a deal with ya," Dunleavy was saying from his spot upon the floor. I could see his member still flopping outside his fly, in an obvious state of disappointment. I stumbled past him, panting, toward the door. I could hear Josef Beck tripping after me, but Dunleavy's voice said, "Forget it, will ye, let 'im go, it ain't worth it," and I was able to escape down the hallway and into my own cubicle.

Once inside I simply grabbed Oha by the hair and pulled. He woke with a great "Ah!" and sat up in the top bunk.

"Knife," I gasped to him, my throat still sore from where it had been gripped. "Where's your knife, I need it—" I threw open his trunk and was pulling objects out at random, throwing them behind me. At last I found the knife, at the bottom of the pile, but Oha was suddenly behind me, blocking me when I turned.

"What you are doing? What iss happen, why you want Oha's knife?"

"Dunleavy and Beck," I panted, "I went to the toilet—" I felt the hand that held the knife shaking badly; I trusted that it would be steady, however, when I thrust the blade into the Irishman's heart.

"Give me knife."

"Get out of my way, goddammit—"

"You give me knife." He could have tried to force me, but he must have known that in my present state I'd be a match for him. So instead he hulked there before me, not moving, but also not allowing me to move.

"You are angry. You do not think right. You kill them, you do murder, captain hold you until we reach England, and then you go to jail, and maybe they kill you. Iss not that importante."

"Get out of my way."

"Sit down. Clear your head. Tell what happen. You still think then to kill

Dunleavy ond Beck, we go kill them together. They be there. We are at sea. They have no place to run."

This seemed fair enough.

I stood trembling for another moment, and then groped toward the bed. I sat down on the bunk, and placed the knife beside me. I could feel the sweat trickling off me, but I was suddenly freezing, and threw my blanket about my shoulders.

Oha, meanwhile, had returned to his trunk, from which he pulled his flask of whiskey. He uncorked it and offered me the bottle, but I pushed it away.

"Drink some."

"I don't want it."

"Drink some, it help the nerves to calm."

I did not necessarily want my nerves calmed, or my senses dulled. But then again, I did not want the picture of Francy Dunleavy on the washroom floor to remain before my eyes, so I took the flask and managed a long pull from it. I am no champion drinker; the taste was as foul to me as ever, but as always I was grateful a minute later when the whiskey's heat caused my fingers to tingle, and my racing mind to slow somewhat.

Oha managed to fold himself beneath the top bunk and position himself on the bed next to me. He took the flask from my hand and drank, then passed it back and waited, his elbows on his knees.

"Now, what happen, Aw-bree?"

I sat for perhaps a full minute, sipping from the flask, before deciding I could trust myself to speak rationally.

"Francy Dunleavy and Josef Beck attacked me in the toilet." My voice was unsteady; I swallowed to calm it.

"Attack how? To beat you?"

"No. No. To—" My tongue froze. I could not say it. Such things cannot, do not, happen in the right world. It was not only grotesque but shameful to be the recipient of such an attention; it hinted at some easily exploited flaw of character.

Luckily I did not have to be more specific. Oha nodded, and I knew he'd taken my meaning.

"They mean to force you."

I sipped and swallowed again. "Yes, I think so. They didn't do it, they didn't get that far, they just—Dunleavy just—I knew what he was doing, and he said—" I took another deep breath. "He and Beck, they said they wanted a deal with me, I think they meant if I agreed to it with them, they were going to go after one of the other boys, and then—" I stopped, not wishing to continue with such a repellent recitation. I rocked back and forth slightly upon the bed, the action somehow calming to me.

"Iss wrong, what they do."

"Oh God, yes."

I shut my eyes, feeling the rage drain out of me, to be replaced by a sensation which made me wish—as a final ignominy—to cry instead. I absolutely refused to yield to this, and the feeling passed after a moment. I continued to breathe deeply; I handed the flask back to Oha and kneaded the cotton of the blanket with my hand.

After a few minutes Oha said, "Now you are more calm, yes?"

"Yes."

"You see now it's better, yes, that you don't run off to stab them."

I hadn't necessarily discarded the idea. But I did feel the immediate need for action to have been alleviated somewhat. I had the rest of the voyage to plot a revenge against my enemies that would allow me to escape detection, and so I was grateful to Oha for thwarting my initial hotheaded reaction. I condensed all of this into "Yes, I see," and then fell silent once again.

A few more minutes passed thus. Then Oha spoke.

"Iss wrong to force. Iss no love there."

"Love!" I laughed harshly into the darkness. "Of course there's no goddamn love. Vile. Venal. That's what's there."

"Yes. Bad iss there with force, which drive love away."

I opened my eyes to glare at him. "There was nothing to drive away, Oha—I did not even *like* those two bastards before, and they've no liking for me, isn't it obvious. And if it's some Christian concept you're dangling, if you're asking me to forgive them in the name of Christian love, you can forget the idea—"

"No, no," he said quickly. "Do not be angry." He placed his arm about my shoulder, his huge hand kneading my neck. It felt good—it told me, at least, that he did not regard me as filthy for having drawn such filth to myself.

I subsided, and closed my eyes again, allowing the liquor to finish its work.

"Iss different when there iss force, Oha iss saying."

I was not following his train of thought, but there was nothing necessarily new about that where Oha was concerned. I shrugged and tried to allow myself to relax under the pressure of his fingers.

"When there iss love, then force iss not needed."

"Uhn," I said, only half-listening, and wishing he would be quiet.

I might have paid more attention at that point. Had I done so, I might have been motivated to open my eyes. But I was focused upon pushing the sensations of the last half hour from my mind, and so, instead of seeing what was coming, I was taken completely by surprise by the feeling of something being pressed against my mouth.

Now my eyes opened of their own accord. And when they did, it was to discover that it was Oha's lips which were pressed against my own, while the hand at the back of my neck had moved up to stroke my hair. Just at that moment, his other hand made its way to my knee, and began a slow progress up my thigh.

It was too much—it was simply too much to be borne, on the heels of the other—and this was so much more monstrous, for this was *Oha*, my *friend*, to whom I'd confided my misery over just this horror not more than a minute ago.

For the second time in as many hours, I felt my body react of its own accord, usurping whatever rational thought my mind might have wished to contribute. I leapt up from the bed, yelling incomprehensibly. Oha's hands flew from where they had rested, and he reared backward, his eyes wide, his mouth still open.

I wedged myself into the corner of the tiny space before him, crouching, the blanket clutched like armor about me; and then in one motion, I leaned forward and spat directly into his face. It was as much to convey what I felt toward him as to relieve me of the nauseating knowledge that his skin had contacted my own. I drew my forearm again and again over my mouth while I stared at him, my stunned mind still unable to accept that he could be capable of what he had just done. I wanted only to escape through the curtain, but it was closer to him than to the corner into which I was backed, and I feared he would attempt to stop me if I ran.

"Aw-bree—" he said, his eyes wide, his hand reaching toward me. He made as if to rise and approach me; in one motion, I sprang to the bed, grabbed the knife, and backed away once more.

I held the blade before me.

"Get away from me, or I'll kill you."

"Aw-bree—"

"Get away from me." I was shouting now, as loudly as I could. I thrust the knife toward him, and he jumped back, raising his hands palms outward in a gesture of supplication. I edged along the wall toward the curtain, still not daring to turn my back upon him. Then I was through the doorway and into the hall. I ran for the steps, staggering blindly in the darkness, and made my way to the topmost deck.

Once outside, I collapsed with my back against the railing, trying to fill my lungs with the heavy sea air. I was still naked, clad only in the blanket, but I would rather have died than return to the crew quarters, where my tormentors—the three of them—no doubt lay in wait for me.

They were insane. All of them. And God knew how many others on this vile, floating, iniquitous heap. To do what they had attempted, even to think of it—

such things did not occur among men, could not be perpetrated by men upon men, for then the order of civilized life failed utterly—

—the intent was grotesque enough, on the parts of the Irishman and the German. The perversity of it, the sheer impossibility, made it grotesque enough.

But for Oha.

For him. To do as he had.

That treachery reached even beyond the depravity of the act itself.

If I reserved a blade for any of the trio, it should be for Oha, whom I had trusted. Whose perfidy had never—could never have—crossed my mind. But—my thoughts raced—how might I have my vengeance on him here, at sea? His disappearance would be too obvious. Which meant—God—which meant I would be forced to share the confines of this ship with him for the duration of the voyage, would be forced to endure his vile, reeking presence—

I heard a sound to my left, and saw the regular crew's watchman for that hour, a sailor named Billings, heading toward me.

"Everything all right?" he asked, seeing me seated there.

"What do you mean—" I barked, and then I caught myself, and said, "I felt ill. I needed some air."

"Do you need the medic?"

"No." *I need to be left in peace, you prick.*

Billings shrugged. "See that you don't run into any passengers, without no decent clothes on," he advised, and then continued his amble topside.

As soon as he'd passed, I heard more noise to my right, where the stair to the crew's quarters lay. I saw a head emerge, and then another. Then I heard Ibrahim's voice: "Ya, Aubrey, that you? What's goin on here, ya wake the dead in the middle of the night?"

I was about to reply—to tell him to go back to sleep and leave me be—when I heard Aurelio's broken English pipe up from behind him.

"I think maybe the trouble be, he get bit by his dead fly."

And then they both fell to laughing.

I picked up the knife from where it lay beside me, and, without rising, hurled it with all my strength at the deck near the stairway. It sank into the wood a foot from Aurelio's nose, the handle quivering for a moment.

"Jee-sus Christ!" I heard him whistle into the darkness.

"Shit, Aubrey, what ya tryin to do—kill us or somethin?"

"Go to fucking hell."

"What? Eh, what's a matter with ya, boy, what ya so touched over, for God's sake." Ibrahim mounted the remaining stairs and walked toward me, then stopped.

"Ya don't have another knife, do ya?"

"Leave me alone."

He ignored me. He continued walking, and when he reached me, sat himself down cross-legged on the deck.

"What ya doin up here, Aubrey. Mister Sven Oha's down dere in the dreary dark, bangin his head against the floor and tearin up ya room like the wild beast, wakin up the whole goddamn boat, and ya sittin up here bare-assed in the cold, throwin blades at innocent men's heads. What get into ya?" He lowered his voice. "Did ya have a lovers' spat?"

I was upon him instantly. I caught him by the throat and threw him to the deck, delivered a sound punch to his face. But although he was smaller, he was a good bit more experienced than I at combat. He kneed me, flipped me round, and caught me against the railings, where he pinned me with one hand, and administered a hard slap to my face with his other.

"Straighten out, boy, and ya keep ya fists to yaself," he said, breathing hard, and releasing me. "Ya done gone crazy, go see the goddamn medic."

"*Fuck* yourself. You knew—you knew about Oha, it's funny, isn't it—you set me up with him—"

"Oh, ya blamin me for whatever he done? Who told ya to bed with 'im, when ya knew better—"

"I *didn't* know better, goddamn you."

Ibrahim took a step back, regarded me. "Ya mean to tell me ya don't know right off Sven Oha's crazy as a goddamn lunatic, got his mind twisted round like a wet sheet? All ya got to do is talk to him for an hour, ya know that!"

What was Faith's expression, about a story that wouldn't fool a day-old coon? I shut my eyes, the fight gone out of me, and tentatively touched my cheek where Ibrahim's open slap had raised a welt.

"Perhaps I'm merely stupid," I said, my eyes still closed. "You could have told me what you knew. But you did not. Now if you've both amused yourselves sufficiently at my expense, I am asking you, please, to leave me be."

Instead of leaving, Ibrahim said, "It never cross our minds ya don't know. Not that we think ya go that way yaself, but ya have to know about Oha."

"Believe me. I did not."

In answer to this, he squatted back down, took out his pipe and lit it. "First time I sail with him, he talk my ear off, leave me feelin like I got to wash my head out after he stuff it full of his shit. It ain't so much he go for the gents—there's lots, especially in the sailin trade, they don't know what a woman is for, and most all of us do on the sea now an then what we'd not give a thought to on the dry ground, and what's it matter, as long as ya on the right end of the buggerin. Most times everyone get on fine, leave ya be if ya leave them be. But Oha—he's strange beyond strange, comin and goin, and he don't make a secret of it, like he don't make it secret that he take to the boys."

"He made a secret of it to me." I shook my head, rubbed my burning eyes. "Until now."

Ibrahim did not answer, but dragged again on his pipe.

Presently he said, "So he try to have at ya, eh?"

I stared past him. "It was not only him. It started in the toilet, with the Irishman, Dunleavy, and the German, Beck."

"Oh, goddamn," Ibrahim said, giving a low whistle. "What'd they do—just ask ya, or they try some convincin?"

"They attacked me. Got me round the neck. And when I told Oha—" I shook my head.

"Oh, shit. Twice in one night—oh ya, ya, that's bad."

I leaned my head on my arms.

"Well, but ya can't let it eat at ya. It's nothin ya did. Oha likes a comely boy—ya know, he chase Aurelio clean round the deck first time them two sail together. But Aurelio don't take on to kill him, just laugh at him, because he knows the bastard's crazy. Oha got him a reputation fer this sorta thing, ya know, an them two other buggers likely hear of it, and figure if ya keepin company with him, ya must be fair game for them. They are right fuckin stupid, though, for they must know they get they heads opened, acting like that. This ain't the jolly pirate schooner, can't have some bloody animals grabbin at us in the shithouse."

"They told me if I did it—with them—they'd go after one of the boys, and give him to me first."

"Name a God! The bastards! Ya, they need they heads opened, sure enough."

"I'm going to report them to the captain." I hadn't been planning this either, it had simply come out, but now that I'd said it, it seemed like a good idea.

"What?" Ibrahim took his pipe from his mouth. "What ya gonna do a fool thing like that for?"

"What do you mean, a fool thing? They attacked me. The captain should know. They should be punished."

Ibrahim shook his head. "Nah, nah, nah, ain't ya know nothin, boy. The captain don't wanna hear any a this. Ya go to the captain, ya just make things the worse for yaself, and everybody else."

"We'll see."

"Ya gonna tell the captain about ya friend Oha too? Ya gonna go that far?"

"No," I said bitterly. "He deserves worse than the captain could give him."

"Why, eh? He force himself on ya, try to rape ya?"

Rape? I had not yet imagined the word being used in reference to myself, or applied to either of these incidents. It shocked me thoroughly. "No. Of course not."

"What, then—chase ya, wave his prick at ya?"

"He tried—he attempted—" I swallowed. "He kissed me."

Ibrahim's barking laughter rang across the open deck; I remained disgustedly silent.

"Jesus Christ on a crutch, Aubrey, that what all ya fuss be over—ya ought to pity him, the crazy fuck. Look, he pick the wrong time ta pester ya, yes. But a smooch ain't worth dis drama. Go on an yell, give him a kick in the arse, and straighten him out. And then get on with ya. But ya best do it soon, before Mr. Sven Oha rip a hole in the bottom of the boat and sink us all."

I had no intention of merely yelling. I had no intention of going back down into the crew quarters and dealing with Oha in any shape or form, and I told Ibrahim this directly. I did not know what I would do, in the end. I intended to visit Hatpin Bob regarding Dunleavy and Beck; but that was as far as I'd got in my plan for justice. The only other thing I'd decided was that I would have no more association with Oha in any guise, and no matter what else occurred to me, this would remain true.

"Eh, suit yaself, then, boy, but I'm tellin ya, ya just makin a big hill out of a little one."

"We'll see," I said.

Ibrahim and Aurelio offered me the floor of their berth for that night. Aurelio shook my hand, and told me in his heavy accent that he'd meant no insult toward me, that he hadn't known I'd take everything so seriously. I found this astonishing but accepted his gesture nonetheless, for he was, after all, willing to tolerate my presence in his cramped quarters. I returned to the crew deck with them; I was afraid I would be forced to set eyes on Oha, but he had stopped his banging about, and was wise enough to keep to his own space.

It was by now close to dawn. The workday would be starting shortly, and I felt near dead upon my feet. Nonetheless I waited for the morning bell, and slipped into my berth when I was certain Oha had vacated it. I retrieved my clothes, then reported to the galley and asked Albert if he could carry on alone, as I had some business with the captain. He agreed, and I went off in search of Delillo, through whom I made an appointment with Hatpin Bob.

At half past seven, Delillo showed me into the captain's quarters.

"And what can I do for you, sailor," the captain asked, looking up. He was seated at a long hardwood desk, where he'd been making an entry in his log.

"I wish to lodge a complaint, sir."

"Do you now. Against whom, and for what?"

"Against Francis Dunleavy and Josef Beck, for attacking me and attempting an unnatural act upon me."

The captain's eyebrows shot up and he pushed his hands out at me, as if to keep me from approaching him. "Whoa there, lad, whoa, now wait a moment. Perhaps you'd better start at the beginning, if you've allegations of that sort to make."

"Gladly, sir," I said. "I went to the toilet at midnight last night. Dunleavy had the watch, and he called to me. I answered, and the next I knew, he had me round the throat and the arm. Then Beck came over and held my other arm, and told me if I allowed myself to be violated, they would corner one of the other boys, the one named Lucas, and allow me to do likewise on him first, before they had at him as well." I had rehearsed this carefully, so as to allow no hint of rage or irrationality to taint it, and I delivered it as I'd hoped to, in a calm and steady voice.

Hatpin Bob rubbed his eyes. "Such nonsense," he muttered. "You'd think we were on a galleon two hundred years ago. You know," he said, now addressing me, "nobody likes a whiner. Or a tattler, telling tales out of school. I especially do not."

I stared back at him, disbelieving. "I didn't regard myself as either one, sir. I was attacked. There was a plan to attack another. I felt it should be reported."

"You have any marks on you to prove that this 'attack' took place?"

"I do not, because I managed to escape before I was harmed. But that does not negate—"

"Did anyone other than yourself witness this 'attack'?"

"There was no one present except the three of us, sir, otherwise I doubt anything would have taken place."

"So it is essentially your word against theirs."

I felt my temper rising. "So is it any victim's word against any criminal's, sir, when one is robbed or struck or cheated."

"Yes, but in that instance there's no reason to suspect that the victim may have sought to be robbed or struck or cheated. What were you doing naked in the shithouse in the middle of the night?"

Now my face fairly burned, I could feel my stomach clench. It was all I could do not to reach across the desk and grab him by the collar.

"I sought nothing but a *piss, sir*. And for it I was *assaulted, sir*."

"Yes, well, whatever the truth of that, these are matters for you to settle amongst yourselves. You are not regular crew, you understand."

"I thought you would wish to know, *sir*, as morale can be quite disturbed by the threat of assault."

"Well, you've lodged your complaint, then, young man, and I'll keep an eye on your companions. Only do try to stay out of trouble from here on in, yes?"

I turned away, stunned into silence. As I reached the door, Hatpin Bob said, "By the bye, you're the lad who works in the galley, aren't you?"

"Yes, sir." I did not turn round.

"Well, you're doing a hell of a job down there, you and Goodman. Keep up the good work."

"Yes. *Sir.*" I was glad he could not read the contempt in my face, although it might have been evident in my tone.

I exited the topmost deck, my spirits thoroughly depressed. I was now beyond exhaustion; whatever fire had been stoked in me by the anticipation of lodging my complaint was burnt completely out. In the galley I reported to Albert, and told him I could not cook that day, as I was ill. I must have looked it, for he shrugged and told me he'd carry on alone. I made my way back to Ibrahim's berth, dreading a confrontation with either the Irishman or the German or Oha; but no one was about the quarters. The others had all gone off to their various posts to work, and so I crawled into one of the bunks and fell soundly, if bitterly, asleep.

It was almost dusk when I awoke. Ibrahim and Aurelio returned with their usual cacophony of laughter and talk, which they made no attempt to restrain on my account.

"We missed ya at lunchtime, all right," Ibrahim said, not bothering to apologize for the noise. "That Albert's a hopeless fool without ya." Seeing that I did not respond, he asked, "So, how went it? Ya get ya audience with His Majesty?"

"Yes."

"An what he say?"

I reported the exchange faithfully and listlessly, and when I'd finished, Ibrahim heaved a long sigh. "Well, I'm sorry to have the chance to say I told ya so. But I did. Ya done what ya had to do. So let it go now, and with any luck, maybe the rest of the crew don't hear of it for a while."

"Why the hell should I care whether they hear of it or not?"

"Like the captain say, boy. Nobody like a tattler."

I did not return to the galley that evening, nor was I able to rouse myself the next day. I truly was sick; I had contracted some sort of infection, and could barely move to the toilet—where I would go only if one of my two bunkmates accompanied me. The ship's doctor came to examine me and provide me with an excuse; he dosed me with quinine as well, and was on his way. Other than him, I saw none of the men, and ate nothing, remaining instead in the cubicle, upon the bed. I lay staring at the bunk above my head, considering at length my ineffectual nature, the elasticities of certain codes of conduct, and my inability—despite past hypocrisies of my own—to accept them.

In this gloomy frame of mind I spent the better part of the entire day. When I was not contemplating my situation thus, I was asleep, which seemed to aid in my recovery not at all. I had no idea how the galley was faring without me—I had other things weighing upon me, and felt in addition that a few bad meals were the least I could manage as a reward for the captain's extraordinary performance.

The dinner hour came and went, and still I was alone, Ibrahim and Aurelio having gone off to participate in some activity or another with our crewmates. I was somewhere between sleep and wakefulness when I heard a commotion which seemed to emanate from near the end of the hall. There were shouts and curses and banging sounds, and the hum of excited voices behind all of it. I had risen up upon my elbows to listen when the curtain of the berth was ripped aside, and one of the younger boys, the one named Will, came rushing into the tiny space.

"Come on, then, Aubrey!" he said, shaking my shoulder none too gently. "Get up with you."

"What's happening? What do you want?" I covered my eyes and squinted, the light from the gasoliers in the hallway burning into my brain like the noonday sun.

"Come on." He yanked at my shoulder so insistently that I rose, despite the ache which suffused my whole body, and followed him.

Will led me down the dim corridor to the washroom. I could see that the space was aglow with lamplight; I entered, and, once inside, beheld the most extraordinary spectacle. All of the itinerant crew and most of the regular one were lining the room's perimeter. In the center of the floor, near the stove, someone had placed one of the huge privy cisterns. Over it towered Oha, who was holding Francy Dunleavy in an unbreakable grip. Dunleavy's hands were yanked behind his back, his head and torso were bare and covered in filth. It took me only a second to realize that Oha had been dunking the Irishman headfirst into the reeking vat.

I looked across the room and saw Josef Beck suspended between Aurelio and Ibrahim. He was watching his companion's humiliation with a resigned dread.

When Ibrahim saw me he yelled to Dunleavy, "Look, here come ya justice now, man." To me he shouted, "Go on, Aubrey—he want a taste of ya so bad, go on and give it to him."

Oha yanked Dunleavy into an upright position and put a knee in his back, which forced him to expose his sickly-white stomach. As he held his captive thus, he gave me a look which reminded me for all the world of a dog presenting a gift to its master. I did not acknowledge it. I stared from Oha to the Irishman. It was all too bizarre, too insane, for which one should I have struck at, given the chance, and how in the world did *Oha* justify holding *Dunleavy* for me to punish?

But then—what did it matter? This was fast becoming my new credo.

I stepped up to Dunleavy and looked him in the eye. He stared back at me, chin raised, without a hint of remorse. Seeing that, I resigned myself to giving my audience their satisfaction. I took a careful boxer's stance, allowed my body to recall its early training, put all my strength behind my arm, and landed a square, solid punch to the Irishman's face. I hurt my hand, but I managed to break Dunleavy's nose as well; I knew his countenance would long bear a reminder of his encounter with me. His head rocked backward at the force of the punch, the skin of his cheek split, blood poured from his nostrils while the rest of the nose began to swell immediately. He reeled for a moment, and then sagged to his knees, unconscious. The other men were cheering and urging me to hit him again, but this seemed redundant, and so I refused.

Whereupon Ibrahim shouted, "Go on, Lucas, he had it in for ya too, so take ya best shot." Dunleavy was just beginning to come round when the boy called Lucas, wiry and perhaps fifteen, stepped forward, egged on by his three mates. "Here's for you, you dirty prick, you don't deserve to call yourself an Irishman." He spat at Dunleavy, and threw a powerful, disciplined punch to the belly. Dunleavy buckled, and Oha let him go, whereupon he pitched forward into the vat, while the other men roared their amusement.

Next it was Josef Beck's turn, but he was not wise enough to submit quietly. He made the mistake of swinging at Ibrahim, who knocked him flat with one sinewy arm. Then Oha picked him up like a pillow, and deposited him entirely into the cistern. Again the men laughed and whooped as he tried to stand and stagger out, cursing us in German. But as soon as he'd reached the floor Oha delivered a kick to his arse which sent him sprawling. Ibrahim took the final shot, administering another kick to his face with a booted foot, so that Beck emerged from his ordeal branded as soundly as his partner.

This appeared to mark the end of the rite. It was left for Ibrahim to pronounce the benediction.

"No hard feelin's on ya, boys," he said, nudging Beck with a toe; Dunleavy was crouched against a wall protecting his face. "Learn ya manners, an don't be lookin ta bugger ya shipmates without they say so." The men sniggered and began to file from the room, and I turned my back on the scene as well, wanting only to exit before it was necessary to acknowledge Oha.

As I walked back to Ibrahim's berth, the crewmen gave Lucas and myself feigned punches on the shoulder, and claps upon the back: "Good lads, you showed the sons of bitches." "They got what was coming to 'em, eh?"

No—not everyone had got what was coming to them.

Within a few minutes, I was back upon Ibrahim's floor, and he and Aurelio had returned, stripped, and slipped into bed. They were still chuckling and rehashing the incident, congratulating themselves and me on a job well done.

I waited until there was a long stretch of silence, and then I asked into the darkness, "Who started it?"

"I told the others one by one today," Ibrahim said without hesitation. "They all get plenty mad, and of course Oha, he already mad."

"Why did you do it, without saying anything to me?"

"I told ya, Bree. Whatever Dunleavy an Beck done, nobody like a tattler. This way, it look like ya call ya friends to stand behind ya first off, so it don't matter so much that ya went to the captain, or what ya tell 'im. It got handled the right way. Ya see?"

"No," I said quietly. "I don't see."

"It ain't fair, but there's how it is." There was a silence. "Feel free to thank me any time for helpin ya."

"Thank you."

"Ya needn't mention it." I heard him chuckle, and shift in his bunk. In another minute he was asleep and snoring, Aurelio falling into chorus with him shortly after.

I did not sleep right away. I rehashed the event of the evening for myself and could find nothing to satisfy me in its execution; as per my sickbed ruminations, the administration of this justice had left me only disillusioned.

The next morning, I was awakened when Aurelio and Ibrahim left for the washroom. I was feeling somewhat less ill, and thought I ought to be getting on to the galley myself, so I arose stiffly and folded my blanket upon the bottom bunk. I opened the curtain—and came face to face with Oha, who stood in the doorway—filled it in fact—his legs planted like tree trunks, his arms hanging by his sides.

In truth, part of my reason for avoiding him had been my fear that, being the animal he'd proved himself to be, he would do violence upon me as a punishment for my vehement rejection of him, and I would be forced to do violence back. But the previous evening had shown me that this at least was not his intent, which left me to wonder just what in hell he wanted.

"Stand off," I snapped, staring at him.

"You talk to Oha."

"No. Let me push it into your thick head: I do not talk to Oha." His jaw clenched; *Go ahead and hit me*, I thought, *it'll give me a reason to crack your skull.* I felt capable of it, my anger toward Oha having not been assuaged in the least.

"Oha come to ask forgiveness." He assumed that doglike look again, then placed his hands together and brought them to his lowered forehead, and for some reason, this ridiculous gesture was even more provocative to me than a threatening one might have been.

"It's done, Oha. You are forgiven. Now go to hell."

He did not move. The sight of him hulking there, like some sort of lunatic pontiff, was repelling and infuriating, and at last I shoved him out of the way and walked by him. "I have work to do," I said as I passed. "Don't approach me again." I stalked off to the galley, served breakfast (noting without surprise that Dunleavy and Beck had failed to appear for it), and ate while Oha stared at me from across the room. As long as he stayed away from me, I decided, he could throw me his evil eye all he liked.

But come lunchtime, there he was, much closer than mere staring distance. He came into the mess, but rather than assume a seat at the plank table, he stood across from me with his arms folded and his head bowed, while everyone else in the room (except Ibrahim and Aurelio, who appeared to be fending off laughter) gawked as if he'd lost his mind. I paid no attention to him. I cleaned up and returned to the galley, where Albert—who had witnessed our performance the night before—was waiting to question me.

"What is the story with that big bloke, Aubrey?"

"I'm damned if I know." It was clear to me that the whole ship knew Oha and I had had some sort of falling-out right after I'd been assaulted, and that I was not on friendly terms with my former berthmate, despite his having aided me in my revenge upon my attackers. I assumed too that they'd all heard the rumors of Oha's strange bent of mind—gossip flies round a ship as quick as round a circle of cosseted old ladies, from what I've witnessed. I hoped my crewmates would presume that Oha's insanity had finally revealed itself in its full measure and got under my skin, whereupon I'd been forced to abandon his company.

"He's wrong in the head, you know," I said to Albert, to lend credence to this version of events.

"You needn't tell me that," Albert laughed. "It's plain enough, and from the looks of him last night, I'd not want to be on his bad side."

I did not want Oha on any side of me. But once again, at dinner, he stood there, eating nothing himself, still as an Indian, a great yellow-haired Indian, casting his shadow over my plate. He was trailing behind me when I returned to Ibrahim's berth to sleep. And he was skulking about the doorway the next morning at dawn, when I awoke to wash.

He stood across from me again when I attempted to eat breakfast.

And lunch.

And dinner.

The other men were now finding this quite entertaining. They'd begun laying bets on how long Oha could last without food, and how long I would last without peace, and whether a full-fledged fight would break out between us. This was something everyone seemed eager to witness. Ibrahim was amusing himself discussing the odds at night, before the three of us slept: my youth and speed might carry the bout, he speculated, but then Aurelio reminded him that Oha had the advantage in terms of sheer size. "Ya, ya, that's true. Ya tall, boy, but he's taller, got reach in them arms, an he know fightin' too—"

"Will the two of you quit this!" I barked from my place on the floor. "I have no intention of fighting him, this has nothing to do with fighting, as you more than know!"

But the next day at breakfast I disappointed all of my constituents by being the first to yield. I could take it no longer, and when Oha planted himself in front of me like some demented carved statue, I finally threw down my spoon and screamed at him: "WILL YOU LET ME BE, GODDAMMIT!" Whereupon an assortment of cheers and groans broke out from the dolts around us.

The men were climbing over themselves in an eagerness to collect on their wagers; I was hardly surprised to see that Ibrahim had been acting as the odds-placer. I could only shake my head that afternoon when I realized he had laid his own coins on Oha, but he shrugged: "Ya held out longer than I woulda, lad, but ya can't beat a madman at bein mad."

This was later, though. In that moment Oha and I were the only two in the mess not moving. "You talk to Oha," he said, over the tumult the other men were creating.

"All *right*," I snapped. "I will talk to you. Now will you please—*please*—allow me to eat!"

That night I met Oha on the topmost deck. Since it was obvious that we were not going to fight, the other men had lost interest in our altercation, and we were accorded some privacy.

I arrived first at the spot where I'd agreed to meet him, a feeling of dread in my stomach. How I wished I'd never spoken to him that first day in the coffee vendor's, for now I might be on my way safely to France, and without having been hounded in this manner.

I saw him clomping up the stairs, his huge form filling the space between the handrails. I seated myself on a rope coil, and turned my gaze out to the sea.

He lowered himself down next to me, assuming his typical posture: both feet braced, hands upon his knees.

"You forgive Oha, Aw-bree," he began at once.

I felt the first flare of intense irritation. "Look here, if you want to talk to me, the first thing you can do is stop referring to yourself as 'Oha.' The word is 'I.' Haven't you ever heard of it—'I'? Who're you, the fucking King of England, that you can't say 'I'?"

He said nothing.

"The second thing you can do is stop ordering me about. Learn how to phrase a question, and stop telling me what I shall do or not do."

There was still no response from Oha, except a stronger setting of his mouth.

So I continued on. "At any rate, I can't. I can't forgive you. I am sorry."

"Oha have—*I*—have—" He seemed to have trouble forming the word. "*I*—have remorse. You are angry, Oha wants that you not be angry."

"That isn't remorse," I said dully. "That is the serving of your own ends."

He shook his head, as if to clear the air of my assertions.

"You betrayed me," I went on, "in the worst moment. In the worst sense. I came to you as a friend, to confide in you, and you turn round and attempt on me the exact thing I'd just suffered. You didn't care a whit for my state of mind, you dared assume I'd share your inclinations, or maybe it didn't matter so long as you got your way. I am on this ship—and friendly with you in the first place, admit it—because you saw an opportunity and seized it to gratify yourself."

"No. No. You are wrong, Aw-bree. Oha think, all the time, that you are one in mind with Oha, for you say you do not touch vooman—remember, you tell Oha that."

I was about to snap at him—and then I realized, I *had* said this, back in New York when I'd sworn not to menace the female sex further, so as to spare them the misery of association with me. "Good sweet Christ. How, from that statement, did you manage to infer that my interests might settle on *you*?"

He stared ahead without answering.

"And anyway, what is this about our being of one mind in casting women aside? Never mind me—*you* spent more money on whores—on *women*, the only *honest* women, do you remember that conversation?—than you did on food, so of what mind were *you*?"

"But Oha do not touch them."

My mouth dropped open. It actually did, I mean no mere figure of speech here.

"Then what in the name of God were you doing with them?"

"Oha never touch their uncleanness. Punish them. Make them to show the body, then to see while—"

"Oh God, shut up with it, I don't need to know."

"—man have pleasure himself—"

"You are out of your mind."

He blundered on, oblivious. "Vooman iss unclean, the beast to swallow him that yield to her. Draw da man with tricks, tit ond cunt, ond man must go to vooman—Oha go but does not yield. Man ond man love equal. Share truth of love. Oha must to give truth to you, Aw-bree. Oha must to show truth and not force, not like them who wrong you."

"Please be quiet. You are making me ill." This was not a figure of speech, either. Oha obeyed me, and we sat in silence for a few moments.

Finally, after some thought, I spoke.

"I cannot begin to understand your mind, or what you aspire to with men like yourself. Therefore I have no basis upon which to deny it to you, or call it wrong.

"But you attempted a—*seduction*—upon me to satisfy your own aims, without thought as to the harm it might do me. And that I call wrong. As wrong as any who'd apply force. It is not my place to judge you perverse, but I can judge you selfish, and I do."

Oha sat pondering his enormous boots.

"You are harsh. If Oha iss done as you say, Oha iss wrong. But he iss not like them who force. He want for himself, but how iss this wrong? Iss only love. He do not offer force, but love. Truth. Goot for Oha, but maybe goot for Aw-bree too. Do you never want someone for yourself, and so tell yourself you do goot for them too?"

This time I was silent for a much longer while.

Oha had clenched his jaw again; something was clearly costing him mental effort. "I—offend you, Aw-bree. I—do not want to, and for that I am sorry. Never do again. You are not Oha, yes? Goot for Oha iss not goot for you. I—ask you forgive, Aw-bree."

The stillness, when he finished, was absolute. The waves slapped against the side of the ship's hull; this was the only sound in the absence of our voices. How black everything was about us! From where we sat, the sky appeared to blend into the sea, the twinkling of the stars and the twinkling of the waves only mirrors of each other.

After a minute I said, "Perhaps you have a point."

And then a minute later, "I forgive you, I suppose." One of us, at least, should have that comfort.

He nodded. Another long moment went by, in which I prayed he would not be moved toward some dramatic conclusion to our discussion.

He tapped his fingers on his knees, and gazed at the sea before him.

Then he said, "Goot."

I went back to sleeping in my own berth. It only made sense; Ibrahim's floor was hard, Aurelio's snoring interrupted my rest. I did not sleep naked, however, or dress before Oha. I could not abide the idea of his gaze upon me, nor did I wish to provide him with the slightest reason to think anything in my stance had altered. He, for his part, kept his distance from me, as a measure of respect, for which I was grateful.

I cannot imagine what our arrangement will be, however, once we make land. We were planning to look for quarters together, as this is cheaper than rooming by oneself, and as Oha is acquainted with the cities of England, whereas I am not. But obviously this cannot serve either of us well, and so I doubt that I shall undertake it for very long, if at all.

Ibrahim and Aurelio, however, are full of nothing but praise for the fact that we appear to have settled our differences. Probably they are just grateful not to be stepping over my prone form on their way to the toilet at night.

I finally saw Francy Dunleavy and Josef Beck a few days after their ignominious thrashings. Dunleavy had had his nose set by the ship's doctor, and Beck was nursing an enormous slash on the cheek which had been stitched closed with catgut. True to form, and now hardly surprising to me, no one in authority set out to discover what happened to them or why, and apparently neither of them revealed it. I continue to marvel at the rules of this game: the rest of the men tolerate the two of them now as if nothing has happened; their reception is not warm, but neither is it hostile. They sinned, bore their punishment, and are now free to reestablish themselves.

How I envy them.

Land ho.

I believe this is the traditional phrase, although no one shouted it from the railings this morning.

The coast of England is in sight. We have made our crossing, without encountering storm or violent sea. We expect to put to shore by this afternoon. What can await me there, I wonder—but I must believe in my own power to make the British soil yield more and better than what I left behind me. Right now I scarcely feel this confidence in myself, but I must try to summon it, as there is no other direction for me to take.

So I suppose we shall see.

Part two

chapter one

June 30, 1861

My dear Miss Leeds,

How odd it seems to be keeping up this association with you through the mails! I feel I know you intimately, as you do me, and yet, laughably, I realize that it is our letters, more so than the length of time spent in each other's company, which cause me to regard you as my dear new friend. Caroline writes nothing but good of you, and I say it again for the thousandth time: that we are all fortunate to have met, for there are enough silly girls in the world to form a small nation, but far fewer of our ilk available to keep each other company.

As you may imagine, I have arrived in New Orleans, after an uneventful (if harried and crowded) passage. My mother—or Maman, as I call her—insisted upon dragging along not only every material object she owns but several living, breathing vassals as well, since she has never trusted the American Negroes to do an adequate job of spoiling her. We are thus saddled with the following: (A) one majordomo; his name is Vivien Dolley, and he is a bile-complected Englishman who has caused the hairs on my neck to lift since my childhood; and (B) two young women from our estates in Provence; one is called Lisabeth, and the other Cici. They are pleasant and sweet creatures, if none too bright, and are thrilled to be having the adventure of their lives onboard ship and Stateside. Besides this there are (C) the lovebirds, Pierre and Aubergine, who've come along equipped with their standing cages, and (D) no fewer than EIGHT coffin-sized trunks holding everything from glassware to foodstuffs (since Maman especially does not trust the Negro—or the American—version of cuisine).

We are settled in at last, despite the difficulty involved in transporting us and our entourage here in one piece, and I must say everything is both exactly as I remember it, and vastly different. I had been dreading witnessing the effects the war might have had upon the home I remembered, but thus far these are remarkably few, at least when considering only the outward, physical contours of the city. It is more the air about the place which is changed—but that is changed utterly. New Orleans is no longer the easygoing lazy port of my youth. There is a tension here which is obvious as much in those topics that are scrupulously avoided as in those which are upon everyone's lips. This war, in one guise or another, is the subject of both speech and silence.

But besides all of this there are those perceptions of mine which are different simply because I myself am different, and these would exist with or without the state of war. I must keep in mind that I have not set foot in New Orleans since entering school as a child of twelve; the spaces which I remember as huge and overwhelming now seem normally sized to me, and the servants—whom I also recall as being exotic and towering—are similarly ordinary. It is wonderful to see them, however; I had forgotten the sensation of that genuine warmth which I and these people have felt mutually toward each other, and I can hardly contain myself at the idea that I am to be able to do right by them at last. One of them was horribly beaten by the louts in these parts who consider themselves the defenders of white citizenry; I shall have my revenge in terms of seeing every last Negro to the free states, or back to Provence with my mother and myself. I have discussed only the outline of my plans so far with our housemistress, but the details are falling into place, thanks in no small part to Caroline's mother, whose friends among the Chicago abolitionists seem endless in number.

I am dying to know all of the news I have not been part of back in London, but I'd urge you not to attempt to write to me until I have concluded my business around the rest of the region, for I shall be traveling about and may be difficult to reach via the mails. I shall write to you, however—I hope you don't bore easily, as I can be less than compelling in my choice of subject matter and description.

How I miss you all—yes, you too, dear, whose face I recall only in its vaguest particulars, but whose spirit is as alive to me as that of any lifelong associate. Please kiss everyone there at least once for me! I have asked that Caroline and her brother do the same to you, so I expect to hear before too long that there has been a frenzy of activity of this nature going on.

May we meet again soon, and the Fates protect us until we do—

—Your newly minted friend,
Louella

July 2, 1861

Dearest Louella,

It is my hope that this letter finds you well, and finally ensconced in your New Orleans abode. (You must surely be there by now! I've had no letter from the United States yet—HINT, HINT!—but I've also had no word of an international incident concerning a shipwrecked Madame and Mademoiselle, so I assume the boat docked safely.) I'm certain you are busy reacquainting yourself with the people and places you've gone to such trouble to reach, and so I shall keep this brief and simple, and urge you to write back at your leisure. (I mean this sincerely, despite the HINTS!)

Perhaps while I await your first missive from America I can sketch a little picture of what has been happening here. Miss Caroline Beckwith has been keeping delightful company with me. She has provided introductions to a number of people whom I believe you are already acquainted with. Firstly, there was a minor flirtation with a Mr. Carter Forbes-Spencer, but that was as brief as his character is deep. Far more interesting have been my associations with Mr. Harlow Beckwith, and a certain Miss Ashe of Hyde Park. I am wondering, Louella: have you any interest in zoology and natural biology yourself, and might you perchance have belonged to Miss Ashe's uniquely informative study group? If you did, or do, you no doubt know of the wonders of her atrium, and no doubt have a key by which to admit yourself. Do tell, please, and I shall enlighten you further as to my own education at Miss Ashe's hands.

Now, what of yourself? Do you find New Orleans much changed, and has the war effected any noticeable hardships upon the city? Above all, are you being exceptionally cautious and careful there? Please say yes to this, even if you are making a reckless fool of yourself. I cannot bear to worry over you, although I no doubt will, whatever you tell me.

I so look forward to your return, Miss Paxton! I feel a kinship with you which I know shall only deepen when we are face-to-face; in the meantime, I should like to thank you again for the manner in which you have taken me into your confidence, and made me a part of your circle. Had I not attended that one horrid Oxonian event, I might be alone and lonely in London, which is precisely the state I was in before that evening. You have saved me from the forced company of my cousins, and, as you know them, you must realize what a tremendous favor you have done me. I shall live to repay you.

All right, then, Louella, I promised I would not rant on, so that you might not have so very much to respond to. I shall close here, and urge you to reply when possible; I await any news you care to send with a bated breath, and til such time as it comes I remain—

—Your devoted,
Arabella

August 13, 1861

Dearest Arabella,

I assume you have taken my advice and decided to wait until I am safely back in New Orleans to contact me, since I have had no word from you. It's just as well: I must tell you, I am as busy as I've ever been, and seem not to have spent more than a single night in any town since undertaking the task of looking after my father's investments. There are lawyers all over the state of Louisiana, and some as far as Texas, who are handling certificates, banking notes, and deeds for my family. I have had to approach every one of them in person, to see to the conversion of certain forms of wealth into the more portable ones of gold coin, or cold cash. Sadly, there are many others with the same idea in mind, and so I find myself always at the end of a queue, or placed midway down a list of names, or facing a harried underling somewhere who has already transacted similar business with a half-dozen people that day.

And everywhere I've gone, I've had to be shadowed by the ubiquitous Mr. Dolley: there are places and circumstances in which my signature upon the line of a document cannot suffice, because I am a WOMAN, *and* WOMEN *are far too incompetent to see to such matters, and so Mr. Dolley must be called in to affix his own signature as well, upon the authority of my father, so that the paper can be regarded as legal. Really, what would we do without the aid of the noble sex! Why, goodness, my tiny hand might drop the pen directly upon the floor were Dolley not there to support my arm!*

I try not to dwell upon all this, for too much anger can make one physically as well as spiritually sick, and I've enough circumstances pushing me toward that unpleasant point. We seem to spend more time inside trains and coaches than out of them—my posterior is sore from sitting, my mind cannot focus upon which day it is, or which town we are visiting. We have an itinerary, and sometimes the only way I can recall where we are is by looking at it, and checking it against the depot stops which roll by our window.

Just now I am negotiating southern Texas. This vast state contains the ugliest countryside I've ever seen, and the people comport themselves like lawless savages. The rule seems to be that one grab all one can and use any means to hold on to it, all the while drawling and smiling. There is no shyness concerning discussion of the war here: the abolitionists and Unionists are devils, out to sabotage the most elite and gracious society to exist west of Europe, but they will all die in the futile attempt. Long live the Secessionist States!

We own land here, vast astonishing quantities of land, as it turns out. I was to sell it off, but right now the cash value is almost nil, and so I've decided to do nothing. We can wait and see if it appreciates; perhaps as time passes and the state becomes more tame, it may draw more of a population, or perhaps there is some wealth within the ground itself—in terms of farming, or coal—which we cannot anticipate as yet.

At any rate, I shall be glad to move on. The hotels are abominable, and if it weren't for Cici the maid (who is a remarkable little soul, and who has done much to see to the comfort of all three of us) I would long since have expired from the sheer ugliness around me, and the want of some civilized diversion.

But enough of my ceaseless whining! (We WOMEN *are given to that, I know.) I shall leave you with my fondest wishes, and the hope that it shall not be long before I hold a communication of yours in my hand. I shall let you know when I arrive back in New Orleans, so save your news, as I'll not be able to get enough of it!*

—Yours upon the rails,
Louella

September 3, 1861

Dearest Arabella,

Such abominable luck! It seems there have been outbreaks of typhus in neighboring towns east of here, and the ensuing panic over the spread of the disease has virtually quarantined me in the town of Parline, Texas. "Town"—that is an overstatement, my dear. The "town" consists of a single street in the middle of a desert. Around it, in widening rings, are hardscrabble farms which will never make their owners more than a pfennig. I am stuck in the one rooming house here, and Cici is in the room with me. Dolley is next door, sandwiched between an itinerant tinker who has taken to drink, and a married couple with a colicky baby who were on their way to Alabama but have now been stranded here. Poor Dolley! As if it isn't enough to lack a houseful of servants to stare down his nose at, as if it isn't bad enough to have me ordering him about and making light of his stuffy habits—now he has descended into the hell of Parline, Texas, to be surrounded by drunks and squalling brats and the threat of dread disease. He has taken to wearing a kerchief about his face at all times, and to fixing his own meals in the woefully inadequate kitchen building outside. He looks as scrawny and sad as a plucked chicken; there is not a place on earth as different from Aix-en-Provence as this one is, and I wonder if Dolley will survive the shock of it all. Yesterday the town's one decrepit bad woman approached him and flicked her skirt above her hardened, browned, and vein-lined ankle; I thought he would swoon.

Wishing dreadfully to be where you are—

—Your loving Louella

September 5, 1861

My dearest Louella,

I had begun to wonder whether perhaps your affection for me had waned, as I'd had no word from you regarding your arrival Stateside, but when I spoke of it to Caroline, she assured me that she has heard nothing either, and so now I am alarmed rather than hurt.

I presume that if you are writing, your letters are not reaching us. Or perhaps you are not writing, as ours have not reached you, and you are feeling completely abandoned. Well, I may not hear a peep from you, but I shall continue to send these missives off, so that if one does chance to get through, you will know of it, and realize that you are uppermost in all our thoughts. Please, please, should you receive a word from any of us, let us know how you fare! We have been unable to contact your brother so as to ask him whether he's had any news of you, so the assurance which will set our minds at rest must come from you.

Know that you are in my thoughts and prayers daily—

—All my love,
Arabella

September 29, 1861

Dearest Arabella,

Well, you shan't believe the exciting news I've to impart to you—it is very nearly a month later and we are STILL HERE. Still in the town of Parline, Texas!!!

If only typhus could be shot at, I would grab the nearest pistol and do battle with it. It is maddening! The stages will run east of here, or north, only for twenty miles, as beyond that point we are now virtually surrounded by a ring of typhus-infected hamlets. How can the scourge travel over this dismal wasteland???

Our business is to the north of here, but it is quite beyond twenty miles. I could, of course, go on horseback, or take an extremely long route around the questionable areas, but typhus is a serious matter, and I've no wish to continue on until word comes that all's clear. I feel relatively safe here. Nobody in Parline has contracted the fever yet, and the town officials are insisting on not allowing any stage stops or visitors from areas where outbreaks are reported. The sensible thing is to wait it out, but in the meantime there is the threat of death by boredom.

Our one amusement is to test the gullibility of the local inhabitants. We have told them, for instance, that in France there is a day upon which everyone is required to go about their business absolutely naked, by ancient decree of the Sun King; we suggested they might like to begin the tradition here in America, and that we would be glad to institute it if we happen still to be here when the appointed day arrives. In some more proprietous place we might be arrested, or locked away, but in Texas they merely look at us uncertainly, as if to say, "Well, perhaps you've an idea there!"

So it goes. May I have something more momentous to report when next I put pen to paper—

—Affectionately,
Louella

October 31, 1861

My dear Louella,

I hope you shall forgive the long lapse in my communications. I have been much preoccupied of late, but perhaps you shall hear the whole story of what has bound me up so when you return safe and sound. I hope, wherever you may be, that this letter reaches your hand, and finds you well and happy.

How goes the war, then: the reports we get here are not encouraging, for it seems that for every step the Federalists take forward, they take two back. Thank God you are not at the epicenter of the fighting! I am sorry for the unfortunates who reside in Washington and Virginia, for it seems the two sides cannot get enough of haggling over that particular piece of the country.

There is no doubt that we shall be spending another Christmas here. I had harbored some secret little hope that I would be home in New Parrish by now, but of course that is an absurd wish. My only consolation is that I am surrounded by my new friends, whom it should have pained me to leave. I shall try to write again before the holidays, but if I am not able, please do not take offense—it only means I am being shuttled between Leeds Hall and Knightsbridge, and am being kept busy with inanities.

I remain your loving and affectionate friend—

—Arabella

November 16, 1861

My dear Arabella,

It seems we are to move from this abominable place at last. I am trying not to concern myself unduly with the reports that typhus outbreaks were reported as far east as Mississippi. Rather, I focus on the good news that the disease has burned itself out in this region, and we are free to resume our travels. We have suffered nothing worse than severe colds, which caused us to spend a few days abed; Dolley and I were quite miserable, but hearty little Cici was not overtaken at all, and was diligent in pampering us, and in supplying those remedies which would shorten the time of our convalescence.

I've begun to wonder what is happening with the mails, for I've sent a number of letters off to my mother and to our housemistress, to let them know where I am, and why I've been delayed, but I've heard nothing back. I have a feeling my notes are rotting in an abandoned stage somewhere, or that they are backed up in some rural post office awaiting delivery, but I am not worried. Our servants are resourceful, and have managed to fare well on their own all of this time, so I've no doubt they are doing splendidly.

As for you, dear, I shall write again as soon as I return home to New Orleans. I doubt I shall have either the time or the inclination to describe the mundane chores I'm about to resume, so hold your breath until the next exciting installment. I hope I shall find a pile of correspondence from you awaiting me when I arrive at home, so that I shall have plenty of interest to occupy me while I make the final arrangements for our servants, and book our passage back to the Continent. I shall no doubt see you soon—

—Your peripatetic friend, Louella

February 14, 1862

Dearest Louella,

I am writing to you upon my birthday. I had anticipated a bit of a busy season over the holidays, but I am shocked at how long it's been since I've seen fit to send you a missive.

Wherever you may be, dear, may you be safe and well! I am now certain that no letter of yours has crossed the ocean, since Caroline took it upon herself to write your father, who is also sick with worry, having had no answer to his own letters to you. But still, I hold out the hope that you are receiving ours, and that you know of the concern with which we await some word from you.

There is a rumor here that the son of poor President Lincoln has taken ill, and may actually have died by now. If this is true, the boy is only another tragic casualty in this tragic conflict. I've come to fear that there will be no end to this war, or, should it end, no recognizable nation to return to. Rather, we shall be two countries, one north and one south, or perhaps only one, a slaveholding territory ruled by the Secessionists.

Nonetheless, I wish that I were there, or that some sort of action would overtake me here. I have the sense that I am waiting, merely marking time, but until what, I do not know.

But enough of these gloomy thoughts. I shall not intrude upon your state of mind with them when there are happier things to speak of. As I mentioned, today is my birthday. I received a number of fine gifts, among them a new journal (you know my fondness for recording the mundane events of my small life), leather-bound and accompanied by its own gold writing pen and inkstand. I was visited by Caroline and Harlow Beckwith, who brought me presents as well: Caroline's was a white winter muff, as she knows I am fond of them; Harlow's was a tiny silver phial upon a chain. You know Harlow's wry humor, and his habits: he explained in his typical manner that the phial is designed to hold smelling salts, but can be used to hold powdered morphia as well, should I find myself with an immediate need for its curative powers. (I have tried the substance only once, but I shall save my description of that experience for when we are again face-to-face.) I quite enjoyed Harlow's little joke, as that bantering tone was absent between us for a time (more upon this later, too) but I hope he does not indulge in any of this kind before my parents, as I doubt they would approve.

Well, Louella, I am afraid I must leave you now, as a second piece of birthday cake beckons me; I offer a birthday prayer to you, dear, and if this is the letter which chances to reach your hand, I urge you to reply, for there is no knowing when this miscommunication may end. I await, as always, some word from you.

Love always,
Arabella

March 1, 1862

Dearest Louella,

I cannot keep from being a creature of extremes. I know I am leaping from silence to loquaciousness in a mere month, but I hope you shall forgive me. I wonder where you are, if spring is arriving in your part of the world, or whether winter continues to hold on stubbornly, as it does here. England is hardly the most cheerful of abodes even in the summertime, but just now its climatic antics are enough to drive one to distraction. Yesterday the temperature reached nearly sixty degrees; I had gone out walking in my heavy traveling coat, fur boots, and muff, only to have to free myself from half my clothing an hour later. Today I thought I would outfox the heavens, and so I left my house wearing only a light spring jacket and silk boots—and was forced to turn round and change my clothes, for the temperature had dropped into the thirty-degree zone, and a mist of something between rain and sleet had begun to fall.

I hope you'll excuse my daring to discuss a subject as clichéd as the weather, but I am quite lonely at the moment. It seems I'm to get a good deal lonelier, too, as I am being abandoned all the way round. A few days ago I heard from Miss Beckwith that she will be making a tour of Scotland and Ireland (of all places) with her mother; they are planning to depart in early summer, and may spend the holidays in that part of the world. Harlow Beckwith will be joining them, at least until the fall, but this will be scant change from the status quo of late: Harlow has been so busy with his classes that I rarely see or hear from him. With the two of them actually gone, however, my social calendar will become a good deal more barren—or perhaps "empty" would be a more accurate term.

I had been neglecting my "studies" at Miss Ashe's atrium for quite a long while, and knew that she had asked after me; I decided I would visit her—not for the usual purposes, but to engage her company, which Caroline has assured me is quite interesting. But when I did so I discovered that, lo and behold, even she is away. She has traveled to Africa, believe it or not—and I believe it, unless her majordomo has got the wrong continent altogether, and meant to say "Wales" instead. Somehow traveling to Africa seems precisely the sort of thing Miss Ashe would do, although why is the question I'm sure will be most interestingly answered. The butler assured me that I may still undertake visits to Miss Ashe's home for the usual purpose, but as I have nowhere to go, I wonder if this would not be a wasted endeavor. I asked him instead if I might come one evening and actually stay, perhaps just to walk about the atrium, and he assured me I would be welcome, as all of Miss Ashe's "students" are, to visit the property in her absence, upon the appointed nights.

So there is that to count upon as a diversion, but little else, and I confess to feeling quite bereft just now. But perhaps that shall soon change! Perhaps even as I write this your letters are wending their way toward me, and I shall have a jolly and great surprise upon the morrow, when they are placed in my hand.

I pray for you, as always.

—All my love and affection,
Arabella

May 18, 1862

My dear Louella,

The tremendous news has reached us—New Orleans has fallen to the Union soldiers! It is a great victory, despite the horrible losses endured at Shiloh. There is hope among all of us here that the tide of war shall at last turn in the Union's favor.

But we can only wonder, despite the jubilation: where are you in all of this? The city is conquered, but the conquerors cannot know of the difference between you and any other Southern supporter. I pray that they are reasonable in dealing with you, that nothing untoward has happened, and that there were no undue hardships which accompanied the fall of the port. These are our people, after all, these "conquerors"—we are all Americans, and surely they shall remember that, and consider what treatment they'd have meted out to their own blood had the battle been fought in their own hometowns. I urge you, Louella, to remind them of your humanity at every turn, to approach them and let them know of your sympathies, for if anyone should benefit from the outcome of this battle it should be yourself.

I must tell you that I spoke with Harlow today, and his shock and concern for you were abundantly apparent. He is mightily angry at your father and brother, but I know what it meant to you to undertake this mission yourself, and so I hold your male relations less accountable than Harlow (being a man himself) surely does.

God be with you—I pray for you always.

—All of my love and affection,
Arabella

October 15, 1862

Dearest Louella,

It has become clear that any suggestion of ending, of truce or victory, is mere illusion, for word of Antietam has reached those displaced Americans such as myself who clamor for news here across the Atlantic.

Twenty-six thousand men gone—missing, dead, unaccounted for—in the course of a single day. Those are the reports. We doubted them at first, but now the photographs are arriving, and they attest to the reality of this most vile and incomprehensible battle.

The Confederacy stopped cold in Maryland, yes, there's that.

But twenty-six thousand lost.

This is more than the sum total of all the people I know, or have ever met.

It is more than twice the entire population of New Parrish, my home in New York State.

I understand President Lincoln has issued a preliminary Proclamation freeing the slaves wherever the Union holds sway. This must surely affect you and your servants; I hope to God it lightens the burdens upon you somewhat. In other minds it may serve a different purpose: it was perhaps necessary, in the wake of twenty-six thousand souls departed, to remind the participants on either side that there is a reason for it all, beyond money and trade.

I offer you my love and prayers, as always.

—Yours, devotedly,
Arabella

October 28, 1862

Dearest Louella,

The reports continue to arrive here from Maryland, the photographs of the scene on their heels. The field, its dimensions hidden by corpses. The grass, shorn into oblivion by gunfire. I wonder if they publish these wherever you are. I wonder if the Federalists are bent upon avenging their dead, despite their having been on the winning side, or whether they fear inflaming the local populace into acts of revenge, and so are lying low.

I cannot imagine it. I doubt, three years ago, that anyone could.

As for the happenings here, they are small, as everything has been reduced in impact just now. Nonetheless, I shall share one of them with you, a discovery I chanced to make quite by accident.

I was sitting alone at breakfast this morning, reading one of the less notable London tabloids, when an advertisement caught my attention. It was touting the services of one Roger Scripps-Boswell, Hypnotist and Necromancer—Available for Private Consortium with the Departed.

Thus did I discover, much to my chagrin, that they are still with us, even here in cosmopolitan London: these postmen-between-worlds, ready to perform the astounding feat of amplifying the misery of the poor and gullible, whilst causing their money to disappear.

The advertisement went on for some time, in the usual vein, with the usual compelling terms employed: communication with the Next World, trained by Romanian Gypsy Spiritualists, *and so on. Followed, of course, by the mention of compensation.*

The more I read, the angrier I became. You will recall that I have some personal experience with practitioners of this chicanery; no doubt I am biased in my opinions, but I adhere to them nonetheless.

It requires a great deal of forethought to fake communication with the dead, and the greatest degree of avarice and callousness to manipulate those in mourning, or those desperate for reassurance and peace of mind regarding some loved one who has passed on. These Spiritualists are therefore the most detestable form of social parasite imaginable. They are self-serving hypocrites, and yet immune to criticism, because they themselves have set the standards by which they are judged.

Plainly speaking, they nauseate me. I have not thought of them in an age, but now, given the scores of newly bereaved with which this war has provided us, I find my contempt reawakened and magnified a thousandfold.

I am certain Mr. Boswell has convinced his clientele that he crosses into the realm of the Dead with the ease the rest of us apply to taking a walk through the countryside.

But with twenty-six thousand new souls clogging up the ether, all of them no doubt desperate to get a word back to those left abruptly behind, I wonder how he shall find his way round, or locate his loyal guide. Or will he perhaps have the corporeal tar beaten from him, by those Departed who resent his intrusion, the mockery he makes of their sacrifice, and their survivors' grief?

It would almost be worth passing on so as to see it.

Almost—but then, of course, I should not be able to reverse my passing, to return so as to expose the fakers in this realm. And so perhaps I ought consider another tack: namely, that of bringing my earthly body to call upon the good Mr. Boswell and certain of his compatriots, to see if I can't catch them at their duplicities, and "enlighten" their clientele as to some realities the Spiritualists would have preferred remain hidden . . . Perhaps I ought assume a new identity for every new investigation undertaken, arriving at this one's home in the guise of the mourning wife, and at that one's as the enthusiastic lover seeking favor with the Spirits; through such brilliant subterfuge, and my clever unraveling of their methods, I shall become, eventually, the notorious, anonymous scourge of the whole lot . . .

But I must not continue in this vein any longer. I realize I've gone off upon a tirade, and may be trying my good reader's patience. Would that I had something more wondrous to tell you, perhaps that some Medium somewhere had been proved the genuine article, and had foreseen the swift end of the war.

Louella, my thoughts are with you. And as always, my prayers also. I feel, in whatever sense it is logical or possible, that we shall meet again, and so send this off to you, again as always, with the hope that that moment shall not be far in the future.

—All my love and affection,
Arabella

January 31, 1863

Dear Arabella

I cannot know whether any letter of mine has reached your hand or those of my family but I assume not. Have heard nothing from any of you and guess the mails failed for it cannot be that nothing was written me. May this letter find you for New Orleans now held by the Union and some order has been restored.

I shall try to be brief. I write to you what I am writing ~~to everyone~~ to the Beckwiths and my family so that if any of you get this you will impart its contents to the others.

My mother is dead. I arrived back in Louisiana December '61, stopped first at my family's country estate. There was typhus and forty-one slaves and staff succumbed.

Then proceeded on to New Orleans. Here to find that my maman and her maid from Provence took ill from poison and passed shortly after I left for Texas.

I cannot describe to you my heartbreak over all of this. I cannot even try else I shall surrender to despair.

I spent many months grieving but have tried to pick up and continue on with the mission I sought to accomplish here. It has taken a long time. There are shortages of medicine and food. The Union soldiers have plundered us in order to support their own numbers. We have survived on the yield from the estate of which we were permitted to keep some. They did not burn our buildings at least.

I sent the majority of the slaves north accompanied by friends of Hester Beckwith's. The final Emancipation Proclamation would have freed them here but I did not know that when I began the process.

Two of the house servants from New Orleans are returning to France with me. There were six I had intended to take but only these two are left. The others are dead or run off.

The properties are now shut down until my father decides what he wishes to do with them. There is no telling what may become of them. They could be razed or confiscated at any time. All other business here is concluded.

We sail on February first. The ship is called the Victorie. *It is expected to dock in Marseilles on the twentieth. I had great difficulty booking the passage but am now assured a space. If you receive this letter please attempt to contact my family and ask them to fetch us in Marseilles as soon as they can. If they do not meet us there I will hire a coach to take us home to Provence.*

May this letter find you and find you well. If it reaches you please copy it and send it to Caroline, Harlow, and Hester Beckwith, and to my father and brother in Aix-en-Provence, France.

God keep you
Louella

Part three

chapter one

FEBRUARY 25, 1863

Louella Paxton is alive.

No better birthday present could I have received than to discover this: she is alive, and for all I know may yet be back in France. At last the details of what happened to her have been made known to me. Her letters, languishing somewhere since the first of them was writ two summers ago, arrived in two thick and weather-beaten bundles.

And such a tale they tell as I could not imagine.

Her mother dead. The servants she had hoped so fervently to aid ravaged by disease. And she alone there, in a conquered city, friendless and without the aid and comfort of her family, when she most needed it. How she endured I cannot fathom. Yet she not only endured but triumphed, accomplishing as best anyone could those aims which had brought her to the divided States to begin with.

Oh, the guilt I now am subject to, picturing what she underwent, as I lie about here wallowing in my own silly affairs, affecting melodrama in my relations with her former beau—as if, in light of what she faced, she had the luxury of normal emotions.

I cringe recalling my letters to her, full of trite tirades and petty observations. I never imagined—never allowed myself to imagine—the circumstances under which she might read them. I thought of her perhaps quartered in her lovely home with her mother and the servants, or at the very worst stranded and bored in some dull but placid burg, where no word of hers could escape and therefore reach us; and I confess, there was that one horrid moment when I wondered if the earth had not painlessly, silently, swallowed her up—if perhaps she had decided never to return to Europe or speak to us again—and if this shouldn't free Harlow from any obligations or feelings for her, so that I in my selfishness might occupy her place.

But that was a brief second, although it haunts me greatly. For the most part I simply never understood the cruelty this war would engender. I deluded myself that the battle was between the soldiers, that the civilian population would be let alone, that horrors like the outbreak of disease or extreme hardship were unthinkable in a conflict comprised of my countrymen upon each other.

I now know better.

I must contact Caroline and Harlow, to see whether or not they have received a similar package of letters. I can only imagine the mingled grief and delight which accompanied its arrival at the Beckwith home, for if I am so affected—I, who knew Louella so briefly and yet found her so compelling—imagine then what they, her longtime friends, must be experiencing.

But before I think any further upon this I must go downstairs and take in the sight of my own Mamee and Papa. I have felt so distant from them of late, as if some chasm has opened between us, but now I wish only to bask in their proximity, in the fact that they are here and whole and not taken from me, so that I may indulge in the pettiness of being at odds with them.

FEBRUARY 26, 1863

I could hardly contain myself long enough to wait out the night before riding to Linton and calling upon Caroline and Harlow. But it is a good thing that my preparations took me some time, for had I left forthwith when I wished to, I should have missed them as they passed, on their way to call on me!

They arrived only minutes before I was planning to depart. I rushed to the door, and there stood Caroline, looking as pale and wretched as I have ever seen her. Harlow was behind her, with the stunned look upon his face of someone who has survived some great shock to the system.

Caroline stared at me, she said, "Louella has written to us—" and then she began to cry. She half-walked and half-fell toward me, and I caught her, Harlow rushing to her aid as well. Her outpouring of emotion unleashed some unsuspected torrent in myself, and as soon as Caroline was safely seated, I began to cry as well—although I caught sight of us in the parlor glass, and was then moved to laugh even as the tears flowed down my cheeks, at these silly sobbing girls who hold up stoically when their friend is missing, and collapse only when they understand she has been restored to them. Caroline had merely to glimpse me in order to begin the same absurd and contradictory performance; she shook her head while attempting to dab at her face with her handkerchief.

"Dear God," she said, when she could speak, and for a time that was the only word we exchanged. Eventually I was able to make clear to them that I had received letters of my own, which I fetched so that we might compare them. Louella had written essentially the same things to all of us, tailoring her sentiments to match the recipient, but imparting her news faithfully to each. It is wretched, every aspect of it is wretched, and Caroline cried additionally for Madame Eugenia Paxton, who, as Louella has said, was a harmless, frivolous soul, deserving of some much less horrible demise than the one she suffered.

Mother came in whilst we were in the midst of discussing all this. She asked Lydia to bring us refreshments, and sat down to join the conversation, and express her relief at finding our poor friend is alive. I must say, Mother has allowed Aunt Jo's vinegared characterization of Louella to affect her less than I thought it would; she has given Louella the benefit of the doubt, and seems sincerely glad that no harm came to her, and sincerely sorry for her troubles as well.

As for ourselves, we are still amazed over it, over both her tenacity and the amount of misery she was dealt. Caroline wishes to write to Louella's father in France at once; Harlow told us he does not trust himself alone with either Thomas Paxton or the father, for he believes this whole episode is the result of their cowardice, despite Louella's insistence that she be granted her autonomy.

For my own part, I realize I must now make the transition from regarding Louella as a phantom to recognizing that she is real. No doubt other Americans here are undergoing the same transformation, and perhaps they are making it in reverse as they discover that loved ones for whom they held out hope to the last are deceased after all, or simply disappeared. What misery this should be, and thank God I have been spared it! I cannot understand why the letters from New Parrish found us while the ones from New Orleans did not, as indeed the Beckwith family's letters arrived from Chicago, attesting to all being calm, if not grand, there as well. But then, Chicago and New York were well removed from any fighting, and the Federalist North has always been recognized as the sovereign United States, while the Confederacy has had no claim upon nationhood, and no system by which to see to its own federal affairs. Perhaps the mails were the first of these affairs to be dispensed with—who can say?

Whatever the reason, the episode is ended, and I await the news which Caroline's communication with the Paxton family is sure to bring.

MARCH 9, 1863

Didn't I have a nasty shock this morning when I sat down to enjoy my breakfast.

I was taking my tea outside. It is still far too cold to make a habit of this, but I've begun sitting in the garden in my flannels and a blanket on pleasant days, so as to take advantage of the pale sunlight. I had just settled myself at the little stone table when Richard appeared in the doorway with a mug, a pot, and a blanket of his own, and proceeded to plop himself down directly across from me.

I gave him a curious look, and he took a loud casual slurp of tea, as if he were accustomed to sitting there every day. And then, without bothering to raise his eyes from the rim of the mug, he said, "I know what you're about."

I did not allow any expression to cross my face.

"Meaning what?" The journal, Harlow, Miss Ashe, the phial about my neck—the list of things I was "about," of which he might know, was alarmingly long, I realized.

"Meaning, I know where it is you go when you leave your Miss Ashe's."

"You know I leave Miss Ashe's?"

"Do not bother looking so shocked—I knew what purpose Miss Ashe's served from the very first time you went there. But that's not the point. It's where you go after that's of importance."

I gazed at him a long moment without speaking, and presently he continued.

"The trouble is, you've grown bold. You believe you are smarter than everyone around you."

"Well." I shrugged.

"But what I know, anyone could know. And what they'd make of it I shudder to think." He paused significantly. "You don't hear what's said about you behind your back."

"By whom?"

"Uncle Charles, mainly. And Aunt Jo. To Mother and Father."

He was no doubt dying for me to ask him what it is they say, but I resolved not to give him the satisfaction of telling it; I can well imagine my relations' disapproval of me in a general sense, and had no desire to hear of it in florid detail.

But since I'd denied him the fun of repeating his gossip, Richard next played his trump card: "By the way, did you hear that Percy is now being called upon by that bug-eyed Brit, Carter Forbes-Spencer?"

I paled, perhaps visibly. "No. I hadn't heard that."

There was another silence.

"So what do you want, Richard? What would you have me do?"

"Do not look at me that way, Berry, as if I am the enemy. It's nothing to do with me, with what I want, I am only concerned for you."

"But you've some suggestions, no doubt."

It was Richard's turn to shrug. "I do."

"Out with them, then."

"The first should be, let me come with you."

I rattled the teacup in my abrupt pushing away from the table. "Absolutely NOT. This is my affair, you've no business—"

"Don't be a deuced idiot, Berry. Think logically. One: with a driver, you'd have more mobility. You'd have reason to take a rig and make use of it all night. Two: you'd have some form of protection, though I'm a twit with my fists. And three: you'd shut Uncle Charles up right quick, for he's nothing to say if we're together."

I glared at him, willing the milk in his tea to curdle. "How did you find out, anyway?"

"I told you: you are getting bold—and sloppy. Last month I saw you with a leaflet. That same night you had me drop you at Miss Ashe's, so I added two and two and decided to follow you. I couldn't understand why you'd want to go where you did, but when I saw how the party broke up it became a tad clearer to me." He paused again. "I still don't really understand it, Berry. Why do you chase these fools when it's dangerous to you? Why do they vex you so? What is it you want—to prove every last one of them a fraud? Would that satisfy you?"

I was prepared to be angry. But the concern in his face, the earnestness in his voice—they touched me to the quick. I decided I owed him a measure of honesty.

"It would. It would satisfy me, for I detest the idea of innocent and bereft people being exploited and downright duped. But you know, Richard, beyond that, I believe I should like to discover only one who cannot be undone, so that I might have some measure of faith in *something* restored to me."

He sighed and placed his hands round his cup, frowned at me from under a wandering auburn curl.

"Will you let me assist you in the ways that I can? Or will you go begging for trouble, as usual?"

The worst thing about Richard's manipulations is that they are underlaid with great affection, and with that tenacity and queer bent of mind I quite recognize. They are therefore irresistible to me.

"All right. You may come with me. *Once.* We'll see how it goes. But keep in mind that I am in charge, and you must obey me to the letter."

"Agreed. When are you next intending to pay a call?"

"Tomorrow night, in Stepney, by the water. We shall leave directly after supper, so be prepared."

"All right, then."

MARCH 10, 1863

At dinner tonight Richard and I stole glances at each other every few seconds; we could hardly sit still through the steak-and-kidney pie Lydia had prepared. It was disgusting, for one thing, as so much English food is, and in addition neither of us had much of an appetite. Earlier in the day, we had smoothly informed Mother and Father that Richard meant to join me at Miss Ashe's for the evening; now that we were but moments away from leaving, I was nervous as a cat, and already regretting my decision to let Richard come along—not because I supposed he would be in any way a hindrance, but because I feared causing him trouble, or entangling him in my deceits. And I could tell he was anxious as well; he has had little cause for deceit thus far in his life, and perhaps was regarding this evening as the first slippery step of his slide into depravity.

But we'd already agreed on it, so as soon as was decently possible we headed toward the carriage house, where Paulus was awaiting his evening's labors between the open shafts of the barouche. I was wearing the clothing I'd had on all day, a gingham dress with a pretty wool shawl Mother had knitted for me—but in the carriage I had hidden what I considered to be my "widow's weeds": the indigo silk dress, with its high neck and sleeves, and a cunning little hat with a black veil for my face. This I believe to be an appropriate costume for these occasions, and besides, it hides my form and features.

I changed my clothes behind the wall of Paulus's stall, whilst Richard looked the other way and whistled silently at the ceiling. Then we hopped into the carriage, and made our escape.

On the way I instructed him briefly in how to behave, and what to be on the lookout for.

"I shall do the introductions for both of us. Follow my lead, and don't give too much away, no matter what you are asked. Remember: we are there only to observe, we are prospective patrons, and we've not decided whether to pay for a reading yet.

"Mind where the Medium tells people to sit, for there may be a cohort, strategically placed. See too that you count the entrances and exits, and memorize their locations for when the lamps are dimmed. That way you'll know where to look if strange noises start occurring. You'd be surprised at what falls out of the stairwells, or the closets, or the traps, when you open one unexpectedly. And note how the guests are chatted up before the 'reading' nonsense is begun. These Mediums can deduce a great deal that way, just by looking at one and gleaning the most basic information."

"Amazing! But how do they predict the future, or reveal names of the patrons' relations that no one could know?"

"Mere guesswork," I said. "The names are easy. You start with the first letter of the most popular ones, and keep trying til you get it right. And the predictions are always suitably vague, so as not to seem too unlikely."

Richard shook his head. "Deuced hard to believe anyone would fall for it."

"You'll see," I said. "Although then again, perhaps you won't—this evening is to be different, from what I understand. This Medium, or whatever she is, has her own methods. They're called 'hoodoo,' or 'voodoo,' but the woman who suggested I visit her wouldn't tell me what they are. She swore by this creature, however. Swore she's the genuine article." I smiled as I said this.

"She's damned hard to get to, anyway," Richard replied. "Perhaps that means something."

We were in Stepney now, and approaching the dockside areas, and I was beginning to feel a bit spooked. Around us were crumbling lodging houses; Orientals and people of some indistinguishable heritage loitered about the stoops, or sat upon crates in the streets. Some of the "buildings" were no more than homemade squatters' shacks set before the actual edifices, hovels of scavenged board covered by bits of metal for roofs. The streets wound about this way and that, and were filled with rickety vendors' carts and bedraggled children; the road signs were almost nonexistent. At last I feared we would lose our sense of direction completely, so I told Richard to pull up, and asked an ancient Englishwoman where the Medium's home might be located.

"Yonder a wise, an left, an two roits, but ye won't say no soin," she told us. After she'd walked away we attempted to translate this, and then set off to find the place.

We were looking for numbered buildings, although the crowded and cramped row houses in the area were haphazardly marked. We finally came upon our destination—207—by narrowing down the location of 206, and assuming we'd find its neighbor in the vicinity.

The building was a dingy brickwork affair which looked as if it might have gone a century or so without any sort of proper maintenance. It was set back from the curb like its attached neighbors; a rickety fence stood in front of its tiny square of a yard, sporting gaping holes left by missing slats. The walkway was covered in trash and debris, and the high windows which faced the street were without curtains. Still, it was a step above its neighbors, for some of them had missing windowpanes over which boards had been placed, or front entryways without stairs leading up to them.

We halted the barouche on the street, securing Paulus to posts near the little driveway, where a dray cart and a dilapidated horse were already tied. I was partially repelled, but intrigued too—I could not imagine Madame Huxley, the society matron I'd met at a reading and who'd directed me here, ever setting foot in such a place. But then, the poor woman was a true—and desperate—believer, one of those who will spend any amount, pursue any avenue, to find answers from the Beyond.

Richard and I stepped up to the unpainted door and knocked.

After some shuffling and clunking sounds, a wrinkled Oriental lady with a cane answered. I said through my veil, "We were sent by Madame Huxley. We are looking for BayBay, who we were told would be holding a ceremony this evening. We're to watch it. Is she here?"

The woman appeared to have caught almost nothing of my speech. But when she heard "BayBay," she nodded, and flicked her head over her shoulder. She held the door wide for us, and we could see that the hall she stood in opened onto a back exit, presumably with a yard behind it. We made our way toward this, followed by the smells of a strange, sweet smoke and some pungent vegetable being boiled, and the mutters of foreign languages from behind thin walls.

"I thought you said we'd be going into a parlor," Richard whispered.

"I told you, I don't know what to expect, as this one is to be different."

"*How* different?"

"I don't *know*, I told you. Would you kindly be quiet?"

The rear doorway led out to a small lot, in the back of which had been erected a rambling barn for animals. In the center of the yard was a circle of dirt, packed down into a hard surface, and arranged all about its perimeter were crates and barrels, to be used as seating. A few lamps had been lit, and there were two torches which provided the circular space with an orange glow by which to see.

It was all highly irregular, particularly since there were people milling about, but the Medium herself appeared to be nowhere in the area.

I stepped down into the yard, and immediately made my way to a crate so as not to have to mingle with anyone. Richard sat down next to me, and we looked the visitors over one by one. There were eleven of us altogether—an unusually large number of guests. And of that number, seven were black—something else I had never seen before.

One of the groups of patrons consisted of a large, dark brown Negro woman with three children. She carried a baby, while an adorable boy and girl of perhaps five and seven clung to her skirts. She was soothing the infant, who was wrapped in some sort of exotic cloth; the woman herself wore a towering headdress of the same material, and her face had a high shine which made it appear to be carved of wood.

Besides her, there were two Negro men, very black with wide noses and full mouths, who looked to be somewhere in their twenties. They lounged on crates; their clothes were ragged and poorly made, dotted with holes here and there, and I could not imagine why any Medium would solicit such patrons, who could hardly have had enough money to pay her.

The last group of people was slightly better dressed, and contained the only whites besides Richard and myself. It was an odd assemblage of three men. One was an older black, short, extremely dark, and rather stocky with biceps as hard and shiny as the Negress's face. He wore a skullcap and a sort of long shirt over his trousers, and—strangest of all—he carried a chicken. Then there was a spectacular giant of a white man with the hair and features of a Teuton warrior. His arms were covered with a blonde down that caught the light like sparks, and he towered over the black man even when he sat. The last man was almost as tall as the blonde but much more lithe. He had a beautiful, carved face and unusual coloring, his hair being black, wild, and long as his companion's, his skin being pale and smooth as marble.

I would not have put any of those men together, nor would I have placed them in the company of the other guests—but then, I can't imagine what anyone would have thought of Richard and myself sitting there upon wooden boxes, looking for all the world like mourning society types who'd taken a wrong turn somewhere along the Thames.

I was considering this when I noticed a flash of white from the direction of the barn. I turned, and saw a young, pretty-featured black woman clad in muslin, barefoot and with a white headwrap, step from behind the shelter. She was of average height and average build, and she carried in either hand the strangest objects I had ever laid eyes on. One was a small statue of stone. It had a round, bald head and the proportions of a bear, but I could tell by the protuberances upon its chest that it was intended to be a woman. In the other hand were a bowl made of some odd material, or perhaps a half-gourd, dried and finished, and a long and very sharp-looking curved knife.

I felt a little thrill of alarm; there was no question that this was the Medium. She had, at least, the familiar bearing, the look of authority, which all such types cultivate. But I had no idea what she carried or why, and I was surprised at the way she moved nonchalantly among her audience, urging us to sit, since she was about to begin.

I was also amazed that nobody had asked for, or in any way mentioned, money.

"What's she doing with those things, what are they?" Richard whispered in my ear.

"Shhh. I don't know. But I've a feeling we're about to find out."

The other guests had taken seats. The woman and her children were arranged next to us on the ground, their backs against crates. Near them were the two black men, and across the circle from us was the group of three. The woman in white—BayBay herself—had placed her three items in the center of the circle. She moved about turning down the lamps, but she left the two torches burning, so that the perimeter of the area was dark while the middle remained bright.

A silence fell over all of us. BayBay swayed into the clearing, and set her little statue—it was about two feet high—upright. Before it she arranged a glass filled with liquid, and in its slit of a mouth she placed a pipe with tobacco. She put the huge knife to one side of the image, and the strange-looking bowl to the other. Then she nodded at the two ragged black men. I glanced over, and saw them take drums from beneath their crates. I had not noticed these, or more accurately, had not known what they were.

The men began a slow, bass tapping on the drums with their hands. The sound of it was indescribable. Who would think that one could be so affected by simple banging upon an object—but it was music, it had the same effect as music, perhaps more so, as I was motivated to keep time with it, to move with it, which I might have done had I not been seated.

BayBay, however, was not seated. Not by any means. As we watched—Richard with his jaw dropping—she began a kind of dance, but one unlike any I've ever witnessed, and one that should have thrown Aunt Jo into a swoon. She raised her arms outward, she shut her eyes, each part of her torso appeared to move in a different direction. Her bosom strained against the muslin and undulated one way, her rotating hips went another, her feet moved in tiny circles, in intricate little steps which seemed unplanned but compellingly graceful. She began to hum as she danced, and then to sing. It was a strange, unmusical chant in a language unknown to me. She called what sounded like a name over and over; it began with a "Ga" sound, that is all I could decipher of it.

The men began to hit the drums with more intensity. I looked across from me, and saw that the stocky Negro, between his two white companions, had shut his eyes, his head moving with the sound. His friends seemed as nonplussed as myself; their eyes never left the woman writhing in the center of the circle.

The black woman next to me was also swaying to the drumbeats, her infant clutched against her. To my surprise, her older children had picked up the dancer's gestures and were flailing about on the edge of the clearing. Nobody made a move to stop them.

The drums became louder, and wilder. The urge to rise and dance was almost irresistible, and BayBay did not resist it. She threw herself about so violently that I feared she risked injury. She yelled into the sky, and the drum players yelled back at her, and from all three of them, occasionally, would burst forth a high wail, like the word "loo" being repeated again and again. It was unearthly, the call of some tortured banshee.

Just when I felt I could stand the increasing tempo of the drums no longer, they appeared to settle into a steady, if fevered, pattern. BayBay's contortions lessened. She was perspiring, her eyes still closed, and appeared to be intensely concentrating, her mouth ajar, her outstretched hands trembling. After a minute or so of this, her eyes flew open. She reached down and picked up the huge knife.

The black guests were still swaying, the white ones still gaping. I felt Richard stiffen beside me. As I stared, BayBay strode over to one of the torches and held the knife blade over the flame. I could see it turning black with soot; still she held it there.

The second she pulled it away the drums began to scream frantically. BayBay raised the knife before her. And then she opened her mouth and thrust her wet, plum-colored tongue against the blade. From a scant two feet away I could see the action perfectly, could hear, as she drew away and then repeated it, the hiss of her saliva on the blackened, sizzling steel. It was no trick—or if it was, it was one beyond the skills of any trickster I'd encountered.

I gasped—I could not help it. Richard whispered, "Good Lord!" and was halfway out of his seat before I pulled him back down. The two white men were staring at BayBay openmouthed.

But she was not finished. She moved the knife down toward her abdomen, while the drums subsided into gently urgent taps. With one hand she raised her chemise, so that her naked flesh showed above her skirt. And with the other she drew the blade across her skin.

I thought I would faint, and drew in a huge swallow of air to prevent it. I saw the gash she opened. It should have hurt—horribly. It should have bled—profusely. Instead, a thin trickle of blood appeared. And then stopped. She dropped the knife and placed her palms against the gash, shut her eyes, swayed to the drum music. When she removed her stained hands from her belly, the gash had become a dry parted line in her skin. There was no further bleeding. Without pausing, she allowed her chemise to fall and then swayed back into the center of the circle.

I had caught my breath and held it, unawares. Whatever this was, it had nothing to do with Mediums, with coldhearted chicanery or even well-intentioned faking.

The drums had picked up again, and now BayBay began twirling even more violently than she had before, stomping at the ground, bending her head almost to her knees, raising her arms and shouting in what appeared to be great joy. The drummers were chanting with her now; the three voices seemed to be calling out a prayer.

Then, with the drums still at fever pitch, BayBay whirled and picked up her knife. She spun toward the stocky Negro man, pointed at him, quivering, and shouted something. The Negro replied in the same tongue. He grabbed the arm of his dark-haired white friend, yanked him to his feet, and thrust him forward. When the white man—I could see that he was actually quite young, perhaps my own age—stood before BayBay, the Negro came up behind him, and placed the struggling chicken on the boy's shoulder. He nudged his young companion, who raised an uncertain hand to balance the bird.

"What in hell are they doing?" Richard hissed over the drums.

"How in hell should I know," I hissed back.

The drums pounded as BayBay stared at the youth and the bird, and then she stretched out her knife before her and pointed it at the chicken.

I watched as the bird—untouched except for the youth's loose hand over its wing—began to bob and lower its head. It tottered, flapped uncertainly, sought to right itself. And then it collapsed against the boy's cheek, its neck thrown forward, its wings splaying out. Its beak moved once, twice, in a convulsive breath. And then it was dead.

"Jesus!" Richard whispered the word aloud. I myself was speechless.

A second later the drums stopped. Stopped completely, leaving us sitting in silence, staring at the tableau before us.

The youth was still standing there, a ribbon of damp hair falling into his eyes. His skin had taken on the green-gray cast of spoiled milk. The dead bird lay over his shoulder, the hand which still held it trembled. BayBay stood motionless before him, the arm with the knife poised gracefully at her side.

She took a few casual steps forward. As if nothing untoward had happened, she picked the chicken off the boy's shoulder and threw it into the dust before the statue. Then she sat on the ground, urging the young man to be seated beside her.

Around me, the other black guests appeared equally complacent. One of the drummers lit a pipe. The woman with the infant wiped at her face and attempted to catch her breath. Her children had run off toward the barn. The stocky black man was sitting quietly with the huge blonde.

But the blonde and the boy seated on the ground—and, I am certain, Richard and I—looked as if we'd been shot at, or worse.

"Ya got a quay-stun tonight?" BayBay said to the boy. She did not look at him. She was pulling the bowl and the chicken toward her.

"Yes, I have a question," the boy answered, and then paused. He had a strange accent: lilting, but precise, a cultivated voice. I was trying to place it when Richard whispered, "He's an *American*."

"No."

"Yes. He's a Southerner. An educated one. I'm positive."

I would never have guessed this myself. I had heard that lilt infrequently, and would have been hard put to identify it. And besides, the boy did not look American at all. He was far too exotic, an unusual combination of rare blood, I imagined, and I'd expected to hear something much more complicated emerge from his lips.

He appeared to be waiting for BayBay to focus on him, but she did not; she was busily plucking the chicken's feathers.

The boy started again. "I would like to ask—"

"Don' say it aloud. Just think it an I answer ya."

The youth stared at his hands. BayBay plucked. Then after a minute or so she picked up her knife again. I shuddered; something ugly had followed each time she touched the thing, and this time was no exception. Abruptly she plunged the blade into the chicken's belly. I was horrified to see an arc of blood strike her white chest, while another smaller arc hit the youth on the cheek. He flinched, then drew a handkerchief out and wiped himself, grimacing.

BayBay, meanwhile, had reached her naked hand into the bird's open body cavity. She pulled the hand out, full of bright red viscera. I thought I would vomit. I tried to tell myself she was doing only what the butcher does every day, but this calmed me not at all.

The boy looked as ill as I felt. He stared while BayBay dumped her handful into the bowl, and then proceeded to push the bloody bits around with the knife. Everything was still for perhaps a minute. Then BayBay looked up, wiped her hand on her apron, wiped the knife there as well.

"Da woman dead," she said matter-of-factly to the boy. "Da one ya think of, she dead. Go fin' where ya belong, the res a ya people, an fin' some peace."

The boy swallowed, blanched as if she'd struck him. His eyes were enormous. BayBay was cleaning her utensils, making as if to rise, but he grabbed her arm. "Wait," he cried, "which woman? Where are the rest of them?"

"Gaybara ain't seh which woman. Da one ya think of, dat's all she tell BayBay. Ya family where ya think dey are. Go fin' 'em, little pup."

Now the boy became positively frantic. He grabbed the Negress's shoulders. *"What did you call me? What did you say?"*

BayBay pushed his hands from her, and stood. "Go on now, boy." She threw a look to his two friends. They rose and bent over him, urging him to get up, then pulled him back to where they'd been sitting, apparently trying to convince him to leave peacefully.

There was no doubt that the evening was over. The drummers had put their drums back in the crates at their feet, while the black woman had risen in search of her children. BayBay was bearing her knife and bowl back to wherever she'd got them. When she had exited, I saw the stocky Negro unhand his friend and walk over to the little statue. He removed some paper money from his pocket and placed it in the figure's lap. BayBay returned, picked up the money, and counted it. Then she divided it, placing half in her bloodied apron. The other half she tore up. She tossed the little scraps over the head of the statue. Then, shaking the Negro's hand, she smiled a few words at him, picked up the statue, and retreated.

I did not trust my legs to carry me. I noticed Richard hadn't got up either. He was still sitting there, not moving a muscle, staring at the little group across the clearing from us. When he turned toward me, I saw that the centers of his eyes were huge and black, and the dark beauty marks on his cheek—which I have as well—shone even darker than usual. I imagined that beneath my black veil I must have appeared exactly the same.

"Let's go," Richard whispered. "I want to leave here. *Now.*"

"Help me up," I said, and he offered me his hand.

The two whites and the stocky Negro were crossing the clearing and exiting the building. As soon as they were out of sight, I took a tentative step forward; I did not wish to meet them in the hallway. The other Negroes, I noticed, had stayed behind, and were now sharing a drink of something with BayBay. None of them looked in my direction or spoke a word to me, but neither did I get any feeling of hostility from them.

"Tell me it was all a trick," Richard muttered at me as we tottered up the rear steps and into the building. I was relieved to see no one before us in the hall.

"I don't know what it was. I've never seen anything like it, and I never want to again."

"Her tongue—it wasn't burned, but that knife was blazing hot, I'd swear it—"

"You needn't convince me. I was two feet from her nose."

We were at the front door. We stepped through, and I was about to congratulate myself on a clean escape when I realized the three men—the whites and the black—were standing just outside in the shadows, leaning up against the wall of the building. Or rather the dark-haired youth was leaning. The other two appeared to be supporting him.

"I *told* ya," I heard the black man say as I passed. I was attempting not to look at them, but I was thinking that whatever he'd told his young friend, it hadn't been enough. Nothing which failed to prevent one witnessing this spectacle was enough. Whatever the night had been about, it was far from my area of expertise. There was no business for me here, nothing for me to do except depart this horrible place, and perhaps allow myself to wonder over it later, in the reassuring light of day.

I practically sagged with relief at the sight of Paulus still tied to his post a few yards away. I climbed into the barouche behind Richard and was smoothing my skirts when I heard him say, "Look, Berry."

I looked up. Richard was staring toward the row houses. The three men had paused on the sidewalk; the blonde and the Negro had let go their friend, and he appeared to be struggling to stand for himself. But as we watched, he took a single step, then crumpled and fell backward, hitting the rocky path headfirst before either of his companions could catch him.

"I'd not like to be him tomorrow," Richard breathed. "He'll have a deuced headache."

I was still watching. The boy on the ground didn't move. The Negro and the blonde knelt down by him, shouting something that sounded like "sea" or "tree." Then they began arguing. The blonde kept reaching for the young man, the Negro kept pushing him away, shaking a finger in his face. Then they both rose. The Negro took hold of the boy's legs, turned his body so that he lay in the grass in the tiny yard rather than on the walkway. And then—incredibly—some decision having been come to, he and the blonde man turned and ran off, fast as lightning, down the road.

"Richard!" I cried. He was pulling on his gloves, preparing to pick up the reins. "Richard, they're leaving him!"

"Not much use as friends, are they?"

"But he's hurt, obviously!"

"Either that or he's dead, in which case he's probably not hurting much."

"But if he's alive—what are we going to do?"

Now he turned and faced me. "What the deuce do you mean, what are *we* going to do? We're going to leave. We're going to go home, and pretend we never saw any of this bloody mess in the first place."

"No, we are not. I can't just leave that poor man lying there. I at least have to go and see if he's all right."

"Oh Christ, Berry, don't do it! You don't know who that lad is. He could be in cahoots with that witch back there—didn't you tell me they all have stooges, and helpers, and various ways of duping one out of one's money! How'd you know it's not just a ruse to make you come over, and then the others jump us, and make off with our money and the rig?"

"Don't be an idiot. If they wanted to jump us, they could have waited behind the carriage, which would have been much more convenient. And besides, his friends ran off in the other direction." I was climbing down to the ground. "If you won't come with me, at least get down and stand there in case I need you."

Richard glared at me, but he dropped the reins and stepped down, and I ran over toward the young man on the ground.

He was not awake, but he was alive. I could see his chest rising and falling. But he had struck his head hard on the stone of the walkway. There was a terrible gash on one side, and his hair was matted with blood.

"Oh God, Richard," I cried, "he's alive and he's hurt. What in God's name are we going to do?"

Richard picked his way over and stared down at the youth. "Why don't you knock on the door and tell that black witch to come out and get him? She's responsible for this, after all, and if she can cut her guts out and lick hot metal, maybe she can revive him."

"Oh, don't be ridiculous. I wouldn't leave a dog in the hands of these people. We have to take him somewhere, he needs a doctor." I turned to stare at Richard. "Uncle Charles!" I cried.

"Are you mad? He's already got it in for you—what are you going to tell him? That we were minding our own business when we came upon this fellow on the streets of Knightsbridge, somewhere between our house and Miss Ashe's, and charitably decided to drive all night to Leeds Hall, so he could be examined? And what about the distance—by the time we get him there, he'll be dead, if he isn't dead five minutes from now."

I put my hands to my temples, then remembered my veil and tore it off as I tried frantically to think of an alternate plan.

"We have to take him someplace. I know—we'll bring him to Miss Ashe's, she's sure to have a doctor somewhere nearby."

"I thought you told me Miss Ashe is still in Africa."

"She is, but her butler will admit us, and most likely will know of a doctor to summon. At any rate, it's a place to take him, without having to offer explanations as to who he is or where we found him."

"Oh Christ," Richard said, but he followed my lead, and bent to pick up the boy's legs, while I put my arms beneath his shoulders.

But an uncooperative human being—especially a tall and muscled one—is difficult to move, which was something I'd not have realized without trying it. "He's heavier than he looks," Richard gasped, and a moment later we were forced to put the boy down again, for his head flopped back upon his neck, and I feared we'd be doing him more harm than good if we continued trying to carry him.

"Go get the carriage," I said, "and bring it round. If it's a bit closer, perhaps we can hoist him into the rear seat without causing too much damage." While Richard went off, I knelt over the boy and slapped his cheek, hoping that he might awaken and provide us with some measure of assistance.

"Sir!" I called to him. "Wake up, sir, or nod if you can hear me." At first there was no response, but then he seemed to revive a bit. He opened his eyes, and I found myself staring into orbs which glittered a brilliant green against the dark lashes. The lids closed again quickly, however, and his head fell to one side. I sighed in exasperation, and then the carriage pulled up beside us. Richard jumped out, and we attempted together to sit the boy up. We managed this, and managed as well to drag him to the barouche; and then, through a combination of sliding and lifting, we attempted to tumble him inside without further cracking his skull.

Why are you doing this, I wondered to myself, even as I panted and perspired beneath the weight of the boy's inert body. But I felt I had no choice. It was something to do, perhaps, with his expression as he'd listened to Bay-Bay, or the fact that he was an American, as out of his element here as I was, or perhaps I just could not imagine leaving him by the side of the road to perish.

At long last, we were able to secure him on the forward-facing seat of the barouche, under the top. He did not look comfortable. His legs hung off the cushions, onto the floor, and his shoulders were squeezed against the door. But he was in, and his head was held upright, and he was still breathing. "Go," I said to Richard, and he signaled to Paulus, turned us round, and headed at a canter down the road from which we'd come.

It seemed to take us eons to reach Miss Ashe's house. I'd started off in the seat facing the boy, but then we'd taken a bump and he had nearly fallen over, so I climbed down to steady him. I sat on the floor, arranging him so that he was curled on his side, and held him straight as we jounced over the rutted roads. When we finally reached Knightsbridge and pulled up before Miss Ashe's gate, I breathed a silent prayer of relief. Then I jumped from the carriage and ran to the door.

Mr. Nevins, Miss Ashe's crepey-necked butler, answered at the first knock. He listened, with one furry eyebrow cocked, to my dubious story regarding the son of a friend of Miss Ashe's. No doubt he knew every friend of his employer's, and their sons too, but he also knew I was a protégée of Caroline's and therefore something of a pet of Miss Ashe's, and besides, I was looking at him with the most woebegone expression I could muster. So he sent a coachman and a stableboy out to the barouche with me. They carried a canvas sheet with them; they dragged the poor young man from the carriage and placed him upon this, then lifted either end and, with Richard keeping the boy stationary, carried him to the house.

Once inside, he was brought to an upstairs bedroom, and the two litter-bearers departed. Richard and I stared down at him, and then Richard said, "Well, now what do you suggest?"

I was about to reply when the ancient butler entered the room. He took one look at the dirtied, bloody body on the bed and said, with typical British understatement, "You'll want a physician."

"Yes," I said, "yes. Can you find one at this hour of the night?"

"There is Dr. Sipperley. He is a family friend, and is additionally suitable because he resides only three doors down."

"Can you call him for me, please?" I was gritting my teeth: the man was slow as molasses in January, with no sense of urgency about him whatever.

"Of course, Miss. I shall send Samuel round for him. It shall take but a moment."

He shuffled off toward the stairway, presumably to look for whoever Samuel might be. I wondered how long a "moment" might last at the pace Nevins set.

Richard was tugging at my sleeve. "All right, Arabella, you've secured help for him, you've delivered him safely here, now let us get home before any more trouble befalls us."

"I cannot just leave him here without explanation. Suppose he wakes up?"

Richard heaved a loud sigh. "Suppose he does. That mummified butler's about, he'll have a doctor soon, and then he can be on his way."

"You are so coldhearted," I snapped.

I decided I should leave the young man a note. I skipped down the steps to Miss Ashe's drawing room and found a paper and pen, an inkpot, and a straight pin. Then I raced back upstairs again.

"What did his friends say his name was?" I stood frowning beside the boy's bed, my pen poised in the air.

"They didn't. At least not that I heard. Let's be *off*, for God's sake."

"Yes they did, they called to him. It was something with an 'e.' "

" 'Pete'?"

I scowled. "I assure you, this young man's name is not 'Pete.' If there is one thing he looks nothing like, it is a 'Pete.' " There may be exceptions, but the few Petes with whom I'm acquainted have been lumpen, unextraordinary beings, and had our guest been so called, my opinion of either him or the name would have had to change drastically.

"Never mind," I said to Richard. I scrawled a note which included, I felt, all the pertinent information regarding the young man's accident and present whereabouts; I further asked him not to leave Miss Ashe's house until I'd had a chance to see and speak with him the next day. Surely he could not object to spending the night in such comfortable surroundings, and then tomorrow I could return and assure myself that all was well with him.

I pinned the note to his shirtfront—this way, I thought, he would be sure to see it—and then I followed Richard from the room. "Good-bye," I called to the inert form upon the bed, just in case he could hear me. But Richard rolled his eyes and yanked me away before I could say anything else.

What a night this has been! I can only hope the remainder of it passes quickly, so that I can return tomorrow and check upon my charge. As to the rest of it—BayBay, the chicken, the knife—I am trying hard to push it from my mind in order that I might sleep.

Jesus God, Gran.

I have awakened in a rich person's house.

I can tell it by the smell, for there is no smell—no reek of trash or bodies—and wherever I look I behold something lovely, something rendered beautiful just for its own sake, the likes of which I have not seen since leaving St. Charles Avenue.

I am in someone's bed, a carved mahogany bed whose posts resemble climbing vines heavy with insects and budding blooms. It is high, and canopied in lacy white—but not frilly lace—with a feather mattress which wraps about my body—unaccustomed these long months to comfort—like a caress. Jesus God—the sheets are fresh but soft, and bleached—they smell of bleach, and of the outdoors where they were dried. Beyond the bed there are pieces of inlaid furniture, exotic hangings on the walls, strange carved masks. Globe lamps glow against the green-striped satin paper which covers the walls.

Oh *Law.*

I have no idea where I am, or how I came to be here. I do not know what time it is, or what day, for that matter. My head is pounding so horribly that I can hardly breathe.

There is a note pinned to my shirt.

Dear Sir: You are in the home of Miss Elizabeth Ashe of Hyde Park. You had an accident earlier in the evening, in Stepney, and injured yourself. Your friends abandoned you, so my brother and I brought you here. A doctor shall be coming to examine you, or may have done so by the time you read this. Please do not concern yourself with his fees, as they have been seen to. There is a butler about should you need anything. Do rest this evening, and remain at Miss Ashe's home until I have returned to speak to you. I shall be back tomorrow morning, at which point I shall be happy to drive you wherever you may need to go. I hope this note finds you feeling better—

Yours truly,

Arabella Leeds

Tomorrow? In relation to what? Who is Arabella Leeds? What evening is she talking about? Abandoned by what friends? Where is Hyde Park? What "accident"?

Think, Aubrey. Lie down—you cannot sit up properly, at any rate—and think.

All right. Begin with the last things first.

I remember this: Oha and I had finally agreed to see the vodou woman, the friend of Ibrahim's who lived only a short distance from our hovel by the docks.

Ibrahim had been trying to arrange it for a week, ever since hearing that my own grandmother was a practitioner.

"Ya ain't sayin it right, that's the first thing," he inisisted. "Not 'vodou.' Voodoo. Bubu. It was my people that brought it to Ghana. The Ewe. E-W-E. My people, that's their gods, the gods a voodoo. Got nothing to do with Haiti. Or Christian Saints, or Jesus, or fortunes. Ya come and see Behbeh, ya see real voodoo, not the Haiti kind."

"My family is two generations removed from Haiti," I said, just to needle him.

"Ya still Frenchies, smart boy."

"Besides, I thought you were a Muslin. What happened to that?"

"*Muslim*. Ya, ya, I find A-La, but the Ewe, most of 'em, they follow voodoo still. My own family was voodoo. Dey powerful gods, even when ya don't believe in 'em. Ya ask me about Africa, ya want to know about Africa, come and see Behbeh." It had surprised me to learn that there was a whole community of free blacks from Ibrahim's home country here—in fact that had been one of his reasons for traveling to England. This Behbeh was only one of the acquaintances with whom he intended to reestablish ties.

"What would we have to do?" I asked him.

"Ya don't have to do nothin. Unless ya want to ask somethin from the gods, then ya make what ya call an offerin, an Behbeh, she'll talk to 'em for ya. She follow one god mostly, a lady. Gabara. Gabara looks after love or somesuch, an she's a bit of a girl on the town—likes her rum now and then, and a pipe, and nice fresh cash. Ya got a question, Behbeh pray to Gabara for ya, an maybe give ya an answer."

"I thought you said African vodou has nothing to do with fortunes."

"Dis ain't no fortune, this here is guidance, practical advice."

"You're making rather a fine distinction. And besides, I doubt any of us here will receive a fig of favor from the goddess of love."

He finally talked me into it, though. We invited Oha and Aurelio to attend as well, but Aurelio declined. He was to meet a young lady from our own dwelling—a "dollymop," Ibrahim called her, working now and again at prostitution—on the night in question. He told me I might enjoy a romp with her pretty companion, but I have no taste left for indulgences with whores. A prostitute is a sad, bought thing, much too nearly a slave; there is no smug pleasure to be had in such purchases once one has experienced the point of view of the merchandise.

So Oha, Ibrahim, and I left our fetid lodging house (which Ibrahim had found us, and which had eliminated the problems I'd anticipated with Oha, since each of us had enough money to secure a tiny room for himself), while Aurelio waved us off happily from the stoop. We carried with us the cash which Ibrahim said he would give Behbeh to secure her intercession on my behalf. We were also to bring an "offering," a chicken which Ibrahim intended to purchase on the way. I was quite surprised that he was willing to pay for all of this, but he said it was his pleasure, and so I accepted graciously.

Behbeh lived about a mile from our own alleyway, nearer the water than we were. We had decided to walk, as cabs are scarce in this part of town, and no one we knew had access to a cart. We passed through our section of the indescribable wretchedness that is London's East End, encountering along the way the denizens with whom we share our misery.

We first overtook two of our neighbors, a pair of toshers off to dredge the sewers beneath the city in their search for coins, castoff jewelry, or the dead body of a swell with money in his pocket. Ibrahim made a show of holding his nose as we passed, and the smaller one of the pair threw us a nasty glare.

We then stopped among the costers, with their carts selling everything from used rags to half-rotten vegetables, who reside—often whole families to a room—on the upper, cheaper floors of our building. We purchased a skinny chicken from one of them, and set off again.

And, inevitably, we were accosted by the prostitutes, who in this city are so numerous that one begins to suspect there are no females left who've not gone gay. They solicit any male old enough to ogle them, but there is no money to be had hereabouts. The smarter ones move west at night, to haunt the lush Argyle Rooms or the squalid Haymarket. Then they return, like Aurelio's engagement for the evening, with money enough to have whole rooms to themselves on the enviable second floors of houses like our own.

I recall my mood as we set off through the smelly, teeming streets, toward the docks: I smiled at Ibrahim's jokes, I talked and listened, but there was no joy in it. I neither looked forward to our adventure nor dreaded it. Lurking behind my ordinary demeanor was the sensation I carry with me always, of sadness, and a dullness of spirit which refuses to lift. I long to savor each moment and drink it in, to feel myself whole within it, and yet there is always a portion missing, from the experience or from myself.

I recall turning to glance at Oha, who trudged along like a draft horse, and at Ibrahim, with his tight little cap, and wondering: what am I doing amidst these people? These are my associates, my companions, and yet there are such gulfs between us. I cannot express what is left of my soul to them, nor can I find kinship in what they reveal to me of their own.

In the following instant, which seemed to have nothing to do with the one before it, I had decided that I would indeed ask Behbeh a question, and see what Gabara had in store for me. I decided I would not think about the question until I got there.

I next remember our reaching the near-crumbling house where Behbeh lived. We entered, and were taken out back to the yard, where she greeted Ibrahim with a screech and a great hug. I recall thinking that Behbeh was pretty in an African manner, being dark-skinned and round-featured. She did not look like a priestess to me, and she did not act like one; except for her lilting English and extravagant headwrap, she might have been any lively young Negro woman. She took my hands and smiled widely at me when Ibrahim introduced us, but I noticed she did not do this to Oha. She only made a quick bow, as if she had already developed an antipathy toward him, or knew the reception her touch would have received.

"Ya wantin any favors tonight?" she asked Ibrahim.

"Ya, ya, my friend here, he's wantin one." He nodded toward me.

"What ya bring for Gabara?"

Ibrahim held up the chicken, who blinked stupidly at Behbeh.

"Ya, that's good!" she nodded. Turning to me she said, "Ya fit to be before Gabara?"

I shrugged. "I haven't any idea. What would I have to do to be fit?"

"It's more what ya not done. Ya eat any goat meat in the last fortnight?"

"Definitely not."

"Ya lie with anybody?"

I felt myself blush. "No."

"Ya heart and mind are pure, yes?"

Ibrahim began to laugh loudly at this, and Behbeh slapped him on the arm, also laughing. "Shut ya mouth, ya infidel, it ain't funny." Turning back to me, she said, "Ya don't have to be a saint, boy. Just carry no evil intent with ya."

"No, I haven't any evil intent toward anyone." I smiled. "Except maybe Ibrahim."

"Ya, but don't we all," Behbeh grinned.

After this seriocomic conversation I was not expecting much from the evening except perhaps a mild entertainment, but as we were walking away Ibrahim said to me in a sober tone, "One thing, Bree, no matta what she tell ya, just listen and then be quiet. Do not ask her to explain nothin, because she won't do it. Ya see?"

"Yes, all right." I shrugged again.

We sat on crates at the edge of a dirt-packed circle. There were other people arriving now: a few shabby-looking blacks, among them a woman with little children, and two very well-dressed whites—a boy, and a woman hidden by a veil—who appeared to be in mourning. Rather a disparate group, but Behbeh seemed used to it, and paid no more mind to one set of visitors than to the next.

I remember her leaving for a few minutes, and then returning with some objects, and drums being beaten, and the ceremony beginning. And her dancing, which made the blood rush to places in me where it had not been in a long while.

And I remember the sick feeling in my stomach when she started to do the most incredible and horrible things, like licking a red-hot steel knife and then using it to make cuts in her skin which did not bleed.

And then what happened?

This is where my memory blurs.

Oh, yes. Oh, God, there was the chicken. She killed the chicken on my shoulder by pointing at it.

And the blood. She pulled the bloody insides out of it.

And then I asked my question, but she told me only to think it, and not to say it aloud.

And she gave me an answer—yes.

That the woman I thought of was dead.

But this was not really an answer, for the question I had asked was: which of my family was alive and well, and when would I see them? So I asked her, *which woman*, for it's to you I tell my every secret, Gran, and it is Mama who consumes me when I am angry, and Faith is never far from my mind, nor even Lila, or Louella . . . She told me next to go on. And I was on the verge, whatever I'd seen, of doing just that, and dismissing it all—

But then she called me "little pup."

Or at least I thought she did.

How could that be? How would she know to call me such a thing?

You would not have been surprised to hear it, would you, Gran?

But Ibrahim had warned me that Behbeh would refuse my questions after this, and so she did.

Beyond that point I remember nothing more.

Except that once I opened my eyes, or dreamed that I opened them, to find the face of a lovely white-skinned woman bending over me. But that was surely a dream—a wish on my part—for what lovely white-skinned women have been anywhere about me of late?

Then I awakened, truly, to find myself here. Wherever "here" is.

And to wonder: did she say it, or did I only imagine it?

It is much later now.

I must have fallen asleep, for when I next opened my eyes, I was again on my back staring up into a face—but this was no lovely miss. Instead it was an old man, wrinkled and jowled, with a dour, pursed mouth. I wondered if I had left the beautiful dream house I'd awakened to earlier, but then I recognized the canopy and the green walls behind the old man's head. After determining that my surroundings had not evaporated or changed, I deduced that I was looking at the butler the woman had mentioned in her note. I wanted to sit up, having no wish to be viewed in a position of helplessness, for I know all about servants, and the glee with which they condescend when it's possible. But I feared another attack of pain or nausea, and so I remained where I was.

"You're feeling somewhat better, *sir*?" the old man addressed me. I could barely detect the irony with which he directed the "sir"; he knew perfectly well I was no gentleman, knew it by my filthy clothes and long hair, but for some reason he had been presumed upon to treat me civilly.

"Yes," I said, with less force than I would have liked. I searched with my right hand for the note which had been pinned to my chest. It had fallen to one side of my pillow. "Can you tell me—is Miss Ashe available? The mistress of the house?"

"She is traveling, sir."

"Well, can you perhaps explain to me how I was brought here? I beg your pardon, but I do not know where I am, and have never heard of any of these people before tonight."

He looked at me for such a long moment that I wondered if he'd understood what I said. At last, however, he replied. "Your benefactress is a young lady named Arabella Leeds. She is a—student, of sorts, of the mistress of this house. She has asked me to see to you for the evening, and has engaged a doctor for you."

"A doctor," I repeated.

"Yes, he's already been and gone, sir."

"Gone when? If you please—what time is it now?"

"It is nearly six o'clock in the morning."

At this I was truly startled. I now attempted to raise myself up in the bed, and only when I did so did I realize I was naked. Someone had stripped my clothes from me and got me situated beneath the sheets, all without my having the slightest awareness of it. Not only that, but my head felt strange. It did not ache, but a throbbing was there, as if the ache were suppressed somewhere, and trying to free itself. I raised my hand to the left side of my skull, above my ear, and there beneath the hair I discovered a neat line of knobby catgut stitches, which made me think of Josef Beck's sewn-shut face.

I also realized that I was in the midst of the floating calm, the warm and treacherous embrace, afforded by laudanum, or by morphine. How they had got it into me without my noticing was beyond me, but there seemed to be quite a lot I had not noticed of late.

Even as I sat up in the bed, the old man was reaching across me to place a basin at my side. He took an extra moment while extending his arm, and when his jacket fell away I saw the cracked chestnut leather of the ancient holster he wore, and within it the polished sheen of the gun's handle. He noted my gaze, and looked at me as if to question whether or not we understood each other. I didn't suppose I could blame him—he an old man alone in this wealthily appointed house, and me a stranger—a scoundrel, a thief or murderer, for all he knew. I was saddened nonetheless, though; at least as *LouisPaxton'sNegroservant-Aubrey* I'd had legitimate business in the great and gracious manses of the rich.

"I thank you for your kindness," I said coldly to the old servant. "If you will return my clothes to me, I'll be on my way and trouble you no more." I had my doubts as to how well I should be able to carry through on my intentions, but if I collapsed a foot from the door of this place, it would be better than languishing here with a thundercloud of suspicion above my head.

"I am sorry, sir, but your clothing was unsalvageable, most of it, and has been disposed of. The sun is very nearly up, and Miss Leeds who brought you here has asked that I offer you our hospitality until she returns, so may I suggest you wait for her, as she may have some solution to the problem of how you shall be attired."

I did not wish any longer to wait for Miss Leeds. I had wondered about her earlier, but now I felt I was getting a clearer picture of what had happened to me. My saviour was more than likely one of those bloodless self-congratulating morality crusaders of the type which abounded on the streets of New York. Who else would drag a complete stranger from the alley, and make such an issue of caring for him? What other sort would so enjoy the chance for an obvious display of "charity"? I did not fool myself that said charity would last one instant past the point when I refused to be recruited as a Christian soldier, or a temperance orator, or whatever this probably priggish Miss Leeds and her like-minded friend Miss Ashe might be.

On the other hand, I had no clothes. And every time I moved, my head reminded me of its injured state with that weightless sensation which threatened to become a full-blown faint.

I was not going anywhere, in other words. It seemed this strange adventure was destined to play itself out a bit longer, and so I lay back down to await confrontation with my rescuer.

And here I am still. I can see the faintest light appearing through the heavy velvet drapes, and can hear too the dismal patter of rain against the window. It must be six-thirty by now. I wonder how early Miss Leeds rises from her chaste bed. What does it matter; there is no point in trying to remain awake. I may just as well sleep in comfort while I can, and gather the strength I will need to depart this place later on.

MARCH 11, 1863

Although it was raining this morning, I fairly bounced out of bed—I sleep without nightdresses now, the better to indulge myself in little rituals, which I've already mentioned at length—dressed quickly, and ran to the kitchen to hunt up some morsel before leaving. There were warm muffins on the sideboard. I grabbed one and made for the front door, but Mother came round the corner and peered at me.

"Where in the world do you think you are going with that?" she asked crossly.

I did not stop moving—I knew if I did I should be held there indefinitely. "I left something at Miss Ashe's last evening, and I must retrieve it," I called from the hallway. Richard was descending the stairs at the same moment, and gave a wicked chortle. "You've left something, all right, but I wonder if it's still where you put it."

"Oh, will you be quiet," I hissed at him, and then I slipped out onto the front entryway, and ran to the corner, from whence I hoped to hail a cab.

I was still sleeping when a small commotion erupted outside in the hallway.

"You mustn't go in, Miss, he's quite indecent," I heard the butler's querulous voice saying.

And a woman answered, in a muffled but playful tone.

Then there was a knock upon the door, and the butler swung it wide without my leave. I sat up, realizing more hours must have passed, and then the old man said, "Miss Leeds to see you, sir."

Miss Leeds. She entered the room in a swirl of gingham and ringlets.

She is not pinched and sour-looking.

Or a temperance worker, or morality crusader, from what I could tell.

She is fresh and lovely. And something else.

There are those women, as I see it, who attract by acting as fixtures, or as hiding places for energy. They seem to draw it from the air, or from the man seated next to them, and swallow it into a great black void, from which nothing emerges but quiet control and coy gestures.

But then there is another kind of woman who seems to exude vitality, as if it is manufactured inside of her—she makes the air fairly hum with it, and one cannot help but be pulled toward its source, as if toward some illuminating sun.

Faith was of this latter kind. And so too is this Arabella Leeds; I knew it before she spoke a word or made a single gesture. I sat up in the bed, clutching the top sheet about me to cover myself, and stared at her, speechless, for what could I say to such a creature, in my present circumstance, which would not embarrass both of us horribly?

She stood filling the doorway, and smiled at me. Her teeth were small and white and even, and I realized she was not an Englishwoman, although the tawny complexion and masses of free-falling brown-red curls could have told me as much. She took me in with a frank and level gaze, hiding neither her curiosity nor her concern.

"Good morning," she said.

In a second I placed the speech: she was an *American*. A Northerner.

"Good morning," I replied, suppressing a bitter laugh. For here before me was the first attractive and well-spoken young lady who had deigned, in a year, to take note of me. She was from my own country, no less. And how did I receive her? Naked and dirty in a strange bed, with my hair to my shoulders and two days of beard on my face. Of just such repellent ironies does my life consist.

"Are you feeling somewhat better today?"

"I am, thank you." I fumbled for the means by which I might express my gratitude. "Truly, I do thank you, Miss—for I've no idea what happened, but I know you are responsible for bringing me here, and I owe you a great deal." Indeed I did—for was it not an act of the purest charity to take in a stranger from the alleyway?

"Oh, you found my note, then." She smiled again, and I thought that, to see this expression aimed at me without derision, I would tell her whatever she wanted to hear, even if it didn't happen to be true.

"Yes, I found it. It was most informative, although I'm a bit hazy on some of what you mentioned, as I've no recollection of the evening."

"Not to worry, I shall be happy to explain all of it to you, only first we should introduce ourselves properly." She strode toward the bed, and I fairly cowered; God knew what a depressing sight I would present up close.

But she did not flinch. Rather, she held out her hand straight before her. I grasped her fingers, then looked past them into her eyes. They were brown, I now saw, and clear. They looked upon me without pity or condescension. And such a soft hand she had! Such a warm hand! Her fingers on my palm exerted a pressure like her gaze: insistent, yet not intrusive.

"I am Arabella Leeds." Again, the smile.

It was not until I saw the expectant flick of her brows that I remembered I was to say something back.

"Aubrey." I had to pause and think a moment. "Aubrey Bennett. I have always been called Bree, though—it's a kind of pet name—" I wondered why I added this, for what could she care for my small personal history?

"Oh, *Bree*!" she said. She appeared to suppress a laugh, withdrawing her fingers as she did so, and I tried to smile back, although I was puzzled.

"You must excuse me," she said finally. "I mean no disrespect. It is only that my brother and I heard you called something by your friends, and we could not figure out—we thought you were a 'Pete,' although I told my brother—his name is Richard, did I mention that?—I told Richard that—oh, honestly, I'm sure this makes no sense to you." A blush stole across her cheeks, and she pressed her fingers to them. "You've a lovely name, sir," she finished. "I am relieved to discover that you are not a 'Pete.' "

Well, of course he isn't a "Pete," perhaps you could move on now, and stop blathering like an idiot.

Aubrey.

Aubrey.

It would be something like that, wouldn't it—I'd heard the name before, of course, but had never taken particular note of it. It somehow matched his startling eyes, which now he was awake were the more startling, and evincing intelligence, as opposed to the previous night's disorientation. He looked back at me as if he were hungry to behold everything he gazed at, to know it completely; yet the effect was not in the least off-putting—rather, it made me wish to continue being looked at, to let him have whatever knowledge of me he sought.

"I am relieved not to be a 'Pete,' then," I said, and thought: is that your attempt at humor, Aubrey? Or is it your attempt at flirtation? You are equally unused to both and should therefore revert to being sensible.

She was still smiling, and I was attempting a fair job of it myself, but then I thought to ask, since I truly wished to know: "Perhaps you could explain to me—if I could so prevail upon you—where was I that you chanced to see me, and what was the accident which you witnessed?"

She seemed to debate for a minute, and then she said, "I saw you first with two friends, a black man and a white, at a ceremony in Stepney. It was a"—she struggled for the word—"an exhibition of 'voodoo,' by a Negro woman. Named Behbeh, or something of that sort."

I stared at her. "You were there? At Behbeh's?"

"I was. I take it you remember that portion of the evening, then."

"Yes, but I do not recall—" It dawned upon me in the same instant. "Wait—you wore a veil. You were the woman who appeared to be in mourning."

"Yes. But I was not actually mourning anybody. I was—well, that is another story, and a long one, which I'll spare you."

I rather wished not to be spared—for I could not imagine her in such a place as Behbeh's and was mightily curious as to why she had been there—but her tone made it clear that she intended to proceed with the answer to my question.

"At any rate, you left the ceremony, or whatever one would call it, and I passed you outside the house, as my brother and I were proceeding to our carriage. You appeared to fall into a faint, and you must have struck your head upon the sidewalk, for you did not rise again or respond to your friends' calls. So they moved you over a bit, and then they turned and ran off, and left you there upon the grass. Whereupon my brother and I agreed that we could not simply drive away and abandon you, and so we examined you, and determined that you were badly hurt, and placed you in the buggy and brought you here."

But at some point before that, you tried to awaken me, didn't you, and I opened my eyes, and saw you leaning over me, and imagined I was dreaming. I struggled for a picture of the rest of that hour, in which I had been left most heartlessly by my so-called friends—and this I could scarcely credit, there must be some explanation for it—but I could recall none of it. Only the moment when I had awakened to behold her.

That, and the priestess's parting words to me.

"I see" was all I said.

I expressed again my appreciation for her treatment of me, the reasons for which I still could not fathom. "You have gone far out of your way, Miss Leeds, and I mustn't burden you further. I thank you profoundly, and if you could only return my clothes to me—the manservant took them, and although he claims they were beyond repair I am certain they are about here somewhere—I shall be on my way, and trouble you no more."

"You mustn't think it was a bother, Mr. Bennett," she replied, and then frowned. "And I am afraid you may have to rest here a bit longer. For you see, Doctor Sipperley left instructions for you." She withdrew a slip of paper from the folds of her skirt. She was about to speak its contents aloud, but I said, "May I?" and extended my hand, and she rose to give it to me.

" 'Severe blow to head,' " I recited. " 'Internal damage possible, do not aggravate, sit still for day; if dizziness or nausea, put cold compress on wound, and call at once."

I looked up to find Miss Leeds watching me. I realized after a moment that she had been waiting to see whether or how well I was able to read. She must have known I'd deduced this, for she colored rather dramatically, then cleared her throat and said, "Yes, there's that, and also, it seems your clothes were truly unsalvageable. They were caked with blood, Mr. Nevins tells me, and so he had them burned with a pile of rubbish this morning."

"He *burned* them?" I tried to keep my face impassive.

"I'm terribly sorry, but yes, that is what he told me."

There went the remnants of Thomas's suit at last, I thought. And with it one of my few changes of clothes, for I had only the trousers and shirt I'd brought from New York remaining to me.

I noted his discomfort at once, although he was at pains to hide it. "Perhaps you've some other garments that could be brought you, if you'll tell me where I may fetch them," I suggested.

"No, it's too far." He hesitated. "I live in the East End, you see."

The East End?

I was puzzled. I could not place this young man one way or another. For on the one hand, he had appeared in the company of what looked to me to be rather rough companions, and his clothes, although well cut, had been quite shabby. Yet he had the manners and speech—and the gaze—of an educated gentleman, and there was about him not a trace of the uncouth or the boorish. What, I wondered, might his circumstances be, why had he come to London, and why might he be residing in one of the seediest and most dangerous sections of the city?

And so there it was: I might as well have said, "I am Mr. Paxton's Negro servant Aubrey," for the revelation of my address was sure to have the same effect upon my listener. It served me right, of course, for somewhere in my mind I had presumed an equality with this young woman. I had not apprised her immediately of my circumstances, for I had wanted to enjoy those few moments of inventing myself afresh, those moments before I was doomed to become once again what I am. I waited for her face to close upon me like a gate, for the warmth and familiarity to leave her voice.

I should have liked to ask him directly what he was doing there, but he avoided my eyes, which gave me to know I must not embarrass him by prying into his affairs. After all, I had only just met him. And so I shrugged and said, "Yes, that is certainly a distance. Let me think a moment, for there must be someplace closer from whence I could borrow you a suit of clothes." It was the least I could do for him; after all, Nevins had destroyed his property without his leave, and he could not very well walk out of Miss Ashe's town house clad in a sheet. Moreover, I got the sense that the loss of the clothes was a significant setback for him. I should have liked to replace them, without making it appear too great a charity.

I looked back at her. A suit of clothes? Was she offering this to me—was there to be no change in her demeanor? It was too extravagant a gesture, accompanied by too much kindness, and I was unsure whether to be suspicious or amazed.

I cast about through the alternatives. Richard was too small. He was not quite as tall as Mr. Bennett, and narrower through the shoulders. Father was tall enough, but too broad, although that should not have stopped me necessarily; but the trouble with Father was that he would no doubt wish to know why I required a set of his cast-off clothes.

There was one person, however, who would be close to a perfect fit, and who would likely not raise an eyebrow at any unusual request of mine: Harlow Beckwith. And Linton was an easier ride away than the East End. It seemed a reasonable idea. Of course Harlow might not be at home, but there were bound to be some clothes of his hanging about, and I knew I could prevail upon anyone there to lend them to me, until such time as I could explain why I might need them. I would have to ask Mr. Nevins to send Miss Ashe's porter, however, for I had no carriage of my own. Nor did I think it a good idea to leave my patient.

She explained all of this quite matter-of-factly, and although it was an outrageous suggestion, I was hard put to reject it. For any alternative I offered—aside from walking stark naked from this place back to Ibrahim's rooming house, and securing directions en route, since I had no idea where in hell I was—would have meant more bother for her than her own plan.

At last I was forced to accept, protesting all the while that she had been much too kind, that I should never be able to repay her, and so on. She shrugged, and said that if I were to chance upon her in the roadway someday, she would expect me to stop and render a similar level of assistance, and by the bye, if I needed to secure clothing for her, she would prefer silks to cottons.

Why, what is that sound—is it me, actually laughing? It has been so long since I've done it spontaneously, I'd forgotten what it sounds like.

She said she hoped I would not be too greatly inconvenienced, but it would probably take until well into the afternoon for the porter to run his errand and then return. But at least I would be spending the time resting, which was a good thing, since that had been the doctor's advice to me anyway.

I tried not to appear too pleased at the manner in which I was to be so "inconvenienced."

With that business out of the way, I decided I should attempt to secure some nourishment for Mr. Bennett, and told him I would return in a few minutes. Out in the hallway, I called to Nevins, explained the mission upon which I wished to send the porter, and asked that he have a small meal prepared and placed upon a tray. He looked at me with even more disdain than he'd evinced when I insisted upon entering Mr. Bennett's sickroom, and replied, "Very good, Miss, although you understand I shall be forced to explain all of this to Miss Ashe, and I cannot be responsible for her reaction to it."

"I shall bear the responsibility for whatever I ask of you. And may I also add how very much I appreciate your cooperation on my behalf." I actually fluttered my lids at the old coot, and although his prune of a mouth did not unpurse itself an iota, he nonetheless turned without any more protest to do as I'd bidden him.

The porter, the cherub-faced Samuel, came round to see me a few moments later, and I sent him off to Linton with a short note of explanation. Then I went back to the kitchen, where Miss Ashe's cook, Mrs. Adams, had laid a cold breakfast out upon a tray.

She knocked again a short time later and entered, bearing a tray with a pot of tea, some fresh bread, and cold sliced ham upon it. I had not known I was hungry, but at the sight of the food my appetite reasserted itself.

She bore the tray over to the side of the bed. I realized I would have to drop the sheet in order to balance it properly, and was reluctant to impose myself upon her in this manner. But she gave me another of those frank stares, and so I let go the material and sat back against the pillows, while she placed the tray on my knees.

I saw her looking with great curiosity at my shoulder. The mottled scar of the bullet wound bloomed there, and beneath it, on the bicep, the Oriental's sun, with its message emblazoned on the face.

She cocked her head. "You were injured somewhere?"

"Yes." She remained still, and I felt obliged to go on. "It was—it was an accident. From a long while back." Years back, I wanted to add. Lifetimes ago.

She nodded. "And what is that mark there, underneath it—it looks like a design of some sort."

"It is called a tattoo."

"Is it drawn there? Does it wash off?"

"No, it will never come off. The ink is beneath the skin."

Her eyes widened. "Beneath? But how is it done?"

"With needles."

"Needles!"

"Actually, a great many pokes with the same needle."

"May I touch it?" She was leaning closer; I could feel her breath upon my shoulder.

"Of course. If you like."

What I mean is, yes. Oh, yes, you may touch it. I extended my arm, and then her fingers were lightly tracing the design, and I looked down into the brilliance of her hair and thought, *What an unusual girl you are*, and I wondered how much time had passed since I had been the recipient of a touch I welcomed.

It was as much the texture of his skin as the design I felt compelled to experience—I am no stranger to this compulsion, and how easily I yield to it!—and I wondered what he must think, but I placed my fingers against him nonetheless. The ink-strokes were not raised, although they were bold enough to make me believe they would be. They lay, as he'd said, beneath the skin, impervious to my attempts to rub them off. His flesh was cool—so smooth, its hue so unusual, that I struggled for a comparison. What came to mind was *crème fraîche* blended with a droplet the color of olives.

The design, I noted, was not only a rendering, but also a word.

" 'Faith,' " she breathed. "What is the meaning of it?"

I could not think of an answer.

He shook his head, and so I drew back, believing I had intruded enough upon him, and prepared to let him eat.

No, don't, I wanted to say. *Don't move away,* but she had pulled a chair to the foot of the bed and was nodding, with a smile, at the tray, and so I picked up what was on it and ate carefully, and watched her from the corner of my eye while she watched me.

It took until nearly three-thirty for Samuel to return from his errand.

We filled the time by talking, and I was able to draw some history from Mr. Bennett, who quickly insisted that I call him Aubrey, or Bree. I agreed, and confided that I had a pet name of my own, and that if "Arabella" proved too tedious, he should revert to "Berry," but never to "Bella," which remains odious to my ears. He laughed outright at this, and asked how my favored name had been given me. When I explained, he told me he thought it a very fitting moniker indeed, as a berry is a bright and lovely-hued and sweet sort of fruit.

It was then his turn to share a fact or two with me. As it turns out, he is from New York. He acknowledges that he was born in the South, but did not say where, and told me only that he left the United States via Manhattan. I was delighted to come upon this information, however. I explained that I was from a town in the north of New York State, and took the opportunity to ask him how the region fared, whether the war had exacted a great toll on the life-quality of its citizens.

No, he said, the North was surely faring far better than everything south of Washington, and I mustn't fear for the health or well-being of my relations.

That established, I asked him question after question about the rapidly growing city on Manhattan Island, for I hear it shall soon rival even London and Paris as a center of dealings.

Aubrey only laughed at me, and declared that New York is a fabulous city for the wealthy, but a wretched one for the poor, that it is rougher and more hurried than London, although newer, and that I should be glad I had never been forced to set foot in it.

I replied that it is no doubt better to be rich in any city, and from what I had heard of New York, I should relish the excitement of it, as opposed to the dreary stuffiness of London.

We went on in this vein for some time, and then found ourselves discussing our respective families, but again Aubrey managed to fill the space with anecdotes and a wealth of trivia without revealing much of import. I gather he is estranged from his parents and has no siblings. His mother he left behind in the States, and his father he supposes to be somewhere in Europe, but he did not say how they came to be separated, or whether it was by choice.

Once we were beyond the subject of our pasts, however, we laughed and chatted away so easily that we might have known each other for years. It's a strange thing about people, that even among those with whom one shares a language there can be an absolute failure of understanding, so that one is left with the impression that a peek into the other's mind would yield an utterly unfamiliar world. And then there are those who seem to have been born knowing or feeling the same things, so that the kinship is instant, and natural. I could tell that Aubrey was no stranger to strangeness and "impropriety," that he somehow understood the need to find one's own path, to dwell upon the outskirts of popular opinion, for which he looked to have no more patience than myself. And he seemed to appreciate that quality in me—indeed, I was reminded of the sensation I'd first experienced in Harlow's company—for he encouraged its expression, and laughed at every feeble bit of humor I displayed, and picked up the threads of my ideas wherever I dropped them.

Indeed, so uncanny was her understanding of even the subtext of my words that I found myself on the verge of being thoroughly honest with her. Having revealed myself through my ideas, I was close to revealing the circumstances which had formed them. But the fear that this ease could not last weighed upon me, and so I contented myself with the delightful sensation of honesty and revelation regarding the present, while indulging once again in the tedious sin of omission regarding the past.

At length I heard carriage wheels pulling into the drive, and realized our talk was at an end. For it could only be Samuel returning, and I hoped he had completed his task successfully, even if it meant I should have to part company with Mr. Bennett.

I was surprised to hear, however, an additional masculine voice accompanying Samuel's into the house, and as it became louder I recognized it: it was Harlow's. It drew closer, and I made a little gasp. I had not expected that he would come to Miss Ashe's himself, and felt a sudden pang, as if I'd been caught at something nefarious—but whether by Harlow or Mr. Bennett, I didn't quite know.

"—can't imagine what the blasted girl is up to, Nevins, but if you lead on I've no doubt—" The voice progressed up the stairs, and then the door was opening, and Harlow strode in, bearing a traveling case and grinning at me.

"All right, Miss, perhaps you could explain what mysterious use you'd have for—" He turned, and was caught short by the sight of Mr. Bennett there upon the bed, and quite naked from the waist up.

The young man blinked at me, and I looked back at him. He was blonde and tall and fine-featured, and it took not a second for me to determine as well that he was American and rich—casually, complacently rich, in the mode of Thomas Paxton—and that there was some great familiarity between himself and Miss Leeds. He betrayed not a hint of discomfort, however.

"Oh, hullo," he said calmly, his eyebrows raised.

"Hello," I said calmly back.

He turned to Miss Leeds. "Arabella, there is a naked American in Miss Ashe's bed."

"Really," I said, "do tell. One never knows where they shall turn up, does one? Mr. Bennett, allow me to introduce my friend, Mr. Harlow Beckwith. Harlow, this is Aubrey Bennett, late of New York City. He is recuperating at Miss Ashe's after an accident, and I'm afraid he's been dispossessed of his clothes, which is why I was forced to ask you for yours."

"Is that so." The young man gazed at me with interest. "Pleased to meet you," he grinned, and then strode over and extended his hand.

I had been prepared to dislike him, but he seemed so genuine that I could not sustain my ill feeling, and shook his hand back.

"So you are visiting from New York?" he asked.

"No, not visiting, actually. I am settled here permanently."

"Oh, a resident, then. Whereabouts are you staying?"

"In the East End," I interrupted, and when Harlow looked as if to question me I shot him a glance that said *Don't ask anything further, I'll explain another time*. He took my meaning and turned back to Mr. Bennett. "Well, welcome to London, friend. We Americans are a small mob here, so don't hesitate to seek us out, and we'll help you get acquainted with the strange ways of the natives."

"You might start by showing me what you brought with you," I said, "for

I've been trying to explain to Mr. Bennett that the English are a delicate race, and that he can't run about in the nude here as we savages are accustomed to doing in the States."

Harlow opened the little case he'd brought with him and pulled out two suits of clothes. One was an elegant ensemble of trousers, a herringbone vest, and suspenders; the other was a pair of workaday pants, a woolen sweater, and a soft cotton shirt. "You weren't terribly specific, so I confined myself to these, which ought to cover most contingencies. If you'll be needing tails and a morning coat," he said, turning back to Aubrey, "I'm afraid you'll have to wait until I can go back and fetch them."

"I suppose I could forgo a few formal engagements" was Aubrey's reply, and I smiled, but then his tone sobered. "Really, you mustn't leave all of this for me. I only have need of something to travel home in, which I can return to you immediately—"

"Oh, nonsense. Take all of it. It's moldering on the shelves, as I'm not getting any use from it."

I bridled at his generosity, which I knew I should never be able to repay. For the clothing—I could tell it from a distance—was finely tailored, and far better even than that which I had stolen in New York. I protested further, but they would not hear of letting me refuse the proffered gifts, and so at length I said: "This is far, far more than you need do, but I thank you. Both for your kindness, and the trouble you've gone to."

"Chalk it up to American largesse," the young man grinned. Then he suggested that Arabella clear the room, so that I could see if the items he'd brought would fit me. "Unless you suspect you could be of help in dressing him." He cocked an eyebrow at her, and I saw another of those mischievous glances pass between them, which somehow made me wish to interrupt the moment and turn away at the same time.

Arabella brushed by him, however, saying, "No, I think he'll be able to manage it himself," and left.

I swung my legs out of bed and stood up. Almost at once I was overcome by a wave of dizziness, and I noted that Mr. Beckwith took a step as if to aid me were I to fall, but I recovered, and bent to pick up the sweater, shirt, and workpants.

"I didn't think to bring you underthings, but I suppose you can survive flopping about a bit until you're home."

I pulled the clothes on. They were a fine fit, only the shirt being a bit tight about the shoulders. My own boots seemed terribly worn in comparison to these handsome things, I thought, but I was fortunate that Nevins hadn't decided to burn those too.

"Here, take the rest of this." Mr. Beckwith began stuffing the items I had not put on into the case.

"I can carry them, you needn't pack them away—"

"No, no, take the case too, I've another set."

How delightful, I thought, to know that there would always be another set. More of this or that to take for granted—as I always had, up until the day I left New Orleans.

Miss Leeds reentered the room, and gave me a brilliant smile upon seeing me dressed. "Oh, that's wonderful," she said, "but you mustn't wear those right away. You must have a bath before you go, and a barbering. I can borrow a razor from Nevins."

Again I protested, but Mr. Beckwith was already out the door to find the butler.

He returned a moment later, and set to pulling on his gloves. "Well, I shall be off now, if this is all you require for the time being. Where are you headed, Arabella—will you be accompanying Mr. Bennett home, or do you need some cash for a hansom?"

"Oh, I can drive him," she said quickly, and I was secretly pleased at this.

"I'd stay to see to it myself," Mr. Beckwith said by way of apology, "but I'm due elsewhere this evening." I was secretly pleased at this too, and hoped my relief did not show upon my face.

"All right, then," Arabella replied.

"It was a pleasure, Mr. Bennett." Mr. Beckwith offered his hand yet again, and I shook it, thanking him yet again. "I'm sure I shall be seeing you about," he added, and although I was equally sure that my path and his would likely never cross, I nodded. Then he was out the door, and his quick footsteps receded down the stairs, accompanied by a light whistling. As I watched him retreat, I experienced a sudden flash in which I imagined that I recognized his name from somewhere, but I am certain this is mere wishful thinking. There is little possibility that I would have happened on Mr. Beckwith upon his own turf, and even less that he would have willingly traveled to mine.

Ah, but to be him, I thought. To move gracefully and naturally through the world that contained himself and Miss Leeds, and throw her that familiar and knowing glance.

Such heady dreams you dream, Little Brown Pup, in the wake of your one day's outrageous fortune.

The butler had drawn a bath for me, and Arabella led me to it. What a luxury it was, to bathe in hot water, with scented soap, to wash my hair and have a shave before a proper glass! I took an unseemly amount of time, as much as any primping woman, and returned dressed in the new clothes, feeling at least a thousand times better than I had upon awakening that morning.

"Are you quite sure you're well enough to travel?" Arabella asked me.

"Oh yes, I've no doubt of it. I feel quite fine, thanks to your ministrations."

"You look quite fine too. All right, then, if you'll only tell me where we are going, I shall borrow the carriage and deliver you there."

We exited the house, and I tried not to stare at the richness of the furnishings, or at the grand exterior of the building, or at the pristine beauty of the neighborhood itself. There is a graciousness about the old city of London which I admire, and nowhere was it more evident than here, upon this quiet street.

Miss Leeds pulled the calash round, and I made as if to step up and take the reins, but she protested. "I shall drive, Aubrey. You must be still and not tax yourself, only keep your eyes open when we're more into your territory, so that we might find your home. What sort of place is it, incidentally?"

"It is a lodging house. I apologize in advance for where I must take you, but it was the choice of my friends, you see, and the best I can afford at the moment. I'm lucky to have them to share expenses with—"

I stopped, noticing that she had pulled back on the reins to slow us.

"Your friends?" she asked. "Do you mean those people who were with you yesterday?"

"Yes."

"You are returning to *them*?"

"Well, I—"

"Mr. Bennett. You surely cannot be asking me to deliver you back into the hands of the same rogues who left you so callously last night."

"I'm afraid I haven't any choice. It's where I live, and besides, I'm certain there is some reasonable explanation as to why they ran off. They're not bad sorts, you'll see that if they are at home when I return . . ." I trailed off, for she was staring at me in wide-eyed rebuke.

"Really, Aubrey. I know this is forward of me. I've only just met you, and I don't mean to insult you or appear mollycoddling. But I must say, I'm most uncomfortable with the whole idea of your returning there."

"You mustn't bother yourself about it. You've been leagues beyond kind already, and I assure you, I can handle myself."

"I've no doubt of that. Only—" She stopped, and said nothing further, for she knew I was not about to yield on this point, and even if I had wished to, there should have been no other place for me to go.

We ended up taking far less time to reach the loathsome slums of the dockside than I would have liked. Miss Leeds was right; she was an excellent driver, and excellent as well at direction. Since I could give her no help in navigating, having no idea where we were, she simply backtracked to Behbeh's decrepit street—the sight of which depressed me utterly, reminding me, as it did, of the entire evening past and the priestess's words to me. From there, however, I was able to recount the route Oha, Ibrahim, and I had taken from our own hovel, and we reached it just a few minutes later.

The lodging house looked even worse, if possible, than it had when I'd left it the day before. On the stoop loitered the Chinese occupants, of whom there are so many in this quarter. They screamed at each other incessantly, Chinese being a language which lends itself to volume. The gutter in front of the house was littered with scraps of refuse and horse manure, the buildings to either side were as haphazard as shanties, the skinny dogs and skinnier toddlers running about out front being indicative of the overall status of the residents there. I tried not to act as embarrassed as I felt, for if Miss Leeds had been clinging to any illusions as to my station in life, this sight was sure to dispel them.

I almost wished that I could bid her farewell in the carriage, and thus retain a last shred of dignity, but she appeared unmoved by the squalor of the place, and insisted upon carrying for me the case with the clothing. This I would not permit, so she said she would relinquish it if I allowed her to follow me to my door, to see to it that I made it with no trouble. There was no need to knock, as Nevins had also had the foresight not to burn my key or other personal effects. I let myself in through the entrance, wincing at the stink which assailed me at once, and then began the climb to my cubicle on the third floor.

I was praying all the while that Arabella would stop and announce that she must leave me here, but she did not. She marched up the filthy, rickety steps before me, pausing now and then to kick a stray fish bone or turnip head from under her heel, or to step over one of the louse-eaten bodies of the children who, lacking a penny for a night's lodging in an attic room with a dozen others, had paid a ha'penny to sleep upon the hallway floor. She turned to me, her expression pained and horrified. I, being dulled to the sights about me, was thinking only that her beautifully tailored gingham and clear, clean complexion looked as out of place here as if she'd been from the moon. She resolutely ignored the gawkings and resentful glares aimed at her from the adults whom we passed on the stair, and I did my best to shield her, moving alongside her whenever the narrowness of the dirty hall did not prevent me from doing so.

I further prayed that Ibrahim and Oha would not be at home, but the moment I entered the dark, rancid third-floor hall, Aurelio's door flew open, and his head popped out.

"Jizzus bloody Christ," he swore upon seeing me, and I winced. "Where you been, Aubrey! Oha and Ibrahim, they go just about crazy out their minds looking round for you!" Then he saw Arabella behind me, and his whole demeanor changed so abruptly that I would have laughed, had I been in any way inclined toward humor just then. "Ay," he whispered, and I thought his eyes would pop out of his head from staring at her. Arabella did not look a bit perturbed. She stepped forward gracefully, and I realized she was expecting a continuation of the social niceties in which we'd been engaging all day.

"Aurelio," I said, wishing there might be an excuse for avoiding the introductions, "this is Miss Arabella Leeds. She was kind enough to see to driving me here."

"How do you do," Arabella said, but Aurelio only repeated, "Ay, *niña*," and kept gawking at her. Then without any warning he bawled at the top of his lungs, "SVEN OHA. IBRAHIM KASSINDJA. GETCHER ASSES OUT HERE."

Oh goddamn it, I thought, but two doors on either side of the hall opened, and out they both came. Ibrahim had obviously been sleeping. He wore no shirt, and his pants were undone. God knew what Oha had been doing, but at least he was dressed. When they saw me they both erupted into a frenzy of backslapping and exclamations.

"There ya are, I'll be damned! What happen to ya, boyo! Ya scare the livin shit out of us, ya bastard!"

"Why do you leave! Oha iss looking everywhere for you, Aw-bree—why do you leave!"

I had not even replied when they both turned, and in the same instant noticed Arabella.

Ibrahim sucked his breath in sharply. "This gal with you?" He backed up a step and folded his arms to regard her. "Ya clever dog, Bree, how ya fool into ya company such a fine whi—" He caught my look and stopped. His tongue froze in midsyllable, where I prayed it would remain.

Oha said nothing. He appeared outraged, his mouth open, his eyes scowling.

I wondered why the blonde cretin dared glare at me so coldly, but I am certain I did not look a good deal happier than he. For here they both were, the two heartless beasts, in the flesh. I was horrified by the abject misery of the place, it being dreadful that Aubrey or any other human being was forced to reside here, but at the sight of these two I felt pure disgust. I was determined to remain as neutral as possible, however, for after all I had no wish to embarrass Aubrey.

"I should like you to meet my companions," he said. But the face he wore made it evident that if he *should* like it, he didn't, at all. "This is Miss Arabella Leeds," he addressed them.

The black man took a step forward and extended his hand to me. "Eebraheem Kessinja," he said, or at least this was what it sounded like. "Charmed," I replied without much enthusiasm, and handed him the tips of my fingers, which he grasped in a courtly manner whilst making a low bow.

The blonde man just stood there. After a moment Aubrey said, "This is Sven Oha." But he still made no move toward me, and I made none toward him. A few more awkward seconds passed, and then the blonde barked, "Awbree iss home now. We take care of him. You may go."

"Really?" I did not bother to comment upon his appalling lack of manners. "You'll take care of him, sir? It's a funny thing: you were with him last night when he fell, which is where I found him, and you did not appear to be willing to take care of him then."

I saw the black man glance over at the blonde, with the good sense to appear troubled.

"Now, let me explain that to ya," he said to Aubrey. "I know ya might be wonderin about it."

"It crossed my mind."

"Well, ya fell, boy, an we see ya head busted open, bleedin like ya drain out in a minute, an I've seen enough of that at sea to know: ya never move a man out cold from the head without the doctor's say-so. They come round fine, but then later they go in and out, and stop makin sense, and sometimes they die. So I figure, we'll get ya out of the line of traffic, and I'll run back home to find a doc, and Oha go find a cab or someone with a cart, and then we fetch him. Home was not so far, and it was late, I'm thinkin nobody gonna pass by there then, so ya be all right. Well, we come back in a quarter hour, boy, an ya gone, not a trace of ya cept the bloody ground, an we went an ask BayBay if she move ya or saw who did, but she seh no. We run through the whole neighborhood last night, an got no sign of ya, so we can't do nothin but come back and see if ya show up."

"You might have asked your friend BayBay to watch him while you were gone, or one of you might have stayed behind, did neither of you think of that?" I asked.

The accused pair threw me a look as if to say, "Who are you to interfere," but I cared not a fig. Then they turned to each other and exchanged rather sheepish glances.

"We might not a been thinkin too clear just then," the black man said to Aubrey. "Ya know, dere was so much blood, an we worried ya might bleed to death before we could help ya, I figgered it's best to get the doc and the cart at the same time, if we can, and haul you off."

"It's all right," Aubrey said. "I'm here safe and sound, am I not, so let's have an end to it." The black man nodded; the blonde cretin flashed me a nasty, smug glance. I would have been much less gracious than Mr. Bennett in the same instance, but since it now seemed Aubrey himself wished me not to interfere, I remained silent. He seemed terribly subdued, however, not at all the animated being he'd been back at Miss Ashe's. Well, no wonder. Who would wish to return to such depressing circumstances, and such depressing company?

Nonetheless, I was back, and this was where I belonged, and sulking would not help it any. I realized the interlude this day had brought me was ended, and so I said to the trio of men, "*Excuse* me," and drew Arabella to the end of the cramped, gloomy hall, where we might have a moment's precious privacy. To his credit, Ibrahim herded Oha and Aurelio back into their rooms, and made for his own.

"I thank you again, Miss Leeds, for all you've done for me," I told her. "I'm afraid I cannot keep your friend's gifts, as they're much too extravagant, but I shall borrow them until I am able to replace my own things." I had finished this little speech when I had a sudden moment of inspiration. "Perhaps if you leave me his address, and yours, I can contact you in order to return them."

"Oh, of course," she said, and I dashed into my cubicle to get my only nub of a pencil. I tore a sheet from a *Pall Mall Gazette* I'd had lying about, and gave it to her. She filled in the addresses in a strong, slanting script, and when she was done, handed it to me. I was about to pocket it when she said, "Why do you not write your own down as well and give it to me, in case I come across some item of yours left behind at Miss Ashe's."

Idiot, I said to myself, *why didn't you offer to do this yourself?* Because, came the answer, I hadn't imagined she would wish ever to be near this place again, however well we'd got on for an afternoon. I fairly snatched the pencil and paper from her.

When we were through this exchange, I could think of no more reason to hold her. "I undoubtedly owe you my continued good health. And I thank you for your company, which provided me with the finest afternoon I've had in years."

"The feeling is mutual, Mr. Bennett."

"You flatter me, I think." I hated to come to the end of these gentle civilities. "Well, good-bye, then."

"Good-bye. And good luck to you, sir."

"And to you, Miss Leeds."

Neither of us moved.

Oha stuck his head from his room and glared at us, then drew back in, and slammed the door shut behind him.

"Good-bye, Mr. Bennett," Arabella said again, and this time she turned on the stairs.

I listened to her descend all three flights, and then I rushed to the other end of the hall, where there was a grimy window, and watched as she exited the crumbling foyer. She turned once and looked over her shoulder, but knew not which window I might be at, and therefore had already turned away when I thought to raise my hand in a wave. Then she climbed into the glistening carriage, and in another moment it and the colorful flashes of the girl inside were around the corner and gone from the street, leaving it a thousand times drearier than before.

I looked down at the scrap of newspaper in my hand. In what ridiculous frame of mind had I secured it? For how should I ever have occasion to use it? I had the young man's address too. When I wished to return his clothes and bag I could do so directly, without bothering Miss Leeds. There was no pretext upon which I could claim to be just "passing through" her lovely neighborhood, past her no doubt lovely home.

The chances that I might run into Miss Leeds again were about as great as my chances of returning to New Orleans tomorrow, and so I put the slip of paper away in the rickety trunk provided by the boardinghouse and tried to forget, lest it pain me too greatly, the day and the young woman it was sure to remind me of.

The carriage ride back to Miss Ashe's seemed interminable to me. I returned the calash to Samuel the porter—who was itching to be off on some business and barely looked at me—and then took a hansom home.

There it is, then. Mr. Bennett is safely returned to his life, such as it is, and I am en route to mine.

I am aghast that I actually left him in that place, that any creature could endure it for a day.

But beyond even that, I am amazed to find that I miss him. A person I have known for a few hours. Although I knew Louella for only a few hours, and yet a friendship ensued. But that was different; Louella and I had reason to pursue our association, having met under normal and encouraging circumstances, and having our respective backgrounds in common.

This business today is not the same sort of thing at all, and I am surely being ridiculous even to consider it in that light.

For all I know, Mr. Bennett may be a criminal, a violator, or a fiend. He could be hiding from the police, which would explain why a person formerly of some means and education has wound up in the wasteland of Stepney, with a distinct unwillingness to reveal his past.

But I cannot talk myself out of my feelings. Whatever his background, however we met, I believe myself to have everything in common with Aubrey Bennett in the present moment. With his manner, his attitude, his intellect. Perhaps it is the gentlemanly veneer which engages me—but I think not. I am no longer necessarily fooled by good manners, the stamp of class. It is what I suspect lies beneath these which has got me wound so tight. An intensity glows there, as though he had crammed a lifetime's lessons into years not many past my own.

And I may as well admit it, he compels me with his handsomeness, so striking and impossible to categorize.

Is this terribly callow, and shallow, of me? Would I be as quick to recognize in Mr. Bennett a kindred spirit if he did not cut such a fine figure?

But then, is it not that way everywhere—we seek out what is attractive to us, what is familiar, and surely I am not so awful for doing likewise. Some other young woman might well find Aubrey's oafish blonde friend a compelling creature, whereas I do not—this is simply a matter of taste, and I am as entitled to mine as anyone.

I have only the scrap of newsprint now, but I shall guard it most carefully, and avail myself of it often, so as to remind myself of the day, and the young man in whose company I spent it. What I cannot figure out is how it might be utilized, for I am not at all sure Mr. Bennett would take to my haunting his neighborhood, seeing as he asked for my address, but did not offer his own until I suggested it. And on what flimsy excuse could I possibly turn up there? None, that is what. Or so it appears to me just now.

But the worst moment of this day—aside from leaving Aubrey at his landing—was arriving home just in time to glimpse Richard in the foyer, drawing on his overcoat and saying to Father, "All right, then, I am going right this minute, but I told you, I know she is there, I just don't know what she left behind. I'm certain she only stayed on to visit with Miss Ashe and they probably went for a drive—"

"Just be off with you," Father ordered him, "and if you are not home with your sister in one hour, I will be coming to fetch you myself."

This was the opportune moment I chose to enter the room. I could not avoid it, as I had to pass through to get to the stairs.

Father absolutely trembled at the sight of me. I doubted that joy at my return had overcome him.

"You stand right there, Miss. Do not even entertain a thought of moving." Evidently Father was onto my recently acquired habit of brushing right by Mother and himself as they spoke, and responding even while proceeding to wherever I was headed. "Charlotte!" he called to Mother.

"Must you necessarily—" I began, but Richard, standing behind Father, widened his eyes at me. Not soon enough, though—for Father fairly exploded. "*Not one word.* Not *one*. I can barely converse with you civilly as it is, you've put this household in such an uproar."

Mother entered the room. "I wish everyone to hear this," Father said, in a low voice which I disliked even more than his shouting. "Where did you go today?"

"To Miss Ashe's. I told Mother. I forgot my—ah, my journal, in which I take notes."

"You are lying. We went past Miss Ashe's at four o'clock and her butler told us neither you nor Miss Ashe was there."

"But he must have told you I was there earlier!" Damn Nevins, I thought; he could have come outside when I returned the carriage, and warned me my father had been round. At least he'd told them nothing more, though—or so I hoped. "We went—"

"Do not bother, Arabella. I am certain whatever you say is likely to be a lie, and I don't wish to hear it. Let me make this clear to you, however: if you ever dare again to disappear this way, and to lie about it, I shall pack you off to Leeds Hall, and I shall tell your Uncle Charles to assign someone to watch you twenty-four hours a day, and keep you in their sights upon the grounds. I will not have this. Not your selfish, crazed behavior, or the dissent it brings to this house."

"You may have your rage, but if you order such a thing I won't go," I replied. Mother gasped. Richard closed his eyes and covered them with his hands. I was even a bit shocked at myself.

"What did you say to me?"

"I said, if you order such a thing I won't go. You are being unfair. I did nothing wrong, merely had a day out of this house without a chaperone. I am turned nineteen years old, but you treat me as though I were twelve. Well, there is no law which says I may not move about. I am an adult. I wish to be treated as one."

"You have the effrontery—" Father began, but Mother cut in.

"Your father has taken an interest in your upbringing which few fathers take, and this is how you repay him! With insolence and threats! You cannot say we have not been liberal in our treatment of you, Arabella. We have allowed you far more leeway than many of our peers feel is respectable or in any way beneficial to you. And you have repaid us by behaving more and more outrageously, so that we are forced to rescind that tolerance, and consider confining you."

"I thank you for your limitless tolerance. However, it is not your place any longer to allow or disallow me leeway. Or to confine me."

"It is my place so long as you are my charge, and live beneath my roof," Father barked.

"Then perhaps I should not live beneath your roof."

My entire family went as silent as if they'd just seen Cromwell's ghost.

"I cannot listen to this insanity any longer," Father said. He turned away, and seemed to sag into a smaller man before my eyes; and this frightened me, as it had when he'd cried before my birthday the year they'd threatened to lock me away—for the very same sin, as I'm able to see in reading my own words over again.

I wished at once that I'd not gone so far, but I could not unspeak the words. Mother gave me a horrified stare, and even Richard was gawking at me, as if to say, "You've stepped beyond all reason this time."

I suppose I have, but I am so awfully sick of it: of the subterfuge, the askance glances, the whisperings, and over what? If Richard were to do the same things as I, no one would bat a lash; in fact they'd be delighted at his show of mettle. It's all so ridiculous, and I cannot stand it another day. I've no idea where I would go, but if it came to being remanded to Leeds Hall, I truly would leave. Better upon the street than there. Mr. Aubrey Bennett has apparently survived some great plummet in his station, and so, no doubt, would I.

MARCH 12, 1863

And yet, today, at breakfast, it was as though the previous day had never happened. Just as they laughed and cavorted at my birthday that year,

Mother and Father seemed to have backed completely away from their positions of extreme anger. They were merely cool to me this morning, and no one said a thing about Leeds Hall, or my departure from the household. This is how it works, invariably: there is a great commotion in which the most extreme words are resorted to, and then the next day it seems all of us wish only to forget them, and return to our previous good humor. I am beginning to think this serves nothing, that perhaps it would be better to be less extreme at the outset, and then reverse ourselves less in the aftermath, but rather try to discuss logically the disagreement we are in the midst of.

Yet today I am as guilty as anyone of this cowardly conduct. I found my anger diminished to a mere simmer; what was uppermost in my mind was my recollection of the day I spent with Mr. Bennett.

I cannot cease thinking of him. It is not only the deepest horror at his circumstance which haunts me, but he, he himself. My cousins would no doubt find this quite natural—they would, after all, convince themselves they were rapturously in love after a single night, if the match were enviable. But such a fancy is not natural to me.

And yet—every move of his, every word, replays itself in my memory, a stage drama in the second day of a long run. Or I reread what I wrote of it: he said, I said. He did, I did. And that moment when I traced the design on his arm.

What can it amount to, though—I've still no means by which to go after him, to see whether another meeting would yield a different outcome, whether the affinity I believe we felt is, on my part, the result of a sudden inclination toward romantic delusion.

Ibrahim has made it clear he can take no more of my sulking, at any rate, and has abandoned the kind approach for the stern one.

"Ya know ya have to throw this from ya mind," he said, after he'd caught me moping about the front steps, staring across the street at the crumbling row of buildings there as though they interested me. "It can't come to nothin, there's money, an color, an a thousand other things against ya.

"It's the whole lot got ya twisted up, seein fancy people again, how they livin. It's not just her. Take my word on it, Aubrey, if ya met the same lass on the street corner here, outta the pretty frock, ya wouldn't still be moonin over having a poke at her."

"I am not interested merely in 'having a poke,' as you so crudely word it. And you are wrong: I have asked myself the same question, whether it is only the trappings surrounding her which attract me, and I'm quite satisfied I know the answer. Were I to meet her here, so long as she were the same person, with the same inclinations, I would feel exactly as I do."

"Cowshit," he replied, and stalked off.

Oha, naturally, is even less verbal, and more direct. Yesterday he sat across from me on a crate outside the entryway, eating an apple. I chanced to remove the newspaper sheet from the pocket of my borrowed workpants—for I carry it with me, despite my best intentions—and was idly thumbing it. Oha caught the gesture at once. He hurled his gnawed apple core at my chest; then he got to his feet, and stomped into the house without a word.

They are surely right, though. I must throw it from my mind, for there are more immediate things to consider. My payment from the voyage is running out by the day, and I've secured no work here; and what of my intention to depart for France? Was that not the ostensible reason for all of this? I must focus myself upon something else, lest I drive myself out of my head.

MARCH 20, 1863

I hit upon an idea some days back, and as it seemed awfully extreme, I dared not mention it, but rather let it stew a bit in my brain, to see if it had merit.

And having determined it did, I approached Harlow two days ago. I had sent him a calling card and received one back saying he would be in, so I knew he was expecting me.

I have been lying low as my parents and I attempt to forget the harsh words we exchanged. I have tried not to cross them with any more alarming behavior, and they have tried to turn a blind eye to the short forays I make from the house. But that day, I announced my intent to call upon the Beckwiths, and although there was a good deal of that hand-wringing I so detest, they did not dare forbid it. I tried to soften the blow by adding that I would leave at noon and be back by four, which at least put the outing into some acceptable time frame.

Once at Linton (where the surely fictional Hester Beckwith once again was not in residence), I sat down with Caroline and Harlow, and launched into an explanation of my plan.

"You must be joking," Harlow sputtered before I'd gotten even halfway through it.

"I assure you, I am not."

"What has got into you, Arabella—if I didn't know you to be a sensible girl, I'd guess you were quite smitten, that you'd put yourself out so for a man you met but once."

"Perhaps you don't know me as well as you think."

His eyebrows shot skyward at this, but I saw the smile playing about his mouth, and knew I'd got him at least half won over.

"Well, that's a fine thing you're about, Miss, throwing me over and then asking me to be the procurer of your next paramour. Have you no regard for my feelings?"

"It's interesting you ask," I retorted, "seeing as you haven't given a second thought to me or anything else since you discovered Louella is well, and arrived safe and sound in Marseilles. Do not lie, sir, your red cheeks give you away."

"Well, besides that"—Harlow deftly steered the subject elsewhere, for his cheeks were indeed red—"how in the world do you know you're not making a mistake with this lad, Berry? He could be any sort of ne'er-do-well, this city abounds with them. Have you any idea the risk you are taking, making such overtures to a total stranger?"

"You met him, Harlow. You must have formed an impression for yourself."

"On the basis of that meeting alone I'd say he seems a fine lad, but then, on the basis of one meeting, every lying cadger in this city seems a fine lad—they work at it, Berry, they can smell a dupe a mile off, and adjust their countenances accordingly."

I shook my head. "No. I know there is something lurking in his past, some misfortune or fall from grace, if you will, otherwise he would not be in the circumstance we found him in. Yet I'm convinced it's nothing to do with meaning harm to anyone. If such were his intent, he had a dozen opportunities, of which he did not avail himself. And if his scheme were to play us for a grander reward, he'd have to be awfully sure of himself, for although he secured my address, he's not turned up here, nor did he wangle any promise of further communication between us, which is a curious way to ingratiate oneself with a potential dupe."

Harlow was frowning. "Even if I were to concede his character, what makes you think he'd go along with us?"

"You didn't see the place where I was forced to leave him. He does not deserve it."

"I shouldn't think that the million or so souls in this city who endure similar conditions could be said to 'deserve' it," Caroline murmured.

This stung me, being precisely what I'd considered for myself, and I had no answer to my guilt, except my good intentions.

"I cannot aid a million souls just now," I said, "however I'm inclined. But I can aid this one, and should I not on account of the rest?"

"Even so, Arabella, if he's half the gentleman you believe he is, there's the chance that his pride will preclude his being 'aided,' " Harlow said.

"That is why it must be done in a certain manner." I was glad to return to the specifics of my plan, all of which I felt I'd worked out grandly. "He needs only a hand up, I'm sure. It would have to be something other than manual labor," I said, "to be appealing, and the offer would have to come from you, Harlow, as it might appear to be a manipulation or, worse, a charity, if I bring it up. Believe me, I've thought it all over. Let me explain the rest of it, don't interrupt me, and when I'm done I think you'll agree I've hit on something suitable, if you'll only go along with it."

I was returning from a dull forage amidst our local costers' carts, carrying a day-old fish and some spongy beets, when I looked up and saw the shining carriage, a sparkling bay in its shafts, parked before the crumbling lodging house. As I drew closer I recognized the young American reclining in the front seat, his feet propped up, head resting against his hands. I did not know whether to laugh or cry.

He saw me in the same instant. "Hullo there," he called, and sat up, waving, seemingly unaware of the commotion his presence on that street was eliciting from its natives. "Aubrey Bennett! Over here, it's Harlow, Harlow Beckwith." As if I'd forgotten. I approached the carriage on leaden feet, for I assumed he'd changed his mind about the loan of his property, and I felt myself horribly remiss for having made not the slightest attempt to return it. I'd intended to, truly, but that would have meant the end of my one slim chance at laying eyes upon her again, and so I'd put it off . . .

"I apologize," I began, "I've not had time to come by and return your things—"

"What? Oh, that—for the love of Christ, forget it. I certainly have—I told you, you're to keep all of it. No, there's something else I wish to talk to you about."

"Me?"

"Yes, have you a moment?"

No—the urgent business of a dead fish beckoned me.

"Yes, of course, only let me bring this to the kitchens."

I hurried to the house. Before slipping in, I turned, and was just in time to see Harlow digging about in his pocket and handing a coin to a dirt-encrusted, barefoot girl of perhaps six. She stared up at him for a moment, openmouthed, and then spun on her heel and ran off, as if fearing that he'd made a mistake and would attempt to grab the coin back.

When I returned he smacked the seat beside him. "Hop up." I was heartily grateful he hadn't asked to go inside and talk, but then, perhaps he hadn't as strong a stomach as Miss Leeds.

"This is somewhat embarrassing," he began. "You see, I was talking with Miss Leeds—you know, that young lady through whom we met—and she chanced to tell me that she'd got into quite a conversation with you that day she aided you after your accident, during which you'd mentioned having a first-rate education. She told me you even managed to decipher an old doc's handwriting, and that's some feat. And as I noted your penmanship when I copied your address, I know your ability in that area is outstanding. Now, here is the problem. I'm at school, and faring well in my classes—astronomy is my field, did I mention that?—at least in the ones that require mathematics. But the papers give me the most damnable trouble. My spelling is atrocious, my scribbling is illegible, and half my ideas go out the window because I cannot manage the grammar on paper. So my question to you is, how would you assess your own compositional skills, and how comfortable might you be in tutoring me a bit—say, temporarily, just for a few weeks, until I'm up to standards with things?"

"You have come *here* to ask *me* to tutor *you*?" He was as transparent as a windowpane. It was absurd; he must pity me or, more likely, the lovely girl had put him up to this, because of what she thought she saw: a compatriot, a fellow white American, educated, and fallen upon some awful tragedy. In need of a leg up from some others of his own former station. All of it a charming misperception which I'd failed to correct. All except the affinity with herself, which she thought she'd witnessed in the tragic young man.

"What school do you attend?" As if this had anything to do with anything.

"Oxford."

Oxford. Where Thomas Paxton had supposedly gone off to matriculate. Whether he was still there I had no idea. Nor did I wish to know, for I had no desire to negotiate Thomas before finding his father. I had no intention of asking Harlow Beckwith whether he'd heard of such a person, and I felt safe in assuming he hadn't, for Oxford is a big university, and lawyering is as distant a field from astronomy as one could hope for. Still, it was uncanny that I should run across someone with even the remotest connexion to my own past.

"I see," I said. I pretended to think. "I doubt my own skills are up to Oxford's standards. And it's been some time since I was forced to call upon them, as you've no doubt figured out."

"Look here, Mr. Bennett, I've no wish to pry—I'm sure there's some reason why you've sought refuge in these surroundings, and it's yours to keep to yourself. But I assure you—*my* skills aren't even up to the standards of the first form, and you are almost undoubtedly in a position to aid me. Besides, I think we'd get on well together. Why not see how it goes, and if you truly feel you can't be of service, we can cancel the arrangement at any time."

"Why not just hire a tutor from the university?"

"What, and embarrass myself, have it get out that it was necessary? Besides, I know a few of them, they're largely condescending bores, and I'd be battling myself every step of the way, placing myself in their hands."

"What would the arrangement be, then—I could travel to your home perhaps once a week, though I haven't a mount—"

"Oh, that wouldn't do at all, I need a good deal more help than that. No, what I had in mind was that you might live on the estate where I'm residing. Temporarily, of course. That way we could work as needed. This would necessitate a move on your part, I don't know how you might feel about that. But I'd supply your room and board, and pay you a salary—oh, perhaps ten pounds a week, say."

Ten pounds a week? In addition to room and board? I knew now he must have been put up to this—or perhaps have something unsavory up his sleeve, for nobody is simply offered ten pounds a week out of the clear blue sky. I should have exposed him, and stalked off in high dudgeon. At the very least I knew I ought to be wary, for if I was not what he thought I was, then he might not be what he appeared either, and I could end up regretting too hasty a decision.

On the other hand, what else was I doing, and where was I doing it? Even a week in this man's employ, at the outlandish ten pounds a week, would make me as rich as I'd ever been in my life. And if his intent were to lure me to some uncertain fate—well, how much worse could it be than what I'd already endured?

And then there was the girl, Miss Leeds, and the chance of being somewhere in her vicinity, that I might meet her once again.

"All right," I replied to the young man, at last. "If you truly feel this would benefit you in some way. It would be a fine opportunity for me, I must admit."

"Good! It's settled, then. Will it take you long to collect your things?"

"What, you mean now?"

"Well, yes, we may as well get started, since it's only a temporary thing. Why waste time?"

I glanced at the American's smiling face, and then at the reeking facade of the lodging house. I glimpsed the little girl to whom Harlow had given the coin:

she was squatting upon the ground, her pinafore hiked up, carelessly urinating in a stream before whoever might happen to pass.

"I'll only be a moment," I said, turning.

In my airless cubbyhole I stuffed my few belongings into the gift of a travel bag. I glanced up, and saw before me the scratchings on the wall left there by some long-departed former occupants: *Irish Jenny, gone back to Dublin and thanking God for it. One Eye Jimmy & his moll here '61 to hide or hang fur muzzling a peeler*. How I longed to add my own final piece of history to theirs, to depart this place, nevermore to ruminate over the fate of Irish Jenny, or the lovers who'd killed the policeman in '61! I picked up the bag and carried my greatcoat with me. Then I knocked on Ibrahim's door. He blinked at me when he saw my possessions in my hands.

"Where—"

"The American has come to call on me. He offered me some work, and I'm going with him. My room's paid up to the end of the month. I'll be gone only for a few weeks, but I've got to hurry off. Say good-bye to Oha and Aurelio, and tell them I'll be back round in a couple of days to explain it in person."

"A couple of days, eh?" He offered me his hand. "Good luck to ya, Bree Bennett. Keep yaself well."

"Thank you. I'll see you shortly, Ibrahim."

"Ya, boyo. Of course ya will."

We arrived at Mr. Beckwith's residence, Linton Manor, later in the afternoon. So: it was real after all. I was not to be kidnapped and sold to a coal mine, or diced up and fed to racing dogs.

I was nearly light-headed at the sight of the place; it is a grand old English estate, although Harlow says his family does not own it, but has only been using it at the invitation of the owners, who are elsewhere.

I was even more light-headed when I saw what were to be my accommodations. There are two guesthouses on the property, and the smaller of these—which has a mere six rooms—is to be my own. I hung my greatcoat up in the entryway, where it clashed horribly with the beauty of everything else inside, and asked Harlow to show me my quarters. You're standing in it, he said, it's all yours, there is nobody else here in the house but you.

Now something else hit me: a squeamishness at being the recipient of this unasked-for consideration, for what would I owe? What prone position of gratitude would I be forced to assume? I had to remind myself that Harlow Beckwith had offered me employment, nothing more. If this was the way people of his status treated their tutors, then so be it. I would perform my job as best I could. I would allow him to be responsible for the offer he'd made me, and try to believe myself worthy of it.

"Come round the main house when you're finished looking about. I want you to meet my family, and the staff, so they're not alarmed at the sight of you gallivanting about the lawn."

I practically jumped for joy at the sight of the carriage pulling into the drive with the two figures seated in it. I'd known I was pressing my advantage with Mother and Father, going visiting at Linton twice within two days, but this made the effort well worth it.

"It's him," I cried to Caroline, "he came! Wait until you meet him, you will fall in love with him on sight—he's that dazzling to look at, and so interesting, so sweet, on top of it all—" I realized I was doing a fair imitation of Cousin Constance in that moment, and tried to curb my gushing enthusiasm, but it was difficult.

Caroline only smiled and patted my arm. "Yes, I'm sure he's all of that, dear."

Once Harlow had gone, I inspected the lower floor briefly, still overwhelmed by this bizarre twist in my fortunes. Then I mounted the stairs to the two bedrooms, chose the largest for myself, and unpacked my things, which took all of a minute.

Upon finishing this task, I set off on the pathway across the vast green manicured lawn, toward the main house. I knocked upon the gigantic vaulted door and was received by a maid in black-and-white uniform, who led me through several huge and fabulously decorated rooms to a back parlor.

The first thing I glimpsed upon entering this space was the girl herself: Miss Leeds. Of course, I had suspected she might be behind the incredible chain of events which brought me here, but I had not dared believe it, for that would have presumed some great interest in me upon her part, and an interest won as much by what I hadn't told her as what I had. But here she was, and what other conclusion could I draw except that she had quite intended to be present on my account—and if that were true, how could I undermine the thrill of it by convincing myself that she'd been engaged merely on false pretenses?

My heart literally danced in my chest at the sight of her. How glorious she looked, her hair thrown over one shoulder, her bright brown eyes shining back at me. "Miss Leeds," I said, trying to appear calm. I inclined my head toward her. "It is a pleasure to see you again."

"Likewise," she said, and smiled her radiant smile.

Only then did I take note of the other people in the room. Mr. Beckwith was there, leaning against the mantelpiece. And seated next to Miss Leeds was another young woman. This girl was flaxen-haired and pink-skinned, dressed in blue and white; she was a fleshy, creamy confection, and in another lifetime had been the sort of female who filled my wanton dreams. But I found myself gazing past her, to rest my eyes again upon Miss Leeds. I barely noticed Mr. Beckwith was speaking, until I saw the ladies incline their heads toward him.

"Allow me to present my sister, Miss Caroline Beckwith," he was saying. The blonde girl rose, and offered me her hand. She eyed me directly, but there was something odd in the glance, something cursory, as if she were not the least bit interested in me—or was even somewhat perturbed at my presence. For one sickening moment I imagined that she saw quite through me, that she had somehow detected the presence of Negro blood in my features or demeanor; but then I told myself this was ridiculous. I grasped her fingers and nodded.

"A pleasure," I said.

"Quite," she replied. She quickly withdrew her hand and resumed her seat.

I wondered at her abrupt manner, but, knowing Caroline to be a mercurial creature, decided to let it pass. I admit I was relieved to see that Mr. Bennett's gaze did not linger upon her, for some tiny, tiny part of me had still feared that he might be a callow romantic, or a cunning libertine whose sport lay in wooing the newest pretty face to cross his path.

Within a moment, however, his eyes had met mine again, and were alight with such obvious appreciation that my last misgivings were put to rest. He was every bit as comely as I'd remembered, and in addition looked a good deal healthier and heartier than when I'd last beheld him. We were both at a loss for words, however, and now stared at each other awkwardly, until Harlow came to our rescue.

"Aubrey's agreed to be my tutor," he announced, "so I hope to see a great improvement in my papers before too long."

"Oh!" I said, rather badly feigning surprise. "How wonderful! Mr. Bennett, I hope you don't mind that I shared some of the details of our conversation with Harlow."

"No, no—I was taken by surprise, I must admit, but my funds were running low, and I welcome the chance for some gainful employment."

We exchanged smiles, and then Harlow began chatting away about his classes, and what he hoped to accomplish with the aid of a tutor, and so forth. Caroline joined in, managing, in a somewhat friendlier tone, to question Aubrey about his education, and his departure from the States. In this way an hour or so passed—during which Aubrey and I were hard-pressed to look anywhere but at each other.

At last I decided I must tear myself away and return home, so as not to excite my parents' wrath any further. I rose and announced that I ought to be going.

"Aubrey," Harlow said nonchalantly, "why don't you walk Miss Leeds to her carriage? It's waiting round back at the stable. She knows the way."

I thought this awfully decent, if somewhat confusing, on his part, but I did not argue. I waited for Miss Leeds to brush past me, and then followed, with a nod to the siblings. Once outside upon the path, we walked beside each other, and I found it impossible to maintain the farce any longer.

"I get the sense that Mr. Beckwith is only marginally in need of tutoring," I began.

"Well, no, I shouldn't put it that way; his composition skills really are atrocious."

"He went awfully far off the path, wouldn't you say, to search me out in the East End in order to engage a competent tutor."

She shrugged, and I could see amusement playing at the corners of her mouth. "It's not so very far, if you've a decent driver."

"You put him up to it, didn't you, Miss Arabella Leeds, whom I mustn't call 'Bella.' "

"I did." She strolled along, not looking at me, and I could see the amusement bloom into a full-fledged grin.

"You've wounded my pride horribly, you must know that. Though of course I am grateful to have become the object of your charity."

"Oh, I wasn't merely being charitable. The arrangement will serve both of you, and so it's not a charity, but a clever exchange of services."

She was smiling widely, and so I laughed aloud, I could not help it. We stopped on the path to the stable and regarded each other.

" 'Clever exchange' indeed," I said. "Really, I had hoped to set eyes on you again, but under conditions that would allow me to maintain my self-respect."

"Please don't be insulted." Her expression became serious. "I saw the chance to do you a good turn, and so I acted upon it. It is not purely manufactured; you truly will be helping Harlow. And besides, I could think of no other way to contact you and maintain *my* self-respect. I was not even certain you desired to see me again until you just now acknowledged it."

So—there it was, and so bluntly put!

"You are an unusual girl, and so very forthright."

"Does it bother you?"

"God, no, it does not bother me, so long as you are forthrightly saying the things I wish to hear—for instance, that I've managed to engage your interest somehow."

"You've managed. Indeed, yes."

So there can be no mistaking it: it was not a fluke, this seeming instant affinity between us, and I was not presuming too much in noting it, and acting upon it. I walked quite far out on a limb, to be sure, but I am overjoyed at the result.

Indeed, I cannot stop smiling; I am tripping about as if on air, and over what? Over a chance meeting which, a month ago, I'd no idea was around the corner.

I have shared the details of this amazing turn of events only with Richard, and if he is somewhat bemused at them, he has the good grace not to tease me unduly.

"I've never seen you like this," he told me wonderingly. "You are quite shaking my faith in your good sense, Berry."

"Oh, let me alone," I scolded him, "for I've had the most damnable luck in the whole enterprise of romance, and I think I am entitled to some unadulterated bliss."

Yet still I cannot get over it, that the course of my life has changed in an instant, and in a manner so uplifting that it feels like a daydream, which must dissolve upon waking.

MARCH 30, 1863

Each day since his first at Linton I've spent, at least partially, in Aubrey's presence; I have been quite forthright in informing Mother and Father of my calls to the Beckwiths' lodgings, neglecting only to add that now it's neither Harlow nor Caroline with whom the all-too-brief visits are spent. Little has been made at home of my disappearances, so perhaps some corner has been turned in my attempts to be recognized by my parents as an autonomous adult.

In the meanwhile, my regard for Bree has grown a thousandfold, for there is not a discordant note struck between us, not a point which causes me to draw back, to question my headlong plunge into his company. We share a most uncanny closeness, yet I am equally excited by what we do not hold in common, for I feel I have a world to offer him that he has not beheld, while his is one which I can only glimpse through my association with him.

Outwardly he is contained, masterful, yet there runs just beneath his surface that vitality which drew me from the first. He is quick to sense even the subtlest shift in my moods; I mentioned this talent to him once, while we lolled before the fire in his cottage at Linton, and he said it is the result of being raised in a houseful of women and obliged to anticipate their whims, but that while it was a burden then, it is a skill he treasures now.

He would tell me little more of his origins, however, and that one thing still disturbs me mightily: that he shares so easily his mind and heart, but not the facts of his past, which are just that—past—and therefore can no longer harm him. In his reluctance lie my only reservations, for I cannot help but feel that whatever he is hiding must be terrible indeed—at least from his point of view—and I cannot push from my mind the picture of that moment when he finally reveals it.

I have tried to encourage him by sharing the adventures most worth mentioning in my own past, for example the ones involving Miss Ashe, whose house I'd brought him to seemingly a million years ago.

We set each other to laughing uncontrollably, she by telling me the outrageous purposes for which that lady's house is used, and I by describing who and what I thought she and Miss Ashe were before actually meeting her.

But of course I soon found myself come upon the incident of Madame Zunia, and ultimately, Jeffrey Price. One day I relayed the entire tale, and he listened in his typical observant fashion, with keen interest, interrupting only when he wished me to expand upon a detail or two. When I had done, I held my breath, wondering what his response should be, while he sat for a moment without speaking.

Finally he asked, "This Jeffrey Price—what became of him?"

"Nothing." I recognized the bitterness in my voice even all of these months later. "Nothing became of him. He simply left our town, and is no doubt moved to some other, and probably still fancying himself the great seducer."

Aubrey looked up at me sharply. "I would not call what he perpetrated a seduction, Berry. I would call it a rape."

I blinked, for this word had often crossed my mind but never my lips, as I believed I would have been roundly scolded for hurling such a term at anyone save a savage caught directly in the act. But Aubrey went on quite matter-of-factly: "It would seem he has performed a rape upon innocents, and for that he is a criminal, to my mind, and ought to be hunted down and punished as one." He looked me squarely in the eye. "There is surely no crime more odious than to force one's attentions upon others, and then attempt to implicate them in one's own decision to do so. It is an act of barbarism. You should be proud that you sought to expose him for what he is."

I sat back, surprised and gratified not only by this assessment of Jeffrey Price which so nearly matched my own, but by the extent of Bree's outrage, which surpassed even Harlow's upon being told the same story.

"I thank you," I replied, "and I do indeed try to take pride in my actions. But I attempt it in the face of considerable opposition, for mine was not the popular position in New Parrish."

"I am not the least surprised to hear it." His expression clouded just a little as he said this, and I considered pursuing the remark further.

But I did not wish to waste all of our precious and hard-won time together on these dismal subjects, and so I turned the conversation elsewhere.

He checked himself, and then looked up at me, brightening a bit. "But I suppose at any rate that your Madame What-is-her-name explains your fascination with the Spiritualists."

"Oh, them—well. You mustn't call it a fascination. I'd engaged upon a crusade against them, I suppose, although I did not realize it until recently." I gave him a long, sly look. "The whole business has come to seem rather less important to me of late."

He smiled. "And was that why you searched out BayBay? Were you seeking to expose her as a part of your crusade?"

"I suppose I was. But there was nothing to expose, as she seemed neither insincere nor greedy, as are most of those I've had the displeasure to meet. I still don't know what to make of the experience, or of her, I should say."

"Nor do I, although she's not the first of her kind I've come across."

"Is that so! Where in the world might you have encountered others?"

"In New Orleans, where I grew up. Her religion—voodoo, 'vodou,' it's called, in the form I'm speaking of—has found a following there. Its adherents mainly practice it sincerely, as I believe BayBay does. On the other hand, though"—he winked at me here—"there were those who were not averse to tweaking it into more entertaining forms, strictly for the benefit of nonbelievers who sought to be amused."

"Oh?" I was intrigued, for not only were his words interesting, but they were the most he'd given out to me of his past.

"Yes," he went on, "quite so. I knew of a woman, a priestess, who was a popular performer as well. She cast spells for a price, and conducted séances. She could make a table appear to rise from the floor, even with her hands and feet held fast by her clients. It was only a trick, to which she freely admitted, but her audience found her so convincing that they returned again and again."

"How did she do it?" I was wondering if I'd hear of a method I'd not come across before.

"She had a special table of balsa wood round which she seated her guests. When it was time to call upon a Spirit, she would snuff out the lamps, and ask those on either side of her to grasp her hands and step on her toes with their own feet." He grinned. "They assumed she hadn't any limbs free with which to hoodwink them. But then she would feign some convulsive trance, during which she'd slip her feet out of her shoes and slide them round the center pole of the table, to toss it about."

"Ha! Precisely the sort of fakery I'd expect."

"But she acknowledged as much," Bree went on, "so you mustn't hold it against her. Besides, there were the other exercises she undertook which were not fraudulent at all."

"Like what?"

"The true religious ceremonies, they were always genuine. Sometimes in the course of these she was asked to intercede with the gods for a special favor, a request she always treated with the utmost seriousness. At other times she sought to predict future events, or guess the details of a supplicant's life. She claimed she could not summon these insights at will, but when they came to her they were reputed to be quite accurate. Sometimes uncannily so, as I recall."

In fact, Gran, Mama claimed you were far better a seer than any of those vodou renegades who collected money for their services, and I hope you do not mind me expounding upon your gifts, or taking license with Mama's few recollections. I am sorry I made an amalgam of you and your own Maman, for I know well enough you never performed her table-raising trick, given your own sentiments regarding truth and falsity, and the sanctity of your Faith. But I wished Arabella to know something of you, and the premonitions you ascribed to the Saints or the ancestors, and so I hope you can forgive me my creative lapse of honesty.

I considered what he'd told me. "Is that what brought *you* to BayBay's, then?" I finally asked him. "Do you practice her faith—this 'voodoo'? Were you searching for some familiar form of guidance?"

"No. I am not a practitioner—more an observer, if anything. And I did not seek Behbeh out. She was only a friend of Ibrahim's, whom you met," I answered her. "He wanted me to experience something of his culture, since he is a native of Ghana, and the woman practices a form of the religion common to that portion of Africa. Perhaps I thought I would see something reminiscent of New Orleans," I added, "but believe me, I was as shocked as you, for what took place there resembled little of what I'd witnessed at home."

And then, because the opportunity had presented itself, I continued.

"But there was something about that evening which I've been thinking of since it happened. I wonder, Berry, did you chance to catch what the priestess said to me before she ended the ceremony? She called me a name—did you overhear it?"

I had put this question to Ibrahim and Oha (who, as I'd expected, had been of no help, having been too far off to hear Behbeh's words). And from the first day I met her, I had considered posing it to Berry, but had been unable to make myself do it. Now I feared she might have forgotten what she'd heard if she'd caught it all, but she answered me quickly, if without enthusiasm.

"Yes, I heard. And I remember it. It was 'little pup.' I recorded the whole evening in my journal, and I recall writing that down: 'Little pup.' "

I would have preferred not to answer him, for I knew perfectly well that this was the phrase which had caused him such distress when it was uttered. But he had asked me directly, and I could not lie.

Indeed, it affected him similarly this time; he nodded at the ground, and was silent.

"What does it mean," I probed gently.

"It was a term familiar to me, which she could not have known of. It was not something I'd shared at any time, with anyone." His luminous green eyes searched my own. "It was a pet name given me by my grandmother."

"A pet name." Her tone softened.

"Yes. It came from a child's book, which was read to me aloud. It was written in French—the story of 'Little Brown Pup.' "

I saw now why his eyes had darkened so.

For on the one hand, what implications the voodoo priestess's vision had, if it were judged credible! How magical to imagine it, the words wafting across the endless oceans upon a grandmother's loving breath, and BayBay bending, straining, to catch them upon what gossamer intuition!

But if she were credible on that count, what of the others? I recalled well enough that pet names were not the only things she'd imparted to Aubrey that evening.

She must have read my thoughts exactly, for now she said, "Oh, Bree, you mustn't take on over it. There could be a thousand explanations—'pup' is a common enough term for a young man in this country, it is likely mere coincidence."

"But she said 'little' as well, Berry."

"All right, that may make it the more uncanny, but still you needn't pursue the most far-fetched interpretation over those most likely and logical. And even if you concede her one point, you are hardly obligated to accept the rest, and fret over them."

"And what if they are all to be conceded?"

"Then either you shall discover that, or you won't. In any case, you cannot know how you shall feel until it's a certainty, and worried speculation can add nothing to your understanding, but only plague you in the present moment."

He still appeared doubtful, and so I grasped his fingers, and drew him down upon the new spring grass in order that he might lie beside me.

"Look, now. If you cannot master the circumstance, you can at least choose how you'll regard it, do you see? There is a good deal to be said for taking comfort in that present moment, Bree, particularly when it is a warm and sunny day, and your fond companion has just discovered what may be the season's first bloom."

And so saying, I directed his eye to where a buttercup had poked its head above the dirt.

He smiled at this, finally, and then reached over to pluck the blossom from its stem. He entwined it in a wandering curl of mine, and tucked it securely behind my ear.

I am not certain I yet understand her approach, or trust it, but how I long to! In anchoring the blossom to her gleaming hair, I sought as well to force all worry from my mind, for I so wish not to be troubled, and to think no more upon trouble, but only of her.

I have never had such a sensation in the presence of another person, that of being both known and unknown, a mystery worth investigating and yet a compatriot in spirit. I feel she tells me everything in the most direct terms, and understands my thoughts before I speak them, and yet she is so intoxicatingly female, so immersed in the most wonderful aspects of her sex, that I alternate between lust and fellow feeling. Lust generally wins out, despite my vow before leaving the States to engage in no more of it. But then, I have quite thrown out that vow as unnecessarily confining, although I take pains to indulge my fantasies regarding her only when alone. I have no wish to bring that aspect of my interest into the open too quickly.

For if Ibrahim is a man most compelled by the thought of a "good poke," to be had any way one can manage it, I am the sort who desires the complete attentions of a woman; I realize this about myself. I have had enough of contempt, of rejection, of barter, and convincing, and guilty seduction. I wish only to know myself to be as wanted as she whom I want. Only here can there be the clean exchange, the sublimation in affection I desire; anything less is less than enough.

In truth, there is a tiny, guilty part of me which wonders why the woman I desire must be permitted to roam the streets at will, why we men do not simply tie our beloveds to a bedstead, feed them by hand, dote upon them generously, and then lock them in at night, safe from the temptations and lusts of all other masculine countenances. That devil on my shoulder would happily see Arabella make of herself a willing slave, so that I might know her every move, and be reassured of her unswerving loyalty. But there is no such thing as a willing slave, and a woman aspiring to be one could never be the woman I seek.

So I resist the temptation to rush headlong into some physical expression of my feeling toward her, until I can be certain that she would enter into that contract willingly. And I wonder how that can ever come to be, for among her class and station there is no impetus toward such behavior, and more than every reason to avoid it.

But I should like nothing better than to take his face between my palms and kiss it recklessly, splay my fingers so that his hair might sift through them, put my mouth upon the mark at his shoulder so as to better savor it. And at times I am on the verge of doing exactly these things—and for their own sake, without heed for anything save the feel of them. But I contain myself, for although I sense that he would welcome them, and welcome that within me which compels me thus, he seems compelled as well by notions of gentlemanly behavior, upon which I do not wish to impinge too quickly.

There are only two things which give me pause, and both of them concern not her behavior, but my own. The worst of these is that I am far less than honest with her regarding the details of my background, for she is so clearly, wholly truthful concerning her own.

But why must I disabuse her of her fancies, say the words that will force her to consider me in a new light—or rather, that old one under which I have labored for most of my life—and most likely abandon any interest in me?

I recall the way she unhesitatingly grasped Ibrahim's hand when she met him, and every word she says indicates to me that she has nothing but tolerance for each strain of the human race. But abstract tolerance is one thing, while the knowledge that I would bring her to is very much another. I know I cannot keep this from her, that to do so undermines the very frankness I relish between us, and yet I cannot bring myself to reveal it. At least, not yet.

The other misgiving I feel within myself has to do with her closeness to Harlow Beckwith, which is obvious, and which excites the greatest jealousy within me whenever I witness it.

As it turns out, the plan and the offer Harlow laid before me are legitimate, and having begun my lessons with him, it's become evident that his assessment of his language skills was also on the level—they truly are abominable, and I believe I can aid him greatly in improving them, so that my claim to the position of his tutor—however it may have come about—will be justified.

Our sessions are productive, but they are also a source of pleasure to me, for I feel Harlow to be not only an employer, but a friend whose company I look forward to. I had feared him to be yet another variation on the person of Thomas Paxton, and I have been wary in allowing myself to feel any sort of kinship with him. I cannot know what sort of prejudice lies within him, or how it should erupt when and if my own truth becomes known. But I feel I am on the way to divining even this without revealing myself, and in the meantime he has quite convinced me of his sincerity, and of his unique character. He is not merely a member of the spoiled upper classes; he is immersed in his field of study, hopes to make a mark upon its history, and yet has confided that his own laziness troubles him, and is a constant source of distraction. In short, he is a man of some insight, willing to acknowledge his own faults, and his humor and good grace in doing so mightily appeal to me.

And yet I cannot help but writhe when I see him in Arabella's company. It is so apparent to me what they share, which Arabella and I do not: a status, a heritage, a frame of mind. He rests a hand upon her shoulder, or they exchange a knowing glance, and it is all I can do to resist knocking that hand aside, or coming between them in some obvious way, so as to interrupt that flow of understanding from one to the other. It is a constant effort to hide my agitation, and it occurs to me that perhaps I should not hide it, that I should ask her straight out what is between them, and satisfy myself that it is nothing at all, the better to go on enjoying what draws me to each of them.

But this too I shall have to think upon, and reserve the decision for another day. For at the moment I am Aubrey Bennett, my secrets are secure, my friendships untainted, the object of my affections engaged; I wish only to relish this instant, and do nothing which may cause it to vanish prematurely.

APRIL 15, 1863

There is to be a gathering at Linton in four days, consisting of exiled young Americans—friends of the Beckwiths—and their families. It's to be quite a mixed-about evening, as we are asked to dress formally, but will be dining outside upon "American cuisine." Harlow and Caroline have assured me that at last I shall meet their phantom mother, although I shan't believe this until the woman is standing before me. In addition, they say they've a surprise planned, but would not give out another word as to what it might be.

I think it shall be a rippingly good time, however, as there is to be dancing, reels as well as waltzes, and barbecue—imagine, in the middle of London!—such as we've had none of since leaving the States. I've implored Mother and Father to go, but they maintain they've "other plans" for the evening, and that they shan't be attending. Nor shall my cousins; apparently the Beckwiths enjoy too much of a dubious reputation for Aunt Jo to allow any of her children to be tainted by it.

Richard is to be permitted to go, however. But I told him he must find another young lady to engage for the dances, as I intend to be spoken for.

I am still somewhat reluctant to accept Harlow's invitation.

For one thing, I have not yet made good my promise to return to the East End of London and let Ibrahim and Oha know what's become of me, and I therefore feel guilty traipsing about to parties and enjoying myself. If I am to make time for anything, it ought to be for the acknowledging of my friends, and yet the way back to Stepney seems so much longer than the way out of it.

For another thing, I wonder how I will be looked upon by the other company the Beckwiths have invited, for if cats may look at kings, it does not follow that they may dine and dance with them.

"Oh, nonsense," Harlow said when I mentioned this to him. "We are Americans, not bloody Brits, we don't stand on that sort of divisive nonsense amongst ourselves."

I might have reminded him, then, of the cause of our exile from our own country, but I knew what he meant, in his good-hearted way, and had no wish to spoil the moment.

"Now," he went on, "we ought to take those wages of yours and fit you up with something halfway decent to wear, as you'll no doubt be spending a good deal of time twirling Miss Berry about, and will want to be at your best."

Would I? Would I be the one to "twirl Miss Berry about," thus receiving an answer to the question of what place Mr. Beckwith occupies in her affections? Would I actually mingle with these creatures as, if not an equal, at least an acceptable underling? I wonder if God will actually permit the great Order of the Universe to be usurped by allowing Mr.Paxton'sNegroservantAubrey to enter the halls of Linton with the fair-skinned Miss Arabella Leeds, of the Knightsbridge Leedses, upon his arm.

Well, let us see.

APRIL 19, 1863

There is never any telling, is there, when one's fondest fantasies may be dashed by something entirely unexpected.

By this afternoon we were ready to set off for Linton. Richard looked positively dashing—very nearly a grown man—and was in a near-faint over the idea that Caroline Beckwith might allow herself a few turns around the floor with him.

I was dressed in my scarlet gown, and had drawn my hair up simply. Mother was gracious enough to lend me her pearls, although I knew she was rather of two minds over having allowed us to attend the party at all. We were permitted the brougham and the luxury of being driven, and all the way there were absorbed in our private thoughts: Richard, no doubt, was in a rapture over dreams of Caroline, while I could scarcely wait to see how Aubrey would look, and what it would be like to appear with him in public at last, after these weeks of meeting each other, if not in secret, then at least discreetly, at Linton. Everyone there would no doubt know he is Harlow's tutor, and I realized I didn't care a fig whether or not they approve of his presence.

At Linton we were announced at the door, and finally—finally!—there before me stood our hostess, Mrs. Hester Beckwith, with her children.

Nothing is quite what you think it shall be, that is for certain; and Mrs. Beckwith was my first surprise of the evening. I had imagined her a tall, grand, sweeping figure of a woman, somewhere along the lines of Miss Ashe, but I discovered now that she much more resembles Caroline, being small, exquisitely pretty, fair, and dimpled. Her gaze, however, was everything I'd thought it might be: the dimples notwithstanding, she looked me over with a directness which bespoke a formidable intelligence.

When Caroline introduced us, she drew me into an embrace. "So—you are Miss Leeds, the very Miss Leeds I've heard so much about! I'd begun to think I might never meet you, that we'd be dispersed to the four corners of the States before ever setting eyes upon each other!"

"I'd thought so as well," I said, laughing. "For I've never heard of a woman as much on the move as yourself, Mrs. Beckwith, although I greatly admire you for it."

"Oh, I suppose I get around a bit, but then, there are those who make even more of a habit of loose feet than myself. You have become acquainted with my dear friend Miss Ashe, have you not?" She winked at me, her startling blue eyes alight with mischief.

"Yes indeed," I smiled back.

"Well, you'll find no more seasoned world traveler than Miss Ashe. If you are ever in need of information regarding any obscure smidgen of the globe, go directly to Miss Ashe, for if she hasn't been there, chances are good she's studied it near to death."

I laughed again, and then Mrs. Beckwith said, "I am glad that my children have happened upon such a rare good soul as yourself, Miss Leeds. Please, come in, dance, enjoy yourself, and let us be certain to talk at more length later on."

Richard and I passed through the foyer, and then into the ballroom, which had been cleared of furniture for dancing. The orchestra was already setting up, although before the evening's entertainments we were to be dining outside, in the rear of the house.

We continued through the ballroom out into the formal gardens and patios. It was cool there, but not overly so, and the topiaries were alight with torches and lamps, and decorated with fresh flowers. Tables had been set up, and laid with silver and china plates in red, white, and blue. And the English cooks had labored to produce something akin to an American barbecue, which I thought Aubrey would especially enjoy, given his childhood in the South.

I was desperate for a glimpse of him. So desperate in fact that when he finally emerged into the garden, I gave a little start. For not only was he there, he was there in a splendor that I could not have anticipated. I had wondered how and in what manner I might introduce his name round the Leeds dinner table, how I would arrange a meeting between him and my parents so that he might make a favorable impression. Why, oh why, I thought, could they not have joined us tonight! Had they been here, they would have been won over instantly. The sight of Aubrey would have blasted any lingering thoughts of Carter Forbes-Spencer from Mother's mind, and his lovely manner would have further assured a positive outcome to the introduction. In his coat and collar he looked positively regal; he moved in evening clothes as if he had been born to wear them, as if he were the prince of some exotic foreign land who only now felt himself to be back in his element.

In fact the stiff formal clothes felt so like the butler's uniform that I found myself adopting, once again, the controlled and careful manner of the house servant.

My discomfort vanished, however, when I glimpsed Arabella. She was a vision, in scarlet which blazed beneath her hair. She seemed to fairly glow from within, and I could scarce keep from placing a kiss upon her bright lips. Instead I said, "You look splendid." I had collected a corsage of fresh flowers from a little coster waif just returned from Covent Garden, and I presented them to her. They were white roses; I made as if to pin them to her breast, but as I did so the pin scratched the flesh of her bosom, and drew a drop of blood there.

"Never mind," she laughed, and wiped it away with a finger.

But the garnet earrings, and the blood they drew, are never far from my mind, nor is the deceit which accompanied them, and which I practice upon Arabella, although to a different end.

"Oh, don't look so chastened," I said, "roses are expected to have thorns, and I shan't die from lack of blood. They are beautiful, Bree, and I thank you."

I presented Aubrey to Richard, and they shook hands, Richard commenting, "You look a deuced bit better than the last time I saw you."

Caroline and Harlow had left their mother to do the receiving, and joined us outside. Caroline was ravishing in yellow silk, and Harlow just as dashing in his evening clothes. I wished there had been a portrait artist there to render a photograph, or indeed a *carte de visite* of our entourage, but alas, such perfect moments are usually doomed to pass uncaptured.

We fell to talking, and then other invitees began to arrive, so that Harlow and Caroline were compelled to circulate about and introduce us to them. Some of the guests I recalled from that long-ago event at Mersy Hall, but others I'd never set eyes on, and I was surprised at the number of Americans who had found themselves stranded in London during the conflict at home.

When the gardens had grown quite crowded, with sixty or seventy people strolling about, Mrs. Beckwith arrived out-of-doors and announced that, as most of the party was present, we should sit for dinner and enjoy ourselves. "Eat well," she advised us, "but don't gorge, for you'll want to be in fine fettle for the dancing later on."

We took a table with Caroline, Harlow, and two others, a young woman named Patricia Harrison and a young man called Paul Davis, who were both natives of Pennsylvania. The meal was a most amusing mix of the casual and the formal. Pitchers of beer were placed upon the linen tablecloths, while the first course consisted of chowder. Then slabs of barbecue, a salad of potatoes, fresh corn, and biscuits were served upon the fine china. It was wonderfully familiar. How Hester Beckwith had managed to find the necessary items, never mind oversee their preparations, was beyond me. I ate and drank myself silly, the beer making me quite tipsy, until it seemed that the conversation making its way round the table was the most witty and sparkling ever indulged in.

Yet however much I drank—and I drank quite a bit—I could not flood away a certain bitter nostalgia, for the smell and sight of the food brought back memories of everything I had left behind me, and served to remind me of the uncertainty of my future; and so I found myself becoming more and more subdued, even as the conversation around me grew yet livelier.

Midway through the meal, Mrs. Beckwith, who had been seated at a table with other guests, came over and whispered something in Harlow's ear. He nudged Caroline, and then the two of them rose and departed, leaving me, startled, in midsentence. I quickly forgot about it, however (no doubt helped along by the beer), and got up from my place next to Aubrey to talk to Miss Harrison, who was seated across the table.

I could not see the entrance to the main house, as it was to my back. Arabella had moved to the opposite side of the table and was chatting away with the other girl seated with us; she therefore was facing the double doors when Harlow and Caroline must have come through them. I was listening to Arabella when I saw her glance up over my shoulder.

Her face changed in an instant from gaiety to shock. Her eyes widened; she covered her mouth with both hands, and began a series of little shrieks, while half-rising from her seat. I felt a movement behind me, and turned to see what had caused this extraordinary commotion.

It was Louella.

Dear God, did I not feel every particle in my body turn to ice.

To stone.

I could scarcely believe it. "You monsters," I cried to Harlow and Caroline, "keeping this from me until the last minute! How could you!"

"Surprise!" Harlow shouted, and he and the rest of the table laughed. Louella and I hugged, and then I drew back to have a good look at her.

It seemed to me that I frantically studied every pore upon her skin, and compared it to my memory of Louella, and then attempted futilely to wrench my gaze away.

No. How could it be? It couldn't be. I must be mistaken, or drunk, or demented.

And yet it was.

Louella Paxton, who should have been somewhere in New Orleans, or in Aix-en-Provence, the south of France, or anywhere on earth but here, stood not five inches from my shoulder.

And all of these people—Harlow, Caroline, and Arabella—seemed well acquainted with her, seemed thrilled beyond words to see her.

I should have known it, should have known that they'd have come upon each other, wealthy Americans in a foreign land, attending the same schools, moving, out of all the dozens of cliques in London, in the same small circles—

And in a second I recalled why, upon first meeting him, Harlow Beckwith's name had seemed familiar to me: because it *was*. Because these were Louella's boarding-school friends from overseas, whom she had mentioned in passing once or twice on her visits home.

She saw me in the same instant, and startled so hugely that her glass tipped and spilled a few drops, but then she was forced to turn at once to Arabella, who had run to her side, and the two of them embraced long and lovingly.

"You are finally here."

"Yes, dear, I am finally here."

Harlow set about introducing her to whomever at the table she did not know, namely, Mr. Davis, Aubrey, and Richard.

And that was the curious thing: for when Aubrey rose to take her hand, the strangest expression passed between them—the one I had perhaps expected to see on Aubrey's face upon meeting Caroline—as if he could hardly tear his eyes away from her.

It was not a long look, and there seemed to be no flirtation in it, but I noticed it, and felt a tiny stirring within me, for wouldn't it have been poetic justice if Louella—whose beau I had trifled with in her absence—were now to compel the one person in the world whose affection I'd felt certain of.

"And this is my tutor, Aubrey Bennett, I've just engaged him, and a good thing too—" Harlow was saying, and then Louella was reaching to give me her hand.

We stared at each other; I willed my expression not to betray the weakness in my body. *My God, it's you*, our eyes said silently. Please, I begged her just as silently, please give me one more hour, one more minute, before you unmask me. Please, please, spare me that, do it later on, I won't put up a fight.

But all I saw in her eyes was shock, and the shine of moisture there, although the smile remained plastered on her face; and she did nothing extreme, only said in a trembling voice, "Charmed, I'm sure." Then Caroline was pulling her off in another direction, to bid hello to the other guests present, whom she also obviously knew.

Something had changed, although I had no idea what. We sat at the table talking, Louella recounting for us her journey from Provence to London. I wanted to give her my full attention, and yet the atmosphere had gone strained and strange. At length the orchestra began to play, and Caroline suggested we hasten into the ballroom, as there would be plenty of time to catch up with each other later on.

Aubrey danced with me, seeming, if anything, more attentive than ever. He drew me to him, and when we waltzed, held hard to my hand as if fearing I might fly away. But as everyone else cavorted through the reels, as the rest of the party indulged in what was likely the most fun they'd had in months, he became positively melancholy, and nothing I could say or do seemed to bring him relief.

Throughout the evening I watched from the corner of my eye as Louella watched me. I felt myself moving as if through a mist—and mist it all was, for with the moment of her arrival Aubrey Bennett had ceased to exist. I wanted only to keep Arabella close to me, to breathe her in, to remember the smell and sight and feel of her, for these hours would likely be the last in which we were the same to each other.

Louella made no attempt to speak to me, nor did I to her. But toward the end of the evening, when I relinquished Arabella for a dance at Harlow's insistence, I saw her staring at me from the edge of the ballroom, near the exit which led to the gardens. Our glances met; she tilted her head ever so slightly at the double doors, and then went through them.

She meant for me to follow her. I picked my way through the crowd, attempting to appear nonchalant, while a hundred waiters accosted me to see if I were in need of anything. Finally I was through the doors, and glimpsed Louella in the shadows of the topiaries.

I approached her leadenly, having no idea what to expect, and then we stood before each other, saying nothing.

"It is really you, then, Aubrey," she whispered, after we had regarded each other for a long moment. She wavered first and then began to cry, and I was speechless, for there was no fury in her gaze, only wonder.

She turned back to me, reached up in the shadows, placed her long hands upon my cheeks, and held my face in them.

The warmth of her palms burned against my skin, which had gone icy.

"Mademoiselle," I finally choked. "You must let me speak with you. You must let me explain—"

She was shaking her head, putting a finger to her lips. "No, no, not now. We cannot talk here. I am staying at Linton, for three days. Where are you staying?"

"Here," I croaked, beside myself. "In the stone guest cottage."

She blinked at me in astonishment, then recovered herself. "I'll meet you there tonight. We've a great deal to say to each other. Go back inside now." Without another word she drew up her skirts, then passed by me to return to the light and warmth of the hall.

I saw him leave the dance floor as Harlow spun me round, and only then did I look about and realize I could not find Louella. A few minutes later she entered from the same place where I'd seen Aubrey heading.

I must be imagining things. It simply cannot be that he went to have some private word with her out upon the lawns. But what else could I conclude?

The party broke up late in the evening. Richard and I thanked Mrs. Beckwith, and Richard bowed low to Caroline, whose single waltz with him appeared to have left him more smitten than ever; Caroline was polite, if amusedly so, to him. And I said good night to Harlow, and then to Louella, and we made arrangements to meet the following day for luncheon, so that we might have a more relaxed visit. I welcomed her home, and hugged her fervently, but again there seemed something so odd in the air. I noticed Caroline watching us, and Aubrey too.

"I will see you to your carriage," Aubrey said stiffly.

"All right," I agreed, although I wished only to be home, with the oddity of the evening behind me.

I sent Richard, grumbling, on ahead. When he was safely in the carriage, Aubrey pulled me off the path and into the manicured shrubbery that lined the house.

There in the shadows, he took me by the shoulders, and without a word, pulled me toward him and kissed me.

He was so much the right person, but it was not the right moment. I flushed as his lips found my own, yet within an instant that sensation was replaced by anxiety, for this was not at all the manner in which I had longed for the exchange to happen. Every day since meeting him had I dreamed of what it would be like to kiss that mouth, and yet here we were, and everything about it felt wrong. The evening preceding it, Louella's appearance, and the strange doings which seemed to have been provoked by it—all of it, wrong. Even his air as he held me—wrong. For he should have been happy, overjoyed, lost in me as I'd wished to be in him, but I could sense through his very fingertips some sort of dread, a sadness that chilled me to the core.

He stepped back, and regarded me with a desperation I'd never seen upon his face. "What is it," I asked, but he shook his head.

"Nothing. It is nothing. You were unsurpassingly beautiful tonight, Arabella. Go home—good-bye—good night, and sleep well."

He released me and, feeling suddenly ill, I turned and ran toward the waiting carriage.

Once back at my own cottage, I sat in the darkness of the little parlor, a cold dread spreading throughout my limbs and organs. I could taste still upon my lips the sweetness of Arabella's skin; but she had not relished that kiss, had she, had not wanted it. Did not, perhaps, any longer want me. Would not, surely, in another day.

Louella.

It was nearly three o'clock in the morning before I heard the gentle tap at the door. I had left no light burning. I opened the latch and saw her there, hidden in the shadows.

I held the door wide, and she entered. Only when I had led her through the foyer and into the sitting room did I light a lamp.

We chose seats across from each other. I was certain she could hear the sound of my heart, smell the fear upon me, and behind it, the resignation.

"So it's really you, Aubrey," she began, just as she had in the gardens earlier.

I was silent.

"Do you know—I rehearsed for months what I would say if ever this moment arrived, I told it over and over to myself. And it flew from my mind the instant I recognized you. I was pacing the floor for hours before coming here, hoping I could retrieve some of it, and not appear before you overwhelmed and speechless."

Overwhelmed and speechless—yes, I could understand precisely how she felt.

"I could have fainted when I set eyes upon you," she continued. "You've no idea how it shocked me. I thought, no, it can't be, I must be mistaken, but of course I knew it was you, and when Harlow introduced you—you see, I'd been thinking maybe I had mentioned the Beckwiths to you, that perhaps you'd somehow remembered them and sought them out, knowing they might have some word of me, but when I heard you called Aubrey Bennett, I realized you must have found them through some incredible coincidence."

Sought them out? So as to *find* her?

She paused, and I realized she was waiting for me to offer some explanation as to how I'd come to be here, but I remained mute. At length she resumed speaking.

"I thought never to see you again. I looked and looked—everywhere in New Orleans, and I sent out bulletins all along the Railroad to the emancipated States, so that if anyone had helped you, word would get back to me. But I heard nothing, and so I assumed finally that you must have been killed, or run someplace where you would never be found—but here you are."

I finally managed to recover my tongue. "You must let me explain. I am begging you, please at least hear me out before you have me arrested—"

"Arrested?"

"Your mother—" I faltered. "The maid, the girl Lisabeth—"

Her face clouded. "What are you talking about?"

"Is that not why you sought me out, and what you should do if you found me?"

"Good Lord, Aubrey. Is that what you are expecting?"

"I don't know what I expect," I whispered.

Now she raised a hand to her forehead, muttered more to herself than to me, "Good Lord, of course you don't know." She addressed me once again. "Listen now, I must explain this to you right off. There are things you could not have found out, as they happened after you left us. I never blamed you for any part of the deaths in New Orleans. I heard all of the rumors surrounding them after I returned home, but the true story emerged through a thorough investigation."

The true story? "You began an investigation?"

"Yes, of course. Your mother helped me, she was invaluable."

Oh God, *Mama*. So Mama had been alive when Louella arrived home. What "true story" had she helped to uncover after I had departed New Orleans in Thomas's stolen suit?

"Look here, Bree," Louella was saying, "let us start over again. We ought to get this settled between us. Tell me what you know about the death of my mother. Go on, tell it honestly, don't be afraid, and then I will tell you what I learned. We can begin there, and set each other's minds to rest."

I closed my eyes. I would have wished never again to revisit that evening and its misery, but of course this was not to be. Better get to the bottom of all of it now rather than later. This might be my only chance to tell the tale without interruption, it might be the only moment at which Louella or anyone else might be willing to listen.

"You recall Faith," I began.

"Yes. The little maid, the new one."

"She was afraid. Afraid Madame—your mother—would not allow her to travel with us when you returned. It was because of me that she was afraid."

I relayed the facts of Faith's pregnancy, and my callousness toward her, and then all the events leading up to and including the days of Madame Eugenia's illness; and I saw the shadows pass over Louella's face, which I would have spared her had it been possible. And I told her what had happened upon my final evening in the Paxton house, how Faith had confessed to me, how she'd meant to hurt no one. How I'd sought to save her. And failed.

When I finished, she looked up at me and nodded.

"I see. Now let me tell you the things I know, which you do not."

"All right." I could not look at her.

"By the time I arrived back in New Orleans, my mother and Lisabeth had been buried. And David and Cheney were dead."

I jerked my head up. "They are dead?"

"They ran just after the poor child's murder. Your mother confronted them upon the lawn—she had my pistol, and when they saw she meant to use it, they turned tail and fled. Onessa didn't chase them then. She knew you'd been shot, and you were her first concern. She dragged you to the carriage house, and she locked you in, for, as she told me, she feared you might awaken and panic, try to wander off and risk further harm. Then she rode for a doctor. Of course, when she returned, you were gone. She knew you had run, and said it broke her heart, but nonetheless she wanted you to have a head start. So, much as she yearned to see David and Cheney caught, she waited to report them. When she did, though, she blamed them for everything—my mother and Lisabeth, the murdered yellow girl, Adeline and yourself driven off at gunpoint. Lila confirmed her story. The sheriffs believed it, thank God, and arrested the pair in town, somewhere on Dryades, where they were attempting to pass as Creole freemen. They were tried and hanged within two days." How fitting, I thought, and yet I could feel no joy in knowing these two had met the end they'd designed for another.

Louella went on. "Your mother felt this was the only solution which would punish those who had actually done murder, and spare those who were innocent.

"She told me what truly happened, though. And said further that she believed the girl Faith had intended no harm, and had not caused the majority of it. You see, Onessa had searched out the substance fed to my Maman and Lisabeth—she was certain it was no more than a type of ipecac."

"Ipecac! But ipecac is not deadly."

"No. It is not. Yet they'd died, and so we were left with the question of what killed them. Your mother wanted my help in determining this. She said it was important that the members of the household be cleared of wrongdoing, so that no whiff of suspicion would linger on in my mind.

"Your mother was my strength in those days, Bree, I must tell you that. Vivien Dolley was as useless as an infant, my own Maman was gone—but your mother never faltered. Each time I felt myself on the verge of collapse she supported me, each time I found myself without direction she pointed the way for me.

"At any rate, we began an investigation. It was not an easy matter. The city's leadership was in disarray, and no one among our own authorities was the least interested in reopening a matter for which two Negroes had already been tried and executed. It became a question of money, and I was fortunate in that I had the resources to pursue my ends on my own. I hired an apothecary, and a doctor who had arrived with the Federalists, and paid them to advise me. Your mother wrote down every detail she could remember about the illness my Maman had suffered. How wise she was—she had saved everything in their rooms intact, every phial, every bottle, everything in the kitchen and pantry with which they could have come into contact. We went over each item, and gave samples to our investigators.

"We suspected there might have been an infection of some sort. There was a virtual plague of typhus about, which I shall come to presently, and so we needed to rule that out. We asked finally for permission to exhume the bodies at our own expense—that was the hardest for me, I almost hesitated at the last minute. But your mother said I owed it to my Maman to discover the truth, and set her spirit to rest. So I agreed.

"I thought I would go insane from hearing the matter discussed over and over, every hideous detail. But after all of the work had been completed, after everything had been scrutinized and analyzed, the story emerged as to what had happened to them."

"And what was it?" I asked, still wide-eyed.

"They were poisoned."

"But you said Faith—"

"It was not Faith's doing. They were poisoned by arsenic and lead."

"*Arsenic* and *lead*? But where did it come from? Who did this to them?"

"It was a chain of events, one upon the other, which killed them."

I could only stare at her, and wait for her to explain.

"You know how particular my Maman could be, Bree. She was so afraid there would be nothing to eat in New Orleans, that she would become ill from the cooking there after having been so long away from it. She insisted on taking a whole market's worth of food with us when we left France. She even brought her own starter bread, so as to have the same yeast we used in Aix. Do you remember—the trunks upon trunks that day you met us at the pier—" She hesitated, and I saw her breath catch in her chest. "At any rate, she decided that the usual means of packing perishables would never do for us, so she sought out some men to take special pains with the process.

"But these workers—I remember them, hirelings from the docks—they did the job improperly. Or perhaps they'd lied in telling her they knew how to do it at all. They built special casks of wood, to protect the food from vermin. And then they lined the casks." She paused.

"With lead."

"Yes. With lead. And inside they placed parcels, contained not only in china or glass but wrapped in paper, or in cheesecloth. And all about the parcels they stuffed hay as a packing, and in the hay they sprinkled the insecticide, a powdered arsenic. And then they sealed the casks. But not well enough. We did not realize this, for there was very little spoilage, but the end result was that nearly everything was laden with poison. It had seeped into the foodstuffs. Even the wine was fouled, having been improperly corked."

I shuddered, recalling the elaborate dinners arranged upon the arrival of the Paxton ladies, and Madame's insistence on accompanying them with the repellent "dainties" and vintages from overseas—which none of the rest of us could abide.

"It was only by chance that the other members of the household avoided illness. Except for Lisabeth," Louella added. "Lisabeth had always enjoyed mimicking my mother's affectations. No doubt she was eager to turn up her nose at the local fare, and dine upon her mistress's own cuisine. And fancy herself a great lady, pampering her delicate constitution alongside Madame."

I could see shiny silver trails down Louella's cheeks, but she did not sob, merely fell silent. I would have comforted her had I not been busy myself, comprehending this new version of the events which had altered my existence.

At length she resumed. "Your little Faith's ministrations only added insult to injury. The child had put her purgative in the tonic of valerian and mint which Maman liked to drink before bedtime. Adeline must have made it up for her, out of her collection of herbal remedies. The apothecary identified it immediately, just by the smell and the color. Your mother had been right, it was senna mixed with ipecac. It would have caused Maman and Lisabeth a few days' discomfort had they been healthy. But they were already so ill, you see."

"And when they began to sicken," I said slowly, "Madame would eat none of the local food at all. She relied completely on her own supplies, and Lisabeth followed her example."

"So you say. Your mother as well. Which means the emetic only pushed them toward the inevitable. They would have passed anyway, the doctor told me, for by the time they began to feel the effects of the poisons, they had already consumed doses large enough to kill. They would have met the same end at the same time, only—" She faltered. "Only perhaps they would have been spared a measure of pain."

She stopped again to wipe her face.

"But the point, Bree, is that I got to the bottom of the affair. And I do not blame you. Or anyone in the household. Only Cheney and David bore any responsibility, for their part in the murder of that poor little girl."

I was absorbing this when she continued on.

"You may credit your own mother with the triumph of fact over suspicion. And there is something else, too, which you should know. Onessa never stopped searching for you after the night you left. She never stopped hoping to find you alive. We agreed not to depart for Europe until she'd exhausted every avenue of pursuit. Her only thought was for your well-being."

I spoke at last. "She may have convinced you of that, Mademoiselle, but you were misled. More than likely she was relieved to have me gone. I have never been innocent in her eyes, she has assumed the very worst of me from the moment I entered the world. Her last act before I left her was to call me a murderer."

"What do you mean—when did she say such a thing to you?"

"When she came upon us outside in the yard, at the moment when Faith was killed."

"Oh no." She shook her head. "You are mistaken. I don't know what you heard, Bree, but she indicated no such sentiment to me. She knew you had nothing to do with any of it. Not Maman, or Lisabeth, especially not Faith."

She leaned over then, and attempted to rest her hand upon my own. It was the second time this night that she had touched me, and the strangeness of it caused me to flinch. "I know there has long been enmity on your part toward your mother. Let it go, Aubrey. All these draining and rancorous convictions you harbor—let them go. I've had to relinquish so much myself, but it must be done, else you shall be poisoned from within."

I was silent for another long moment.

"But what of you, Miss? Why did you look for me? Why did you do any of it, risk yourself and your mother to come to New Orleans, for a passel of slaves?"

She did not hesitate.

"I would have done for the others anyway. I would have found a means by which to free them and provide for them. But as regards yourself and your family, Bree, I am sure you can guess at what compelled me. I came because I could not leave my own flesh and blood behind."

Her eyes did not waver, they regarded me unblinking, green and luminous in the dim light.

"So. You know all that I know." I turned away. Wished never to meet that level gaze again.

"Yes. I do."

I pulled farther still from her, fixed myself in a rigid posture where I would not be forced to confront the sight of her as she spoke.

"I know—" Louella began, but I thrust an arm out toward her, as if to ward off her words.

"Please, wait," I whispered.

She began again after a few moments, gentle and insistent. "I know what you know. Although I am certain you realized it before I did myself. I believe I had always suspected, but when Onessa wrote to my father to tell him of the danger all of you were in, I felt I could push it to the back of my mind no longer.

"I confronted my father. He confirmed in so many words that it was true, although he would not speak of it in any detail. And I realized then someone must come for you.

"I determined I would not bring the issue to light until we were all safely away from New Orleans, and able to discuss it calmly. But when I returned to the city house after seeing to our family's affairs, and found the situation as it was, I wondered if I would ever have the chance to right things. There was no sense in holding back at that point.

"So I revealed to Onessa what I'd gleaned from my father, and drew the entire tale from her. She told me you suspected as well, that regretfully the hiding of it had been an issue between yourself and her and her own mother, Evangeline, for most of your life, though she had desired only to protect you."

Regretfully? Protect me? I felt my stomach heave. Mama should live to know the meaning of regret. To bear witness to what her *protection* had wrought. I took a breath to calm myself, and forced my concentration back upon Louella.

"How could you stand even the sight of us," I asked her. "How could your mother agree to return for us?"

"Maman never suspected a thing. And even if she had known, why in the world would she have held it against you?"

"Not against me, perhaps. But my mother."

"But your mother was an innocent girl. Had Maman known, I am certain she would have agreed with me, that you both deserved our acknowledgment and our compassion. If there is to be ill-feeling, I should imagine it would be on the part of your family against mine, not the other way round. It was we who allowed our own kin to be enslaved in our household, after all."

How many times had I told myself exactly this; yet the sentiment, coming from Louella, seemed unfathomable, utterly out of place.

I did not question her further, however. This was not the time, and I did not wish to delve into any more detail, for both her sake and my own.

"So you came to rescue your brother" was what I finally managed to say.

She gave a harsh, sour little laugh. "Yes, I suppose you could describe it that way, although that's not exactly accurate—it doesn't do justice to the complexity of the situation, does it?"

"No. It surely does not."

She was leaning toward me, her voice urgent; I thought she might touch me again. "Listen to me, Bree—I know how it must strike you, hearing all of these things at once. We've suffered, we've both sustained losses. But we have also gained, because we are reunited under different circumstances. As a family."

"A *family*?" I could not hide my incredulity. "Who—you and Thomas and your father, and me and my relations, all gathered round the table for Christmas dinner? Forgive me my tone, but is that how you see it? Can you believe for a moment that anyone else under your roof will be anxious to claim my kinship?"

"Don't mock me, Aubrey. Do not force me away, or think it so far-fetched. You shall sit at *my* table. You shall be *my* family." She was fierce. "I am not naive, but neither shall I be tethered to conventions I abhor. When the war is won by the Unionists—and they will win, it is only a matter of time—then the notions which divide us shall be dead."

"Oh, I doubt they shall ever be dead."

"They are dead to me already. There are amends to be made, and I must begin with my own flesh and blood. It won't be difficult, as I already feel great love for them."

It made me writhe to hear this. I was so long used to my anger, to my carefully honed sense of injustice, that I did not know how to discard it in the face of Louella's insistence.

"You know, Bree, I love Thomas because he is my kin, the product of the same parents, and because I grew up alongside him. But were I to meet him today, without that connexion, I cannot say I would like him much, or choose to know him. We have little in common in terms of our ideas. I believe he has retreated into callowness and bluster in order to maintain a false picture of our history, and this makes it impossible for me to share my thoughts with him.

"Whereas you have been always of the same bent as myself—I saw it in your character long ago, and I doubt you have changed so very much. You have always been more the kin of my heart than Thomas, Bree. I defy you to deny that you thought of me the same way."

I looked at her. And in her face I saw, as I had from the day of her return to New Orleans, the irrefutable proof of our connexion, the one she now so shocked me by acknowledging.

"I cannot deny that," I said in answer to her question. And why would I wish to? Let it go, she had said, and I thought, indeed, that perhaps it was possible to let this portion of it go. I reached for her hand of my own accord, amazing myself, and then she wound her fingers about mine, held them fast.

Awkward as it was, we were reluctant to separate, to let the emotion of the moment dissipate. But it was so new to both of us, and we needed time, I think, to regard it separately.

At length we released each other, and then Louella said softly, "Now you must tell me, Bree—how did you come to be here? How on earth did you find these people—Harlow and Caroline Beckwith, and Arabella Leeds?"

I was relieved, I admit, to turn my attentions from all which had been revealed to me to a history more recent. "I did not find them. I suppose you could say they found me. Or Arabella Leeds did."

"Tell me," she said, and so I did tell it, the whole story from the moment I'd left the Paxton house to the moment earlier that night when I had turned to find her over my shoulder. I was brief; it was only the time since my arrival in England which I wished to dwell on at any length, for it was only here that I could find happy events to relate to her.

She listened, openmouthed, interrupting me to ask a question or two. And when finally I reached the end of my tale, she sat back and regarded me. "Providence is an odd thing."

I smiled a little at her. "Yes, indeed."

After a moment she said, "There is a great deal between you and Miss Leeds, isn't there."

I colored. "Yes. There is. Do you disapprove?"

"Do you mean on account of your heritage, and hers? No. I understand why you fear I would, but I should be the greatest of hypocrites if I did, don't you think?"

I shook my head. "It's almost certainly ended now. One way or another. It was founded upon deceit, and as such must end."

"But why?"

"It was my first thought when I glimpsed you: that it was time for me to be revealed as the liar I am, that you were here to undo me, so I might as well shake Arabella's hand and bid her farewell that very second, since she was already lost to me. But even if you shan't be the means of my undoing, I cannot go on this way. I cannot go on deceiving her, or any of these people, and I cannot ask you to conspire in my lies and cover up for me."

"I will say nothing without your permission," Louella said. "But I must tell you, in my opinion you would be wise to spill everything. I do not think you should consider Arabella lost—I took to her as quickly as you did yourself, for she's possessed of a remarkable and flexible mind. I cannot lie to you—it doesn't follow that things would go easily between the two of you if you attempt to court—but I am near certain Arabella will not turn from you based upon your background."

"I would like to believe that."

"Then do. But by all means, right things quickly. If anyone else learns of what we know before she does, the consequences, for her, could be dire. You are putting her at risk by keeping from her the knowledge that would allow her to protect herself, to make her own decisions where you are concerned. Make a clean breast of it, and let her appreciate your honesty. Do not toy with her any further."

I could not help myself; I thought of Faith, of what had come of that toying which Mama had lectured me so severely upon. I brought my fingertips to my eyes, dropped my head upon my arms.

"My advice has disturbed you."

"No. I was reminded of something else."

After a long while, I raised my head. "Faith and her child," I said, "they died for no reason."

"They did."

I stared off into the darkness, at nothing.

Eventually Louella said, "I cannot redeem their deaths, Aubrey, or ascribe purpose to them. They were needless. As were my mother's, and the maid's—"

She paused for a moment.

"—and all the other deaths as well."

All the others?

I realized she had spoken the phrase deliberately. And knew from the heaviness of the pause between us that she had left it up to me to determine whether I should catch it, so that it might provide the entrée into something she'd meant to impart all evening.

And I suspected too what that thing might be, for throughout the night I had listened with one ear for the mention of other names, vital ones, which should have been central in the recounting of histories, being central in my affections, but were conspicuously absent.

"What others?" I asked, because I knew it was time, the question must be put, though I prayed to be spared an answer.

Louella was not looking at me. She was looking out of the windows, where a chill breeze shook the budding branches of the trees overhead in the darkness. "It is so late, Aubrey. I needn't continue."

"No, go on now."

"There was typhus," she said.

"Yes, you mentioned it."

"I am sure you've already guessed this, but your mother is alive, Bree. She returned to Provence with me when I left. So did Lila."

Again she waited.

Ah, God, do not stop there, with only those names spoken.

"It struck hardest at the Old House, at all the lowland plantations in fact, perhaps because of where it originated. And it hit the older people and the weak ones worst."

No.

"Amos did not survive it, Aubrey. Neither did Evangeline."

No. No. No.

The woman ya think of, she dead. Little pup.

I was falling from the chair; the room threatened to tilt, perhaps the whole house was moving, capsizing, like the *Artemis* upon a rough sea.

I felt her hand covering my own once more.

"I am so sorry, Bree."

And so it was that I found it out, Gran, that I was informed at last of what had become of you.

All of these many years, from the day Mama and I departed your cabin up to this very wretched second, I had pictured you there, in the warmth of your home among your homely objects, securing me fast to my own vision of a future. That picture had been more tangible to me than any photograph, had loomed in my mind's eye as religious icons do in other minds.

For you were the example I called upon to remind myself that love could exist and aim itself at me, pure and unqualified, and be moved by my own affection in return.

Your letters to me had confirmed that our bond would endure, despite our lack of contact. So had I drawn our connexion round and into me, felt it pure and pervasive as air—a resource to inhale at will, which would bring us into lightheaded, happy communion.

And so too had I forced from my mind the ominous words of the vodou priestess, and their worst interpretation. For such a thing could never be: that the air itself could be drawn from the earth without catastrophic effect, without fanfare, without my knowing or feeling it. Had I lost you, I thought, there would have been some signal sent to body or mind: a crushing pain, an epic nightmare striking at the moment you breathed your last, something which would let me *know* it.

Yet in a few sentences I was given to find that there had been nothing. Disease had ravaged you as though you were ordinary flesh, and had made no warning so that I might save you from it. I'd had not time to race to your side, to offer you my comfort as you have been mine. I had not even the solace of a farewell. Instead you are turned to dust and decay, even as I lay picturing you still vibrantly alive.

So that all these months of waiting, of believing that every moment I endured would be survivable because I would tell you about it upon our joyous reunion, had been for naught.

For naught, that was my first thought.

I would awaken every day from this day hence to the realization of your absence. Dead today, you would be dead a day longer tomorrow. For all the tomorrows to come. And in your absence, the bitter facts of my life were not merely bitter but rendered meaningless.

Yet I could not cry.

I was certain I would, and so I turned from Louella as the shock in the depths of me became a stranglehold at my throat. I encouraged it, longed for the release in that instant, waited to be borne away upon it, so that I might express some degree of my desolation.

But it was a strange thing, that I could not cry, because I could not feel the fact of your absence to be true.

As I struggled for tears, I thought: it was not for naught that I held you so close to me. I could not believe that. And although I have accepted that I shall never behold you again upon this earth, never feel your arms about me, or the unquestioning fervor of your love envelop me, I still do not believe it.

For I feel you near me yet. Watching me, hearing me, guiding my steps. You are, as much as the air still is. In what manner you survive I cannot know, but I can trust without knowing.

And perhaps that is what is behind the outrageous twist my fortunes took: it was you, Gran, reaching to turn me a bit this way, a little that, so that I might walk into safety and happiness seemingly by accident.

That is what I believe, and that is why it is still to you that I address my thoughts, dedicate my acts, lift my eyes. Still to you, Gran. Wherever you surely are.

Presently Louella spoke, from behind my shoulder. "All night I have looked for the words to tell you this, and dreaded speaking them. For your mother and I discussed at length the feeling you and Evangeline sustained for each other, though I had never guessed at it til then. I know this cannot take the pain of it away, Bree, but I can tell you that your mother and your grandmother were reconciled before she died. Your mother cared for her, she cared for Amos, for the sick ones at the Old House. She risked her life, Aubrey—"

"Who told you that?" I asked, straining to resume my place in the present moment. "Did my mother tell you that herself?"

"Not only her. Lila too. Lila was with her. They both behaved as heroines, when all around them the ill were abandoned by their own families."

I nodded. There was no point in arguing, what did it matter. Mama the heroine. Mama the Valiant. According to—Mama. What did it matter. It was important only for the comfort it might have given you, Gran. Let Mama have her accolades, so long as a scintilla of it was true: that she attended to you, provided you with some modicum of peace and solace as you lay ill, and as you died.

With that thought came at last the tears I'd expected. I wiped at them with my fingers, but it was no good, I could not hold them back. They became a torrent which forced me to yield. I felt Louella press her handkerchief into my hand, and I put it to my face, but the sweet scent of it only pained me further. Ashamed I was, and so I remained turned away, but even shame failed me eventually, for it seemed trite and unsuitable in the face of my grief.

I lay upon the arm of my seat, my face pressed to the windowpane, my cheek sliding against the cool glass. Presently my own numb hand recognized Louella's warm one covering it still, as it had all this time. I made no attempt to pull it away, but rather sought to draw some solace from her, so that I might calm myself.

When the worst of it had passed I fell back against the cushions, and only then gently removed my fingers from beneath hers. We sat so, beside each other in silence, until Louella broke it by saying again, in the quietest tone, "I am so sorry, Bree. Tell me what I may do for you, how I may console you."

"There is nothing I would ask of you now. Only that this miserable night be over."

I realized upon saying this that I was to be granted my wish, for it was night no longer. The sky was brightening, and in an hour it would be fully morning. I was exhausted beyond all telling.

"I understand," Louella had replied. She rose, and moved the heavy drape aside, observed for herself the coming sunrise. I took the long moments she spent at the window to recover myself: I wiped my face, brushed damp strands of hair from it, folded her wet handkerchief neatly. When she turned round to me once more she said, "I shall leave you now, although it pains me. I ought be back abed before my absence is noticed. But should you need anything, do not hesitate to call upon me."

I rose stiffly to see her to the door. When we reached it, she turned once again. "Will you be all right, left to yourself?"

"Yes. You mustn't be concerned."

"What shall you do from here, then?"

I shook my head. "I've no idea."

"Remember what I said of Miss Leeds, Bree. She may be a great comfort to you now, if you deal with her fairly."

"I shall," I replied, and meant it. I would not put Arabella aside. For far from paling in light of the blow I had been dealt regarding you, Gran, my connexion to Arabella now shone more vital than ever. Only she might possibly replace just a little of that consuming affection I'd lost with you, which I yearned to give and receive once more. It was a matter of even greater import that I reveal myself to her as Louella had suggested, so as to see whether such a happiness could lay before me.

"I shall take all you said to heart. And I would wish, Miss—" I began, but she stopped me.

"Louella. I am Louella to you, Bree, not 'Miss' ever again."

"I would like very much—Louella—to see you before you go. But I don't feel I can be in Arabella's company, or in the Beckwiths', until I've cleared the air. Perhaps we could meet alone at some point."

"Of course we could. But tell me, why do you not speak to Arabella immediately—and then when I leave here, in a few days, you can come with me. Back to France."

I startled, my hand rattling the doorknob it held. "Back to France? With you? In a few days?"

"Not for good, of course. But it is time, I believe, for us to resolve all of this. Your mother is in Provence. So is my father. And Thomas, having taken a leave of absence from school. It is time to have it out, and over with. Come back with me."

My mouth was dry. I shook my head: "I cannot—that is, a few days is not—" Just the thought of it filled me with the most abject terror. Face Mama? And Paxton, and Thomas—upon the heels of the news of your death— *Too much, too much*, my mind screamed, and I shook my head harder. "I cannot. Don't ask me, Louella, not just yet. Not now."

"All right," she said. "I shall leave you the instructions for finding us, though. And I shall see you again, before I go, in some capacity."

I nodded. She reached up, placed a kiss upon my cheek, grasped my hands to squeeze them. "Good night, Bree. Try and sleep. For whatever it can mean to you, remember, you are not alone in this. Your sister awaits you, whenever you are ready to claim her."

My eyes clouded once more. I felt myself on the verge of becoming mawkish, so I murmured, "Thank you," and bent to kiss her swiftly upon the cheek, then withdrew inside.

APRIL 20, 1863

I was unable to sleep for even an hour last night. I lay stiff upon the mattress, sat by the window as the first light was dawning, and rose with a pall of misery about me. This yielded to an anxious anticipation, for today I was to meet Caroline and Harlow and Louella—and Bree—for luncheon. I assumed that whatever strange ill feeling had manifested itself in the previous night would be resolved in the light of day, one way or another.

But when I arrived at Linton, it was to discover that Aubrey would not be joining us, in fact was not even about.

"Damnedest thing—I went to rouse him this morning, and he'd already gone," Harlow said, bewildered. "He left a note—said he had something urgent to see to in Stepney, and asked me to give you his apologies." My stomach—already sick from the night's alcoholic revelry and the lack of sleep—twisted further, for I could only believe that here was undeniable proof of some bizarre and monumental shift in his regard for me.

"Oh, he asked me to give you this, Berry," Harlow said, as an afterthought, handing me a piece of paper.

I unfurled it under the table, my hand shaking as I did so.

Lovely Berry-not-Bella, will you meet me beneath the Oriental temple at the entrance to the Cremorne Gardens, tomorrow at three o'clock. There is something I must talk to you about. Send your reply through Harlow. Yours ever, Bree.

Here it was, then. The *something* I had been sensing, and dreading, from the first. I wadded the note into a ball, and stuffed it into my bag.

Louella appeared at table, looking quite wan but cheerful; now, of course, it was time to visit at length. She was asked questions, and all of those things which had been broached lightly the previous evening were discussed in depth. Except for the death of her mother. The servant girl, the poisoned food, the pointlessness of it—we had all got the full story of that through her later letters, and there was no need to go over those sad facts again.

And of course there was no mention of her having met Harlow's young tutor, or of what she might have needed to say to him in the gardens beyond the earshot of the other company.

Harlow practically bent backwards over himself trying to see to her every possible whim before she troubled to express it. Caroline and Mrs. Beckwith alternately beamed and clucked over her, passing her plate after plate of food and commenting on how thin she'd become, and how she must build up her strength.

And I sat beside her feeling positively tortured, for although I should have been celebrating her return to us, which I had so eagerly awaited, I could only study her whilst thinking miserably, *What have you done, this has all to do with you, and what can I make of Aubrey and his strange note, and why is he not here?*

I lay down upon my bed and waited to be delivered from my torment by sleep, but of course this is precisely the sort of moment when that mystical state proves most elusive. I shut my eyes, but my mind refused to quiet itself; I was unaware for some time that I was crying again, but when I realized it, I made no attempt to stop. I feel I've cried more in two years than any man can by rights do over a lifetime and still call himself a man, but what does it matter? There was no one there to see it, and it was the only comfort I could afford myself.

I knew I could not remain there, in the curtained bedroom, with the dirty dawn searching me out. I was due to lunch in a few hours with the Beckwiths, Louella and Arabella, just like a gentleman, thank you, and knew that I could not do this, either. So I arose and bathed, changed quickly, and left a note for Harlow, stating with regret that I had business to attend to in Stepney which I'd just recalled, and could not join them.

And I enclosed a note for Arabella, asking her to meet me tomorrow at Cremorne Gardens, whereupon I shall tell her all of it. Then I rushed from the cottage before I could change my mind and tear the second note to pieces.

I decided I really would go to Stepney. It was true I owed to Ibrahim and Oha the courtesy of a visit nearly a month after I'd promised to make one, but this was hardly why I undertook the journey at that precise moment. I dreaded approaching the dockside territory again, but I dreaded more what was behind and ahead of me, and wanted desperately to be as far away from Linton, from the genteel neighborhoods which were not my own, as possible. The misery of Stepney, I thought, would be a fitting counterpoint to my own abject misery. It would be a safe place for me to hide, to abandon myself to my melancholy without need of pretense or fear of notice.

Let me tell you about it, Gran, and that shall make it all easier to bear, I thought, as I always do while I narrate my day, filter the world through your forgiving eyes.

I shall when we next meet—and then I caught myself, and the shock of it, the unfairness, brought me to tears that morning, and a hundred times that day, as it's likely to do for a hundred thousand days to come.

But I called upon you anyway. For I know you were beside me as I sought out the coach, and viewed the city coming into focus and then falling in upon itself, into the warrens and rookeries of the slums, while my own black thoughts likewise drew in upon themselves.

At length I pulled up before the lodging house and paid the driver, and was accosted by the usual little mob which, mistaking me for a swell, was determined to beg every last penny off me. I pushed through them, and through the inevitable Chinese screamers, and used the key I had not returned to open the front door. Then I proceeded to the third floor, came first upon Ibrahim's room, and knocked at it.

The door opened a crack, and a greasy, toothless Englishman somewhere in his middle age stuck his head out. "Oo 'r you, then," he snapped at me.

"Where is the black gentleman," I sputtered, "the one who resides here?"

"*I* reside here. There ent no 'black gennelman.' "

"You? When did you take the room over? Are you sharing it, or letting it from a Negro?"

"I'm lettin it fair an square from the landlady, an if there was a nigger hereabouts, I'd know it. Now get off with ye."

"But could you tell me—"

"Fuck off," the man snarled, and the door slammed in my face.

I knocked next upon Oha's door, and this time found myself face-to-face with a slatternly, worn-looking girl of seventeen or so. She stood on the threshold and peered at me, her lips compressed into a hard line. In the tiny space behind her I could make out the shapes and sounds of several small children. "I ain't no gay," she snapped, before I could open my mouth. "You're lookin for a poke, try elsewheres. I'm an honest girl, I am."

"I am not looking for a woman," I sighed. "I am looking for the man whose room this was. A big blonde man, a Norwegian. Sven Oha."

The girl's expression did not change. "I ain't knowing nothing about no men. This 'ere's my room, mine an them what's with me. Has been for a week, an before that I ain't knowing nothing."

"Thank you," I said quietly. She retreated inside without replying.

I did not have to knock at Aurelio's door. The moment I turned, I saw a shabby man and woman emerge from the room and lock it up behind them, giving me to know that Aurelio, too, had moved on.

I made my way, dejected, to the first floor. The landlady, Belfast Kate, lived there, in the back apartments. Perhaps she could tell me what had become of Ibrahim.

I had been a bit frightened of the landlady from the first. She was a huge, squat woman who claimed to be "handy with me mauleys," and indeed I suspected that a punch from her meaty fists would have knocked the breath out of even Oha. But she had always had a soft spot in her heart for Ibrahim, who was a steady customer, and brought other paying tenants with him as well. She kept a decent house compared to some; there were rooms with doors, at least on two floors, and adequate beds, few bugs, and a privy, instead of the common gutter in use in the alleyway. I knocked at her door, and waited through the panting and scraping sounds which told me she was answering.

"Oh, it's you, then!" she huffed upon seeing me. "Well, yer too late, I let yer room already, since I ain't 'eard a word from you. Ye ain't gettin your rent back, you paid on it, and ain't my problem you weren't 'ere. And don't be thinkin a usin your key to burgle neither, I'll know it were you, and I'll track ye down, sure enough—"

"No, no," I interrupted her, "I don't need the room anymore. You may have the key." I took it from my pocket and handed it to her. She whisked it out of sight quickly, looking surprised. "I only wished to inquire—where is Ibrahim, the black man, you know who he is—and where is Sven Oha, the big blonde who was our friend?"

"Ibrahim is shipped out, kiddy. Left amost a fortnight ago. And the other one, that big one, he lit out a week ago, just walked off with 'is bag and the little bloke, the Spaniard."

"But where did they go?"

"Ibrahim's off to Portugal, I 'eerd him say it. Ain't knowin where the others got to."

"Did they leave any word for me? Anything at all?"

She shrugged. "Not 'ere they didn't. But then, why would they, seein as you ain't been about, is you?"

No. I hadn't been about. I had not returned, hadn't visited, hadn't had even the decency to send a note. Why should I be surprised that they had left without a word to me?

"If it 'elp ye any, the big one, he's still abouts in London, I 'eerd him tell the Spaniard they'd be best off lookin fer work farther in the west."

"Thank you."

I retraced my steps through the dingy building. I had half-thought, upon arriving here, that I might let another room for myself, that I would run from the tantalizing promise of Arabella, the havoc wrought by Louella's presence and all she'd confronted me with. I would disappear back into the morass which had swallowed me once, ship out with Ibrahim, forget the Paxtons for good, declare myself through with all of it.

I had known even as I fantasized that I would not do it. I am too much spoiled, too desperate for comfort, to throw it away twice. But I had not expected to have the choice made so finally for me, to find my friends departed, no shred of my nameless existence among the underclass left me.

There was no place left to go except back to that beautiful universe where everything most desired and most dreadful awaits me.

APRIL 21, 1863

I dressed slowly today, taking great pains with my costume. I wished to be at my best even if I were about to have my heart yanked from my chest and stomped upon.

I wondered if perhaps she would not appear, but at three o'clock I ran up toward the Garden entrance and spotted her before I'd come within a hundred yards of her. She was dressed in green-striped silk and carried a parasol, and the freshness of her, the splendor, even at that distance, made me despair, for how could I bear to lose it? I cringed at the lack of care I'd taken with myself. I was at least clean and in decent clothes, but not shaven; and my hair, which I've not cut properly since arriving here, was flying about my face, since I had neglected to tie it back.

Suddenly self-conscious, I slowed my pace, and approached her at a walk. She was turned in the other direction, looking for me no doubt, and jumped back with a little "Oh!" when I touched her upon the arm.

"Arabella," I said.

"Hello, Bree."

How I hated the sudden awkwardness between us, the stiffness which made us peek out at each other, instead of boldly seeking each other's eyes, as we had done throughout the month previously.

He looked tired, disheveled even, and it occurred to me that whatever mission he'd undertaken yesterday, it must not have been a pleasant one. Yet he also had about him that exotic air which I'd found so compelling upon first setting eyes on him, and I could not wrench my gaze away.

I was searching as well for any clue as to what he was about to say. But his eyes—his general appearance—told me nothing, beyond the obvious fact that he was in some great distress.

"I am so glad you came," I said.

"Did you think I would not?"

"I wasn't certain. I know—" I was about to tell her I knew she was disappointed in me of late, that I had been acting strangely over the last two days; but as this would segue directly into what I wished to say to her, I stopped myself, and suggested we find a more private place in which to talk.

I took her by the hand with some trepidation, wondering whether she would allow this, but she did, and so I led her away from the crowded thoroughfares, away from the kiosks and the menagerie, where there were so many strollers and young people such as ourselves. We found an isolated spot beneath the elms, and sat down upon the soft grass. Nobody was about here; the picnickers had packed up in order to get an early start upon their suppers, and the shadier denizens of the Gardens had not yet made their after-dusk appearances.

We did not look at each other for a few moments. Then she raised her head to me—always forthright, Miss Arabella—and said, "Well. What is it you wish to speak to me about? It's to do with Louella Paxton, isn't it?"

"No—yes—but only some of it—" I stammered, taken aback for the dozenth time by her frankness.

There was no point in dragging it out; we might as well get to it, I thought. And he must have agreed with me, for he turned, and drew in a deep breath.

"I believe I am falling in love with you," I said miserably.

It was not what I'd intended to begin with. At all. I saw her eyes widen.

"I—" she began, and I did not know whether she meant to dissuade me or encourage me, but I bade her stop before she said another word.

"Please—let me go on to the end, for if you interrupt me, I shall never reach it."

"There's *more*?"

Oh believe me, yes. "Yes, there's more."

She sat stock-still, and I collected myself.

"Because of my feelings—because of how I feel about you—how I think I feel, given that I haven't had much experience in feeling what I think I feel toward you—"

Step back, you idiot. You are confusing even yourself.

"Let me start over again." I took another deep breath. "There are things I haven't told you about myself. Not because I wished to deceive you, but because I was afraid of what you would think of me. But because of what I feel toward you, I want to say them now. I want to believe that you share my affection, but you may not when I've done, and I won't try to influence you. It shall be up to you to decide what to make of any of it, and I shall hold you completely blameless if you decide you cannot any longer trust me or associate with me."

She was still staring at me, in that rapt, attentive attitude.

Take a breath. Don't look at her or you won't say it.

Plunge in.

"I am a Negro."

Silence. I wondered whether she'd heard me.

"I beg your pardon?"

"I said, I am a Negro."

"A Negro?" She furrowed her white brow. "Is that some sort of club, some alliance I've not heard of?"

"What—no—a *Negro*. Arabella—I know perfectly well that you know what a Negro is."

"You mean a *Negro*? As in an *African* person?" She was staring at me now as if I'd lost my mind. "You believe you are a *Negro*?" She frowned at me. "Is this some sort of joke?"

"No. It is not a joke. I realize I don't look the part particularly, but I am not insane, nor am I playing with you."

I was too shocked to do anything but stare, and perhaps that was a good thing, for as he'd said, he might not have gone on had I spoken.

"Please hear me out. Do you know what an 'octoroon' is?"

She nodded dumbly.

"That is what I am. An eighth Negro. It seems irrelevant in England, thousands of miles away from home, it seems silly to contemplate it when I am with you, when I am amidst the Beckwiths, but it was not irrelevant where I was born and raised." Go on. Keep going, don't let yourself think about it. "Back there, I was believed—erroneously—to be in possession of even more black blood. A quadroon, one fourth of me Negro. Enough to ensure that I would be enslaved."

No. He was not joking. No one would joke about such a thing. We were in the midst of the outdoors, yet I felt there was not enough air for me to breathe.

"I was a slave in Louisiana."

I felt myself some sort of awful executioner, every word of mine a blow sure to cause her the greatest distress, til I delivered the final one. I wondered how fast I could do it, get it all out, so as to be mercifully quick.

"My name is not Aubrey Bennett. It is Aubrey Paxton." She gasped; I ran on, seeking to finish it while she was still numb and reeling. "You asked me if any of this had to do with Louella, and it does for that reason, because I know her—more than know her, I share her name, you can guess the rest of it—her family owned mine, my grandmother, my mother and me, and in fact I am related to her, for her father is my own."

There.

I had done it.

I could safely pass the game to her, wait for her reaction. It was so hard not to rush on, not to beg for understanding and clemency, but I felt I ought to let her set the pace just then.

She had not moved a muscle, and did not for a full minute. Gradually her eyes resumed their normal proportions, and she trained them on a spot directly in front of her.

I had feared that she might simply get up and leave. Or slap me, or scream, and then run away. I was thoroughly amazed that she'd done none of these things. But then she began to giggle.

Please, please don't accuse me again of joking, don't make me convince you I am not. I watched her, speechless, as she put a hand to her mouth as if to suppress her mirth.

"Do you know what I thought?" she asked when her laughter had subsided a bit.

"No."

"I thought perhaps that Louella was a lover or an enemy from your distant past, or that you were some sort of lunatic who goes about falling for girls at first sight, and were instantly smitten by her. I thought that was what you'd asked me here to tell me." She gave me a small smile. "But none of those things come close to the story, do they?"

"No," I said. "They don't."

Abruptly she stopped smiling. "And you haven't given me much of that story, either. Just the barest bones. Isn't that the truth?"

She shifted round to face me.

"I want you to tell me everything, Aubrey. Everything about how you came to be here."

I balked; she could see it, and continued. "You have put into my head a completely new picture of who you are. Actually it is the only one I have, except for the opinion I'd formed as to your character in the present moment, for I knew so little of your past. As long as we've reached this juncture, you may as well make a clean breast of it, Bree, and tell me all of it now."

"All of it."

"Of what is important, yes. What is there for you to lose? Tell me—I want to understand it. If I am to consider you in a different light, you owe it to me to give me the details to be considered. In other words, all of it."

She made a case for the idea. But the thought of actually doing it made me recoil. There was no use attempting to hide anything, though—much of it she knew through Louella, and what she did not she would only ask about at some point. If I wished to climb out from beneath the pall of dishonesty I'd cast over myself, if I wished her to remain even civil to me in light of what I'd revealed myself to be, had I not better take the opportunity, as I had with Louella, to tell my history as I might want it told?

Besides—I had to admit it—there was a portion of me which wondered what it would be like to be naked before judgment, a known quantity, whether an accepted or rejected one, after such a long period of subterfuge.

I would need more than a deep breath this time. I thought wistfully of a glass of beer, a draught of morphine, but those comforts are temporary, and besides were not to be had here. I would have to content myself with the abundant air alone.

I fixed my eye on a point well past us, where a blonde girl in pigtails romped with a little dog upon a lead. "My great-grandparents were the bought servants of the Paxton family," I began.

So there they were, the dread secrets, revealed at last—and as I'd thought, offensive to the mind of the bearer, but only pitiful to that of the listener.

No police chase him.

There is no abandoned female, no trail of wanton conquests.

None of that.

I was hard put to keep my wits about me and contain my reactions, for to have it before me was so much a relief and yet so much worse—for him—than I had imagined.

It came to me in a new and poignant manner: the nature of the war at home.

What did I know of it—I'd met, in New Parrish, exactly one person of mixed race: Mrs. Audrey Stanton's little maid Christina, who happened, like Bree, to be an "octoroon." I had never questioned how she might have come by that remarkable heritage, or why it should have been common knowledge among the townspeople although the girl herself appeared as white-skinned as I. And I'd had not the slightest inkling what the term had bequeathed her—it was only a word, something people knew of her, as they knew I was the daughter of Harrison and Charlotte Leeds. Yet how could I have escaped the knowledge that *octoroon* was the reason why white-skinned Christina was condemned to a life amidst dirty laundry and the beatings of her mistress, while white-skinned Arabella was to dance at cotillions?

But it became clear now as Aubrey spoke. His words were an incantation which removed me from the noisy Gardens, from the district of Chelsea in London, England, and flew me back to the sanguine and genteel city of New Orleans, which I have never seen in my life. Finally I could behold his boyhood, and what a difference that makes in the knowing of any person or circumstance, to connect what you've learned of them with where it must have come from.

At some points I wanted to laugh, at others to put my face in my hands and apologize, as if I'd had to do with any of it. But mostly I was wide-eyed, set down to wander amidst an unimagined, alien landscape. And at the last I was rendered speechless, for when he reached the story of the word on his arm, I found there was nothing I could say that might adequately express my feelings.

I should have been compelled in any case by the subject of the girl who'd known my beloved before me. She could provide a window to his past, whether remembered with fondness or venom. But this story was different, and so too was the young woman, called Faith. She reached past idle curiosity to touch me to the quick. I recalled her death through Louella's description of her mother's passing, and moved through that history as through a terrible morphia dream, arriving damaged but alive on the far shore of the tale, as Aubrey himself had. He seemed a thousand miles away, staggering beneath these needless burdens, and I wondered how he'd managed to crawl out from under them long enough to engage me, to take pleasure in my presence.

When he told me what he'd learnt only two nights ago, I was tempted to cry, *Enough!* For I'd come in a few hours to feel for the characters of his life's drama. To discover the loss of his grandmother, to see upon his face what it had wrought within him, was an intolerable injustice. Only

Louella's acceptance of him lifted my spirits somewhat—and I recalled the second instance in which I'd sold her short, my discomfort at table with her the previous day. *I am sorry, Louella,* I said to her, wherever she was so that, as usual, she could not hear me.

But mostly I was sorry for him, sorry beyond words for his life, and for his reluctance to tell me of it. Sorry I could change none of it, and served only to complicate it further. But "sorry" did not begin to help.

I saw it upon her face, that she was sorry for me. And this disturbed me, for I had not meant to play upon her sympathies, however preferable that might have been to engaging her anger. I cannot bear to be the object of her pity when I'd hoped to be the object of her passion. I knew I'd had my chance at explanations, that she had listened well and closely to every word I'd spoken, that I had now to place my trust in her character. So I endeavored to come to an end, that her concentration might be diverted away from sympathy for me, and back onto the question of what my revelations would mean to her, and to us.

The one point of view which I had thus far neglected was my own. As Aubrey drew at last toward the close of his story—it was pitch-black, the supper hour long since past, the Gardens filling with its nighttime players—I knew I should have to consider it: what was I to do with any of this? How was I to fit it—and him—into the place I presently inhabited? It was all too astonishing, too rich with repercussions, to be digested in a sitting.

Were I to love him now, it would have to be completely, knowing all I knew and anticipating that others should come to know it, and that once it were revealed, it would affect me irrevocably.

How romantic a notion it would have been to throw myself forward without consideration—what a temptation, to blame fate for bringing us to each other, and therefore place myself in its hands, blind to any influence I might have had upon my own path.

But such was a childish notion as well, and I was of a mind to leave childhood behind. I had reached the age of reason, I had argued for my autonomy upon that basis, and so reason must form part of my perception, even of love.

I recalled how disappointed I'd been that the anticipated meeting between Mother and Father and Bree had not taken place two nights ago. Now I thanked God it had not.

He had reached the end, had long since forced down the catches in his voice, had added one last thing—"Louella felt I should come with her when she leaves"—and now he was silent.

So there it all was. And so had I become Aubrey Christian Paxton once again, in the span of a few short hours. And I had told all of it, but not to the audience I had so long anticipated, and not with the promise of understanding that you might have provided, Gran.

If earlier on I had had to refrain from speaking, I was now all but drained, and had so little an idea of how she might respond that I could think of nothing further to add.

She was silent as well, her expression sober, as it had been for a long while previously.

Then she said to me, "What was it you began with? The first thing you told me, when we sat down?" She did not wait for me to answer. "You said you believed you were falling in love with me. Did you say it so that we might explore it further? Did you mean it?"

"Of course I meant it. More than any words I've spoken in my life."

"I believe I feel the same," she said simply.

I thought I knew better than to be elated just yet.

She did a strange thing then: she reached over to trace my features with her hand. Her fingers scampered over my eyebrows, down the bridge of my nose, to my lips. She paused there, and—out of what yearning, what instinct?—I took the tip of her pinky into my mouth, kissed it, bit lightly at the smooth nail.

"I know you now," she said, and took the finger gently from my lips. "I know you, and I cannot but love you. It would be different had you revealed yourself to be a murderer, or to have done intentional and grievous harm in your past. But such a story as this—how can I do otherwise than to love you better? You must have known I would not hate you for your parentage. Or for any portion of your life which proceeded from it. It is this which makes you as you are, all of what you are, and as such ought be a source of pride. What a foolish thing, that you are obliged to regard yourself so myopically, and with such loathing! You must have known I would not.

"And yet—" Her eyes dropped here, and I felt my soaring hopes do likewise. "And yet it changes things, for the future I imagined before I knew any of this is not the same one I must contemplate now. You must know that too, Bree."

I did know it. Although I had not allowed myself to think upon it. No; I had concentrated on the idea that she might storm and rant and cease to love me or never start, in which instance there would be argument to make and fall back on. But I had not dared examine the worse alternative: that she might love me anyway, but that realistically, in terms of the drastic effect it would have upon every facet of her life, to act upon that love would be a sacrifice beyond any I could ask of her. In which case argument was useless, for I had no answer to that problem, no means by which to fix it. I had nothing to offer her to compensate her for the losses she would endure on my account.

"I understand."

"You must give me a while to think upon it, by myself," she said.

I nodded.

"You mustn't imagine you're to be thrown aside, in any event, for I love you more than I did a day ago, and I loved you quite a lot then."

How easily she said those things—said "love," as if it were natural, and painless—and how easily I listened, fell into the rapture of believing them, and what a misery it was to pull myself back.

"But on the other hand," I forced myself to say, "you may not be able to go it any farther. For which I cannot blame you."

"Don't put it that way, Bree. Let me think on it."

We sat contemplating the grass at our feet for a few more moments.

"You know," she said, after we'd been silent for a time, "you kissed me the other night." I marveled that she'd brought it up, that the idea of having kissed an octoroon was not a repellent memory of which she wished to rid herself.

"Yes, I know. You're very observant. Nothing slips past you unnoticed, does it, Miss?" I saw the rounded curve of her cheek as she smiled a little. "You seemed not to like it, or perhaps it was just a reflection of the whole strange evening."

"Precisely the latter."

I thought I knew her mind well enough to say, "Perhaps I should try it again, then." We were at either the beginning or the end of our association; either way, our affection was intact, so what was the point in forgoing this?

She was already leaning toward me, and when I was finally able to take hold of her, I succumbed to that loss of contact with everything about me which I remembered from my brief collisions with bliss. Her kiss was not Clara's strange, purchased one, nor was it Faith's innocent fumbling; hers was an eager and knowing revelation. She caught my bottom lip lightly in her teeth and licked it, and I explored her with my own tongue, and of their own accord, my hands found themselves tangled, at last, in that mass of hair, and then about her waist, so tiny I thought I might encircle it, but firm too. And I thrilled to the sensation of her own fingers, sure, unhesitating, along the ridge of my back, then at my neck, then brushing my cheek. In my head I heard her, although she was not speaking, saying the words over and over again: "I know you now. I know you."

This time it was everything I had hoped it might be—now in this most poignant moment between us!—for he seemed to revel in every advance of mine, and answer it with something unexpected but delightful of his own, and the degree of urgency as he pressed against me matched mine exactly, as if we had established an instant communication of the senses, or a mutual approach to sensuality.

I wished never to stop it, and that in itself told me that I must. I placed my hands firmly upon his chest and pushed away from him, breathless.

I could hardly catch my own breath. I sought her eyes and probed them, wishing to make sure that I was not alone in this state. She regarded me with her lips parted, her face a strange mixture of sadness, pleasure, and surprise, and I knew her expression mirrored my own. I could not let go of her—I knew it was right that she'd forced us apart—but I could not stand the idea of it, and instead of making it that much easier for her, I drew her closer, so that her cheek rested upon my chest. I put my arms about her, and gazed out over the top of her auburn head; protected and enfolded she was, yet I was the one as much protected, her trust in me, her affection, a shield between all that was wretched and myself.

I decided we would simply remain like this for the rest of our lives. Nothing should follow this moment, which would stretch into infinity. We would not get up, brush ourselves off, depart—become weary with the world, bored, short-tempered, angry, complacent. We would grow old here upon this spot, die quietly, and collapse into the dirt, to fertilize the trees and soil.

We fit together so exactly, as if that spot upon his shoulder had been designed with the contours of my face in mind, as if my height and weight had been exactly calibrated so that I would nestle perfectly into the niches of his body. I might close my eyes and be content here forever—indeed, to move would be to defy the gods, who'd gone out of their way to create an ideal melding of two forms.

I shut my eyes, breathed him in. He smelled faintly of peppermint. Of Harlow's toilet water, I realized. On Harlow it was sweetish, soothing. On Aubrey it took on a lively bite, as if it had mixed with the essence of some foreign spice. I opened one eye, explored the minute weave of the fabric from which his shirt was made.

Then I allowed my gaze to widen, to take in a fraction of the lawn beyond us.

I felt her startle in my arms, and then all at once she was sitting up, peering round me, at something over my shoulder.

"What is it" I asked, startled myself.

She shook her head and continued to stare, as rigid as a hunting hound prepared to flush its quarry from the bush.

After a moment her body relaxed somewhat, and she took a breath.

"What is it, what did you see?" I asked her again.

"Nothing. It was nothing. Only—someone I thought I knew, but I couldn't be sure."

At least I wished to believe I wasn't sure. That it could have been anyone running by, anyone's black head turning to look at me with what—recognition?—apparent in the eyes, before being drawn away by the escort.

That it didn't necessarily have to be Cousin Percy and—who else?—her new conquest, Carter Forbes-Spencer, out "slumming" in the Gardens, perhaps so as to have an interesting tale to tell the ever-eager Aunt Jo over dinner at Leeds Hall.

I hadn't gotten a very good look at either of them. Which meant they couldn't have gotten much of a look at me, hidden as I'd been behind Aubrey. Unless, of course, they'd seen us long before the moment I glanced up. Seen us kiss, and draw together, and waited for me to raise my head, so that they might be sure it was me.

Forget it, I told myself; but the mood had been broken for me, and—returned to my senses—I knew Bree and I must leave each other, for tonight, at least. I wished only to gaze upon him one last time before releasing him.

She backed away from me, took my face in her hands. I gently covered her fingers with my own. "You must get home."

"Yes, I know."

I got to my feet, pulled her up beside me. She smoothed her dress, brushed some errant strands of hair from her eyes, retied the sash at her waist. I watched, in an agony of indecision as to whether I should say something more, attempt to wrest some final comment from her.

When she looked back at me I found I could not help myself.

"Arabella—what is to happen from here? When shall I see you? Or hear from you?"

"It shan't be that long. Give me a few days, and I will send you word."

"If I do not hear from you—"

"You shall hear from me. Rest assured, you shall."

I made my way home in the hansom Bree had called for me. I watched him even as we drove off, stuck my head from the window to have a glimpse of his retreating form as he stood there amidst the prostitutes and merrymakers now swarming about the gaily lit Garden entrance. I stared until we rounded a corner and his dark head was lost from view.

Then I turned to face forward, twisted my gloves in my hand, massaged my temples. My heart was beating so rapidly I wondered that the driver did not hear it, and check to be certain I had not exploded upon the seat. My head was throbbing, and I was at once bone tired and yet so anxious, so possessed of a nervous energy, that I could not sit still.

A thousand thoughts flashed through my mind at once, a great river of them from which I attempted to snatch an individual drop or two. It was no good, though. No sooner did I latch onto some particular aspect of the evening than it led me into a hundred avenues of speculation. At length I found myself drawing a blank, staring from the window at the passing scenery, content not to have to think at all.

I stumbled into the house at last, and as I passed the parlor where Mother and Father and Richard sat reading from the newspaper, I saw them all glance up and stare at me. But no one said a single blessed word—absolute miracle!—so I merely popped my head in, announced I was tired, and proceeded up the stairs to my room.

So it is that I am alone, once again, with myself, no great evil having followed on the heels of honesty.

It is enough to make me reconsider, to make me wonder if perhaps it is not better to renounce Aubrey Bennett, to be Aubrey Christian Paxton and let things fall where they may, to find some consolation—nay, some dignity—in the truth of my origins, the refusal to hide, the refusal to—how did she put it—regard myself myopically, and with self-loathing.

Yet I do not trust that perception entirely.

The world is just not like that, and my good fortune may not hold forever.

Arabella, I hope you have got home all right, I hope you are asleep in your bed, dreaming dreams of a lovely future. I cannot imagine how I shall continue to be a part of it.

APRIL 22, 1863

I slept badly again last night, which surprises me not at all, given the state I was in upon arriving home.

This morning, at promptly nine o'clock, I heard some rumpus downstairs, and got out into the hallway to see what it might be. Mother, Father, and Richard were scurrying about completely dressed, while Lucy and Lydia made ready with bundles and packages of food, which they placed in the waiting barouche outside.

Mother spied me upon the landing, but strode by without a trace of acknowledgment.

"Don't expect us until late evening, or perhaps even tomorrow morning," she said through tight lips.

I walked directly into her trap by asking, "But where are you going?"

"You've forgotten, of course. You were undoubtedly busy somewhere with affairs of your own, which is why you needed to disappear for an entire day. But had you bothered to think on it, you might have recalled that we made arrangements for a luncheon at Leeds Hall."

Now she mentioned it—oh, dear—I did recall it. And she was right, I had forgotten completely, in the wake of the past few days' events.

"If you wait, Mamee, I can be dressed and ready in a few minutes—"

"You needn't trouble yourself. We've grown accustomed to your absence from family functions. I doubt anyone shall bother commenting upon it." And with that she turned upon her heel, snatched a wicker basket from Lucy in a most unusually rude way, and clicked across the marble foyer to the door.

She shut it—hard—behind her, and from the hall window I saw her climb into the barouche to sit across from Father and Richard, whereupon Phillip gave Paulus and Jenny the mare a good smack with the reins, and they set off.

Well, hang them all. It's just as well they're gone, for I am in no mood to deal with any of them. Except perhaps Richard, who, if he'd stayed behind, might have provided some company and useful advice regarding my present situation.

I have done nothing but pace and stare, wander and fidget, as indeed I did nothing last night save toss and turn.

What dreams I had were bizarre and frightening, and a relief to awaken from.

Now I know everything I could have cared to know about Bree. Aubrey Paxton, I should say.

And so, what shall I do?

What is it I expect her to say—what is it I want?

If Mother and Father were to find any of it out—the truth is, I have no idea how they'd react. They do not, in theory, hate or look down upon Negroes, or persons of mixed race. On the other hand, they do not, in practice, associate with them.

And I doubt that in their wildest nightmares they ever imagined they would have to confront the notion of their own daughter being in love with one of them.

Which I am.

In love.

I want her to love me. Completely. Only her, and no other.

Ibrahim always thought me a fool for such romantic notions.

It was the company of men from which he drew strength; women were a glorious entertainment A-La had provided in his wisdom.

"What's wrong with ya, boyo—done too much friggin on ya own, got no spunk left for the ladies? Get all the pussy ya can while ya young," he advised me, and although no longer young exactly, he set out the moment we reached England to show me how to go about this.

I could not explain to him why it did not—does not—appeal to me. I could not put it into words for myself. I only know that however much I look and imagine—however many feminine ideals may possess my dreams and guide my hand to solitary and dismal acts upon myself—the pursuit of variety leaves me only emptier, overcome by yearning for what I have not.

What I have not. I have tried to put that lack into words for myself too, but the perfect description eludes me.

The closest I can come when I consider it is this: I seek the reflection of myself in the eyes of a woman whose esteem is worth having. Her opinion of me would be the image I'd trust and carry with me.

Only one woman need provide it. But she must be the right one. This one.

Le coeur a ses raisons que la raison ne connaît pas.

None of what I've learned of him has changed my feelings a whit.

I am in love! Look at how beautiful that appears on paper—I think I shall write it again—

!!!!I AM IN LOVE!!!!

Yet when I think of it—of finding that one, of being possessed and possessing utterly—I realize I am frightened near to death by the prospect.

What do I know of the experience of love? Besides yourself, Gran, who stood before me as a shining example of its realization?

I do not know whether what I feel is what I *should* feel.

Whether it is enough to dream her waking and sleeping, to be enamored of her every particle and movement. To feel in an instant that I have found in one person a dear friend of my childhood and the subject of my grown fantasies. That I've loved and known and cherished her all of my life past, and will do so into infinity.

I am terrified that I will disappear, consumed by the ties I created. Or that I shall fail to live up to the noble sentiments I express. That I am at bottom flawed in character, and that whatever great depth of feeling I imagine I possess, I should not trust it, or dare lay it before anyone, lest it be found lacking.

Can it be natural to feel such cold fear when faced with the fulfillment of one's fondest wish?

It frightens me, intimidates me, but my instincts tell me this is the state I've awaited, however unfamiliar, and with all its unasked questions. I trust those same instincts to bear me forward. I must know what can or cannot come of this, whatever it is.

But my own struggles are beside the point, for beyond them lies still another cold fact: that were I to plunge ahead, the woman of my choosing could surely never love me with equal fervor, or remain with me for long.

For what have I to offer her, what have I made of my life that I might present it to her with any measure of pride? Nothing. What am I—nothing. Mama's yellow bastard. It would be only a matter of time before she realized it.

Surely the more Arabella sees of me, the more my flaws will be revealed to her, until I stand before her exposed as something much less than a man. And *that* would be the image available to me then, *that* would be the reflection I would meet in her gaze.

Better to avoid the whole thing. To dream of it only in some far-off sense.

How easy it would have been had she rejected me out of hand. Then the matter would have been decided for me. I could have wallowed in my misery, and gone on cursing my African blood as the cause of my misfortunes.

Instead she places before me hope, and possibilities, which I must rise to meet.

But I must be aware of the risks.

Aubrey has no family to speak of, is employed practically as a domestic, a tutor (although his salary is more befitting a tenured professor, thanks to Harlow's generous spirit). He has no inheritance, poised to drop into his lap through the benevolence of death. Were we to marry—I am getting ahead of myself, I know—I would be relatively *poor*, unless we agreed to dip into my own inherited funds—which I doubt Aubrey would sanction, lest he be branded a fortune seeker. I do not fool myself that a kiss from my beloved would take the place of a chicken in the pot—even from a distance, a life of want appears miserable, and what sort of person would choose it willingly? What sort of family would happily see their child into such a state? I wonder how I should acclimate to it.

But I needn't even consider these facts just now, as they will pale in the light of other information. For if it becomes common knowledge that I have consorted with an octoroon—and how silly that I must even consider this!—the consequences, amidst this muddleheaded company, may be dire.

I must therefore be either prepared to face them, or prepared to hide our association, or Aubrey's parentage.

Should we do the former, her family, her entire social circle, may disown her, and both of us become pariahs, unwelcome in every segment of society save the basest. I shall lay misery and mayhem at the feet of my beloved, while my own dream of taking on a new coloration will be dead.

Yet I cannot imagine maintaining the pretense of lies. I cannot do it. Whatever the cost, I would have us go forward with honesty.

And if I would ask this of her, I must have something to offer her besides endearments.

This can be no mere flirtation, no little adventure in romance. If I ask her to give up one life, I must offer her another.

I would prefer to make a clean sweep of it, to perhaps have Aubrey meet Mother and Father in person, to have him call upon me in a normal manner, and then let them discover gradually—after having had time to be impressed by him—the less palatable aspects of his history. Surely they cannot be unreasonable when they see the sort of person he is, and how thoroughly I have searched my own heart regarding him. I can employ Harlow as a character witness—well, maybe not Harlow, Mother has always taken such a sour outlook toward him—but Caroline, at least, and Louella—

—oh dear, Louella! When did Bree say she was leaving! And didn't he mention something about her wanting him to accompany her! Well, he surely isn't planning to do that, or he would have told me. I needn't rush my reply to him on that account, but nonetheless I must be certain I call upon Louella immediately, or send word to Harlow that I want to see her before she goes—

I would have a much better notion of my prospects if I met with Paxton—and with Mama, who for all I know may be living with him, or *married* to him, anything being possible beyond the borders of the wanton *la belle* France.

The thought of attempting this sends me into a frigid sweat. God, I cannot do it. The man is my father. If he were to cast me out, to retract what he told Louella—I could not bear it.

And Thomas. Thomas would be there. How can I face *that*?

It will have to be faced sooner or later.

I must make up my own mind as to how serious I wish all of this to become. And if I wish it to move forward, and if she wishes it too, then France lies in my very immediate future.

Which brings me round to the questions again: am I a fit partner for anyone such as she? Do I own my own mind, to feel such fear alongside such elation?

Help me, Gran. Help me to know. So that if she decides to have me I shall be certain beyond any doubt that I am prepared to have her.

—and just wait until Harlow discovers the truth about Bree, the look upon his face will be priceless—

I've so much to do. But I don't wish to rush myself, I think I will wait a few days before I speak to Bree again, just to let things settle in my mind. I shall only make certain I send word to Harlow today, so that nobody departs before all of this can be worked out amidst us. I don't wish to make Bree wait too long, for I could see how much he was pained by my leaving last night, and I am anxious to reassure him that I believe we can move forward if we wish to, that I am prepared for the consequences, and that I have a sound plan.

I lay down upon my bed last night, overwhelmed by these ruminations and expecting to stare at the ceiling until morning, as I thought myself too agitated for much else. But I must have fallen asleep, for when I next awakened it was late in the afternoon, and I only opened my eyes at that point because some racket at the front door had forced me into it.

The noise turned out to be Harlow, banging with the knocker, and running round the side of the house to hurl stones at my window.

I drew a shirt on and descended the stairs, still somewhat dazed with sleep. "I'm *coming*," I shouted, when he began to pound yet again.

I threw the door open. "Finally!" Harlow exclaimed, his fist poised in midair. "I was beginning to think I'd have to break the door down, or send the bloody peelers out to look for you!"

"I was asleep."

"Yes, I can see that. I won't bother asking whether you think it's quite normal to be sleeping at three in the afternoon. What in the name of Christ have you been up to the last few days? You missed lunch on Tuesday, and I was hoping to have you about yesterday, but you were off somewhere until God knows when."

"I had—there were a few things I needed to do—"

"—which you've no intention of talking about. Yes, I can take the hint. Well, you missed an excellent day. I took the girls target shooting—Caroline, and our guest Miss Paxton. You perhaps remember her from the party." He paused here, as if waiting for me to respond.

"Yes. I remember her."

Harlow gazed over my shoulder at the foyer. "Mind if I step in a minute, old boy, or are you in the midst of *other* things you need to do?"

"No—" His presence was, in fact, making me edgy, since I feared his sister and Louella might be nearby, and I had no wish to go through the awkwardness of seeing them. But I could hardly excuse myself without appearing rude. "Of course I'm not busy, come in."

He sauntered in, leaned against the doorframe in an attempt to appear casual. Then he blurted out, with all the subtlety of a schoolboy, "So tell me the truth, Bree—what did you think of her—of Louella? Miss Paxton."

"What? I—I met her only briefly, Harlow. I hardly had enough time to form an opinion."

"Yes, exactly true, dammit, that's why I'd hoped you'd be at lunch, and at home yesterday." He frowned.

"But why do you want to know," I asked, sensing that he was waiting for me to question him, and wondering where it might be headed.

"Well, you see—" He blushed crimson. "You see, Louella and I—we were—you might say, *involved*, a while back."

I blinked, so as to keep the mingled relief and surprise from my face.

"It ended badly," Harlow went on. "And then she went to the States, and all manner of awful rot befell her—I don't know if you overheard any of that. Anyway, now she's back, I find I'm more infatuated than ever. I've learned a good deal more of—of romance, and of myself, than I knew at the last go-round, and I want to bring up the whole business again."

However I was feeling, I could not suppress a smile at the notion of Harlow and Louella together. Louella would have found a man worthy of her, if Harlow could only keep the fire lit under his backside, and apply himself seriously to his goals. That done, they'd make a perfect match. And Harlow would be out of Arabella's way. And mine.

"So what do you think?" he pressed me.

I shrugged in what I hoped was a casual manner. "I'm in no position to judge, you understand. But offhand, I think it's a fine idea."

"Do you—that's excellent. Now if I can only find the means to speak up—you see, I'm in such a quandary, Bree, I can't tell whether it's a proper time to say something, if she's warmed toward me, or if it's just my imagination. I mean, she has been through so much, she lost her mother in the States, you know—I've no way of knowing if it's just a relief to her to be among old friends, or whether I stand a chance of making it anything more."

It was undoubtedly my own state of mind which caused me to reply without hesitation. "If you are lucky enough to be sure of what you can give her, you ought to act. What can she do but refuse you? Only make your case solidly, think on it before you approach her."

"Good, good—you'll help me with that, won't you? Will you? Perhaps tonight, maybe?"

"I cannot tonight. There is something else I must attend to. What about tomorrow—"

"All right, but tomorrow it must be, for she's due to leave two days hence, and I must corral her before then."

Due to leave—I had nearly forgotten. Would I be going with her or not? If only everything would fall the way I wished it to over the next three days, I might be on my way with her, the whole story out before Harlow, Arabella prepared to wait and see what I resolved for myself in France—

Or it might fall apart completely. Arabella lost to me. In which case I might as well leave with Louella anyway, and swallow all my bad fortune in one dose.

"—so you must promise to set the time aside, agreed?" Harlow was saying.

"Yes. Yes, I agree to it, I'll be here."

He brightened. "All right, then, old boy—I've things to attend to myself, are you sure you won't come to dinner tonight? No? Well, then, let me be off, and I shall see you tomorrow, around noon, say, and I'll tell Caroline to entertain Miss Paxton herself, and afford the men some privacy."

"All right."

He gave me a brisk clasp of the shoulder, and then trotted down the path, taking the stairs at the end two at a time.

I had not been merely putting Harlow off. I did indeed have plans for that evening. I had awakened knowing what I wished to do; perhaps it had come to me in that murky state which precedes sleep.

The moment Harlow disappeared from view, I leapt up the stairs, washed, and pulled on some clothes. Then I rolled some paper money into a wad and stuffed it into my pocket.

I have never got used to the idea of having money upon my person. It still surprises me, what a simple piece of paper entitles one to, although Harlow has assured me it is the gold behind the paper which is truly important. At any rate, I forget that I am not pretending the part of a swell, that in fact I have almost become one by virtue of the wage I am paid, and that my autonomy is increased a thousandfold because of the fact.

Thus it was that I was able to hire myself a cab to carry me back to Stepney, and was able to purchase not one but two squawking chickens from the few shabby carts prowling the waterfront, which I then carried to the decrepit house where the voodoo woman, Behbeh, resided.

It was well after dark when I knocked upon the rickety door. I cast a glance about the weedy walkway, recalling that it was here my association with Arabella had begun; but even this thought could engender no fondness in me for the place.

The door was opened by the Chinese landlady. I believe all women in this position have attended, perhaps, a vast academy which teaches nothing save landlady etiquette, for they are all suspicious, wary, grizzled, whatever their race or age. The Chinese woman peered at me as hard as Belfast Kate was likely to do, and at the mention of Behbeh's name changed her expression not an iota. She flicked her head backward and stepped aside, indicating that I should look for Behbeh in the dirt yard behind the house.

She was out there, seated upon crates with some cronies of various races, puffing on a pipe and gaily conversing. My eyes were drawn to her rounded breasts, obvious and outlined against her yellowed cotton chemise as she threw her head back to laugh. How she could look so vibrant, or wrest any morsel of happiness from her life amidst this squalor, was beyond me.

I stopped at the edge of the yard, the bound chickens beneath my arms, reluctant to call to her. A black woman seated next to her noticed me, however, and put a hand to her eyes to make me out better in the light from the house.

"Ya lookin for somebody, sir?" the woman called.

Behbeh turned in that instant, and I nodded at her. She cocked her head, as if debating, and then nodded back. Taking another pull on her pipe, she got to her feet and approached me.

"Ya lookin for me?"

"Yes, I am. I should like to engage you for a reading."

"A reading? What ya mean?"

"A—ceremony. Of the sort you do. A vodou—voodoo—ceremony."

She glanced down at the two birds I was holding, and then looked back at me. "Don' know watcha mean, sir. Don' do nothin like that here."

"But you did—" I stammered, taken aback. "I was here— Look, I am a friend of Ibrahim's, Ibrahim Kassindja. I was here some weeks ago for a ceremony, with Ibrahim and a big white man. I asked you a question—"

I saw a sly smile creep over her face, and then recognition came into her eyes. "Ohhhhhh," she said, grinning so that her white teeth were visible. "Yeh. Now I remember ya. I thought ya look familiar." She eyed my jacket and new boots. "Look like ya come up in the world some since ya sit before Gabara."

"You might say that."

She nodded. "Good, that's good. Ya see? Gabara always kind to them that got a pure heart."

I might have asked her why she was still stuck here, that being the case, but I had no intention of pressing my luck.

"So—you'll give me an audience, then?"

"Nah. Not tonight. Gabara sleepin tonight."

I struggled to keep my composure. "What might it take, exactly, to wake her up?" I released the two chickens, who flapped about the yard and set to mindlessly pecking in the dirt for food. Then I put a hand in my pocket, withdrawing it just enough to let her peek at the roll of notes.

Her eyebrows flicked, but she nonetheless shook her head. "It ain't a matter a money. It just ain't the proper night, is all. Come back—"

"I *cannot* come back," I fumed, my patience exhausted at last. "I'm here *now*."

She sighed and folded her arms. "Ain't no need to take on. I'm tellin ya, ain't nothin I can do about Gabara, but mebbe ya have a reading with me."

"With you?"

"Ya, there's other ways I answer ya quay-stuns, that what ya want."

I considered it a moment, then nodded. "All right. What would you require as payment?"

"De birds be enough."

Whatever else she was, I thought, BehBeh was at least not overly greedy. She indicated that I should follow her into the shed beyond the yard. She picked up a lamp at the entrance and lit it, then led me past a table where she kept her knives, an assortment of feathers, a drum. Beyond that, inside a little stone niche excavated from the wall, I saw the statue, adorned now with flowers, and with a little silver cup of some dark liquid before it.

We continued into a small back room, where Behbeh set down the lamp and lit several candles. There was a barrel, which served as a table, and two mismatched chairs, where she indicated I should sit; and then she went to a bank of shelves along the wall and withdrew a metal box.

Seating herself before me, she removed a deck of cards from the box and began to shuffle them. "Tarot," she said. "Ya know the tarot?"

"No."

"Well, it ain't de best, can't vouch for it, really, but it better than nothin. So," she said, still shuffling, "what ya wanna know?"

"You want me to say it aloud?"

"Well, a course, I ain't no mind reader."

"But the last time—"

"The last time ya talkin to Gabara. Dis time ya talkin to me."

"I want to know—" I struggled for the proper words, feeling ridiculous. "I came here to speak to someone who's—passed on. I'm certain—I believe she spoke through you—through Gabara—the last time I was here, and I wanted to ask her— There is a young woman. I believe she loves me, but I'm not certain she shall have me, as I revealed to her some information which she must now ponder for herself. And—"

"—and ya want me to fin' out if she gonna come roun, or how ta make her."

I shook my head. "No. If she's to come to me, it must be in her own time, of her own accord. No, what I wish to know is whether what I feel toward her is as it should be, if I am in the right frame of mind or even the right person—whether any good can come of my pursuing her—"

Behbeh stopped her shuffling. She looked up at me.

"*That's* what ya want? Ya gonna bother the Other World for *that*?"

"Well—" I huffed.

"Let me tell ya somethin, boy." She put the deck down. "Ain't no cards, no spirit, or Gabara either, gonna tell ya that. Ya got to know it for yaself, an if ya don't, nothin in the world can decide it for ya. What, ya want ya own heart be all set up–like by someone else, ya get ya money back if it don work out? Huh." She snorted. "Ya want, I ask Gabara to bless ya in love, but if ya ain't certain of ya own self, don't expect much."

My keen disappointment must have showed in my face, for her gaze softened. "I can't help ya here, boy, an I'd run from anybody dat seh they could. I been lucky in love myself." She smiled genuinely, coyly, and I wondered what on earth she meant, since I'd seen nothing to indicate this. "But that's 'cause I trust me own min'. Don' expect it ta go perfect, but I know what I think an what I don', an how I wanna see it, an how I don'. An that I be deservin a what I want." Her smile remained, and I saw that one of her incisors was capped in gold, the metal winking in the lamplight.

"So you aren't going to read the cards."

"Nah. Ain't no point in it. Cards give ya things dey can know, answer quaystuns there's answers to. But what ya wantin—nah."

I watched her slowly open the metal box and replace the cards. She hesitated a moment before shutting the lid and returning the box to its place upon the wall.

"Ya can take the birds back if ya like."

I sighed, and stood up. "No. You keep them. I haven't any use for them."

"I thank ya, boy. I'm sorry, ya know, that I ain't help ya more."

"It's all right. I'm sure you did the best you could."

Lucky in love, I scoffed to myself as I made my way home. I dwelled on it as I watched the Thames go by, its black water reflecting here and there the twinkling of stars or overhead lamps. The yellow splotches of lamplight recalled for me the shine of Behbeh's golden tooth.

Who was she to regard herself as lucky at anything?

But then I answered myself: she had simply decided she was, and so she was.

Why not me?

Why could I not choose to make my point of view whatever I wished it? God knew it was the one thing I could control absolutely.

By the time I reached the drive to Linton, I realized I had made up my mind. If Behbeh in her miserable circumstances could decide to trust her perceptions, then so could I. If this is how I love, then this is how I love, and if I trust it, then all the more reason for Arabella to do so. She knows her heart, after all, and shall inspire me to greater confidence in that regard. If I've made nothing of my life so far, well, it is not over yet, and I've still time to change what remains of it. And if I cannot shower her with riches just now, she has known this from the day we met, and has not so far been discouraged by it.

In bed I found myself yielding for the first time in days to the deep and pleasant sleep of the untroubled. My final thought before I lost consciousness was that my arrival in this restful place had been well worth the price of a pair of chickens.

APRIL 23, 1863

Mother and Father and Richard are still not arrived back from Leeds Hall. I cannot imagine what's held them up for so long, but I am now more glad than ever that I decided to remain at home. I should have gone mad were I forced to endure a protracted visit with my cousins—although it might have been interesting to needle Percy a bit about whether or not it was she I saw in the Cremorne Gardens. For now I think of it, she should be just as worried that *I* spied *her* as vice versa, and I'm certain that fact will prevent her from spilling the news to Aunt Jo.

I am feeling much less anxious today, and a good deal less fidgety. I wrote out a card to Harlow and Caroline, telling them to reply as soon as they receive it, and not to let Louella leave before I've had a chance to speak with her again (which I'm sure she intended anyway). I mentioned tomorrow as a possibility, and it only remains to see whether they've any other plans.

I shall have to fill you in on their response later, however, for the porter only left a few minutes ago, and besides, I think I hear a carriage at the end of the road. It may be my own family, returned from a no doubt splendid visit with our relations.

Harlow awoke me this morning—or should I say this afternoon, at exactly twelve—with his usual assault on the knocker, and dragged me from bed so that we might discuss at length his plans for snaring Louella.

I wonder that he has no better comrade in whom to confide besides myself, but he assures me that his friends from university—whom I have never met—are bookish sorts with little use for the messy business of human interaction.

He then, without irony, proceeded to lay out his ideas with that very bookish precision of a scientist explaining the latest theorem. This is here, that goes there, the result of A plus B is C.

Being as I was feeling considerably more optimistic (and no doubt more willing to yield to a fair amount of romantic foolishness) than I'd been the day before, I told him straight out that his approach struck me as rather dry, hardly the means by which to engage a sweet young thing's heart.

"But you told me to think on it," he said, looking injured. "And besides, the last time around, she said I was directionless, and dispassionate, and that she's soured on the idea of marriage altogether. I thought I should make a well-pondered, intellectually sound case for myself to win her over."

I was about to reply that he might be misinterpreting my suggestions and the girl I knew so well, but I caught myself just in time.

"Miss Paxton is soured on marriage? Why?"

Harlow scowled. "Oh, she's been spending too much time around my mother. And that oddball Miss Ashe—you never had the pleasure, did you? Well, they've all taken up the banner, not only as Abolitionists, but as Feminists, as they call themselves."

"Feminists?"

"Yes, crusaders for the rights of women. The suffragist movement, civil liberties, that sort of thing. Louella has come to believe that marriage might confine her in some way. My mother may not be one to plant such an extreme suggestion, but I've no doubt that fanatic Elizabeth Ashe surely would. That one's slotted marriage just under Negro slavery, and she's got Louella thinking along the same lines. To say nothing of my sister. And"—he grinned at me—"Miss Arabella Leeds as well. We'd best keep our wits about us, friend, or all three of them will be marching over us with placards in their hands."

We chuckled at this.

"Not that I don't support them, to a large extent," Harlow continued. "I'm not one to think women ought to shut themselves up in a bandbox, God knows. But let us be frank—why carry it to extremes? Louella would be mistress of her own home, and any man not a fool acknowledges the supreme reign his wife enjoys there. What need has she with other spheres of influence? There is nothing Louella ought fear from me—I am no saint, but neither am I inclined to whore and drink and thieve, and I believe myself progressive as regards most domestic affairs. I should think I'd make a most benevolent master to any mistress of mine."

I was about to mouth some glib assent when I recalled my lot amidst the Paxtons.

"A benevolent master," I finally replied, "is a master nonetheless."

"Well!—but what's to make us men at all if they're to chase their own aims, maybe form their own bloody government?" Harlow grumbled.

"I'm sure I don't know." I grinned back at him. "I squirm at the prospect as much as you. But I doubt we've some God-given mandate to prevent it."

"You're a fine lot of help. So what am I to do, then?"

I shrugged. "Perhaps you could speak to Louella frankly about her concerns. And find some concrete means of addressing them."

"I don't follow you."

"Perhaps a solicitor. Someone to examine legalities—for that is where freedoms are contracted, and yielded—so that she may secure those things she fears forfeiting in marriage. Her money and liberty, for instance."

He blanched. "Well—by God, Aubrey—you are as insane as Miss Ashe! I've no wish to embroil us in such a radical action as rewriting the laws of matrimony."

"I am not even sure it's possible. But you know, even if it is not, it may be as important to Miss Paxton that you look for a solution as that you actually find one."

"I shall think on it."

"Imagine it were you in her place," I was surprised to hear myself say, for what man finds this position comfortable? "That should give you an easier time of thinking."

He nodded as if the subject were closed, but I gave him a stern glare.

"Spare me your smug acquiescence, my friend. There are still those issues to which you've begged a resolution."

He groaned. "I seem to have forgotten where we started."

"Well, let us see—you were telling me how Louella described you when last you proposed to her. What were the terms—*directionless? Dispassionate*? Yes, I believe I've recalled them correctly. She has quite the aim, hasn't she, when it comes to shooting you through the heart."

His face fell. "So what—you think all of that is true?"

It might have appeared true, I thought, for a variety of reasons—not the least of which were the pokes he administered himself with greater and greater frequency, and the corresponding languor which resulted. I recalled my increasing hunger while in the grips of the Soldier's Disease, and wondered if much of Harlow's reserves of passion had not been thus diverted. But I had only my own experience as a point of reference—not enough to justify my interfering with Harlow's appetites.

"Let us just say that based on what you've laid out here today, I doubt you'll convince her it *isn't* true. You are not directionless—I am sure of that—but you've hardly made a case for your own passion."

"Thank you," he snapped. "What might you suggest, if you know so bloody much about passion?"

I shrugged. "You've made a plan. Good, now bugger the plan. Intellectual exercise is not passion, after all. It appears to me you've left no room for spontaneity, for something heartfelt. Let your imagination speak for you."

"Why don't I let your imagination speak for me. You seem to have a better one."

"No, I am no Cyrano. You'd best do your own talking. Only—be willing to risk yourself, to allow her to see that you care for her. Quit being blithe and witty and cold. Make an ass of yourself, if that's what it takes."

"Oh, splendid idea. You think women are favorably impressed by asses?"

"I think *Louella* would be. By a particular breed of ass, anyway. She is—she seems—a very smart and free-thinking girl. Who would appreciate your willingness to reveal yourself before her. She said as much to you—and that's passion, isn't it, the exposure of your enthusiasms? Trust it a little, and yourself as well."

" '*Trust* it,' " he mimicked me. " 'Trust *yourself*.' Oh, what a lot of horseshit. You sound like a bloody minister." He stood up and crossed the room, straightened his lapels. After a moment he turned, looking pained and resigned, but also determined.

"All right," he sighed. "How does this strike you, then—"

It was evening by the time Harlow felt he'd got his approach to courtship where he wanted it. We were both exhausted, and I was certain that his rounds of practice would have quite stamped out any spark of spontaneity by the time we encountered Louella. But our efforts had lightened my mood, so that I was not minding as much the prospect of seeing her. I would be asking her silence, her cooperation, for only a short time longer, and then the awkwardness would be past. In one way or another.

Harlow invited me to dine with his family and himself. Louella and Caroline had returned from a day out among the grounds at Linton, and Caroline explained that they had taken a trip to what was called the Observatory—which I had not even known existed. It is somewhere on the far edges of the property, she says, and apparently a fine place for spending an afternoon, to say nothing of an evening, watching the sky.

I was attempting to participate in the conversation, but it was difficult for me to speak up, as I was quite overcome by the particulars of this gathering.

Mrs. Beckwith sat at the head of the grand table, as servants (who I noticed seemed at ease and comfortable with her, to the extent that English servants are at ease with anyone) delivered and cleared the consommé, fish, and lamb we'd been gorging on. I knew hardly how to take to being waited on—I attempted to anticipate each action, and reach for a plate, or lift one, but the help glared at me as though I were the most boorish of beasts, and at length I gave up and suffered their attentions—a slave amidst servants.

Harlow was at the other end of the table, and Caroline across from me, both of them exquisitely dressed for the meal. Next to Caroline sat Louella—and that, to my mind, was also awesome and strange: that I was sitting at a table not only with the Beckwiths, but with Miss Paxton, dining in her company, instead of pouring her wine.

"The observatory's a lovely old building," Caroline Beckwith was saying. "Very isolated, and the perfect spot for a fairy-tale tryst, if you were ever of a mind to arrange one. You must go and see it sometime." Then her eyes narrowed; at the same time she gave me a dazzling smile. "Harlow took Arabella Leeds up there on one occasion. Didn't you, Harlow?"

He smiled just as dazzlingly. "Yes, I did, dear. She enjoyed it thoroughly, too. What a shame you've had no occasion to visit yourself, that is, until Louella arrived here."

Mrs. Beckwith interrupted them to direct a question at me. "Tell me, Mr. Bennett—we've had so little time to speak since I arrived home—how exactly did Harlow discover you? He thinks the world of your tutelage, and I am glad to see what a friend he's made of you, but I've wondered—how did you chance to meet?"

"Miss Leeds introduced us."

I wanted very much to leave it there, but Caroline's eyes narrowed further, and I felt my awkwardness increase tenfold. "Oh come now, Mr. Bennett. There's a good deal more to it than that," she chirped. "Actually—"

Louella cut her off. "*Really*, Caroline." When I looked over at her I saw she was smiling, but her tone did not match her expression. "I'm sure when Mr. Bennett wants to explain his own story he will do so, and it will be the more amusing for your mother to hear it from his own lips."

Caroline attempted to arrange her features into something resembling remorse. "Of course. I am sorry, Mr. Bennett. I'm certain you are best suited to the task of telling your own tale."

"No harm done," I said.

But what flitted across my mind was a word which rarely enters there: *bitch*.

It is an ugly thought, I don't like to have it of her, but there is something smoldering, angry, within the girl, I am certain of it now. She dislikes me, has from the first moment she set eyes upon me. I cannot understand why, as I've been nothing but respectful in her presence, but I can sense her annoyance, or resentment, or *something*, toward me each time I encounter her. She seems to struggle with it, but I feel it, and it stings me, evoking as it does the withering looks of all those fine young beauties given to staring down upon or away from me in the past.

I tried to ignore her, focusing instead upon her mother, whom I like very much, and who I believe would have heard any tale—even the one Caroline had attempted to embark upon—with gracious good humor. After all, she is an Abolitionist, and a Feminist, and perhaps a number of other "ists," and she had invited her son's tutor to her own table. Apparently she was no poseur, or hypocrite.

"I should be happy to tell you all about how we met sometime," I smiled at Hester Beckwith.

"Well—there's certainly no rush." She glanced from me to her daughter to Louella, perplexed at the little whiff of tension that had evinced itself, but determined to fend it off. "Here," she said, "you may help yourself to some more potatoes, Mr. Bennett. They'll be cold by the time I call Abbott in to serve them. And you take some as well, Louella, you're still not filled out enough for our tastes."

I saw Louella throw me an unreadable glance, and then she turned toward Harlow, who was off upon some other topic.

Dessert arrived—pear halves in a wine sauce, and whipped cream—and then we were finished eating, and the kitchen help began to clear. As we were preparing to rise, Harlow said, with a significant look in my direction, "Louella, I should like to speak to you privately tonight. Before you retire, if you don't mind."

She gave a surprised little "Oh!" but before she could answer, Caroline said to her brother, "Don't go making any plans with Louella for tomorrow, Harlow. We received a card from Arabella today."

I took in a breath and held it.

"She asked that Louella visit before she leaves. You and I are not to let Miss Paxton depart, in fact, until they've seen each other."

"Fine, fine, we'll all go over."

"All right, then, I shall send a response."

"No, don't do that, let's surprise her. What're your plans for the morrow?" Harlow asked me briskly, in between trying to herd Louella toward the door.

"Oh—I cannot. I'm busy, I'm afraid." I was shaking my head. I assumed Berry wished a visit alone with Louella, which might or might not be on account of me; but had she anything to say to me directly, she would surely have sent word.

Harlow frowned at me as he passed. "You're awfully damned *busy* these days, Bree." When I said nothing, he shook his head, then prepared to guide Louella out of the room by an elbow. She caught my eye and widened both her own, and then disappeared down the hallway with Harlow behind her.

I said my good-nights to Caroline and Mrs. Beckwith, thanking them for a delightful meal and—with only half-sincerity—the pleasure of their company. Then I started down the hall toward the front entrance, from which my own cottage would be more accessible. From somewhere in the recesses beyond the hall I heard the murmur of low voices, but I could make out none of the words, and so I silently wished Harlow luck and departed.

I was still awake and sitting in my little parlor some three hours later—wondering, in the dark, why Arabella had sent no word to me, and what would happen when she saw Louella the next day—when I heard a scratching sound at the entryway. I crept into the foyer, alarmed, in time to see a piece of paper being slid beneath the door.

It must be her, I thought. I rushed to the window, but whoever had left the paper had disappeared into the vegetation.

I picked the note up eagerly. But it was not from Arabella after all.

Aubrey—

I am wondering if you spoke to Miss Leeds—if this is why you have been absent the last two days. I'll say nothing to her when I see her, rest assured, unless I have your leave. You and I will talk again tomorrow night at your cottage. I'll see you around one A.M.*, please expect me or give word if you shan't be home.*

Yours, Louella

APRIL 24, 1863

I cannot fathom why I've heard nothing from Linton. It is already nine in the morning, I surely should have had some word by now. I hope Louella has not changed her plans and decided to leave the Beckwiths early, without seeing me again. But that is ridiculous—of course she would never do such a thing. Nor is it likely that Aubrey would depart for a foreign country without telling me. I must stop worrying over such nonsense. But how annoying that I've no idea what Louella's plans are! I mightily hope she expects to visit me this afternoon—I've so much to say to her, and I wish, at the end of it, to leave word with her for Aubrey, so that he'll not be fretting.

Oh well. If I hear nothing within the next hour, I shall take a drive or a walk by myself, and if there is still no message when I return, I shall set out for Linton myself. I had rather hoped to see Bree alone next time we meet, but I don't care to risk missing Louella by standing on ceremony.

I would have liked to ask Richard to accompany me outside, but he is not here. He did not return home with Mother and Father yesterday. He elected instead to stay at Leeds Hall, where Father says he and Henry intend to make a day of pursuing—naturally—some wild game. The massacre of small animals has never been Richard's idea of play, but then, I suppose I cannot hold it against him that he wishes to draw a bit closer to his cousin. He lacks sorely for male companionship, and if Henry is the only reasonable facsimile available, then at least Richard is to be commended for trying.

I doubt it would be a good idea to ask either Mother or Father if they would care to come along with me. They seem to have had an argument of some sort. Mother is wandering about teary-eyed and reproachful, and Father has put on his resolute and stalwart face, and appears to be avoiding her as much as possible.

Harlow, Caroline, and Louella did not set off today until after two. I had plenty of time to obliquely tell Louella that I had indeed spoken to Arabella, but that nonetheless I did not feel she should refer to the conversation, seeing as Harlow and Caroline would be in tow.

Just before the party left, I made sure to pull Harlow aside, and asked simply, "Well?" He answered me with a frantic shrug of his shoulders. "I've no idea where I stand with her," he whispered. "I can't explain now, it'll have to wait." His sister called him to the carriage, and then with a shout to the horses, Harlow turned them down the drive and out of sight.

I assumed I would see no more of them until later in the evening. I was therefore quite surprised when, only a little before four, the carriage once again appeared in the drive, and Harlow handed the reins over to his groom, then helped each of the ladies down in turn.

I was outside my door and trotting down the path in an instant; even given the distance from the cottage to the drive, I could tell something was wrong. The three figures were huddled together in a small formation; their voices were hushed, and their speech punctuated now and then by a shake of the head.

When they saw me approach, they glanced away and fell silent.

"What is it?" I looked first at Louella and then at Harlow.

Harlow shook his head. "I just don't understand it. Arabella isn't there."

"Not there?" I shrugged. "Why is that so unusual? Maybe she was out. You meant to surprise her—perhaps she made other plans, since she'd no idea you were coming—"

But Louella interrupted me. "No, Mr. Bennett, you are not taking his meaning. Miss Leeds was not merely out. She has gone."

I felt the air rush from my lungs as if I'd been punched. "Gone?" My voice emerged as a whisper. "Gone where? Who told you this?"

"A housekeeper met us at the door," Caroline Beckwith answered me, for once without a hint of enmity in her voice. "She told us—I'm quoting here—that Miss Leeds was in need suddenly of a change of locale, and is not expected back any time in the near future."

I stared at her, openmouthed.

"We thought at first that the whole family was departed, and we asked when they had moved, but the housekeeper told us it was only Miss Arabella who'd gone. We then asked for an address where we could contact her, but the housekeeper refused to give it to us," Harlow said.

"Yes, so I asked to speak with Mr. or Mrs. Leeds, whom I get on with well enough," Caroline put in, "and the woman told me they were at home, but were not taking any callers."

"You see what I mean, I'm sure," Harlow said. "Damned queer. We just received her card yesterday, and she asked us to let her know about visiting today—she knew Louella would be leaving, that was the whole point—where in hell would she go between then and now? And why didn't she say anything?"

"It is thoroughly unlike Arabella. One doesn't make plans on Wednesday and then decide to leave the vicinity on Thursday," Caroline added. "Something is not right."

Harlow was nodding in agreement, but I could only stare down at my boots. I did not dare look at any of them, least of all Louella. No, something was not right, but neither was it a mystery to me; it was fairly obvious what had happened.

She must have decided to put as much distance between me and herself as possible. She must have wanted to say a last good-bye to Louella before they both departed. But because she'd gotten no response to her note, she'd decided not to wait any longer. She'd simply gone.

It had been that important to escape me.

I turned, dazed, and began to walk back to the cottage. I had gotten only a few steps when Harlow trotted up beside me.

"See here, Aubrey, I know you must be taken aback. But there must be an explanation, so don't assume it's something dire, or that she means never to return, or that she shan't contact you. It's nothing to do with you at all, I'll wager. Probably some unexpected business she needed to see to, and we'll hear from her any day."

"Yes," I said, still walking, "I'm sure you shall."

"Look, don't take on, all right? Come back to the house with us. There's nothing to be gained by sitting within your own walls by yourself."

"Thank you," I said, "but no. I think I would prefer to be alone for a while just now."

She betrayed me.

How foolish I was after all. Had I learned the lessons my life offers me, I would have seen that this outcome was inevitable.

Still, I thought it was you guiding me, Gran, placing the vodou girl in my path and urging me to reexamine my last visit with her, to let myself believe a little. Why did you allow me to raise my hopes only to see them dashed? You must have known what would come of it.

But perhaps you are not prescient, even from your height. Or perhaps you are punishing me, or allowing me to be punished for all the sins, acted upon and merely imagined, of which I'm guilty.

But what if there is another explanation, I thought, as I sat alone waiting for evening to overtake the estate and bring Louella's visit with it.

What if this is a test of my fortitude? Then I must not give up so easily, I must not allow myself to sink into self-pity, or regard myself as Mama's unlovable son. There may be another reason for her defection besides a change of heart, or a lack of love for me.

The more I considered it, the more likely—and chilling—this possibility came to seem. Suppose there was something terribly wrong, and I—too occupied with wallowing in my misery—failed to see it, and come after her?

At exactly one in the morning there was a light tapping at the door, and I opened it to find Louella standing before me, as promised.

"Bree," she said, and reached up to kiss me upon the cheek.

"Hello, Louella."

"You've not been sitting here in the dark, I hope." She frowned as I lit a lamp, and then we sat. I perched on the edge of a chair, my face in my hands, attempting to hide my distraction and failing miserably.

"I cannot blame you for being upset, Aubrey," Louella said, leaning back in her seat, "but you mustn't decide you know what's happened unless you really do."

"I don't see that there are many alternatives."

"You said you spoke to her. What did you tell her?"

"Everything."

She nodded. "And how did she react?"

"She said she needed to think upon it, but she assured me—*promised* me—that she cared for me, that she only needed time to consider what it would mean, and that she would contact me within a few days."

"And so you felt you left her upon a hopeful note?"

"As hopeful as I could want under the circumstances." I paused. "What do you think, Louella? What could have happened? I am torn between believing that she would never break her word—in which case something dire must have befallen her—and believing she simply reversed herself, and hadn't the courage to face me in person."

"I don't know. She could have had some sort of accident, though I do not understand why her family would refuse to tell us. But on the other hand, though it seems completely out of character for her to have run away, God knows one could not blame her, considering what you have just revealed of yourself."

"How reassuring." My face fell farther into my hands, and she bit her lip, looking chastened. I sighed. "I am sorry, Louella. You're quite right, and I don't mean to vent my frustration upon you just because you are being honest. What I was thinking, though"—I wondered if she would find it a stupid idea—"was that I ought to see if I can't discover more, perhaps go to her house myself and ask some questions."

She nodded. "I think that an excellent idea, if you're willing to do it."

"Oh, I am willing. The only thing which would give me pause is if Arabella had left of her own accord, if by her decision I knew she was asking me not to question her further. Then I would let things lie. But until I know that, there is no reason for me to hesitate in pursuing this. What does it matter what I do or how I look, if it brings me nearer to understanding her?"

I felt obligated, after we had tossed this topic about a good deal longer, to take a brief pause, during which I inquired after Louella. On any other occasion I would have been eager to find out more about herself and Harlow and the talk they'd had last evening; I was only less so tonight because the business of Arabella was foremost in my mind. But I felt I should not allow my own distraction to keep me from at least asking. After all, tomorrow she would be gone, and we had spent quite enough of our time together dwelling upon my situation.

"I'd no idea, when I saw you back home, that you'd a beau here," I told her.

Her clear, transluscent skin took on a pink hue that spread from her neck to the tips of her ears.

"You know now, of course," she said. "And don't think I'm fooled any—I recognize your stamp all over what he had to say the other night, I know he went to you."

I shrugged. "For moral support, yes. But whatever he presented was his own sentiment, I'd nothing to do with that."

"You are a fine friend, Aubrey, but a terrible liar. I know Harlow too well to believe he has suddenly sprouted a radical sensibility, or a poetic one. He told me he wished to support my 'political objectives.' And he recited *Byron* to me, for God's sake."

I managed a small smile and shook my head. "That's none of my doing, I assure you. Had he taken my advice, he would have steered clear of that gloomy fop, and spun you round in a reel." She smiled back at me, and at length I asked, "So what have you decided to do from here?"

"I don't know. That is what I told him, that I didn't know. I realize my affection for him is undiminished, even after the time we've spent apart. And I long for a companion, perhaps children, a family life. But there are other things I want—an existence of purpose, so that when it is over I will not regret having lived it. I am so reluctant to own this, for Maman was appalled by it, Father considers me an oddity, and at times everything I believe strikes me as the greatest selfishness. It's only when I am able to draw courage from other sources—from Caroline, and other friends wrestling the same demons—that I feel at peace with my convictions. I do not trust that Harlow understands this, or that he is the sort of person to stand beside me—" She caught herself, and halted. "But I mustn't go on like this, thinking aloud. And your masculine sensibility should not find much of interest in this subject, should it?"

I smiled again. "Certainly not. I only indulge in it so as to humor you."

She laughed at this, and then added, "Anyway, Bree, I have not had the best examples of wedded bliss set before me to incline me toward the condition, you must admit."

"No, I don't suppose either of us has. But surely you aren't going to let that sour you on your chances. I am trying not to let it influence mine. Besides, Harlow told me what you'd said to him the last time round"—she blushed even more deeply at this—"but I believe I've met a different person than the one you left."

She sighed again. "I don't know, Bree. I must wait and see. And think."

So many thinking women, I said to myself. I hoped her deliberations would bear a different fruit than Arabella's had.

The conversation then turned back to how I would proceed, and Louella got down to the point on which I'd known she was sure to dwell this evening.

"You must decide what you're to do about returning to France with me," she said at last. "Now, do not cut me off—I know this business with Arabella presents a problem, but you may yet resolve it quickly enough. Or you may not, you may be forced to wait for more information. Either way, I believe you are afforded an opportunity to see to other important things which may greatly influence your chances with Arabella, should there be a chance, and should you desire to take it."

"I had already come to that conclusion myself. But I cannot come with you in the morning—not when all of this remains up in the air. I must see to it first, and unearth whatever I can."

"I understand. But by the same token, I believe you should set your plans quickly, whatever you learn, so that you arrive in Aix upon my heels. Do not wait. All of this is fresh in my mind and in yours, and we Paxtons are at our most impassioned when things are fresh to us. Do not wait until you've strategized, and meandered into making excuses not to leave. Go now, and have it over with."

I looked at my hands. I did not wish to meet her eyes, which I knew would be full of that familiar feminine energy. It was too easy for me to get caught up in her fierce optimism, to let myself ignore pitfalls which would give me pause were she not pulling me blindly along.

Women, after all, are not the only ones who need solitude to make their determinations.

I shook my head. "I cannot promise you anything. As to when I will go, at least. I can only tell you that I am of a mind to do it, and I shall. But you must leave tomorrow, regardless, and I must pursue my instincts and call upon Arabella's family. And then, after that, we shall see."

The next morning, Louella departed for the railroad station and the ferry, as planned. I gave her a cool handshake in the drive, before the Beckwith family, for we had already said our more emotional and heartfelt good-byes the evening before. I had in my possession the railroad and ferry schedules, the travel timetables and directions, that Louella had saved for me. She had also given me one of her Aix-en-Provence calling cards, and an itinerant artist's photograph of one of the many fountains in the village, by way of drawing me there quickly. I had asked her to promise that she would say nothing about having seen me until I knew my own plans, and she had agreed.

She hugged the Beckwith women, and Caroline's blue eyes brimmed with tears. But her longest embrace was saved for Harlow, who whispered something in her ear as he held her to him. It was Caroline who urged them apart, reminding Louella that she could not miss her connexion to the ferry, and so they released each other, and a moment later, Louella had been helped into the carriage.

Then it started slowly down the drive, and Louella was borne away, as surely as she had swept back into my existence the night of the party. I sent my thoughts with her, and told her silently that I would meet her again and soon, and that this time there would be no need for subterfuge, no denial of the mutual past we shared.

My eyes did not leave the carriage—nor did Harlow's hand drop, or Caroline's tears cease—until the last flashes of her had disappeared from view.

Barely an hour later, I'd donned the finest of my recently purchased clothing, astonished Harlow by asking for directions to the Leeds home, and—since it was my wish to travel with the utmost speed—arranged for a mount to carry me there.

It had been a long while since I had ridden astride, and the seventeen-hand roan mare whom I'd borrowed from the Linton stable did little to instill any joy in me at the prospect. So buoyant and jarring was her trot that I could neither sit it nor post it comfortably, and so I ended up pushing the beast into a canter upon the flats and easier stretches, and merely walking her the rest of the while. Once I reached the thoroughfares near Knightsbridge, however, the traffic became so thick that I could not have cantered had I wanted to, and at any rate I was forced to slow my pace in order to follow the directions I'd been given.

I finally found Arabella's street, which turned out to be one of the more elegant of some very elegant blocks. Elaborate facades graced the multistoried, crenellated dwellings, their huge windows reflecting the afternoon sunlight. I counted down the numbers until I came to 118. The house was of white stone, with a high black wrought-iron fence surrounding it, and broad steps which led up to an arched entryway and a carved, scrolled door.

It looked like precisely what it was, the home of an angelic and exceptional personage.

The gate was not locked. I tied the mare to the hitching post outside it, and slipped through. I hoped no one would spy me there upon the walkway and confront me before I'd had time to prepare myself.

Once at the foot of the steps, I took in a deep breath, closed my eyes, and conjured in my mind the picture of Arabella's face when I had kissed her at the Cremorne Gardens. That was what I'd told myself to trust, that was the reason for my presence here. I must not let myself forget it, or be distracted from my purpose. I opened my eyes, straightened my collar, and then mounted the steps to the entrance. At the door, I picked up the heavy brass knocker, letting it drop twice for good measure.

Instantly I heard footsteps from within the house. My pulse began to race; I took another deep gulp of air to calm it.

A moment later the door opened, and a gray-haired, matronly woman of around fifty stepped into the space before me. She was trim and pleasant-looking, dressed in simple dark blue. No doubt she was a servant of some sort—her costume and carriage told me this, and even if they hadn't, this was not the sort of home where the master or mistress was likely to answer the door.

"Yes?"

She squinted out at me, discovered she did not know me, and took just the tiniest step back into the foyer.

I drew myself up to my full height—hardly necessary, since I was already quite a few inches taller than she—and gave her a smile that was friendly, but not at all obsequious.

"Good day. I am looking for the Leeds family. I trust I've reached the right house. I am expected—would you mind letting Miss Leeds know I've arrived?"

"Miss Leeds?" The woman's expression clouded a little, and I saw her right hand reach out to smooth a section of her unwrinkled skirt.

"Yes, Miss Arabella Leeds." I took a tiny step of my own toward her, not enough to cause her to back away further, but enough to let her know I was not about to be easily put off.

"Miss Leeds is not at home. You'll have to come back during calling hours."

"Why, how strange—you see, I had an engagement with her for this very day, and she'd given no word to either myself or our mutual friends that she wished to cancel. Where has she gone, exactly?"

The fingers of the hand twisted a knot in the fabric of the skirt. "Miss Leeds is—is not in residence here at the moment."

"Not in residence! Why, this is positively bizarre, I must tell you. I cannot believe that Miss Leeds has simply up and removed herself without warning. Especially as you yourself just advised me to come back during calling hours—for what would I be returning, pray tell, if she's not in residence?" I smiled at her, as if I were merely bemused by all the contradictions, and this, combined with the interrogation, had the effect of causing her to stammer in an attempt to backtrack.

"I don't know—that is, I—"

For a moment I regretted causing her to squirm. For she struck me as one of those simple, good-hearted spinster-housekeepers who devote themselves to "doing" for their employers, with little hope of ever being done for.

But the regret passed when the woman backed into the door and began to close it, saying as she did so, "Miss Leeds is not here. She has gone away, I do not know where. If you desire any more information you must come back during calling hours. I do not know when. Truly, I am sorry. Good day to you, sir."

"Just a minute." I lunged forward and placed my shoulder into the diminishing space so that she could not close the door upon me. I tried to forgive myself the fear in her eyes. "Look here, I traveled a long way to keep an engagement, and all I've gotten from you is this strange story. Surely if you haven't any information, you can summon somebody who does. Go and get your mistress or master."

"There is no one else at home."

I set myself more stubbornly against the door's frame. Then I folded my arms in contemptuous disbelief, and assumed a stance which said I'd no intention of budging until she obliged me.

She raised her chin. "Just a moment," she quavered, and then, since she could not slam the door on me, made a show of turning her back instead.

There was another door at the far end of the white marble foyer. She went through this and closed it behind her, so that I could not see into the rest of the house. I was left to wait, and now my attack of nerves returned to assault me in earnest. For I am expert in bluffing servants—I know their lot, and their loyalty or resentment toward their masters is generally easy to assess and exploit. But I was at a loss when it came to the heads of households. I was as used to being lorded over as my fellow domestics, and I doubted I would be able to sustain my gentlemanly airs in the face of the genuine article. Besides all that, the person who came through the door next would likely be Arabella's own flesh and blood, and what would they make of me?

I was breaking into a cold sweat when the far door opened and another woman entered the foyer.

She strode toward me, her fine silks rustling as she moved, the stiff crinolines beneath them keeping the skirts in a graceful motion about her ankles. Her little satin boots clicked on the marble floor, reminding me for one brief instance of Mama's boots upon the parquet in New Orleans.

"May I help you?"

The voice was low, well modulated, controlled in a way that Berry's was not. The woman was not tall but finely proportioned, and she moved with a graceful surety. Her hair, simply pulled from her unlined face, was a rich woodsy brown, her irises a deep blue.

But I recognized the familiar curve of the jaw, the bright, slanted eyes, alight with a keen intelligence—the clear skin, tiny dark beauty marks dotting it like stars, and, especially, the overall impression of comeliness, of a creature finely put together, secure in her attributes and enjoying the peak of her moment. All of this told me that the woman before me could only be Arabella's mother.

"Lucy tells me you are looking for Arabella."

Her words returned me to myself, and served to renew my courage somewhat. After all, she had come to the door, which was more than she'd done yesterday, when the Beckwiths and Louella—people she knew—had called upon her.

"Yes, I am looking for Miss Leeds. I hope you shall pardon the intrusion, Madame. Your maid seemed not to have much information, and so I asked to speak to the mistress of the house." I ventured a small smile. "Whom do I have the pleasure of meeting?"

"I am Arabella's mother, Charlotte Leeds."

I grasped her hand. "At your service," I said, but I offered no introduction of my own. "Miss Leeds and I share mutual friends, and I was expected to call upon her today."

"I see," Mrs. Leeds replied. "Well, as Lucy told you, Arabella is not at home. She left unexpectedly, and most likely will not return for a long while. I do apologize for your trouble, sir."

"Might you tell me where I may contact her, then?"

"I am afraid I cannot. It is a private matter, sir. I'm sure a gentleman such as yourself will understand."

I knew that my next move would either make or break the situation. I only prayed I could carry it off.

I took yet another step into the house, and let the front door close a little behind me. I stared down at Mrs. Leeds and allowed the smile to fade from my lips.

"Please forgive me, Madame, but I must insist. My business with her is urgent. I am sure a lady such as yourself will understand."

So well had she hidden her struggle for composure that I had not even been aware of it, but now she lost the battle, and I saw a dozen different expressions flit across her face in the span of a few seconds. She seemed to sway just a little, and her eyes widened. Pain, as well as a certain amount of fright, was evident in them. Her hands, which had been still, now fluttered before her, the fingers of one clutching at the other.

I feared she would call for help or flee the room, and so I thought quickly. She had not reacted with anger at my effrontery, and so I decided the best way to press her was not with force, but with kindness.

"Please," I said, "you may trust me. I am interested only in your daughter's welfare. If something untoward has happened you may tell me about it, and rest assured it will go no further."

She seemed on the verge of either tears or revelation.

But then, as she stared at me, something else came into her eyes, a light of discovery which made her draw in her breath and pull herself straight again.

Her contortions ceased. She held my gaze now, her own steady and cold.

And then she said to me, "You are Aubrey."

I was overcome—strangely—by neither shock nor surprise. Or rather, these emotions flashed through me for only a brief second. Instead it was as though we had reached at last that impasse which was destined to happen, and which I had been expecting, or dreading, in some part of myself.

There was no point in denying it.

"Yes," I replied. "I am Aubrey."

"So." Her voice was trembling now. "*So*. You have the audacity to show your face here. And demand explanations, of all things. Well, you shall have them, then, although you are owed nothing—certainly not civility—by any member of this family. You see, we know all about you. We know quite well what you intended to perpetrate upon our child—"

"I meant to perpetrate nothing, Madame. I love your daughter—" I interrupted her, but she spat back at me with renewed vigor.

"Do not dare to use that word before me, to debase it so. You debased my daughter with your appetites before the entire city, you foul creature—is that what you would call 'love'? Then you know nothing of it, or you pretend it for your own evil purposes. She left here because of *you*—you—*animal*. You uncivilized—panting—*animal*. To avoid your coercion, to retain what you would have had of her. Did you never think of it, what you would have forced her to give up—her future, her dignity—with your demands that she accept you? Or did you simply not care, as you selfishly satisfied your own sickening desires? Oh yes, that's more likely, isn't it—you would have made an *outcast* of her, you would have ruined her *life*—you *fiendish, scheming*—"

Now the tears did come, and as she flung her words, the droplets flew from her eyes as well, landing upon her skirts, and upon me. Every accusation struck at me like an arrow, its truth piercing me, until I could not look her in the face any longer. For she was right, of course, all of her thoughts were my own, and had I been thinking rationally on that long-ago night at Miss Ashe's, I would have anticipated all of this, and spared the girl and myself.

"She left because of *you*," Charlotte Leeds hurled the accusation at me again. "Now let her be, will you. Let her recover her bearings, and save her affection for a *man*, one worthy of the title, and by God do not trouble her any further. I don't expect that you have any shred of decency about you. But if you would pretend to it, you wretch, then locate it within yourself and manage this."

She stood waiting for me to respond in some way, but I could not. I could neither speak, nor look, nor move. I stared at the floor, still and ashamed, my one wish to disappear, to hide from her scorching and righteous gaze.

"You've nothing to say, you coward—I am not surprised. I'd have expected no better from any creature of your ilk—*sir*.

"Now remove yourself from these premises, before I call to have you forcibly removed. You are not wanted here. Not by anyone, least of all my daughter."

And having delivered this, her last blow, she turned her back upon me finally. Her clicking heels carried her back across the foyer, and she opened the door at the end and exited without another glance at me. She did not wait to see whether I would show myself out. She must have known that I would, that I would not dare follow her, or insist upon remaining there upon her property.

But it was another moment before I could unglue myself, and force my legs to turn me round and carry me from the house. I negotiated the steps one at a time—those steps I had climbed so brazenly just minutes ago (for all of this had taken only minutes, although, like some exquisite torture, it felt like an eternity). There seemed to be something the matter with my vision: it had narrowed to an opening just before me, making an abstract blur of everything left or right. I ignored it, found the horse tied where I'd left her, and summoned the wherewithal to climb on and guide her away from Number 118, and back toward Linton Manor.

When I arrived at Linton, I sought out the groom and threw the horse's reins to him without comment. If he resented my presumptuousness, I didn't know it or care. I went directly to my cottage, mounted the steps, continued to the bedroom, and fell upon the bed.

I was only there a few minutes when I heard the click of stones against glass, and realized that Harlow had come searching for me. I did not even bother to descend the steps. I rose, an automaton, from the bed to open the window.

"So what happened?" he shouted up at me. "How did you make out?"

"I learned nothing more than you. Arabella left unexpectedly. She is quite well, she only had some sudden business to see to. No one would tell me what it was."

Harlow shrugged. "Well, I'm sure she had her reasons, although I still say it's damned queer—"

"I have to lie down now," I interrupted him. "I'm not feeling quite well."

"Look, Bree—" he started, but I cut him off.

"I'll speak to you later, perhaps." I withdrew, and shut the window behind me, and then fell upon the bed once again, willing every thought to flee from my head.

A few days later I told Harlow that I wished to take an extended leave from my duties as his tutor.

"What!" he gasped. "You're leaving me before the end of the term?"

"I'll help you write your final papers. But then I'd like some time to travel, if you don't mind. I'm grateful for all the leeway you've given me, and I know it's sudden, but I ask you to indulge me one final time."

"Has this anything to do with Arabella?"

"No."

"But you'll not be here, then, when she comes back—and she has to come back at some point, we have to hear from her, this whole episode is ridiculous—"

"It's business of my own," I said, to steer the subject away from Arabella.

"Well, of course you can go—it's hardly my place to be giving you permission, I mean, you're not a slave, after all—" (And if he noticed my quick swallow here, he gave no sign of it.) "—but tell me, do you mean to come back?"

"Yes, of course," I replied, although this was by no means certain. As of now I could not imagine staying in this place, but I had no wish to abandon him after his generosity toward me, and God knew what would happen to me in France.

"Well, that's a relief, although I hate to see you leave under these circumstances." He seemed quite downcast. "You know, I wish you'd tell me what's happening, if there's something I can help you with." He paused, and when I did not reply, he sighed. "But it's your own business. Where do you mean to go exactly?"

I did not wish to give my destination away, since of course it was the same as Louella's. Once I had imagined that my tie to her would be revealed by now, that I would be basking in the wholehearted acceptance of my friends when I set off upon this journey. But Mrs. Leeds had squelched any desire in me to engage in further folly of this kind, so I said only, "To the Continent. To France, most likely."

"Oh. Well, if you head south, you ought to drop in on Louella. I can give you her address if you like."

"You may give it, but I doubt I shall be visiting that region."

For the next week and a half, I spent almost every waking hour working with Harlow upon his exam papers. It was an arduous job, but one I knew I must take on if I would call myself his friend to any degree. When they were finished, when we were both satisfied that they would pass muster with even his most unyielding professors, I purchased the tickets which would carry me across the English Channel, and thence across the whole of the countryside of France.

I left on a dreary, rainy afternoon, which suited my mood and my sense of order exactly. Harlow, Mrs. Beckwith, and even Caroline had come to see me off.

"You'll write, old man, won't you?" Harlow asked. I assured him that I would, and that he would know of my plans one way or another well before the new semester began. Then I hugged each of the ladies, who wished me well and offered baskets of food which they'd prepared for me, and which were intended to see me through the first segment of my journey. Touched, I thanked the family for their many kindnesses to me, and promised that I would find some way to repay them, and to live up to their good opinion of me.

Then, having loaded my bags—Harlow's bags, actually, since I still had the case he'd given me that first day we'd met—onto the hired carriage, I stepped in, and closed the door behind me.

Linton fell away, and the Beckwiths with it, waving from the wide drive. I watched them as I'd watched Louella, until they disappeared from sight. Only this time, it was I who was moving, being spirited away, toward—yet again—I knew not what. How many times in the past two years had I undertaken similar journeys? The only difference now was that my destination was not entirely unknown. The people, if not their reaction to me, were the most known portion of my life. For I headed toward the embrace of my only family.

The embrace of my family.

I shut my eyes at the irony of it.

Part four

Chapter one

APRIL 30, 1863

My dear friend and companion:

I am so glad that Richard was able to bring you to me hidden in my little colored lap blanket. I must be careful to make no sound as I write lest I disturb Agnes, for she might reveal me if she were to discover this forbidden activity of mine. And then the good Dr. Gregory would surely have you taken away from me.

I write that it is the thirtieth of April, but I am not certain of this. I may have confused several days after my arrival here, and have been unable to correct myself, as no one gives us any information regarding the precise date. I know I was taken on the twenty-fourth, though. That much I am sure never to forget.

That morning, I was waiting for some word from Linton. I was to say goodbye to Louella Paxton, to whom I hoped to give a message for Bree. But no word arrived, and I was debating whether or not to go for a drive when I saw Uncle Charles's barouche pull up to the gate.

I should have known long before this that something was terribly wrong. Mother and Father had been acting peculiar since their visit to Leeds Hall, and, strangest of all, Richard had not returned with them. But even if I'd been suspicious, I could never have arrived at the correct conclusion, could never have imagined what they had in store for me.

Uncle Charles came to the door, and I heard the murmur of voices in the foyer as Mother and Father let him in. I was surprised to see two more men alight from the carriage; I did not know them, but assumed they were associates of my uncle's.

Then Father was calling me. "Will you come down here a moment, Arabella?"

I descended the stairs, and my first thought was that some tragedy involving Richard had occurred. Mother had a look of absolute misery on her face, and Father seemed to be struggling to contain some strong emotion. Uncle Charles stood, bulky and immobile, at the foot of the steps, and the two strangers hovered behind him to form a gloomy little band.

"How are you, my dear?" Uncle Charles asked me. His fleshy cheeks were pink from some exertion, but that did not prevent him from assuming his usual haughty take-charge air.

"I am well, thank you," I replied, looking about me. I waited for my parents to address me and explain whatever was happening, but it was Uncle Charles who continued.

"Arabella." He cleared his throat and took a little step toward me. "I shall not delude you as to why I am here. I have come to take you on a trip of sorts, which your parents have arranged, and which the family agrees would be in your best interest."

I stared at him, disbelieving, robbed, for a moment, of words. "A trip? What sort of trip would that be? When is it supposed to take place, exactly?" I finally managed to ask.

"Immediately. Today."

Now unease and outrage descended upon me in equal measure, and I turned to Mother and Father. "What is he talking about? Tell him, please, I've no plans to go anywhere, either now or at any time in the near future."

Neither of them spoke a word.

"*Tell* him," I said again.

Father was wringing his hands. "I urge you not to resist us in this, Arabella. We have put a great deal of thought into it, it is not a decision to be taken lightly. But in view of what you are doing to your life—the rash decisions you are making, which tell us you have no doubt come under evil influences—we felt we had no other choice."

"What are you talking about," I gasped, although I was beginning to think I knew.

Father shook his head, and Uncle Charles jumped in. "You have been engaged in nefarious activities for months now, despite your parents' attempts at intervention. Most alarming of all, you are keeping company with a young man."

Percy. It had been Percy in the park after all. But Uncle Charles was not finished.

"He is not only beneath your station in every respect, but is also racially compromised. Possessed of Negro blood."

I gasped again—I could not help it—for how could he have known that? The only ones who knew it or had spoken of it were Aubrey, Louella, and myself. Percy certainly had not given him that tidbit of information. But somehow he had acquired it, and it was obvious from Uncle Charles's gratified expression that he was glad to have ambushed me with it.

"Why you choose to consort with such a creature was a question we debated at length, Arabella. And we have concluded that while there might be a variety of causes, the important thing is that you be removed from the presence of this barbarous seducer at once, for your own well-being."

My heart had begun to pound, and I fought to control my voice. "I am sorry for what you know. And I thank you for your concern. But I tell you again: I will not go with you. Whatever you wish to discuss with me, you must do it here, and with respect for my decisions, which I assure you were not influenced by any fiend."

"Do not make our job any more difficult, Arabella," Uncle Charles said. "Spare your parents that at least. You will be going to a place which shall afford you every comfort—a spa overseen by an associate of mine—so I urge you: come with us of your own volition."

Mother began to cry. "Please, Berry. Please go, it will be for only a little while, dear, and the fresh air and sunshine will do you good—"

A spa. A sanitarium, no doubt. They were doing it—actually doing it—my parents were attempting to have me locked away.

"You would have this happen?" I turned on Father. "You are having me committed against my will? You think that will somehow solve something?"

"I believe it will prevent something. Something you may be glad I prevented in the future." He was crying now as well, and could barely look at me.

I began to back away toward the stairs. "I am sorry, but I cannot cooperate with you. I must beg your leave, as I've things to see to—"

Even as I moved, one of the strangers darted in front of me and blocked my path. I looked over at Mother and Father. "What is he doing," I said, staring into their eyes. They turned away—turned their faces from me—and I felt the beginnings of panic in my throat.

I then looked toward the door to the foyer. Uncle Charles and the other man were before it. The stranger stood at the steps. The only other means of egress was past him, down the hallway, to the rear of the house. I turned slowly to Uncle Charles, as if I planned to give in.

And then, before he could take my elbow, I raced in the other direction, past the man at the stairs. I flew down the hallway, bumping into the framed portraits, knocking into the walls. I was almost at the kitchens when the stranger caught up to me. He did not call, or gently stop me; no—he leapt upon me, and threw me to the ground.

I began to scream. I had no awareness of doing so, it simply happened. I swore at him, I kicked him, but now the other one was there as well, yanking my arms behind me, and I could hear Uncle Charles running down the hallway, crying, "Gently! For God's sake, don't hurt her!"

"You *bastard! You* mean to hurt me!" I shrieked. He gasped—no doubt at my language—and I was able to think to myself that this was the turn it had come to: I lay upon the ground, wrestling with hired thugs, on the verge of kidnap, and he had the temerity to be shocked by a word.

I could hear my mother sobbing in the background. "Don't come in," Uncle Charles yelled back behind him, "there's no use in your seeing this." To me he hissed, "You will not prevail. Be smart and spare all of us this scene."

As an answer, I kicked at him with all the force I could muster. He gave me a look of pure contempt—my own uncle, although I had long suspected this to be the opinion he harbored of all who threatened his glib perceptions—and then he turned and exited, leaving me at the mercy of the two men.

"Behave yourself, Miss," one of them hissed to me.

"*Damn* yourself," I snarled.

"My God, you are a lunatic," he smiled, and then bent my arms so far behind me that I cried out. The line had been crossed, I knew it from all I had seen in years past: that there is no justice based on one's simple humanity. I had broken rank, was a lady no longer. I swore, and consorted with Negroes. No holds would be barred.

If I allowed them to take me from the house I could expect much, much more of the same. My only hope now lay in struggling with all my might. Perhaps if I caused enough commotion, I could induce my parents to see the reality of what they had condemned me to.

I swiftly turned my head and sank my teeth into the arm of the tormentor before me, the one holding my shoulders. He cursed and released me; then he opened his long coat—which I now saw contained the tools of his trade—and withdrew a stout leather strap. In a single motion he had fastened it about my waist, and looped it around my hands, which the other thug held behind me. In another moment a second belt had been produced, with which my ankles were tied. And then, despite every motion I could make, despite the use of every ounce of my strength, and my most piercing screams, the first man managed to slip a hood over my head, so that I could see nothing, and had no idea which way to fling myself to avoid them. Then one lifted me beneath the arms, and the other took me by the legs.

And this was how I was removed from the home of my family: trussed like an animal, less than an animal, for no one of us in my household would have treated an animal thus.

I could not know whether my parents had remained in the foyer to see me wrested from them this way. But as we passed through the house's interior, I screamed to them, made one last appeal to their sanity, and their love.

"Look what you are doing—look at it! Is this what you intended, is this what you think I deserve! I do not—I do not! Don't let them do this, Mamee! Papa! Don't let them take me from here—they will hurt me, can't you see it—they hurt me now when you're here, don't you see what they'll do when I'm without you—"

But nothing I said evoked any response. I heard no cry as I was dragged outside. No one protested, no one came to rescue me. Instead I was lifted into what I knew was the carriage. And then Uncle Charles's voice came quite close to my ear: "I asked for your cooperation, Arabella, and I am sorry that you did not give it, and that this was the result. I should not have liked to see you like this. It was so unnecessary."

I will harm you someday, I thought. I said nothing. I was crying despite myself, and was glad of the hood just then, for I wanted him to see nothing of my feelings.

Now I knew there was no point in fighting. My audience had not intervened. I was on my own. Struggling would only justify more horrors being perpetrated upon me. So I sat making not a sound, and the carriage began to move off.

We drove for the better of the day. After a long, long hour or so, in which every idea including a suicide beneath the carriage wheels crossed my mind, Uncle Charles told me he would be glad to remove the hood and foot manacles if I would give him my word that I would behave.

Behave.

"You may do as you wish," I told him. "I've no intention of struggling and providing you excuses for more barbarism, if that is what you want to know."

There was a flutter of air, and the hood was suddenly pulled from my head; it yanked my hair along with it, but Uncle Charles's criminal lackeys seemed beyond caring whether or not they caused me pain.

I saw that I was sandwiched between them, and that Uncle Charles was across from us, apparently feeling he was entitled to a seat to himself, or that I required the presence of not one but two guards.

"I know you must be terribly angry just now," Uncle Charles said, "but I hope you will come to realize in future days that your parents and I took this action for your own good, to spare you far greater unpleasantness. It was of the utmost importance to remove you from the presence of that creature before he could compromise you any further."

"You are all so ignorant. Aubrey is no 'creature.' You know nothing of him."

"On the contrary, Arabella. We know a very great deal of him."

"Oh yes, that's right, my cousin spotted us beneath a tree. And someone, most likely your wife"—I could not bear to refer to her as "Aunt Jo"—"has no doubt been spying upon me. Yes, I'm sure you've unearthed *bushels* regarding Aubrey's character."

"As a matter of fact," he said, and here he gave me a smug curl of his lips, "it was through none of those means that the information was dispensed. It was one of the creature's own associates who sought *us* out."

One of Aubrey's associates?

I said nothing, determined not to show my surprise, and after another self-satisfied pause Uncle Charles resumed speaking. "It is my hope, Arabella, that however you view me now, you will come to thank me later. After all"—he adopted an injured tone here—"this was a difficult process for me as well as you. I've no wish to play the ogre, you know."

I stared at him, thinking of how little I knew him, had truly known any of my family and what they were capable of in light of a threat to their conventions—which, I saw now, were far more important to them than any well-being of mine.

Uncle Charles was still talking. "Now, what do you say to putting your anger aside, so that we may be friends again?" He appeared to expect some sort of reply from me. When I did not give one, he leaned in toward me.

And then, saying, "Hm? What do you think of that idea?" he reached forward and chucked me beneath the chin.

The gesture was so unpardonable that I did not even plan my response. "*Keep* your hands from me," I spat, and turned my chin so as to slap him away.

He reared back into his own corner of the barouche's seat, and the two lackeys exchanged glances. All of the false camaraderie fled Uncle Charles's face. "Your father has hopelessly overindulged you. Although I'd wager there must be a good deal else that's awry in your mind as well. Well, no matter. You are due for a correction, and you shall have it."

He did not exchange another word with me for the rest of the long, long ride.

We arrived around nightfall at our destination—whatever it was. I'd been unable to see the road signs over the heads of the lackeys, and had no idea whether we had traveled north or south, east or west. I knew only that we were far removed from London, out in the countryside, where buildings had become more and more infrequent, so that by the time we stopped it had been what seemed like a quarter hour since we'd spied another dwelling.

We had to pass through a gate, set into a spiked iron fence which was at least eight feet high; I had rarely seen one so imposing, or so well suited to its function. It chilled my blood to see that fence, to imagine myself en route to any place which required it. But then, I was already horribly frightened, had been feeling even more so since discovering that we were close to disembarking.

Once through the gate, I could see buildings at the end of a long, straight drive. They were estatelike, huge, imposing. Old trees girded them on every side. There appeared to be two main structures: before us was the domicile, its windows ablaze, its architecture of some ancient sort. Behind it was the shadow of a larger, less ornate edifice.

Uncle Charles instructed the driver to pull up to the estate house, and then a moment later, one of the lackeys was grasping my still-bound arms, and I was being "helped" from the carriage. A thousand questions ran through my mind, but I was too frightened to put my anxieties into words, and in the end could only follow behind Uncle Charles as he made his way up the steps and banged at the door. I noticed a plaque there: it said—NORTH VALHALLA HOME FOR WOMEN, and I thought, how evilly, eminently appropriate: Iphigenia has come home at last. Then someone was opening first the door, and then the iron bars beyond it, and I was being pushed through into the building.

It appeared to be a Papist sister of some sort who had opened the door. She wore one of the familiar black-and-white-robed habits, and her face was partially obscured by a stiff wimple and veil. She moved aside, her voluminous skirts whispering, as we entered. Then, taking us in, she murmured, "You must be here to see the doctor."

"We are," Uncle Charles said, staring down his nose at her. "Charles Leeds, and his niece Arabella. We're expected."

Expected, I thought—meaning, the plan to spirit me away in this manner had been in the works for a long while.

The nun bobbed her head, then wafted off down a long, darkened hallway.

I took this opportunity to peer quickly about me. We were standing in a huge, empty slate-floored room; there was no foyer, this space lay directly beyond the front door. Its walls were of plaster; at its far end were several heavy oaken side chairs, and a round matching table with a small vase of flowers upon it. The windows were without curtains, and I could see now that they were grated in the same manner as the door. An archway in the center wall led to the hallway down which the nun had disappeared, while at either end of the room were sliding wooden panels which I guessed opened off into other portions of the ground floor.

There was nothing threatening or foreboding in sight, and yet neither was there anything warm or personal. I had the sense of a space designed to give the illusion of a home with none of its comforts.

A moment after she left, the sister returned, following on the heels of a well-dressed man who I assumed was the doctor she'd referred to. He was thin, tall, with swept-back dark hair and alert, intense eyes. He did not look unfriendly—but then, I was placing little stock in looks these days.

When they reached us, the doctor's face broke into a smile. "Charles," he said, moving to clasp my uncle's hand. "Michael," Uncle Charles blustered, leaning into the greeting.

These niceties completed, the doctor deigned to notice me. "And you must be Miss Leeds. I welcome you to the Valhalla Home. I am Dr. Gregory, founder and administrator. I hope we shall be able to be of service to you."

"You will excuse my not offering my hand," I said, without a shred of sarcasm, "but it is bound behind my back at the moment."

The doctor exchanged a quick look with Uncle Charles, and then said, "Well, we shall have to see to that, won't we." He gestured to the two thugs. "You'll untie her, please." The lackeys nodded, and then obliged.

When I was free, the doctor grazed my fingers with his own. Then he said, "Wait here a moment, please," and drew Uncle Charles off into a corner for a conference. I could not overhear them, but after a minute they shook hands once again, and I realized Uncle Charles was preparing to leave.

Despite the seething hatred I felt for him, I also experienced a pang at the notion of his departure, for it meant I was truly to stay here, that there was to be no last-minute reprieve. But the pang dissipated, and then I thought I should be glad to see the last of him, that if he intended to leave me here he should damned well get on with it.

The two men walked back toward me. "I hope you shall remember your upbringing, and comport yourself as the gentlewoman you've been raised to be," Uncle Charles said to me. "I think you shall find that your time here will be easiest if you take the proper attitude from the outset." I did not even look in his direction. "Good-bye, Arabella. I wish you well."

"I wish you what you would earn," I replied, still facing the opposite wall.

From the corner of my eye I saw him don his hat. Then the sister unlocked the door for his little party, and he was gone.

"Well, now," Dr. Gregory said after a second. He rubbed his hands briskly together as if washing them. "Why don't you follow me to my office, Miss Leeds, and I shall explain a few of the basic tenets of operation, and of life, here, and then we shall get you situated."

I followed him, thinking that thus far the place was not what I had anticipated, and that perhaps I need not fear being physically abused here. I had arrived in manacles, it was true, but that seemed to be more the doing of Uncle Charles and his two thugs than the policy of the doctor. I was now quite free, and unescorted, the sister having departed when the doctor had asked me to his office.

There were no shouts or screams of misery emanating from anywhere in the building. I saw no filthy hallways lined with straw, no lunatics lying about in their own waste. Not only that, but the doctor was speaking to me in a respectful and normal manner, as if I truly were a visitor at some pleasant, if austerely appointed, spa.

His office was just down the dark hallway. It was a large, well-furnished room, with an Oriental carpet and mahogany desk, and a high velvet-draped window on one wall. He gestured me into a leather-padded chair, and then sat behind his desk and regarded me with his hands folded.

"So," he began, "you have been remanded into our care by your family. Have you any questions for me?"

"Yes. Quite a few."

He waved with a gesture which said, ask away.

"I was not 'remanded' here so much as abducted. I was dragged from my home, and told nothing as to where I was being taken. I trust this is not the usual manner in which people arrive here."

Dr. Gregory leaned back in his chair. "Our guests find us at the end of a number of different paths. There are times when one's course must be interfered with for one's own good, particularly when the moral purity and future happiness of a young woman are at stake. And so occasionally extreme measures must be taken, with the knowledge that the ends shall justify the means."

Now I felt a little of my earlier relief beginning to fade. "And what exactly are the means? What sort of place is this?"

The doctor seemed pleased with the question. "Valhalla House is committed to restoring the eroded moral sensibilities and compromised mental faculties of its guests. We accept a variety of young women, from those who have lost their claim upon Christian virtue to those who have suffered some grievous injury to their thinking minds. What most of these unfortunates have in common are well-regarded and caring families who have eschewed traditional methods of treatment in favor of what is offered here."

In other words, I thought, you service the daughters of *wealthy* families: either those who seek in your establishment a way round the insane asylum (so long as there is money to purchase it), or those whose relations disapprove of them for one reason or another—or perhaps were embarrassed by them—and so have deposited them here, where they will be out of sight and mind. My optimism was melting away by the minute.

"You shall find here a haven, in the strict daily schedule of prayer and meaningful work combined with voluntary self-discipline and introspection," the doctor was saying. "I am very proud of the fact that the vast majority of our guests leave here with their places amidst their families and social spheres restored."

HOW LONG DOES THAT TAKE, I wished to ask, but I knew quite well that I should not put the question to him in those words. In fact I was getting the sense that it would be pointless to continue the interview, as the doctor appeared to regard it as an opportunity to present his prerehearsed speeches to yet another captive audience. I decided that I would try a different tack, and see what it might gain me.

"I am certain you do a world of good for your—guests. However, I am also certain that those who benefit most are those who are truly in need of your services. I, on the other hand, am not. Please understand, Dr. Gregory, I am here against my will. Fine as your course of treatment may be, I do not care to take advantage of it. I must tell you quite frankly that I do not intend to stay."

He was nodding and smiling still; I did not find this encouraging. "Yes, Miss Leeds, I understand that you arrived under less than ideal circumstances. And I can understand why you might wish to depart. But I assure you, that is quite impossible. Your presence here may not be voluntary, but it is now a matter of legality. You were remanded here by your legal guardians, they who are responsible for your welfare, and in whose house you dwelled—"

"I am an adult, sir," I cut in. "I am not a little girl beholden to my parents. And at any rate even a little girl has certain powers of consent—"

"Consent is one matter, my dear, whereas legal autonomy is another. May I remind you, you are a female with neither husband nor income. You reside with your father, who provides for all your monetary and material needs. Under the law, Miss Leeds, your father has the power of attorney over you—he is well within his rights in sending you here. And"—his tone changed, and I felt my stomach clench—"we are well within our rights in preventing your flight. This is not an asylum, Miss Leeds, in terms of its approach to the difficulties of its guests. But we are regarded legally as a medical facility, the rules of involuntary commitment apply, and right-thinking men will not hesitate to enforce them."

I suppressed a shudder. "Is there to be no inquiry into the reasons for my *commitment?*"

"You are a danger to your own welfare, and by any account a wayward young woman." He now referred to a sheaf of papers before him—to which, I was stunned to note, my father's easily recognizable signature was affixed. "According to your father, your behavior has been erratic and bizarre for many months now. You have undertaken nighttime trips to dangerous areas of the city of London, you have indulged in scandalous behavior with various male accomplices. And most recently—most alarmingly—you embarked upon a liaison with a person who can only be regarded as profoundly unsuitable. To put it bluntly, Miss, you were found to be consorting with a Negro."

I felt my temper rising. "I must correct you on that point, Dr. Gregory," I snapped. "The young man is not a 'Negro' per se. He is one-eighth Negro—" I was about to plunge on, but then I caught myself: this distinction was hardly relevant, and besides, my words betrayed Aubrey and his heritage. "At any rate, what does it matter whether he is the Prince of Wales, or recently arrived from the Dark Continent and black as a lump of coal? Is it a crime here in England to choose a consort from outside one's own race? Or is romance without familial approval now to be interpreted as a form of insanity? If it is, then I submit that half the young women in the country would risk internment in hospitals."

"Your sentiments are quite interesting," the doctor replied, not unkindly, "but I am afraid they wander from the point. It's a question of consistency,

Miss Leeds, and of what is considered normal and appropriate under certain circumstances. And no judge, no court of law, will find it normal and appropriate that a girl of good family, and formerly of good character, raised in a Christian household, suddenly embarks upon a distinct course of lasciviousness and wanton behavior with socially and morally inferior elements."

He leaned back once more in his chair, and I shuddered again, for the picture he'd painted for me was only too clear. I could well imagine it—a hearing before some magistrate of approximately the same ilk as the doctor himself, the well-respected Leeds family on one side, and me—with Aubrey, the octoroon former slave and itinerant tutor—on the other.

I felt myself falling into a black, bottomless pit, for it seemed there would be no way out of this place, save the one I undertook by my own hand, and by stealth.

There was nothing left to say to the doctor; we understood each other now, I knew. I was silent, and after a moment he concluded the meeting in the same honeyed tone he'd adopted through most of the discussion. "I would suggest you make your stay with us no more difficult than it need be, Miss Leeds. Allow this place to benefit you. Yield to it. You shall be the happier for it, I assure you."

Still I remained silent, and after another few seconds the doctor rose, and opened the office door. "Come, let us get you settled in. I realize you've no luggage as of yet, but your family shall no doubt be supplying you with some within a few days. In the meantime, we shall provide you with whatever basic accouterments you need."

"Are there to be visits with my family, then?"

"Why, of course!" The doctor seemed injured at the idea that I'd think otherwise. "Of course! We wish your family to see your progress, and to assist in your rehabilitation."

He held the door wide for me, and I followed him out of the office and down the hallway, toward the rear of the building.

At the end of the hall was another thick door, covered by another iron-barred grate, which the doctor opened with a key upon a full, clanking ring. I now saw that beyond the door was a large courtyard, a pleasant grassy space with paths and a little fountain at its center. And beyond that, surrounding the courtyard on its other three sides, was another building. Unlike the one we'd just left, this structure was ugly and unadorned. It was five stories high, and shaped like a U, its smooth walls interrupted by slitlike windows which, I now saw, were barred as heavily as the doors. I realized this must be where the doctor's "guests" resided. It was a far cry from the country-house exterior one viewed upon rolling up the inviting driveway.

The doctor led me across the courtyard, and opened another barred, locked door. He gestured me inside. "This is where you shall be living," he said, with obvious pride. The room we stood in was bare, plank-floored, with unpainted, unupholstered wooden chairs scattered about, and wooden benches before a large hearth. I peered round, but the lamps were out, and at any rate the doctor was urging me onward. He took me to a door which opened on the left side of the U, and locked it behind him.

I saw a flight of stairs before us, and we ascended. On the third floor, the doctor halted, opened the inevitable grille with his keys, and beckoned me through. At each passing of a locked gate I'd found myself becoming more and more apprehensive; as this one closed behind me and was secured again, I felt the sudden welling of tears in my eyes. I took a deep breath, determined not to allow myself a moment's vulnerability until I was alone.

We entered a wide hallway, which was lined with little locked doors. Each door, I saw, had a tiny square cut in the top, through which one might peek at the occupants of the rooms beyond. The hall was dimly lit; at the end of it, I could just make out another row of bars. Behind them, in a large cubicle filled with latticed glass cabinets, a desk, chairs, and cots, was a sister, who sat going over some figures in a ledger. On one of the cots was a man—a guard, no doubt, employed to watch over the women—and so observe their every intimacy, in this place which prided itself on propriety.

"Good evening, Sister Raymond," the doctor addressed the nun. She looked up, the man on the cot did as well, and then the sister rose to unlock the door from the inside. "This is our new visitor." The doctor indicated me with a hand.

The nun and I regarded each other. She was tall and plain-featured, one cheek sporting a brown mole with hairs sprouting from it. She wore pince-nez, and the flesh of her face seemed to be oozing forward from beneath the tight wimple which contained it. "Well. Welcome to Valhalla House," she said without warmth. "I am Sister Raymond Marie. You are"—she glanced at some paperwork on her desk—"Miss Arabella Katherine Leeds." Once again I was shocked at the extent to which I'd been expected.

"How do you do," I said in the same tone as her own.

"Take her to 305," the doctor instructed Sister Raymond. "Agnes's room." The sister nodded, and he turned to me. "Well, Miss Leeds, I wish you luck. We shall meet again very shortly. For now, though, I bid you a good night." He waited expectantly.

"Indeed." I could not bring myself to wish him good night in return. He frowned, then retreated back down the hallway from which we'd just come.

In the meantime, the nun had swished by me, taking a ring of keys from the desk and urging the man on the cot to get up and accompany us—most likely to supply force should it be needed for some reason. "Follow me," Sister Raymond said.

When we were halfway down the hall she stopped before one of the little doors and unlocked it. I saw that the tiny, slit-windowed room beyond was dimly lit by a nubbin of candle which stood upon a plain metal nightstand with drawers. In the candle's feeble glow a girl of approximately my age lay upon a metal cot, a Bible propped up in her hands. She wore a white nightcap over her hair, and her round, childish face glanced up at us when we entered.

"You've a new roommate, Agnes. This is Miss Arabella Leeds. Miss Leeds, this is Miss Agnes Starkweather."

"Hello," I whispered.

She looked at me a long moment. Then she said, "Hello," in a toneless voice.

"You'll help Miss Leeds settle herself," the nun said to Agnes. It was more a demand than a request, but the girl's countenance did not change.

"Yes, Sister."

"You'll find a nightdress, cap, and stockings in the drawer of your nightstand," the nun then told me. "You are required to don these after evening prayers and recreations, at approximately eight o'clock each evening. We shall issue you daytime clothing in the morning." With that, she turned and departed, and I heard the click of the door being locked behind her. That click was as loud in my ears as the rush of my blood.

I sat down on the second cot, which was on the wall opposite my roommate's, and only three feet or so from her own bed. I was feeling as disheartened and alone as ever in my life. It was the sound of the door, I realized—I had never been, or expected to be, in a place where I was contained like a wild beast. Yet here I was, when only this morning—only a few brief hours ago—I had been as one in charge of her own life. I was dazed, turned inside out—and the realization that I had now to deal with a complete stranger, with whom I was trapped in this virtual horsestall, caused me nearly to scream. I sat against the wall, my breath coming in short gasps, willing myself not to acknowledge the girl a few feet away from me.

But after a minute I realized this would serve nothing. I could provoke the girl's hostility—which would surely make our confinement worse—or I could engage her somehow, learn all I could from her. I turned to look at her, and saw that she was staring at me as well.

"Your things are in that stand." She flicked her chin at the metal box of a nightstand by my cot. That she seemed about to offer me no comfort caused my spirits to plunge yet again, but I tried to recover them. When I did not say anything the girl added, "There's a bit of candle in there too. You get one a month, and seven matches a week." She turned back to her Bible.

I opened the battered top drawer, with the horrible sense that every movement of mine was an infringement on the girl's privacy, that far from having any pity for me she hated me for interrupting her solitude. I slid out the white nightdress and cap, exact imitations of hers. Then I saw the nub of candle, and four matches tied with string. It was the middle of the week; it seemed my captors had not wished to give me the full match allotment and risk flouting the rules.

I lit the candle, and forced my numb fingers to unbutton my frock. But I could not bring myself to take it off. It was all that remained of my real life; I did not wish to yield it and become a faceless prisoner within these walls.

I searched the other drawers of the nightstand to see what else they contained. There was a worn Bible, also a duplicate of Agnes's, and a small leather bookmark. Nothing more. I noticed a trunk at the foot of each bed; on both were basins and pitchers of water. I cleared these from the trunk meant for me, then I flipped up the lid and peered inside, but there was nothing save a single thin cotton hand towel.

"Excuse me," I said to Agnes. She gave no obvious sign of annoyance, but I thought I imagined her stiffening at the sound of my voice. "Are we provided with nothing else here? A towel for bathing, perhaps? A brush for teeth, or tooth powder? A comb?"

"There's a chamber pot under the bed. You must ring the bell by the door if you need the privy, but the sister does not take kindly to being summoned in the middle of the night. Baths are on Saturday evenings on the first floor. You are given a bath towel just before your turn. Beyond that, you are expected to provide your own toiletries. You may have your family bring them to you." I wondered what happened to the girls without families—but then, I thought, there were probably none of those here, for if a girl had no family, who was to pay for her no doubt expensive stay in Valhalla House?

I sat down on the bed again. I peeked over at Agnes, suddenly desperate for conversation, for anything to distract me from the terrible loneliness I felt overtaking me. But she did not look away from her reading, and I knew better than to bother her again. I lay down, blew out the stubby candle, and stared up at the bare plaster ceiling.

What was happening at home, I wondered—had the Beckwiths responded to my calling card? Would anyone question where I'd gone, or why? Would Aubrey?

Aubrey. He surely would know I'd not left of my own accord.

Mamee, Papa, why did you do this to me? Help me, come get me. But there was no Mamee or Papa to hear my pleas. They were gone. And left in their places were the two unfeeling strangers who had shut me away. I felt the tears I'd managed to hold back all day slide down my face, and into my hair.

I doubted, though, that my parents had come by this insanity of their own accord. Uncle Charles's influence was more than likely behind it: my parents had been worried about me, and at the moment of their greatest vulnerability he must have supplied them with this, his helpful solution. Perhaps he even believed it himself, that kidnap and imprisonment might be beneficial to me.

But that excused none of it. Or them. What, I wondered, would they tell Richard? What lies would all of them they perpetrate? Or perhaps they had told him the truth, and he had taken their side. No, that wasn't possible—they must have anticipated some sort of negative reaction from him, for they'd detained him at Leeds Hall while the dirty work was done. But they could not hide it from him forever.

In the midst of these ruminations, I heard Agnes Starkweather roll over, and a second later her candle was blown out. She had not spoken another word to me, and it was obvious she did not intend to, that she had put herself out quite enough on my behalf. There was no point in attempting to stay awake; at length I slipped under the sheets fully dressed.

I discovered then that my mattress was a thin, stale-smelling pallet of cotton batting through which I could feel the iron platform beneath, while the blanket over it was of a wool so rough it scratched me through the top sheet. There was no bottom sheet.

I arranged myself around these various discomforts, all the while imagining that Miss Starkweather in her prim cap would hardly sanction my failure to change my clothes. But it was my first night, I thought—I could always plead exhaustion, being now too tired and despondent to care whether the automaton next to me approved or not.

But I could not sleep. I lay awake most of the night listening to the odd sounds, the occasional cry, that filtered through the walls. When I did manage to drift off, I awoke a short time later, startled and terrified from nightmares, to find myself still within the nightmare. I cried, stopped, cried some more, swallowing the sound so as not to alert Agnes Starkweather. I wondered whether this wretched night would ever end, and if it did, what would await me on the other side of it.

On the very next day I discovered precisely what awaited me. Ill and exhausted though I was, I was nonetheless jammed into the inexorable, smooth-flowing regularity of Valhalla House.

At five in the morning I was wrenched from my murky sleep by a clanging bell, which the sister in attendance was swinging up and down the hall. The door was unlocked, with that terrible clashing sound, by one of the male attendants. It opened a crack, and a gray pinafore, white chemise, and gray apron—my set of promised day-clothes—was shoved at me.

Agnes—up at the first reverberation of the bell—managed to communicate to me in as few words as possible that we would have a half hour to dress, wash, make our beds, and sweep before being made to leave our cell for the day.

Breakfast was at five-thirty, in the dining hall on the first floor, and consisted of porridge—no coffee or tea, as these are stimulants, *verboten* for young ladies. I was already nauseated; I blanched at having to force the cold, tasteless mass down past the constriction in my throat which made breathing and swallowing a painful effort. I tried to stay near to Agnes—she was the only soul I knew here—but she dodged off into the throng of girls and left me behind, and I found myself alone, seated at the end of a raw plank table, upon a plank bench.

A sister handed me a square of cloth for a napkin, one pewter spoon, and a pewter mug from which to eat. When the other girls began filing out I noticed they took these items with them. There was a long metal trough set up at the end of the room opposite the kitchen. I watched as the others dunked the cup and spoon in the trough, dried them with the napkin, showed the sister, and were then permitted to go. I scarcely had time to do the same; then I was being shooed from the hall and into the chapel, also on the first floor.

Prayers, I discovered, follow breakfast. I sat down trembling in a pew, whereupon the sister in charge walked over to me, grabbed me by the shoulder, and pulled me forward, onto the wooden kneelers before me. I watched as the other girls folded their hands, bowed their heads, and recited, while Sister sauntered by, inspecting each row. I tried to follow her lips through the long, unfamiliar Latin prayers, but I stumbled and faltered, so that at the end the nun's stony gaze was aimed straight at myself. "We were far from pleasing this morning," she intoned. "We shall therefore begin again." I felt the pairs of hot, resentful eyes boring into my back. Five times we repeated the syllables, until they had been robbed of any meaning I might have wrested from them and became mere sounds, and then at last we were allowed off our stiff and creaking knees.

As I attempted to rub the blood back into my limbs, I recalled the many times I'd heard my uncle revile the Catholics and their clergy as heathens and barbarians—hardly a step above the godless Negroes. Wherever he was, I thought, he was no doubt congratulating himself on the magnanimity with which he'd overlooked the Papists' shortcomings, and undertaken the decision to imprison me here.

Work duties—cleaning, cooking, laundry, mending—followed prayer. I was given a partner, a fat, sullen girl named India, and we were ordered to one of the Public Rooms, this one that great bare space next to the dining hall. There we were set to mending a mountainous pile of frayed sheets. "I hope you're better at stitching than you are at praying," India hissed at me beneath her breath, "for I'm accountable for my partner's work, and if we have to do all of these over again I shall get even with you somehow."

"Why do you blame me," I hissed back. "No one has instructed me in a single rule."

"No one instructs any of us, Miss. We all learned the hard way, after having our ears boxed by our housemates for all the extra work our mistakes cost them."

I set my trembling fingers to stitching as finely as possible. At times the work drove pictures of home, of past, from my head, but at one point the scent of a newly washed sheet made its way through the veil of my concentration, and I found myself crying once more, borne back to some exquisitely painful reminiscence of my own sheets, my own bed. I stopped for a moment to gather my wits, but my scowling partner narrowed her eyes and sighed in exasperation.

Just when I thought I could stand no more of the close work and the bend in my back, the clock chimed two. A tea of sorts was served in the dining room, with hot milk and sliced bread. The other girls devoured this meager meal with gusto, but I found I was not hungry. I was hugely relieved to hear, however, that the next three hours were ours to spend as we liked, either in the Public Rooms or outside in the garden. I chose simply to sit; I reclined in a rocking chair so as to appear to be doing something, when in fact my head was empty of any save the most miserable thoughts.

At five P.M. we were rousted again, for the start of Hall Meetings.

Seeing me wander about in confusion, a sister asked me sharply where I was roomed. I froze, suddenly unable to recall the number of my cell; I could only reply that I knew the route back. She instructed me to use it, then, lest I be demerited for tardiness. Agnes chanced to be disappearing round a corner at that very moment, so I followed her and, once arrived on our floor, beheld our fellow inmates gathered on the ground in a circle. The sister, our monitor for the meeting's duration, sat in her chair, her back to her barred refuge, but her keys within easy reach.

I had no idea what to expect of this "meeting." Ostensibly the point was to examine one's behavior, and the progress each girl felt she'd made that day toward eliminating "wrong thoughts" and "inappropriate actions." But it soon became apparent that the inmates were expected either to disparage themselves in the vilest manner, or to tattle and comment upon each other with venomous, soul-crushing thoroughness. I listened as, one after the next, they rose to condemn their own characters, or a cellmate whom they disliked, or the girl down the hall who had committed some silly infraction. The sister nodded sagely to all that was said, adding to the frenzy now and then by soliciting judgments on the parts of the listeners.

By some miracle the hour ended without my having been required to speak, and at six o'clock Sister closed the meeting. We returned to the dining room for the main meal: vegetables, potatoes, bread, milk, and stringy mutton, all of it doled out in niggardly fashion, greasy, barely warm, without spice or flavor. This time I was given a pewter bowl, spoon, and butter knife. I wondered why the other girls rushed their meal so; I realized on my way out the door that they hoped to be first at the troughs, which soon become fouled from the seventy or so sets of plates being dumped and then dunked in them. Naturally I found myself at the very end of the line. I stared down into the putrid water, repelled enough that any pleasure I'd found in satisfying my hunger disappeared at once.

Then I was shooed back upstairs to the hall. I made immediately for my room, which was open. Agnes was sitting upon her bed, brushing her hair. "Please," I whispered—I had got used to whispering after only a day—"what is happening now?"

"You needn't whisper," Agnes said in a normal, impersonal, voice. "We have an hour's recreation period, til eight o'clock when the doors are locked. One may visit from room to room, or talk." I did neither. I had no one to talk to, as Agnes had evidently indulged in all the conversation that her principles allowed her.

Instead I read the Bible in my nightstand. When our attendant came by he was gallant enough to tell me that Bible study is permitted until nine o'clock, when there is a last check for light beneath the doors and all candles must be blown out. I utilized the hour in the appropriate manner, as did Agnes.

Thus ended my first day. And then it began again. Every one exactly, numbingly the same, except that on Sundays there is no work duty, the time left free is devoted to chapel and to the singing of hymns, while supper is served cold.

Not a single gesture here escapes scrutiny, either by the sisters or by the other inmates. And every one which is noted is duly reported to the doctor, who sits in upon the meetings once a week, nodding at progress, shaking his head in dismay at regression.

I believe, despite my instinctive dislike of the man, that the doctor is sincere, that he truly feels he is effecting a "cure" for what he sees as the disease of our minds. I find this the more frightening than if he were merely a charlatan, for, in his zealotry, the doctor is untouched by any appeal made either to his vanity or his corruptibility. One cannot wink and ask him to turn a blind eye to infractions, one cannot avert his stern gaze through flattery. He is single-minded in his devotion to his program and his beliefs; if they chance to provide him with an income, so be it, but I doubt the doctor's motives are either pecuniary or selfish.

The same cannot be said of the sisters or the male attendants who guard us and enforce discipline. While the sisters may not gain financially from their positions here, I get the impression that they are fulfilled in other ways by their tasks of bullying and condescending. Certainly they undertake said tasks with far more relish than remorse.

The male attendants seem even less complicated, from the limited glimpses I've had of them so far. I see them at every turn disobeying the rules they are ostensibly there to enforce: they leer and smirk at us, they steal food, imbibe alcohol (which unsteadies their gait, and causes their breath and perspiration to reek), they smoke tobacco, and trade all of these things with the inmates upon the stairwells or in the yards. Just what they are trading for is less obvious, although I am sure I could hazard a well-founded guess.

I discovered, also within a very few days, what it is that brings eight out of ten of the young women to Valhalla House: they are pregnant outside of wedlock. That is the form their insanity has taken.

My own roommate, Agnes, is among these unfortunates. She is perhaps four or five months along, with a round little belly disguised by the high waist of her dress. It is hard to fathom what she feels or thinks of her condition, as she does not speak of it. In fact it's difficult to know what—or if—Agnes thinks of anything. I've discovered she is as noncommittal toward everyone else as she is toward me, seeming to have no friends among the inmates, and keeping to herself for the most part. What I took for annoyance is, rather, a sort of disconnection with the world, as if she is too absorbed in some internal dialogue to be distracted by what is happening outside of her.

I have met the other residents of the third floor, and they vary widely, from the tall, older, and distinctly strange girl called Julia Hoxley—not pregnant—to the pert child of thirteen, Emily Tarnower, who seems about to deliver at any moment. There are twelve residents on this floor, and we are all on what the sisters call the Reward System: if we pass through a certain number of days without incident and appear duly enthusiastic, we are allowed a reward. These consist of sweets, at the bottom of the list, all the way up to outings about the grounds, at the top. The sisters—and the doctor even more so—consider their Reward System a great advance in the running of the facility, a modern technique far superior to the notion of merely punishing for bad behavior. Of course there is that too. But as punishment is in use everywhere, it is not considered quite so original or progressive an idea.

On the third day I was here, my parents arrived for their first visit. The daytime monitor, Sister Louise, fetched me from the Public Room, where I was hacking at a bit of needlework, and informed me that I had guests. Then I was taken across the courtyard to the ornate building containing Dr. Gregory's office, across from which are small rooms appointed for visiting.

Mother and Father brought my comb and mirror, a toothbrush, some scented soap, and underthings. They must have been shocked at my appearance, as I had already been two days without these essentials. I had been rubbing my teeth with a corner of my towel and untangling my hair with my fingers, but I felt filthy and barely human nonetheless, having had nothing to wash with but water in a basin.

They had also brought me an extra frock, but this I did not need, as I'd already been issued the gray uniform raiments to be worn here each and every day. Thus have I been reduced, like everyone else, to shadows.

What is there to say of that first visit? I was torn in two by it, and so were they, and yet the sight of them, both in tears, as if some accident had befallen me, only served to arouse my rage. "Why are *you* crying?" My voice shook with my own tears. "I am the one who must endure being here, not you. You did this to me. Did you not consider how the result might look?" Father flinched as though I had slapped him, but then met my gaze once again.

"We did what we thought was necessary, Arabella. We love you, and are determined to save you, even from yourself."

"If you wish to save me, then take me out of here."

He was silent a long moment. "Suppose we were to do as you ask. Would you then agree to reside at Leeds Hall, and to discontinue any contact with that—*person?*"

I was equally long in answering him. "I could lie to you, Father. I could give you my word that I would do as you ask, and then I could break that word. But that isn't how I wish to secure my freedom. The answer to your question is no. I would not promise. There is no reason for me to be here, or for me to agree to residing where I know I would be miserable, or to give up Aubrey. Why should I have to make bargains when I've been stripped of my liberty unjustly?"

Father's shoulders sagged; he slumped in his seat.

"How did we ever come to this turn?" He gazed at me with such helplessness that I almost pitied him.

Almost.

"*You* brought us to it. You know nothing of Aubrey, never gave me leave to explain, and yet you've determined that he is responsible for some debauchery you imagine I've engaged in."

Mother and Father exchanged a glance, and then Father spoke again.

"Can you still not see, after all this time, that it is irrelevant what we know or do not know of *that person*? He is *racially mixed*. It does not matter what else he is—this is why you are here, Arabella, because you don't seem to understand the simple truth of it. You've lost all sense of perspective—and it isn't only in the matter of *that person* that you've done so. It's all the rest of it as well—the sneaking about, the nighttime drives, the lies, the keeping company with men unchaperoned—" He put his head into his hands and rubbed at his face. "We should never have been so lenient with you when we saw the signs of your rebellion. All of this began long before we left the States, and we should have attended to it then—"

He fell silent. Mother had not ceased sniffling in all this time, but now she peered up at me, dabbing her eyes with her handkerchief. "You must take advantage of your time here, Berry. You must make it count for something, and learn to be yourself again, to leave this image you have taken on behind you."

"You misunderstand, Mother. I *have* left behind the image I wished to discard. I am becoming who I wish to be."

Her eyes overflowed at this, and we sat so for several minutes, until she raised the basket she'd prepared for me. "I brought you some of the things Dr. Gregory told me you'd need, dear."

"What I need is to go home," I said.

"You are eating properly? You are well treated, I am sure?"

"I am a prisoner, Mother. I am kept here like an animal, in some vain attempt to drive the life force from me. I cannot look beyond that to such trivialities as how the food tastes."

This set her to sobbing once again.

"There is no point to this," Father sighed.

"No. There isn't." I would not soften. "You have done wrong—you *know* you have. If you are not about to undo it and sign me away from this place, then you may as well leave."

There was a terrible silence, and then Father rose. "Come along," he said to Mother. She stood up, her tears redoubled. I stood as well. They were passing by me when Mother reached out to pull me to her.

I allowed a moment of contact, then let my arms fall limply from her. Father gave me a final defeated look, and then escorted Mother, still sobbing, out the door.

The moment they had retreated down the hall, I collapsed back into the chair I'd occupied, leaned my arms and head onto the desk, and cried without restraint.

Two days later they returned with Richard. We all sat once more through the same recriminations, the same stalemate. Then Mother and Father left the room, and Richard and I were alone for the first time since my abduction.

"So." Richard heaved a great sigh.

"So."

"I am so sorry, Berry—" his words came in a rush. "I didn't know. Had I known, I would have warned you, but they wouldn't let me come back and they wouldn't tell me why—"

"Never mind," I told him, "I don't hold you the least bit responsible."

He glanced toward the door, and then leaned toward me. "I brought you something." From a basket he took my folded lap blanket, and placed it on the table between us.

"Thank you. That was sweet of you."

"You might want to unfold it—carefully."

It was when I did so that I saw the two of you, my dear friends old and new, hidden in the folds with your pen alongside you.

"Oh, Richard! Oh, thank you! But how did you know where to find them, how did you get into the trunk—"

"I tore your room apart, and finally there was no place left to look. So I picked the lock on the trunk." I shook my head at him. "It wasn't hard. I read all about how it's done in the *Gazette*. When Agar and Pierce robbed that bullion train in the fifties, it's said—"

"You needn't go into detail regarding your methods. Only—thank you. You cannot know how much this means to me."

There was an awkward pause, and then Richard asked, "So how are you treated here, really?"

There was no reason to vent my rage upon him. "It's bad. But not unbearable. At least not so far. It's mostly that—it's *wrong*, Richard. It's wrong that I'm here."

"I know it is. But—but perhaps if you'd agree to a couple of things, just to go home—after all, Berry, you *did* go much too far this time—"

"What do you mean, too far?"

"Is it true, what they say he is? Did you know of it?"

"What who is? Know what? You mean Aubrey?"

"Is it true?"

"What is true, Richard, is that he is a fine person, and I have come to love and trust him."

"So it's true."

"If it were, what of it?"

"And you knew of it."

"If I did, it would be because he was honest enough to reveal it, and again, what of it?"

"I'm not sure—it's only so— Oh, for God's sake, Berry, it's extreme beyond words and you know it. It's not that I've anything against them, the Negroes, I mean—but when my own sister is involved, and her reputation is at stake—"

"Am I to hear this from you too, then? You met him, Richard. You saw him. Now, what is to become more important—what you yourself thought of him, or what other people make of some fact of his background?"

"I only wish you weren't here, and it seems to me that he is the one responsible for it."

"No. Mother and Father and Uncle Charles are responsible. They put me here. They did it without knowing anything at all of what was happening, they did it based on some irrational bias they harbor. Place the blame where it belongs, Richard."

Before he could reply, there was a knock on the door: our visit was up. We stood, and as we were about to exit we hugged each other spontaneously. "I love you," Richard whispered, and then he rushed from the room and was gone.

On Richard's second visit, there was no mention of Aubrey's failings, or of my having "gone too far." I gathered his good sense had got the better of him.

Instead he began by blurting out, "They all came looking for you—Harlow Beckwith and his sister, and Aubrey Bennett."

I tried not to appear as shocked as I was. "What happened? Were you there?"

"No. I was still at Leeds Hall. It was just after you were taken. I don't know what was said, but I know none of them have returned since I came back."

I felt my stomach drop. "Richard—you must get some word to them, let them know what happened. Especially Mr. Bennett. Please, even if you could send a card—"

"I can't, Berry. You've no idea how they watch me. I can't leave the house by myself, I can't call a porter—for most of the week I am shipped off to Leeds Hall, and then I've got all of *that* deuced crew watching me. They know you'll ask me to carry some message, and they're doing everything they can to prevent it."

"Look, Richard—they have to relax their vigilance sooner or later. They cannot keep you penned up like this forever. When you have a chance—"

"When I've a chance, certainly. But it may be a while before that chance arises."

"So be it, then."

Then it was Mother and Father's turn to enter.

Each of their visits leaves me more heartbroken than the last, as those visits have become mere contests of will, between the members of what used to be a united and loving family.

MAY 3, 1863

Mother and Father have announced that they shall confine their visits to weekends, which I feel is for the best.

That leaves me, for the rest of the time, in the presence of my other "family," the inmates whose company I am forced to share here.

One of the great oddities regarding this place is that there is no division between the pregnant or merely obstreperous girls and the ones who seem in the grips of some genuine insanity. To Dr. Gregory, we are all equally sick or well, all confined as a result of some *moral* corruption, and so all equally susceptible to the "cure" he is determined to work on us. We are therefore all housed together, mixed about on the two floors reserved for dormitories.

Thus it is that all of Three West Hall is forced to endure the presence of Julia Hoxley, who is surely as crazy as any resident of Bedlam. Much of the time she appears quite normal, even docile. In fact she is something of a pet among the sisters, whom she reveres and fawns over as if they were cherished companions. But then for no reason she will claim she hears voices speaking to her; she works herself into tempers, and accuses the rest of us of controlling her thoughts by means of a liquid poured into her ears while she sleeps.

Certain of the sisters appear unable to decide whether Julia is a lunatic, or divinely inspired. But even more bizarre, to me, is the doctor's own assessment of our floormate: he seems to regard her misfortune as a willful choosing of wrong, a personal affront toward himself requiring the utmost punishment.

It is because of Julia that I learned in detail what the fourth floor above us is used for.

Every few days, poor Julia performs some act which the doctor terms a "challenge to order." The sisters wring their hands, but nonetheless assert that "correction" shall benefit her, and so she is hauled, kicking and screaming, through the barred doors, into the stairwell, and up the steps to the fourth floor. Once there, she is subjected to Reformation Treatment. I asked one of the other girls, a conspicuously not pregnant one named Martha Crampton, what this consists of, and she told me: among the various methods in use is "self-contemplation," which in plain language is confinement in a darkened cell by oneself. There is also "hydrotherapy," which consists of being thrown naked in a vat of freezing water until one appears more tractable. And there is caning, which is administered by the sisters on one's hands or posterior, in imitation of that grand tradition followed in the English boys' academies.

I was stunned, for I'd no idea such things went on here; moreover, I was stunned to think they'd be inflicted, if upon anyone, upon Miss Hoxley. My own belief is that Julia can no more help her ranting and delusions than a baby can control its cries, so that punishment can be no more a deterrent in her case than in the case of a hapless infant. Each time the exercise of dragging her upstairs is performed, I shudder within myself, for it seems to me that Dr. Gregory is as deluded in his thinking as Julia is in hers.

On the other hand, it appears so far that the fourth floor is an extreme not often resorted to. I have heard whispers concerning a population permanently hidden there, but this is mere rumor, and I do not put much stock in it. As of yet, I've not seen any of the other inmates of my hall taken upstairs for any reason.

But then, none of these girls misbehave. In the presence of the nuns and attendants they are propriety itself, and if I catch the distinct whiff of rebellion or fury here and there, it is soon brought under control so as not to be seen by the staff.

I myself engage in the same behavior. I have no intention of arousing anyone's ire, or drawing undue attention to my person.

For I have decided that if I am to leave this place, it may well have to be by my own strategizing—in other words, an escape.

I first came to this conclusion after another conversation I had with the abovementioned Martha Crampton. Miss Crampton is as full of bitterness over her confinement as am I myself. As she explained to me one day in the Public Room, she has not even the comfort of a specific date of release to look forward to.

"The girls like Miss Tarnower and Agnes—the Pregnants—they'll be released when their children are born. But those of us like you and me, and even Julia Hoxley—we have no namable problem, nothing as precise as a pregnancy, to set a limit on our incarceration. Julia, for example, has been here almost four years."

I blanched at this, although I knew Julia was hardly representative of the rest of us. "How long have you been here?" I asked Martha, dreading the answer.

"Two years. Since I was eighteen."

I could not help releasing a gasp. "Two years! What precipitated it? What did you do?"

"I took a beau. Unfortunately for me, he was of the wrong spiritual bent. A Jew. From my family's reaction, you would think he'd nailed Christ to the cross himself."

I was finding this story hideously familiar, but I felt compelled to know the rest of it. "What became of him?"

She gave me a sad smile. "I've no idea. My parents sent him packing, and he never wrote, never attempted to contact me. I had letters smuggled out, but he did not answer them for months. When he finally replied, it was to tell me that he believed we'd been young and foolish, that it truly is best for people to keep to their own, and that he wished me well. But so far as my family's circle was concerned, I was ruined. Everyone knew of my liaison, and my parents could think of nothing better to do than to keep me here until some time passed. The Home, of course, is happy to have me so long as the appropriate fees are paid."

I could not reply to this at first, feeling a mix of both empathy for Martha and horror over meeting the same fate. *Two years.* With no foreseeable end to it.

No. I would not submit to that. I would leave here promptly, as soon as I could manage it, if I had to bend the bars on the windows back with my bare hands.

We moved on to other subjects that day, but Martha's words have not fled my mind for an instant, and the thoughts they incited have turned from fantasy to the beginnings of a plan.

I am not certain just yet whether to ask Miss Crampton if she wishes to join me. I sense in Martha a kindred spirit—like me, she refuses, at the daily finger-pointing meetings, to indulge in the ritual of tattling on her fellow inmates, and I can see the bitterness with which she regards the whole business of the Home's "treatment."

But I am not yet certain that I need or desire a companion in my enterprise, or that she is the person best suited to the position. If Martha has not seen fit in two years to depart this place, it can only mean some vital incentive is lacking on her part, and I may be better off entrusting my intentions to no one, or to someone whom I've not encountered as yet.

MAY 7, 1863

Yet another facet of our strange existence here has been revealed to me, and I cannot say that I am certain what to make of it.

Last night Agnes and I were locked into our cramped quarters as usual, and had settled into our hard beds to attempt sleep. Also as usual, said sleep eluded me for some time, and so I was still awake when, after what felt like several hours, the door slid open with nary a sound, and dim light from the hallway fell in a triangle upon the floor.

I was startled and about to cry out, when in the semidarkness I saw Agnes sit up, and turn without alarm toward the source of the intrusion. She seemed to know precisely what was going on, and so I remained still, and waited to see what would happen.

A moment later the night attendant entered the room. He is not the same one as locked me in here on my first evening; this one is a lout named Andrews, a large, unclean-looking person with a mass of oily, colorless hair.

I have never seen Agnes exchange a word or gesture with this man or any other, nor had I witnessed her taking advantage of those favors which are regularly bestowed on inmates by the attendants. Yet this could mean nothing save that Agnes is smarter or more subtle than our housemates; I was expecting some sort of romantic encounter between her and this Andrews, given all I have observed of the interaction between certain of the young ladies here and their guards.

But what happened next was something far removed from any notion of "romance" as I understand it.

Andrews was barely through the door when he began to undo the fly of his ticking-striped coveralls. In the half-light I was quite able to see what he next freed from within their folds. In the meantime Agnes had arranged herself atop the covers, shoulders propped upon the pillow, like a corpse within a casket. As the head of my bed faces the door and the foot of the other cot, I could make out with ease the expressions on the faces of both parties: the brutish Andrews was glassy-eyed, openmouthed, while Agnes appeared serene, her lips a line, her eyes open and unblinking.

In one motion he was beside the bed and atop her. He pushed her nightdress up about her shoulders, he arranged himself over her, then slipped his arms under her thighs, and parted them.

During all of this, and during the few minutes that followed, Agnes did not utter a sound. She moved voluntarily only once, raising her arms behind her head to cushion it, but otherwise she was still, even as her torso was rocked about in time to the attendant's pumpings. After an interval which seemed rather brief to me, his contortions ceased; he released her legs, rose up on his arms, and stiffened. Then a moment later, he collapsed onto her breasts, and another moment after that he was standing up again.

I watched, fascinated and repulsed, as he wiped himself, tucked himself back into the coveralls, pulled down his shirt, and straightened the suspender straps. He took a casual look down at the bed as he ran his hands over his hair to smooth it. Then he moved out the door as silently as he'd entered it.

Just before the sliver of light from the hallway disappeared, I glanced over at Agnes's face once again. She had not moved, her eyes were still calm, and she made no attempt to cover herself or change her position. She smoothed her own hair back with a hand, and replaced her nightcap. Then the light was gone, the door once more locked upon us by our trusted guardian, and we lay as we'd been in the dark stillness, my even breaths and Agnes's the only discernible sounds.

The entire incident had taken perhaps ten minutes. In the ensuing blackness it was possible for me to believe that it had never happened at all, that the attendant's appearance had been a figment of my dreaming imagination. But then I heard Agnes rise and drag her chamber pot from beneath her bed; I could just make out the black hump of her form squatting over the enamel jar. A thread of scent—pungent, dense, familiar—drifted over toward me, the lone bit of evidence that I had not in fact been dreaming. Then, after another minute, I heard the jar being replaced, and the squeak of springs as Agnes reclined upon the bed once more.

I fell asleep eventually. The next morning, at the sound of the breakfast bell, the guard Andrews completed his duties by unlocking the door of our chamber. Agnes said not a word to him, and he not one to her, as if nothing out of the ordinary had transpired between them.

But then, what exactly did transpire? Of course, I know what it was, but what noun would best describe the exchange? Was it an "encounter"? A "tryst"? A "rape"?

There was no knife or gun wielded. I recall, however, that Mr. Price had no need of those, his mantle of authority being enough. On the other hand, in this instance, Agnes did everything she could to ensure that the process went smoothly, even if she appeared not to enjoy any part of it.

Agnes herself has given me not a clue as to how she regards the incident. If she believes herself violated, or is on the verge of collapse, I should not know it. I am more inclined to think she is willingly trading her favors for some privilege of which I have no knowledge. In which case, I am inclined not to interfere with her arrangement, because there is enough backbiting and tattling within these walls as it is, and I should like to see a sister inmate succeed in manipulating her circumstances favorably.

What I do not like, however, is that I was forced to bear witness to the event. I am angered by the participants' intrusion on my privacy, even as I am amazed at their boldness. Why do they choose to conduct their affairs three feet from my bed, and thus risk my disclosure, when they could make use of any of the illicit trysting spots on these grounds? I mightily hope they choose never to behave so again. I have no desire to view once more his huffing, grunting exertions, or her deathlike stupor, whatever the motives behind them.

MAY 8, 1863

Today at Hall Meeting I was the cause of a dressing-down, delivered in the inimitable style of this place. It began when Emily Tarnower accused me of being "haughty."

"You've a superior attitude," she cheeped in her tiny voice, "and I do not care for the way you march about here, as if you are head and shoulders above the rest of us."

"What have you to say for yourself, Miss Leeds?" Sister Raymond intoned.

"I am sorry Miss Tarnower thinks I'm haughty."

The sister narrowed her eyes. "I believe you'll find that noncooperation merely lengthens your stay here. It is high time you accept the mandate of this place, and take the opportunity we afford you to scrutinize the flaws within yourself."

"Thank you, Sister, but I prefer to do exactly that. Scrutinize within myself."

"I did not ask you what you prefer. This is the Hall Meeting. At Hall Meeting you shall examine your flaws with diligence before your fellows. Is that understood?"

I kept my eyes to the floor, but did not answer.

Coldly, and with evident great pride in her "mandate," Sister Raymond ordered me to say twenty Hail Marys on my knees in chapel tomorrow. Aloud. Then she addressed the gathering at large, in a manner better suited to a colonists' warden than a Bride of Christ.

"You had all best take heed of a lesson here. It is addressed not only to Miss Leeds, but to any of you who might be tempted to follow her example. You are no longer in your snug homes, your mothers' darlings, your fathers' little princesses. You are under our auspices now. Valhalla House shall set the pace. You shall march to it. You needn't question why you are required to obey a particular rule, for its merit to any singular one of you is not at issue. It has been decided upon by those in authority, and for that reason it shall be obeyed. That is as much as you are required to know. Nor will your individual whims be allowed to interfere with the group's progress. There is a propriety to be maintained here, and it shall be preserved at any cost. My hope is that you shall realize this, and be made ready to take your eventual places in that process of preservation. Have I made myself clear?"

There was not a sound from the gathering upon the floor.

The sister resettled herself in her seat. "Now then. Let us continue." Her watery blue eyes swept over the group. "Miss Starkweather. What have you to offer up for perusal?" Agnes took a breath, and then began a long recitation of her own faults and failings, a virtual litany of self-loathing, for she is one of those compelled to tattle only on herself. It was all I could do to keep from rushing over and slapping my hand across her mouth to silence her.

But I could not help but note her failure to include "unchaste" anywhere upon her list of shortcomings. In the same manner, none of the girls spoke up to say, "I let the attendant in the Public Room run his hand under my skirts, and he gives me oranges." Or "I smoke tobacco at the far end of the garden whenever I have the opportunity." And nobody revealed these grave crimes when hurling accusations at another. It seemed there was a tacit understanding that the truly punishable wrongs, the worst of what is done and said, never be acknowledged, or used as a weapon.

I cannot decide whether this is a brilliant system of subversion, or a kind of deliberate blindness, a disease specific to these circumstances, which overtakes every inmate at once.

MAY 12, 1863

My parents continue their visits, and their visits continue to pain me, mainly because of my opposing desire either to take them in my arms or to strike them.

Always there are the predictable questions and answers, always the proffered gifts of food or some other material object: a ribbon for my hair, a new pair of stockings. For whom do they imagine I would don ribbons? Or take the pains to notice that my stockings are torn?

Today, as on other occasions, I attempted to confront them with the reality of this place, with the various hypocrisies and indignities that make up life in this twisted and unnatural environ.

"If it was your wish to protect me from the effects of lust," I began, "I must tell you, you have chosen a most unsuitable shelter for me." I then went on to describe the spectacle I witnessed in my own room, involving Agnes and Andrews.

When I had finished, Mother and Father exchanged a glance. Then Father said, "You have quite the lurid imagination, Arabella."

"What?" I gawked at him.

"The doctor warned us that you might begin spinning fabrications of this sort. You must face facts: you needn't bother telling us these tall tales, as we will not be manipulated by guilt into removing you from the Home."

"Have you lost your reason? Does it not occur to you that perhaps what I report is real, and that it is you and the good doctor who must 'face facts'? Can you truly believe that I am making up tales, or lying to you?"

"It would not be the first time, would it, Arabella?"

This stopped me cold. It was quite clear to me then what the problem was.

It is Madame Zunia and Mr. Price and all of it all over again.

MAY 13, 1863

It seems to me that when I consider my parents these days—my present disillusionments aside—their union is bathed in a harsh new light.

They had always loomed in my mind as the perfect pairing, the ideal upon which I would base my own marriage; I do not know when my perceptions began to change. But I am certain now that, however well their arrangement has served them, it is not the one I desire.

For it appears to me—and I admit, I have neither the wisdom nor the life experience to know whether this observation is sound—that they are complicitous in maintaining a system of falsehoods which bonds them to each other. The lies extend not only to their view of themselves, but to the world at large.

Thus Mother pretends, before Father, to be fluttery and indecisive, and Father pretends to be convinced by her deceptions, although he knows as well as she—as well as I—that it is Mother who rules the household, who is likely to be at once inflexible and capable, in direct opposition to the picture they would paint of her.

And Father, for his part, pretends at mastery, independence, wisdom, when in fact he is apt ten times a day to rush to his wife to secure her opinion, or to misplace his keys or his pocket watch or his snuff case. Mother will gently relay her advice, or recover the lost items for him, never letting on that she has done so, and so she participates in his charade as he does in hers.

And outside our home, these false faces are the ones they are apt to present, and again, each supports the other, like the secondary player in a drama, helping the act to appear seamless.

Oh, it is not all an untruth. Father does possess a marvelous head for business, he is in many ways the *paterfamilias* he aspires to being. And Mother truly has the greater tendency toward tears, toward flights of silliness or fancy. But why are these qualities the ones they choose to magnify in each other, to the detriment of the others?

It smacks of gamesmanship to me. I've no wish to mother a man who feigns a disdain for that treatment even as he cultivates it. Nor do I wish to be spoiled and pampered in exchange for the maintenance of a frivolous facade. If we cannot be all of who we are to each other, my mate and I, on what basis are we mated?

But perhaps I do not know enough about the state of marriage, about the arrangements one makes in order to sustain a union of more years than one had lived unwed.

Mother and Father at least are friends to each other, companions who take joy in their pairing. This in itself, I believe, is rare, even as it is held to be the ideal of marriage. So there is yet one lesson I may aspire to taking from my parents, and I believe I had better take it—else I may find myself in the shoes of Aunt Jo and Uncle Charles, who treat each other with polite disdain, and never miss an opportunity to expose each other's flaws before outsiders.

How I miss my regard for my family, though. My illusions. But most of all, I miss trusting them. Feeling them my faithful allies, even though we might exchange harsh words. At times it seems a sacrilege to recall that feeling in all its vividness.

But I remind myself there is yet love, although it is imperfect. There are yet parents, although (like me!) they are also imperfect. I must accept what is, but there is no shame in holding them in some special place still, and in fact I feel I must allow myself to be distracted, for were I to exist solely within the parameters of what is before me just now, I truly would lose my mind, and become the mad creature I am suspected of being.

MAY 14, 1863

My one reason for looking forward to the visits of my family is the appearance of Richard, and with him the possibility of some word from Aubrey, or from the Beckwiths.

But thus far there has been nothing. Richard tells me I must be patient, as the restrictions upon him have not yet been relaxed, and he cannot hope to communicate with any of my companions until they are. I understand this, but impatience gnaws at me—I worry every minute I am awake about what Bree must be thinking, what he's made of my disappearance, what was said to him when he came looking for me. If only I could have some word, just one word, to let me know that he maintains his faith in my affection, that he realizes I would not betray my promise to him.

Aubrey, how I long to behold you once again, to make certain you were flesh and blood! The loss I experience each time I awaken without you is the loss of the dreamer who, in sleep, has laid her hand upon the exact and perfect thing.

Oh, Richard. You must not tarry a moment beyond that time when mobility becomes possible on your part. You must bring me some news, carry some message, for all that is around me is strange, my relations have become strangers; and my connexion to a person so recently entered into my existence has become the most reliable source of my strength.

MAY 16, 1863

It has happened again, and under circumstances even stranger than those of the other time.

Last night I was lying abed, once more awake long into the wee hours, when I heard our chamber door being unlocked from the outside. I was confused: Andrews was not on duty. It was his counterpart, Henry Thurston, the oaf I'd met the night I arrived, who'd been left in charge for the evening.

But when the door opened wide, I saw that there was no need for confusion: it was indeed Henry Thurston who stood upon the threshold.

And I did not need to wonder long why he was standing there, for, aside from the change in personnel, the next ten minutes were an exact reenactment of what I witnessed last week. As soon as she realized her "visitor" had arrived, Agnes went through the same motions she'd undertaken with Andrews: she threw off the sheets, lifted her gown, and lay perfectly still. Thurston managed to match Andrews in terms of speed—he was shed of his coveralls and down to his business in record time, and finished in much the same fashion. The only difference between the two beasts, so far as I could tell, was that Thurston preferred to kneel over Agnes's supine body; perhaps he found her bulging belly too much of an impedance to the act.

Once again clothes were soon rearranged, the door opened and relocked, the silence maintained. Once again Agnes slid her chamber pot from beneath the bed, performing some ritual over it which I could not make out in the darkness. Once again morning arrived to see the ravisher and his accomplice stand face-to-face at the opening of the chambers. And once again neither of them acknowledged each other, or me, or any aspect of what had been undertaken only hours before.

What *is* this?

Whatever it is, it must stop. It makes me literally sick to my stomach—I, who would embrace pleasure in all its variety—but this is not pleasure, and I cannot bear having its grotesque imitation forced down my throat. For some reason, neither party seems to have the slightest compunction about performing these horrid intimacies in front of me. But it must stop, and I must be responsible for making it so.

MAY 17, 1863

I made up my mind, during our afternoon recess, to attempt a conversation with Agnes Starkweather regarding her nocturnal exercises. I had by this time formed the opinion that Agnes is simply, uncaringly, promiscuous, and wise enough to keep the fruits of her labors well hidden, and so I approached her with what might be regarded as a certain rancor. I asked her to accompany me to an isolated corner of the Public Room for the purpose of discussing some needlepoint techniques; once there, I came swiftly and bluntly to my argument.

"Look here, Agnes. You are entitled to behave in any manner you choose. I shall not judge or condemn you for it, nor will I reveal it to anyone else. But I must ask—I must insist—that you consummate your arrangements in some other manner, when I am not present."

She gave no sign of understanding, so I went on. "If you will agree to it, I promise I'll do all I can to oblige you. I can use the lavatory whilst you're occupied, if you'll only give me some warning. Or I can speak to Sister on some pretext or other, and leave you the room for however long you need it." I paused. "Well? What say you to that—I think it's fair enough, don't you?"

Her expression did not change an iota, and her voice, when it emerged, was as flat and empty as her eyes. "I've no idea what you are talking about, Miss Leeds."

My mouth popped open. Did she mean to embarrass me by forcing me to say it in so many words? "Why—what I am talking about—perhaps it's not to be mentioned aloud—well, I beg your pardon, Miss, I've a grievance, and I *must* mention it—I am asking you not to *fornicate* with the night attendants two feet from my eyes, Miss Starkweather—it's a total invasion of what little privacy we are afforded—"

Before I could babble on any further, she'd reared backward in her seat, her formerly bland features now arranged into the very picture of outrage. "How dare you use such language in my presence? How dare you aim such an accusation at me, Miss—you must be absolutely raving mad!"

Was *she* absolutely raving mad?

Whatever the case, it was plain our discussion was over: Miss Starkweather leapt to her feet and, in highest dudgeon, stalked off toward the other end of the room. I was too astonished to follow her. In any event, I doubted it would have done any good, as I was not about to deny the evidence of my own eyes, and she was not about to acknowledge it.

I could scarce bring myself to enter our quarters that evening, so addled was I over the treatment Agnes had meted out to me. I was loath to look in her direction, and she avoided me as well, climbing straight into her bed, and pulling the covers up about her face. I did likewise, not even bothering to take advantage of the hour or so of free time we are afforded before the mandatory extinguishing of the candles.

I lay there upon my back, knowing I might well pass the night wide awake. I was still seething when, perhaps a half hour later, Agnes's small voice cut through the stillness.

"They'll never come after you," she said.

I startled at the unexpected sound, and it occurred to me that perhaps she was talking in her sleep.

"Are you awake?" I whispered.

"Yes. I am speaking to *you*, Arabella. I said, they will never come after you."

"I don't understand."

"The night attendants. You needn't be afraid of them. They will never touch you."

She was not making sense, and so I did not reply, wondering if she might reach some comprehensible point were she allowed to keep talking.

"You are not with child. Therefore you could be *got* with child, and then they would be suspect, and caught, as there are no men here but themselves. That is why they take up only with those of us already debased: that which is dead cannot be killed again. Do you see?"

Oh, yes. I did indeed see now, she was indeed making sense.

"Agnes—I did not know. Tell me what to do—"

"There is nothing to be done. They do not care who sees. If you tell, you will not be believed. Nothing will happen to them. They will only know that you acted against them, and they will make your life an agony in return for your folly."

"But there is surely a means by which—"

"There is no means." She spat out the words as if defying me to dispute them. "You need fear nothing if you sleep soundly and well. So sleep well, Miss Leeds."

Then I heard the sound of springs giving, and realized she had turned her face to the opposite wall, with the same degree of finality she'd mustered when stalking off earlier this afternoon.

Nothing to be done.

I found I was miles farther from any notion of sleep than I had been an hour before, and so I waited until I was fairly certain Miss Starkweather had fallen into her dark dreams. Then I lit my stub of a candle with one of my precious matches, and began this entry, which I am just now upon the verge of finishing.

She is wrong, though. There is always something to be done, once one takes up the burden inherent in determining what it might be. There are, at the opposite ends of the spectrum, at least two options: revenge and escape.

Tomorrow I shall approach Miss Starkweather again. Now that the ice is broken, my presumptions shattered and far worse facts established to take their place, I feel she shall talk to me. And there is a good deal more I wish to know.

MAY 18, 1863

But she did not care to enlighten me. Today in the Public Room it was the same as yesterday.

"Agnes," I began, when I'd corralled her alone in an empty corner of the room, "I have been thinking of what you told me—"

"What I told you when?"

"Last evening. When we spoke."

"I'm afraid you're mistaken, Miss Leeds. We did not speak last evening."

"But of course we did, before we slept, when you said—"

"I said nothing before we slept. Last evening I slept, that is all. We had no conversation."

Again I was brought up short. And again felt anger bubbling up into my throat, making me wish to impale her with words, force her face into expression. How dare she play such idiotic games with me—but then I noted the pupils of her eyes, which had widened to obscure the blue iris; I noted the vein pulsing in her forehead.

"Perhaps you have forgotten," I said more gently.

"I have forgotten nothing. I said nothing to you. We had no discussion. I went to sleep, and so did you. Perhaps you had a dream in which we spoke."

"Perhaps I did."

She returned my gaze. Then she nodded. And rose, without another word, and left the room.

And tonight, when I again lay examining the dense blackness, her voice cut through it once more, although this time I did not startle, as I was not so surprised.

"You must promise that you will do nothing, and say nothing else. Please promise. Aloud."

"I don't understand, Agnes. Why must I, why do you wish me to? There is no need for you to shame yourself, if we attempt—"

"You keep a book," she interrupted me.

"What book?" I whispered.

"The one you write in. I have seen you, and I know where you hide it. If you breathe a word, I will reveal you, and it will be confiscated, and you will be severely punished." She said all of this as though reporting upon the weather.

"But Agnes—why do you threaten me this way? I wish to help, does that mean nothing to you?"

"I ask you again for both our sakes: promise me you'll do nothing. Nor speak of it again."

My frustration overcame me at last. "I cannot promise. I've my own sanity to think of. My obligations. What's done to you is done before me, will be done to some other. I cannot live with myself if I turn tail and hide from it."

"You are not noble, then. You are selfish."

"And what are you if not selfish? You let yourself be used, taken without a murmur—for what, for the sake of martyrdom? While you hang from the cross do you never think of the girl who'll sleep in this bed when you are gone, who'll endure the same treatment whether she wishes to or not, because you did nothing?"

She was silent. Such a long time passed in the darkness that I was certain she was finished, but then she spoke once more.

"Some things are noble endeavors and some things only foolish. You would be wise to learn the difference, Miss Leeds. And to sleep soundly from now on."

MAY 21, 1863

At last at last at last—oh thank you God thank you angels—thank you, Richard!

Word has at last been sent to the Beckwiths regarding my whereabouts. During our visit yesterday, Richard explained how he managed it, how he finally arrived at the obvious solution: though practically imprisoned at Leeds Hall, he has been permitted both to call upon and write to a Miss Wentworth, a young acquaintance of his in Mayfair. He posted a note to the girl, which was allowed past the censors; within this he'd enclosed a letter for Harlow, and a request that Miss Wentworth send the missive on to Linton via porter. Utterly simple, and brilliant!

He has had no word back as yet—he only sent his message two days ago—but he urged Harlow to reply via the same young lady, and I am sure it shan't be long before a letter arrives. In the meantime, I must begin one of my own, to give to Richard when he next visits.

At last, I shall have made some contact with the outside world. At last, someone shall know where I am. And that will be the beginning of the end for this place, for I know that my friends will not abandon me, and that their affection will lend me strength.

I think of you every moment, Aubrey—I shall write all of it down now, and pass it on to Richard, so that you shall know it unconditionally.

I feel renewed in myself, and that has helped me to come to a decision regarding Miss Starkweather. That situation has been tormenting me for days, for I feel torn between a responsibility toward the greater good of all the inmates here and the personal wishes of Agnes herself. But I believe I've hit upon a solution that shall serve both ends.

I have decided that I shall ask to be moved from her room. The excuse I'll give is that the door is being constantly opened at night by the attendants, which disturbs my sleep. I shall say nothing of what happens after the door is opened. It's my hope that just this revelation will be enough to arouse suspicions, which shall then be investigated. There will be no repercussions for either Agnes or myself, and I shall not have betrayed either my principles or my roommate's wishes.

It is not the solution I would have wanted, but one cannot fight every battle, and besides, the war itself looms upon my personal horizon just now.

chapter two

(MAY–JUNE 1863)

The journey got off to an inauspicious start, as the weather caused me almost to miss my train at London Bridge. I'd barely time to secure a compartment and stow my baggage when the locomotive began its chuffing departure for Dover and the Ostend ferry. I watched as London presented itself again for my perusal: steeples, river, lamps, pedestrians, carriages, all an incoherent mass passing by the window, which was lashed with raindrops from the dark clouds overhead.

But at Dover the rain began to let up somewhat. We passengers waited for the tide to adjust itself and the baggage to be loaded down the chute onto the steamer's belowdecks, and during this interim we were treated to a glimpse of the sun through the parting gray.

It seemed a good omen, and I allowed myself to be cheered.

The ferry ride itself was uneventful (although the choppy waves revived my tendency toward seasickness), but I felt a sudden surge of anticipation as we docked at the other side of the English Channel: I was in France. I had dreamed of this moment, wished it, wished it away, a thousand times since New Orleans, and now—after all that had come between—here I was, ready at last to set foot upon French soil.

In Boulogne my bags were unloaded by the crew of the Compagnie Chemin de Fer du Nord, which runs the train to Paris. I marveled at the pure, happy sound of their shouts and curses—how good it was to hear French spoken again! On the train I sank into the velvet-covered cushions of the compartment, and noted that the sun was now fully out, shining down upon the track, the men, the ladies with parasols ready to embark, the whole bustling, congenial scene.

Then we departed for the Gare du Nord, and Paris.

Paris.

I had thought London beautiful because I had not seen Paris.

In London the buildings, although lovely, seem swathed in a mantle of gray exuded by the clouds. The people hurry about, rendered colorless by the lack of sunlight and contrast; they draw their coats about their necks and proceed stiffly on their way, their faces closed.

In Paris all predetermined notions of citydom fall away. The light seems to strike everything at a different angle. Even beneath clouds, it is pearly, aglow with pinks and yellows and ambers. When the sun shines upon it, it explodes into a panoply of color—flowers, awnings, windows, and people. Especially people, and what people! They are vivid, expansive, dressed in colors of every sort—even the men—preening and parading about as if to be seen and admired is a daily national rite. Their chatter strikes the ear everywhere, so refreshingly gay—they sound as if every moment is a headlong rush toward pleasure of some sort, and in this place, are they not correct?

This city, it seems, is laid out according to whether or not it will please aesthetically, and every sense is engaged: the eyes by the architecture, the exquisitely planned boulevards, tree lined, flower bedded, immaculate; the nose by the contrasting scents of fine perfume, coffee, and delicacies of every sort; the ears by the song of the language; the skin by the freshness of the air, the gentleness of the breeze; and the tongue by the pleasures of the food.

Oh, the food. That in itself could cause me to rhapsodize for days. I secured my hotel room for a fortnight stay, then thought better of it and paid in advance for another week; if I was to squander my money, this should be the place to do it. I then at once availed myself of coffee and fresh bread with sausage at a tiny café, and I did not stop eating from that moment til the morn when I set out for the region of Marseilles. I had barely time to view this jewel of a city, and I did it by carriage and on foot. I rode the length of the Champs-Elysées, and walked it, I explored the Seine and the denizens of its Left Bank, I wandered among labyrinthine back streets and main boulevards with equal interest, and on every one of them, I found something to eat. I devoured herring and fresh oranges in the backs of taxis, dandelion salads and vichyssoise, lamb and croissants, oysters and *crème fraîche* at tables grand and humble. All washed down with wine and more wine, red and white, and especially brut Champagne, the pride of French vineyards. I absorbed food and drink as if it were the life-elixir of the populace. I felt full and happy despite myself; I smiled at strangers, and they smiled at me, and we greeted each other with the music of French. *Bonjour! Bonsoir! Bon matin, mon ami!*

My smiles faded only when I thought of Arabella. And I thought of her every other moment there.

Oh, Arabella. No wonder you did not like London. You must have suspected that there was this place, this nation, which would suit you so very much more.

London, with its rigid, misty beauty, its populace wanton behind its mannered veneer, was my city. One as gray and repressed as my spirit in those days before you found me. But this wondrous Paris belongs to you—wild and refined in the same instant and proud of both extremes, as swirling with energy as are you yourself.

How I should have liked to show you this place, to watch your face open with the joy of it. You would have loved it here. You would have loved *me* here. Here in Paris, where I find myself weightless and ready to act, infused with a sense of mastery that I have denied for so long.

Why did you abandon me when there could have been this?

How I hated to leave Paris for Marseilles, even as I knew that the point of my coming here had been the journey ahead.

My route south would take me through the whole of the French countryside, which unfolded itself like a golden dream before me. Nothing could match the grandeur of Paris, but the varying scenes of Auxerre, of Macon, of Lyon, enticed and entranced me, even as I grew more and more anxious to reach Aix-en-Provence.

At last the final leg of the journey lay before me. On May 20, I arrived here, in Salon-de-Provence. I am residing in a small inn in the center of the village; upon settling in, I sent a messenger off to Aquitaine, which is the name of the Paxton estate—or, I should say, the Denis estate, since Madame's family owned the place for generations before it passed to her husband—in Aix-en-Provence.

I asked only that the messenger secure some word as to who would be at home at Aquitaine to receive a traveling visitor. I made no mention of my name, or what business I had with the family. The fellow returned to tell me that the Paxtons—Louella, Thomas, and Louis—are traveling in the Côte d'Azur, but are expected within the week.

I did not ask about the presence of a woman named Onessa Lee Paxton.

So now I must decide what I shall do. Should I wait until the return of the Paxtons? Or should I venture to Aix right away, and confront whatever may greet me there?

Just the notion that Aquitaine is before me—just a few miles to the south of where I now sit—is enough to cause my blood to alternately boil and chill.

I am here at last.

Somewhere beyond the low hills, the verdant countryside and purple horizon, Mama and Paxton, Louella and Thomas and Lila, all have made a home for themselves. The same sun which strikes me here in my white-curtained room also shines over them. Their lives have gone forward, without me, in ways which I cannot know, just as mine has unfolded without them.

They are so close—I am overcome. So much crowds for space inside me at the thought of them, at the thought of what I cannot know until I reach them.

How I wish you awaited me at Aquitaine, Gran. Then I would feel no confusion, I would rush toward you, lighthearted, assured of a warm welcome, a safe haven, at last.

This morning I decided it. I can be patient no longer. Whatever shall happen to me in Aix, I must know it. I have packed my bags and engaged a coach, which shall leave tomorrow at eight in the morning, and bear me right to the door of Aquitaine. If they are there I shall see them, and if they are not I shall wait.

Today is May the twenty-fifth.

We set off as the sun was climbing beyond the hills to the east, burning through the morning mist with a clear-blue intensity.

It was already warm, and so I'd dispensed with my coat, and remained in my finest shirt, pants, and boots. I want to look, above all, successful. To appear upon the doorstep of the estate not as a beggar but with confidence.

If I were truly confident, though, I would not be shaking. I would not be alternately fanning myself and wiping my forehead with a linen handkerchief, with my palms damp and my fingertips freezing.

God, let the carriage stop bouncing over the ruts in the road; it is nauseating me, causing every morsel I ate this morning to strike the walls of my stomach. God, can we not just get there—the driver insists upon resting the horses, taking a bite of lunch, having a sip of wine. Would I care for some—no, I would not, I would care to be on my way, please.

We pass into Aix itself, and I note the fountains everywhere—Louella had told me to be on the lookout for them, and they are just as she described. Then we are through the beautiful town, heading down a straight, well-traveled road. I begin to notice smaller drives which angle off into the countryside; there are white wooden roadside signs which indicate where they might go. After perhaps forty-five minutes we reach one which says AQUITAINE in simple black lettering.

We turn; it is a lovely road, edged with flowers and meadows, with grand old trees planted every few yards to form an archway over the path itself. We ride on for a few minutes, and then arrive at a high, scrolled black iron gate which is bordered by hedges and blocks our passage. The driver gets out and swings it wide; I am relieved to know it is not locked. Now the road is graveled, is clearly part of the property, and we round a corner to the right. We enter the far end of a circular drive, the bottom of a slight hill.

And then it is before me. At the top of the hill, laid out on an expanse of flat land, its turrets rising into the air, is Aquitaine. It is huge, a palace. A fairyland apparition. It is hewn of some yellow-colored stone, and story after story, enormous window after window, sparkles golden in the sunlight. It juts off into two wings on each side, but its main entrance is reached either by traveling the round driveway we are on or cutting through the verdant oval at its center, down a path leading through a lawn and hedges, two fountains which merrily trickle water, random beds of flowers which bob in the breeze.

I am staring at it, openmouthed. Paxton *owns* this, I think, and am overcome by the notion of how much he must possess in order to keep it this way: not in some fallen-down condition, but in that edge-of-wildness perfection which takes constant care. There is an almost tropical beauty about the place, and indeed I see that little palms wave here and there amidst the foliage in the central garden; no expense has been spared in its upkeep. Evidently the fortunes of my former owner have not been on the wane.

We reach the front entrance. The carriage driver halts the horses, clears his throat. "Aquitaine, Monsieur," he says, with great understatement. I step down to stand beside the coach; I am reaching into my pocket for payment when a little commotion at the far end of the left wing catches my attention. A door opens there, and two figures exit, a man and a woman, on their way out for the day. They are finely dressed, and even from the distance of perhaps a hundred feet I can hear the sound of their laughter as they amuse each other. I pause in my task to watch them.

It is amazing how beauty registers upon the brain. Not through conformation, but through a carriage which tells you the bearer has divined its secret: that somewhere out there is at least one person—and perhaps many more—who will find them the ideal of all ideals, and so they comport themselves every moment with the assurance that this day or the next, they shall happen upon that person. The woman I watched reveled in her own confidence. Even at this distance, I could see the coy turn of the head, the shaking of the black curls, the sway of hips beneath red stripes. I had no trouble identifying any of it.

It was Mama.

My hand froze upon my purse. *No. I can't—I'm not ready*. I would have run if my panicked brain had had its way, but I was rooted to the spot.

She laughed again—they were fooling with her parasol, it refused to open—and I blanched. *What did you expect?* I asked myself. Had I thought I'd find her sitting in a heap of ashes, consumptive and guilt-ridden, swathed in rags? Or walking the halls of the great manse in a black veil, wringing her hands?

No. This is Mama, after all. She lands upon her feet, and falls upon her gifts, which are always untouched. Adversity only strengthens her. I should have known it.

The man with her should have been Paxton. But again, I could tell with only a glance that it was not. This man was blonde-headed, meatier. He looked up, and in my direction, and now for the first time noticed the carriage, and me standing beside it.

He nudged Mama, and now she looked up too. Raised one gloved hand to her forehead, the better to see who had arrived. They did not recognize me; the man called, "Good morning." I did not call back. Only stared. So they began to walk toward me.

I watched Mama approach. She seemed all business now, and perhaps a little disconcerted by the appearance of a stranger. Her step was confident as she prepared to dispense with me, and then be on her way.

When she had gone perhaps ten feet, I saw her falter. She stopped, raised her hand again. And then began to move in a different manner. She seemed to have forgotten the man beside her. She was hurrying now, the seductive display gone, and then she was running. As she loomed larger and larger before me, I could hear her; she was calling something. Calling my name.

"Aubrey?" It was a question, and then as she must have become more certain, it became a statement. "Aubrey. Aubrey." When she was perhaps five feet away, she stopped. Her hands flew to her mouth. I could see that she was crying. She said, "Bree," in a hoarse voice; and then, with no other warning, her hands dropped, she tottered and fell to the ground.

I could not unglue myself in time to catch her. The man had run up behind her, and he was frantic, calling: "My God—Onessa! Onessa!" He looked up at me, and I unstuck myself at last, rushing over with the carriage driver to where she'd fallen.

The blonde man had bent down to roll her over, cradle her in his arms. "Onessa, darling," he crooned to her. "It's all right, wake up. Wake up now." A thin stream of saliva ran from her mouth; he brushed it away with his glove. I raced back to the rig, rooted about a moment, and found my coat, the driver's bottle of wine, and a skin filled with water. I rolled the coat up and said, "Lay her on this." The man eased her gently to the ground, her head propped up on the coat, and then I handed him the water, with which he splashed her face.

Her eyelids fluttered, and she peered up at him. "It's Jules, darling," he said. She called, "Aubrey?" and then fell back upon the coat. The man continued to stroke her forehead, hold her hand.

He looked up at me. "*Are* you her son?"

He had heard of me, it seemed. "Yes."

Then she awakened again, and this time turned toward me. She stared, and her eyes filled. "Mama," I said. Her breath caught, and she sobbed. The man called Jules helped her into a sitting position. She did not take her eyes from me. I glanced away for a moment, realized the carriage driver was still standing there. I reached into my pocket for my purse, withdrew a fistful of notes, determined without looking that there was more than enough. "Here," I said, thrusting them at him, "you may go."

"She's all right, then?" He looked back at Mama, wrung his hands.

"Yes, she will be fine," I snapped, thinking, *Dolt, if she were ugly you would have been off ten minutes ago*. He reached down to retrieve his water skin, emptied my bags from the rig, and then was gone.

Mama was still staring at me, her tears, of which she seemed unaware, now running down her cheeks. "Bree," she said.

"It's Bree, Mama."

She reached out her hand, placed it upon my arm.

I knew the feel of that hand. Oh yes. The memory of it was embedded in my flesh, rather than my mind.

But so rarely had it been laid upon me in this manner.

Her fingers sought mine; she twisted herself about me, would not let go.

"It's all right, Onessa," Jules soothed.

She turned to him. "It's Aubrey," she said. "Look—it's Bree." She turned back, as if afraid to let me out of her sight. "Look how beautiful he is—is he not the most beautiful thing you have ever seen—"

"No, I rather think you are the most beautiful thing I've ever seen"—the man winked at me, over her head—"but he certainly takes after his mother."

She managed to smile, but then she was sobbing again, and squeezing my hand, repeating my name, and leaning forward to touch my face.

I did not realize until I felt her fingers brush my cheek that my own face was wet as well.

After a few minutes, the man called Jules asked her if she felt well enough to rise. She nodded, and he said, "Why don't we get you inside, then," and took her beneath one arm, indicating that I should take the other. We walked her toward the door out of which they'd come only a few minutes ago. Our progress, slow in order to keep pace with her, was further impeded by her insistence upon stopping to look at me.

We entered the house, and passed through a foyer, sitting rooms, gaming rooms, ballroom, all exquisitely appointed, airy and bright. Frescoes peered down from the ceiling and walls; sheer drapes fluttered at many of the windows.

Then we reached a large hidden staircase, and we helped Mama up, and through a carpeted hallway. Jules pushed open the heavy door to a chamber. I saw it was a bedroom and large sitting room, all of it minty green, pink and white, the huge bed canopied, and made up in satins and fresh crisp cottons. Expensively mounted paintings hung upon the walls, and photographs in silver frames sat upon a side table. Fresh flowers bloomed everywhere from china vases.

It was Mama's room. I knew it at once. Jules and I laid her upon the bed, arranged pillows behind her. "Do you need anything?" he inquired, and she shook her head.

He retreated to the door. "Well, now. This is quite the miraculous moment, and I'm sure you both need some room to recover. Why don't I leave the two of you alone, then." Neither of us protested. "I shall be about if you want me, Onessa. Ring, and Paulette or Michel will find me."

Paulette. Michel. Servants, for whom Mama—most decidedly not a servant—might ring.

When the door shut behind him, I took a seat in the satin-tufted armchair by the bed, and Mama and I regarded each other.

She had composed herself somewhat, and now we found ourselves inhibited, awkward, she as well as I. We assumed some silly veneer of propriety; on Mama's part it seemed necessary so that she would not become unhinged.

"I did not expect to see you," she began, and then smiled, shook her head at the absurdity of the statement.

I was speechless. There was too much to wonder over, too much I did not understand, and most of all I was overcome by the way she had responded to me.

Oh, I had enacted the whole scene in my head. How I would come upon her, perhaps at dinner with Paxton, playing the lady of the manor, and how she would rise, furious at having her fantasy, at last realized, interrupted; and how I would confront them both—"Yes, it's me, returned from the dead!"—and demand my due.

Or how I would discover her guilt-ridden and shamed, a harlot hidden in the back rooms, overcome with loss and the debasement she had fallen into. Then I would redeem her, forgive her with magnanimity, but only after hearing her confession and her plea for absolution.

What a very bad and overwrought playwright I would have made.

I had not the slightest idea what to do with the reality of her. She was glad to see me. Not just glad. Overwhelmed. And she seemed something else: opened somehow. Changed.

I had never seen her cry. Not ever. And I had never allowed myself to cry before her, past a certain point. It had been a contest of wills, which I refused to lose. Yet here we were, sobbing over each other like protagonists in an opera. It unsettled me. I realized that what I wished to feel was anger—familiar, reassuring—but it had gone, it seemed to have no place here, and I was at a loss as to how to behave without it.

"You look so different," Mama said.

"Do I?"

"You are so much older. You're certainly not a little boy anymore—" With that she began to cry again, sought about her nightstand for a handkerchief, wiped instead at her eyes with the back of her hand.

"You look the same, Mama." I tried to make it a joke. "You never grow any older."

She wasn't having it, though. "How did you get here, how did you ever find us?"

I shook my head. "It's a very long story. I'll tell you this much: I met up with Louella, in England. By accident. She told me how to get here."

"Louella! You've spoken to Louella!"

"Yes."

"But she never mentioned it—she never told me—"

"I asked her not to. I did not know when I'd come, or if I would, and I wanted to do it in my own time."

"But why would you keep yourself from me—why would there be any question—oh, my poor baby, you must have thought we'd abandoned you, Aubrey, but you must have been told it wasn't so. I looked for you everywhere—everywhere, in the States, I tried so hard not to leave without you—but things were getting so bad, and so much had happened to Louella, I knew I could not risk all our necks any longer. She said that if I did not go, she would not, and then it would have been a matter of her own life as well as mine. I never gave up, though, even after we arrived here—" She stopped herself. "How much did she tell you of this?"

Now I felt the slightest flicker of it: anger. *My poor baby*—what was this? What had happened to "yellow bastard"? The memory of what I had come here for reasserted itself. "Everything, Mama. She told me everything."

But she did not appear perturbed. On the contrary, she looked almost relieved. She nodded and then said, "I was so afraid you had been killed—" This brought a fresh wave of tears, and she gestured me over to the bed. I sat down on the edge, and she said, "Let me look at you some more," and then she threw her arms around me and stroked my hair.

She had not hugged me this way since I was a little boy. Since before I became the wretch she beat with the open palm of her hand. I had not sat on a bed with her since those long-ago afternoons when she would curl up with me while I napped, spinning fantasies of what would become of us: "Perhaps you'll buy up your own business, Bree, and become as rich as Mister Paxton, and we'll live in a Big House of our own—"

"I want to hear everything, every single detail about how you came here. But—Lord, I haven't even thought how tired you must be—I've got to have a room made up for you, we'll have to settle you in—" She now became more herself, leaping up, pacing, planning. "Oh my God, Lila is here—I must call Lila! When she sees you—*mon Dieu*, I hope she doesn't do as I did, and fall into a faint, or worse—"

"Mama," I interrupted her, just as she reached for a little bronze beetle attached to the pull cord which summoned the servants. "If you don't mind—please, don't call anyone just yet. Especially not Lila. I don't know that I'm ready to see anyone else—I would rather you and I talked for just a little while."

She stopped in midpull. "Of course, my lamb, anything you wish. Only let me call a maid to have a room made up for you, and you'll let me have something brought for you to eat, won't you?"

I hesitated. *My lamb? My poor baby?* I wished she would stop these frothy endearments; they sounded so wrong issuing from her and aimed at me.

She noted my hesitation. "You are staying, aren't you?"

Was I? I hadn't thought of it. But—where else was I going? I had left my room at the inn, taken my bags, and settled my bill. Apparently, somewhere in my mind, I had assumed I was staying.

"I suppose so," I stammered, and relief flooded into Mama's face.

"All right, then, let me attend to this, and then we'll sit, just us, Bree. You know," she rushed on, pulling the cord, and then brushing a curl from her face as she awaited the maid's knock, "I suppose it's just as well Louis and the children are traveling, it'll give us time to speak—but when they come back, won't there be a surprise waiting—"

I was caught short again: *Louis and the children?* Since when? On what new and casual basis were all of the figures of my past now relating to one another? And what could she mean by a "surprise"; did she think any confrontation I might have with Thomas would amount to mere "surprise"—I wished she would slow down, that all of it would slow down, for there was too much being piled upon me at once.

My confusion was interrupted by the appearance of the maid, a rosy-cheeked creature, indisputably white, who greeted Mama by curtsying and inquiring, "Yes, Madame?" *Madame?*

"Paulette, dear, step in. There's someone here I wish you to meet." The girl did as she was told, and her gaze fell upon me with interest. "Now, Paulette, do you have any idea who this handsome young man might be?" She shook her head, wide-eyed. "Let me introduce you, then. This is my chambermaid, Paulette Seviroux. Paulette, this is my son. Aubrey Paxton."

The girl's pink hands flew to her cheeks. She gave several little staccato gasps, and then chirped, "Oh, Madame! Oh, how wonderful for you, your son has come back to you! You've found him!"

"*He* found *me*, Paulette. Let us give credit where it's due. But yes, it is wonderful." She beamed first at the maid and then back at me. "Aubrey will be staying, of course, so we need to ready a place for him."

"Of course, Madame. Which of the rooms do you wish made up?"

"Why, I suppose we should leave that up to Aubrey, shouldn't we? He's a grown man, I think he should have something to say regarding his own accommodations." With that, Mama nodded toward the door, put her hand upon my shoulder, and indicated that we should follow the maid, and have a brief tour of the available lodgings.

"Mama," I began, as I followed her down the hall, "are you certain it's acceptable to give me a room here, will Paxton allow—"

"Mister Paxton does not allow or disallow me, Bree. This is my section of the estate."

"Your section? Do you mean to say that all of this is your living quarters?"

"Yes, well—not exactly. I'll explain it to you later on."

I had no time to question her further, as we had stopped before a set of heavy double doors. Paulette grasped the ornate handles and swung them wide. "Perhaps this will do, sir, as it's rather more complete than a single room." She beckoned me in, and I saw that I was standing in the foyer of an apartment within apartments. There was a living space, a dining room, a tiny office, a lavatory, and a staircase which led to a balconied bedroom.

"What do you think, Bree? Will this do?" Mama asked, turning to smile at me.

We left Paulette to see to the making up of the quarters. Mama led me downstairs, and into a dome-ceilinged room, which was painted white and lined with books. There were settees strewn about, and a desk in the chubby-bodied French style, painted white and adorned with carved flowers, with an armchair behind it. "This is my study." Mama urged me onto a sofa, then took one across from me and pulled her feet up underneath her.

"So," she began, and I thought the million questions I had would come tumbling out of their own accord, but instead I found myself near speechless. I managed to say, "So," in faint imitation of Mama, and then I fell silent.

She filled the space between us then. Filled it with talk of the estate, its rooms and gardens, the yield of the vineyards, how she would show me about later on, how wonderful life was here, how much I would enjoy it. Lila was her cook, she confided, although she could have chosen to do nothing at all for all that Mama cared. She was called upon only occasionally to fix a light meal, which she and Mama more often than not ate together. She insisted on this function, though, saying she was used to taking orders from Mama, and wouldn't know what to do with herself without them.

Mama laughed as she told me all this. But she also leaned forward now and then to touch me upon the knee, or the elbow, as if to assure herself that I was not an illusion.

And she asked me questions, asked and asked, her eyes often spilling over; she wanted to know every detail as to what had transpired since the night I had abandoned New Orleans.

But about that night—about everything preceding it, about every relevant thing after—we exchanged not a sentence.

It was almost a relief to sit here in this strange dreamworld, with this strange version of Mama, everything suspended between us. For as long as it could last, it was a delightful and seductive delusion, and I sank into it with gratitude.

While we were indulging ourselves thus, the man named Jules knocked on the door and peeked into the room, causing Mama to clap a hand to her head in mock horror, and declare that she'd forgotten about him, and could he ever forgive her.

He did, of course, forgive her, and came in to sit, inquiring as to whether we were all right, and then introducing himself properly as Jules Begnard, of Aix-en-Provence. He shook my hand, and told me that my mother spoke of me every day, and it was surely a miracle which had reunited us. And I agreed, and smiled, and continued on with my bleached and scrubbed version of the story of my life since New Orleans, and then Paulette entered with tea and proper little sandwiches and cakes, which we ate from dainty china plates.

And eventually Mama said that she must call Lila, she could not in good conscience wait any longer, and a few minutes later came the knock at the door, and then Lila was there, dressed in clean white linen, looking for all the world like someone's fine dowager aunt. Mama said, "Come here a moment," and Lila stepped farther into the room, then emitted a scream and rushed headlong at me, causing Mama and Jules to laugh indulgently. She placed her hands everywhere upon me, on my face, my shoulders, my waist, a doubting Thomas before the risen Christ. "It's me, Lila," I kept repeating, and if in my mind's eye I was seeing her as she'd looked that last night—standing wild-eyed over Madame Eugenia's bed, her apron still spattered with the gore from Lisabeth's body—if I saw that picture, I pushed it cleanly away, to that place where all other images and questions had been relegated for the time being.

"Oh, Aubrey," Lila kept moaning as she touched me and cried. "I thought never to see you again. Never, never." She turned to Mama. "It's a miracle, Onessa," to which Mama nodded and beamed and dabbed at her eyes. And then we sat again, and I continued to answer their questions, to tell my silly story, until the maid called us for dinner. And then we moved—we, the lords and ladies of creation—into the dining room in these quarters of Mama's, and were served by servants—Mama's servants—whilst she introduced me to each of them, explaining that I was her son, which caused them all to cross themselves and give thanks to God, as if they were personally acquainted with every nuance of my history.

When at last this strange, strange day ended—when Jules had announced that he must leave for town, when Lila had gone off to her quarters, when Mama had left me at the threshold to the rooms she'd had made up for me—left me with a kiss upon the forehead—I lay down upon the feather bed and fell asleep at once, falling from dreams into dreams, as if I'd been surreptitiously drugged.

We both knew this interval could not last. And, indeed, by the next morning it was over.

I had awakened with unreality still clinging to me; the maid had roused me and told me my mother was waiting in the dining room, and I'd found her there, with breakfast already laid before her.

She began at once to prattle on—we would visit the vineyards today, if I liked, and she would take me into Provence later—but the fog which had enveloped me since the previous day was evaporating, and so I interrupted her.

"We must talk, Mama."

She laid her fork down and stared across the table at me.

"Yes, I know it." For the first time, her buoyant expression faded, and her eyes took on that feline expression which made her instantly Mama to me again. As fast as that look crossed her face, though, it was gone, and she tilted her chin up, to regard me.

"You didn't come here to rejoice with me. Did you, Bree. You came here to be angry."

"I don't know anymore what I came here for."

"Start anywhere you like, then. Go ahead and ask, and I'll tell you anything you wish to know."

I took a breath. And started where I felt it was easiest.

"Who is Jules, Mama?"

"He is a merchant in Aix. He distributes our wine to buyers all about the country, his father owned their business before him—"

"That's not what I meant, as I'm sure you know very well. What I'm asking is, who is he to you?"

She stared out of the window for a moment, and then looked back at me.

"He is my companion. He has been a great comfort to me, Bree—"

I gave a mirthless chuckle. "Is that right—are things so cool between you and Paxton, then, that he allows you to have a *companion* here? Or doesn't he know about it?"

She stared at me. "What do you mean?"

"I mean, what is your station here, Mama? What do you *do* here? What *is* all this? How did you come to occupy this house like you own it, what are you to Paxton—a concubine? A wife? What are you to Thomas and Louella—who am I supposed to be now—" I broke off, felt my cheeks flush, my voice catch.

She raised a hand to her lips to pat them with her napkin. Then she said in a low voice, "What did you mean yesterday, Bree, when you said that in London Louella told you everything?"

So there it was. What lay between us, coiled like a snake beneath a stone, about to be exposed to the light at last.

"I meant everything. I know it all, Mama. I know about you and Paxton. I know he is my father."

I saw her flinch, just a tiny bit, the smallest movement of the head betraying her.

"Louella never told you that."

"She didn't have to. I've known it all along. She only confirmed it for me."

"No. She never would've done that."

"*Why*? Why shouldn't she have, Mama?"

"Because it isn't true."

Now it overwhelmed me, white-hot and pure, that wave of rage which I knew so well. I leaned against the table, pushed it so hard that the china rattled.

"Will you *lie* to me? Even now? After all of this, when you know that I know—"

"It isn't true, Bree. You can rant at me, or you can let me tell you what you need to hear."

I sat back, panting, feeling that I could rise up in an instant and strangle her if she made so much as a false move, all the *bonhomie*, the ebullience, of the previous day forgotten.

"What do I need to hear?" I hissed at her.

"Louis Paxton is not your father."

"You are lying. Louella told me we are blood relations—"

"You are. But Louis is not your father—"

"Then what is he, goddammit," I shouted at last. "Who fathered me? And don't give me that nonsense of yellow servants and tragic love; don't lie to me or I swear it, I'll hurt you—"

"All *right!*" She rose forward to scream back at me, and we faced each other, as if ready to engage in mortal combat. She was the first to turn away, take her seat. I waited for her to speak again, and at last she did, her voice much softer now.

"I shall have to recount some events which predate your conception, Aubrey" was what she said.

"Do not play games with me, Mama. I'm warning you, I will not stand for it."

"I'm playing no games. You asked me to tell you who fathered you. I'm telling it. I've planned for a long time how I'd come to it, and this is where I'm starting."

I watched her, still panting, but went silent, and Mama, satisfied that I was listening, resumed. "I should like to begin by recounting to you how your Gran got her cabin at the Old House."

I waited, to see where she might be leading with this.

"You probably think she earned it by virtue of being the nigger doctor. But that isn't all of it. No. She was given a private and comfortable space so that she could visit easier with my own father.

"Not the overseer, Aubrey. There was no overseer. That was a lie I told you. My father was the old master. Master Leland, Louis's daddy. Master Leland Paxton."

I turned away from her. Felt the air rush out of me, and knew right then that I did not want to see her eyes, or hear the rest of her forthcoming tale. Her speech took on an odd cadence, almost a singsong. It was a voice I remembered from bedtime books, soothing recitations of past events. A story voice, which presumes to go on at length uninterrupted. But this story was not meant for comforting.

"Yes. Leland Paxton. I'll tell you how it happened.

"My mama—your Granevangeline—she caught Leland Paxton's attention at the Old House, as a pretty little yellow gal. When she was fifteen she became his concubine, with the blessing of her mother and father. They exchanged her for ten dollars. In gold, you see. Your Gran says her own mama—your great-grandmama—wrapped the coins in a kerchief and kept them in a jam jar on her bedstand, she was so proud of them. I never saw them, though, since my grandfolk were dead by the time I was old enough to remember anything.

"Anyway, this is why Leland Paxton installed your Gran in that big comfortable cabin by herself, so that he could have a visit with her whenever he pleased, away from any prying eyes.

"Paxton had other women. And of course he had his wife, the old mistress, Hattie—I doubt you remember her. For a time, though, your Gran was her master's favorite, and he made no secret of it.

"But of course this high placement was not without its pitfalls. It was said among the colored folk that Leland Paxton dispensed with his colored mistresses once they were with child. Even to his white wife and their son, Louis—your own Master Louis, he was around eight at this point—he supposedly scarce gave the time of day. So your Gran and her mama were at pains to keep Gran out of trouble, lest she fall from favor or be sold off.

"They were very smart—smart enough to last at it for four whole years, til your Gran was nineteen. But then they slipped. Your Gran got in a family way. And sure enough, the second he found out, Leland Paxton quit her cold. She said she thought herself lucky, for the most part—he allowed her to keep her cabin, and she wasn't treated any worse, but he was through with her, just like that. He took up with the next of his girls in line, one as wasn't with a child.

"So your Gran was left alone, and she went on to have her lying-in, and as you might imagine, this is where I entered the family history.

"Later on, your Gran told me that she wondered at first if I'd ever meet Leland Paxton face-to-face, given how he treated his legitimate son. But the master surprised everyone. Right off, he makes a pet of me. Didn't bother hiding it. Once again he chose a favorite from my family, and I cannot remember a time when I didn't know it was me. Hattie must have known it. And Louis. They never said a word, no one dared, but it was plain as the nose on anyone's face; I had stuffed dolls and a rocking horse, and my own little four-poster bed that the master gets made for me, and got tutored in the Old House kitchen.

"All those privileges—they caused such a row between your Gran and myself. We fought like cats and dogs, because Leland would send something down to our cabin—a ribbon, or a dress, say—and your Gran'd send it back up, tell him, 'Onessa has enough, she doesn't need another ribbon.' Which would get me so riled, I'd scream at her and tell her my daddy wanted me to have those things, and she better let me have 'em.

"Oh, I knew he was my father like I knew my own name. Oh, yes. Your Gran made that clear from the get-go. But Leland Paxton never called himself my daddy, and I never mentioned it in front of him. I called him Masta Lee, just like everybody else did. But still, I had my airs.

"I used to prance around in front of the other Negro children in my new dresses, with my new toys. 'Masta Lee gave me this. Masta Lee bought me that. My mama put the gree-gree on Masta Lee, and he'll do whatever we say. So you better not call me names or I'll tell Masta Lee.' Those children, they hated me something awful. But no wonder.

"And Louis—God knows I tried to provoke him too. Didn't care any who he was, that just made me bolder. I fanned my tail at him every chance I had, I'd show off all the new things I'd got. From our daddy. He had every reason to hate me. But if he did, he never showed it. Never rose to the bait. Later on I realized he must've guessed his father's bent before any of us."

She paused here, her lips parted, her gaze aimed somewhere past my shoulder. I longed to spit out some cutting or stupid remark, one which might interrupt the inexorable flow of her narrative. But I was still, and after a moment she continued.

"Things went on like this til I was halfway through my fourteenth year. I remember it was March—the ground was drying out, it was already getting hotter. There came this day when Masta Lee called your Gran up to the Old House. When she came back she said she had a job doctoring a baby at another plantation. She packed up her bags and her herbs, and left me in our rooms by myself.

"It got dark, and long about an hour after there was a knock on the door. When I opened it, there was the master. My father. Smiling and saying, Onessa, you must be some scared, being out of the way here in this cabin, with your ma off on her rounds."

She stopped. When she resumed, her voice had gone dead, flat, like her eyes when they took on that catlike slant. My own mouth went dry. The blood fled my stomach and fingers, leaving them cold.

"What a fool I was, Bree. Thinking all that time I was his favored daughter."

I shut my eyes.

"He was still in the doorway. His hand was in his pocket, and there was something in the gesture—right then I knew his mind, although I am not sure how. I actually cried some—I tried that first—then I thought to fight him; I couldn't believe he would do this over my protests, within yards of his other blood. He hit me even before my hand could rise. In the face. I recall he bent my arm behind my back—without anger, just to make me stop, like you'd muzzle a dog. All the time, he was silent, with these wide eyes, this kind of wonder in them, as if he just could not understand why I'd raise such a fuss. I invoked all of the foolishness I could think of to turn him. Decency. God's commandments. The laws of nature. I called him Daddy. Papa. But of course I couldn't touch him, was not a person before him in the way you think of a person. Whatever I said—it must have been just noise to him, like the calls of birds, or cows.

"Think of it, Aubrey. Imagine it. To bide your time that way, through fourteen years. Not pretending to yourself, or to anyone else, that this is foreign flesh you're looking on, but knowing all along what it is, and what you'll have of it. It must've been in his mind each time he laid eyes on me, and I believe that was very much the point of it. That he knew."

She fell silent. I thought she was crying, but she was not. She was staring out of the window, her black eyes as impenetrable as marble.

I waited for her to say something else. I might have waited a minute—or maybe it was an hour, or a lifetime, for time was doing that strange thing I'd wished it would do when I sat in the Cremorne Gardens with Arabella: it had stretched its smallest unit out into an infinity, as if in the knowledge that I would not be able to go forward into the next second, having heard all of this.

"It's hard to own, I'm sure," Mama said at last, in that same toneless voice. "Unless you've been considering it for years—decades—as I have."

She turned back to face me.

"When your Gran got home that first night, I acted the same as always. I didn't say a word. Not that time. Not any of the other times after. I went on for a year and a half before I was got with you, Bree. And when it happened, I told your Gran it was a boy from the quarters. But she didn't believe me. She found the money, you see. We fell out a dozen times about it, she shook me stupid—and she never hit, you know your Gran was never one to strike a child. But she wanted me to say it, and I never would, out loud. Because that was the point, Bree, right from the start: that I not ever say it, not to her, and after a time, not to myself either."

"I am sorry, Mama," I rasped, "please, you do not need to explain—"

"Yes I do. You have to let me. For I have thought a long, long while about that, Bree. About why it was I did that. I believe it was because here all along I'd had this illusion, that I was adored just for existing, being a part of him. And I could not bear to have everyone know what he had really been about. I couldn't bear to know it myself. After I was got with you, he left me alone, he never came near me again, so I fooled myself I wouldn't have to think on it."

I stared at my fingers, laced and rigid in my lap. I thought that if I moved my head I might vomit.

Mama had already pressed on. "But Louis knew. The whole time it was happening, almost from the first, he knew. When I passed him anywhere on the property, he watched me, and it was something in his face—I could tell it. But he was never smug. Or vicious. And never turned toward doing as his father had, like some of these sons of bitches will. He looked at me like we shared something. The same misery. Him and me, and his mother, Hattie, and your Gran. And the more I felt this, the worse it got between him and his father, and then between Hattie and Lee.

"I got scared then for all of us, but especially for you. And of how it would be when you came.

"I meant to love you, Aubrey. But I did not know that I would. And I was afraid of how you'd turn out—I couldn't imagine a child conceived in such a manner coming to any good. I feared you'd be an imbecile.

"Or a girl.

"But you were a beautiful, perfect baby. And smart, smart as a whip—and then I was afraid of what would happen if we stayed round Lee. Right off I could see him in you. You'd turn a certain way in a certain light, or your eyes would have a look, something arrogant I imagined you got from him—later on I wanted to slap it out of you, I know I tried it. But right then I was more scared than anything else of where it might lead, for when I recalled myself as a child, and how Lee treated his son by his own wife—God knew what he'd do to the two of us.

"Louis had gone to Europe after you were born. He'd been courting Madame for a while, and he married her, and returned home. His father gave them the property on St. Charles Avenue, likely at Hattie's request, and they established themselves there.

"And just after that, when you'd started walking and talking, Louis asked that all of us—your Gran, and me, and you—be given to him and Madame, that we be permitted to leave the Old House and move to the city.

"Lee said he was welcome to you and me. But he wouldn't allow your Gran to go. She was the doctor, and he needed her. Your Gran told me to leave, she said she would be all right, and we would see each other.

"And so I did it. I felt I had to, for your sake. I did not want to fear for you every second. And I did not want you knowing any of it. I felt Louis would protect you. And that I'd have a better chance of keeping the truth of it from you in New Orleans.

"Of course your Gran advised against this. She said she'd always wanted me to know how I came to be so she and I wouldn't have secrets—but then, it wasn't the same thing, her and Leland Paxton. Not the same as for me.

"So I took you to Louis's. And shortly after, Hattie died, and just after that, so did Lee. Which is the way sometimes—you're bonded in hatred with someone, but then the hate disappears, and you don't know what to do with yourself, there's nothing left to do but die." I looked up at her, but her expression was neutral. "The Old House passed on to Louis and Madame. Your Gran could've left if she wanted, and come to stay with us, but by that time she and I—we were falling out. I lived to keep you safe then, Bree, and what she wanted you to know—it was dangerous. I truly believed that. I hope you can understand."

She stopped, perhaps to give me time to place myself within the story, to reflect; but instead, in the silence, I inadvertently began those mental computations which she'd warned me she'd been at for years.

The man whom I'd thought of as Louis Paxton's father, and later, my grandfather—an anonymous figure dead before I'd even known he was alive—

This was my father.

Also the father of Louis Paxton. And of my mother. My mother, whose immersion in love, I'd imagined, had precluded her understanding for an instant the depth of my pain.

I meant to love you.

My owner Louis Paxton was my half-brother. And also my uncle.

His children were my cousins. And also my nieces and nephews.

My mother was a half-sister to me.

This was who I was. My family tree. A strangled, festering rot of black and white and yellow.

Breezes blew outside. It appeared to be a warm day, the sun shone. We could hear mourning doves cooing in the trees and then taking flight, their wings beating with that odd whistling sound as they rose. On the mantelpiece a clock ticked; it was Mama's pride, she'd told me last night, an antique, its flowered face supported by gold figures of horses and nymphs.

"Why are you able to tell me these things now?" I asked finally.

"You left me. Your Gran passed. Louella came back to New Orleans. She knew everything. Brought it into the open. She had already done so with her father, and then she did with me. She had lost her mother, was having no more of pretending, and I knew then I was finished with it as well."

She leaned over the table to me.

"I want to be clear with you now that I am sorry—"

"No—do not apologize." I stepped upon her words, for I had a dread of hearing her say these things. Of having nothing left to do afterward but die. "Don't let's discuss it anymore—" I wanted, in fact, to slap my hands over her mouth, or over my ears.

"No. Let me finish." She was implacable. "I regret especially what went on after Louis brought us to New Orleans. He and I had a bargain. Uneasy and unspoken it was, but a bargain. We were his servants. Nothing more, however we were treated at times. Those were the terms. I was afraid you wouldn't understand them, that if you learned the story, thought yourself other than a slave, you would cross a line with Louis, and there would be an end to all of it.

"But there is no excuse. I am only asking you to accept my apology."

"I accept it."

I could not look at her. She was not Mama. She was weakened somehow, diluted, in what she no doubt thought her strongest moment, the one which had taken all her mettle to get through. I could see it all now, and I did not want to see it, did not want to know her reasons, experience her agonies, at the expense of my own.

"What is to happen now?" I rasped, mainly to shift the focus of the discussion. "What is it you and Paxton acknowledge to each other these days?"

"All of it."

"And he has no difficulty with that."

"Some things do not change. There was no discussion between us. When we arrived here he introduced me as his half-sister. He gave me a share in the management of this estate. Not ownership. In the event of his death his children will inherit the equity outright. But I cannot be evicted from the property, nor can it be sold without my consent. I would receive a quarter of the proceeds of any sale. There is also a trust. Reparation—that is how it is termed. Wages due. A bank in Marseilles is the executor.

"I refused it all initially. Louella convinced me to reconsider. Thomas, however—Thomas has raised certain objections. I don't know how he will react when he discovers you here."

I did not make any reply to this, only contemplated the ground. I was no longer nauseated, for my body had gone numb all the way to my knees. Gradually, though, a picture began forming in my mind. It was of Mama, in her fine dress, affixing her signature to certain weighty documents. And Thomas, compelled to bear witness. I felt my lips curl of their own accord.

I looked up at Mama, my smile spreading.

"Mama. You are a wealthy woman."

"Yes, actually, I am." She attempted a smile of her own, tiny and uncertain.

I began to laugh. It was a strange laughter, it sounded strange to my own ears, but I could not stop it.

I picked up a dainty teacup from the service. Before I knew what I was doing, I'd dropped it on the floor. It shattered into pieces, the shards skittering across the polished floor, the tea spreading into a pool.

"Don't mind it," I giggled, "you can buy a new one. Call the maid to clean it up."

Mama's smile had vanished. "Aubrey—"

"Tell the fucking maid to clean it." I picked up the matching saucer, hurled it with all my strength against the wall.

Mama was up, behind me, in an instant. She laid her hand upon my arm, and I grabbed it away, and before I knew quite how it had happened, my hand had snapped back, struck her across the cheek. She grabbed at my wrist again, restrained it, and I allowed it this time, despite my greater strength, the ease with which I could have thrown her off—could, in fact, have hurled her against the wall. Instead I sat down upon the floor, amidst the broken pieces of china.

She held fast to me, followed me to the ground, and I allowed this as well. A moment later she wound her fingers around mine. Then we sat wordlessly, the ticking of the nymph clock assuring that the minutes would continue to flow smoothly, one upon the other.

A little later, I pulled myself onto my knees, and set to picking up the pieces of china.

"I'm sorry, Mama," I said, although the mark on her cheek had already faded.

"Never mind." She set to wiping up the stain upon the floor with a napkin.

I did not care to walk the estate with her that day, or the next, or to see Lila or anyone else. Instead I wandered about by myself. I was not hungry, or thirsty, or hot or cold, or desiring of anything. In my head I was breaking down the events of my life and reassembling them according to the new information I possessed; it was an arduous task. I felt I had become vapor, as if the very particles which formed me had separated, and would blow off in different directions at the slightest breeze.

I was lying in bed two days later, preparing for sleep, when someone knocked upon the door. It was Mama. She swept into the room in a flowing gown of some diaphanous material; she had already mentioned that she wished me to accompany her to Aix so that her tailor—who sent to Paris for his patterns and fabrics—could make some proper clothes for me. I was not surprised at the speed with which she had adapted to her new status. She had been around wealth her entire life, after all, participating in the amenities it provided even if from behind the veil of servitude. She therefore knew its nuances as well as any heiress to the manor born.

I noticed she was carrying two large accordion-pleated folders, one beneath each arm, which were stuffed to overflowing.

"I have something for you," she said. "I had intended to wait to give these to you, until we'd discussed a few more things, but I think now is the time—considering."

I furrowed a brow at her. She placed the folders on my knees.

I opened one, and felt my throat tighten.

It was the collection of letters from you, Gran. The ones you'd written me after our separation, which Mama had stolen, and I'd recovered, and had left behind in New Orleans.

Except that it had to be more than that, for there were many, many other papers, a whole second folderful.

"When she was dying," Mama said, never one to soften her speech, although her eyes were soft, "she told me about the rest of these. I came to the Old House to take care of her and said I knew you were alive—I wasn't sure, of course, but it seemed important for her to believe that—so she kept writing, near to the day she died.

"I haven't read them," Mama added. Then she turned and exited the room, her gown swishing behind her.

I stared at the door long after she'd closed it. Then I lit the two other lamps in the room—the ink had faded, and in some places your penmanship had yielded to the racing of your thoughts. I picked with care from amidst the papers, and then, when I had a small pile before me, I settled myself back in my bed.

August 16, 1847

My dearest Bree

Nothing in the world not even the triles we face over the last year could make me forget that this is a Special day. Happy Birthday my little man my little brown pup! How glad I am that you are growing up but oh how sad I am too Bree for this is the first birthday I don't spend with you. I will not be there to see you eat your birthday cake or get your growing pinch or your presents. Maybe this is the year Mister Louis will give you the poney he promised. I am sure I shall hear about it if it happens.

I do not know whether you get the basket I made up or anything else I send you but today on your birthday I have settled on something. I will write to you anyway and tell you all about the thoughts I have of you so that someday And it may not be for a very long time but I can wait! you will know how beloved you are always. Here is your very first letter!

Believe me Bree I would be with you if I could. Your Mama and I have a falling out but that does not mean my afection for you has gone anywhere. It is right here waiting for you and will be yours as soon as your Mama thinks we can be family again. Mean-

time I have left your Sitting Corner just like always. Your chair is already some too small. We must get Jesse to build you another. But your books are here and your paints. I have not finished the Saints faces for they need your Special touch. Each night I light a Candel for your return!

Please be well and mind your Mama and if you wish send me a little note or a picture you made or anything at all. And may your birthday be the happiest ever!

I sit in the Sunshine of my thoughts of you and send a Sunshine Beam your way. There do you feel it. That was me!

All my love to you beloved
Your own Granevangeline

May 8 1852

Dearest Aubrey

I spent last night in the Quarters looking after Mavis and Bucks son Tilden. I do not know if you remember Mavis and Buck for they are feild workers and I doubt you have even heard of Tilden. He is only a year old and you havent visit much over the last year and when you are here your Mama just takes you straight to the Old House and then straight home. Tilden is a precious little basketful but he will fuss because Mavis is so rough with him which I try to tell her without making her mad. I get him drinking and slip a bit of poppy tea to him. Then I said to Mister Walsh that Mavis ought not go to the feilds tomorrow or the next day so that she could care for him and I guess she was grateful for that though there is always so much bad feeling between the Quarter folk and myself. They are afraid of your Grans gree-gree and Frenchy ways though I pray to Jesus just like them. I dont blame them but it hurts me just the same.

Today was one of my Candel days so I lit one for you to Our Lady of Charity. I also asked an extra favor of her that we might visit each other before the end of the year. She watches over both of us and keep us safe and I know she will do whats best so let us hope this is the year we are brought back together!

I miss you every moment of every day Bree.
Your devoted—Granevangeline

August 16 1855

My dearest Aubrey

Once again it is your birthday and I am thinking on all that has happened over the last year. It is hard to believe that you are twelve years old today and near grown. I can tell from the little I see of you that you are tall and comely as I knew youd be. I can only hope you are nobel and good at heart as well since that is far more important.

On this birthday Bree I have made a decision which has to do with both of us. I have been asking and praying for help to see where we are going you and I and now I think I have been told. It come to me in a Dream whats ahead and what I must do.

It pains me so to say this but it may not be give to me to hold you close ever again. I pray it is not so and that God change His mind but right now this is what He is showing me. So it also come to me that I must find another way to tell you important things about yourself for I have known all along that this is my duty toward you. Those things have been in my mind a long time. I long to say them but did not because they are more than you can take in as a boy. You must know them someday though. So I decide to write them to you in letters as I wrote other letters but these I will not send. I will put them away for that day way ahead when you will be ready for them and get them to your hand somehow.

Today like always I think of our separation and I am sad. You may not remember someday hence that once upon a time we were Special Friends who share ourselves in a way I think is rare between children and grown people. You may not remember why that friendship ended or you may have a wrong picture of what happened and so I feel I have to talk on it and tell you my side of the story.

I am kept from you because of an argument between your mother Onessa and myself. The argument is over a secret I am sure she have not told you but what I have always felt it would be best for you to know. I will tell it to you now and I hope you forgive me if this is the way you come to it for the first time. I will start at the front of the story though so that you know why I place this truth on you and why I believe it to lighten you rather than crush you once you understand it. Whatever you feel please remember that what I do is out of love for you. Bear with me and promise now before you read another word that you shall not quit me until you read the last one my dear.

Your great grandma and grandpa Delia and Francois who was called Frank here were longtime servants of the Paxtons. Maman was born in Haiti and when her own mother died she was bought by Jean-Tomas Paxton. He was a widower but still hearty and like his gin and cards and ladyfriends. He had two sons the older called Leland and the younger Evan. Papa was Creole born in New Orleans and also bought by the Master as a young man. He and Maman were very high yellow Negro and start off at the Old House as Maid-of-all-work and Footman of Master Jean. They married late in their lives and I am their only child.

Maman was very beautiful. She was slim with high cheeks and thin nose and her headwraps of bright cloth rose up into the sky. Nobody else on the plantation looked like my Maman. She got good schooling in Haiti and spoke English but like French better and fell into it when we were by ourselves. From the first she was very much favored by Master Jean and then by Master Leland who let her follow Vodou as she had in Haiti and hold her services on the property.

In fact the Masters think so much of her that they took to having her perform just for them. She knew fortune telling and necromancing and other things that are not only of Vodou and oft conjur for Master Jeans guests at parties and balls. But this was just for show and she was smart about it. No white folk ever hear bad news from Delias Spirits. No ones poppet ever had a pin stuck in it or bad luck hex onto it.

Maman also knows herbs and cures and medicines so over time she come to be the plantation doctor. This made her even more valuable to the Masters. When she doctored she wore her own skirts or wrapped cloth and ropes of apple seeds and one of tiny bones which hung from her neck. Around her waist she had a rosary with a silver crucifix and a velvet bag with her Fortune Stones in it. These things passed to me now and you may remember them from our visits Bree. Maman worked hard at keeping the black folk on the Paxton property healthy in body and spirit and thus she had run of the place and did mainly as she liked with her own time.

Papa worked in the house with the Master. He was tall with a soft face and quiet except when he and Maman argued which they did on many a day and night. They are all sparks and gunpowder when they fight and then they made up just the same way with kisses and crying. Like all the other house servants Papa could read and write. The Masters believe that for high-yellow Negroes most of all learning is important as a smart slave could better serve his owner. I myself was taught by my parents and sometimes by the Paxtons own white tutors. They like that I was quick with learning though I know I do not write as well as you or your Mama. But I do well enough reading and sometimes I recite from the Bible before the Masters company even as Maman call the Spirits in the next room. The Paxtons were very free with us in some ways which put them on the bad side of a few of their neighbors and I believe Maman and Papa felt a debt to them for that reason.

Maman most of all was loyal to the death to our Masters and she expected me to be so too. She had a great future planned for me. Greatness to her was the post of Vodou healer after her. She wanted to teach me all of her secrets quick as she could and I was more than happy to learn. The days we spend to practice the Spells of Protection called the Makutos and walk about the forest for herbs and plants were some of the sweetest of my girlhood.

Maman and I lived in a cabin in the Quarters back then. It was set away from the feild workers huts and was much nicer than theirs but not anywhere nice as the one I have now. Papa slept in the Old House the better to serve Master Jean. He come to our cabin late at night and on Sunday which is the only times there is no work to be done. Remember Bree when Master Jean and then Master Leland run the Old House it was a real cotton plantation not like now and there are chores sunup to sundown.

Still and all though we have privilege and we knew it specially when we stood our lot longside that of the feildhands. I always hate sunrise when we lived in that cabin near the Quarters. I could hear the feild workers—men and women—get up and make ready for the day. The first one awake rang a bell outside by the water pump and soon after come the other voices and the sound of the overseers horses. Then they set off with the workers singing to keep themselves in step. That singing made me want to cover my ears. It was so terrible even the songs about Redemption and Heaven. I know those people are wed to the feilds and that it be the same year in and year out til the day they up and died.

And this was on a GOOD plantation mind you where there was little beating and plenty of food and warm living quarters and day of rest.

But good or no I hate hearing the gangs go off to the hard boredom of their days and I was always glad when the singing fades and I could go back to sleep for an hour until Maman awakened me.

Maman was very strict with me while I grow up. I was not allowed any truck with the fieldhands or with the blackskin Negroes whatever their jobs who she think beneath us. There were no yellow children about so I was very lonely but Maman says this is the price of my station. She was very proud that we are so light we sometimes taken for white ourselves. She saw a day coming when we might even buy our liberty and live as free coloreds though this was not high up on her list of plans. She thought freemen had a rough time of it and most of them end up worse off than if they stayed on a plantation and that with all our privilege there would be no point in trading a good soft life for a hard one just so we could call ourselves FREE.

But she settled herself on one point that I should set my sights to MARRYING UP and get a husband among the yellow free class or even among the local house servants so long as he was a higher yellow than myself and could add a good part of white blood to the mix in my veins.

When I was nine Old Master Jean was killed in a terrible carriage accident and Master Leland and his wife come to be the owners of the Old House and all the property. By now they had a son your own Master Louis who was just a babe. The wife Miss Henrietta who was called Hattie did not like my Maman and so we found ourselves with less business at the Big House though my mother kept on as plantation doctor and herb woman and Papa keep to looking after Master Leland.

Then when I am thirteen Master Leland all at once took an interest in me. Up to then he mayhaps patted my head once or twice in a year but since we are no longer at the Old House very much even those pats had stopped. When I turn thirteen though he began hiring my mother out to neighbor plantations to doctor and charge for the service and come to our cabin himself to give her her appointments and directions. I never understand why he did not just send these messages with my father or call for my mother to come get them but my mother seemed glad for the new job and the visits so I figured there must be something good she expected to come of them.

Anyway Master Leland get to know me by name and took to calling me Little Bit Evangeline and spoke a few words to me whenever he come to the door. Maman on her part started to find reasons to call on him at the Old House and she would bring me with her most every time. This went on for a year or so and though I didnt much like it I hadnt any idea what it was leading to.

But then my mother starts hinting at what she had in mind. Old Master Jean had liked me quite a lot she said and it seemed Master Leland did too. What a wonderful man he was so rich and handsome. She admired him so for the way he ran the plantation and for the fine manner in which he held himself.

I did not think Master Leland was much to admire. I thought he was full of himself and petty and I saw the triles he put upon his own family. He was pure horror to his son Louis. Stepped round him like he is a piece of wood on the ground or else said the cruelest things to him. Mainly that he was not to be spoiled soft by his mama but must learn to be a man and know that men take the punishment of life. It was not life that punish Louis though. Twas Master Leland with the back of his hand. Sometimes I would spy Louis hiding in the brambles near the Quarters when his mama and daddy fought, and many a time I saw his face marked up and tears upon it. Likely the only thing that saved Louis was Master Lelands brother Evan who come to visit each week and took a shine to the poor child. God did test Louis not only with his father but also because he was very handsome and later on could have spent his wrath upon the gals black and white what chase him. But God also give him a righteous heart for he never fell that way. Or maybe it is because of how he sees his mother suffer.

Master Leland act worst to Miss Hattie. Maybe this pleased me a little at first for Hattie did not like my family and it seemed her comeupince that her husband be so hateful toward her. But Master Lee was so bent on misusing her that in time I come to pity her.

She accused him of having women amongst the slaves and mistresses amongst the free coloreds in the city.

And he never denied it but instead ask what she expected when she was his fathers choice of a bride and not his own and married him for his money without a thought to how they might get on.

Miss Hattie took to whisky and fits and what she called accidents. She once drank a half-bottle of laudanum which my Maman had to help her puke up. But soon as its out of her stomach Hattie turned and shoves Maman away and curses her to hell. Maman said Master Leland hears that and rush in then and tells Hattie that the next time she better finish the whole bottle or by God he will ram it down her throat himself and so she picks up that bottle and pitches it at him.

Maman always took Master Lees side in the arguments. She said Hattie was a crazed bitch of a drunkard who got what she deserved. A man is not about to plant his feet down and let them take root she said not unless he has a powerful reason like love for his wife to do so. Most marriages are not for love though and so a wife should not expect her husband to be Martyr or Saint but know that he would roam and ask only that he come back to her bed in a decent span of time. Gals are just bound to chase a fine man like the Master Maman said and Hattie ought be happy that she bore the Masters name and had bore him a son instead of nagging him into an early grave. She winked at me and told me she would not have minded a toss with him herself though of course I was not to tell my Papa she said so.

Then she asks what about me? What did I think of Master Lee she wanted to know.

I was still some shocked that she would betray my Papa so easy so I told her I had no thought about the Master one way or another so long as he was never mean to me.

But she asks me that question again and again and soon it was no longer a question but a list of Master Lees fine points and of all the things he said about me or the ways he showed interest in me. At the same time Maman was pointing out how few suitors there are for me to choose from. She cut down every yellow boy we know for miles around. I told her that maybe I could meet with more of them if she took me along more often on her doctoring but this fine idea only caused her to do the opposite. She made sure I never rode along with her even when she could have used my help.

That was a bad and black year. I look to my Papa to stop my mothers scheming but he didnt seem to notice how put out I am. He had the idea that he and Master Leland was more birds of a feather than owner and slave and so in his mind too I suppose the Master could do no wrong not even against his own daughter.

I was just past my fifteenth birthday when Maman stop circling round me like a vulture and land on her point.

I was to be give to Master Lee. She had consulted the Stones and it would be for the best. He wanted me and Maman knew it and what he wanted he would take for we belong to him and always will. So she wanted I should give in quietlike and think myself lucky to be picked from all the women he has his choice of.

But I would not agree. No I say I will not do it. They could not make me. I would run away or kill myself first. I have my virtue to think of and want a mans love and proper husband and family. I would not play the harlot with a married man one who spit in Gods eye by owning his fellow human beings and shame his wife under her nose. I would not ruin the dreams I have for myself. Not for Maman or for anyone would I do this. And sure enough not with Master Lee.

Well that was fine Maman said she would tell the Master and he would likely sell me off but before that he was bound to come in here and rape me just for the thrill of it and if any of us raised our hand he would have us whipped or hanged. She told me it was time that I wake up and know I have no choice Your Royal Highness. I cant refuse lest I wish to be sold or dead and my virtue is worth nothing less the Master wants it. Then I can be smart and turn it into something worth trading and give it as a gift instead of force the Master to take it as from a common feild slut.

If you act like a squalling sow then that is how he will treat you Maman said to me. He will have you anyway and leave you quicker with less than what you start with. But if you act like a Queen while you give in to him then he will believe its a Queen he is having and who knows where that may lead.

What swayed me though are her tales of what may happen to Papa and her if I am difficult and beyond that what good might fall to them if I am not.

You must not think Bree that I went happy or willing into Master Lees arms. I surely did not. But neither must you think I hate my parents for how they jump to place me there. In my mothers mind this was a chance and there are so few to grab at. She showed me many valuable things and though in this I believe she was worse than wrong I dont hold it against her. For in a strange way I can see her side of It.

I never know what talk took place between Maman and Master Lee but somehow they decide that I would go to him in the Old House. Miss Hattie was away visiting her sister and the house slaves were kept busy so that I could make my way to him not seen. Or rather everyone would see but also act like they had not.

I was get up for my rendezvous with Master Lee as if for my wedding night. Truly this was how my mother looked at it for even after all the terrible things she said she still thought there was no finer match to be made than this false one with her precious Master. When the great day come it was June and muggy and we spend all afternoon to ready me. Maman filled the tin tub in our cabin not once but twice so I could bathe and rinse myself proper. Then she poured over my head water in which she has steep rose blossoms. She cleaned my nails and buff them all the time working her Prayers and Incantations and pulled two pieces of string tight and spun them over my forehead so my brow is smooth. She rubbed charcol stick neath my eyes and used a berry die on a rag to color my lips and give some bloom to my cheeks.

My hair was then done up in a big round bun at the back of my head with a long shiny bone needle to hold it in place. Maman always loved showing off my hair. Her own was coarse and nappy the blackest part of her which she kept under her head-wraps. But she called my curls the blueblood at work and so she left them down and flowing. Tonight though I am to start out with my hair up and out of sight and then at the right moment which she made us practice a dozen times I am to pull the pin and shake my head so that the curls fall down over my shoulders.

Then she got out a corset which she had saved for a moment like this and slip it about my waist and pull it tight. It very near squeezed the life out of me. I had never wore one and thought to myself that if this was what fine ladies have to put up with each and every day it was no wonder they were miserable and give to faints. But even so there was a kind of thrill to the pain like I am being gusseyed up for Royalty maybe to meet with a King who could turn me to a Princess. And when I saw myself in the glass which was another Special thing Maman was allowed to have I smiled though part of me did not want to. For the gal staring back at me almost was a Princess so pretty under the paint that it was easy to forget what she was headed for.

When I had done with preening Maman had me to step in the white muslin gown with the tiny pearl buttons in front. She made this herself with Magdalenes help and though it was plain in style it was cut to fit me exact and covered in fancy needlework and looked for all the world like a piece from a grand ladys wedding finery. It would come off with just a tug of the buttons the main thing being that it look good whilst it fall to the ground.

Last off Maman stuck tiny balls in my ears. She had give me rings when she pierced me long ago but these she said are Gold and sure to catch the Masters eye.

When she was all finished with her busy work she stepped back and look at me.

You are every inch a Queen she told me and then she hugged me to her and slipped a Makuto charm in the bodice of the dress which was the dried heart of an owl. She was crying and though I hugged her too I wondered if she cried out of knowing the wrong she did or out of some twisted up sadness akin to what the brides mama feels.

We let go each other and then it was time to talk over some last minute lessons.

I was to go to his door meek as a child for that was what I must show off just now in my freshness and innocence. I must not make the first move Maman warned me. Be proud resist a little but do not fight him straight out only make him work a bit. Later on you may tease him but this first time you must not appear too confident. When he is ready act like you are won over however you truly feel. You must expect that it will hurt some and you may cry afterward so as to make him pity you a little bit but do not scream for that will only annoy him.

When he is done make certain you flatter him but not too much so that he is left wanting more of you. When you go leave him as a woman not as the little girl you are when you come. You may switch your hips some but dont overdo or he will think you uppity. You are my brave girl she said and kiss my forehead and tell me you will be a great lady and hold a great man in the palm of your hand.

We went into the Old House through the kitchens in the back. Once we had got up the servants stairs Maman said a Prayer and left me and it is up to me to walk alone down the long dark hall to the Masters bedchamber.

I am shaking and freezing and I recall my mouth was so dry and my knees knock together. I was scared half to death of what was to happen and of what might go wrong and of spoiling my only chance to please the Master.

I brought my hand up slow and knocked upon that big black door.

Go in as a child I hear Maman tell me and so I make big eyes and stick my lip out and waited for the door to be opened.

But it was not so I had to knock again harder which scared me because already it seemed that things are going wrong and I was acting much more uppity than I plan to.

At last I heard the Masters voice say Yes what is it.

When I go in he was stretched out on his giant bed in his silkin robe looking through the newspapers he read each day.

Now I would be lying if I did not say that Master Lee was a handsome man in his time though by this point he started going to drink and bloat and his face had lost that young look. Still he had his high color and blue black hair and light eyes which stood out so among a crowd of men. He had long fine muscles from which clothes hang just right and he was clever at dressing and grooming and playing up his good points without seeming to work at it. When I come in he looked that way there on his big bed. Just so but not trying to be. Like his hair just fell perfect over his brow. Like that robe just opened by itself right at the chest to show the muscles and the curly black hair in the middle.

I stood there swallowing and flushed and dont need act the childs part as I felt just like what I was.

Master Lee looked me up and down and then went back to his reading. Fix me a whisky from that sideboard he ordered me and did not bother to watch while I did it.

I felt my heart banging. It was all so awful wrong. I had dreamed he would sweep me into the Candelite and whisper shameful words to me. He wanted me Maman was telling me. Instead he was acting like he had no interest in me at all and I was fixing him a drink as though we are in the dining room.

I put the whisky on his night table and stand there not knowing what to do with myself.

He put his paper down then like he remembered I was still there.

He stared at me and said What is it you want to see me about Little Bit.

I near fainted when I heard that. See him about? I say to myself and I cannot think straight. It is trouble enough I am to be ravished. To bring up the subject myself was a thing I had scarce imagined.

I start to backing off to the door. I whisper Nothing. Its nothing Master Lee sir. Good night sir. and hope I can get out of there without tripping on my own feet.

But he called to me Come on back here Evangeline. I dont want to but I stop and turn slow and walk back.

You are all done up Little Bit. Now why would you be coming here at night all done up in this nice new dress to see me hmm?

I just look at him Bree and then I get so very angry. For I know right then what he is doing. Here he had ordered me to him like a Christmas ham on a platter. But he would play this coy game with me and later on after he sent me away he would tell himself it was all my doing. That I come flaunting myself to throw at him and he only obliged me.

I am so stirred up in my mind that for a second or two I could not think clear so I dont try to play along with him. Instead I just stated what was true. My mother told me you sent for me. If she was wrong and if you want me to go I shall.

He scrunched his brows like he did when he was bothered but when I again made as if to leave his tone had turned as if he were a little sorry and laughing underneath. Now now Evangeline dont be peckish I am not telling you to go. Of course you can stay if you want.

I felt that anger lick at me again Bree. For I see that no matter what I say he would twist it round to make it look that I am the one that want to come to him.

I walked back to the side of the bed and at last he seemed to get that I was not clever enough to try the game but only enough to know the insult in it. He went a different way then and look at the gold beads in my ears and asked teasing how I come by them. I try to follow Mamans lessons but in a clumsy way and later than she told me. I start with being sassy and cute but it come out all flat and stiff which was just how I feel. Up close the Master was not handsome or dashing. There was something use up like rot about him and whatever little fool thrill I give in to on the way to his rooms had been chased off now by dread and a sickness inside me.

He must have seen this for he set to dimming the lamps and then he poured me whisky which I had never tasted before. He switched hats again and now turned kind and fatherly patting the sofa beside him so I would sit while he asked me questions about myself. How old was I again was my mother really teaching me to doctor and could I read and write and what sorts of things did I do to amuse myself. I answered him stiff with all the manners I could muster for I was trying to be like Maman had called me every inch a Queen.

Back then I thought it was this air I put on which made things go as they did but now I know better. The Master was just the sort who need to think he does not force for he is so grand a gal cannot resist him. He liked to make believe the girl start out saying no and then end up wanting him to ravish her. But if it did not turn out so he was not above dealing a black eye or split lip along with the ravishing for Master Lees make believe went just so far.

The liquor went quick to my head and the Master come to my aid. I must make myself more comfortable he told me. Like he is doing me a favor he helped me loose my corset and take off my shoes. He dished out the sweet talk which I swallow up like the hungry little minnow that I was. Whilst the whisky burnt my brain I forgot my anger at him. I talk myself into the fool notion that in my comeliness I have great power namely the power to break his heart. He went on over my charms and begged me not to spurn him and then when he has whipped himself into a like fit of passion he finished the farce by setting me to test myself. I hear Mamans lessons in my head once again saying fight him just a little and so when I was giddy as I ever been and my nerve was up I yawned a big fake yawn and told him I feel tired and wish to go to my bed. I got up and made a drama out of stretching and then pulled that pin from my hair and toss my head. Whereon Master Lee took his cue and grabbed at my hand and groaned like a lover Have you any idea how you afect a mere man my lovely Evangeline? And then he pulled me to his lap so that I might know just what that afect was.

He kissed me hard and from then on oh I am like a babe in the ocean pretending to swim but really just fling about to keep from drowning.

Of course I made mistakes.

I did not yell at the right moment. Instead I yell like the Devil all the way through. Cant help myself for he hurt me like the Devil thinking he will force the camel through the eye of the needle and I am the needle. He took no mind of me only did for himself and then asked me when he was done do I carry on because I feel so good. I am so crazed for a second I forget to agree with him and just look at him bug eyed that he can hear me yell and still ask me this. I made a face at the sticky mess that come out of me and wiped a handful of it on the Masters clean bedsheets. And I forget to switch my hips when I left.

But in spite of all this I did good past my Mamans wildest hopes.

I come home to her on tottery legs my mouth all a red bruise my head aching and my heart full with remorse once the liquor dried up. But she drew a warm bath and washed me gentle and let me cry and then she wrapped me in blankets as if I were again her little gal and put me to bed crooning to me while she brushed my forehead.

I heard nothing from Master Lee but after two days Maman and Papa were called to the Old House. They come back laughing and praising God and as it happened they come back rich for Master Lee had given them ten dollars in gold which he jokes and calls a dowry payment. But Maman said that I ought be thrilled for no greater compliment could he have payed me than to say to the world or at least the Quarter that he saw me in the same light as a bride. Gold was the greatest of prizes and whoever was given it important indeed.

I was just in a daze. I looked at Papa to see if there was any bit of shame in his eyes for I felt sick with it but he was smiling from ear to ear and told me he was proud of the way I wound the Master round my little finger.

So I watched my whores ransom take a place of honor on the little table by Mamans bed. It was not all they got. Their work hours were cut back and more and better food sent them from the kitchen and also castoffs from the Old House like a down quilt and a painting in a frame.

A little while after that I forget how long some of the hands set to work beyond the side of the Old House opposite the Quarters. It turned out they were busy gusseying up an empty overseers cabin by the little copse of fruit trees that led to the meadow. Master Lee soon come to tell us that when it was ready it was to be my new home.

I was partways glad of this for my room until now had been a tiny corner of the cabin cut off with a curtain Maman hung from a beam. But this new place was so far away from everything. I could not see the Quarters at all since they lay down a hill from the Old House. And I could not even see the Old House itself very well because of the fruit trees that hid me.

But the new cabin that same one where you visited me Bree and where your own mama grew up was wonderful and huge with three big rooms like a small house and I was given furniture and got to make and take whatever I wished to get it nice. And the view from the back of the rolling meadows and the hills in the distance was so beautiful it made me smile and feel light inside whenever I look at it.

I thought it was grand as a palace but later I found out that Master Lee had got other of his Negro mistresses quarters of their very own in the city.

Once I move to my new cabin my visits with Master Lee come just like clockwork. He saw me twice or thrice a week and in not very much time it was almost like we are betrothed right down to the fact that we are laying with each other just as most Quarter couples did well before they jump the broom or had Maman sing Prayers over them.

I know in the back of my mind that he had done for me not to make me happy but to suit himself yet at times I let myself go off in the dream that we are lovers of a sort. You see I was scared that I might never know love and that this fakery may be my only truck with it. Sometimes I could not help pretending.

But the shine wore off quick enough. I dont mean to boast but I know I tire of the Master well before he tired of me. It wore on me that he has to make his visits to my doorstep look to be my doing and wants me to pretend the same. But the worst of it come to be his whining. If at first he want me for my innocence it turned round quick so that he come to be a pouty child at my feet and I his comforting elder.

He fussed about women that we are all alike wanting to pin him down and all greedy and eyeing his purse while flattering his person. He fussed about his brother Evan that he was their parents favorite while Leland had been left the Old House only because he was the first son. He fussed about his own child Louis that Evan had turned the boy against his father so that Louis set to ignore everything Leland tried to teach him.

To myself I called all this complaining the Poor Lelands and after I heard it over and over I found myself so bored that I feared I turn to stone. So then I would make up songs in my head or lists of tasks for the morrow and rouse myself only every few minutes to toss out a nod or a word like a pebble into a river so he thinks I am listening.

In time though I come to know that witches pot of lies and crossings which you so often find in big spreadout rich families like his. And then I felt a lick of sorrow for him for I could see small pieces of the man he might come to been. He had fine money sense and was a clever judge of people. And he had the long view of what was to come in Louisiana and all about the South and was sure it will not include the bondage of Negroes. He said the idea made him sad and no wonder. But the state ought ready itself a little at a time for the change. He was roundly scorned for that but I believe he was right. I still sometimes wonder what Master Lee could have made of his life if he take himself half serious and had gone into government.

But instead he went to liquor and selfpity and left room for little else.

Even our pleasuring come to be less important than the Poor Lelands despite the tricks that Maman taught me and which I practiced on the Master to his at first endless delight. It seems in time that Master Lee wanted more a mother than a mistress and I found myself at seventeen a matron without ever I bore a babe.

But we still did lie together and for a long while I was able to toy with him so that close as Maman figured we are not abed on the days I was most likely fertile. She had warned me I must take care for the Master turned on his women once they became mamas to his children. This made me hate the Master even more and it made me madder at Maman too for she give me to such a fool and ran me in a race I was bound to lose. I did what she said though. I always use the excuse that I had my ladies time to avoid the Master. When I really had it I use other excuses or made up some mad lustful game so that he did not notice.

But at last Maman or I made a mistake or maybe the Lord felt twas time. So that after four years of us together in which I had come to know the Master likely better than Miss Hattie ever did I find I am with child.

Blind as Master Lee was about so many things he was sharp as a bloodhound when it come to his mistresses being in a family way. He knew about me near before I did and from that minute his interest in me was fled. Maman said she could help me get shed of the child even though it was dangerous but I told her I wanted it no matter what it meant. She said she hoped I would not regret it.

I was some scared then but everything went on just as it was. I kept my cabin and Maman and Papa kept their privileges. Master Lee come to say hello to me or to sit in the sitting room but he never touched me again. I was so happy like a weight was off me! I told Maman if I knew this would happen I would have prayed for a baby the very first night.

But Maman got mad and told me I then likely would have met a different fate. She knew of other women Master Lee had taken who were not so lucky. They were got with a baby much quicker, or the Master lost interest in them much sooner, and when he was through with them they were sold. Maman said she had turned me into a clever bedmate, one who stays before her King so many nights that she squeezed some drop of love from his heart. She kept my belly flat long enough to keep my head on my shoulders.

Bree the baby I bore was of course your Mama Onessa. She was a beautiful child. She was so light when she come that no one would have guessed she had even a drop of Negro blood in her. Maman thanked the Spirits on her knees for this but I did not. I was long past the point of caring whether a skin was yellow or brown or pink. I was sick of loving whiteness when all that was evil had been put on us by that color. I had seen one of them up close and he was no more great or godlike than I myself. I was sick of hearing the Negroes rant against the white man and then argue among themselves as to whose gal had more yellow. I would have loved my baby no matter what color she come in and I was mighty put off by my own mothers crowing but by that time Maman was ill with consumption and I know she had not long to live so I let her spoilage of Onessa pass without a fuss.

Maman loved to point out the sameness between the Masters looks and the babys but I never thought of your mother as the Masters child. She was mine all mine from the moment I knew she was there inside of me. She was the gift of my life and however I got her it only goes to show that there is goodness waiting to come up from even the worst things.

What struck me funny though was Master Lee took note of Onessa right from the outset. He even wanted her named after him but I knew by this time that I could say no to him if I go about it a certain way and so Lee come to be your mamas middle name. All this favor excited Maman but I did not trust it. Master Leland was not one to do right for rights sake. If he decided to favor something it had to be because it was good for him in the long run.

Besides I did not want the Master needling his wife and son with the favor he showed to his mistress and her daughter. Things were shakedy enough what with Hatties evil eye upon us. I want to lie low out of its reach.

But I never hid from your Mama that the Master was her daddy. I know she would hear of it sooner or later and I thought it best that she hear it from me. I did not find fault with him before her but I let her know that I had been with him because I had to be and that though he is father to her by blood he is more the Master and we ought beware his favor for whatever he did was mostly apt to serve himself.

She did not believe me though. Who can blame her? I surely dont. She was a child.

Her father set to spoil her and make a pet of her and what child does not wish to believe this could only come of his Special love for his daughter?

His gifts and attentions looked to bear this notion out and she showed them off whenever she could. She screamed at me when I sent the gifts back to the Old House and said I am jealous when I told her that she must take her father with a grain of salt. She lorded herself over the other Negroes who did not understand the awful fix she was born into. I tried to step in but in the end the older folks hate her and the other slave young ones whose friendship I hope she would have taunt her silly instead.

We come to fight over everything. Vodou is the source of my Spirit and my Refuge as it was my Mamans and I long to pass it on to Onessa as it was passed on to me. But she want nothing to do with it. She called it witchcraft and would not touch the tools I show her.

And she took no interest in healing with or without Vodou. The medicine plants had no Special fix for her. She rather dress up in her dresses. And while I allowed as she was surely pretty and ought feel proud of herself I wished she might take interest in learning so as to have something which she had done herself instead of just what was Gods to give and someday to take away.

But then my parents died in two years of each other first Maman and then Papa. I was swallowed up by sadness and could not rouse myself from it even for your Mamas sake. So she took all the more to Master Lee who was her only source of afection and who gave it mainly for her comeliness. This set the stage for a rift between her and me and when in time I got my wits about me and again took up trying to keep her at safe distance from her father our battles come to be more and louder than ever.

This was the state we are in when I begin taking over Mamans patients visiting the Negroes within the parish homes and doctoring them as she did.

Master Lee kept the same terms with me that he had with Maman. He gave me half of what the Masters pay me for my services and keep half for himself. The money add up quick and I used it to buy toys and such for Onessa in the city so that she did not feel so much the loss of the presents I send back to her father.

At first I took Onessa on my rounds with me but as she grew older she would stay home by herself to do lessons or set dinner for us or see to other chores about the cabin.

It was surely while I was out on my doctoring that Master Lee first come to her.

I never knew how it started for your Mama never said a word to me. I noticed her changing for she got stormy then quiet and keeping secrets but then she was turned fourteen and fifteen and those are rough years for any girlchild. I did not suspect the truth of it until long round her sixteenth birthday.

She had put meat on her bones and her face seemed puffed to me and the bodices of her dresses look to squeeze her tight. I told her we would have to let them out for she was filling out and she started to cry but mad tears which she held back and rose up from the table without a word. It struck me right then how blind I was. That she was not filling out. She was having a baby.

I got up at her and demand to know if it is true. She did not say yes or no she was just quiet. I raved and ballyhooed and did all which no mother should do and every mother does when she finds herself in these shoes. I threatened and begged. I even shook her some though I never put a hand to her before this all so she would tell me whose child it was. But still she said nothing.

The months pass and she grew big like any gal will and through it all I try to coax a story from her. But she never talk about it and act like I was not talking. She seemed to think her belly will go down if we pretend not to see it. But I did not want to pretend. There was a baby coming. That baby was you Bree. I was to be a grand-mama. I had Magdalene sewing tiny baby things for you and I had Jesse building you a crib with spools and curlicues all over it. I want only to love you and to see you born into honesty so that there will be no cobwebs and mystery or no evil secrets around you.

But as the day you are due to come got close I begin to have Visions of the reason for your mothers quiet. I know it in my heart and tried to keep it from my head but the Spirits and my own good sense will not let me. They tell me where to look and I find money beneath her mattress which he must have given her but she lies and says she stole it from me and will not reveal the truth. So while she was laying in I had only pictures in my mind which come to me when I throw the Stones or lay in bed with my eyes shut and Mamans rosary between my fingers.

Then you are born and in the midst of my great happiness I find that my Visions have told me true. I know it the moment I saw you for you look so much not only like Onessa but like Louis too. Snow white with a head of black hair and silver blue eyes that come to be not black but green instead. So there can be no doubt.

You have been fathered by Master Leland.

Oh Bree. I love you so and fall on my knees happy that you are born and sound and yet still I want to cry and tear my hair to murder him dead to shake your mother and pull her to me and scream away the foulness of it. To cut my own flesh over this evil for it is happened right before my eyes and I do not see it.

This is why she kept her tongue until you are born and then conjures stories of secret nights with yellow boys. Why she did not carry herself proud in her laying in or ask my advice about the birthing or spin out dreams of her new life with her child like any mama will do.

And this is why she and I do not speak today and why you have been taken away from me for so many years upon years. Because your mother never wish to hear the facts of your begetting spoken of and would not let me tell them to you but instead serve up those ghost tales of wooing and betrayal.

I am sure this is a great great shock to you.

In fact I cannot think of any news which can hit harder.

Maybe you ask why then why I choose to tell it. Believe me I ask the same question of myself. I started even before you are born. What should I do if my Visions told me true I ask? Why do I wish you to know a thing so bad and why tell it with all my own feelings and thoughts mixed up in it? Why when I try to walk that honest path with my daughter only to see it lead to disaster?

This is my thinking. It was not my honesty that fail Onessa but the deceit of her father which claim her because it is so great. Even now she would run from it or battle wrong with more of itself. I do not blame her in her awful hurt. But I shall fight to win her back to truth for it is the secret and the lie told to keep it hid which fouls what it touches and eats away at trust and love.

I cannot leave you at the mercy of those dark things.

You are who you are Bree your fathers son. That much is true and cannot be changed. But you may take a different path for you now hold all that was good in him. I can see it and with all the faith in me I trust that you will find it in yourself. Now you know the truth you can hate and rage at will but I hope I BELIEVE you will let that fire burn itself out and use the ashes to build a greater good. What fortunes shall await you then!

From the very first time I set eyes on you Bree I love you so that I can only think how Gods feeling for us is greater than we ever dream and that the more awful evil we invent the more good that God will make it give out if our hearts are keep open to that good.

But our hearts cannot be open when they are guarding lies.

Forgive me any pain I bring you my dear one my beloved.

Your—Granevangeline

August 16 1858

My little pup

I know I should not start my letters to you this way. You are not little anymore. You are fifteen today and well on your way to manhood. How did such a thing happen? I know thats what every gran or mama ask when she sees her baby boy grown big.

I think of what you must be doing every day and knowing you are fifteen I can guess you are not any more playing pirates or poppets. I am sure one thing you notice much more these days is young ladies. So on this birthday I write you another letter that is meant for your grownup eyes for I wish to speak to you about Love.

I know I tell you that after Master Lee I was afraid I never have the love of a man something I wish for and plan for even as a tiny child. For a long time I thought God had forgot that wish of mine or decided it was not to be. After all I am near to the end of childbearing and where would I meet a man seeing as I know every one of them for miles around and not one has caught my eye or me his?

But dont you know God was only waiting for the right man and the right time to put him before me.

Near to two years past I hear there was to be a Christian camp meeting outside of New Orleans with famous preachers and Negro singers that travel all over the Southern states. Many of the Masters who take a free hand with their servants give out passes and let their black folk go. Of course your Master Louis is among these and Mister Walsh writes out permission for the Paxton slaves and them who are not Vodou or Catholic line up to get them.

I like to have gone myself but I know the feeling would run against me for those who see Vodou as the Devils doing outnumber us here at the Old House and were sure to raise a fuss over my coming. So I plan to stay at home but Jesse promised he will tell on everything that happens that is if his addled brain did not let it slip away before he got back.

Then just a few days before the meeting I hear that preachers are going about the countryside looking for permission to visit the slaves maybe to round us up for the big event. Early the next morning one of these show up at the Old House.

I see him come and see the black folk gather round but I know I am not welcome at their prayers and so I stay in my cabin. But that afternoon I hear a knock on the door and when I open it there stood the minister.

Oh Bree he was quite the man! Tall and dressed nice with his hat in his hands and his boots shiney. He was round my own age maybe a little younger. I was so shocked to see him I just stand in that doorway gawking.

He told me he come because he heard there was Vodou and a conjur woman on the grounds. The other darkies pointed out my cabin. I backed off a little then and told him that I am Vodou but if he come here to talk against it he is wasting his time for I know God and Jesus the Savior and the gods of Vodou too and find nothing wrong in that.

The minister laughed and says no he has no wish to talk against anything he only hears I know a good bit about the subject and as he knows little and could find no one in New Orleans willing to share it with him he wondered if I might do so.

He took me by surprise and so I asked him in and from that day to this Bree we have not been apart in Spirit even when there are many miles between us.

His name is Will Outlaw and I would wager that he is among the finest men God made in his image. Will was a widower five years when we met and had courted a cou-

ple gals. One changed her mind about him and one he changed his mind about so he never remarried. He is a freeman and makes his wage by traveling about bringing Gods word to black folk. But true to his promise he said nothing against Vodou that first day and never has since.

That first meeting we talked long into the evening and I find myself open up to him like I never was to a man. At first I was nervy as a cat for I never had any man visit my house except Master Lee and I keep telling myself that this one shall have no interest in me even as I wish the more I look at him that he would. He was that kind and gentle drawing me out and listening and with never a word of judgment. He told me the hard lessons of his life as well and they were many. Parents sold on the block and three children lost to yellow fever and his struggle to buy his family free only to have his wife die just a few years after. He said he come to be a preacher because the evil of bondage was so great that he feels it his duty to offer his people hope not of pie in the sky when you die but of pride in this earthly life.

Will told me something else he believes. That of all the bad which come of trade in slaves the worst evil was the hate of a people for all that is theirs a hate which takes them over and make them more slaves in their hearts then they are on paper. He say that instead what is of the black races of Africa must be held close to free the black ones here from the curse of inslavement. The Isrealites know bondage in Egypt Will says but they do not yield to despair because they stand fast as Gods people and never embrace the ways of their capters over their own ways.

When I heard this I blanch some for I am as high yellow as any and I wonder if he was pointing a finger in some way at me. And much as I know I do not judge color harsh neither do I think it ought be the source of our pride for we cant help the skin we are born to and if you look back far enough we are all come from Adam and Eve and therefore all brethren.

I say this and Will told me he wasnt speaking of false pride but of the pride born of knowing selflove as Gods creature. Isrealite might love and marry Egyptian he says if each loves his or her own as well as what belong to the other and remember above all that both is Gods child first.

This comforted me being what I believe myself and further raised my spirits since it left the door open for Will to find himself drawn to me. For you see Bree he is a very dark black Negro and told me his wife and children of whom two yet live are likewise. I dont know what your Mama might think of such a suitor for me but I know my own Maman is pitching about in her grave. But then perhaps in Heaven she has learned a few lessons she could not get into her head on Earth. I like to think so.

Anyway I feel after this that I could talk to Will on Vodou like he asked me in the first place and so I began knowing I am spilling precious knowledge but sure it is the right thing to do in this case. I think it right to tell you some of these things too for I dont know how much you remember of the Faith and you should know it if you would know all that you come from.

I tell it as it is passed to me best as I remember. When the Negroes of the tribes of Africa called Fon and Ayway and Yoruba come as slaves to Haiti and to Jamaica and Cuba the white folk force them to pray as Catholics. But the Africans are clever. They hide their old gods behind the faces of the new ones so they look to be good Christians when they kneel at prayers or leave offerings at the painted Statues. In time the new Gods and the African ones mix together so much that they are called different sides of the same coin though some take on the new religion only to hide the old while some accept Jesus in their hearts.

In Haiti the Africans know their faith by the old name of Vodou. This is where my Maman learned it. In Jamaica some call it obaya. In Cuba where many slaves are come from that part of Africa called Congo they follow the Orishas who are the many gods and mix them with the Christian ones to make the Way of the Saints or the Santeria in the Cuba tongue. And in Cuba too are the dark ones who turn the Orishas and the Saints to evil and follow the way of the Paylo Mayombee which is used only for ill.

But as my Maman taught it to me Jesus in the form of the Trinity Father Son and Holy Ghost is Lord of all Creation. His Saints along with the Angels good and bad dwell on the next plane between us mortals and the hand of the Father. The African gods of Vodou are part of that plane too.

Maman made sure I learned to call the gods our family has served back in the African lands. Now I tell them to you Bree so you know them and do not forget them though we have traveled far and come to Christ. Mawu the Creator is above all the others. Beneath him sits Gabara who watches over Love and Flimani Koku the Healer and Mamy Watu she who brings Wealth and Heviyosi the Thundermaker. There are many more but these are our family gods. They must not be worshiped as they are not divine for only God is divine and only Jesus is Lord. But as Catholics we know the Saints can be called on to bring our prayers to God and grant us favors and watch over them that pass on. The old gods of Vodou are just the same.

The gods can be used wrongly too for just as some pray to the Devil and do his bidding some will summon Spirits for their own dark ends. But Vodou knows no sin or Satan. Vodou can be used to make evil but it is not made of evil or only to do wrong.

Will was some surprised when I told him all this for he never met any slave with knowledge of the tribes of the African lands such as I have. He wanted to know how I come by all this and I say that my Maman told it to me as it was told to her by her own mama and so on. He laughed at the notion that he being so dark of skin has to hear of Africa from a gal who looks to be near white. He said he never thinks that that could be the story of Vodou for he was from Virginia where even Catholics are called witches and heathens.

He asked if I ever try to raise the dead and if I make blood offerings and I say no for I dont believe in spilling live blood and no Christian can raise the dead even if she can talk with them now and again. I allow as there are many who do these things for my own Maman did them but I do not and that made him happy. He said that had anyone explained Vodou to him as I did he would no longer be scared or willing to paint us all with the same brush.

As I say we are together from that day to this and what I know is that I have been happier in Wills company and in his bed than at any other time save at the births of your Mama and yourself. He cannot fill the space left empty by the two of you but then he does not try. He has made a space just for himself and I have had to grow some to fit it in me which is all to the good.

We have not married proper because this would make him family and I must have the blessing of all my family meaning you and Onessa to take that step. But Will and I made our lives with each other. We had to think long on this for we do not wish to be adulterers and hypocrits before God or ourselves. But we decide that God joins man and woman in love and that this love is our bond which shall be kept strong and true. If we promise ourselves to each other then we are promised whether Earthly beings know of it or not. So we held a ceremony in the orchard here for just us two. We wrote our vows and each say them aloud. Will wore his finest black suit and I a red dress which Magdalene and I sewed together just as she and Maman sewed the muslin I wore the night of Master Lee. But what a different night this one was from that!

We have not kept our afection a secret from the servants here or in your household so some may have guessed it. I do not ask for their silence but hope I shall be the one to tell your mother of it. Will makes his home in the French Quarter and I use my passes to visit him. He travels many months at a time for he is still called to his preaching but returns here always at the end of his journeys with a tale or gift or song he come upon in some city or town.

He is set on buying my freedom though I have explained this is not a matter which money can take care of. I would not wish it for myself unless you and your Mama are granted it too and I am afraid to bring that up before your Master Louis.

I so pity Louis Bree. He has not escaped the ruin born of falsehood though he has tried. I believe he seeks to do right by your Mama and you but cannot truly come to right and free you from bondage. So long as you stay slaves you are apart from him and he can treat you well to make up for some of what was done to you. But if this is taken away then he will have no choice but to see you full as his kin. And I think this is what he knows and fears more than anything for he knows the sins which join you to him. So I dont wish to test the waters by having Will go to him. Besides what would any of us do as freemen just now? I live well here and come and go as I like though I know Will would care for me were I free. And I know you are well treated in the city.

But when you reach your majority Bree then it will be another story. For you must have a chance to make of your life something besides toil under a Master and by then maybe your Mama and I will have joined forces to be ready for the change.

So that is the story of my life with Will and I hope you will find joy in my joy and be happy for me that I am so blessed with him.

I know you will be blessed in love someday too. But right now Im sure you burn just like any boy your age and you may have to learn a few lessons before you make peace between your body and your heart.

So here is the next part of this letter where I will talk to you plain and try to help you as best I can for I do not know who else is about you to take on the task.

First off Bree you must know some truth about gals. Do not think a girl is less apt to lust because of her nature for much as you hear that it is not true. A gal in her full womanhood is one in need of a man and she should have the blessing of her kith to find and enjoy one. A girl who tells you otherwise is lying so as to look proper or has not bloomed yet or maybe never will and so can never be the companion of your body. Lust has its place God knows and must be satisfied whether one is lady or gent. So look to a girl of fire to match your own not for one who sees your fire as sin and would throw water on it to put it out.

But lust will burn itself off so do not be fooled by it else you and your gal shall be shed of each other soon enough. Lust greases the wheels of love but later on love must be pushed uphill. You must work to see what you love in your chosen one at times and you must work to know each other full but then you must know where to leave off so as not to tire of each other. Make a companion of your wife Bree not mama housemaid or burden and she will be your finest company. Flee lies and fornication for this will destroy the peace between you.

If you are moved only by lust or by that which is untried then you shall likely stay a child wanting new toys and not a man. But you are free to choose this and if you should then I advise you do not marry.

Take care in any case where you spend yourself. Beware women who trade on lust for they can bear disease.

And beware what sadness you would bring to the lives of others. You know the hardship of a fatherless youth and I am sure you would not have that for your own blood. Each woman you would be with could well bear your child so ask yourself whether you wish to raise that child with her and if not how she might raise it alone. If your answer does not please you then isnt it wise not to bed with her and put the whole question to rest. Yes this means you must forgo your pleasure but learn to do it for no gal was placed on this Earth to be your amusement as you were not placed here to be anyone elses and it is your innocent child who suffers most in the end.

These are the rules of kindness and you may be thinking they sound too simple and things are often not so easy but I have learned that just as often they are not so hard as we would make them either. The simplest rule is the Golden One to do unto others as you have them do unto you and if you follow it then I believe you shall find your hearts desire my precious boy for you are all goodness and will draw goodness to you.

Such things as this a man should be telling you but maybe one already has or maybe by the time you set eyes on this you will have figured them for yourself. But it cannot hurt for me to say them to you Bree and hope they do not make you blush and to tell you again that you are always in my thoughts my plans and Dreams.

Be well upon your birthday my fine man. Seek your happiness and you shall find it.

I love you always and with all of me
Your Granevangeline

November 16 1861

My beloved Aubrey

What harsh times have fallen upon us but only serve to make life more precious. If God sees fit to take me in this fever I am ready for it. He has always guided my steps and will not fail me now I know. If I have not been granted my deepest wish to set eyes upon you and hold you in my arms once before I depart there must be reason for it and I shall find it out when I face Him at last. He has warned me this might be His wishes and so I accept His will. So much has been given to me even in these bad days that I know the Lord and Our Lady still watch over me. I lay beside a beloved companion and have seen my child restored to me. These are my Miracles which make my time near complete.

I am well cared for by your Mama and Will and Miss Lila. How changed I find your Mama. But she is my Onessa still and if I saw you my dear I would know you too however changed you are.

So terrible this scourge has been. There are so many whose Earthly bodies are left untended. Mister Walsh Timmy Walsh Magdalene among them. I long to go to the dead to bless them and guide their Spirits to God. I cannot rise but if I do not pass then I shall be better soon I pray to continue that work. In the meantime Will does it and so I know my people here are sure to enter the Kingdom redeemed and cleansed.

I tire so easy I must set down my pen til tomorrow. Pray for me as I pray for you each day Bree. May God protect you and keep you safe in His love. May mine touch you wherever you be my dearest one. Families rise and fall and I know you shall be the raising of this one for you and your Mama possess the best of it. I shall look down on you always whatever the next morn brings.

chapter three

Some mornings later I consented to a walk with Mama through the vineyards, which were heavy with new plants, with green leaves and the beginnings of fruit. I had long since finished my lugubrious indulgence in tears. But my eyes still itched, they were puffy and sore, and the bright sunlight caused me to squint, or peer at the ground as we strode along.

Mama kept glancing at me as if expecting an outburst, or as if wondering whether to address me. I decided to alleviate some of the tension by speaking myself.

"Did you chance to meet a man named Outlaw when you returned to the Old House?"

"Ah, yes. Will Outlaw. I suppose she wrote about him." She seemed relieved that I had begun here.

"Yes. What did you think of him? What was your impression?"

Mama shrugged. "Oh, I can see him and your Gran having a meeting of the minds. He was like her, to a large extent, full of mystic holy talk, God this, and heaven that, very proper and principled, but soft, too. A softhearted sort of man." She curled a lip. "He was surely not the type I would have given a second look to, even in his younger days. Black as the bottom of an iron pot, for one thing, and very—quaint. Old-world. He was educated, at least to the extent a Negro country preacher might be, but—well, that's how I saw him, really, as a quaint, old-world Negro holy man."

"But do you think Gran was happy with him?"

"Happy? Oh, yes. That much I'll grant him without qualification—he surely did make her happy. He was brave, he cared for her, nursed her as much as I did, those last weeks. He was very loyal. Very steadfast in his affections." She smiled. "Of course I'm sure it was all quite bloodless between them, probably nothing more than holding hands and simpering in the moonlight like a couple of children will do."

I glanced over at her, but said nothing—it will be our secret, Gran.

"But you know," Mama went on, "she was happy by nature, she was that type. Simple. If one loves the Lord and follows the Good Book, then even in adversity it shall all work out. And no matter how it works out, well, it was God's will, and probably happened for the best. She would've whistled on her way to hell."

"Which I take it you found somewhat irritating." Now I was smiling.

Mama smiled back. "It worked my nerves, I'll admit it. To have her always seeing the best side of things. That speck of gold in a field of manure. She didn't hide from ugliness—it wasn't her way, we both know that—but she had this means of making something else of it, refusing to let it be as ugly as it was. Sometimes I wanted to shake her, tell her it's not so easy, you must let people have their hurt. You can't always sweet-talk it to death. Smile in its face until it gives up and rolls over. Only now—" she trailed off. "She had her ways, Bree. I don't feel anymore that she was trying to talk me out of mine."

"Mmm."

"The last few days, when I was at the Old House—" she resumed, but I interrupted her.

"Please, Mama. Not right now. I'm sure someday I'll need to hear about it. But not just now."

"All right." We walked on.

"Where has your friend Jules been over the last few days?" I asked presently.

"Oh, he's no doubt giving us some time to adjust to each other. That would be like him." Her tone didn't change. "Or maybe he had some obligation to attend to with his wife."

"Jesus God, Mama."

"Don't get on a high horse, Bree. Would it help if I told you she has a companion of her own, and they haven't lived in the same house for years?"

"How convenient. Perhaps she is also a lunatic, or their marriage was never consummated, so it's not really a marriage—honestly, Mama. I am not a fool."

"But it could all be true!" She was laughing. "They haven't any children, come to think of it. And it is a convenience, merely that, what's between them. A family matter."

"But enough to keep him tied, so he can't be free for you."

"You're assuming I'd want him to be free for me."

"I should hope you'd think enough of yourself to want that."

"I think enough of myself to admit to what I want, and have it."

We were rounding a corner in the endless rows of vines curling upon their poles, and Mama stopped to question two workmen who were culling leaves. When we'd gone a little farther she said to me, "You know, I would forgo him if you were desperate for me to do it, Bree. If it pained you so much that it would come between us."

"Don't be absurd, Mama." Especially, I thought, in light of what had come between us until very recently. "However I feel about it—and I'm not certain of how I feel yet—I would never ask you to do such a thing."

She merely nodded, though I could sense her relief.

"But thank you for offering," I added.

We were having lunch served us two days hence—Mama, Lila, and I—when the hooves began their clattering on the circular drive beyond the house.

"They're home," Mama said, brushing a crumb from her lip with a pinkie.

We allowed them time to unpack, to see to their settling back in. That in itself was an enterprise. I watched from the windows in one of the front parlors as the family emerged from its carriages, while house servants and porters unloaded the extra vehicles bearing trunks.

Louella looked stately as always, and was very much in charge of the domestic arranging, directing the servants here and there with their burdens. She had more than filled Madame's shoes, I thought: Madame had not had a tenth of Louella's presence or wherewithal even in her best moments.

And there came her father, Mister Paxton. Emerging from a landau, he held his back straight, as usual, his blue-black hair, still merely flecked with gray, swept from his forehead in the longish style I recalled so well. He looked scarcely older than the last time I had seen him.

And finally, there was Thomas. His mousy-brown head appeared last of all, but I had no trouble recognizing him. It struck me still, how much Louella and Thomas resembled not their comely father, but their mother and each other. Yet Louella was so distinctly, appealingly handsome, while Thomas was so much not; his essence shone through to render him as unattractive outside as whatever he nursed within.

I watched him follow behind his father, squinting in the sunlight and looking churlish, as was his wont. I had expected to be overwhelmed with anxiety at the sight of him—at all of them—but for whatever reason, I was calm within myself, registering only a profound sadness as my eyes followed them through the doors.

It was different later on, though, when Lila had run off (to the extent that she could be said to run) to announce my presence, being unable to contain herself a moment longer.

She was back less than an hour later, with Louella following behind her. I could hear Louella's quick steps approaching through the halls, while she sang out over Lila's head, "Where is he, then—where are you, Bree?"

I stepped out of the dining room, where I'd sat with Mama, and strode down the long hall to greet her. "Here I am, Louella."

She ran to me with a little cry and hugged me, which once more took me aback, and caused me to stiffen a bit. She seemed not to notice, clutched me by the shoulders, and stood off to look at me. "So you came! You devil!"

"Yes. I came."

"Welcome, Bree. Welcome to Aix, and welcome to Aquitaine!" She fairly beamed at me, then sobered. "But what happened? You were so adamant about waiting—why did your plans change? How did you get here—*when* did you get here?"

"One question at a time, if you please. As to why: I had certain other—arrangements in London which did not work out."

Her face fell. "Miss Leeds?"

"The same."

"But what—"

"Not now, I shall tell you all of it later. As to your next question, how: I came into Paris, followed your most excellent directions south, *et voilà*, here I am. And as to when: five days ago."

"You've seen your mother, then?" she dropped her voice.

"Yes. It's been all right. We've spoken. I suppose you could say we've made a beginning. At any rate we straightened a number of—misunderstandings."

"But why did you not warn me," she scolded. "I did exactly as you asked, I said not a word, and now I feel such a scoundrel, for here you show up with no announcement, you give me no time to explain about London, not to mention that you might have shocked your poor mother into an early grave—"

"No, Louella, I survived him." Mama had come out of the dining room and walked toward us. Louella released me to rush to her, and they kissed each other's cheeks, and embraced.

"Oh, Onessa," Louella said, "I hope you can somehow forgive me for keeping quiet. You see, he may have told you—we found each other accidentally in London—it's quite a story, but Aubrey wished me to say nothing until he decided to come here—"

"Yes, I forgive you, dear. He owned up to making you promise your silence. The important thing is that he is here."

Louella smiled, relieved. "I suppose that is always the important thing." She turned back to me. "And so"—her smile lost a bit of its ease—"how have you been faring, Bree, what do you think of your Mama's new lodgings?"

"Very impressive." I was finding it hard to look at her. Here on the Paxton property, with Mama gazing on, it was as though London had never happened; it seemed we were back in New Orleans, and I felt compelled to place my hands behind my back, bow, and address her as "Miss."

"It's quite a turn of events, I know," Louella was saying. "I'd have told you of it while we were in England, but we never got the chance to discuss it. It seems I am guilty on both ends of failing to prepare all of you properly."

"No, it's only a little difficult to adjust to, but surely not your fault."

"Well, Bree, I must not compound the mistake by failing to prepare you and the rest of the family for your reunion." She said this a bit too brightly, and looked at me sidewise.

"You have something in mind, no doubt." I was unable to manage even a false smile.

"Well—I don't think you've the luxury of taking your time with it, is all. Lila is in the main rooms right now, she fairly exploded with the news that you were here. The cat is out of the bag, in other words. I would suggest that perhaps you and Onessa might come by later this evening, after Papa and Thomas have had a chance to rest a bit from the journey."

"But of course, I'm sure they need to rest," Mama chimed in.

Yes, I thought dismally. Rest. And prepare for the inevitable. As I would need to do myself.

The walk from the west wing to the main rooms, as Louella's portion of the family home was known, seemed to go on for miles. Mama had nitpicked over my attire as if dressing me for my wedding—or for my burial. She seemed as nervous as I; it was obvious how much she wished this meeting to go well, but I had tried to clear my head of expectations. I thought of you, Gran, your courage in the face of all that had happened to you, and this gave me courage as well. The Paxtons were only people, and what would pass between us only words. I would survive them. Nervous I was, but not afraid.

Louella met us at the end of the hallway which connected the wings. She stood by the louvered doors and smiled at us, beckoned us on. We passed through a series of rooms until we came upon a carved entryway. There was an inscription above it in Latin—some banality regarding God and knowledge—but I'd forgotten too much of that language to understand it. I could see the wooden shelves filled with books, however, and knew it was a library.

I breathed deeply, followed Louella in—and there before a man-high fireplace saw them seated: Louis Paxton and Thomas.

Mister Paxton turned to see me first. We froze into a strange little tableau, which Mister Paxton disturbed by rising. "Aubrey," he murmured. He walked toward me.

My first impression of him had been somewhat misleading, I now saw. He had indeed changed, if not in terms of aging then at least in those of world-weariness. He had the bearing of one who has been beset with troubles; his eyes had a hollow look to them, and his hair was grayer than it had appeared from a distance. But there was an openness in his face which encouraged me.

He held out his hand to me. I took it—how strange the gesture felt, this simple one between two free men. I started to speak—but what was I to call him? "Mister Paxton" no longer existed. "Louis," I said, feeling even stranger. I was struck, now I knew everything, by those aspects of his form I could identify in my own.

The legacy of our father.

"Welcome to Aquitaine," Louis said. Oddly, I got the sense he meant it. "You look well, Aubrey."

"Thank you." I stopped myself just in time from adding "sir." "You do also. I know—I know you've had many years of trouble. And I offer you my sympathies. For Madame Paxton. And the others who were lost at the Old House."

"I offer mine as well, Aubrey, for the loss of your grandmother. And for—" He stopped there, his mouth open in midsentence. I stepped in, before he completed the thought.

"Thank you."

We stood awkwardly, until Louis waved his hand at the sitting area. "Well—come in, take a seat, there's much to discuss, isn't there."

I followed his gesture, which brought my eyes back to rest upon Thomas. He had not risen or said a word, and now he gazed back at me without the least bit of friendliness or interest. Two years had passed, and he looked at me thus. I returned the stare, felt my heart jump a bit, for something in me still so wanted to see some evidence of kinship, some spark of the memory of our boyhood closeness. But in Thomas's eyes I found none of that, only a smoldering anger, which I now realized had long lain beneath that smug gaze and studied indifference.

He would not have addressed me, I knew, except that Louella, standing by Mama in the doorway, spoke up. "Aren't you going to say hello to Aubrey, Thomas?"

"Hello, Aubrey." He managed to look at Louella when he said it.

"Thomas," I replied, looking out the window.

I sat down. Mama and Louella did likewise on sofas behind us. There followed a long, shifting silence, which Louis Paxton broke. "Well, Bree. It is still Bree, isn't it? You haven't taken to being 'Aubrey' among your peers, have you?"

"No. I am still 'Bree.' "

"A good thing. Your grandmother stuck that name to you, did you know it?"

"No, I didn't. How did she think of it?"

I heard a sigh from the corner where Thomas occupied an overstuffed chair.

"Oh, she didn't think of it. You more or less did that yourself, as a baby. You were desperate to pronounce your own name, but the 'bree' was all you could manage. You never tired of yelling it, though. You could go on for hours, and so that was what your grandmother called you. We all eventually fell into step."

He was smiling, and I laughed with him, astonished not only at his recollection of this homely story, but at his obvious pleasure in repeating it. This from the man who had held a deed upon me for nearly the whole of my life.

"You know, you gave us quite a shock turning up here as you have. It was the last thing I expected to hear when Lila attacked us in the hall. Moving, by the way, faster than I'd ever seen her. I thought certain the grounds were afire." His smile faded a bit. "Louella has since filled us in on some of the details of how you managed it. But tell me . . ."

He launched into a long series of questions then, one upon another, which I answered as best I could. How had I managed to get past the Rebel soldiers in New Orleans? How had I wound up in New York, what had I seen of the war-torn country on the way there, how had I found my way to England, how had I survived there, on what money, in what manner, how had I happened to meet Louella, and so on.

I had some questions of my own for him, but I recalled all that I'd just learned, and kept them to myself. I would have the whole of the future in which to ask them, after all.

Still, we ended up engaged in conversation to the point that I forgot we were rudely ignoring the others. Out of the corner of my eye I saw Thomas rise and stalk out of the room—"*Do* excuse me," he muttered under his breath, and his father barely interrupted himself to nod an acknowledgment. But I was unaware of the moment when Louella and Mama exited. It seemed like only minutes after we'd sat—but in fact it had been two hours—when we turned to see that they were gone.

But we were in the midst of something important. When Louis saw that we were by ourselves he paused for a moment, and then said, "I should never have allowed Eugenia and Louella to travel to the States alone."

I could not in good conscience assure him this had been a sound decision, so I was silent. He went on: "You must understand, there was the chance that either myself or Thomas might have been conscripted into the Confederate services, or caught in New Orleans without a means of egress. And Louella made such convincing arguments. No one knew it would become as bad as quickly as it did, for there was so much doomsaying about, how could one be expected to consider it seriously?" He gazed past me, then continued. "The emancipation of your fellows, however—the colored servants—I suppose there were certain opportunities of which one could have availed oneself, so that it might have been accomplished earlier."

I hadn't anything to add to this either. For there was so much turmoil Louis could have saved us had his conscience assailed him at the death of his father, rather than all those many years later. Yet I knew what he himself had endured. I said the one thing I thought true, if trite:

"We all act in error. Whatever the outcome, the deeds are done, I suppose we can only go forward vowing never to repeat them."

"I suppose so." He met my gaze. "I am so very pleased to see you, Bree, to know you survived." He shut his eyes, as if to avoid a painful picture before them, then opened them to stare past my shoulder.

"I offer you my sympathies as regards your young lady. The one from the islands. What was her name—"

"Faith."

"Yes. Faith. She was intended only as a distraction, you know. Something to flounce about and occupy your attentions. We did not anticipate the circumstances you found yourselves in."

We? Who else had been part of the idea? I tried a bluff. "I'm sure Mama regrets the whole affair as much as you do."

"I know that she does. It was wrong to use a child in such a manner. Yet I recall upon first seeing the girl that I thought—she oughtn't to have been laboring as she was, she seemed in need of—" He caught himself, veered away. I considered the others he must have inspected, their skins less fair, and hair less silken, who had failed to move him and thus lived on. "Onessa was certain you *would* be merely distracted," Louis added. "It was not anticipated that you would attempt more than a flirtation right under her nose. But people and actions are not always predictable, are they?"

"Surely not." Ah, Mama. I will try to forgive you. Knowing the thin ice you felt you walked. Whether I can forgive Louis remains to be seen. Whether Faith forgave any of us I cannot say.

I wondered, after these veiled admissions from Louis, whether he meant to come near what we knew was most painful.

What he said next was: "There are certain provisions which have been made for you, Bree. They were made for your mother, and for you as well, separately, in the unlikely event that you lived on and we someday saw you again."

There. He had gone where he dared.

I would have had it otherwise. Perhaps if he were given more time. "You needn't rush yourself, we can speak on all of this, at length—"

But he was not to be engaged so. "No, no. This ought be resolved now, and set to rest. Excuse me while I fetch the papers."

He rose and exited before I could protest further, and returned a minute later with a leather-bound ledger full of official-looking documents. "Louella does not know of this. For once I've succeeded in keeping something from her." He riffled through the ledger's contents, pulled spectacles from his pocket and peered over them. "Let us see, let us see . . ."

I sat, then, as he consolidated, organized, categorized—a zealous priest at the sacrifice. At first, I could not focus upon what he was saying. But within a few minutes the stunning realization hit me: this orgy of unburdening was making me rich. In an instant. Without my having lifted even a pinky or engaging in the least intellectual exercise. There were deeds. Small plots of land here and there. In Texas. On the Côte d'Azur, in France, where the Paxtons had just been. And shares in American companies.

And ten thousand English pounds sterling.

How much money was that? It meant nothing to me, and everything, for it struck me that with such a fortune I should be able to buy shoes and a shirt whenever I desired.

Louis meticulously listed my new holdings as he had the grocery orders he'd gone over with Mama: one side of mutton, lean but not too much so, ten thousand pounds sterling, et cetera, et cetera . . .

When at last he was done, it was after midnight. "Good Lord, look at the time," Louis exclaimed, rising and rubbing his back. When I stood my legs ached; I hadn't moved in hours.

"Take these with you and examine them." He handed me the ledger full of documents. My fingers brushed his own, and he drew them away, cleared his throat. "We shall put all of this in a safe for you when you've finished, for there are certificates there which are original copies. You mustn't lose them."

"All right."

We walked to the door together. At the threshold, I started toward the hall which would lead back to the west wing, but Louis stopped me. He once again held out his hand. "I welcome you," he said, unsmiling. This time he squeezed my fingers. And drew me closer to plant a kiss on either cheek, in the manner of the French. His eyes, when I gazed into them, were opaque. Then he turned, and strode down the hall to his own quarters.

I stood in the hallway for a moment, idly touched my cheek where he'd kissed it. I had never been kissed by a man before—except for Oha, whose contact with me I did not care to dwell on. Never in this manner, I amended. There had been no father, no brother, no uncle, to do it. It felt strange. Awkward. Wonderful. I could not know then—and did not struggle to know, for it would come of its own accord—where this sensation might take my heart. I started down the hall toward my own quarters.

I was dog-tired, but it seemed my trials for the evening were not over. For as I turned a corner, I looked up to see Thomas headed toward me. I wondered if he'd been waiting somewhere to see how long his father and I would talk together, or to ambush me when we finished.

He'd set his face into a mask, and was prepared to hasten by me. Without thinking, I caught his elbow as he passed.

"This is ridiculous, Thomas," I blurted out.

He snatched his arm away and drew back. But I'd cornered him, and so I continued on.

"We are not to be friends any longer, that is evident. But are we to cross each other's paths each day as enemies?"

His flat green eyes blinked at me. He raised his chin.

"You misunderstand, Aubrey. As you have always misunderstood."

I waited; he brushed at the sleeve of his jacket where I'd handled it.

"You once engaged my attentions, yes. In the manner not of a friend, but of a pet. Which I outgrew, in the way that a child inevitably does. You've now no place in my universe. And I assure you I shall never stoop to enter yours. I've no interest in where you've been, or what you've done, or what you ever will do. I simply do not care. Whether you live or die is of no consequence to me. So we are not enemies. For that would presume some equality of footing which does not exist. You are nothing to me at all."

"We are of the same blood, Thomas."

Now a malevolence stole across his features. "No. You misunderstand that as well. My father chooses to elevate you thus, but I do not. Yes, I know some scintilla of your flesh is in the technical sense the kin of mine. But a cupful of blood does not a gentleman make. Your presence here is a fluke, if not an outright abomination. You are the bastard result of a privilege of ownership, so let me correct myself: you are less than nothing to me—you are an insult without name, you have no claim to one.

"Rather than seeking to turn my mind, then, perhaps you'd do better to seek some other venue for yourself. One more befitting the place to which I'd consign you."

He straightened his shoulders, prepared to take his leave, and I reached for the wall, dizzy before this onslaught of hate; it took my feet from under me. What had I done, to have earned this? What would I do?

I tried to right myself, so that I might face him squarely.

And in that instant made my choice.

"I understand you, Thomas" was what I said. "And I know that nothing shall change your mind. Indeed—blood does not a gentleman make. But you are no longer my concern. I am here. I am not leaving. Make of it what you will, it is not my affair. I wish you luck in grappling with it."

And then I brushed by him. I gave him my back. He might have been cursing me silently, he might have been foaming at the mouth or doing nothing at all, but I did not see it.

I proceeded toward the west wing, the papers his father had given me in my hands, feeling the tiles firm beneath my feet, the louvered doors wide open before me.

The next day, Mama and I sat spreading everything Louis had given me out upon her dining table. We puzzled and furrowed our respective brows, but it was hopeless. Most of the documents were in a legal language so dense that only a solicitor would be able to figure it out.

Mama quit first, shaking her head at the monument of the task. "Whatever it is, Bree, it is enough. Believe me."

I did.

Louella came looking for me in the afternoon. I owed her an apology for the previous evening, I thought, and so I was additionally happy to see her. She took me to the stables, showed me the enormous Percheron draft horses they used here for heavy work, and the Arabians kept for hunting. When she opened the last of the paddock gates, I startled. For there inside, contentedly munching grass, were Soleil and Lumi—the carriage team from New Orleans. They raised their heads, looking as at home as if they'd been born in the south of France.

"They are valuable." Louella shrugged at my raised eyebrows. "We could not leave them behind to become a supper for ravenous soldiers. They very nearly did not survive the journey, though. They were horribly sick. We had to quarantine them in Marseilles for a month, and even then they had to be transported here in drays, rather than driven or ridden. But they seem well now, don't you think?" Indeed they did. I called to them; they snuffled the air, and then their ears twitched, and they made for the railing as if remembering me and the adventures they'd borne witness to. I scratched Lumi's cheek, blew on his nose.

"You managed to thoroughly disquiet Thomas yesterday, you know," Louella was saying. I knew she was smiling without looking at her. "Your return was shocking enough, but what else did you say to vex him so?"

"It was not my intent to vex him." Lumi butted me with his head, the better to facilitate my pats.

"I know it, Bree. I do not mean to tease. I am certain his behavior pains you, and I am sorry. But please consider the source before you take his ill feeling to heart."

I promised her I had already done so, and would continue in the same vein. She then asked me to explain at length why I had left England, and what had happened between Arabella Leeds and myself to bring me here.

I told her all of it, and she shook her head. "I am so terribly disappointed, Bree. I would never have thought Miss Leeds the type to abandon you thus. She seemed so forthright to me—I cannot imagine what happened to turn her so."

"I should not have misled her. I did not tell her the entire truth when I had the chance, and I suppose once she considered it—well, the choice was inevitable."

We patted the horses a final time, and then strolled toward the main house.

"What shall you do from this point, then? Will you make your home here with us, at least for a time? You would be welcome—for the most part—of course."

"Thank you. I know as much. I've no plans to go, for all I am connected to is here, there is no reason to be elsewhere. But still—"

"But still it is not home to you."

"Not yet, although I suspect that will come in time. And one could not ask for better surroundings from which to feel estranged in the meanwhile."

"Trust me, there is much to build upon here. I'm certain that with the passage of less time than you'd imagine you shall be whole and happy."

"I do trust you, Louella. Particularly when you are telling me something I should like to believe."

We entered the house, and stopped in the front foyer where Louella collected a bundle of post deliveries from a metal box by the doors. The receptacle was filled to overflowing; the mails had continued during the Paxtons' holiday, and were awaiting the attentions of their addressees.

Louella sighed as she flipped through the many-colored envelopes, separating out a number of plain white ones on which her name was printed in a strong if somewhat illegible hand.

"Harlow," she said, holding one up and frowning. I frowned myself, for I knew I should one day have the unpleasant task of explaining to Mr. Beckwith exactly where I was and why, and that I would not be returning to help him scribble his term papers for the upcoming year.

"What does he write?" I could not help wondering if she had softened any in her regard for her determined suitor.

Louella sighed again. "Oh, the usual, I'm sure. Have I thought over our discussion in England, may he come to Aix and visit me, and progress reports, on what he has done, and what he expects to accomplish within a week or a month."

"You don't seem terribly pleased."

"Oh, well—it's not so much that I am not pleased. But in the first place, I don't know how I should reply, for I do care for him, but I've not made up my mind, and don't wish to make it up because I was pressured. In the second place, I must tell you, Harlow is a terrible writer of letters. He forgets what he's said in the last one, and repeats himself, and goes off into grandiose schemes to which I cannot possibly respond."

"I cannot believe he's as bad as all that."

"Well, you ought take my word on it, Bree, but since you don't—here, let us see if he's managed to improve any since my holiday began."

She opened one of the letters, scanned it, rolled her eyes. Then she picked up another, slit it expertly, prepared to perform the same cursory inspection.

Only this time, her eyes did not lift from the paper. This time, her expression changed midway down the first paragraph.

"What is it?" I asked.

She waved me away, grabbed for the second page.

When she was finished, she looked up, her lips parted. Without a word, she thrust the letter at me.

Brace yourself, Louella dear, it began, *I've the most astonishing news regarding Arabella Leeds—*

chapter four

So it was that I found myself en route back to London.

I'd had a family for a week. In the blink of an eye, I was taking my leave of them, to trek across the Continent once more.

For no sooner had I absorbed the news Harlow had imparted than I knew I must leave France, and return to England for Arabella.

How Louella and I cursed ourselves over that letter! We should have known, we told each other. We should have known that she would not have quit us in such a manner. That something was dreadfully, horribly, wrong.

I felt a cold anger overtake me at the thought of her mother. To lie to me as she had—to spew with such righteousness the most repellent falsehood, perhaps the one she wished were true, without batting an eye.

And what she had done to her daughter! What manner of people were these, who would prefer to see their child in such circumstances rather than acknowledge her choice of a beau they disapproved of? For my one-eighth of African blood—and any of you, you proud and smug Leedses, might find something similar coursing through your own veins, if you look back far enough, and it should be a source of pride to you—they had deemed an institution the proper punishment.

I would confront them if it was the last thing ever I did. I would get to their daughter if they stood an army between us.

She cared for me still—she had relayed this news to her brother, who had smuggled it to Harlow, who had told it to Louella, on the "off chance" that I decided to visit her in France. She had not abandoned me—she thought of me yet—every dream I'd had of her in Paris I could now indulge in without melancholy, every longing that had stirred me I could now imagine satisfied. Such a remarkable change overtook me that I was amazed at it myself. I had forced my feeling for her down into the depths of me in the hope that it would disappear, but it seemed only to have grown stronger in its isolation.

I decided I would leave at once to go to her. Louella decided likewise; we would have the journey to contemplate what we would do when we reached London.

Mama was aghast at the idea that I was departing. She sputtered and cried, but I explained to her that only the most urgent emergency could have budged me, and this was surely it. It involved a girl, I began, and got no farther—for Mama's eyes had assumed my least favorite expression. "Well, I suppose I should be relieved," she snapped. "At least you're not to become a shriveled old bachelor before my eyes."

What in the hell is this now, I wondered.

"What color is she?" Mama went on.

For the briefest second, I was twelve again, or fifteen or seventeen, searching for the answer she might deem least offensive. But I shook off this sensation.

"I find that a pointless question, and one I'd rather not answer. You of all people ought to know from delineating along those lines."

She drew herself up, but then deflated. "I of all people," she repeated, under her breath.

I knew I'd not heard or spoken the last on this subject, but I hadn't the patience to dwell on it. Instead I elaborated on the reasons for my going. Mama did not stop crying, but she grudgingly wished me well on the journey, and good luck in obtaining the liberty of the young lady in question, and a speedy return, or communication.

I packed my belongings, and would have been ready to set out that very afternoon, but there was one thing I needed to see to first, so that I might leave Aquitaine with my conscience clear—and my pockets lightened.

I had decided to return to Louis the "provisions" he had given me. Oh, how it pained me to do it! I sat with the documents, petted and crooned to them, as a means of saying good-bye to the delights of affluence—but good-bye it had to be.

I had tried on every possible justification for keeping this tidy fortune, for I dearly wished to do so. Yet I could not. It rubbed me wrong, a hairshirt many sizes too small. I'd had the great good luck, after all, not to have been born my father's daughter; I'd escaped one form of whoredom, and so ought not yield to another.

I returned to Louis the cash and the deeds, likewise the shares in American holdings. I consented to keep, however, the French properties, including the plot of land on the Côte d'Azur. For these had passed directly to Louis through the death of Madame Eugenia; they had been in the possession of her family, not his, and so had bypassed the taint of Leland's hand.

Louis was crestfallen at my refusal. He told me he would keep the returned instruments safe for me should I change my mind; they were mine in name and would become my responsibility automatically upon the occasion of his death, but—given the circumstances—he understood my feelings, and did not begrudge me them.

I told him I would be leaving shortly, and that Louella would be accompanying me, for an emergency had summoned us to England. At this he became even more disheartened, once he'd gotten over his surprise. I assured him we would return—both of us, and maybe a third, with any luck—but even so I could see him scramble to move his displeasure behind a wall of aloofness, so that he could bid me a civil and proper farewell.

I did not bother apprising Thomas of my plans.

I'd tied my loose ends together, however, and so I was off with my heart and mind pure. As the priestess Behbeh and her Gabara (and you as well, Gran) would have it.

Louella and I had Louis's own driver take us as far as Aix, from whence we would catch the next stage. As luck would have it, said stage was driven by none other than the very lout who'd hired himself out for my trip to Aquitaine.

"How does the lovely Spanish mademoiselle fare," he asked, recognizing me at once—probably as much because of the huge tip I'd thrown him as because of Mama's beauty.

"She is not Spanish," I snapped. "She is partly of African blood. And at any rate she is fine." Louella raised her brows at this exchange but the driver seemed uncaring as to Mama's origins. He nodded his deep satisfaction that she was well, and bore us to our next point of leave in Salon-de-Provence without another word, for which I was heartily grateful.

Louella and I were ostensibly on the same mission, and therefore on the same side of righteousness, but almost from the moment we left Aquitaine we found ourselves at odds.

We were already uneasy, given our reasons for setting out. And we were both recovering from the upheaval caused by my visit. I knew Louella must still be miffed that I had not written to her ahead of time. And I on my part was still seething over Thomas's cruel dismissal, which perhaps I was wont to avenge, unfairly, upon his sister.

Whatever the causes, though, we had fallen out of step with each other, and sparred over issues great and small. It was my first experience with discord amidst my new relations, and the feeling was a novel and uncomfortable one.

Our worst argument occurred when we were a good way along our route, outside Lyon. We were once more crammed a scant foot apart in a carriage, having done without lodgings or a proper bath for the better of two days so as to save time. We were hot and tired and irritable, and fed up with jouncing along the roads and being thrown against the walls of the coach. The driver had stopped twice to mend his axles—inadequately—and I felt myself at the end of my tether.

We had been bickering over the causes of Arabella's imprisonment. I was wont to see it as the result of color, and of blood—for was it not my ancestry that had provoked all of this? But Louella viewed it as a tragic folly of gender: the same fate would never have befallen a young white man who consorted with an octoroon female.

The subject was a sore one for both of us, and we had agreed to disagree, as neither was bound to be won over to the other's side. But Louella was determined to have the last word, and waited until I'd sunk into silence to slip it in.

"By the bye," she said peevishly, after we'd sat for a few minutes, "I must take issue with the fact that you insist upon referring to yourself as a Negro. After all, Aubrey, you are a good deal more white than black, as you must realize every time you face a glass. You're also quite willing to shut your mouth and be presumed so when it suits you, and therefore have hardly endured the suffering of those Negroes truly on the black side of the color line."

I answered her just as peevishly. "May I remind you, Louella, that it was your own people and their rules of law which first determined me Negro. And enslaved me. If I reserve the right to refer to myself thusly, it is surely the fault of your compatriots, who accorded my few drops of black blood such undue and disastrous weight."

After this exchange, we both decided the scenery outside was worthy of closer scrutiny.

Nor was the mood between us improved any by our arrival at our destination. When we disembarked in Lyon, Louella looked around for a porter to carry our cases, and was quite annoyed to find there were none. I, for my part, wondered at the incredible spoilage of the inheritance-wealthy: never having lifted a finger toward their own security, they took for granted that there would always be a body to bear their burdens—all because of the presence of the money in their pockets. Even Louella, most likely the least spoiled of all of them, fell prey to this odious presumptuousness. She searched every cranny of the coach depot for a soul willing to tote our things to an auberge or hotel; finding none, she settled for standing in the midst of the bags and fuming.

"We might try picking up our own suitcases with our very own arms," I pointed out to her. "Think of the blow you'd strike for those of your *gender*, after all, by attempting such an exertion."

"And think of the one you'd strike for those of your *heritage* by refraining from it."

"Here," I snapped, "just give me all of them, and let's have done with it."

"Oh no you don't. Spare me your patronizing. I'll carry my own things." She picked up her suitcase (which was heavy, I'd have granted her that) with one furious yank, took her train case in the other hand then stormed past me without waiting for me to grab my own belongings. But because I was behind her, I was able to bear witness to the difficulties that ensued: as she leaned into the weight of the suitcase, Louella's hems touched the ground and tangled under her feet, causing her to trip at every other step.

We had gone a hundred yards or so—and she very valiantly at that—when she at last lost her temper and threw the suitcase down.

"God curse these skirts!" she screamed in English, in the middle of the street. "I'll wager you ten to one some cursed *man* fashioned them, just so some woman'd never be able to run more than a few feet from him!"

I caught up with her. "Point taken." I smiled. "Now, why don't we be sensible: you let me have the larger bags, and you can carry our train cases."

"Why don't you stuff your sense in your pipe and smoke it," she suggested, and picked up the suitcase again.

We marched thus to the closest boarding establishment.

I was still nettled, even after we'd secured rooms. "I was merely attempting chivalry," I huffed at her. "You needn't have bit off my head."

"You were not being chivalrous. You were being condescending."

"Is that so—such fine distinctions must elude you at times, Louella. For I've seen you solicit that very *condescension* you just refused, when it suits you. You ought not complain of how the trappings of ladyhood burden you, if you'd don them when they fit your purpose."

She sat down on her settee and rubbed her temples.

"Touché, Aubrey."

We wisely decided to drop the matter there in the interest of getting some much-needed rest.

Our letter, fortunately, had reached the Beckwiths before we did. We had included in it a brief explanation as to how I'd come to be ensconced at Aquitaine, and of my connexion to Louella and the other Paxtons residing therein—but of course brevity was not enough to overcome the pop eyes and clamoring questions Harlow and his sister had for us when we arrived at Linton on the morning of June the twenty-eighth.

We were barely down from the carriage when they ran out, accompanied—I nudged Louella—by the porter. "So it's true," Caroline exclaimed, "you are got here together!"

"Well, we wouldn't have intended such a thing as a joke, dear," Louella assured her, rushing to give her a kiss.

Harlow gawked at me as if at a ghost, then grasped my hand and shook it with such fervor that I feared he would detach it. "My god, what a turn this is, all of it! Come along. Bree, you are welcome to your old lodgings, although you may have a room in the house if you wish it. Louella, you are in the Rose Room, as per usual. Now, settle in quick, and nap if you must, but then come to the trophy room when you're ready, for we've much to discuss."

I had never seen Linton's trophy room before, and found it a disquieting setting for a meeting. From the deep-green walls the glass eyes of beheaded wildlife bore down on us. Even from the floor we were spied upon, for a tiger glared up from atop the Oriental carpet.

Harlow and Caroline seemed at home here, though, and Harlow allowed as Arabella had quite taken to this room, once he'd explained that the animals were long dead, and that neither he nor anyone yet alive was responsible for their demise. "She once said she felt their spirits might be watching us," he laughed. "She is surely part heathen, that girl!"

"I wouldn't have credited Arabella with putting stock in such a notion," I offered, a little stung that Harlow had this knowledge of her which I did not.

He grinned. "Apparently, spirits sit fine by Miss Leeds. Need I add that it's the spiritualists she can't abide?"

We laughed at this, for of course none of us had forgotten the means by which we'd met.

But then we were reminded of what had become of her, and were quickly sobered.

As if not to leap to that topic too soon, we spent the next several hours discussing the other news: the relationship between Louella and myself, how it had come to be, and all of the misery and subterfuge the facts of its origins had wrought.

Harlow and Caroline perched on the edges of their seats and stayed there. The greatest incredulity was unleashed by the story of my seeing Louella in England for the first time, and the chicanery she and I had employed to keep the Beckwiths in the dark. The most leaden moment was reserved for Faith. Harlow asked if she was the inspiration for the strange marking on my arm, and I allowed as yes, she was, I'd done it so as never to forget the trouble I'd caused her, her bright spirit, or the fact of her brief, sad life.

But I *had* forgotten, I added. At the end of it all, there lay the inescapable conclusion that Arabella was the second woman to care for me and suffer for that sentiment. Would I never cease torturing them—never accept that each female I brought myself into contact with would come to grief on my account? Would I never embrace my solitary fate? Would I quit—would I yield—

"Would you leave *off*, for God's sake!" Caroline snapped. She rolled her eyes heavenward, and Louella quickly chimed in.

"Yes, really, Aubrey. Do shut up. That is the faultiest bit of logic I've ever heard, and if you indulge in it further you'll bore us all to tears, and sink too far into self-pity to be useful to Arabella or anyone else."

"If you cannot understand—" I began, but Harlow cut me off to address them.

"You could allow him his moment of wallowing, for God's sake."

"No, we cannot allow it—for Arabella's sake," Louella replied. "What happened to her is the fault of no one in this room, and every one of us may be needed to reverse it. We don't need one of our number moping about and undercutting his own efforts to that end. Especially when that one has such a vital interest in the outcome."

"You think, then, that there is something to be done—by us—about this circumstance?" Caroline asked Louella.

"Of course we do," I jumped in, despite (or because of) the lambasting I'd just received. "Why else would we have rushed here? To commiserate in person?"

"But what do you suggest? If we go once again to her parents—" Harlow started.

"No, forget her parents," I said. "They are odious beyond description."

"Oh, they aren't really," Caroline chirped, "they are only somewhat wrong-minded—"

"Do you suppose you could refrain from contradicting just one sentence of mine?" I snapped at her. "The Leedses are the people who placed her where she is. They are hardly going to supply us with the means of her release, however delightful you've found your visits with them. Remember, you went to them once before, and it did no good at all."

"So what have you in mind?" Caroline asked, no longer chirping.

"I think we must get her out. By whatever means necessary, which may involve simply going and taking her. But I hope we can come up with a more subtle plan."

"You know, we were moving along those lines ourselves," Harlow said. He then began to elaborate on some of the ideas he and Caroline had come up with. They were not necessarily bad, but Louella and I saw the holes in them at once.

So we laid our own thoughts on the table—only to see that the Beckwiths were just as sharp at catching our mistakes.

The four of us stared at each other. It had grown very late, and we were at a loss.

"She has been imprisoned there two months already," Harlow sighed at last. "And the second month has been far, far worse than the first. Whatever we are to do, we must do it soon, and plan it soundly. If we've run short of ideas, perhaps we should bring some others in on our plot, and see what they can contribute."

"Who would you suggest?" I asked.

"Arabella's brother Richard," Harlow said. "He went to a good deal of trouble to get us word of her, and the more time we've spent with him, the more he's come round to Berry's way of thinking—and ours. Besides, he's a very clever lad. And the only one of us to have seen the place where Berry is being kept."

We all agreed that Richard Leeds should be made privy to our plans.

"Who else?" I asked.

"My mother," Caroline offered next. "And Miss Elizabeth Ashe."

She was so eager to present the names that I wondered whether she'd been thinking of including them all along, or whether they were simply the first, and smartest, people to occur to her.

"I agree your mother would be a fine addition anywhere," I replied, "so long as you are sure she'll take our side in the matter, and not that of the Leedses. But as to this Miss Ashe, it's true I've been a guest in her fair home"—I smiled here—"but have never had the pleasure of an introduction. What makes you think she'd bring anything to the endeavor?"

"As to your first point, Bree, Mother would have sided with us anyway, but the fact that you were formerly enslaved will have her championing you to the grave. She is positively rabid on that subject. And as to your second point, Miss Ashe was the source of my mother's infection, and tends to froth even more heavily at the mouth. She too is both Feminist and Abolitionist, and I can assure you there is no quicker tongue and no steelier mind in the world than hers." *Except maybe yours, Caroline,* I wanted to say. At least where the tongues were concerned.

"I'm afraid I can vouch for that," Harlow sighed. "It's a shame Miss Ashe is so damned smart, otherwise I'd discount her out of hand. She hasn't the slightest use for us men."

How delightful, I thought. That'll make two of our co-conspirators whose barbs I shall have aimed at me, the other being the divine Miss Beckwith.

But—"Go on then, bring her aboard, by all means," I said, for if it would serve Arabella, then I could develop a thicker skin.

The next evening we were sitting once more in the trophy room, beneath the gaze of the animals. I had to admit I'd come to see Arabella's point: I could almost imagine the beasts had decided to champion us. I only hoped that in death they were perhaps wiser than they'd been in the lives that had seen them speared and shot.

The room was crowded this time, for we'd been joined by four other bodies. It ought to have been three, but Richard Leeds had come with a girl in tow, a comely little blonde mite of a child whom he introduced as Miss Amelia Wentworth. Miss Wentworth had been the postmistress between Richard and the Beckwiths, and was also the excuse by which he'd managed to leave his own house to be present. He therefore thought it only fair that she be included in whatever plans we made, since her further assistance might prove necessary. I thought this a sound line of reason, but knew a more likely one was to be found in the girl's well-formed bosom and tilted nose, which Richard peeked at often, if subtly. I hadn't had time to talk to him—or to anyone, for that matter, for I'd only just arrived when Harlow suggested we find seats for ourselves.

Hester Beckwith presided in the largest chair, being the lady of the manor. But it was clear that the ruling head and voice would belong to none other than that nemesis of the male sex, Madame Elizabeth Ashe.

This lady swept into the room just behind me, wearing a costume so bizarre that one's first inclination was to laugh. But then we saw the ease and the seriousness with which she sported it, and didn't dare.

She was covered head to toe in a garishly red, patterned cloth, which she'd wrapped around her body like a winding sheet. The material was pinned in two places, at the bosom and at the waist, with toggles made of bone. And the effect thus achieved was positively scandalous, for it was evident she wore no petticoats, no skirts, no corset, beneath this flimsy raiment, which clung to the contours of her figure, making her appear a pillar of fire. Only her shawl was of the usual cut; it looked ridiculously out of place atop the rest of this ensemble. Her feet were covered with strange, square, flat leather sandals—without question the ugliest feminine footwear I'd ever seen—and dangling from her neck and her ears were strands of multicolored beads.

I wondered how she'd managed to arrive here without being arrested. But then, Miss Ashe was another of that moneyed inheritance set, and so would never be hauled off the street—or rather, out of her private carriage—for appearing deranged.

"I see you have taken note of my dress" was the first thing she said to us, when we fell silent at her entrance. She gazed around the room, as if daring anyone to challenge this tremendous understatement. "I am glad, for I should like the opportunity to explain it to you. I am wearing the traditional garb of the Mass-eye people of Africa, whose territory I recently visited. The Mass-eye are great herders of cattle and workers of beads and feathers. Their dress is quite comfortable, and I believe you would all be converts after a day or so in it."

Harlow was trying to catch my eye, his lip twitching in mirth, but in fact I had suddenly become interested in Miss Ashe's little speech. After all, she had been to Africa. She was only the second person I'd ever met—the first being Ibrahim Kassindja—who could make this claim. Whatever the woman's eccentricities, I thought it quite courageous of her to undertake such a journey alone, and adventurous indeed to give consideration to the natives' dress and customs. I decided to reserve my judgment of Miss Ashe until after I heard what she had to contribute.

She took a chair by Caroline, who beamed at her. I could not help noticing that when she sat, her garment parted, exposing a good bit of her calves. She appeared not to care at all, however, and went on chatting to Caroline, and, on the other side of her, to Hester Beckwith.

After a few minutes, Harlow cleared his throat, and spoke up from his place by the mantel. "Well, I suppose we had best get down to business." The rest of us fell silent. "Introductions are in order, I would imagine." He made them, and when he came to me, I nodded to the gathering, and wasn't surprised to see Miss Ashe give me a dry, appraising stare back.

"We know why we are here," Harlow went on. "A dear friend is being kept against her will, under horrendous conditions, in an experimental institution for wayward women. Being as she's done nothing to deserve this treatment, and has sent us back reports of terrible abuses, we've come to the conclusion that, as her comrades, we must act against the wishes of her family and find a means by which to free her. Having said that, I think I should yield the floor to Mr. Leeds, since he's the only member of Berry's family present, and also can report upon the manner in which she's being held."

I glanced over at Richard Leeds, who looked pained at this mention of his relations and the intentions of the group toward them. From what I'd seen and heard of him I'd been inclined to like him a good deal; I only hoped he would prove worthy of his sister's trust. He paused, as if contemplating his own betrayal of his parents, and then stood up to speak.

"I don't suppose I'd be here if I didn't think there was a deuced good reason. You mustn't judge my parents too harshly, for they're decent people. They've only come under some queer influences, namely, my Uncle Charles—not that he's not decent too, but he's some strange ideas, and he and Berry didn't precisely hit it off where ideas are concerned, and—well. Enough of this, I should just tell you what I've got to tell you.

"Berry is in a place called the Valhalla Home for Women. It's run by a Dr. Michael Gregory, who fancies himself a pioneer in the business of subduing unruly girls. He is a friend of my uncle's, who talks him up as if he's God Almighty. He has got my sister shut in some sort of punishment bin. She says it's a plot. She'd asked to change rooms because of disturbances in the night, but really it was because the girl she shared with had men into their chambers for—well, for *indecencies*." He glanced here at his friend Miss Wentworth. "But the men are guards, and when they discovered her complaint they became afraid she'd say more. So they lied to the doctor, told him Berry was violent and dangerous. The nuns who help run the place knew otherwise, but not one of them opened their mouths to help my sister. They turned a blind eye while the men beat her. And now where she's held, they are allowed to torture her. She told me they throw buckets of waste at her, then stick her in freezing baths. They take her food away, or tie her up and leave it where she can't reach, or lock her in a room by herself, in restraints, in the dark, for a week at a time." I closed my eyes, wished I could convince myself he was exaggerating, but knew he was not.

"Each time I see her—and I see her less now, because part of her punishment is that she's allowed fewer visits—but each time I go, she has fresh bruises, she is nothing but bones and seems more and more broken, and they have forced her at—at other things too—" He broke off, took a moment to gather himself.

"She's told all of this to my parents, and to the doctor, who claims she is having delusions or lying, and advises my parents to ignore her. The bruises are explained as the result of her assaults on the guards. Or as self-inflicted. Bids for pity. And my parents swallow this medicinal horseshi—uh, nonsense—I'm sure because my uncle is spooning it to them, and because they don't wish to know otherwise. Which is just what Berry said. That they would think what they want, no matter the evidence.

"But I know she is telling the truth. And I know we must do something, because I believe what is happening to her could kill her." He stared a last time round the room, and then was quiet.

In the silence I could hear the steady hammering of my own heart. If I came upon this Dr. Gregory, I thought, I would murder him. Or the uncle. He ought to be murdered, too. And the guards. And the fucking nuns. In fact, the finest solution might be just to kill them all and lead Berry out over their dead backs.

"Now, here's the thing," Harlow was saying. "Louella and Aubrey and Caroline and I have wracked our brains looking for a means of going about this. We believe we shall have to abduct Arabella from this place in secret. We've learned a little about the layout of the buildings, the best route back to London, the schedule maintained, but—"

"—but you may as well forget it all, for that approach will lead you exactly nowhere." Miss Ashe had risen from her seat, and she spoke up now, cutting Harlow off at the knees with the finality of an expert.

"There is simply no way," she went on, "that you will be able to effect an abduction off a grounds filled with obstacles without being found out and foiled at some point. There is no way to go about this surreptitiously."

"What might you suggest, then?" Harlow asked. "You no doubt have an opinion on the matter."

"Indeed I do." She pulled herself even straighter and sucked in a breath, giving us to know that she intended to be on about her opinion for a while.

"Generally in such circumstances," she said, "I'd advocate either the direct approach, or the legal one. The direct approach consists of simply marching in en masse, demanding to see her, and taking her out. You'd be surprised how you can cow these doctorly types in many instances. They fold like a house of cards when faced with a bit of spine.

"But it so happens I know the reputation of this Dr. Gregory. He is a devotee to his cause, he knows the law concerning incarceration, he cannot be bribed or bullied. He has deprived many a young woman of her God-given freedom by crossing all of his T's, and is not the type to yield to a mob, however determined.

"So I suggest we take the second tack. Pursue him through his own territory. Check into the legal means by which we might free Miss Leeds."

"But none of us here are experts in the law, Elizabeth," Louella said. "Unless you are yourself—and even then, since you are not a solicitor, what can you possibly do?"

"Allow me to look into the matter, dear. I am not without resources. I shall call in some favors, and lean upon a few old friends. Miss Leeds was an apt and ready pupil of mine, and I am as determined as any of you to do right by her.

"I suggest that all of us convene back here two nights hence. That should give me enough time to establish a few lines of attack, which we shall then examine with the legendary fine-tooth comb, so as to come up with a flawless plan. Agreed?"

In the face of such determination, there seemed nothing to do but agree, and so all of us did.

Two nights later we were again reassembled in the same fashion. This time I was able to have a few words with Richard, and was relieved to find that he seemed not to hold me responsible for what had overtaken his sister. He had even carried a note to me. He explained that it was over a month old, having been written when Berry was still in the less restrictive part of the home; he had forgotten, in the midst of all that was happening, to bring it to our first conspirators' meeting. I thanked him and took it, my fingers fumbling to unfold it. It was scrawled in pencil, and obviously in haste.

Darling Bree, if this note finds you, let it remind you of my affection for you. Do not believe what you'll hear regarding my departure from London. It is sure to be a pack of lies. I am held here against my will, I long to see you again. If Richard should find you, I beg you please respond, and believe in me. I shall find a way to get out from here, and be reunited with you. Yours in love, Berry.

I shoved the paper into my pocket. Later, when I held it against my cheek, I imagined it gave off the faintest scent of her.

I could not think on it further just then, however, for Miss Ashe had once again made her entrance.

This time, she had come attired in silk robes that fell to the floor. The sleeves were long but bell-like, and about her waist was a wide sash with a bundle of some sort at the back. On her feet were bizarre black sandals like little bridges, and beneath these she wore thick white ankle-high stockings.

Once again we were all rendered speechless.

"Keemono," Miss Ashe announced to us. "Zoree, and tabby. The dress of the people of Nippon. Very comfortable, and practical summer and winter. If only the men weren't so abominable toward the women, I should rather embrace the entire culture. Clean, they are, very clean. Certain Europeans would do well to follow their lead."

Miss Ashe then lowered her Orientally clad posterior into a chair, our meeting was brought to order, and all of us gave our attention to the woman in the "keemono" to hear what she'd unearthed. Hester had asked that Cook prepare a light cold supper, and so we all selected from trays and balanced plates while we listened.

"I believe," Miss Ashe said between bites of cucumber sandwich, "that I have found a solution." She paused dramatically and then smiled, her taut skin drawing away from fine white teeth.

"The primary problem we face is that Arabella is under the legal jurisdiction of her parents. Arguably, the girl may be subject to that statute which makes a child the ward of its family. Without question, she is subject to the one which makes a female the ward of her closest male relation. Either way, the Leedses have a claim upon their daughter; having established as much, they are entitled, under the law, to make decisions regarding her liberty, and the one they have made is to incarcerate her.

"We have, however, been left a loophole, which may prove very useful to Miss Leeds." She looked smugly round at all of us, and I wished she would quit pausing for effect and get to the point.

"There is one position on the social ladder which, in the eyes of jurisprudence, can outrank even a father's. And there is one means by which even a child in the care of her parents, or a girl in the care of her father, may attach herself to that position, and so select for herself a new guardian."

Her eyes came to rest on me.

"The age of consent, in England, now stands at twelve. In this most civilized of nations, where an unmarried woman of any age is forever the ward of her father, a twelve-year-old may consent to lie with a man. And she may give her consent in marriage. And once she is married, the power of attorney passes from her father to her husband, so that his word becomes law on all matters concerning her. That is the sort of world we inhabit, ladies and gentlemen. But in this instance the obscene shall do the bidding of the noble.

"Miss Leeds cannot free herself, but according to the letter of the law, she is not a criminal, nor is she insane. She is held at what her captors term a spa, not technically an asylum or a prison. And she is thankfully over twelve. So she is able to give her consent to marriage."

I now understood why Miss Ashe stared at me. Indeed, everyone else in the room was doing so as well.

"Well, Mr. Paxton," Miss Ashe threw it down, "what say you to the task?"

What did I say?

Poor and foolish though I was, my hand was a very desirable commodity, at least in certain peculiar instances. Once before I'd been reluctant to give it.

I would not hesitate a second time.

"I say I shall do it." I met Miss Ashe's gaze. It was not how I might have wanted to be wed to Arabella, but want her I did, and this was the way that would most benefit her.

"I shall do it," I repeated more firmly.

But of course that was not to be the end of the discussion. Not by a long shot. For, as Hester Beckwith pointed out a second later, "We must still figure out a means by which this marriage can take place. And I doubt the good doctor will lend us Miss Leeds for a day, so that we can perform the ceremony."

"Well, of course he won't," Miss Ashe boomed. "There's still a good deal of plotting to be done, but not to worry. I've already got on it."

"Oh dear," Hester said. "Please keep in mind, Elizabeth, that my children are involved in all this."

"Honestly, Hester, you can't be implying that I'd place them in any danger. When have I ever advised us badly?"

"Well, when we were traveling about Barcelona, in fifty-nine—"

"Oh, bollocks to Barcelona, that was eons ago. I've become a good sight better at dealing with firearms. Now, as I was saying—we shall indeed have to make use of some bullying, but we shall have the power of the law behind us, and the power of the clerical collar ahead of us. See how this suits all of you."

The upshot of Miss Ashe's plan was that we would all travel to the Valhalla Home, for it was here that the marriage would have to take place. We would be accompanied by Miss Ashe's solicitor, a Mr. Grenville, and by an acquaintance of hers, a Catholic priest named Father Bouchard, whom she described as a "right-thinking chap—for a Catholic," who owed her "a favor or two."

We would maintain that Arabella had asked for a priest. Richard, as the family representative and the one person among us who could actually see Berry, would secure a paper from her attesting to this, to be presented when we arrived upon the grounds. According to Mr. Grenville, clergy had the right to travel anywhere at the behest of the incarcerated. Even gaols and asylums could not refuse a prisoner the right to visit with a religious advisor—although they regularly did refuse, when there was nobody to force them to obey the law. Thus Mr. Grenville would be with us, so as to read the very statute to anyone who barred our entrance. The rest of us would be accounted for as follows: Harlow and I would be posing as altar assistants, and Miss Ashe and Louella as intermediaries by which family (as represented by Richard) and clergy (Father Bouchard himself, of course) had been introduced. The presence of the nuns was sure to help us; they would be reluctant to support any decision which went against the wishes of the priest, their automatic superior.

Once we were admitted and had been brought to Arabella (or had had her brought to us), the good Father would perform his part, namely, Berry's hasty and unorthodox conversion to Catholicism, so that her request for a Catholic service would withstand any scrutiny. Then would come the marriage itself. The papers would be prepared ahead of time, all would be ready, and only the vows would have to be given and witnessed, and signatures affixed to the documents. It would be over in a matter of minutes, after which Mr. Grenville, armed with the legal sword, would demand Arabella's release into her husband's custody. If Gregory refused, we would wait with Arabella while one of our number summoned the constable.

It was a good plan. Yes, there were things which might go wrong with it, but that was true of anything we might think of; it was forthright, it avoided illegalities like trespass, and it swept Arabella out of the hands of her tormentors by a means which would stand in any court of law.

"At least you're already of that faith which suits our purposes, Mr. Paxton," Miss Ashe winked at me.

"I was raised a Catholic. My master saw to that. As to how much I embrace the faith, let us see what it lends to our plans."

It was decided that Richard would smuggle the plan and the request for the priest to Berry when his family visited her that Saturday. By then we would have set a date for the undertaking, and Richard could give her that as well. It would all come to pass, I thought, there was no way it could not, for the formidable Miss Ashe had covered most every eventuality, and had summoned what looked to be her vast network of resources to aid us.

When the meeting ended we were all in high spirits. I was going over our scheme with Harlow and his mother when I heard Miss Ashe call to Caroline.

"My dear, there are quite a few loose ends I must see to, papers to draft and whatnot. I wonder if you might come home with me this evening and lend a hand."

"Do you mind?" Caroline asked her mother. "I suppose I should have to stay overnight."

I hoped Hester did not mind. It would be a relief to have Caroline and Miss Ashe off where they could do no damage to my fragile masculine sensibility.

"No, no, you go on ahead, Caroline," Hester said. She heaved a little sigh. "Children are such a trial, Mr. Paxton," she told me, tweaking her son's cheek. "One is forever trying to keep them in one's orbit. But I mustn't go saying that with your wedding looming on the horizon. You shall find it out soon enough for yourself. And be assured, children will be the joy of your life, no matter how much you fret over them."

"Aubrey is probably wondering how you managed to have any offspring," Harlow said, "seeing as your husband is generally a continent away."

"Your father and I are a love match, Harlow dear. Never doubt it. We have only discovered that our love remains the more fresh for being tested by distance."

With that, Hester sashayed off, and Harlow winked at me, obviously feeling he'd had a joke on his mother—but I rather suspected the joke was on him.

I rose early the next morning and wandered about my room, anxious and agitated.

I had opted against my old quarters in the cottage, feeling the need for less isolation than usual, and was therefore ensconced on the second floor of the main house. My room was called the Yellow Guest Room, for obvious reasons: someone had had the time and inclination to scout out yellow lamp-globes, yellow bedclothes, and yellow-striped wall papering, not to mention yellow tile for the bath—and yellow soap with which to wash. At least, I thought, it was cheery. But it was not relaxing; the effect of all that yellow was to make me jump about even more than I might have under the circumstances.

For I wanted us to be undertaking our plans immediately. Now. This minute. Every day that passed was another day that Arabella spent locked away; the thought of it sickened me. Today was Thursday. Caroline would be returning with the date decided on by Miss Ashe and her cohorts, and Richard would be passing that information to Berry on Saturday. I only hoped it would not be long from then, for I should not be able to bear the wait.

Nor could I bear to pace anymore in my yellow chamber, so I left it and wandered downstairs, thinking I might visit the animals in the trophy room. I was just at the landing of the stairs when the front door opened, and Caroline entered. She turned to wave off Miss Ashe's driver and shut the door behind her. She had not seen me and, thinking herself alone, she leaned against the doorframe and shut her eyes, gave a rapturous sigh. I imagined she was either very glad to be home or thinking of something else entirely, but in any event, I had never seen her look so radiant—perhaps because my own presence and the dislike it engendered in her precluded her appearing so before me.

I intended to turn into the hall and avoid her, but just as I reached the bottom of the steps she opened her eyes and spied me.

"Oh, Aubrey! You are awake." She walked toward me, and I saw, to my amazement, that she was still smiling.

"Yes, I am up. So, how went your evening with Miss Ashe? Has she decided on a date for our mission?"

"Indeed she has. It is to be July the eighth. Three days from Saturday. Her driver is on his way to little Miss Wentworth's right now, to pass the message to her. She shall send it to Richard at once."

I felt my stomach flutter. How close that day seemed! And yet I could only imagine how slowly the time would pass for Arabella.

"Did you discuss things any further? Were there any details she left out while she was here?"

Caroline was still smiling her dreamy, faraway smile. "What? Oh—no. We took care of some of the paperwork, and Elizabeth used—well, she has a special method for determining important dates, so she figured this one, and then we lay down. That is to say, we went to bed. To sleep. Around eleven."

"I see. Well." I turned to go. "I am relieved to know that it's all set. We'll tell Harlow and Louella when they awaken. But now I think I shall perhaps look for some breakfast, if you'll excuse me."

"Wait a moment, Bree," Caroline said—and then she shocked me silly by catching me about the wrist.

I turned and peered at her, wondering whether she was quite well.

"I should like to talk to you, if you have a minute."

"Yes, of course."

"I would like to tell you—I should like, actually, to apologize to you."

My eyes widened, but I did not interrupt her.

"I feel I have been rather abominable toward you, a bit backhanded without meaning to be, and I am genuinely sorry. I never disliked you, Bree. I only—only wondered if you would do right by Arabella, for being as she is my great friend, I suppose I am possessive of her. But that is no excuse for the way I behaved. I regret it, and at any rate I am now certain you and she shall make an excellent match. And I want you to know that I wish you well, and that I intend to make up for my previous rudeness so that you shall know I am sincere." She beamed at me, and I wondered how many men had been smitten by this expression, for Caroline in good spirits was quite irresistible. "Do you forgive me?"

"Of course I do, Caroline. I am sure you only meant to be loyal to Arabella's interests."

"No, you mustn't make an excuse for me. But I am so glad you accept my apology. For now we shall be good friends, and I can put all of my past silliness behind me."

And with that she reached up and bussed me upon the cheek, and then skipped up the steps toward her own bedroom, leaving me standing bewildered in her wake.

Richard was scheduled to report to us on Sunday, after his meeting with Berry. The entire household trod on eggshells during the intervening couple of days, for we were all wondering whether something would go wrong, whether the Leedses would get wind of our plot, or Richard fail to have his solitary visit with his sister on Saturday, or some other disaster prevent him from getting out from under his parents' noses and riding to Linton.

But come Sunday—a thundering, rain-soaked mess of a day—Richard appeared on the doorstep promptly at three, sopping wet and irritable, but otherwise in one piece.

We assaulted him the moment Caroline opened the door. "You're here! Did anyone see you? Did you talk to Arabella? Is everything set?" We would have dragged the information from him then and there, had Hester Beckwith not reminded us that the poor lad might be more forthcoming once inside and dry.

When he'd seated himself in the front parlor and been given a cup of tea, we began more gently to direct our questions to him.

"Well?" Caroline asked. "Were you able to visit her alone?"

"Yes. I'm fairly sure we weren't overheard, for we were in a room by ourselves, and Mother and Father were kind enough to leave us be. It's a good thing I'd set a precedent by seeing her alone during all my visits, for no one batted an eye at us."

"Did you tell her of our plan? Did you give her the date?" I jumped in.

"I had to begin by telling her you'd arrived here," Richard answered me. He shook his head. "She very nearly swooned. I was almost afraid to deliver the rest of the message."

I held my breath.

"But I did."

I exhaled. *"And?"* Talking to Richard had suddenly become like dealing with Miss Ashe: he seemed awfully reluctant just to spill it.

"And—she refused the plan as it was."

"What?"

I nearly exploded, only faintly aware of the gasps of the others behind me. "Refused it? What did you say—don't tell me—"

"Would you let me finish!" Richard cried. "I said, she refused it as it was. She requested that you make one change, and she was very clear on the reasons. Now, if you'll let me explain them to you, and if you all agree, then we are still set with our plan, for I told her she'd only hear back from me in the event you didn't accept her suggestions."

"Well, out with it, then, man," Harlow said.

We argued back and forth—I, especially, and loudly—but in the end, we all agreed to Arabella's request, which meant that our date was ready and set for the eighth. If I had been worried that too much time would pass before we were to act, I now worried that there was too little in which to finely polish our plans. Why, when one looked at the list of things yet to be done, the eighth seemed to loom just over the horizon.

"It isn't that much to do, Bree," Richard pointed out. "We need only a last strategy meeting to wrap things up. I think you're giving way to nerves."

I sighed. "I suppose I am. I can't help but think how dire things will become for Arabella should something go wrong. This will be our only chance, we'll not get a second one, I'm sure. If we fail, your parents will likely move her someplace where she'll never be found."

"Try to settle yourself, Bree. You mustn't get overwrought between now and then," Louella said, patting my shoulder.

Richard announced that he had to depart; he'd had a "deuced" time getting out of the house in the first place, and his flirtation with Miss Wentworth was beginning to draw attention to itself. He so often used her as an excuse to disappear (and he really did stop at her house each time, so that her parents would support his alibi) that the Leedses were warning him not to tarry at so young an age before a single girl's shrine.

"If you've a moment, Richard," I said as he was drawing on his sodden boots, "there's something I've been meaning to ask you."

"Of course, let's have it."

"How did your parents find out about me in the first place? About my ancestry, I mean. They couldn't have learned it from any of their spies, as only a few people knew of it."

"I'm not completely sure," Richard said. "But I'll give you my best guess. A man called on us a while after you moved to Linton as Mr. Beckwith's tutor. Our maid answered the door and fetched my father, who claimed the fellow'd got lost and was seeking directions. I would've forgotten all about it, but I'd got just the barest glimpse of the man, and he seemed familiar for some reason. It wasn't until later—until after my parents had begun to act strangely, and Berry was taken—that I finally placed him. He was one of those with you at the voodoo woman's. The strapping one with the blonde hair. The more I thought on it, the more sure I was that I recognized him. I believe now he may have revealed you during that visit."

I remembered the apple core hitting my chest on the boardinghouse steps. And the little piece of newsprint which had provoked the missile.

If I saw him again—

No, don't think on it now. It can serve no purpose.

"Of course, I can't be certain of what he said," Richard told me.

"I've no doubt your conjecture is correct."

"But would he wish you ill?"

"It saddens me to think it. But it appears he would."

Richard was ready to go. He was slinging his bag over his shoulder when he remembered something.

"Oh—it very near slipped my mind with all this deuced fuss—I brought some things of Berry's out with me yesterday. I don't know how she managed to hold on to them, as they were contraband from the first—but somehow she did, clever girl, and smuggled them back to me, so that they might be got safely beyond the doctor's clutches."

He reached into the bag and withdrew a package.

"She asked that you look after them."

He handed me the bundle, which was wrapped in a little knitted lap blanket. I uncovered it. It was a drawstring pouch of velvet, and inside were a gold pen, and a small bottle of ink. Along with a fat, worn book, covered in battered chintz, and another, newer, bound in leather.

"They are diaries," Richard said.

Later that night, when the rest of the household had taken their beds, I wandered downstairs to the trophy room, the books in my hands.

I arranged myself on the tiger's back and stared at them.

Why had she given them to me to hold? So that I would read them. Because she trusted I would not.

I flipped the pages of the one bound in chintz. The writing was bold, neat, distinctive.

Contained in here was Arabella as she was to herself. That portion of her unrevealed to any other.

I wanted to know it, whatever it might be. I did not wish to violate her, to pry into the private moments of which I should have no part, but of her character, her mind, her heart—I wished to know.

I looked up at the heads upon the wall, waiting for them to offer advice. They stared back, mute.

I lifted the cover, waited—*Would she want this?*—then let a page fall open.

I glanced down at the neat script.

Monday, April 23, 1860

Dear Journal:

I am beginning to think it may not be such a dull week after all . . .

Perhaps an hour had passed when I heard voices raised somewhere quite near me, in one of the front parlors.

I fell backward into the present. And wondered if the voices were not a god-send, pulling me out before it became impossible for me to leave.

"I am only trying to help you—" I recognized Harlow's voice, and then Louella's. It seemed they had not retired earlier either.

"By pushing me? By insisting? Do you suppose that helps me? That my ambivalence is something you can convince away?"

"What in hell is it, then, if not that?"

"Let me be for the time being. That is all I ask of you. I've too many things on my mind already. At least wait until after we go for Arabella—"

"No. I wish to know now. Must I explain to you why—"

Louella said something else I could not make out. Then there was silence, and then footsteps—a single set—mounting the stairs.

A moment later I heard footfalls coming toward me as well, and a moment after that, Louella burst into the room. She gave a startled little cry upon seeing me laid out on the floor.

I sat up, having had just enough time to shove the diaries beneath the tiger-skin before she entered.

"I didn't realize you were awake, Bree. What are you doing here?"

"Thinking."

"No doubt Harlow and I interrupted your efforts," she said, coloring a little.

"I didn't hear much. And at any rate, from what I did hear, you didn't say anything so very awful."

She seated herself in one of the plush chairs and leaned her head upon her arm. "I am only asking for time. You understand that, don't you?"

"Yes, but I also understand why it's on his mind, given what we are about to undertake."

She nodded, and was silent a moment. "You know, Aubrey, I've meant to tell you for some time that I am sorry you and I fought on the way from Aix."

"So am I."

"Shall we make up, then, like a good brother and sister?"

"Or like a good uncle and niece?"

I thought perhaps I'd gone too far, but she smiled. "Whichever you prefer."

"Just so long as our détente is sincere."

She rose, and squeezed my shoulder. "It is. Good night, Aubrey."

"Good night."

As soon as I heard her lighter step upon the stair I reached beneath the tiger's pelt once again.

"Well, my friend, have your feelings toward this folly of ours changed any overnight?" Harlow asked me the next day.

We were seated at breakfast. It was a late one, given that everyone had been up into the small hours. I was having difficulty raising a morsel of food to my lips.

For in fact my feelings toward everything—not least of all Harlow himself—had changed, and changed back, a half-dozen times in the previous evening.

"No," I answered him. "We must do as we planned. We must make it work. I am more determined than ever to see it through."

chapter five

The morning of July eighth would be hot and overcast. I knew it though the sky was still dark when I arose.

It was five A.M.; we were all to assemble at Miss Ashe's by eight, and proceed by carriage westward to the Valhalla Home, which we expected to reach by sometime before noon.

I wanted no breakfast, but knew I should eat something, since it might be a long while before I'd have another opportunity. I washed and dressed with care—after all, a wedding is a solemn occasion, however it is undertaken—and neatened my yellow bed. By then I had wasted enough time to hear Cook clanging about in the detached kitchens where she worked when it was hot, so I made my way downward in the half-light.

A short time later I was joined by Hester, Louella, Caroline, and Harlow. Hester would be going only as far as Miss Ashe's, where she would help ready the "Bridal Suite"—the spare room where I'd first been brought by Arabella so many months ago. The others would, of course, be going to Valhalla, and as it turned out, they'd chosen to dress in much the same manner I had: in attire which suited both formal occasion and running away. Louella had on a crisp blue ensemble—and gardening boots. Harlow had donned a cutaway coat and his hunting breeches.

But Caroline had gone to the greatest extreme: she wore a man's formal coat, and beneath it a skirt which came barely to the ankle, without hoops or supports beneath—rather like Miss Ashe's African garb. Under this were flat polished riding boots, whose outline, along with that of her legs, was plainly visible beneath the fabric.

Hester shrieked when she saw her. "What on earth has come over you? Are you mad—they shall lock you up in Arabella's place if they see you like this!"

"Oh, for heaven's sake, Mama, it is only a piece of cloth. I fail to see what is so shocking. I thought it would be easier to move about in."

"It certainly would be that," Louella muttered.

Caroline twirled, opening the coat.

"Good Lord—your legs—" Hester ran over to shield her.

"I thought you would approve of it, Mama, being as it is quite freeing. Elizabeth wears her skirts this way all the time. In fact, she lent me this one."

"Well, perhaps you should give it back to her," Harlow snapped.

"Caroline, dear, this is not the time to draw attention to yourself. There shall be enough of that happening today as it is. You must learn to pick your battles," Hester advised her. Caroline sighed, but retreated to the stairs and the selection of another outfit.

I dreaded seeing what Miss Ashe would turn up in.

But when we arrived at her gate, we found her in proper English gentlewomanly dress: a somber gray snood, driving gloves, and parasol, and a suit which buttoned high on the neck. She looked every inch what I'd once assumed she was: the crusading moralist, in whose company any young woman would undoubtedly be much too safe.

"Welcome," she said when we were all assembled in her parlor. She looked us over with approval: Caroline and Louella in proper dresses (the boots hidden so long as they did not move), Harlow, Richard, and I in our odd combinations.

Little Miss Wentworth was there too, but she was staying behind with Hester, and therefore need pass no particular muster.

Then it was time for us to meet Miss Ashe's hand-picked players. She first introduced all of us to Mr. Grenville, the solicitor. This short and well-fed chap sported a top hat, a fine formal suit, silk collar, and gold pocket watch and chain. His sideburns were barbered into reasonable muttonchops, and he carried a leather briefcase bulging with law journals, the pages of which were marked so as to invoke the relevant statutes on the rights of prisoners, should they be needed.

He was every inch the solicitor, I thought, the most apt inches being those composing his mouth. He took a deep breath and addressed us in curlicued language for several minutes, then allowed as how it was a great honor to make our acquaintance, and kissed all of the ladies' hands. For Miss Ashe he had a regal bow—I wondered what service she had rendered that Mr. Grenville owed her this one and undertook it with such good grace, seeing as it was to be had *pro bono*.

Next we were to meet Father Bouchard. He struck me as somewhat fey for a priest; he had about him more the sleek air of a dandy than the suffering one of a martyr. His hair was a brilliantined blue-black flecked with gray, and he was tall and comely, and had arranged even the unflattering black robes he wore so that they flattered. But he led his own parish, in Mayfair, and he carried the tools of his trade: white collar, holy water, Bible, incense, host, and chalice, in a leather bag. His hand, when he shook mine, was as limp and cold as a dead fish.

I dearly hoped there would be no running to be done, for I doubted the solicitor and the good Father would be up to it.

When the introductions were complete, Miss Ashe got down to assigning us the various posts we were to man once we entered Valhalla House, as well as what we were to do, where we were to be at such and such a time, and why. Then she handed each of us a whistle upon a cord.

"These are our means of communication when we are out of sight. One blast shall mean that you are asking to be advised of danger. Two will mean that the way is barred, or that there is trouble. Three shall mean that the way is clear." She looked at Caroline. "Go on, dear, test it, you'll find it quite effective." Caroline did, and the resulting wall of sound very nearly deafened us.

"Now—are there any questions?" Miss Ashe paused, but nobody raised their hand. "Anyone who would like to go home?" We smiled; no one moved.

"Very well, then. Let us be off, my compatriots—and Godspeed!" She raised her umbrella high above her head, a Joan of Arc wielding her sacred sword.

"I thought I was supposed to say that," I heard Father Bouchard grumble behind me.

The ride to Valhalla was interminably hot and sticky, as I'd figured it would be. We had taken two coaches. Richard, Caroline, Miss Ashe, and the Father were in one, while Louella, Harlow, Mr. Grenville, and I rode in the other. My group was second in the caravan, since Richard was our navigator.

As we rolled through the countryside, Mr. Grenville regaled us with tales of his courtroom exploits. The world of the bailey and barrister was quite different in England than in the United States, but it did not lack for drama, as the portly man's stories illustrated. Interesting though he was, however, I wished he would be quiet, for my nerves were raw, and I longed for silence in which to collect my thoughts. In time I found myself able to drift off, to leave the carriage and its garrulous occupant behind, and become lost within myself, whilst still appearing to pay attention.

In the privacy of my mind, I set to bidding my good-byes to Arabella as I had known her. For by the time I'd completed my reading of the diaries that evening, she had become quite someone else: more complete, certainly more unique in character.

I had therefore almost considered calling this entire exploit off, or postponing it until I'd had time to rework certain elements, but then I realized it was all set in place, it must be now or never. To sit in this carriage with Harlow next to me, however, was proving a trial.

And he, mistaking my mood for a reaction to Mr. Grenville, leaned over to say to me, "Don't worry, it shall yet work itself out, by tonight you shall be seated next to Arabella, and that shall make all the difference."

"Yes." I was grim. "It shall."

And then, after what seemed double the hours that had passed, we were turning into the drive of Valhalla House at last.

I winced at the iron gate erected all round the place—what sort of hardened criminals did Dr. Gregory imagine he was confining? I worried for an instant that it might remain locked and our plans foiled at once, but Miss Ashe dismounted directly, strode over, and spoke a few authoritative words to the gatekeeper. He allowed us through without comment, and we rolled toward what appeared to be the main building.

Once at the doors, we came to a halt, and Miss Ashe began positioning us.

"All right, Caroline, you understand your instructions."

"Understood. I am to wait with the horses at the ready until called upon."

"Exactly. Let us go, then."

The rest of us moved off in a little mob, Miss Ashe and I ahead with Richard, who was leading the way. The others stayed behind a ways, so as not to be noticed immediately.

Our first obstacle came in the form of a nun who met us at the barred front door. She was a fleshy, cold-eyed creature with a faint moustache; I expected nothing good from her, and got it promptly. Recognizing Richard, she informed us that guests of the fourth floor were not permitted visitors on weekdays, and at any rate Richard had just been here last Saturday. What did he mean by returning, when he knew he could come but two weekends a month? And who were these other people—Dr. Gregory's rules—

She got no further, for Miss Ashe had stepped up to the grille.

"My good Sister. Thank you for your concerns, but they are unnecessary, I assure you. This is not an ordinary visit. We shall speak to Dr. Gregory at once, please, and then shall be happy to introduce ourselves properly." And then she stood there, looking impatient.

With deliberate slowness, but no further haughtiness, the nun drew the grille away and permitted us inside, her eyes going wide at the unsuspected size of our band—for Harlow, Louella, Father Bouchard, and Mr. Grenville had now caught up with us and entered as well.

We did not have to seek the doctor out, as he came striding toward us from down a long hallway. "Here now, what in the world is all this commotion—" He stopped upon seeing us. "Who the devil are these people, Sister Theresa?" Then he spied Richard. "Mr. Leeds—what are you doing here?"

Again we were silent as Miss Ashe took the lead. She strode forward to grasp the doctor's hand. "Elizabeth Ashe," she announced. "And you are undoubtedly Dr. Gregory, founder of Valhalla House."

"I am, Madame." The doctor, I saw at once, was not going to be an easy mark. He had recovered his equilibrium, and was now attempting to outstare Miss Ashe.

She surprised me by breaking into a wide smile. "You are all the talk among the medical community of London, sir. I've heard a great deal about your exemplary methods, Dr. Gregory, and I congratulate you."

"Well! I am pleased to know—" He puffed up at once, almost bit the bait, but then caught himself. "Yes—that is, I thank you. Now, exactly who might you be, and what business brings you to Valhalla?" He peered at her more closely. "Are you and young Mr. Leeds here arrived together?"

"Indeed we are, sir. You will forgive the intrusion, but there was no time to call ahead. Mr. Leeds informed me only yesterday that his sister has made a request, one with which I was able to offer assistance. She has asked—no doubt due to your fine example, Sister—to speak immediately with a representative of the Catholic faith, regarding a conversion. It happens I am friendly with a local parish Father—may I present Father Anthony Bouchard, Dr. Gregory"—and she had them shaking hands just like that—"and knew that I could impose upon him for this one day to grant an especial favor to an old acquaintance."

Dr. Gregory was smart enough not to drop his civility a notch just yet. "Well—I am certain you've come a long way, but I must tell you, this is highly irregular. Were you expecting to see Miss Leeds in person *today*?"

"Oh yes, quite. We shall be brief, as the Father's time is precious."

"But I'm afraid that's completely impossible. Young Richard here should have explained to you that his sister is the recipient of special treatment, and her contact with outsiders is limited. Even her parents have abided by the restrictions, which must be enforced to the letter. I do hate to send you away empty-handed, though, as you've no doubt had a long trip. Perhaps you'll stay to tea."

"Oh, I'm afraid we can't, and that I must insist upon disrupting your schedule a tad, Doctor. Allow me to reiterate, this is a matter of religious privilege."

"So you say, but I'm certain I can do nothing without Miss Leeds's having submitted a written request to that effect."

"We have that," Miss Ashe said crisply. She withdrew Arabella's letter from her carry-bag, and handed it to the doctor.

I caught the twitch of an eyebrow as he made a show of looking it over. "I am sorry, Madame, but this must be submitted to me in advance, and the meeting scheduled."

That was it, I knew. Miss Ashe was ready to call for her troops.

She pulled herself up eye-to-eye with the doctor. "Let me remind you, Dr. Gregory, that visits with clergy are a right guaranteed to all the incarcerated, whether criminal or medical, voluntary or involuntary, by royal decree, upon whatever terms they are arranged."

"Now look here—"

"My solicitor, Mr. Grenville, Esquire—" (Grenville gave a low bow.) "—has looked into the matter extensively."

Whereupon Mr. Grenville withdrew one of his leather-bound books with a flourish, and allowed it to fall open. "If you'll permit me, sir—and I quote—'Section Fourteen, subsection A of the revised Manuals of Incarceration: Being that said party—' "

Mr. Grenville was still reading, and giving no sign of stopping, when Father Bouchard turned to the nun. "Certainly, Sister, you observe the papal decrees and the royal ones in equal measure here—for they do so even in the New Gate Gaol—do you not?"

"Why—" she fluttered, "I'm sure that we do—it's never happened before—" She blinked at the doctor, who was trying to appear unmoved by Mr. Grenville.

"Here," the solicitor said, proffering the book, "if you wish to look it over for yourself—'Subsection B: if said party upon presentation—' "

"That will do!" the doctor snapped. "You needn't read the entire thing. I was unclear on a point or two," he sniffed, "but they are resolved to my satisfaction, and you may proceed—but I must insist that you be brief, as promised."

"Splendid!" Miss Ashe clapped her hands. "Now, if you can show Father Bouchard to Miss Leeds's quarters—" At that we all moved off, except for Miss Ashe and Louella.

"One moment!" the doctor barked. "Miss Leeds may confer with the priest. Alone. The rest of you may wait here."

"Oh, no," Father Bouchard said with a patient smile. "I'm afraid the gentlemen must accompany me. These two here are my altar assistants, and Mr. Grenville shall see to it that no British law is trodden upon, and a family member must be present so as to see to the honor of the young lady, since unmarried men are on hand. You understand, of course, Sister. Perhaps you could explain to the doctor."

"Never mind," Dr. Gregory seethed. "You must be taken through the back route, though, like any visitor to the fourth floor. I do not allow my young ladies to be exposed to the presence of strangers, priests or no. And you shall use the fourth-floor visiting chambers. There is to be absolutely no physical contact between any of you, and you shall confine your visit to fifteen minutes. Which I expect you to monitor, Sister, as you are still under the jurisdiction of this establishment." He gave the nun a hard stare, and then sent us off behind her. As we turned I could hear Miss Ashe introducing Louella—calling her Miss Fornsbury or some such—and then addressing the doctor in her hearty bass: "Now, you must explain the history of your remarkable research to me . . ."

"So far, so good," Harlow muttered under his breath.

I craned my neck as we moved toward the hallway where the doctor had appeared. I could make out a room next door, a big one, for the door was open just a crack. I glimpsed seated female figures who appeared to be working, but we passed them too quickly for me to note their expressions. Thankfully, though, they all looked healthy, and I heard no cries of misery; I had already noted that so far the surroundings were attractive if plain, and spotlessly clean. Perhaps it was not as bad as it had been rendered—

But then we were down the hall and through a courtyard, and I saw behind this building a much less grand one, with tiny barred windows blasted into it at regular intervals.

The living quarters, no doubt.

These contained a side entrance. A padlocked barred door opened into a dark, cramped staircase.

"Is this the way you usually take?" I whispered to Richard.

"Yes," he whispered back.

So we were really going to her—she was really here, somewhere just yards away—my pulse was galloping, although thus far everything had gone smooth as glass. Exactly as planned.

Please let it continue, I prayed, please let her be all right, please let it be over soon—

We reached the fourth floor, and the sister admitted us with her huge key ring. The other doors had been made of wood with a barred grille, but this one was of solid iron. I stepped through it, and as soon as we had all passed, the sister locked it again, with a terrible metallic clanking.

I turned to find myself in a narrow windowless hallway floored with rough wooden planks. Lamps were suspended on the plaster walls, which were sooty from years of lightings and lowerings. Having come up a back staircase, I realized we were also in a back hall; down its length I saw a few doors, all padlocked.

But to my right was an open room. When I looked in I saw that it was filled with tin bathing tubs. There were man-high lockers inside too, which I realized were new-fashioned ice chests. Of course. For the ice deliveries—for the cold baths. There was another exit at the opposite end of the room, from which I could see another hall, running parallel to the one we stood in. The main hall, no doubt. Where the "patients" were.

But the sister had no intention of letting us wander about at will. She shooed us along until we came to an inconspicuous door also on our right. It had a little wooden sign on it which said VISITORS. The sister unlocked it, and we were led into a very strange chamber. For there were bars which divided the room in two: we were on one side, and on the other was the remainder of the space, with another door through which the "patient" would likely come.

I felt my face blanch.

"Please wait here. I shall be a moment in fetching Miss Leeds." With that, the sister swished out of sight, closing the door behind us.

The minute she was gone I grabbed Richard's arm. "Do you notice anything wrong, for Christ's sake!"

"Jesus, I forgot—I forgot the deuced bars—"

I sank into a chair with my eyes closed.

"Shit." Harlow slapped a hand to his forehead. "Bloody goddamn horseshit."

"Now wait a moment, lads," Grenville interrupted us. "This complicates things a bit, but let us not lose hope. For if there's a way for her to get in, there's a way for us as well, and we know it is down the main corridor."

I opened my eyes. "And we can reach that, too, the tub room we passed is unlocked at both ends."

"Yes, I noticed," Grenville winked.

A moment later Richard had slipped out of the room, leaving the four of us alone. It was stifling in the chamber; I was covered in perspiration, but assumed I would have been thus even if I'd been suspended in the ice bath.

And then, after a seeming eternity, the door behind the bars opened.

And Arabella was there.

If I had passed her on the street, I should not have known it. So changed was she. She wore a gray shapeless pinafore that was stained and wrinkled, and I got the sense that she had just now donned it hastily, for it was inside out. If ever it had fit her, it had now assumed the proportions of a sack, so utterly without flesh was she. The bones of her fingers, her wrists, her arms, lay directly beneath the skin.

Her hair was knotted, and plastered to her head. At the corner of her mouth was a crust of blood. And a purple bruise was fading beneath one eye. She moved with an agonizing slowness, and I wondered what lurked beneath the formless dress, what other evidence of torment.

The nun stood behind her. When I was able to wrench my gaze from Arabella, I found myself moving toward that black-and-white habit; my mouth opened. "You—" I started, but before I could go any further, Harlow had pulled me back by the collar of my coat. I recovered myself and was silent.

I looked back at Arabella, and now she looked at me. And her eyes sparked, then glittered, and in case I'd somehow missed all that, she delivered a sure, slow wink.

"You may leave us, Sister," Father Bouchard said.

"I'm afraid I must interrupt after fifteen minutes." She fawned in the face of his priestly authority, and shot Arabella the barest, coldest glance, having no shame whatsoever. Then she retreated behind the other chamber's door, to observe us through a small glass window.

I wanted to run to Arabella, to touch her. Since I could not I said, without moving, "We're here, Berry. Don't worry. Nothing will go wrong."

She was not speaking, only nodding and crying; it frightened me that I had not heard her voice. "It's all right, Arabella," I whispered.

"I know it," she said clearly, and I felt relief flood through me.

Grenville stepped up to her, and his words came soft and fast. "Listen now, child. Your poor brother, he forgot to tell us about the bars."

I saw her eyes go wide.

"No, no, do not worry, we've sent him round the corner to keep a passage open for us. When we are finished here you must leave this room the way you came in, with that creature, but find a way to tarry in the outer hall. We shall meet up with you at the far end, from the direction of the baths. Do you understand?"

She nodded. I prayed she had the wherewithal, after all of this, to carry out some simple ruse.

I had not even noticed that the others had gone to their tasks hard upon the nun's exit. Harlow was holding the Father's bag open. The priest was withdrawing the necessary artifacts. Grenville went back to readying his papers, and now he touched me upon the arm to help him.

A moment later, Father Bouchard stood and called to Arabella. "Come right up to the bars, my dear." She stepped up, and the rest of us followed suit, so that only the iron barriers lay between us.

"Do you accept the Catholic Church, all of her teachings, the sanctity of the Blessed Trinity, and the divinely ordained leadership of Our Holy Father, the Pope, and do you vow to pursue instruction following to this baptism *in extremis*?" the priest intoned.

"I do."

I gazed into her brown eyes, which still flashed, as she answered. I knew then that she would manage to stay in that hallway—and do whatever else was required—if she had to kill herself in the process.

"I baptize you in the name of the Father, Son, and Holy Spirit." Father Bouchard sprinkled water on her forehead, made the sign of the cross over it, all without touching her.

"Are you prepared to receive, *in extremis*, the Holy Host, the body and blood of Christ?"

"I am."

He blessed the host quickly, in Latin, broke it, and handed a piece to Arabella, who swallowed it.

"Now repeat after me . . ."

When they had completed the Apostles' Creed together, the Father declared, "I confirm you as a member of the Holy Roman Catholic Church . . ." and in a record three minutes, Miss Arabella Leeds had become a servant of His Holiness, the Pope.

"Very good, here is your baptismal certificate. Please sign." He handed pen and paper through the bars, and I saw the nun's eyes narrow, but the door did not open. Arabella's hand wobbled, and the ink left a huge blot, but she signed, and then Father Bouchard did as well.

"Now then: to business," the priest said. He exchanged his holy water for a missal. "We haven't time for the service, we shall only note the presence of the appropriate intent." We were already dead quiet; somehow, we managed to get quieter, and I felt the room contract.

The priest beckoned the Bride closer still.

"Do you take this man to be your lawful wedded husband, before God, in sickness and health, til death do you part?"

I imagined she hesitated just a second. When she spoke, her voice was a whisper so soft it could scarce be heard.

"I do."

And then—inevitably—it was the turn of the Groom.

"Do you take this woman to be your lawful wedded wife, before God, in sickness and health, til death do you part?"

"I do," said Harlow Beckwith.

I had shut my eyes, not wanting to look at them when they spoke the words. When I opened them, Grenville was already leaping forward with the documents to be signed, even before the priest had finished: "By the power vested in me by the Holy Roman Catholic Church, and by Her Majesty Victoria, Queen of England, I now pronounce you husband and wife."

And then the papers were going round quick as shuffled cards: Grenville and I witnessed the marriage and the conversion, Arabella and Harlow signed their

Certificate of Marriage. And Harlow placed a plain gold band in Arabella's hand, which she slipped upon her finger.

It was done.

And not a moment too soon. For the nun yanked the door open a minute later—just as Arabella was folding her documents—and stood imperiously in the doorway.

"Your time is up," she rasped at Arabella. Then, in a sugared tone, she addressed us: "Please wait here until I come to fetch you."

Grenville stepped up to the bars. "Good-bye, my dear." He gave Berry a long look, and she nodded back, glanced once more at me. Then the cursed bitch of a nun was hustling her away, and again I was on the verge of screaming and ripping the bars from the walls. But the second they passed from view, Harlow was grabbing me—"Let's go, man! Hurry up!"—and I was shocked to see Grenville move like lightning out of the chamber and down the hall.

We were through the tub room in a flash. And there on the other side—where I now heard the moans and screams I'd dreaded, where I saw, through a door at the far end of the hall, a virtual cage with wretched, clawing forms within it—there was Arabella, struggling between the nun and her brother, the nun screaming invectives, while Richard shouted, and Arabella made a sound far bigger than her worn-down body should have managed:

Aubrey—Aubrey—

That the nun was a woman did not enter my head. I knocked her down with such force that she rolled along the floor; I snatched Arabella under the arm in a single movement. I would have carried her the entire distance, but she was upon her feet and racing away beside me, with Richard just behind us.

"Why in the hell did you swat that creature!" Grenville panted at me as we all ran back toward the rear stairs. "We've the law on our side now, she would've yielded!"

"No—she deserved it," Arabella cried, and I thanked myself for losing my temper.

"We must make haste," Grenville urged us. "She's surely up and heading toward the doctor as we speak." We clattered down the narrow flights of steps, taking them two at a time, Harlow and I lifting Arabella off her feet when she could not force them to go fast enough.

But the nun must have had a much shorter distance to travel than did we, or some quicker means of summoning help, for we were met at the foot of the stairs by two large men with rings of keys: the attendants. They crouched low, aiming for a fight.

"Stop right there," one of them snarled. "Unhand the inmate, and get yer arses off this property before you have them flattened."

"Sorry, lads," Grenville panted. "You're too late. This lady is being removed from the premises by order of her husband." He flourished the paper. "Take one more step, and it'll be your posterior in gaol, when the authorities haul you off for interfering with Mr. and Mrs. Beckwith's legal rights."

The louts looked at each other. And then the first one turned back to us. "We'll take our chances with the peelers, mate." And with that he threw a punch to Grenville's middle, which set off a general melee.

Grenville covered himself gamely. I jumped in to throw his attacker to the wall, while Harlow leapt at the other one. I had got my victim pinned against the brickwork when I glimpsed Arabella, frozen on the steps. "Don't wait here," I shouted at her. "Run! All of you, run toward the front—Miss Ashe is there." They sped away. Harlow and I struggled with our opponents for as long as it took us to realize we'd be wiser just to run ourselves; I gave mine a shove and was off, with Harlow behind me.

But they began shouting for reinforcements, and within a second they were after us—while at the other end of the courtyard I heard two earsplitting whistle blasts, and saw our compatriots running back *toward* us, instead of to the exit. I could hear Arabella—she was in the lead, and she was screaming.

"My uncle," I heard Richard shouting behind her, "my uncle—"

And then I saw, behind our band, the doctor and a tall, corpulent figure whom I realized must be Charles Leeds—the bastard who'd started all of this. And behind them came Elizabeth Ashe, and finally Louella, blowing on her whistle for all she was worth.

It was impossible to know who was chasing whom at this point, and so we all stopped where we were, in the middle of the courtyard. Arabella rushed at me, grabbed my arm, would have run back from whence she'd just come except that I pulled her to a stop. "There he is!" she screamed when she'd turned. "There!" Her thin hand thrust out at the big man who stood wheezing alongside the doctor.

"It's all right." I shoved her behind me—but the attendants were there, menacing her from that direction. I pulled her to me once more, and held her close. My comrades joined me, while the nun, the doctor, and Leeds blocked our escape through the front. From somewhere in the distance I heard another whistle blow—two short blasts—and knew it must be Caroline, warning us of trouble, but of course we had already met it.

Now we were all face-to-face, we were frozen, as in that moment just before something drastic occurs. None of us knew what it should be, though, and so nobody moved.

It was Arabella who decided it.

She broke away from me and tottered toward her uncle. I could have stopped her—any of us could have—and yet no one raised a finger. It had somehow become a private issue, this one between blood relations. She reached him, and halted. Then she drew back her fist, and in a single sharp movement landed the knuckles on his cheek. He took a stunned step backward, and she hit him again, open-handed. She was shouting, but since she wasn't facing me, I could not understand her. At last they turned round in their strange dance, she advancing, he retreating, and now I could hear what she screamed at him; it was just one word.

"Enough."

She slapped him with each repetition.

"Enough."

Her fury at last burned itself out. She stood still, panting, and then she turned from him and walked back to where I stood, her head lowered, wisps of dirty hair swinging wild about her face.

The courtyard was as still as any City of the Dead. Miss Ashe broke the silence. "Yes," she said, from her place at the edge of the crowd. "I do believe it's been enough."

She made her way toward the doctor, signaling Grenville to come forward as well. He'd lost his hat, and his few stringy locks had come unglued from his scalp, but he carried himself with no less dignity for it.

Now the doctor decided—now, at the end of the game—to be irate. "What is the meaning of this? Who are you people? You realize you shall all be arrested, for assault and the abduction of this girl—unhand her at once, this has gone far enough—"

"No one is being abducted," Grenville said. "Miss Leeds gave her consent to wed in a Catholic ceremony, performed legally and witnessed properly on these premises. Here are the papers. They are in order. It is the wish of Arabella's husband to remove her at once, and so you shall let your former patient pass, and trouble us no further."

The doctor's jaw dropped. He peered from one of us to the other. But Leeds, taking in the sight of Arabella standing against me, my arms wrapped about her, now proceeded into full apoplexy.

"You," he bellowed, thrusting a finger at me. "So it's you behind this. I know who you are, you vermin, you don't fool me. You've sullied her—and her brother too—how could you, Richard—" I saw the boy turn away, then Leeds whirled, and shouted at the priest, his face gone crimson: *"Do you know what you've done, you idiot? Do you know you've married her to this golliwog, this half-monkey fortune-hunting bastard-born nigger?"*

The doctor grabbed Leeds by the arm. "Then it surely isn't legal—there must be prohibitions—" he hissed *sotto voce*.

"As a matter of fact there aren't," Grenville broke in. "But even if there were, I'm afraid Miss Leeds is not married to the, ah, golliwog here. She is married to this other one." He pulled Harlow forward. "Mr. Harlow Beckwith. Of the Chicago Beckwiths, late of London."

Leeds and the doctor peered at Harlow, Leeds now appearing more confounded than enraged.

Miss Ashe took over from the solicitor. "As Mr. Grenville says, Mr. Beckwith wishes to remove his wife at once. You know, sirs, that there is nothing to be done to stop him. They are legally wed. Be assured that if you create any more of a ruckus, we shall be the ones sending for the authorities. Please do not make further discomforts on anyone's part necessary."

Leeds stared into Arabella's face. It cheered me to see that she'd drawn blood from his lip, so that it now matched her own. Too bad she hadn't had her full strength, and blacked his eye as well, I thought—especially after I heard what he said next. Was he moved to apology, to remorse by the sight of what had been wrought on his niece? Indeed not.

"Everything that could be done to help you has been done. If you shall now fall into ruin, it is by your own hand, and you shall do it alone, for I shall advise my brother to have no further contact with you. I pity your poor parents, girl."

In answer Arabella clung more firmly to my shoulder, then rested her head upon it and looked at him no more.

The doctor knew he was beaten. He straightened his lapels and turned to his cohort. "One cannot save the world, Charles. One must acknowledge that there will be failures." He looked back at the rest of us. "Go on, then. Get her out of here. You shan't be interfered with." And with that he gave us his back; he strode off toward his sanctuary, and after a moment Leeds followed suit, with a last furious glance over his shoulder.

The attendants and the nun drifted off, giving us venomous glares of their own, and then the path before us was clear. We were free to traverse the hallway, and then to leave. For good.

"And so we triumph," Grenville said, raising his arms to indicate the empty yard. I hugged Arabella now, really held her, for the first time and without care for who witnessed it. But I had no wish to spend another moment in this wretched place, and so, when Louella touched me upon the shoulder, I gently put Berry's hands from me, turned her round, and half-carried her toward the elaborate main building, and the way out.

The ride home passed in a blur of jubilation—for the rest of us, at least. Berry, overcome at last by the day's events, collapsed upon the carriage seat, at first crying without interruption, thanking us over and over again, and then, when I'd comforted her the better part of an hour, falling into sleep. But her hand held fast to my shirttail. She clutched it with such determination that even in her sleep I could not pry her fingers open. I'd meant to arrange her across the seat, to make her more comfortable, but at length I let her dream on as she wished; it was a pleasure to feel her there.

We'd been joined in the carriage by Louella and Caroline and Richard, while Harlow, Grenville, and the priest had ridden with Miss Ashe. But our coaches traveled side by side whenever possible, so that we could talk freely. We'd taken the tops of the landaus down, for the sun was shining and a breeze had come up, and we were loath to shut it out.

Caroline was describing to us her horror at seeing the strange surrey arrive and hearing Leeds announce himself to the underling who answered the door. She'd blown the whistle right then, to warn Louella and Miss Ashe that something had gone amiss. Leeds had been startled half out of his mind, but Caroline had batted her eyelashes and explained that she was only signaling her friends, who were inside on business and wished to be reminded of the time.

Louella picked up the story from there. "We were doing our best to keep Gregory busy—or rather Elizabeth was."

"And a simple task it was, for he'll talk into the next century about his beloved convictions, and what he's done to force them down the throats of others," Miss Ashe put in.

"But then we heard the whistle," Louella continued, "and we saw a man coming through the door. And then Gregory was calling him Charles, and started exclaiming that wasn't this a coincidence, Arabella had just been called to an impromptu meeting with a priest, and here was her uncle. It seems that Leeds had stopped by because he was visiting a patient in the area. It was just plain bad luck that he happened to appear. But once he heard Arabella had callers—well, he was furious, wanted to know what was happening. He guessed right away that something was amiss, especially because Richard was with us. In no time at all he was demanding the doctor go up and find all of you, or swearing he would himself—and at just that moment, I saw Richard running through the hall doors from the courtyard. So I blew the whistle, and thank God, he understood, and everyone turned round. But then the doctor and Leeds gave chase, and of course we were right behind them."

"Thank God I turned round is right," Richard muttered. "I'm amazed I managed to do anything properly, after that fiasco with the bars."

"It was an understandable mistake," I told him. "And I am sorry if I was harsh with you." I then explained the nasty surprise of the barred room, and our fear that Arabella would be swept out of sight without our being able to get hold of her.

"But Grenville was on his toes, as I imagine he always is. Tell me," I said to the solicitor, "have you ever invoked that Manual of Incarceration before?"

Grenville chuckled. "Actually, my boy, there is no such thing."

We all stared at him—all of us except Miss Ashe.

"Do you mean to say you made all of that up? About the right to clergy and so forth?"

"Well, yes."

He chuckled again at my outraged expression. "Part of a barrister's wisdom, Mr. Paxton, is knowing when to have all the facts before you, and when you need only convince someone else that you do. I apologize for the deceit, but this way, you had every confidence we'd prevail, and so we did."

"But what if he'd called your bluff," Harlow asked.

"Oh, I could have found a statute or two to back our contention, or to raise enough doubt in anyone's mind that we'd have been allowed to proceed." I thought Grenville might be bluffing now as well, but what did it matter?

"And what about you," I asked Father Bouchard. "Have you bent the Church's statutes a bit as well?"

"I've perhaps set a precedent," the priest shrugged. "But the Church is flexible in terms of how one comes to her. It was an extreme situation; it called for an extreme solution, and rules are meant to be broken now and again. Even the Holy See would have confirmed as much, I'm sure, had there been time for a consultation." He gave me his fey little smile, and I smiled back at him, grateful for his rather liberal interpretation of Catholic doctrine.

"Well, we had some bracing moments, didn't we," Miss Ashe said with relish, and then we all began again recalling and exclaiming over them—except for Arabella, who slept through our self-congratulations, oblivious to the status we'd accorded her: the jewel, inert and helpless, now smoothly, successfully thieved.

It was just as well she stayed asleep.

chapter six

AUGUST 10, 1863

It is the act of writing which makes me heal, I am certain of it. It was only after I had taken hold of you, friend, and begun to mark you once more, that I felt returned to myself, enough to believe that my freedom is tangible and permanent, that all which has come with it—Bree, of course—is also real.

I wish to God I had been my own salvation, and perhaps in time I would have been. How wretched to have wound up the damsel in distress, beholden to kindnesses from without, for it's as though I failed—failed myself—my pretensions of independence aside.

And yet I might as easily have died. And must not hold it against myself that in dire straits I chose instead a rescue not of my own making. Had I stood upon the ledge of a burning building, would I have refused the helping hand on principle? Surely not—and would I not offer my own aid to Bree, or to any of my beloved friends, had they been in my shoes? I would—fully and unconditionally, as did they.

AUGUST 12, 1863

I try to eat as much as possible, and my flesh remembers where the curves and hollows are to go. Sleeping is more difficult, for of course I dream of the place. How wrong I was to ignore the rumors of that portion of the fourth floor, which no one saw. In my dreams I again reside there; I sleep naked on the ground with the others, our straw-strewn cell open to the world, observed every hour and in every intimacy, and beaten bloody for any sign of infraction. And taken to the office of the sisters, or to the tub room by the men, for those services which shall not get me with a child, but which, if unrendered, shall land me in the darkened cell for day upon day, where I was certain I would go mad and die.

I am neither mad nor dead, though. And I applaud myself that I am not, and heap no shame upon myself for what I did to make it so, but rather send my persecutors to hell.

But that is not enough. Until I have made peace with it in my own mind I will not speak of it. Once I am ready, however, I shall shout it louder, and again, until I am heard and heeded.

AUGUST 13, 1863

In my dreams I cry out for my mother and father, who even there abandon me as surely as they did, and do, in waking life.

Perversely, though, they maintain that it is they who've been abandoned.

For they say that on top of all else, I (O fickle and disloyal daughter!) have turned my back upon my blood for the sake of an outsider, a mere suitor, and in my ignorance cannot realize how sorry I shall be when infatuation fades and my folly reveals itself as such.

But I do not see it so. I have chosen not one connexion over another but rather myself above all—my truest self, as I am in my own thoughts, where I need not censor or censure.

It is Aubrey who embraces that self—every aspect of her—and so it is Aubrey whom I embrace.

My parents send letters full of condemnation, or threat, or plea, through Richard. And I write them back, as always, the truth: the direct, unadulterated truth of what became of me, of what becomes of me now, which in their next letter they acknowledge not at all.

I have done the best I can do, by them. I would turn my attentions to myself now.

AUGUST 14, 1863

I close my eyes each night in the bed where I first brought Aubrey; this comforts me. Miss Ashe has a finely tuned sense of irony, in this instance and in many others. I had not suspected the depth of her humor, even when I was in the midst of taking advantage of her "study groups." I also had not realized the depth of her character.

But I sleep here chastely, for while Bree comes every day, he does not stay into the night. I believe it has to do with my frailty, which if extreme is now fast disappearing. But besides that, I believe it has to do with Harlow.

Father Bouchard has advised me that the annulment may perhaps take a while, and until such time as the paperwork is completed I remain Mrs. Harlow Beckwith.

And of course I cannot—will not—even think of consummating my affection for her under these sundry conditions.

She is not well, that is the main thing. She is on the mend, surely, but not well, however much she insists that she shall be back to her former self in a day or two. She screams at night; I hear her, for I wait in Elizabeth's study after Berry has retired, to see if the situation has improved any.

But most every night is the same. Elizabeth and I talk. We are often joined by Caroline, who sticks quite close to Elizabeth, but has been infinitely kinder to me, as she promised. Elizabeth shows us the photographs she has taken on her jaunts round the world—and many they are, for she is near sixty, she has told me, not the forty she appears—or we indulge in a game of chess (which by some miracle I win about half the time), and just as we are settled in, the yelling (or banging, for she falls out of bed sometimes too) begins. And I am on the verge of running up and waking her when it stops—or Elizabeth stops me, for she has got this theory that dreams are the mind's attempts to resolve its unfinished waking business, and that they must therefore not be interfered with.

It is too soon to expect that this business shall be finished, although I wish it. Passionately.

I am tormented night and day by my imaginings of the place, and imaginings they remain, for she will tell me nothing of what went on there. But whatever it was, until it has released her, until it no longer haunts her sleep—or at least not so severely, for I doubt it shall ever leave her—I shall not believe her whole, and restored to me.

So there is that.

But there is also the matter of Harlow. I cannot deny it.

Each time I grasp her hand, or am about to kiss her lips, it rises to my thoughts, that she is wed to him not only in name, but in flesh as well—and then the kiss lands on a cheek, for I cannot free myself from the notion that he taints our every intimacy, that he too needs to be resolved and departed before Berry and I are restored to each other. His presence as a husband hangs over our enterprises, for it is the piece of paper binding them that keeps the authorities, the parents, and me at bay. She belongs to another, and I cannot forget it; I torture myself that she does not either, that in some secret place she cherishes knowing he was first in all things, and takes a tiny bit of satisfaction from bearing his name at last, and forever being, if under the most inane circumstance, his first wife.

I am rather ashamed of feeling as I do, for I know it is ridiculous. Harlow is my closest friend, this business of feminine chastity and sheer jealousy defies my rational beliefs—*le coeur a ses raisons*, but that is no excuse—and I can see that Arabella is keenly frustrated.

"Do you not understand why it could not be you?" she asked me, before she had lost her patience for it.

"No."

"I could not wed you as a device, Bree. It would have ruined everything for me. Bad enough I could not effect my own escape, but to have my marriage be the means of it—as it is, I shall be forever reminded that I was delivered from one man's authority by virtue of another's. If that must be true, at least let the marriage be one undertaken solely for that purpose, one which I arbitrate myself, and then dispense with. It is a matter of principle. I wish my vows to you to be spoken freely, and for the sake of affection.

"Besides, it would have ruined things for you too, if you think on it. You would have given yourself under pressure, which might someday have become an issue between us."

"But don't you understand, I wanted to do it?"

"For someone else, perhaps. That is what I believe. You cannot restore Faith to the world, Bree. Moreover, what befell her was not your fault. She forgives you from wherever she is, I am sure of it—can you not do the same? Otherwise her death shall occupy a greater portion of your considerations than did her life, and I doubt that would please her."

"At least you are willing now to acknowledge that the dead may live on somewhere."

"I've no trouble with the concept of another realm, Bree. It is the residents of this one that frustrate me."

"What makes you think she forgives me?"

"Because I would have. And she seems a person I'd have been of one mind with."

"But why Harlow?" I whined.

"Who better than he? Who else was in a position both to know the whole story and assist us? We are lucky he agreed to it."

"So—you now suggest I should feel *lucky* that Mr. Beckwith has assumed my place?"

"He has not assumed your place."

"You are *married* to him."

"On paper—why does it vex you so, when you know very well the truth of it! Look, Bree, can you trust, please, that it's you I wish to be with, and remain with. But I feared that, had our marriage begun upon a false note, all that came after it might have been colored."

"And yet you do not fear that being wed to Harlow Beckwith will strike a false note, and color everything that comes after," I shouted.

"We are going round in circles." She folded her arms in disgust.

A few days later the rest of it came out as well.

"You read the journals, didn't you?" I asked him one night as we lay on the bed in each other's arms, held close, but stiff, fully dressed, a million miles apart for all it mattered.

There was a long silence, which made his eventual "yes" merely redundant.

"I knew that you would. I must have wanted you to, I suppose, or I'd not have left them with you. There were times when I was truly certain I would die, and you would never know me, know the things I thought of you when I had all of the liberty in the world to express them. I wanted you to have me with you."

"And that was why I read them. I did not mean to intrude, Berry. I agonized over it, often wondered if I ought to stop, to preserve your privacy and my sanity. But then I thought of how you would be revealed to me, and I had to know."

"And?"

"And it made me wish I could rethink our plan," I wanted to say, "for I loved you far, far better once I'd finished, but after what I had learned the idea of seeing you joined to Harlow Beckwith for any reason at all made me ill." But I did not say this.

"And I loved you the more for seeing you more fully. You must know me better than to think I'd have done otherwise."

"I hoped for as much. But what you read—it is also the reason for this uproar concerning Harlow, is it not?"

I felt him stiffen further beside me.

"Can you blame me? Am I to have no feelings, knowing you not only carry his bloody name—"

"—but am marked as his forever through my deeds? How conventional of you after all, Bree."

"Oh, don't twist my meaning. It's nothing to do with your sullied virtue—what concerns me are your own words, for they gave me to see, through your very eyes, every sigh, every fancy, every goddamn second you shared with him. And now, to top it all off, you're his wife. On paper. How can I be sure that some spark of interest does not yet remain in you, however you protest? To yourself you had no cause to be other than honest, and I saw the words you chose to tell it."

"Really—then what did you make of the rest of my words—the end of Harlow, my affection for you? Did you not read those? Were they not honest? Or do you push them aside, so you may wallow in your injuries, and go on refusing to trust my heart?"

He made no answer. After a long while he said, "I am doing the best I can. I am only telling you it would be easier were there not this constant reminder hanging over my head. When the annulment is valid I am certain I shall feel differently."

I waited a while myself, still seething. "And if you do not feel differently?"

"I know that I shall."

"I'm not certain I trust *that*," I said.

He glared at me but I went on. "Suppose I could not let go my contemplation of the women you were with. Or the fact that I compete with a ghost for your attentions."

"Don't be ridiculous, that is completely different. I did not love Faith in the first place, that was the very nature of the wrong I did her—and besides, you haven't some glaring symbol of our attachment, or my own written words, to haunt you—"

"Oh, but I have both. You thought enough of Faith to have her tattooed on your very flesh, and you've made no move toward erasing her."

"A tattoo cannot be erased, for God's sake. This is absurd—"

"It is exactly as absurd as you sound yourself."

He rolled over on the bed so that his back was toward me.

"The point being, Bree," I continued nonetheless, "that in the end I must trust you in some things, and grow to accept others, and so must you."

Another long while went by, during which I imagined he was rallying his forces to foment fresh arguments, but when I heard the deep, even breaths beside me, I realized he had fallen quite asleep.

The situation has eased, however, since those first tumultuous arguments, and continues so in little measures with each passing day, and so I am hopeful.

AUGUST 16, 1863

Today was Aubrey's birthday, and such a celebration we had for him! He said he had not seen the like since the days of his extreme childhood, when he was fussed over disproportionately. Of his last few birthdays he claims there is little to recount, for he recalls being mainly miserable, and so I decided we would have to make up for those dismal years in some appropriate manner.

I found it all quite overwhelming—the meal, the guests, the Champagne, and the slightly listing three-tiered cake made by Caroline and Berry, which had them shrieking with laughter in Elizabeth's kitchen for the whole of last night. I had quite forgotten what a to-do we are wont to make of our entry into the world when there is no pressing business to distract us.

On the heels of this thought my mind turned for the first time in many months to the States, to the war there. The tide has turned against the South since Gettysburg, and there seems little doubt that the Federalists shall carry the day. What has become of the populace I scarcely can imagine.

I wonder sometimes about returning, should the end of the conflict arrive soon. Do I not owe it to myself to claim the opportunity denied me, to force restitution from the Confederacy which trod upon Constitution and Christian duty?

But I would return to a graveyard.

I would venture, therefore, only to a part of the country I had not seen before, west or north or south, so long as it is new and without associations.

Berry noted me reflecting while Harlow argued with the other guests over which parlor game we might play, and offered me a penny for my thoughts. So I put the question to her, to see what she might say.

I thought on it, for the same idea has occurred often to me. But, like Aubrey, I know that I should find everything changed even as I am changed, and so I replied to him that just now I prefer to look forward rather than back, to make secure my own self so that when I do return it shall be with confidence, rather than bittersweet longing for the unhaveable.

She then said she would permit no more ruminations of this kind to dampen my mood, and took me by the hand to lead me to the pile of presents my friends had so kindly bought for me.

Her own gift was the one I shall treasure above all. It was a silver pen, carved to resemble a staff with various creatures adorning it, and a leather-bound book, very much like the one already so familiar to me.

She had inscribed the cover on the inside: *To Beloved Aubrey, for what you dream of. Your Arabella.*

I thank her most for her confidence that I shall fill it.

AUGUST 31, 1863

Things have loosened quite a lot between Harlow and Bree, due on no small account to Harlow. He has shown up here so many times wringing his hands over Louella that even Bree can see we are hardly wallowing in our "married life." Yesterday, in fact, Bree even asked if he would consider coming along when we leave England for the south of France, which is the plan we've decided upon.

"Oh, Louella would never invite me," Harlow said, disgusted. "She is a hard taskmistress, believe me."

"But you see, you needn't rely on Louella, for I can invite you," Bree replied. "Rest assured, there's enough room for you in my mother's quarters. Or"—he wore a wide smile by now—"you can stay in a cottage, on the property. And once you're arrived, we can see to planning another assault on that hard heart of Miss Paxton's."

I was amazed at the offer. For of course Louella shall be making the trip, and lately Bree has been making noises about asking Elizabeth to come along. (It seems she has quite fallen from grace here in London. She will never again be the staid former tutor to London society; her secrets are out, her learning circles disbanded, for what good can they do anyone now? Bree thinks a trip might be just what she needs, although in fact I wonder, for she has never seemed livelier, according to Harlow and Caroline, and my own eyes.) And Aubrey suggested in so many words that if Elizabeth came, we ought to ask Caroline, and, well, we could surely extend the invitation to Hester. But I knew that he felt Harlow to be a great obstacle, for if all of the others were to be asked, of course we couldn't leave him out.

And how would Bree feel having him haunt us all the way to France, where we are ostensibly to begin afresh with each other?

Something must have budged in his mind, though, for he sewed up the whole question by inviting Harlow before any of the rest.

It may have to do with the plans we've been working on with such earnestness. We laid the deeds out a few nights past, and discovered, much to Aubrey's surprise, that he owns not one but two pieces of property. He did not realize he'd been given control of a holding company, a small incorporation which exists for the purpose of easing taxes. It was Louella who explained this to us. The company has two properties, she pointed out, a piece of land on the Côte d'Azur and a villa on a good amount of acreage in a place called Midit d'Or.

We could barely find the latter locale on the map—it is a tiny hamlet in the countryside just outside Paris. "What is a Midit?" Bree was mystified.

"Who knows," Louella laughed, "but it seems there's one outside of Paris that's made of gold. You can tell me if it's earned its name once you've been to inspect it."

The more we plot and our conjoined future takes shape, the more remote the past becomes, to both of us. And I believe it is this which has caused an easing of Bree's concern over Harlow.

But it has not helped *my* cause any that Mother and Father have entered a Penitent phase, as I knew they would. They come to the door now themselves; they have appeared there twice, and each incident has been excruciating for me.

Aubrey always handles them, though. No doubt he takes a vengeful delight in it.

For I am able to stand in the doorway of Elizabeth's fine house (where I now reside, in another of the guest rooms, much to the horror of old Nevins the butler; the trek from Linton each day was just too impractical) and look down on them. And tell them, in a tone kind but firm, that yes, Arabella is here, she fares well and is recuperating, but no, she will not see them.

They were polite to me the second time we met. The first time they fairly swooned. The mother, recognizing me, could only stammer, "What are you doing here? Where is her husband—where is this man she married—" whereupon I called to Harlow, who happened to be visiting as well, and asked would he please come here?

Which he did, explaining with complete calm that yes, he and Berry were quite married, but expected an annulment very shortly. Which had the parents gawking even more strenuously. They figured it out soon enough, though, when they saw us both standing there, friendly as can be, our arms about each other's shoulders. And then they appeared so despairing and defeated that I almost pitied them.

But not quite.

For the next time, I found it just as pleasant to announce that no, Berry still did not wish to see them. She had asked me to tell them she loved them, and would keep her whereabouts known to them, but just now she felt she could not talk to them, and asked that they understand. I said all this dripping with sympathy, for I knew that would sting them more, to receive pity from myself. But I try not to be too cruel, or enjoy it too much, for there is Richard to consider; he is to be my brother-in-law, and I like him immensely, and wish to do nothing to alienate him.

Residing with Elizabeth is something of an experience, but it has this one added bonus to it—this small-minded vengeance I exact upon the Leedses—and that makes it easier to put up with Nevins's exasperated looks, and with Elizabeth's oddities.

SEPTEMBER 6, 1863

Last night we were lying together upon my bed in the dark, as we always do, having one of our usual inane presleep conversations. This one was about what letters of the alphabet we would switch if we had the chance so as to create a new language for ourselves. (You see, I told you they are inane.)

We had set ourselves to laughing uncontrollably—of course it doesn't sound funny now, but I assure you, to us it was hilarious. When we stopped, we were still smiling at each other, and then Bree leaned over and kissed me.

It was our first real kiss since the one in the Cremorne Gardens. The first one I felt flip my head about as that one did.

I hadn't meant to do it, which perhaps is the finest part. It overtook me, and I hadn't a single thought of Harlow Beckwith, or anything else that might have sullied it. The edge of her hair still has that fresh, distinctive scent which would lead me to her in the dark; her mouth on mine was as ripe and as exciting as I remembered it. And my mind was a wonderful, utter blank, consumed only by the business before it in that moment.

SEPTEMBER 18, 1863

I told Bree that he must reveal to me at last what he discovered during his visit to Aix-en-Provence. He has been putting it off since we arrived here, doing much as I've done with my own secrets, telling me the palatable portions of the story and promising the rest when I am "better." But I said to him that I felt it was time, and last night he finally agreed.

He came to my room as usual, and had brought with him a folder full of papers.

"What are these?" I asked.

"They are letters from my grandmother. My mother gave them to me when we saw each other."

"But I thought you said there was no contact between any of you."

"There was not, for the longest time. My grandmother kept some of these back, and only gave them to my mother in the last days she was alive, when they'd made their peace to whatever extent they could. And others were sent to me, but my mother had held them from me. You remember. They were the ones I found in the carriage house as a child."

"Goodness." I touched the filmy papers; I pictured Bree receiving these, and how he must have looked as he sat reading them into the night, struggling to see how it all came out, as he had with my journals. Except that his grandmother's story had an ending, while we were still writing mine.

"Take this one first," I said, and gave her the one in which you reveal Leland Paxton.

"Why?"

He blushed quite red, and confessed to me that while I keep a journal on paper, he has always kept one of sorts in his head, that he speaks to his grandmother near every day, about every important thing that happens, and so he wished me to know her, and thought she could explain the situation better than could he himself.

So she began. I watched her face in the lamplight as her eyes ran across the pages. She was at first eager, glancing up at me on occasion and then returning quickly to the words. But within not much time I saw her flinch, and then the pleasant curve of her lips vanished, and she seemed to lose all awareness of where she was. Her eyes slowed, and she no longer took them from the paper. And by the time she finished a long while later, any hint of mirth was gone from her.

She looked up and out and not at me, the papers resting in her lap. "There is nothing I can say that will not be too little. It is beyond comprehension." She was shaking her head, struggling for words and failing to find them.

For there weren't any, of course. How could this be? How did one wake up in the morning and live the day with it?

If ever I had thought I understood Bree, or his circumstances, I now knew I'd understood much too little.

"What do you do with this?"

"I cannot change it. And so I suppose I work to accept it. I believe my Gran was right: that it is better to know what's there to be known. And it did not hurt to see what she was able to make of herself even in adversity, that she was able to find some happiness and a means of guiding me toward it."

"She was able to find some happiness?" For if that were the case, it was not apparent in the pages I had just finished.

"Well, you see, you mustn't stop reading, that is only a single letter. Here, you must also look at the rest of these—"

Which, fortunately, I did.

In time she was commenting as she read, and then we were going over various passages together—"What did she mean here, do you remember this?" and so on.

We laughed over your descriptions of the pukey babies, the proud mamas, the impossible patients you described so well. I pronounced aloud the names of the gods of our family—*Flimani Koku, Mamy Watu*, how musical those strange sounds seemed, tripping from my tongue for the first time. Berry rhapsodized over your romance with Will—as I'd known she would—particularly the idea that you had written your own vows to each other and read them aloud at your "wedding."

"We should do the same!" she cried. "Oh, let's do, Bree, that is a real wedding. When the two who undertake it also author its terms."

"Of course," I said, for I thought it a splendid idea as well. I had gone so far for this girl, and wished my sentiments toward her to be my own, for if birth, death, and marriage are the most important events in a man's life, then there is only one in which he may wield any influence.

"But we ought have some sort of official sanction too, and congregation as well, so long as it is based upon good principle."

"We shall make our own sanction. Choose our own congregation. We shall do whatever we wish." I was smiling at her. "Perhaps we oughtn't get married at all—we could adopt each other instead."

"What—and saddle myself with two fathers to obey? I'd be freer with a husband." She frowned. "Though I'd rather something entirely new, for I've seen enough of contracts which constrict me."

As had I. "Well, then, write a wedlock proposal of your own. So as to keep your autonomy even as my wife."

"You know my mind too well, Bree—would that it were possible."

"But certainly it is. Have Grenville draw it up with you. He's a solicitor, after all, he can see to the technicalities."

"What a perfectly outrageous idea—wherever did you happen on it?"

"It's my own. It came to me when Harlow sought my help with Louella."

Her eyes went wide. "You are quite serious."

"Well, aren't you? I would ask only that we hold our ceremony—whatever its specifics—in Aix-en-Provence, before my family, for mine will be the first marriage among the colored Paxtons in three generations, and I should like my own blood to witness it, however strange that gathering would be."

"Of course—it is a fine idea, for the place holds no unpleasant memories for me. And we shall have Louella there, and Harlow, and Richard, if he'd only agree to it, though I know he shall be loath to vex my parents further—"

"—and Elizabeth and Caroline—"

"—and your mother—oh, goodness, Bree, I am terrified at the thought of her!"

"As you ought to be, for she'll devour you alive."

She was laughing now; and then she picked up your letter again, and said, "Look here—look what your Gran says of this Gabara, goddess of love—why don't we marry in her name? She can be our sanction—she is already among your family gods, and wasn't it she that the voodoo priestess invoked the night we met?"

"Yes, yes, it was Gabara—" I laughed, caught up in it as well, for though her eyes danced, I could see there was a seriousness in them too, and I thought, why the hell not? Would it not be the perfect thing?

And that was how far we traveled from the initial shock your letters brought her—all the way to the point where we were plotting and planning together, and you were there every step of the way, Gran—I have no doubt it was you that turned it, for if ever I believed you watch over me still, I knew it then, felt it to the core of me.

I wondered if it were sacrilege, that I could go so soon from horror to gaiety, but Bree seemed not to mind, and I thought, if he has found a way to get by it, why should I not follow him? I felt quite strongly—and strangely—that it was his grandmother's letters which had done it, as if she had been speaking the words to us herself, urging us past the dark facts of his conception to the rest of the story.

Indeed, by the time I had finished all of her missives, cried over her death, and rejoiced in her strength, I felt I knew her; it was as though she had befriended me, and now sat in the room to laugh and scheme with us.

But when I had gathered the papers together, when I had folded them with care and replaced them for safekeeping, then I felt you depart, Gran, and close the door behind you, so as to leave us decidedly alone.

He returned from his room empty-handed, and it seemed something had changed, had either fled my quarters or entered it—we both felt it at once. For though we had been within these same walls, alone with each other every night, it had not been like this, this curious new awareness between us.

I knew the instant I sat down upon the bed what was to happen, for the right moment is simply right, and nothing stood any longer between us and it.

She was lying with her knees drawn up atop the covers, in her chemise and pantalets, and when I saw her there, beautiful beyond any picture, beyond my ability to describe it, I did not hesitate. I eased over beside her, pushed a curl of hair from her cheek, and kissed her.

Is there anything as wonderful as a kiss that is wonderful? It is like the act of passion in miniature, and the better, for a woman possesses a tongue as well as a man does a mouth, and each can explore the sensation from both perspectives. You must see the other's face, taste him, absorb and be absorbed. There are many things more lusty, but they are less intimate, and can be done while man or woman is indifferent, or dishonest, or filled with hate.

But a kiss returned is love.

And if I have at times been frozen in place, and longing to stay that way, in other kisses with Aubrey, if he has been too, this time I knew we would not. I recognized the heat of him the moment his lips found me.

I could not take her in fast enough, or prolong each second sufficiently, wanting, as I did, both extremes at once. I wondered whether I had learnt anything in my past excursions into passion, and decided then and there it ought be a conversation rather than a monologue, and so I forced myself to back away a bit from my own inclinations, to see where she might be in hers, whether she wished me faster or slower.

And what helped me immeasurably—even as I fought a pang of guilt, for what other lover has a manual to follow to his beloved's most private space—was the journal: all I'd read in it, what she expected, what she had done, and liked, and disliked.

For I should never have known, had she not exposed me to this shocking news, that she could expect the rapture that I did, and have it—or that I might give it to her, rather than plunge alone into that brief and bottomless bliss.

And I thought—wickedly, perhaps, but nonetheless with satisfaction—that this was one place she had not been with Harlow Beckwith, that I knew this but he did not, and that I would bring her there with me, and share a secret with her which would exclude him forever.

And if there was anything more exciting than the overwhelming evidence of his need, it was the fact of his holding it back, which I could sense at once, in the way he touched and then waited, satisfied himself, and yet observed my satisfaction, and then confined himself to the things I appeared to like best.

So that when his hand slipped beneath my chemise, to caress first breast then nipple, he was eager and rough, and then, when he discovered an action which caused me to catch my breath and push against his hand, which made the skin beneath his fingers contract and the tiny nipple condense itself, the better to absorb this wonderful sensation—when he noted this, he stopped, and raised the chemise over my head, and then laid me on my back, and applied his tongue so subtly, so expertly, to the same morsel of flesh that I thought I might scream from the paining pleasure of it.

I expected him to tarry longer there, but he seemed to have got an idea, and before I knew quite what was happening, he was running his tongue across my belly, causing the flesh upon it to waken, then proceeding, with a brief and interesting pause at the navel, to the edge of the pantalets, which he pulled down around my hips. He stopped there a moment

to catch my breath, for I could not believe I was at last looking at her in this manner, the subject of my unending fantasies, stretched before me, divinely, entirely mine.

She had skin the color of apricots. I had beheld that strange fruit in a market once, and its dusky orange—less peach than tawny—had intrigued me. And now here was the color again, and the texture as well. The tiny blonde hairs upon her forearms, her thighs, her belly, glinted in the lamplight; between her legs the dark wedge sparked a deeper red than the long curls over her shoulders. She raised up upon one elbow, gloriously aware of her effect upon me, I thought. I had to look away from her for, had I proceeded right to it, I might have got ahead of myself, and reached a state in which I would not any longer be able to consider her.

I continued, a degree cooler, a second later.

I had got the idea because of my own experience with pleasure of this sort—and I was applying the rule that what I enjoyed, she might as well, since her own words had implied as much—but I was also eager for the sight of her this would provide me, and with the novel thought of knowing a woman this way, which would be a first, I was sure, for both of us. After a moment I continued on, drawing the pantalets off her legs one at a time, easing each little foot—which I caressed and kissed, while I watched her face, to see what it would do—through the openings.

He then knelt before me; he drew my foot down the length of his body, pressed it against him, and then replaced it on the bed. He ran his tongue, then his hands, over the little bone of my ankle, then over my calf and behind my knee, and then to the inside of my thigh, where he lingered, whilst I, now realizing what he meant to do, wondered whether or not to stop him.

In the end I forgot why I'd had misgivings. I forgot to think at all, for his tongue wound its way across my thighs and then to where it knew it should stop and linger.

The taste of her, salty and slick, was as much only hers as her words had been, something I knew of her which no other did.

He teased me, withdrawing, and then so lightly licking, circling about again, so that if at some point I had imagined wanting him to stop, I was now reduced to begging that he not. I drew my knees up, and put my hands in his hair, pulled him to me. He settled into a steady rhythm, moved upon me with greater force, and I felt that weightedness descend upon me.

She became more liquid, more ocean than shore beneath me, and moved me about like the ocean too, and when I felt her pace quicken, I slid out from between her legs

and then entered me with a finger, and then applied his tongue, and alternated them, so that I did not know which to gasp for next, until that liquid weight tipped over itself, became a torrent rushing the other way, pulling me with it, drawing him into me.

She made a sound I had not heard before, a soft, quick panting—another delight to me—and then a little cry, and I knew what she experienced, for her back arched from the bed, she held me so tight about the neck with one hand that I could not have moved had I wished it, and I felt the flutter of her about my fingers, even as she grew almost too slippery for me to remain inside her.

I felt it went on and on and on, but at length the Orgasm finished itself, having made a universe of my body, blocking my awareness of anything outside of it. And then it released me, so that I might know I inhabited the earth once more. I returned, felt once again the bed beneath me, and my hand wound in Aubrey's soft, lush hair.

I looked down—somewhat embarrassed now—and he raised his head, gave me such a delighted, lascivious smile that I could only smile back at him, and then shake my head, and then laugh, and fall back, panting, upon the pillows. He could have asked anything of me in that instant—that I leap from a cliff, follow him into the fires of hell—and it would have been his, for having revealed myself this way, I now felt more attached to him than ever, as if he had created the capacity for such pleasure in me, which was his alone to give.

He allowed me a moment, that my breath might return to some normal cadence, and then he raised himself up, settled atop me, pulled my mouth to his so that I could taste myself upon his lips.

I love you, I said, when we had ended this kiss. I had not planned it thus, it was just the right moment for that too, and I marveled at how simple a thing it was to say once it was truly meant.

I licked my lips, the experience still upon them; and I replied, I love you, realizing only then that we had never said this before, not in this way, in that joyful rush of feeling that makes it harder to be silent than to speak. We had mouthed the words, and understood them to be true, but I suppose we'd saved the feeling of it up, as we'd saved all of this.

We savored the words in the air between us, but then she shifted beneath me, and my attention was drawn to lust once again. Only then did I think to chastise myself, for perhaps the experience was over for her. Perhaps I had squandered my power to create it for her, and would be left to make my lonely way to my own ecstasy.

Or—oh damnable possibility—perhaps she would not wish to continue at all, now her own ardor had cooled.

"We can stop if you like," I whispered, wishing I could cut my own tongue out rather than say it, while my body screamed that it would never, ever forgive my mind its treachery.

But she looked at me with what could only be alarm upon her face. "Why would I wish to do that?" she whispered back, but she did not give me time to answer.

I thought I knew what he meant, for I'd learned from my survival of Valhalla that a man, once satisfied, is safely barred from commission of the act for a time. But although I'd never tested the idea, I suspected that it would not be the same for me, and I had no inclination whatsoever to stop, and every one possible to continue. So rather than answer him, I pulled him down for another kiss, tested my own appreciation of it—yes, there it was, as vibrant and insistent as it had been before.

I smiled at him, for he was half-dressed, while I lay there naked, and I thought it high time that the situation level itself.

I rose onto my knees, and then applied myself to his undone shirt, which I pulled from him with ease. And then I made him to lie on the bed, so that I could remove his trousers the same way he had mine. And I took a long, slow look at him, and bade him kneel again; and he no doubt noticed the way my eye lingered upon his Penis, for though he blushed, and his breath quickened, he grew ever larger the more I gazed.

"Well? Shall I do?" he smiled.

"Oh, you are quite a lot past doing," I said, honestly, for he was exceptionally beautiful, and I thought he should know it.

He was still smiling when he pulled me to him. "How bold shall you be, then?" he asked me, and I did not answer, but showed him instead, by running a finger along his back, down the curve of the buttocks, and reaching round to the front of him, to tease him a bit as he had me, by brushing my fingers where I knew he was most sensitive, on the little cap the Penis wears, just under the rim of it.

There was nothing shy in her touch, she was no trembling virgin; I gasped at being handled so expertly—as expertly as I handled myself. It was as though she had lived in my body before me, had learnt its preferences and weaknesses, and now was prepared to exploit her knowledge fully.

No sooner had a sound escaped me, though, than she released me, and urged me down upon the bed, kneeling between my thighs, and looking upon my face.

She began there to apply herself again, stroking over my lips, my cheekbones, my collarbone. She leaned forward, allowed her hair and the tips of her breasts to tickle my chest as her hands traced along my shoulders and slid down my arms, at first gentle, then more firmly confident. Wherever I felt her, my attention became concentrated in that area, and I discovered my skin, my shoulder, my wrist—and each one's capacity for pleasure—for the first time. When she reached my hands, she grasped them with her own, lying almost upon me, covering near every inch of me with herself. When I looked into her face, I saw that again she was gazing into mine, and a moment passed between us of such profound communion that I was taken from my senses. I had never been touched in such a manner, had never imagined it even in my fantasies—could not, perhaps, believe myself deserving of such unhurried and obvious indulgence.

I realized I wished to taste him, as he had me, and if I had learned this technique under great duress, so that I'd imagined it would never be other than odious to me, I now discovered the degree to which affection could change even that perception. I sat back, still holding his hands, and then released them; I traced my path back along his arms, down his chest—with more force this time—and then along his thighs. I could see him tense with anticipation, and so I did not satisfy it. Instead I let my fingers play just beyond where they were most desired. Then I lay down. I put my mouth to him, and the rich, spicy scent, the satin slip of skin over muscle, coupled with the stunned and appreciative intake of his breath, knocked me back to the edge of desire, as close as I had been minutes before. I had climbed a hill, slid down the other side only halfway, and now found myself here, with half the distance to go to reach the pinnacle again. It was a fine surprise.

Once more I earned my body's undying enmity, for though I was half of a mind to lose myself right here, I stopped her and pulled her up to me, for I wished to have her face me once more. When I had run my hands over every inch of her, satisfied myself as to the texture of her every particular, put my lips to her wherever I thought I had missed, I slid to the edge of the bed, and, sitting, pulled her onto my lap.

It was unexpected and delightful, the way I fit upon him, so we could not help but contact each other whether we wished to or not. I felt him against me and slid over him, then back slow, so as to intensify this; it was very near Intercourse, but deliciously not, and we kissed each other's mouths while bridling so, just upon the verge of completion.

But I knew I could not contain myself any longer, that I should not, and I desired to act upon her with all the mobility I could. I guided her off me and down upon the bed, and she parted her legs, the strong, firm muscles of her calves flexing to grip me when I lay atop her. And then she

he

was everywhere around

was within

me.

And it was as I had pictured it a thousand times, the start and finish of our separate bodies lost and unimportant.

Just as I had hoped, we arrived at the end not together, but she first, so that her song—unimagined, animal-pure, and lovely beyond words—was the catalyst for my own descent. I lost track of the moment when I joined her, for I did it unawares, the sound forced out of me, the joy of it inexpressible.

So that this thing—lust and its resultant act, pleasure or torment in its own right—was coupled with the contribution of mind, which makes of it transcendence, the triumphant joining of spirit and flesh.

SEPTEMBER 28, 1863

Last night I dreamed of Africa.

Just as I did that first halcyon evening, after we'd lain next to each other, delighting ourselves into the dawn.

"Why do we not keep going," I'd asked him, after we finished that initial exploration of each other, and I lay upon his chest inspecting the smooth twin rounds of muscle there.

"Hmm?"

"Once we have reached the Côte d'Azur, why do we not keep going?"

"Where? Tell me where you wish to go, and I shall take you there," he said.

"To Africa."

Africa? I asked her, mystified. But why would you wish to go to Africa?

Don't you? she asked. Are you not curious about it?

I am, as I am curious about any foreign shore, but I had never regarded the Dark Continent as the seat of my heritage, for if an eighth of me originated there, another seven of those eighths were contributed elsewhere. I'd felt no kinship with that Africa upon the map, with the dwellers in huts and tents, the strange jungles, searing deserts, and bizarre customs of which I know nothing. Whatever connexion I had was with the Africa of your teachings, Gran, the one which existed in your mind and your stories, to be passed down through the arts of vodou and healing to Mama and myself.

Besides, it is not one great "Africa," I told Arabella, not one country, but a vastness of peoples and languages, as different from one end to another as any portion of it might be from Europe.

"But of course it is that—and all the more reason to see it," Arabella said. "It is unlike all that's been known before it. And so I feel it is our place."

I laughed. "I feel it is *your* place, Berry. Like Paris. Much more so than mine. It's Gabara's place, and she would be pleased that you came looking for her in her own home, I am certain of it. I would enjoy seeing you there much more than I would relish the visit for its own sake."

But then I began to wonder if she is not right, if it is not for me as well, and I found the notion of it possessing me—the wildness, the expanse, the places from which old gods set forth. Those places which wait to seduce and yield and reveal themselves, all unlike what has been known before.

I looked down beside me and was glad for her, and for the person I become because she sees me thus: brave, intelligent, strong, upstanding.

And sometimes idiotic, which she gives me to see as well, though I forgive myself for it more easily these days, because she does.

"Then why do we not go?" she was saying.

And he replied that we might ask Elizabeth about it, though this would no doubt lead to a night of hyperbolic stories regarding the allure of the many and varied cultures of the realm.

We again examined our wedding plans, in the same position, she upon my chest, cradled in my arm, I upon the pillows on my back, the perfume of her hair beneath me. We named our children, of which there are to be one of each sex, and invested our fortunes and I told Bree I intended that I should make mine in the writing of Great Truth, whether in book form or as a journalist—perhaps a traveling one.

He quite agreed with me. "You are intended to be a thorn in the side of all convention," he teased. But he added that I must keep open the wellspring of my passions, and just those words—the respect with which he uttered them, the seriousness he accorded them—were enough to firm my resolve.

And what shall I do? I asked, for again I wonder this myself—what shall I do now I am bound no longer to the conviction of my wretchedness? Tend to my new place in society, and my properties? What a dull and pointless existence.

"I cannot answer that," she said, frowning. "You must make your own answer, it is in you, though you've not discovered it yet." She looked up at me, half-smiling. "Perhaps you ought discuss it with your Gran."

And I said that perhaps I would—but since then I've come to think I ought now rely on myself. You, Gran, have helped me enough, have inspired me to seize upon a passion when I had the good fortune to stumble over it; and for that I should thank you forever, and trouble you no more.

Do you suppose every time shall be like this one, I asked him.

I hope not, he smiled, for I would do nothing else, and never rise from the bed, and be dead of exhaustion in a week. But, he said, kissing me upon the forehead, I should happily die that way a thousand times over, believe me.

Yet I expect too that we shall argue, and grow by turns bored and irritated and angry, and we shall fuss over money or furniture or some other mundane nonsense, I told her; and I for one shall welcome all of that. For I am ready for those things, the normal things of life.

Once upon a time I fretted over whether I should ever feel as I do now. Then I fretted over whether I would always feel this way. Now I anticipate that I shall not, and it is all right. You have helped us past that too, Gran, by assuring me that such change is to be expected, and even welcomed.

We fell asleep, and it must have been all of the talk of Africa which overtook me, for that night as I lay in his arms I dreamed I was there.

The landscape I conjured was a verdant jungle, the trees thick with shadows that turned their leaves black in places. Flowers bloomed everywhere, pink and orange blossoms the size of a fist. Their fragrance delighted me, and so I picked them, and handed them to Aubrey. I recall I saw striped horses, zebra they are called, which ran across the open spaces just beyond our leafy glade. And above our heads, clouds rose, mountainous, to share a sky of blazing blue and sunlight, while multicolored birds flocked across that domed expanse, jewels against its brilliant backing.

Our house was made of sun-bleached wood and muslin, and was open everywhere, and rose from the ground on tall stilts, into the tops of the trees.

But I recall most of all our attitude which matched this wondrous place, for we had dispensed with every form of shame and artifice, and lived unconcealed each before the other.

Perhaps there is such a magical continent. For wherever we lead and follow shall become magical to us.

We have entered that realm of which I wrote to myself, alongside all the birds and beasts, and it is much as I imagined. We dwell there, loved and beloved, captives of its music, the ballads of passion, to dance beneath its spell, and to sing for each other those songs which the animals sing.